Death's
End

DEATH'S END

Cixin Liu

TRANSLATED BY

Ken Liu

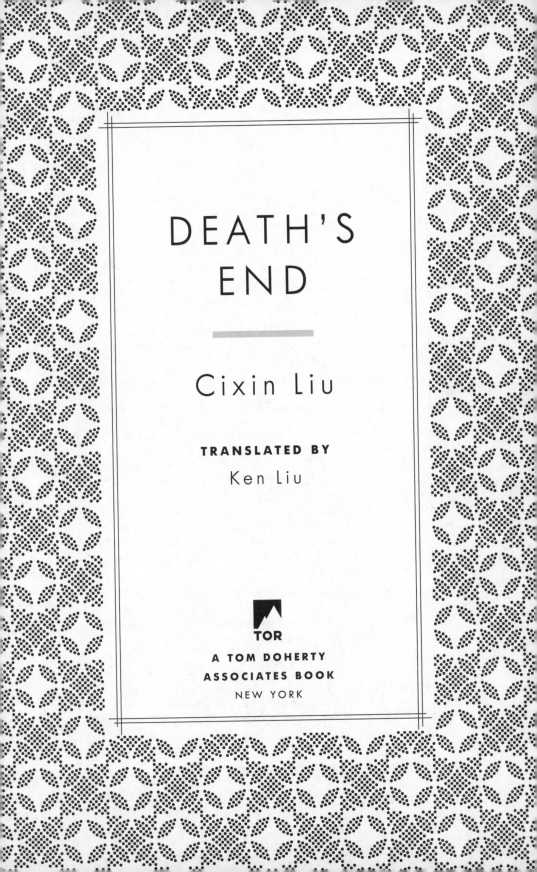

TOR

A TOM DOHERTY
ASSOCIATES BOOK
NEW YORK

DEATH'S END

Copyright © 2010 by 刘慈欣 (Liu Cixin)

English translation © 2016 by China Educational Publications Import & Export Corp., Ltd.

Translation by Ken Liu

This publication was arranged by Hunan Science & Technology Press. Originally published as 死神永生 in 2010 by Chongqing Publishing Group in Chongqing, China.

A Tor Book
Published by Tom Doherty Associates, LLC
175 Fifth Avenue
New York, NY 10010

www.tor-forge.com

Tor® is a registered trademark of Tom Doherty Associates, LLC.

The Library of Congress Cataloging-in-Publication Data is available upon request.

ISBN 978-0-7653-7710-4 (hardcover)
ISBN 978-1-4668-5345-4 (e-book)

Our books may be purchased in bulk for promotional, educational, or business use. Please contact your local bookseller or the Macmillan Corporate and Premium Sales Department at 1-800-221-7945, extension 5442, or by e-mail at MacmillanSpecialMarkets@macmillan.com.

Printed in the United States of America

0 9 8 7 6 5

A BRIEF NOTE FROM THE TRANSLATOR

Chinese and Korean names in this text are rendered with surnames first and given names last, in accordance with the customs of these cultures. For example, in the name "Yun Tianming," YUN is the surname and TIANMING is the given name.

CHARACTERS FROM *THE THREE-BODY PROBLEM* AND *THE DARK FOREST*

(Chinese names are written with surname first.)

Ye Wenjie	Physicist whose family was persecuted during the Cultural Revolution. She initiated contact with the Trisolarans and precipitated the Trisolar Crisis.
Yang Dong	Physicist; daughter of Ye Wenjie.
Ding Yi	Theoretical physicist and the first human to make contact with the Trisolaran droplets; Yang Dong's boyfriend.
Zhang Beihai	Officer in the Asian Fleet who hijacked *Natural Selection* during the Doomsday Battle, thus preserving a flicker of hope for humanity during their darkest hour. Possibly one of the first officers to understand the nature of dark battles.

Secretary General Say	UN secretary general during the Trisolar Crisis.
Manuel Rey Diaz	Wallfacer; he proposed the giant hydrogen bomb plan as a defense against the Trisolarans.
Luo Ji	Wallfacer; discoverer of the dark forest theory; creator of dark forest deterrence.

TABLE OF ERAS

Common Era	Present–201X C.E.
Crisis Era	201X–2208
Deterrence Era	2208–2270
Post-Deterrence Era	2270–2272
Broadcast Era	2272–2332
Bunker Era	2333–2400
Galaxy Era	2273–unknown
Black Domain Era for DX3906 System	2687–18906416
Timeline for Universe 647	18906416– . . .

Death's
End

Excerpt from the Preface to
A Past Outside of Time

I suppose this ought to be called *history*; but since all I can rely on is my memory, it lacks the rigor of history.

It's not even accurate to call it the *past*, for the events related in these pages didn't occur in the past, aren't taking place now, and will not happen in the future.

I don't want to record the details. Only a frame, for a history or an account of the past. The details that have been preserved are already abundant. Sealed in floating bottles, they will hopefully reach the new universe and endure there.

So I've written only a frame; someday, the frame may make it easier to fill in all the specifics. Of course, that task won't fall to us. I just hope such a day will come for someone.

I regret that day didn't exist in the past, doesn't exist in the present, and will not exist in the future.

I move the sun to the west, and as the angle of the light shifts, the dewdrops on the seedlings in the field glisten like countless eyes suddenly popping open. I dim the sun so that dusk arrives earlier; then I stare at the silhouette of myself on the distant horizon, in front of the setting sun.

I wave at the silhouette; the silhouette waves back. Looking at the shadow of myself, I feel young again.

This is a lovely time, just right for remembering.

PART I

May 1453, C.E.
The Death of the Magician

Pausing to collect himself, Constantine XI pushed away the pile of city-defense maps in front of him, pulled his purple robe tighter, and waited.

His sense of time was very accurate: The tremor came the moment he expected it, a powerful, violent quake that seemed to originate from deep within the earth. The vibrating silver candelabra hummed, and a wisp of dust that had sat on top of the Great Palace for perhaps a thousand years fell down and drifted into the candle flames, where the motes exploded in tiny sparks.

Every three hours—the time it took the Ottomans to reload one of the monstrous bombards designed by the engineer Orban—twelve-hundred-pound stone balls battered the walls of Constantinople. These were the world's strongest walls: first built by Theodosius II during the fifth century, they had been continually reinforced and expanded, and were the main reason that the Byzantine court had survived so many powerful enemies.

But the giant stone balls now gouged openings into the walls with each strike, like the bite of an invisible giant. The emperor could imagine the scene: While the debris from the explosion filled the air, countless soldiers and citizens rushed onto the fresh wound in the walls like a swarm of brave ants under a sky full of dust. They filled in the break with whatever was at hand: bits and pieces taken from other buildings in the city, flaxen-cloth bags of earth, expensive Arabic carpets. . . . He could even imagine the cloud of dust, steeped in the light of the setting sun, drifting slowly toward Constantinople like a golden shroud.

During the five weeks the city had been under siege, these tremors had come seven times a day, spaced as regularly as the strokes of some colossal clock. This was the time and rhythm of another world, the time of heathens. Compared to these tremors, the ringing of the double-headed eagle copper clock in the corner that represented the time of Christendom seemed feeble.

The tremors subsided. After a while and with an effort, Emperor Constantine pulled his thoughts back to the reality before him. He gestured to let the guard know that he was ready for his visitor.

Phrantzes, one of the emperor's most-trusted ministers, came in with a slender, frail figure trailing close behind.

"This is Helena." Phrantzes stepped aside, revealing the woman.

The emperor looked at her. The noblewomen of Constantinople tended to favor clothes bedecked with elaborate decorative elements, while the commoners wore plain, shapeless white garments that draped to the ankles. But this Helena seemed a combination of both. Instead of a tunic embroidered with gold thread, she wore a commoner's white dress, but over it she draped a luxurious cloak; however, instead of the purple and red reserved for the nobility, the cloak was dyed yellow. Her face was enchanting and sensual, bringing to mind a flower that would rather rot in adoration than fade in solitude.

A prostitute, probably one who did rather well for herself.

Her body trembled. She kept her eyes lowered, but the emperor noticed that they held a feverish glow, hinting at an excitement and zeal rare for her class.

"You claim the powers of magic?" the emperor asked.

He wanted to conclude this audience as quickly as possible. Phrantzes was usually meticulous. Of the approximately eight thousand soldiers defending Constantinople now, only a small number came from the standing army, and about two thousand were Genoese mercenaries. Phrantzes had been responsible for recruiting the rest, a few at a time, from the city's inhabitants. Though the emperor wasn't particularly interested in his latest idea, the capable minister's standing demanded that he at least be given a chance.

"Yes, I can kill the sultan." Helena's quiet voice quivered like silk strands in a breeze.

Five days earlier, standing in front of the palace, Helena had demanded to see the emperor. When guards tried to push her away, she presented a small package that stunned the guards. They weren't sure what she was showing them, but they knew it was not something she should have possessed. Instead of being brought to the emperor, she had been held and interrogated about how she had acquired the item. Her confession had been confirmed, and she was then brought to Phrantzes.

Phrantzes now took out the small bundle, unwrapped the flax cloth, and placed the contents on the emperor's desk.

The emperor's gaze was as stupefied as those of the soldiers five days ago. But unlike them, he knew immediately what he was looking at.

More than nine centuries earlier, during the reign of Justinian the Great, master craftsmen had cast two chalices out of pure gold, studded with gems and glowing with a beauty that seized the soul. The two chalices were identical save for the arrangement and shapes of the gems. One of the two was kept by successive Byzantine emperors, and the other one had been sealed along with other treasures into a secret chamber in the foundation of Hagia Sophia in 537 C.E., when the great church was rebuilt.

The glow of the chalice in the Great Palace that the emperor was familiar with had dulled with the passage of time, but the one in front of him now looked so bright it could have been cast only yesterday.

No one had believed Helena's confession at first, thinking that she had probably stolen the chalice from one of her rich patrons. Although many knew of the secret chamber under the great church, few knew its exact location. Moreover, the secret chamber was nestled among the giant stones deep in the foundation, and there were no doors or tunnels leading to it. It should have been impossible to enter the chamber without a massive engineering effort.

Four days ago, however, the emperor had ordered the precious artifacts of the city collected in case of Constantinople's fall. It was really a desperate measure, as he understood very well that the Turks had cut off all routes leading to the city, and there would be nowhere for him to escape with the treasures.

It had taken thirty laborers working nonstop for three days to enter the secret chamber, whose walls were formed from stones as massive as those in the Great Pyramid of Cheops. In the middle of the chamber was a massive stone sarcophagus sealed shut with twelve thick, crisscrossing iron hoops. It took most of another day to saw through the iron hoops before five laborers, under the gaze of many guards, finally managed to lift the cover off the sarcophagus.

The onlookers were amazed not by the treasures and sacred objects that had been hidden for almost a thousand years, but by the bunch of grapes placed on top, still fresh.

Helena had claimed to have left a bunch of grapes in the sarcophagus five days ago, and as she had declared, half of the grapes had been eaten, with only seven left on the stem.

The workers compared the treasures they recovered against the listing found on the inside of the cover of the stone sarcophagus; everything was accounted for except the chalice. If the chalice hadn't already been found with Helena, and without her testimony, everyone present would have been put to death even if they all swore that the secret chamber and the sarcophagus appeared intact.

"How did you retrieve this?" the emperor asked.

Helena's body trembled even harder. Apparently, her magic did not make her feel safe. She stared at the emperor with terror-filled eyes, and squeezed out an answer. "Those places . . . I see them . . . I see them as . . ." She struggled to find the right word. ". . . open. . . ."

"Can you demonstrate for me? Take out something from inside a sealed container."

Helena shook her head, dread stilling her tongue; she looked to Phrantzes for help.

Phrantzes spoke up. "She says that she can only practice her magic in a specific place. But she can't reveal the location, and no one must be allowed to follow her. Otherwise the magic will lose its power forever."

Helena nodded vigorously.

"In Europe, you would already have been burned at a stake," the emperor said.

Helena collapsed to the ground and hugged herself. Her small figure looked like a child's.

"Do you know how to kill?" the emperor pressed.

But Helena only trembled. After repeated urgings from Phrantzes, she finally nodded.

"Fine," the emperor said to Phrantzes. "Test her."

Phrantzes led Helena down a long flight of stairs. Torches in sconces along the way cast dim circles of light. Under every torch stood two armed soldiers whose armor reflected the light onto the walls in lively, flickering patterns.

Finally, the two arrived at a dark cellar. Helena pulled her cloak tighter around her. This was where the palace stored ice for use during the summers.

The cellar held no ice now. A prisoner squatted under the torch in the corner; an Anatolian officer, based on the way he was dressed. His fierce eyes, like a wolf's, glared at Phrantzes and Helena through the iron bars.

"You see him?" Phrantzes asked.

Helena nodded.

Phrantzes handed her a sheepskin bag. "You may leave now. Return with his head before dawn."

Helena took out a scimitar from the bag, glinting in the torchlight like a crescent moon. She handed it back to Phrantzes. "I don't need this."

Then she ascended the stairs, her footfalls making no sound. As she passed through the circles of light cast by the torches, she seemed to change shape— sometimes a woman, sometimes a cat—until her figure disappeared.

Phrantzes turned to one of the officers: "Increase the security around here." He pointed to the prisoner. "Keep him under constant observation."

After the officer left, Phrantzes waved his hand, and a man emerged from the darkness, draped in the black robes of a friar.

"Don't get too close," Phrantzes said. "It's all right if you lose her, but do not under any circumstances let her discover you."

The friar nodded and ascended the stairs as silently as Helena had.

That night, Constantine slept no better than he had since the siege of Constantinople began: The jolts from the heavy bombards woke him each time, just as he was about to fall asleep. Before dawn, he went into his study, where he found Phrantzes waiting for him.

He had already forgotten about the witch. Unlike his father, Manuel II, and elder brother, John VIII, Constantine was practical and understood that those who put all their faith in miracles tended to meet with untimely ends.

Phrantzes beckoned at the door, and Helena entered noiselessly. She looked as frightened as the last time the emperor had seen her, and her hand shook as she lifted the sheepskin bag.

As soon as Constantine saw the bag, he knew that he had wasted his time. The bag was flat, and no blood seeped from it. It clearly didn't contain the prisoner's head.

But the expression on Phrantzes's face wasn't one of disappointment. Rather, he looked distracted, confused, as though he was walking while dreaming.

"She hasn't retrieved what we wanted, has she?" the emperor asked.

Phrantzes took the bag from Helena, placed it on the emperor's desk, and opened it. He stared at the emperor as though he was looking at a ghost. "She almost did."

The emperor looked inside the bag. Something grayish and soft was nestled on the bottom, like old mutton suet. Phrantzes moved the candelabra closer.

"It's the brain of that Anatolian."

"She cut open his skull?" Constantine glanced at Helena. She trembled in her cloak like a frightened mouse.

"No, the corpse of the prisoner appeared intact. I had twenty men observe him, five men per watch, keeping him in their sight from different angles. The guards at the cellar door were also on extra alert; not even a mosquito could have entered the space." Phrantzes paused, as though stricken by his own memories.

The emperor nodded at him to continue.

"Two hours after she left, the prisoner went into sudden convulsions and fell down dead. Among the observers at the scene were an experienced Greek doctor and veterans of many battles—none could recall anyone dying in this particular manner. An hour later, she returned and showed them this bag. The Greek doctor then cut open the corpse's skull. It was empty."

Constantine observed the brain in the bag: It was complete, showing no signs of damage. The fragile organ must have been retrieved with great care. Constantine focused on Helena's fingers grasping the lapels of her cloak. He imagined the slender fingers reaching forward, picking a mushroom nestled in the grass, picking a fresh blossom from the tip of a branch. . . .

The emperor lifted his gaze up toward the wall, as though observing something rising over the horizon beyond. The palace shook with another pounding from the gigantic bombards, but, for the first time, the emperor did not feel the tremors.

If there really are miracles, now is the time for them to manifest.

Constantinople was in desperate straits, but not all hope was lost. After five weeks of bloody warfare, the enemy had also suffered heavy casualties. In some places, the Turkish bodies were piled as high as the walls, and the attackers were as exhausted as the defenders. A few days ago, a brave fleet from Genoa had broken through the blockade of the Bosporus and entered the Golden Horn, bringing precious supplies and aid. Everyone believed that they were the vanguard of more support from the rest of Christendom.

Morale was low among the Ottoman camps. Most commanders secretly wanted to accept the truce terms offered by the Byzantine court and retreat. The only reason the Ottomans had not yet retreated was because of a single man.

He was fluent in Latin, knowledgeable about the arts and sciences, skilled in warfare; he had not hesitated to drown his brother in a bathtub to secure his own path to the throne; he had decapitated a beautiful slave girl in front of his troops to demonstrate that he could not be tempted by women. . . . Sultan Mehmed II was the axle around which the wheels of the Ottoman war machine revolved. If he broke, the machine would fall apart.

Perhaps a miracle truly has *manifested.*

"Why do you want to do this?" the emperor asked. He continued to stare at the wall.

"I want to be remembered." Helena had been waiting for this question.

Constantine nodded. Money or treasure held no allure for this woman; there was no vault or lock that could keep her from what she desired. Still, a prostitute wanted honor.

"You are a descendant of the Crusaders?"

"Yes." She paused, and carefully added, "Not the fourth."

The emperor placed his hand on Helena's head, and she knelt.

"Go, child. If you kill Mehmed II, you will be the savior of Constantinople, and be remembered as a saint forever. A holy woman of the Holy City."

At dusk, Phrantzes led Helena onto the walls near the Gate of St. Romanus.

On the ground near the walls, the sands had turned black with the blood of the dying; corpses were strewn all over as though they had rained down from the sky. A bit farther away, white smoke from the giant cannons drifted over the battlefield, incongruously light and graceful. Beyond them, the Ottoman camps spread as far as the eye could see, banners as dense as a forest flapping in the moist sea breeze under the lead-gray sky.

In the other direction, Ottoman warships covered the Bosporus like a field of black iron nails securing the blue surface of the sea.

Helena closed her eyes. *This is my battlefield; this is my war.*

Legends from her childhood, stories of her ancestors recounted by her father, surfaced in her mind: In Europe, on the other side of the Bosporus, there was a village in Provence. One day, a cloud descended on the village, and an army of children walked out of the cloud, red crosses glowing brightly from their armor and an angel leading them. Her ancestor, a man from the village, had answered their call and sailed across the Mediterranean to fight for God in the Holy Land. He had risen through the ranks and become a Templar Knight. Later, he had come to Constantinople and met a beautiful woman, a holy warrior; they had fallen in love and given birth to this glorious family. . . .

Later, when she was older, she had found out the truth. The basic frame of the story was true: Her ancestor had indeed been a member of the Children's Crusade. It was right after the plague had swept through the villages, and he had joined in the hope of filling his belly. When the man had gotten off the boat, he found himself in Egypt, where he and more than ten thousand other children were sold as slaves. After many years of bondage, he escaped and drifted to Constantinople, where he did indeed meet a woman warrior, a holy knight. However, her fate wasn't much better than his. The Byzantine Empire had been hoping for the elite troops of Christendom to fight off the infidels. Instead, they received an army of frail women as poor as beggars. The Byzantine court refused to supply these "holy warriors," and the women knights became prostitutes.

For more than a hundred years, Helena's "glorious" family had barely eked out a living. By her father's time, the family's poverty had grown even more acute. A hungry Helena picked up the trade practiced by her own illustrious ancestor, but when her father found out, he had beaten her, telling her that he would kill her if he ever caught her again . . . unless she took her clients back home so that he could negotiate a better price and keep the money "for her."

Helena left home and began to live and ply her trade on her own. She had been to Jerusalem and Trabzon, and even visited Venice. She was no longer hungry, and she dressed in beautiful clothes. But she knew that she was no different from a blade of grass growing in the mud by the road: indistinguishable from the muck, as travelers trampled over her.

And then, God granted Helena a miracle.

Even then, she didn't model herself after Joan of Arc, another woman who had been divinely inspired. What had the Maid of Orléans received from God? Only a sword. But God had given Helena something that would make her into the holiest woman besides Mary. . . .

"Look, that's the camp of *el-Fātiḥ*, the Conqueror." Phrantzes pointed away from the Gate of St. Romanus.

Helena glanced over and nodded.

Phrantzes handed her another sheepskin bag. "Inside are three portraits of him from different angles and in different clothing. I've also given you a knife—you'll need it. We need his entire head, not just the brain. It's best if you wait until after nightfall. He won't be in his tent during the day."

Helena accepted the bag. "You remember my warning."

"Of course."

Don't follow me. Don't enter the place where I must go. Otherwise the magic will stop working, forever.

The spy who had followed her last time, in the guise of a friar, had told Phrantzes that Helena had been very careful, turning and looping back on her own path multiple times until she arrived in the Blachernae quarter, the part of the city where bombardment from the Turkish cannons was heaviest.

The spy had watched as Helena entered the ruins of a minaret that had once been part of a mosque. When Constantine had given the order to destroy the mosques in the city, this particular tower had been left alone because, during the last plague, a few diseased men had run inside and died, and no one wanted to get too close. After the siege began, a stray cannonball had blown away the top half of the minaret.

Following Phrantzes's admonition, the spy had not entered the minaret. But he had questioned two soldiers who had entered it before it had been struck by the stray missile. They told the spy that they had intended to set up a watch station on top of the structure but gave up after realizing it wasn't tall enough. They told the spy that there was nothing inside except a few bodies that had rotted until they were practically skeletons.

This time, Phrantzes didn't send anyone to follow Helena. He watched as she made her way through the soldiers thronging the top of the walls. Among the dirt-and-blood-encrusted armor of the soldiers, her bright cloak stood out. But the exhausted soldiers paid her no attention. She descended from the walls, and, without making an obvious effort to throw off anyone who might be following her, headed for the Blachernae quarter.

Night fell.

Constantine stared at the drying water stain on the floor, a metaphor for his vanishing hope.

The stain had been left by a dozen spies. Last Monday, dressed in the uniforms and turbans of the Ottoman forces, they had sneaked through the blockade in a tiny sailboat to welcome the European fleet that was supposed to be on its way to relieve the siege of Constantinople. But all they saw was the empty Aegean Sea, without even a shadow of the rumored fleet. The disappointed spies had carried out their duty and made their way back through the blockade to bring the emperor the terrible news.

Constantine finally understood that the promised aid from Europe was nothing more than a dream. The kings of Christendom had coldly decided to abandon Constantinople to the infidels, after this holy city had withstood the tides of Mohammedans for so many centuries.

Anxious cries from outside filled his ears. A guard came and reported a lunar eclipse: a terrible portent. It was said that Constantinople would never fall as long as the moon shone.

Through the narrow slit of the window, Constantine observed the moon disappearing in shadow, as though entering a grave in the sky. He knew, without knowing exactly why, that Helena would never return, and he would never see the head of his enemy.

A day passed; then a night. There was no news of Helena.

Phrantzes and his men stopped in front of the minaret in the Blachernae quarter and dismounted from their horses.

Everyone was stunned.

Under the cold, white light of the newly risen moon, the minaret appeared complete: Its sharp tip pointed into the starry sky.

The spy swore that the last time he had been here, the minaret's top was missing. Several other officers and soldiers, familiar with the area, corroborated his testimony.

But Phrantzes gazed at the spy in cold fury. No matter how many witnesses testified to the contrary, he must certainly be lying: The complete minaret was ironclad proof. However, Phrantzes had no time to mete out punishment; now that the city was about to fall, no one would escape the punishment of the Conqueror.

A soldier off to the side knew that the missing top of the minaret hadn't been destroyed by a cannonball. He had found the top half of the minaret missing one morning two weeks ago. There had been no cannon fire the previous night, and he had recalled that there was no debris on the ground around the minaret. The two soldiers who had been with him that morning had both died in battle. However, seeing the look on Phrantzes's face, he decided to keep quiet about it.

Phrantzes and his men entered the bottom of the minaret. Even the spy who Phrantzes was sure had lied came along. They saw remnants of the corpses of plague victims that had been scattered around the ruin by feral dogs, but there were no signs of anyone living.

They ascended the stairs. In the flickering torchlight on the second story, they saw Helena curled under a window. She appeared to be asleep, but her half-closed eyes reflected the light from the torches. Her clothes were torn and dirty and her hair unkempt; a few bloody scratch marks crossed her face, perhaps self-inflicted.

Phrantzes looked around. This was the top of the minaret, an empty, cone-shaped space. He noted the thick layer of dust covering everything, but there were few marks in the dust, as though Helena, like them, had arrived only recently.

She awoke, and, scrabbling at the walls with her hands, stood up. Moonlight falling through the window turned the messy hair around her face into a silvery halo. She stared, wide-eyed, and seemed to return to the present only with effort. But she then closed her eyes again, as though trying to linger inside a dream.

"What are you doing here?!" Phrantzes shouted at her.

"I . . . I can't go *there*."

"Where?"

With her eyes still half closed, as if to savor her memory like a child holding on to a favorite toy that she would not give up, she answered, "There's so much space there. So comfortable . . ." She opened her eyes and looked around in terror. "But here, it's like the inside of a coffin, whether I'm inside the minaret or outside. I have to go *there*!"

"What about your mission?"

"Wait!" Helena crossed herself. "Wait!"

Phrantzes pointed outside the window. "It's too late for waiting."

Waves of noise cascaded over them. If one listened carefully, two sources could be distinguished.

One source was from outside the city. Mehmed II had decided to launch the final assault on Constantinople tomorrow. At this moment, the young sultan was riding through the Ottoman camps, promising his soldiers that all he wanted was Constantinople itself—the treasure and women of Constantinople would belong to his army, and after the fall of the city, the soldiers would have three days to loot everything they desired. All the soldiers cheered at the sultan's promise, and the sound of trumpets and drums added to their glee. This joyous din, mixed with the smoke and sparks rising from fires in front of the camps, covered Constantinople like an oppressive tide of death.

The noise coming from inside Constantinople, on the other hand, was lugubrious and subdued. All the citizens had paraded through the city and gathered at Hagia Sophia to attend a final Mass. This was a scene that had never occurred and would never occur again in the history of Christianity: Accompanied by solemn hymns, under the light of dim candles, the Byzantine emperor, the Patriarch of Constantinople, Orthodox Christians of the East and Catholics from Italy, soldiers in full armor, merchants and sailors from Venice and Genoa, and multitudes of ordinary citizens all gathered in front of God to prepare for the final battle of their lives.

Phrantzes knew that his plan had failed. Perhaps Helena was nothing but a skilled fraud, and she possessed no magic at all—he preferred that possibility by far. But there was another, more dangerous alternative: She did possess magic, and she had already gone to Mehmed II, who had given her a new mission.

After all, what could the Byzantine Empire, teetering on the brink of ruin, offer her? The emperor's promise to make her into a saint was unlikely to be fulfilled: Neither Constantinople nor Rome was likely to declare a witch and a whore a saint. Indeed, she had likely returned with two new targets in mind: Constantine, and himself.

Hadn't Orban, the Hungarian engineer, already been an example of this? He had come to Constantine first with plans for his giant cannons, but the emperor had no money to pay his salary, let alone finance the construction of such monstrous engines. He had then gone to Mehmed II, and the daily bombardments had served as a constant reminder of his betrayal.

Phrantzes looked over at the spy, who immediately unsheathed his sword and stabbed at Helena's chest. The sword pierced her body and got stuck in a crack in the wall behind her. The spy tried to pull the sword out, but it wouldn't budge. Helena rested her hands on the sword's hilt. The spy let go of the weapon, unwilling to touch her hands.

Phrantzes left with his men.

Throughout her execution, Helena never made any noise. Gradually, her head drooped, and the silvery halo formed by her tresses fell away from the beam of moonlight and faded into darkness. The moon's glow lit a small patch of ground in the dark interior of the minaret, where a stream of blood flowed like a slender, black snake.

In the moments that preceded the great battle, noises from both inside and outside the city stopped. The Eastern Roman Empire welcomed its last dawn on this Earth, at the intersection of Europe and Asia, of land and sea.

On the second story of the minaret, the woman magician died, pinned to the wall. She was perhaps the only real magician in the entire history of the human race. Unfortunately, ten hours earlier, the age of magic, brief as it was, had also come to an end.

The age of magic began at four o'clock on the afternoon of May 3, 1453, when the high-dimensional fragment first intersected with the Earth. It ended at nine o'clock on the evening of May 28, 1453, when the fragment left the Earth behind. After twenty-five days and five hours, the world returned to its normal orbit.

On the evening of May 29, Constantinople fell.

As the bloody slaughter of the day was coming to its inevitable end, Constantine, faced with the swarming Ottoman masses, shouted, "The city is fallen and I am still alive." Then he tore off his imperial robe and unsheathed his sword to meet the oncoming hordes. His silvery armor glinted for a moment like a piece of metallic foil tossed into a tub of dark red sulfuric acid, and then vanished.

The historical significance of the fall of Constantinople would not be apparent for many years. For most, the obvious association was that it marked the final gasp of the Roman Empire. Byzantium was a thousand-year rut behind the wheels of Ancient Rome, and though it enjoyed splendor for a time, it finally evaporated like a water stain under the bright sun. Once, ancient Romans had whistled in their grand, magnificent baths, thinking that their empire, like the granite that made up the walls of the pools in which they floated, would last forever.

No banquet was eternal. Everything had an end. Everything.

Crisis Era, Year 1
The Option for Life

Yang Dong wanted to save herself, but she knew there was little hope.

She stood on the balcony of the control center's top floor, surveying the stopped particle accelerator. From her perch, she could take in the entire twenty-kilometer circumference of the collider. Contrary to usual practice, the ring for the collider wasn't an underground tunnel, but enclosed within an aboveground concrete tube. The facility looked like a giant full stop mark in the setting sun.[1]

What sentence does it end? Hopefully only the end of physics.

Once, Yang Dong had held a basic belief: Life and the world were perhaps ugly, but at the limits of the micro and macro scales, everything was harmonious and beautiful. The world of our everyday life was only froth floating on the perfect ocean of deep reality. But now, it appeared that the everyday world was a beautiful shell: The micro realities it enclosed and the macro realities that enclosed it were far more ugly and chaotic than the shell itself.

Too frightening.

It would have been better if she could just stop thinking about such things. She could choose a career that had nothing to do with physics, get married, have children, and live a peaceful, contented life like countless others. Of course, for her, such a life would be only half a life.

Something else also bothered Yang Dong: her mother, Ye Wenjie. By accident, she'd discovered on her mother's computer some heavily encrypted messages that she had received. This aroused an intense curiosity in Yang.

Like many elderly people, Yang's mother wasn't familiar with the details of the web and her own computer, so she had only deleted the decrypted docu-

---

[1] *Translator's Note:* The Chinese full stop punctuation mark looks like this: ∘

ments instead of digitally shredding them. She didn't realize that even if she had reformatted the hard drive, the data would still have been easily recoverable.

For the first time in her life, Yang Dong kept a secret from her mother, and recovered the information in the deleted documents. It took her several days to read through the recovered information, during which she learned a shocking amount about the world of Trisolaris and the secret shared by the extraterrestrials and her mother.

Yang Dong was utterly stunned. The mother she had depended on for most of her life turned out to be someone she didn't know at all, someone she couldn't even have believed existed in this world. She didn't dare to confront her mother, never would, because the moment she asked about it, her mother's transformation in her mind would be complete, irrevocable. It was better to pretend that her mother was still the person she had always known and continue life as before. Of course, for Yang, such a life would be only half a life.

Was it really so bad to live only half a life? As far as she could see, a considerable number of the people around her lived only half lives. As long as one was good at forgetting and adjusting, half a life could be lived in contentment, even happiness.

But between the end of physics and her mother's secret, Yang had lost two such half lives, which added up to a whole life. What did she have left?

Yang Dong leaned against the banister and stared at the abyss beneath her, terrified as well as enticed. She felt the banister shake as it bore more of her weight, and she stepped back as though shocked by electricity. She dared not stay here any longer. She turned to walk back into the terminal room.

This was where the center kept the terminals for the supercomputer used to analyze the data generated by the collider. A few days ago, all of the terminals had been shut down, but now a few were lit. This gave Yang Dong a bit of comfort, but she knew that they no longer had anything to do with the particle accelerator—other projects had taken over the supercomputer.

There was only one young man in the room, who stood up as Yang Dong came in. He wore glasses with thick, bright green frames, a distinct look. Yang explained that she was here only to retrieve a few personal items, but after Green Glasses heard her name, he became enthusiastic and explained the program running on the terminals to her.

It was a mathematical model of the Earth. Unlike similar projects in the past, this model combined factors from biology, geology, astronomy, atmospheric and oceanic sciences, and other fields of study to simulate the evolution of the Earth's surface from past to future.

Green Glasses directed her attention to a few large-screen displays. These did not show scrolling columns of numbers or crawling curves on a chart; instead, they showed bright, colorful pictures, as though one were viewing the continents and oceans from high above. Green Glasses manipulated the mouse and zoomed in on a few places to show close-up views of a river or a copse of trees.

Yang Dong felt the breath of nature seeping into this place that had once been dominated by abstract numbers and theories. She felt as if she were being released from confinement.

After the explanation from Green Glasses, Yang Dong retrieved her things, politely said good-bye, and turned to leave. She could feel Green Glasses staring at her back, but she was used to men behaving this way, so instead of being annoyed, she felt comforted, as if by sunlight in winter. She was seized by a sudden desire to communicate with others.

She turned to face Green Glasses. "Do you believe in God?"

Yang Dong was shocked by her own question. But considering the model displayed on the terminals, the question wasn't entirely out of place.

Green Glasses was similarly stunned. After a while, he managed to close his mouth and ask, carefully, "What kind of 'God' do you mean?"

"Just God." That overwhelming sensation of exhaustion had returned. She had no patience to explain more.

"I don't."

Yang pointed to the large screens. "But the physical parameters governing the existence of life are utterly unforgiving. Take liquid water as an example: It can exist only within a narrow range of temperatures. Viewing the universe as a whole, this becomes even more apparent: If the parameters of the big bang had been different by even one million billionth, we would have no heavy elements and thus no life. Isn't this clear evidence for intelligent design?"

Green Glasses shook his head. "I don't know enough about the big bang to comment, but you're wrong about the environment on Earth. The Earth gave birth to life, but life also changed the Earth. The current environment on our planet is the result of interactions between the two." He grabbed the mouse and started clicking. "Let's do a simulation."

He brought up a configuration panel on one of the large screens, a window filled with dense fields of numbers. He unchecked a checkbox near the top, and all the fields became grayed out. "Let's uncheck the option for 'life' and observe how the Earth would have evolved without it. I'll adjust the simulation to be coarse-grained so as not to waste too much time in computation."

Yang Dong glanced over at another terminal and saw that the supercomputer was operating at full capacity. A machine like that consumed as much electricity as a small city, but she didn't tell Green Glasses to stop.

A newly formed planet appeared on the large screen. Its surface was still red-hot, like a piece of charcoal fresh out of the furnace. Time passed at the rate of geological eras, and the planet gradually cooled. The color and patterns on the surface slowly shifted in a hypnotic manner. A few minutes later, an orange planet appeared on the screen, indicating the end of the simulation run.

"The computations were done at the coarsest level; to do it with more precision would require over a month." Green Glasses moved the mouse and zoomed in on the surface of the planet. The view swept over a broad desert, over a cluster of strangely shaped, towering mountain peaks, over a circular depression like an impact crater.

"What are we looking at?" Yang Dong asked.

"Earth. Without life, this is what the surface of the planet would look like now."

"But . . . where are the oceans?"

"There are no oceans. No rivers either. The entire surface is dry."

"You're saying that without life, liquid water would not exist on Earth?"

"The reality would probably be even more shocking. Remember, this is only a coarse simulation, but at least you can see how much of an impact life had in the present state of the Earth."

"But—"

"Do you think life is nothing but a fragile, thin, soft shell clinging to the surface of this planet?"

"Isn't it?"

"Only if you neglect the power of time. If a colony of ants continue to move clods the size of grains of rice, they could remove all of Mount Tai in a billion years. As long as you give it enough time, life is stronger than metal and stone, more powerful than typhoons and volcanoes."

"But the formation of mountains depends on geologic forces!"

"Not necessarily. Life may not be able to uplift mountains, but it can change the distribution of mountain ranges. Let's say there are three mountains, two of which are covered by vegetation. The one that is nude would soon be flattened by erosion. 'Soon' here means on the order of millions of years, a blink of an eye in geological terms."

"Then how did the oceans disappear?"

"We'd have to examine the records of the simulation, which would be a lot of work. However, I can give you an educated guess: plants, animals, and bacteria all have had important roles in the present composition of our atmosphere. Without life, the atmosphere would be very different. It's possible that such an atmosphere would not be able to shield the surface of the Earth against solar winds and ultraviolet rays, and the oceans would evaporate. Soon, greenhouse effects would turn the Earth's atmosphere into a copy of Venus's, and then water vapor would be lost to space over time. After several billion years, the Earth would be dry."

Yang Dong said no more as she stared at that yellow husk of a planet.

"Thus, the Earth that we live on now is a home constructed by life for itself. It has nothing to do with God." Green Glasses held out his arms in mock embrace of the large screen, clearly pleased with his own oration.

Yang Dong was not really in the mood to discuss such matters, but the moment Green Glasses unchecked the option for life in the configuration panel, a thought had flashed into her mind.

She asked the next terrifying question: "What about the universe?"

"The universe?"

"If we use a similar mathematical model to simulate the entire universe, and uncheck the option for life at the beginning, what would the resulting universe look like?"

Green Glasses thought for a moment. "It would look the same. When I talked about the effects of life on the environment, it was limited to the Earth. But if we're talking about the universe, life is exceedingly rare, and its impact on the evolution of the universe can be ignored."

Yang Dong held her tongue. She said good-bye again and struggled to put on an appreciative smile. She left the building and stared up at the star-studded night sky.

From her mother's secret documents, she knew that life was not so rare in the universe. In fact, the universe was downright crowded.

How much has the universe been changed by life?

A wave of terror threatened to overwhelm her.

She knew that she could no longer save herself. She tried to stop thinking, to turn her mind into empty darkness, but a new question stubbornly refused to leave her alone: *Is Nature really natural?*

Crisis Era, Year 4
Yun Tianming

After Dr. Zhang's regular checkup on Yun Tianming, he left a newspaper with him, saying that since Tianming had been in the hospital for so long, he should be aware of what was happening in the world. There was a TV in Tianming's room, so he was puzzled, wondering if perhaps the doctor had something else in mind.

Tianming read the newspaper and came to the following conclusion: Compared to the time before he was hospitalized, news about Trisolaris and the Earth-Trisolaris Organization (ETO) no longer dominated everything. There were at least some articles that had nothing to do with the crisis. Humanity's tendency to focus on the here and now reasserted itself, and concern for events that would not take place for four centuries gave way to thoughts about life in the present.

This wasn't surprising. He tried to remember what was happening four hundred years ago: China was under the Ming Dynasty, and he thought—he wasn't sure—that Nurhaci had just founded the empire that would end up replacing the Ming, after slaughtering millions. The Dark Ages had just ended in the West; the steam engine wouldn't make its appearance for another hundred-plus years; and, as for electricity, one would have to wait three hundred years. If anyone at the time had worried about life four hundred years later, they'd be a laughingstock. It was as ridiculous to worry about the future as to lament the past.

As for Tianming himself, based on the way his condition was developing, he wouldn't even need to worry about next year.

But one item of news attracted his attention. It was on the front page:

The Special Session of the Third Standing Committee of the National People's Congress Passes Euthanasia Law

Tianming was confused. The special legislative session had been called to deal with the Trisolar Crisis, but this law seemed to have nothing to do with the crisis.

Why did Dr. Zhang want me to see this news?

A fit of coughing forced him to put down the newspaper and try to get some sleep.

The next day, the TV also showed some interviews and reports about the euthanasia law, but there didn't seem to be a lot of public interest.

Tianming had trouble sleeping that night: He coughed; he struggled to breathe; he felt weak and nauseous from the chemo. The patient who had the bed next to his sat on the edge of Tianming's bed and held the oxygen tube for him. His surname was Li, and everyone called him "Lao Li," *Old Li.*

Lao Li looked around to be sure that the other two patients who shared the room with them were asleep, and then said, "Tianming, I'm going to leave early."

"You've been discharged?"

"No. It's that law."

Tianming sat up. "But why? Your children are so solicitous and caring—"

"That is exactly why I've decided to do this. If this drags out much longer, they'd have to sell their houses. What for? In the end, there's no cure. I have to be responsible for my children and their children."

Lao Li sighed, lightly patted Tianming's arm, and returned to his own bed.

Staring at the shadows cast against the window curtain by swaying trees, Tianming gradually fell asleep. For the first time since his illness, he had a peaceful dream.

He sat on a small origami boat drifting over placid water, oarless. The sky was a misty, dark gray. There was a cool drizzle, but the rain apparently did not reach the surface of the water, which remained as smooth as a mirror. The water, also gray, merged with the sky in every direction. There was no horizon, no shore. . . .

When Tianming awoke in the morning, he was baffled by how, in his dream, he was so certain that *there*, it would always be drizzling, the surface would always be smooth, and the sky always a misty, dark gray.

———

The hospital was about to conduct the procedure Lao Li had asked for.

It took a great deal of internal discussion before the news outlets settled on the verb "to conduct." "To execute" was clearly inappropriate; "to carry out" sounded wrong as well; "to complete" seemed to suggest that death was already certain, which was not exactly accurate, either.

Dr. Zhang asked Tianming whether he felt strong enough to attend Lao Li's euthanasia ceremony. The doctor hurried to add that since this was the first instance of euthanasia in the city, it would be better to have representatives from various interest groups present, including someone representing other patients. No other meaning was intended.

But Tianming couldn't help feeling that the request did contain some hidden message. Still, since Dr. Zhang had always taken good care of him, he agreed.

Afterwards, he suddenly realized that Dr. Zhang's face and name seemed familiar—did he know the doctor before his hospitalization?—he couldn't recall exactly how. The fact that he hadn't had this feeling of recognition earlier was because their interactions had been limited to discussions of his condition and treatment. The way a doctor acted and spoke while performing his job was different from when he spoke as just another person.

None of Lao Li's family members were present for the procedure. He had kept his decision from them and requested that the city's Civil Affairs Bureau— not the hospital—inform his family after the procedure was complete. The new law permitted him to conduct his affairs in this manner.

Many reporters showed up, but most were kept away from the scene. The euthanasia room was adapted from a room in the hospital's emergency department. A one-way mirror made up one of the walls so that observers could see what was happening inside the room, but the patient would not be able to see them.

Tianming pushed his way through the crowd of observers until he was standing in front of the one-way glass window. As soon as he saw the interior of the euthanasia room, Tianming was seized by a wave of fear and disgust. He wanted to throw up.

Whoever was responsible for decorating this room had made quite an effort: There were new, pretty curtains on the windows, fresh flowers in vases, and numerous pink paper hearts on the walls. But their well-intentioned attempt to humanize the situation had achieved the exact opposite: The frightful pall cast by death was mixed with an eerie cheerfulness, as though they were trying to turn a tomb into a nuptial chamber.

Lao Li was lying on the bed in the middle of the room, and he appeared to be at peace. Tianming realized that they had never properly said good-bye, and his heart grew heavy. Two notaries were inside, finishing up the legal part of the procedure. After Lao Li signed the documents, the notaries came out.

Another man went inside to explain the specific steps of the procedure to Lao Li. The man was dressed in a white coat, though it was unclear whether he was really a doctor. The man first pointed to the large screen at the foot of the bed and asked Lao Li whether he could read everything on it. Lao Li nodded. Then the man asked Lao Li to try to use the mouse next to the bed to click the buttons on the screen, and explained that if he found the operation too difficult, other input methods were available. Lao Li tried the mouse and indicated that it worked fine.

Tianming recalled that Lao Li had once told him that he had never used a computer. When he needed cash, he had to go queue up at the counter at the bank. This must be the first time in Lao Li's life that he used a mouse.

The man in the white coat then told Lao Li that a question was going to be displayed on the screen, and the same question would be asked five times. Each time the question was displayed, there would be six buttons underneath, numbered from zero to five. If Lao Li wished to answer in the affirmative, he had to click on the specific numbered button indicated in the on-screen instructions, which would change randomly each time the question was asked. If Lao Li wished to answer in the negative, he just had to press zero, and the procedure would stop immediately. There would be no "Yes" or "No" button.

The reason for the complicated procedure, the man explained, was to avoid a situation where the patient simply continued to press the same button over and over without thinking about his answers each time.

A nurse went inside and secured a needle into Lao Li's left arm. The tube behind the needle was connected to an automatic injector about the size of a notebook computer. The man in the white coat took out a sealed package, unwrapped layers of protective film, and revealed a small glass vial filled with a yellowish liquid.

Carefully, he filled the injector with the contents of the vial, and left with the nurse.

Only Lao Li was left in the room.

The screen displayed the question, and a soft, gentle female voice read it aloud:

Do you wish to terminate your life? For yes, select 3. For no, select 0.

Lao Li selected 3.

Do you wish to terminate your life? For yes, select 5. For no, select 0.

Lao Li selected 5.
The process repeated twice more. And then:

Do you wish to terminate your life? This is your last prompt. For yes,
    select 4. For no, select 0.

A surge of sorrow made Tianming dizzy, and he almost fainted. Even when his mother died, he didn't feel such extreme pain and anger. He wanted to scream at Lao Li to select 0, to break the glass window, to suffocate that voice.

But Lao Li selected 4.

Noiselessly, the injector came to life. Tianming could see the column of yellowish liquid in the glass tube shorten and then disappear. Lao Li never moved. He closed his eyes and went to sleep.

The crowd around Tianming dissipated, but he remained where he was, his hand pressed against the glass. He wasn't looking at the lifeless body lying within. His eyes were open, but he wasn't looking at all.

"There was no pain." Dr. Zhang's voice was so low that it sounded like the buzzing of a mosquito. Tianming felt a hand land on his left shoulder. "It's a combination of a massive dose of barbitone, muscle relaxant, and potassium chloride. The barbitone takes effect first and puts the patient into a deep sleep, the muscle relaxant stops his breathing, and the potassium chloride stops the heart. The whole process takes no more than twenty, thirty seconds."

After a while, Dr. Zhang's hand left Tianming's shoulder, and Tianming heard his departing footsteps. Tianming never turned around.

He suddenly remembered how he knew the doctor. "Doctor," Tianming called out softly. The footsteps stopped. Tianming still didn't turn around. "You know my sister, don't you?"

The reply came after a long pause. "Yes. We were high school classmates. When you were little, I remember seeing you a couple of times."

Mechanically, Tianming left the main building of the hospital. Everything was clear now. Dr. Zhang was working for his sister; his sister wanted him dead. No, wanted him to "conduct the procedure."

Although Tianming often recalled the happy childhood he had shared with his sister, they had grown apart as they grew up. There was no overt conflict between them, and neither had hurt the other. But they had come to see each other as completely different kinds of people, and each felt that the other held them in contempt.

His sister was shrewd but not smart, and she had married a man who was the same way. They were not successful in their careers, and even with grown children, the couple couldn't afford to buy a home. Since her husband's parents had no room for them, the family had ended up living with Tianming's father.

Tianming, on the other hand, was a loner. In career and personal life, he wasn't any more successful than his sister. He had always lived by himself in dormitories that belonged to his employer, and left the responsibility for taking care of his frail father entirely to his sister.

Tianming suddenly understood his sister's thinking. The medical insurance was insufficient to cover the expenses for his hospitalization, and the longer it went on, the bigger the bill grew. Their father had been paying for it out of his life savings, but he had never offered to use that same money to help Tianming's sister and her family to buy a house—a clear case of favoritism. From his sister's point of view, their father was spending money that should be hers. Besides, the money was being wasted on treatments that could only prolong, but not cure, the illness. If Tianming chose euthanasia, his sister's inheritance would be preserved, and he would suffer less.

The sky was filled with misty, gray clouds, just like in his dream. Looking up at this endless grayness, Tianming let out a long sigh.

All right. If you want me to die, I'll die.

He thought of "The Judgment" by Franz Kafka, in which a father curses his son and sentences him to death. The son agrees, as easily as someone agreeing to take out the trash or to shut the door, and leaves the house, runs through the streets onto the bridge, and leaps over the balustrade to his death. Later, Kafka told his biographer that as he wrote the scene, he was thinking of "a violent ejaculation."

Tianming now understood Kafka, the man with the bowler hat and briefcase, the man who walked silently through Prague's dim streets more than a hundred years ago, the man who was as alone as he was.

Someone was waiting for Tianming when he returned to his hospital room: Hu Wen, a college classmate.

Wen was the closest thing to a friend from Tianming's college days, but what they had wasn't friendship, exactly. Wen was one of those people who got along with everyone and who knew everyone's name; but even for him, Tianming was in the most peripheral ring of his social network. They had had no contact since graduation.

Wen didn't bring a bouquet or anything similar; instead, he brought a cardboard box full of canned beverages.

After a brief, awkward exchange of greetings, Wen asked a question that surprised Tianming. "Do you remember the outing back when we were first years? That first time we all went out as a group?"

Of course Tianming remembered. That was the first time Cheng Xin had ever sat next to him, had ever spoken to him.

If she hadn't taken the initiative, he doubted if he ever would have gotten the courage to speak to her for the rest of their four years in college. At the outing, he had sat by himself, staring at the broad expanse of the Miyun Reservoir outside Beijing. She had sat down next to him and begun talking.

While they talked, she tossed pebbles into the reservoir. Their conversation meandered over usual topics for classmates who were becoming acquainted for the first time, but Tianming could still recall every word. Later, Cheng Xin had made a little origami boat out of a sheet of paper and deposited it on the water. A breeze carried the boat away slowly until it turned into a tiny dot in the distance. . . .

That most lovely day of his time in college held a golden glow in his mind. In reality, the weather that day hadn't been ideal: There was a drizzle, and the surface of the reservoir was filled with ripples, and the pebbles they tossed felt wet in the hand. But from that day on, Tianming fell in love with drizzly days, fell in love with the smell of damp ground and wet pebbles, and from time to time he made origami boats and placed them on his nightstand.

With a start, he wondered if the world in his peaceful dream had been born from this memory.

But Wen wanted to talk about what had happened later in the outing— events that did not make much of an impression on Tianming. However, with prompts from Wen, Tianming managed to recall those faded memories.

A few of Cheng Xin's friends had come by and called her away. Wen then sat down next to Tianming.

Don't be too pleased with yourself. She's nice to everyone.

Of course Tianming knew that. But then Wen saw the bottle of mineral water in Tianming's hand and the conversation shifted.

What in the world are you drinking?!

The water in the bottle was a green color, and bits of grass and leaves floated in it.

I crumpled some weeds and added them to the water. It's the most organic drink.

He was in a good mood and so he was more loquacious than usual.

Someday I may start a company to produce this drink. It will surely be popular.
It must taste awful.

Do you think cigarettes and liquor really taste that good? Even Coca-Cola prob-ably tasted medicinal the first time you tried it. Anything addictive is like that.

"Buddy, that conversation changed my life!" Wen said. He opened the card-board box and took out a can. The outside was deep green, and on it was a picture of a grassland. The trademark was "Green Tempest."

Wen pulled the tab and handed the can to Tianming. Tianming took a sip: fragrant, herbal, with a trace of bitterness. He closed his eyes and was back at the shore of the drizzly reservoir, and Cheng Xin was next to him. . . .

"This is a special version. The mass market recipe is sweeter," Wen said.

"Does it sell well?"

"Sells great! The main hurdle now is cost. You might think grass is cheap, but until I can scale up, it's more expensive than fruits or nuts. Also, to make it safe, the ingredients have to be detoxified and processed, a complicated pro-cedure. The prospects are fantastic, though. Lots of investors are interested, and Huiyuan Juice wants to buy my company. Fuck them."

Tianming stared at Wen, not knowing what to say. Wen had graduated as an aerospace engineer, but now he had turned into a beverage entrepreneur. He was someone who did things, who got things done. Life belonged to people like that. But people like Tianming could only watch life pass them by, aban-doned and left behind.

"I owe you," Wen said. He handed three credit cards and a slip of paper to Tianming, looked around, leaned in, and whispered, "There's three million yuan in the account. The password is on the note."

"I never applied for a patent or anything like that," Tianming said.

"But it's your idea. Without you, there would be no Green Tempest. If you agree, we'll just call it even, at least legally. But as a matter of our friendship, I'll always owe you."

"You don't owe me anything, legally or otherwise."

"You have to accept it. I know you need money."

Tianming said no more. For him, the sum was astronomical, but he wasn't excited. Money wasn't going to save him.

Still, hope was a stubborn creature. After Hu Wen left, Tianming asked for a consultation with a doctor. He didn't want Dr. Zhang; instead, after much effort, he got the assistant director of the hospital, a famous oncologist.

"If money were no issue, would there be a cure for me?"

The old doctor brought up Tianming's case file on his computer, and after a while, he shook his head.

"The cancer has spread from your lungs throughout your body. Surgery is pointless; all you have are chemo and radiation, conservative techniques. Even with money . . .

"Young man, remember the saying: A physician can only cure diseases meant to be cured; the Buddha can only save those meant to be saved."

The last bit of hope died in Tianming, and his heart was at peace. That afternoon, he filled out an application for euthanasia.

He handed the application to his attending physician, Dr. Zhang. Zhang seemed to suffer some internal, moral conflict, and did not meet Tianming's gaze. He did say to Tianming that he might as well stop the chemo sessions; there was no point for him to continue to suffer.

The only matter that Tianming still had to take care of was deciding how to spend the money from Wen. The "right" thing to do would have been to give it to his father, and then let him distribute it to the rest of the family. But that was the same as handing the money to his sister, and Tianming didn't want to do that. He was already going to die, just as she wanted; he didn't feel he owed her any more.

He tried to see if he had any unfulfilled dreams. It would be nice to take a trip around the world on some luxury cruise ship . . . but his body wasn't up for it, and he didn't have much time left. That was too bad. He would have liked to lie on a sun-drenched deck and review his life as he gazed at the hypnotic sea. Or he could step onto the shores of some strange country on a drizzly day, sit next to a little lake and toss wet pebbles onto a surface full of ripples. . . .

Once again, he was thinking of Cheng Xin. These days, he thought of her more and more.

That night, Tianming saw a news report on TV:

> The twelfth session of the UN Planetary Defense Council has adopted Resolution 479, initiating the Stars Our Destination Project. A committee formed from the UN Development Program, the UN Committee on Natural Resources, and UNESCO is authorized to implement the project immediately.

The official Chinese website for the Stars Our Destination Project begins operation this afternoon. According to an official at the UNDP resident representative office in Beijing, the Project will accept bids from individuals and enterprises, but will not consider bids from nongovernmental organizations. . . .

Tianming got up and told his nurse that he wanted to take a walk. But as it was already after lights out, the nurse refused to let him leave. He returned to his dark room, pulled open the curtains, and lifted the window. The new patient in Lao Li's old bed grumbled.

Tianming looked out. The lights of the city cast a haze over the night sky, but it was still possible to pick out a few silvery specks.

He knew what he wanted to do with his money: He was going to buy Cheng Xin a star.

Excerpt from *A Past Outside of Time*
Infantilism at the Start
of the Crisis

Many of the events during the first twenty years of the Crisis Era were incomprehensible to those who came before and those who came after; historians summarized them under the heading of "Crisis Infantilism."

It was commonly thought that Infantilism was a response to an unprecedented threat to the entirety of civilization. That might have been true for individuals, but it was too simple an explanation when applied to humanity as a whole.

The Trisolar Crisis's impact on society was far deeper than people had imagined at first. To give some imperfect analogies: In terms of biology, it was equivalent to the moment when the ancestors of mammals climbed from the ocean onto land; in terms of religion, it was akin to when Adam and Eve were banished from Eden; in terms of history and sociology . . . there are no suitable analogies, even imperfect ones. Compared to the Trisolar Crisis, everything heretofore experienced by human civilization was nothing. The Crisis shook the very foundation of culture, politics, religion, and economics. Although the impact reached the deepest core of civilization, its influence manifested most quickly at the surface. The root cause for Crisis Infantilism may well be found in the interaction between these manifestations and the tremendous inertia of human society's inherent conservatism.

The classic examples of Crisis Infantilism were the Wallfacer Project and the Stars Our Destination Project, both international efforts within the framework of the United Nations—initiatives that soon became incomprehensible to anyone from outside that period. The Wallfacer Project changed history, and its influence so permeated the course of civilization that it must be discussed in another chapter. The same elements that led to the birth of the grand

Wallfacer Project simultaneously conceived the Stars Our Destination Project. That project, on the other hand, quickly faded away after launch and was never heard from again.

There were two main motivations for the Stars Our Destination Project: first, to increase the power of the UN at the beginning of the Crisis; second, the genesis and popularity of Escapism.

The Trisolar Crisis was the first time that all of humanity faced a common enemy, and it was only natural that many placed their hopes in the UN. Even conservatives agreed that the UN ought to be completely reformed and given more power and more resources. Radicals and idealists pushed for an Earth Union and for making the UN into a world government.

Smaller countries, in particular, favored elevating the status of the UN because they saw the Crisis as an opportunity to get more technological and economic aid. The great powers, on the other hand, responded to this coolly. In actuality, the great powers all invested heavily in space defense after the Crisis. In part, this was because they realized that contribution to space defense would become the foundation for national strength and political status in future international relations; it was also because they had always wanted to invest in such large-scale basic research, but the domestic demands of their citizenry and constraints imposed by international politics had made such efforts impractical in the past. In a sense, the Trisolar Crisis provided the leaders of the great powers with an opportunity similar to the opportunity given to Kennedy by the Cold War—similar, but a couple of orders of magnitude greater. While all the great powers were reluctant to place their efforts under the aegis of the United Nations, due to the rising tide of calls for true globalization, they were forced to cede to the UN some symbolic, political commitments that they had no intention of honoring. The common space defense system advocated by the UN, for example, received little substantive support from the great powers.

In the history of the early Crisis Era, UN Secretary General Say was a key figure. She believed that the time for a new UN had arrived and advocated transforming the institution from what was little more than a meeting place for the great powers and an international forum, into an independent political body with the power to genuinely direct the construction of the Solar System's defenses.

To achieve this goal, the UN needed sufficient resources, a requirement that appeared impossible to meet given the realities of international relations. The Stars Our Destination Project was an attempt by Say to acquire such resources for the UN. No matter the results, the very attempt was a testament to her political intelligence and imagination.

The basis for the project lay in the Space Convention, which was a product of pre-Crisis politics. Based on the principles enacted in the Law of the Sea Convention and the Antarctic Treaty, the Space Convention was negotiated and drafted over a long period of time. But the pre-Crisis Space Convention was limited to resources within the Kuiper Belt; the Trisolar Crisis forced the nations of the world to set their sights farther out.

Since humans had not even been able to set foot on Mars, any discussion of outer space was meaningless, at least prior to the expiration date of the Space Convention fifty years after it was drafted. But the great powers viewed the Convention as the perfect venue for political theater and amended it with provisions regarding resources outside the Solar System. The amendment provided that the development of natural resources outside the Kuiper Belt, and other economic activities regarding them, had to take place under the auspices of the United Nations. The amendment went into excruciating detail to define "natural resources," but, basically, the phrase referred to resources not already occupied by nonhuman civilizations. This treaty also offered the first international law definition for "civilization." Historically, this document was referred to as the Crisis Amendment.

The second motivation for the Stars Our Destination Project was Escapism. At the time, the Escapist movement was still in its early stages, and its consequences were not yet apparent, such that many still considered it a valid choice for humanity in crisis. Under such conditions, other stars, especially stars with their own planets, became valuable.

The initial resolution proposing the Stars Our Destination Project would have the UN auction off the rights to certain stars and their planets. The intended bidders were states, businesses, NGOs, and individuals, and the proceeds from the auction would be used to fund the UN's basic research into a Solar System defense system. Secretary General Say explained that the universe had an abundance of stars. There were more than three hundred thousand stars within one hundred light-years of the Solar System, and more than ten million within one thousand light-years. A conservative estimate suggested that at least one-tenth of these stars had planets. Auctioning off a small proportion of these would not affect the future of space development much.

This unusual UN resolution attracted wide interest and attention. The permanent members of the Planetary Defense Council (PDC) mulled it over, but each decided that adopting it would not lead to adverse consequences in the foreseeable future. On the other hand, voting against it would incur a heavy cost under the prevailing international political climate. Still, debates and compromises followed, and the final version of the resolution that passed was limited to stars more than one hundred light-years away.

The project was halted almost as soon as it began for a simple reason: No one bought the stars. In total, only seventeen stars were auctioned off, and all at the minimum reserve price. The UN earned a grand total of only about forty million dollars.

None of the winning bidders ever revealed themselves. People speculated on why they spent so much money to buy a piece of useless paper—even if the paper was supposed to be a binding legal instrument. Maybe it felt cool to own another world, but what was the point when you could see but not touch it? Indeed, some of the stars were not even visible with the naked eye.

Say never thought of the project as a failure. She claimed that the results were just as she predicted. Fundamentally, the Stars Our Destination Project was a political proclamation by the UN.

The Stars Our Destination Project was quickly forgotten. It was a classic example of the irregular behavior of human society at the beginning of the Crisis.

Crisis Era, Year 4
Yun Tianming

The day after making his decision to buy Cheng Xin a star, Yun Tianming called the number listed on the website for the Chinese office of the Stars Our Destination Project.

Then he called Hu Wen to get some basic information about Cheng Xin: contact address, national ID number, and so forth. He was prepared for any number of reactions from Wen in response to his request—sarcasm, pity, exclamation. Instead, after a long silence, all he heard was a soft sigh.

"No problem," Wen said. "But she's probably not in China right now."

"Just don't tell her I'm the one asking."

"Don't worry. I won't ask her directly."

The next day, Tianming got a text from Wen with all the information he had asked for, but nothing about Cheng Xin's employment. Wen explained that no one knew where Cheng Xin had gone after she left the Academy of Spaceflight Technology last year. Tianming saw that there were two mailing addresses for her: one in Shanghai and another in New York.

That afternoon, Tianming asked Dr. Zhang to give him permission to leave the hospital and run an errand. The doctor wanted to come with Tianming, but he insisted on going alone.

Tianming took a taxi and arrived at UNESCO's Beijing office. After the Crisis, every UN office in Beijing had expanded rapidly, and UNESCO now took up most of an office building outside of the Fourth Ring Road.

A giant star map greeted Tianming as he entered the spacious office of the Stars Our Destination Project. Silver lines connected the stars in constellations against a pitch-black background. Tianming saw that the map was displayed on a high-definition screen, and a computer nearby allowed for zooming and searching. The office was empty except for a receptionist.

Tianming introduced himself, and the receptionist excitedly went away and returned with a blond woman.

"This is the director of UNESCO Beijing," the receptionist explained. "And also one of the people responsible for implementing the Stars Our Destination Project in the Asia-Pacific region."

The director appeared very pleased to see Tianming as well. She held Tianming's hand and told him, in fluent Chinese, that he was the first Chinese individual to express an interest in buying a star. She would have preferred a ceremony to generate as much media coverage as possible, but she refrained out of respect for his wish for privacy. She seemed quite sorry to lose out on a wonderful opportunity to publicize the project.

Don't worry, Tianming thought. *No other Chinese will be as dumb as me.*

A middle-aged, well-dressed man wearing glasses came in. The director introduced him as Dr. He, a researcher at the Beijing Observatory. The astronomer would help Tianming with the details of his purchase. After the director left, Dr. He asked Tianming to sit down, and called for tea to be served.

"Are you feeling all right?" he asked Tianming.

Tianming knew that he didn't exactly look healthy. But after stopping chemo—which had been like undergoing torture—he felt much better, almost as if he'd gotten a new lease on life. Ignoring Dr. He's question, he repeated the request he had already made on the phone.

"I want to buy a star as a gift. The title to the star should be registered under the name of the recipient. I won't provide any personal information about myself, and I want my identity kept secret from her."

"No problem at all. Do you have an idea of what kind of star you want to buy?"

"As close to Earth as possible. One with planets. Ideally, Earthlike planets," Tianming said as he gazed at the star map.

Dr. He shook his head. "Based on the figure you gave me, that's impossible. The starting prices for stars meeting those criteria are much too high. You can only buy a star without planets, and it won't be very close. Let me tell you something: The amount of money you are offering is too low even for bare stars. But after your call yesterday, in consideration of the fact that you're the first person in China to express an interest, we decided to lower the starting bid on one of the stars to what you offered." He moved the mouse to magnify a region of the star map. "It's this one. Say yes and it's yours."

"How far away is it?"

"It's about two hundred eighty-six point five light-years from here."

"That's too far."

Dr. He laughed. "I can tell you're not completely ignorant about astronomy. Think about it: Does it really make a difference if it's two hundred eighty-six light-years or two hundred eighty-six billion light-years?"

Tianming thought about it. The astronomer was right. It made no difference.

"There's a very big advantage to this star," Dr. He said. "It's visible with the naked eye. In my opinion, aesthetics matters the most when you're buying a star. It's much better to possess a faraway star that you can see than a nearby star that you can't. It's much better to own a bare star that you can see than a star with planets that you can't. In the end, all we can do is look at it. Am I right?"

Tianming nodded. *Cheng Xin can see the star. That's good.*

"What's it called?"

"The star was first cataloged by Tycho Brahe hundreds of years ago, but it never acquired a common name. All it has is a number." Dr. He moved the mouse pointer over the glowing dot, and a string of letters and numbers appeared next to it: DX3906. Then, patiently, the astronomer explained to Tianming the meaning of the numbers and letters, the star's type, absolute and apparent magnitudes, location in the main sequence, and so on.

The paperwork for the purchase didn't take long. Two notaries worked with Dr. He to make sure everything was proper. Then the director appeared again, along with two officials from the UN Development Program and the UN Committee on Natural Resources. The receptionist brought a bottle of champagne and everyone celebrated.

The director declared that the title to DX3906 was now vested in Cheng Xin, and she presented Tianming with an expensive-looking black leather folder.

"Your star."

After the officials left, Dr. He turned to Tianming. "Don't answer me if you aren't comfortable, but I'm guessing you bought the star for a girl?"

Tianming hesitated for a moment, but then nodded.

"Lucky girl!" Dr. He sighed. "It's nice to be rich."

"Oh, please!" said the receptionist. She stuck her tongue out at Dr. He. "Rich? Even if you had thirty billion yuan, would you buy a star for your girlfriend? Ha! I haven't forgotten what you said two days ago."

Dr. He looked rather embarrassed. In fact, he was worried that she was going to blurt out his opinion of the Stars Our Destination Project: *This trick the UN is pulling was already tried by a bunch of scammers more than ten years ago. Back then they sold land on the moon and Mars. It would be a miracle if anyone falls for it again!*

Fortunately, the receptionist went on in a different vein. "This isn't just about money. It's about *romance*. Romance! Do you even understand?"

Throughout Tianming's purchasing process, the young woman had stolen glances at him from time to time, as though he were a figure from a fairy tale. Her expression had at first been curious, then awed and admiring. Finally, as the leather folder containing the deed to the star was handed over, her face filled with envy.

Dr. He tried to change the subject. "We'll send the formal documents to the recipient as soon as possible. Based on your instructions, we won't reveal any information about you. Well, even if we wanted to, we can't—look, I don't even know your name!" He stood up and looked out the window. It was already dark. "Next, I can bring you to see your star—sorry, I meant the star you bought for her."

"Can we see it from the top of the building?"

"No. There's too much light pollution inside the city. We have to go far into the suburbs. If you aren't feeling well, we can pick another day."

"Let's go now. I really want to see it."

They drove for more than two hours, until the glowing sea that was Beijing was far behind them. To avoid the lamps of passing cars, Dr. He drove off the road into a field. Then he turned off the headlights and they got out of the car. In the late-autumn sky, the stars were especially bright.

"You see the Big Dipper? Imagine a diagonal across the quadrilateral formed by the four stars, and extend it. That's right, in that direction. Can you see those three stars that form a flat triangle? Draw a line from the apex, perpendicular to the base, and keep extending it. Can you see it? Right there. That's your star—the star you gave her."

Tianming pointed to two stars in succession, but Dr. He said neither was right. "It's between those two, but a bit to the south. The apparent magnitude is five point five. Normally, you have to be trained to find it. But the weather tonight is ideal, so you should be able to see it. Try this: Don't look for it directly; move your gaze a bit to the side. Your peripheral vision tends to be more sensitive to faint light. After you find it, then you can move your gaze back. . . ."

With Dr. He's help, Tianming finally saw DX3906. It was very faint, and he had to find it again it each time his attention wavered. Although people commonly thought of the stars as silvery, careful observation revealed that they each had different colors. DX3906 was dark red.

Dr. He promised to give him some materials to help Tianming find the star in different seasons. "You are lucky, as lucky as the girl who received your gift," said Dr. He.

"I don't think I'd call myself fortunate. I'm about to die."

Dr. He seemed unsurprised by this revelation. He lit a cigarette and smoked it in silence. After a while, he said, "Even so, I think you're blessed. Most people don't cast a glance at the universe beyond the world we live in until the day they die."

Tianming looked at Dr. He for a moment, then he looked back into the sky and found DX3906 easily. The smoke from Dr. He's cigarette drifted before his eyes, and the faint star flickered through the veil. *By the time she sees it, I'll be gone from this world.*

Of course, the star he saw and the star she would see were only an image from 286 years ago. The faint beam of light had to cross three centuries to meet their retinas. Another 286 years would have to pass before the light from the star at this moment would reach the Earth. By then, Cheng Xin would long have turned to dust.

What will her life be like? Maybe she'll remember that in the sea of stars, there's one that belongs to her.

This would be Tianming's last day.

He wanted to note something special about it, but there was nothing. He woke up at seven, as usual; a shaft of sunlight fell against its habitual spot on the wall; the weather was not great, but also not too bad; the sky was the same grayish blue; the oak tree in front of the window was bare (instead of, say, hanging on to a lone, symbolic leaf). Even his breakfast was the same.

This was a day like any other day in his life of twenty-eight years, eleven months, and six days.

Like Lao Li, Tianming didn't inform his family of his decision. He did try to write a note that could be given to his father after his procedure, but he gave up because he couldn't think of what to say.

At ten, he walked into the euthanasia room by himself, as calmly as if he were headed to his daily examination. He was the fourth person in the city to conduct the procedure, so there wasn't much media interest. Only five people were in the room: two notaries, a director, a nurse, and an executive from the hospital. Dr. Zhang wasn't there.

He could go in peace.

Pursuant to his request, the room was undecorated. All around him were the plain white walls of a normal hospital room. He felt comfortable.

He explained to the director that he was familiar with the procedure and did not need him. The director nodded and went to the other side of the glass wall. The notaries finished their business with him, then left him alone with the nurse. The nurse no longer showed the anxiety and fear that she had had to overcome the first time. As she pierced his vein with the needle, her motion was steady and gentle. Tianming felt a strange bond with the nurse: after all, she was the last person who would be with him in this world. He wished he knew who had delivered him when he was born twenty-nine years ago. That delivery doctor and this nurse belonged to the small number of people who had genuinely tried to help him during his life. He wanted to thank them.

"Thank you."

The nurse smiled at him and left, her footsteps as silent as a cat's.

Do you wish to terminate your life? For yes, select 5. For no, select 0.

He had been born to an intellectual family, but his parents lacked political savvy and social cunning, and they had not been successful in their lives. Though they did not live the life of elites, they had insisted on giving Tianming an education they thought befit an elite. He was only permitted to read classic books and listen to classical music; the friends he tried to make had to be the kind that his parents deemed to be from cultured, refined families. They told Tianming that the people around them were vulgar, their concerns common. In contrast, their own tastes were far superior.

In primary school, Tianming had managed to make a few friends, but he never invited them home to play. He knew that his parents would not allow him to be friends with such "vulgar" children. By the time he was in middle school, his parents' intensified push for his elite education made him into a complete loner. That was also when his parents divorced, after his father met a young woman who sold insurance. His mother then married a wealthy general contractor.

Thus, both of his parents ended up with the kind of "vulgar" people they had told Tianming to stay away from, and finally realized that they had no moral authority to impose the kind of education they wanted on him. But what had already been done to Tianming was enough. He could not escape his up-bringing, which was like a set of spring-loaded handcuffs: The more he struggled to free himself, the tighter they bound him. Throughout his high school years, he became more and more alone, more and more sensitive, grew further apart from others.

All his memories of his childhood and youth were gray.

He pressed 5.

Do you wish to terminate your life? For yes, select 2. For no, select 0.

He had imagined that college would be a frightening place: a new, strange environment; a new, strange crowd; more things for him to struggle to adjust to. And when he first entered college, everything pretty much matched his expectations.

Until he met Cheng Xin.

Tianming had been attracted to girls before, but not like this. He felt everything around him, which had been cold and strange, become suffused with warm sunlight. At first, he didn't understand where the light had come from. It was like a sun seen through a heavy veil of clouds, only appearing to observers as a faint disk. It was only when it disappeared that people realized that it was the source of all light during the day. Tianming's sun disappeared at the start of the weeklong holiday around National Day, when Cheng Xin left school to visit home. Tianming felt everything around him grow dim and gray.

It was almost certain that more than one boy felt this way about Cheng Xin. But he didn't suffer the way other boys did, because he had no hope for his yearning. He knew that girls did not like his aloofness, his sensitivity. All he could do was to look at her from afar, bathing in the warm light she gave off, quietly appreciating the beauty of spring.

Initially, Cheng Xin gave Tianming the impression of being taciturn. Beautiful women were rarely reticent, but she wasn't an ice queen. She said little, but she listened, really listened. When she conversed with someone, her focused, calm gaze told the speaker that they were important to her.

Cheng Xin was different from the pretty girls who Tianming had gone to high school with. She didn't ignore his existence. Every time she saw him, she would smile and say hi. A few times, when classmates planned outings and parties, the organizers—intentionally or otherwise—forgot about Tianming. But Cheng Xin would find him and invite him. Later, she became the first among his classmates to call him just "Tianming," without using his surname. In their interactions—limited though they were—the deepest impression Cheng Xin left in Tianming's heart was the feeling that she was the only one who understood his vulnerabilities and seemed to care about the pain that he might suffer.

But Tianming never made more of it than what it was. It was just as Hu Wen said: Cheng Xin was nice to everyone.

One event in particular stood out in Tianming's mind: He and some classmates were hiking up a small mountain. Cheng Xin suddenly stopped, bent down, and picked up something from the stone steps of the trail. Tianming saw that it was an ugly caterpillar, soft and moist, wriggling against her pale fingers. Another girl next to her cried out: *That's disgusting! Why are you touching it?* But Cheng Xin carefully deposited the caterpillar in the grass next to the trail. *It will get stepped on.*

In truth, Tianming had had very few conversations with Cheng Xin. In four years of college, he could remember talking with her one on one just a couple of times.

It was a cool, early summer night. Tianming had climbed to the deck on top of the library, his favorite place. Few students came here, and he could be alone with his thoughts. The night sky was clear after a summer rainstorm. Even the Milky Way, which normally wasn't visible, shone in the sky.

"It really looks like a road made of milk!"[2]

Tianming looked over at the speaker. A breeze stirred Cheng Xin's hair, reminding him of his dream. Then he and Cheng Xin gazed up at the galaxy together.

"So many stars. It looks like a fog," Tianming said.

Cheng Xin turned to him and pointed at the campus and city below them. "It's really beautiful down there, too. Remember, we live here, not in the faraway galaxy."

"But aren't we studying to be aerospace engineers? Our goal is to leave the Earth."

"That's so that we may make life here better, not abandon the planet."

Tianming understood that Cheng Xin had meant to gently point out his own aloofness and solitude. But he had no response. This was the closest he had ever been to her. Maybe it was his imagination, but he thought he could

---

[2] *Translator's Note:* Some Anglophone readers may get the impression here that the Chinese name for our galaxy is also "Milky Way." It is not. The actual Chinese name for the galaxy is *Yinhe*, or "Silver River." All Chinese students, however, study English for years.

feel the warmth from her body. He wished the breeze would shift direction so a few strands of her hair would brush against his face.

Four years of undergraduate life came to an end. Tianming failed to get into graduate school, but Cheng Xin easily got accepted into the graduate program at their university. She went home for the summer after graduation, but Tianming lingered on campus. His only goal was to see her again at the start of the new school year. Since he wasn't allowed to stay in the dorms, he rented a room nearby and tried to find a job in the city. He sent out countless copies of his résumé and went to interview after interview, but nothing resulted. Before he knew it, the summer was over.

Tianming returned to campus, but couldn't find Cheng Xin. He carefully made some inquiries, and found out that she and her advisor had gone to the school's graduate institute at the Academy of Spaceflight Technology in Shanghai, where she would finish her graduate studies. That was also the day Tianming finally found a job at a new company founded for civil aerospace technology transfer that desperately needed qualified engineers.

Just like that, Tianming's sun left him. With a wintery heart, he entered real life in society.

He pressed 2.

Do you wish to terminate your life? For yes, select 4. For no, select 0.

Right after he started working, he had been happy for a while. He discovered that, compared to his competitive peers in school, people in the business world were far more tolerant and easier to deal with. He even thought his days of being isolated and aloof were over. But after winding up on the losing end of a few office political maneuvers and bad deals, he understood the cruelties of the real world, and became nostalgic for campus life. Once again, he retreated into his shell and set himself apart from the crowd. Of course, the consequences for his career were disastrous. Even in a state-owned enterprise like his company, competition was intense. If you kept to yourself, you had no chance of advancement. Year after year, he fell farther and farther behind.

During that time, Tianming dated two women, but the relationships fizzled quickly. It wasn't that Cheng Xin already occupied his heart: For him, she would always be the sun behind a veil of clouds. All he wanted was to look at her, to feel her light and warmth. He dared not dream of taking a step toward her. He never even sought out news about her. He guessed, based on her intelligence, that she would go for a Ph.D., but he made no conjectures about her personal life. The main barrier between him and women was his own withdrawn personality. He struggled to build his own life, but it was too difficult.

Fundamentally, Tianming was not suited to live in society, nor out of it. He lacked the ability to thrive in society, but also the resources to ignore it. All he could do was hang on to the edge, suffering. He had no idea where he was headed in life.

But then, he saw the end of the road.

He pressed 4.

Do you wish to terminate your life? For yes, select 1. For no, select 0.

By the time his lung cancer was discovered, it was already late stage. Maybe there had been an earlier misdiagnosis. Lung cancer was one of those cancers that spread fast in the body, so he didn't have much time left.

As he left the hospital, he wasn't scared. The only emotion he felt was loneliness. His alienation had been building up, but had been held back by an invisible dam. It was a kind of equilibrium that he could endure. But now, the dam had collapsed, and the weight of years of accumulated loneliness overwhelmed him like a dark ocean. He could not bear it.

He wanted to see Cheng Xin.

Without hesitation, he bought a plane ticket and flew to Shanghai that afternoon. By the time his taxi arrived at his destination, his fervor had cooled somewhat. He told himself that, as someone about to die, he shouldn't bother her. He wouldn't even let her know of his presence. He just wanted to look at her once from afar, like a drowning man struggling to take one last breath before sinking down forever.

Standing in front of the gate to the Academy of Spaceflight Technology, he calmed down even more. He saw how irrational his own actions of the past few hours had been. Even if Cheng Xin had gone on to obtain a Ph.D., she would be finished with her studies by now, and she might not even be working here. He spoke to the guard in front of the door and found out that there were more than twenty thousand people working at the academy, and he had to know the exact department if he wanted to find someone. He had lost touch with his classmates, and had no more information to give the guard.

He felt weak and out of breath, and he sat down a little ways from the gate.

It was still possible that Cheng Xin did work here. It was almost the end of the workday, and if he waited here, he might see her.

The gate to the academy complex was very wide. Large golden characters engraved into the short black wall next to it gave the formal name for the place, which had expanded greatly since its early days. Wouldn't such a large complex have more than one entrance? With an effort, he got up and asked the guard again. Indeed, there were four more entrances.

Slowly, he walked back to his place, sat down, and waited. He had no other choice.

The odds were against him: Cheng Xin would still have to be working here after graduation; to be at the office, instead of away on business; to pick this door, as opposed to four others, when she got out of work.

This moment resembled the rest of his life: a dedicated watch for a slim, slim ray of hope.

It was the end of the workday. People began to depart the complex: some walking, some on bikes, some in cars. The stream of people and vehicles grew, and then shrank. After an hour, only a few stragglers remained.

Cheng Xin never passed.

He was certain that he would not have missed her, even if she drove. That meant that she was no longer working here, or maybe she hadn't come to work today, or maybe she had used another entrance.

The setting sun stretched out the shadows of buildings and trees, like numerous arms extended toward him in pity.

He remained where he was until it was completely dark. He didn't remember how he managed to hail a taxi to bring him to the airport, how he flew back to his city, how he returned to his company-owned single dormitory.

He felt he was already dead.

He pressed 1.

Do you wish to terminate your life? This is your last prompt. For yes, select 3. For no, select 0.

What would he want as his epitaph? He wasn't even sure he would get a tomb. It was expensive to buy a burial plot near Beijing. Even if his father wanted to buy him one, his sister would probably disagree—she was still *alive*, and she didn't even own a home! Most likely, his ashes would be stored in a cubby in the wall at Babaoshan People's Cemetery. But if he were to have a tombstone, he would like it to say:

He came; he loved; he gave her a star; he left.

He pressed 3.

———

There was a commotion on the other side of the glass. Just as Tianming was pressing the mouse button, the door to the euthanasia room flew open and a group of people rushed in.

In the lead was the director, who dashed for the switch that would turn off the automatic injector. The hospital executive that followed him went and yanked the injector's power cord out of the wall. After them came the nurse, who pulled the tube attached to the needle in Tianming's arm so hard that he winced from the sharp pain as the needle was jerked out.

Everyone gathered around the tube to examine it.

"That was close! None of the drugs went into him," someone said.

Then the nurse began to bandage up Tianming's bleeding left arm.

Only one person stood outside the door to the euthanasia room.

But for Tianming, the whole world seemed brighter: Cheng Xin.

Tianming could feel the dampness on his chest—Cheng Xin's tears had soaked through his clothes.

When he first saw her, he thought she hadn't changed at all. But now he noticed that her hair was shorter—it no longer draped over her shoulders, but stopped at her neck. The ends curled prettily. He still didn't have the courage to reach out and touch the hair that he had long yearned for.

I'm really useless. But he felt like he was in heaven.

The silence seemed like the peace of paradise, and Tianming wanted that silence to last. *You can't save me,* he said to her in his mind. *I will listen to you and not seek euthanasia. But I'm going to end up in the same place anyway. I hope you take the star I gave you and find happiness.*

Cheng Xin seemed to hear this inner speech. She lifted her head. It was the first time their eyes were this close, closer than he had ever dared to dream. Her eyes, made even more beautiful by her tears, broke his heart.

But when she finally spoke, what she said was not at all what he expected.

"Tianming, did you know that the euthanasia law was passed specifically for you?"

Crisis Era, Years 1—4
Cheng Xin

████████

The start of the Trisolar Crisis coincided with Cheng Xin's completion of her graduate studies, and she was selected to join the task force working on the design of the propulsion system for the next generation of Long March rockets. To others, this seemed like the perfect job: important and high profile.

But Cheng Xin had lost the enthusiasm for her chosen profession. Gradually, she had come to see chemical rockets as similar to the giant smokestacks of the early Industrial Age. Poets back then had praised those forests of smokestacks, thinking that they were the same as industrial civilization. People now praised rockets the same way, thinking they represented the Space Age. But if humanity relied on chemical rockets, they might never become a true spacefaring race.

The Trisolar Crisis simply highlighted this fact. Trying to build a Solar System defense system based on chemical rockets was pure lunacy. Cheng Xin had made an effort to keep her options open by picking some classes in nuclear propulsion. After the Crisis, all aspects of work within the aerospace system accelerated, and even the long-delayed first-generation space plane project was given the go-ahead. Her task force was also charged with designing the prototype for the engines that would be used by the plane in spaceflight. Professionally, Cheng Xin's future seemed bright: Her abilities were recognized, and in China's aerospace system, most chief engineers began their careers in propulsion design. But since she believed chemical rocketry was yesterday's technology, she didn't think she would get very far in the long term. Heading in the wrong direction was worse than doing nothing at all, but her job demanded her complete focus and attention. She was deeply frustrated.

Then came an opportunity for her to leave chemical rockets behind. The

United Nations began to create all sorts of agencies related to planetary defense. Unlike UN agencies from the past, these new agencies reported directly
to the PDC, and were staffed by experts from various nations. The Chinese aerospace system sent many people to these agencies. A high-level official offered
Cheng Xin a new position: Aide to the director of the Technology Planning
Center for the PDC Strategic Intelligence Agency. Humanity's intelligence-
gathering work against the Trisolarans had so far focused on the ETO, but the
PDC Strategic Intelligence Agency, or PIA, would focus their efforts directly on
the Trisolaran Fleet and the home world of Trisolaris itself. They needed people
with strong backgrounds in the technical aspects of aerospace technology.

Cheng Xin took the job without hesitation.

The PIA Headquarters was located in an old six-story building not far from the
UN Headquarters. Dating from the end of the eighteenth century, the building was thick and well-built, like a solid block of granite. When Cheng Xin entered it for the first time after her trans-Pacific flight, she felt a chill, as though
entering a castle. The place wasn't at all what she had expected from an intelligence agency for the whole world; it reminded her more of a place where
byzantine plots were hatched through whispers.

The building was mostly empty; she was among the first to report for duty.
In an office full of unassembled furniture and just-unsealed cardboard boxes,
she met her boss, PIA's Technology Planning Center director.

Mikhail Vadimov was in his forties, muscular, tall, and spoke English with
a heavy Russian accent. It took a few moments before Cheng Xin even realized that he was speaking English. He sat on a cardboard box and complained
to her that he had worked in the aerospace industry for more than a dozen
years and had no need for any technical assistance. Every country was eager to
fill the PIA with its own people, but much less willing to give cold, hard cash.
Then he seemed to realize that he was talking to a hopeful young woman
who was growing rather dejected from his speech, and tried to comfort her by
saying: "If this agency manages to make history—a big possibility, even if it
probably won't be very good history—we two will be remembered as the first
to show up!"

Cheng Xin was cheered by the fact that she and her boss had both worked
in aerospace. She asked Vadimov what he had worked on. He carelessly mentioned a stint on the Buran spacecraft; then that he'd served as the executive
chief designer for a certain cargo-carrying spaceship; but after that, his expla-

nations turned vague. He claimed that he had done a couple of years in diplomacy, then entered "some department" that "did the same kinds of things we do now."

"It's best if you don't probe too much into the employment histories of your future colleagues, okay?" Vadimov said. "The chief is here also. His office is upstairs. You should swing by and say hi, but don't take up too much of his time."

As soon as Cheng Xin walked into the PIA chief's spacious office, she was greeted by the strong smell of cigar smoke. A large painting hung on the wall. A leaden sky and the dim, snow-covered ground took up most of the painting; in the distance, where the clouds met the snow, a few dark shapes lurked. A closer examination revealed them to be dirty buildings, most of them one-story clapboard houses mixed with a few European-style houses with two or three stories. Based on the shape of the river in the foreground and other hints in the geography, this was a portrait of New York at the beginning of the eighteenth century. The overwhelming impression given off by the painting was coldness, which Cheng Xin thought fit the person sitting under the painting rather well.

Next to the large painting was a smaller picture. The main subject in the painting was an ancient sword with a golden cross guard and a bright, shining blade, held in a hand enclosed in bronze gauntlets—only the forearm was shown. The hand was lifting the sword to pick up a wreath woven from red, white, and yellow flowers floating over the water. In contrast to the larger painting, this picture was bright and colorful, but it nonetheless radiated eeriness. Cheng Xin noticed that bloodstains covered the white flowers in the wreath.

PIA Chief Thomas Wade, an American, was far younger than Cheng Xin had expected—he looked younger than Vadimov. He was also more handsome, with very classical features. Later, she would conclude that the classical appearance came mostly from Wade's expressionless face, like a cold, lifeless statue transplanted out of the cold painting behind him. Wade didn't look busy—the desk in front of him was completely empty, with no sign of a computer or paper documents. He glanced up as she entered, but returned to contemplating the cigar in his hand almost right away.

Cheng Xin introduced herself and expressed her pleasure at having a chance to study from him, and continued until Wade lifted his eyes to look at her.

Cheng Xin thought she saw exhaustion and laziness in those eyes, but there was also something deeper, something sharp that made her uncomfortable. A smile appeared on Wade's face, like water seeping out of a crack in the frozen surface of a river; there was no real warmth, and it didn't relax her.

She tried to respond with a smile of her own, but the first words out of Wade's mouth froze her face and entire body. "Would you sell your mother to a whorehouse?" Cheng Xin shook her head no, but she wasn't even trying to respond to the question; she was terrified that she had not understood what he said. But Wade waved at her with his cigar. "Thanks. Go do what needs to get done."

After she told Vadimov what had happened, Vadimov laughed. "That's just a line that used to be popular in our . . . trade. I heard it started back during the Second World War. Veterans would use it as a joke on novices. The point is: Our profession is the only one on Earth where lies and betrayal are at the very heart of what we do. We have to be . . . flexible when it comes to commonly accepted ethical norms. PIA is formed from two groups of people: Some are technical experts like you; others are veterans of the various intelligence agencies in the world. These two groups have different ways of thinking and acting. It's a good thing that I'm familiar with both and can help you adjust to the other."

"But our enemy is Trisolaris. This is nothing like traditional intelligence."

"Some things are constant."

Over the next few days, other new PIA staff members reported for duty. Most of them came from countries that were permanent members of the PDC.

They were polite to each other, but there was no trust. The technical experts kept to themselves and acted as if they were on guard against theft every minute. The intelligence veterans were gregarious and friendly—but they were constantly on the lookout for something to steal.

It was just like Vadimov had predicted: These people were far more interested in spying on each other than gathering intelligence on Trisolaris.

Two days after Cheng Xin's arrival, PIA held its first all-hands meeting, even though not everyone had shown up yet. Other than PIA Chief Wade, there were three assistant chiefs: one from China, one from France, and one from the United Kingdom.

Assistant Chief Yu Weiming spoke first. Cheng Xin had no idea what kind of work he had done in China—and he had the sort of face that took multiple meetings to remember what he looked like. Fortunately, he didn't engage in the habit—common among Chinese bureaucrats—of giving long, meandering speeches. Though he was just repeating platitudes about the PIA's mission, at least he spoke succinctly.

Assistant Chief Yu said that he understood that everyone in the PIA was sent by their own country, and so they had dual loyalties. PIA didn't demand, and didn't even hope, that they would place their loyalty to the agency above their duties to their own nations. However, since the PIA's task was the protection of the entire human race, he hoped that everyone present would at least try to balance the two appropriately. Considering that the PIA was going to work directly against the Trisolaran threat, they ought to become the most united of the new agencies.

While Assistant Chief Yu was giving this speech, Cheng Xin noticed that Wade was kicking the table legs and slowly maneuvering his chair away from the conference table as though he didn't want to be there. Later, whenever anyone asked him to say a few words, he shook his head and refused.

Finally, after everyone who wanted to make a speech had done so, he spoke. Pointing at the pile of boxes and fresh office supplies in the meeting room, he said, "I'd like the rest of you to take care of these matters on your own." Apparently, he was referring to the administrative details of getting the agency up and running. "Please don't take up my time or theirs"—here he pointed at Vadimov and his staff. "I need everyone in the Technology Planning Center with experience in spaceflight engineering to stay. The rest of you are dismissed."

About a dozen people remained in the now much less crowded conference room. As soon as the heavy oak doors closed, Wade dropped his bomb. "The PIA must launch a spy probe at the Trisolaran Fleet."

The stunned staff members looked at each other. Cheng Xin was surprised as well. She had certainly hoped to get to substantive technical work quickly, but she hadn't expected such directness or speed. Considering that the PIA had just been formed and there were, as yet, no national or regional branches, it seemed ill-equipped to take on big projects. But the real shocker was the boldness of Wade's proposal: The technical challenges and other barriers seemed insurmountable.

"What are the specific requirements?" asked Vadimov. He was the only one who seemed to take Wade's announcement in stride.

"I've consulted with the delegates of the permanent members of the PDC in private, but the idea hasn't yet been formally presented. Based on what I know, the PDC members are most interested in one specific requirement— and this is something that they won't compromise on: The probe must achieve one percent of lightspeed. The permanent members of the PDC have different ideas about other parameters, but I'm sure they'll come to some compromise during formal discussions."

An expert from NASA spoke up. "Let me get this straight. Given those mission parameters, and supposing we only worry about acceleration and provide no way for the probe to decelerate, the probe will take two to three centuries to reach the Oort Cloud. There, it will intercept and examine the decelerating Trisolaran Fleet. Forgive me, but this seems a project better reserved for the future."

Wade shook his head. "With those sophons zipping about at lightspeed, spying on us constantly, and completely blocking all fundamental physics research, it's no longer certain that we'll make significant technological progress in the future. If humanity is doomed to crawl at a snail's pace through space, we'd better get started as soon as possible."

Cheng Xin suspected that Wade's plan was at least partly motivated by politics. The first effort by humanity to make active contact with an extraterrestrial civilization would enhance the PIA's status.

"But given the current state of spaceflight technology, it will take twenty, maybe thirty thousand years to reach the Oort Cloud. Even if we launch the probe right now, we won't have gotten very far from Earth's front door by the time the Trisolaran Fleet arrives in four hundred years."

"That is precisely why the probe must achieve one percent of lightspeed."

"You're talking about boosting our current maximum speed a hundredfold! That requires a brand-new form of propulsion. We can't achieve that kind of acceleration with current technology, and there's no reason to expect a technical breakthrough within the foreseeable future. This proposal is fundamentally impossible."

Wade slammed his fist down on the table. "You forget that we now have resources! Before, spaceflight was merely a luxury, but now it's an absolute necessity. We can ask for resources that far exceed what was imaginable before. We can throw resources at this problem until the laws of physics bend. Rely on brute force if you have to, but we must accelerate the probe to one percent of lightspeed!"

Vadimov instinctively looked around the room. Wade glanced at him. "Don't worry. There are no reporters or outsiders anywhere near here."

Vadimov laughed. "Please don't take offense. But saying we want to throw resources at the problem until the laws of physics bend is going to make our agency the laughingstock of the world. Please don't repeat it in front of the PDC."

"I already know you're all laughing at me."

Everyone held their tongue. The staff just wanted the meeting to be over. Wade looked at everyone in turn, then returned his gaze to Cheng Xin. "No, not everyone. She's not laughing." He pointed at her. "Cheng, what do you think?"

Under Wade's keen gaze, Cheng Xin felt as if he were pointing a sword at her, not a finger. She looked around helplessly. Who was *she* to talk?

"We need to implement MD here," said Wade.

Cheng Xin was even more baffled. MD? McDonald's? Doctor of medicine?

"But you're Chinese! How can you not know MD?"

Cheng Xin looked at the other five Chinese in the room; they looked just as confused.

"During the Korean War, the Americans discovered that even common Chinese soldiers taken as prisoners seemed to know a lot about their own field strategies. It turned out that your commanders had presented the battle plans to the troops for mass discussion, hoping thereby to find ways to improve them. Of course, if you become Trisolaran prisoners of war in the future, we don't want you to know *that* much."

A few of those present laughed. Cheng Xin finally understood that MD meant "military democracy." The others in the conference room enthusiastically supported Wade's proposal. Of course, these elite experts didn't expect a mere technical aide to have any brilliant ideas, but they were mostly men, and they thought that by giving her a chance to talk, they would have a perfect excuse to appreciate her physical attributes. Cheng Xin had always made an effort to dress conservatively, but this sort of harassment was something she had to deal with constantly.

Cheng Xin began: "I do have an idea—"

"An idea for bending the laws of physics?" The speaker was an older Frenchwoman named Camille, a highly respected and experienced consultant from the European Space Agency. She looked at Cheng Xin contemptuously, as though she didn't belong in the room.

"Well, more like getting *around* the laws of physics." Cheng Xin smiled at Camille politely. "The most promising resource at our disposal is the stockpile of nuclear weapons from around the world. Without some technical breakthrough, these represent the most powerful sources of energy we can launch into space. Imagine a spaceship or probe equipped with a radiation sail, similar to a solar sail: a thin film capable of being propelled by radiation. If we set off nuclear bombs behind the sail periodically—"

A few titters. Camille laughed the loudest. "My dear, you have sketched for us a scene out of a cartoon. Your spaceship is filled with a pile of nuclear bombs, and there's a giant sail. On the ship is a hero who bears more than a passing resemblance to Arnold Schwarzenegger. He tosses the bombs behind the ship, where they explode to push the ship forward. Oh, it's *so* cool!" As the rest of the staff joined in the mirth, she continued. "You may want to review your homework from freshman year in college and tell me: one, how many nuclear bombs your ship will have to carry; and, two, with that kind of thrust-to-weight ratio, what sort of acceleration you can achieve."

"She didn't manage to bend the laws of physics, but she did fulfill the other aspect of the chief's demand," another consulting expert said. "I'm just sorry to see such a pretty girl fall under the spell of brute force." The wave of laughter reached a crescendo.

"The bombs will not be on the ship," Cheng Xin replied calmly. The laughter ceased abruptly; it was as if she had put her hand on the surface of a struck cymbal. "The probe itself will be a tiny core equipped with sensors attached to a large sail, but the total mass will be light as a feather. It will be easy to propel it with the radiation from extravehicular nuclear detonations."

The conference room became very quiet. Everyone was trying to think where the bombs would be. While the others were mocking Cheng Xin, Wade's mien had remained chilly and unmoved. But now, that smile, like water seeping from a crack in the ice, gradually reappeared on his face.

Cheng Xin retrieved a stack of paper cups from the drinking water dispenser behind her and laid them out on the conference table in a line. "We can use traditional chemical rockets to launch the nuclear bombs in advance, and distribute them along the first segment of the probe's route." She took a pencil and moved its tip along the line, from one cup to the next. "As the probe passes each bomb, we detonate it right behind the sail, accelerating it faster and faster."

The men now moved their gazes away from Cheng Xin's body. They were finally willing to take her proposal seriously. Only Camille continued to stare at her, as though at a stranger.

"We can call this technique 'en-route propulsion.' This initial segment is the acceleration leg, and it takes up only a tiny fraction of the overall course. As a very rough estimate, if we use one thousand nuclear bombs, they can be distributed along a path of about five astronomical units stretching from the Earth to Jupiter's orbit. Or we could even compress it further and distribute the bombs within Mars's orbit. That's definitely achievable with our current technology."

The silence was broken by a few whispers. Gradually, the voices grew louder and more excited, like a drizzle turning into a rainstorm.

"You didn't just come up with this idea, did you?" asked Wade. He had been listening to the discussion intently.

Cheng Xin smiled at him. "It's based on an old idea in aerospace circles. Stanislaw Ulam first proposed something like it back in 1946. It's called nuclear pulse propulsion."

"Dr. Cheng," Camille said, "we all know about nuclear pulse propulsion. But those previous proposals all required the fuel to be carried aboard the ship. The idea of distributing the fuel along the spacecraft's route is indeed your invention. At least, I've never heard the suggestion before."

The discussion grew heated. The assembled experts tore into the idea like a pack of hungry wolves presented with a piece of fresh meat.

Wade slammed the table again. "Enough! Don't get bogged down on details right now. We're not evaluating feasibility; rather, we're trying to figure out if it's worthwhile to study the idea's feasibility. Focus on big-picture barriers."

After a brief silence, Vadimov said, "The best thing about this proposal is that it's easy to get started."

Everyone immediately caught on to Vadimov's meaning. The first step in Cheng Xin's plan involved launching a large number of nuclear bombs into orbit around the Earth. Not only did humanity possess such technology, the bombs were already on launch vehicles: the ICBMs in service could easily be repurposed for this use. American Peacekeepers, Russian Topols, and Chinese Dongfengs could all directly launch their payloads into near-Earth orbits. Even intermediate-range ballistic missiles, if retrofitted with booster rockets, could do the job. Compared to the post-Crisis nuclear disarmament plans that required destroying the missiles, this plan would be far cheaper.

"Excellent. For now, let's pause our discussion of Cheng Xin's en-route propulsion idea. Any other proposals?" Wade looked around the room.

A few seemed to want to speak up, but finally decided to remain quiet. None of them thought their own ideas could compete with Cheng Xin's. Eventually, everyone's eyes focused on her again, but this time, the meaning was completely different.

"We'll meet twice more to brainstorm and see if we can come up with a few more options. But we might as well get started on the feasibility study for en-route propulsion. We'll need a code name."

"Since the probe's velocity would go up a level each time a bomb explodes, it's a bit like climbing a flight of stairs," Vadimov said. "I suggest we call it the Staircase Program. Besides the requirement of a final velocity exceeding one percent of lightspeed, another parameter to keep in mind is the mass of the probe."

"A radiation sail can be made very thin and light. Based on the current state of material sciences, we can make a sail of about fifty square kilometers and limit the mass to about fifty kilograms. That should be big enough." The speaker was a Russian expert who had once directed a failed solar sail experiment.

"Then the key will be the mass of the probe itself."

Everyone's eyes turned to another man in the room, the chief designer of the Cassini-Huygens probe.

"If we include some basic sensors and take into account the necessary antenna and radioisotope power source to transmit information back from the Oort Cloud, about two to three thousand kilograms ought to do it."

"No!" Vadimov shook his head. "It has to be like Cheng Xin said: light as a feather."

"If we stick with the most basic sensors, maybe one thousand kilograms would be enough. I can't guarantee that's going to succeed—you're giving me almost nothing to work with."

"You're going to have to make it work," said Wade. "Including the sail, the entire probe cannot exceed one metric ton in mass. We'll devote the strength of the entire human race to propel one thousand kilograms. Let's hope that's light enough."

During the next week, Cheng Xin slept only on airplanes. As part of a task force led by Vadimov, she shuttled back and forth between the space agencies of the US, China, Russia, and Europe to coordinate the feasibility study of the Staircase Program. During that week, Cheng Xin got to travel to more places than she had in her life up to that point, but she didn't get to do any sightseeing except through the windows of cars and conference rooms.

At first, they had thought they could get all the space agencies to do a combined feasibility study, but that turned out to be an impossible political exercise. In the end, each space agency performed an independent analysis. The advantage of this approach was that the four studies could be compared to get a more accurate result, but it also meant that the PIA had to do a lot more work. Cheng Xin worked harder on this project than anything in her professional career—it was her baby, after all.

The four feasibility studies quickly reached preliminary conclusions, which were very similar to each other. The good news was that the area of the radiation sail could be shrunk to twenty-five square kilometers, and with even more advanced materials, the mass of the sail could be reduced to twenty kilograms.

Then came some very bad news: In order to reach the required speed of 1 percent of lightspeed, the mass for the entire probe assembly had to be reduced by 80 percent—to only 200 kilograms. Subtracting the mass reserved for the sail left only 180 kilograms for sensors and communication devices.

Wade's expression didn't change. "Don't be sad. I have even worse news: At the last session of the PDC, the resolution proposing the Staircase Program was voted down."

Of the seven permanent members of the PDC, four voted no. Their reasons were surprisingly similar. In contrast to the technical staff of the PIA with background in spaceflight, the delegates were not interested in the propulsion technology. They objected that the probe's intelligence value was too limited—in the words of the American representative, "practically nil."

This was because the proposed probe had no way to decelerate. Even taking into account the fact that the Trisolaran Fleet would be decelerating, the probe and the fleet would pass by each other at a relative speed of around 5 percent of lightspeed (assuming the probe wasn't captured by the fleet). The window for gathering intelligence would be extremely small. Since the small mass of the probe made active sensors such as radar impractical, the probe was limited to passive sensing, mainly of electromagnetic signals. Given the advanced state of Trisolaran technology, it was almost certain that the enemy would not be using electromagnetic radiation, but media such as neutrinos or gravitational waves—techniques beyond the current state of human technology.

Moreover, due to the presence of sophons, the plan for sending a probe would be completely transparent to the enemy, making its chances of successfully gathering any valuable intelligence nonexistent. Considering the enormous investment required to implement such a plan, the benefits were too minuscule. Most of the plan's value was purely symbolic, and the great powers were simply insufficiently interested. The other three permanent members of the PDC voted yes only because they were interested in the propulsion technology.

"And the PDC is right," said Wade.

Everyone silently mourned the Staircase Program. Cheng Xin was the most disappointed, but she comforted herself that as a young person with no record of achievements, having gotten this far on her first original idea wasn't too bad. Certainly, she had exceeded her own expectations.

"Ms. Cheng, you look unhappy," Wade said. "Apparently you think we're going to back off from the Staircase Program."

Everyone now stared at Wade, speechless.

"We're *not* going to stop." Wade stood up and paced around the conference room. "From now on, whether it's the Staircase Program or any other plan, you do not stop until *I* tell you to stop. Understand?" He dropped his habitual indifferent tone and screamed like a crazed wild animal. "We're going to advance! Advance! We'll stop at nothing to advance!"

Wade was standing right behind Cheng Xin. She felt as if a volcano had erupted behind her, and she cringed and almost screamed herself.

"What's our next step?" asked Vadimov.

"We're going to send a person."

Wade had resumed his calm, emotionless voice. Still in shock at his explosion, it took a while before those in the room understood what Wade meant. He wasn't talking about sending someone to the PDC, but out of the Solar System. He was proposing sending a live scout to the bleak, frigid Oort Cloud one light-year away to spy on the Trisolaran Fleet.

Wade kicked the leg of the conference table and sent his chair flying backwards so that he could sit behind everyone as they continued to discuss. But no one spoke. It was a repeat of the meeting a week ago when he had first brought up the idea of sending a probe to the Trisolaran Fleet. Everyone tried to chew over his words and unravel the riddle. Shortly, they came to see that the idea wasn't as ridiculous as it seemed at first.

Hibernation was a relatively mature technology. A person could complete the voyage in suspended animation. Assuming the person weighed 70 kilograms, that left 110 kilograms for the hibernation equipment and the hull—which would resemble a coffin. But what then? Two centuries later, when the probe met the Trisolaran Fleet, how would they wake this person up, and what could he or she do?

These thoughts revolved inside the heads of everyone present, but no one spoke up. But Wade seemed to be reading everyone's minds.

"We need to send a representative of humanity into the heart of the enemy," he said.

"This would require the Trisolaran Fleet to capture the probe," Vadimov said. "And to keep our spy."

"This is very likely." Wade looked up. "Isn't it?" Those inside the conference understood that he was speaking to the sophons hovering around them like ghosts. Four light-years away, on that distant world, other invisible beings were also "attending" their meeting. The presence of the sophons was something that people tended to forget. When they remembered it, besides fright, they also felt a kind of insignificance, as though they were a swarm of ants under the magnifying glass of some playful, cruel child. It was very difficult to maintain confidence when one realized that whatever plans one came up with would be known by the enemy long before they were even explained to the supervisor. Humanity had to struggle to adjust to this kind of warfare, in which they were completely transparent to the enemy.

But now, Wade seemed to have changed the situation slightly. In his scenario, the enemy's knowledge of the plan was an advantage. The Trisolarans would know every detail about the trajectory of the probe, and could easily intercept it. Even though the sophons allowed the Trisolarans to learn about humanity, surely they would still be interested in capturing a live specimen for up-close study.

In traditional intelligence warfare, sending a spy whose identity was known to the enemy was a meaningless gesture. But this war was different. Sending a representative of humanity into the Trisolaran Fleet was, by itself, a valiant gesture, and it made no difference that the Trisolarans would know the individual's identity ahead of time. The PIA didn't even need to figure out what the spy had to do once he or she got there: As long as the person could be safely and successfully inserted into the fleet, the possibilities were endless. Given that the Trisolarans were transparent in thought and vulnerable to stratagems, Wade's idea became even more attractive.

We need to send a representative of humanity into the heart of the enemy.

Excerpt from *A Past Outside of Time*
Hibernation: Man Walks for the
First Time Through Time

A new technology can transform society, but when the technology is in its infancy, very few people can see its full potential. For example, when the computer was first invented, it was merely a tool for increasing efficiency, and some thought five computers would be enough for the entire world. Artificial hibernation was the same. Before it was a reality, people just thought it would provide an opportunity for patients with terminal illnesses to seek a cure in the future. If they thought further, it would appear to be useful for interstellar voyages. But as soon as it became real, if one examined it through the lens of sociology, one could see that it would completely change the face of human civilization.

All this was based on a single idea: *Tomorrow will be better.*

This was a relatively new faith, a product of the last few centuries before the Crisis. Previously, such an idea of progress would have been laughable. Medieval Europe was materially impoverished compared to the Classical Rome of a thousand years earlier, and was more intellectually repressed. In China, the lives of the people were worse during the Wei, Jin, and Southern and Northern Dynasties compared to the earlier Han Dynasty, and the Yuan and Ming Dynasties were much worse than the earlier Tang and Song Dynasties. But after the Industrial Revolution, progress became a constant feature of society, and humanity's faith in the future grew stronger.

This faith reached its apex on the eve of the Trisolar Crisis. The Cold War had been over for some time, and though problems such as environmental degradation persisted, they were merely unpleasant. The material comforts of life improved at a rapid pace, and the trend seemed to accelerate. If one surveyed people about visions of the future, they might give different answers for how things would be in ten years, but few would doubt that in another hundred years, humanity would be living in paradise. It was easy to believe such a thing: They could just compare their own lives with the lives of their ancestors a hundred years earlier!

If hibernation were possible, why would you linger in the present?

When examined from the perspective of sociology, the biotechnology breakthrough of human cloning was far less complicated than hibernation. Cloning raised moral questions, but they mostly troubled those with a moral view influenced by Christianity. The troubles brought about by hibernation, on the other hand, were practical, and affected the entire human race. Once the technology was successfully commercialized, those who could afford it would use it to skip to paradise, while the rest of humanity would have to stay behind in the comparatively depressing present to construct that paradise for them. But even more worrisome was the greatest lure provided by the future: the end of death.

As modern biology advanced apace, people began to believe that death's end would be achievable in one or two more centuries. If so, those who chose hibernation were taking the first steps on the staircase to life everlasting. For the first time in history, Death itself was no longer fair. The consequences were unimaginable.

The situation was akin to the dire conditions of post-Crisis Escapism. Later, historians would call it Early Escapism or Time Escapism. Thus, even pre-Crisis, governments around the world suppressed hibernation technology more zealously than cloning technology.

But the Trisolar Crisis changed everything. In a single night, the paradise of the future turned into a hell on Earth. Even for terminal patients, the future no longer appealed: By the time they woke up, perhaps the world would be bathed in a sea of fire, and they wouldn't even be able to find an aspirin.

Thus, after the Crisis, hibernation was allowed to develop without constraints. Soon, the technology became commercially viable, and the human race possessed the first tool that allowed them to traverse large swaths of time.

Crisis Era, Years 1–4
Cheng Xin

Cheng Xin went to Sanya on Hainan Island to research hibernation.

This tropical island seemed an incongruous site for the largest hibernation research center, which was operated by the Chinese Academy of Medical Sciences. While it was the middle of winter on the mainland, spring ruled here.

The hibernation center was a white building hidden behind lush vegetation. About a dozen test subjects inside engaged in experimental, short-term hibernation. So far, no one had been put into hibernation with the intent of crossing the centuries.

Cheng Xin first asked whether it was possible to shrink the equipment necessary to support hibernation down to one hundred kilograms.

The director of the research center laughed. "One hundred kilograms? You'd be lucky getting it down to one hundred metric tons!"

The director was exaggerating, but only slightly. He showed Cheng Xin around the center, and Cheng Xin learned that artificial hibernation didn't exactly match its public image. For one thing, it didn't involve ultra-low temperatures. The procedure replaced the blood in the body with an antifreeze cryoprotectant, then brought the body temperature down to minus-fifty-degrees Celsius. Relying on an external cardiopulmonary bypass system, the body's organs maintained an extremely low level of biological activity. "It's like standby mode on a computer," said the director. The entire system—hibernation tank, life-support system, cooling equipment—weighed about three metric tons.

As Cheng Xin discussed possible ways to miniaturize the hibernation setup with the center's technical staff, she was startled by a realization: If the body's temperature must be maintained around minus-fifty-degrees Celsius, then in the frigid conditions of outer space, the hibernation chamber needed to be heated, not cooled. In the long journey through trans-Neptunian space in particular, outside temperature would be close to absolute zero. In contrast, minus-fifty-degrees Celsius was like the inside of a furnace. Considering that the journey would take one to two centuries, the most practicable solution was radioisotope heating. The director's claim of one hundred metric tons was thus not too far from the truth.

Cheng Xin returned to PIA Headquarters and gave her report. After synthesizing all relevant research results, the staff again sank into depression. But this time, they gazed at Wade with hope.

"What are you all looking at? I'm not God!" Wade surveyed the conference room. "Why do you think your countries sent you here? To collect a paycheck and to give me bad news? I don't have a solution. Finding a solution is your job!" He kicked the leg of the conference table, and his chair slid back farther than ever. Ignoring the conference room's non-smoking rule, he lit up a cigar.

The attendees turned their attention back to the new hibernation experts in the room. None of them said anything, but they made no effort to disguise the anger and frustration of professionals faced with ignorant zealots who were asking for the impossible.

"Maybe . . ." Cheng Xin looked around hesitantly. She was still unused to MD.

"Advance! We stop at nothing to advance!" Wade spewed smoke at her along with the words.

"Maybe . . . we don't need to send a live person."

The rest of the team looked at her, looked at each other, and then turned to the hibernation experts. They shook their heads, uncertain what Cheng Xin meant.

"We could flash-freeze a person to minus-two-hundred-degrees Celsius or below, then launch the body. We wouldn't need life support or heating systems, and the capsule holding the body could be made very small and light. The total mass should not exceed one hundred and ten kilograms. For us, such a body is a corpse, but that may not be the case for Trisolarans."

"Very good," Wade said, and nodded at her. This was the first time he had praised one of his staff since she had known him.

One of the hibernation experts said, "You're talking about cryopreservation, not hibernation. The biggest barrier to reanimating a flash-frozen body is preventing cell damage from ice crystals during the thawing process. It's like what happens to frozen tofu: When you defrost it, it turns into a sponge. Oh, I guess most of you haven't had frozen tofu." The expert, who was Chinese, smiled at the confused Western faces around him. "Now, maybe the Trisolarans know techniques to prevent such damage. Perhaps they can restore the body to normal temperature within an extremely short period of time: a millisecond, or even a microsecond. We don't know how to do such a thing, at least not without vaporizing the body in the process."

Cheng Xin wasn't paying much attention to this discussion. Instead, she was focused on one thing: Who would this minus-two-hundred-degree corpsicle that would be shot into deep space be? She was trying her hardest to advance without regard for consequences, but she couldn't help but shudder at the thought.

The latest version of the Staircase Program was brought back to the current PDC session for a vote. Private discussions between Wade and the delegates of the various nations called for optimism. Since the plan, as modified, would represent the first direct contact between humanity and an extraterrestrial civilization, its meaning was qualitatively different from merely sending a probe. Moreover, the person sent to the Trisolarans could be said to represent a ticking bomb implanted in the heart of the enemy. By skillfully using humanity's absolute superiority in tricks and ruses, he or she could change the course of the entire war.

Since the special session of the General Assembly was going to announce the Wallfacer Project to the world tonight, the PDC session was delayed by more than an hour. PIA personnel waited in the lobby outside the General Assembly Hall. During previous PDC sessions, only Wade and Vadimov were allowed to attend, while others had to remain outside, waiting to be summoned if their specific area of technical expertise was needed. But this time, Wade asked Cheng Xin to accompany him and Vadimov to the PDC session itself, a high honor for a lowly technical aide.

After the General Assembly finished its announcement, Cheng Xin and the others watched as a man surrounded by a swarm of reporters passed through the lobby and left the building through another exit—clearly one of the just-revealed Wallfacers. Since everyone from the PIA was focused on the Staircase Program, most weren't interested in the Wallfacers, and only a couple of them left the building to catch a glimpse of the man. Thus, when the famous assassination attempt of Luo Ji occurred, no one from the PIA heard the gunshot; they only saw the sudden commotion through the glass doors. Cheng Xin and the others ran outside and were immediately blinded by the bright search-lights from helicopters hovering overhead.

"Oh my God, one of the Wallfacers has been killed!" One of her colleagues ran over. "I heard that he was shot several times. In the head!"

"Who are the Wallfacers?" asked Wade. His tone indicated no particular interest.

"I'm not too sure either. I think three of them are from the pool of well-known candidates. But this fourth one, the one who was shot, was one of your people." He pointed at Cheng Xin. "But no one had heard of him. He's just some guy."

"In this extraordinary time, no one is 'just some guy,'" Wade said. "Any random person could suddenly be handed a heavy responsibility, and anyone important could be replaced at any time." He looked at Cheng Xin and Mikhail Vadimov in turn. Then a PDC secretary called him aside.

"He's threatening me," Vadimov whispered to Cheng Xin. "He threw a fit yesterday and told me that you could easily replace me."

"Mikhail, I—"

Vadimov held up his hand to stop her. The bright searchlight from one of the helicopters shone through his palm and revealed the blood under his skin. "He wasn't joking. Our agency does not need to follow normal HR procedures. You're steady, calm, hardworking, and also creative; you display a sense of responsibility far above your official position. This is a rare combination of qualities in someone your age. Xin, really, I'm glad that you could replace me—but you *can't* do *quite* what I can do." He looked around at the chaos surrounding them. "You won't sell your mother to a whorehouse. You're still a child, when it comes to that aspect of our profession. My fervent hope is that you will always remain so."

Camille marched over to them holding a stack of paper. Cheng Xin guessed that it was the interim report on the feasibility of the Staircase Program. Camille held up the document for a few seconds, but instead of handing it over to either of them, she slammed it against the ground.

"Fuck them all!" Camille screamed. Even with the helicopters thundering overhead, a few onlookers turned to stare. "Fucking pigs don't know how to do anything except fuck around down here in the mud."

"Who are you talking about?" asked Vadimov.

"Everyone! The human race! Half a century ago, we walked on the moon. But now, we have nothing, can't change anything!"

Cheng Xin bent down and picked up the document. Indeed, it was the interim feasibility report. She and Vadimov flipped through it, but it was highly technical and difficult to skim. Wade had also returned to their circle—the PDC secretary had informed him that the session would begin in fifteen minutes.

Camille calmed down a bit in the presence of the PIA chief. "NASA has conducted two small tests of nuclear pulse propulsion in space, and you can read the results in the report. Basically, our proposed spacecraft is still too heavy to reach the required speed. They calculate the entire assembly needs to be one-twentieth its proposed mass. One-twentieth! That's ten kilograms!

"But wait, they also sent us some *good* news. The sail, it turns out, can be reduced to under ten kilograms. They took pity on us and told us that we can have an effective payload of half a kilogram. But that is the absolute limit, because any increase in the payload will require thicker cables for attachment to the sail. Every additional gram in the payload means three more grams of cables. Thus, we're stuck with zero point five kilograms. Haha, it's just like our angel predicted: light as a feather!"

Wade smiled. "We should ask Monnier, my mother's kitten, to go. Though, even she would have to lose half of her weight."

Whenever others were happily absorbed by their work, Wade appeared gloomy; when others were forlorn, he became relaxed and jokey. Initially, Cheng Xin had attributed this quirk to part of his leadership style. But Vadimov told her that she didn't know how to read people. Wade's behavior had nothing to do with his leadership style or rallying the troops—he just enjoyed watching others lose hope, even if he himself was among those who ought to be in despair. He took pleasure in the desperation of others. Cheng Xin had been surprised that Vadimov, who always tried to speak of others generously, held such an opinion of Wade. But right now, it did look as though Wade took pleasure in watching the three of them suffer.

Cheng Xin felt weak. Days of exhaustion hit her at once, and she sank to the lawn.

"Get up," said Wade.

For the first time, Cheng Xin refused to obey an order from him. She remained on the ground. "I'm tired." Her voice was wooden.

"You, and you," Wade said, pointing to Camille and Cheng Xin. "You're not allowed to lose control like this in the future. You must advance, stop at nothing to advance!"

"There's no way forward," said Vadimov. "We have to give up."

"The reason you think there's no path forward is because you don't know how to disregard the consequences."

"What about the PDC session? Cancel it?"

"No, we should proceed as though nothing has happened. But we can't prepare new documents, so we have to orally present the new plan."

"What new plan? A five-hundred-gram cat?"

"Of course not."

Vadimov's and Camille's eyes brightened. Cheng Xin also seemed to have recovered her strength. She stood up.

Accompanied by military escort vehicles and helicopters, an ambulance departed with the Fourth Wallfacer. Against the lights of New York City, Wade's figure appeared as a black ghost, his eyes glinting with a cold light.

"We'll send only a brain," he said.

In fourteenth-century China, during the Ming Dynasty, the Chinese navy invented a weapon called Huolong Chu Shui, literally meaning "fiery dragon issuing from water." This was a multistage gunpowder rocket similar in principle to antiship missiles of the Common Era. The missile itself (Huolong) was augmented with booster rockets. When launched, the booster rockets propelled the missile toward the enemy ship by flying just above the surface of the water. As the booster rockets burnt out, they ignited a cluster of smaller rocket arrows stored inside the missile, and these would shoot out the front, causing massive damage to enemy ships.

Ancient warfare also saw the use of repeating crossbows, which prefigured Common Era machine guns. These appeared in both the West and the East, and Chinese versions have been discovered in tombs dating from the fourth century B.C.

Both of these weapon systems were attempts to utilize primitive technology in novel ways that demonstrated a power incongruous for their time period.

Looking back, the Staircase Program implemented at the beginning of the Crisis Era was a similar advance. Using only the primitive technology available at the time, it managed to boost a small probe to 1 percent of lightspeed. This achievement should have been impossible without technology that would not appear for another one and a half centuries.

At the time of the Staircase Program, humans had already successfully launched a few spacecraft outside the Solar System and had managed to land probes on Neptunian satellites. Thus, the requisite technology to distribute nuclear bombs along the acceleration leg of the probe's course was relatively mature. But controlling the flight path of the probe to pass by each bomb, and detonating each at the precise moment, posed great technical challenges.

Every bomb had to detonate just as the radiation sail passed it. The distance from each bomb to the sail at the moment of the explosion ranged from three thousand to ten thousand meters, depending on the bomb's yield. As the probe's velocity increased, the timing needed to be more precise. However, even as the sail's speed reached 1 percent of lightspeed, the margin for error remained above the nanosecond range, well achievable by the technology of the time.

The probe itself contained no engine. Its direction was entirely determined by the relative positions of the detonating bombs. Each bomb along the route was equipped with small positional thrusters. As the sail passed each bomb, the distance between them was only a few hundred meters. By adjusting this distance, it was possible to alter the angle between the sail and the propulsive force generated by the nuclear explosion, and thus control the direction of flight.

The radiation sail was a thin film, and the only way to carry the payload was to drag it behind in a capsule. The entire probe thus resembled a giant parachute—except that the parachute flew "upwards." To avoid damage to the payload from the nuclear explosions occurring three to ten kilometers behind the sail, the cables connecting the sail to the payload had to be very long: about five hundred kilometers. An ablative layer protected the payload capsule itself. As the nuclear bombs exploded, the ablative material gradually vaporized, cooling the capsule as well as lowering the total mass.

The cables were made from a nanomaterial called "Flying Blade." Only about a tenth of the thickness of a strand of spider silk, the cables were invisible to the naked eye. Eight grams of the material could be stretched into a cable one hundred kilometers long, yet it was strong enough to securely pull the payload capsule during acceleration, and would not break from the massive radiation generated by the nuclear explosions.

Of course, Huolong Chu Shui was not, in fact, equivalent to a two-stage rocket, and the repeating crossbow was not the same as a machine gun. Similarly, the Staircase Program could not bring about a new Space Age. It was only a desperate attempt that drew upon everything humanity's primitive level of technology could offer.

Crisis Era, Years 1–4
Cheng Xin

The mass launch of Peacekeeper missiles had been in process for over half an hour. Trails from six missiles merged together, and, lit up by the moon, resembled a silvery road that reached into heaven.

Every five minutes, another fiery ball ascended this silvery road into the sky. Shadows cast by trees and people swept along the ground like the second hands of clocks. This first launch would involve thirty missiles, sending three hundred nuclear warheads with yields ranging from five hundred kilotons to 2.5 megatons into orbit.

At the same time, in Russia and China, Topol and Dongfeng missiles were also rising into the sky. The scene resembled a doomsday scenario, but Cheng Xin could tell by the curvature of the rocket trails that these were orbital launches instead of intercontinental strikes. These devices, which could have killed billions, would never return to the surface of the Earth. They would pool their enormous power to accelerate a feather to 1 percent of the speed of light.

Cheng Xin's eyes filled with hot tears. Each ascending rocket lit them up like bright, glistening pools. She told herself again and again that no matter what happened next, it was worth it to have pushed the Staircase Program this far.

But the two men beside her, Vadimov and Wade, seemed unmoved by the spectacular scene playing out before them. They didn't even bother looking up; instead, they smoked and conversed in low voices. Cheng Xin knew very well what they were discussing: who would be chosen for the Staircase Program.

The last session of the PDC marked the first time a resolution had been passed based on a proposal that wasn't even written down. And Cheng Xin got to witness the debating skills of Wade, usually a man of few words. He argued that if we assumed the Trisolarans were capable of reviving a body in deep freeze, then it made sense to assume they were also capable of reviving a bare brain in similar condition and conversing with it through an external interface. Surely such a task was trivial for a civilization capable of unfolding a proton into two dimensions and etching circuits over the resulting surface. In some sense, a brain was no different from the whole person: It possessed the person's thoughts, personality, and memories. And it most definitely possessed the person's capacity for stratagems. If successful, the brain would still be a ticking bomb in the heart of the enemy.

Although the PDC members did not fully agree that a brain was the same as a whole person, they lacked better choices, especially since their interest in the Staircase Program was largely based on the technology for accelerating the probe to 1 percent of lightspeed. In the end, the resolution passed with five yeses and two abstentions.

Once the Staircase Program was approved, the problem of who should be sent came to the forefront. Cheng Xin lacked the courage to even imagine such a person. Even if his or her brain could be captured by the Trisolarans and revived, life afterwards—if such an existence could be called life—would be one interminable nightmare. Every time she thought about this, her heart felt squeezed by a hand chilled to minus-two-hundred-degrees Celsius.

The other leaders and implementers of the Staircase Program did not suffer her pangs of guilt. If PIA were a national intelligence agency, this matter would have been resolved long ago. However, since PIA was only a joint intelligence committee formed by the permanent member nations of the PDC, after the Staircase Program was revealed to the international community, the issue became extremely sensitive.

The key problem was this: Before launch, the subject would have to be killed.

After the initial panic of the Crisis subsided, a mainstream consensus gradually dominated international politics: It was important to prevent the Crisis from being leveraged as a tool to destroy democracy. PIA personnel were instructed by their respective nations to be extra careful during the process of selecting potential Staircase Program subjects and not commit political errors that would embarrass their countries.

Once again, Wade came up with a unique solution to the difficulty: advocating, through the PDC and then the UN, the passage of euthanasia laws in as many countries as possible. But even he wasn't confident that this plan would work.

Of the seven permanent members of the PDC, three quickly passed euthanasia laws. But these laws all clearly provided that euthanasia was only available to those suffering terminal illnesses. This was not ideal for the Staircase Program, but it seemed the outer boundary of political acceptability.

Thus, candidates for the Staircase Program had to be chosen from the population of terminally ill patients.

The thunderous noises and bright lights in the sky faded. The missile launches had come to an end. Wade and a few other PDC observers got into their cars and left, leaving only Vadimov and Cheng Xin.

"Why don't we take a look at your star?" he said.

Four days ago, Cheng Xin had received the deed to DX3906. She was utterly surprised and fell into a delirium of joy. For a whole day, she kept on repeating to herself: *Someone gave me a star; someone gave me a star; someone gave me a star. . . .*

When she went to see Chief Wade to give a status report, her happiness was so palpable that Wade asked her what the matter was with her. She showed him the deed.

"A useless piece of paper," he said, and handed it back to her. "If you're smart, you should drop the price and resell it right away. Otherwise you'll end up with nothing."

But Cheng Xin wasn't bothered by his cynicism—she had already known what he was going to say. She knew very little about Wade except his work history: service in the CIA, then deputy secretary of Homeland Security, and finally here. As for his personal life, other than the fact that he had a mother and his mother had a kitten, she knew nothing. No one else did, either. She didn't even know where he lived. He was like a machine: When he wasn't working, he was shut down somewhere unknown.

She couldn't help but bring up the star to Vadimov, who enthusiastically congratulated her. "Every girl in the world must be jealous," he said. "Including all living women and dead princesses. You're certainly the first woman in the history of humankind to be given a star." For a woman, was there any greater happiness than to be given a star by someone who loved her?

"But who *is* he?" Cheng Xin muttered.

"Shouldn't be hard to guess. He must be rich, for one thing. He just spent a few million on a symbolic gift."

Cheng Xin shook her head. She'd had many admirers and suitors, but none of them were *that* wealthy.

"He's also a cultured soul. Stands apart from the crowd." Vadimov sighed. "And he just made a romantic gesture that I'd call fucking ridiculous if I read it in a book or saw it in a movie."

Cheng Xin sighed as well. A much younger Cheng Xin had once indulged in rose-tinted fantasies that the Cheng Xin of the present would mock. This real star that appeared out of nowhere, however, far exceeded those romantic dreams.

She was certain that she knew no man like that.

Maybe it was a secret admirer from afar who, on impulse, decided to use a tiny part of his vast wealth to indulge in a bit of whimsy, to satisfy some desire she would never understand. Even so, she was grateful.

That night, Cheng Xin climbed onto the top of One World Trade Center, eager to see her new star. She had carefully reviewed the materials that accompanied the deed explaining how to find it. But the sky in New York was overcast. The next day and the day after were the same. The clouds formed a giant teasing hand that covered her gift, refusing to let go. But Cheng Xin wasn't disappointed; she knew she had received a gift that couldn't be taken away. DX3906 was in this universe, and it might even outlast the Earth and the Sun. She would see it, one day.

She stood on the balcony of her apartment at night, gazing up at the sky and imagining her star. The lights of the city below cast a dim yellow glow against the cloud cover, but she imagined her star giving the clouds a rosy glow.

In her dream, she flew over the star's surface. It was a rose-colored sphere, but instead of scorching flames, she felt the coolness of a spring breeze. Below her was the clear water of an ocean, through which she could see swaying, rose-colored clouds of algae. . . .

After she woke up, she laughed at herself. As an aerospace professional, even in her dreams she couldn't forget that DX3906 had no planets.

On the fourth day after she received the star, Cheng Xin and a few other PIA employees flew to Cape Canaveral to attend the launch ceremony for the first batch of missiles. Achieving orbit required taking advantage of the Earth's spin, and the ICBMs had been moved here from their original deployment bases.

The trails left behind by the missiles gradually faded against the clear night sky. Cheng Xin and Vadimov reviewed the observation guide for her star. Both had had some training in astronomy, and soon they were looking at the approximate location. But neither could see it.

Vadimov took out two pairs of military-issue binoculars. With them, it was easy to see DX3906. After that, even without the binoculars, they could find the star. Cheng Xin stared at the faint red dot, mesmerized, struggling to comprehend the unimaginable distance between them, struggling to translate the distance into terms that could be grasped by the human mind.

"If you put my brain on the Staircase Program probe and launched it at the star, it would take thirty thousand years to get there."

Cheng Xin heard no response. When she turned around, she saw that Vadimov was no longer looking at the star with her, but leaning against the car and looking at nothing. She could see that his face was troubled.

"What's wrong?"

Vadimov was silent for some time. "I've been avoiding my duty."

"What are you talking about?"

"I'm the best candidate for the Staircase Program."

After a momentary shock, Cheng Xin realized that Vadimov was right: He had extensive experience in spaceflight, diplomacy, and intelligence; he was steady and mature. . . . Even if they were able to expand the pool of candidates to include healthy individuals, Vadimov would still be the best choice.

"But you're healthy."

"Sure. But I'm still running from my responsibility."

"Have you been pressured?" Cheng Xin was thinking of Wade.

"No, but I know what I must do; I just haven't done it. I got married three years ago, and my daughter just turned one. I'm not afraid to die, but my family matters to me. I don't want them to see me turned into something worse than a corpse."

"You *don't* have to do this. Neither the PIA nor your government has ordered you to do this, and they can't!"

"Yes, but I wanted to tell you . . . in the end, I'm the best candidate."

"Mikhail, humankind isn't just some abstraction. To love humanity, you must start by loving individual persons, by fulfilling your responsibility to those you love. It would be absurd to blame yourself for it."

"Thank you, Cheng Xin. You deserve your gift." Vadimov looked up at Cheng Xin's star. "I would love to give my wife and daughter a star."

A bright point of light appeared in the sky, then another. Their glow cast shadows on the ground. They were testing nuclear pulse propulsion in space.

The process of selecting a subject for the Staircase Program was fully underway, but the effort imposed little direct pressure on Cheng Xin. She was asked to perform some basic tasks such as examining candidates' knowledge of space-flight, a primary requirement. Since the pool of candidates was limited to terminally ill patients, it was almost impossible to find someone with the requisite expertise. The PIA intensified efforts to identify more candidates through every available channel.

One of Cheng Xin's college classmates came to New York to visit her. The talk turned to what had happened to others in their class, and her friend mentioned Yun Tianming. She had heard from Hu Wen that Tianming was in the late stages of lung cancer and didn't have much time left. Right away, Cheng Xin went to Assistant Chief Yu to suggest Tianming as a candidate.

For the rest of her life, Cheng Xin would remember that moment. Every time, she had to admit to herself that she just didn't think much about Tianming as a person.

Cheng Xin needed to return to China for business. Since she was Tianming's classmate, Assistant Chief Yu asked her to represent the PIA and discuss the matter with Tianming. She agreed, still not thinking much of it.

After hearing Cheng Xin's story, Tianming slowly sat up on the bed. Cheng Xin asked him to lie down, but he said he wanted to be by himself for a while.

Cheng Xin closed the door lightly behind her. Tianming began to laugh hysterically.

What a fucking idiot I am! Did I think that because I gave her a star out of love, she would return that love? Did I think that she had flown across the Pacific to save me with her saintly tears? What kind of fairy tale have I been telling myself?

No, Cheng Xin had come to ask him to die.

He made another logical deduction that made him laugh even harder, until it was hard to breathe. Based on Cheng Xin's timing, she could not know that he had already chosen euthanasia. In other words, if Tianming hadn't already chosen this path, she would try to convince him to take it. Maybe she would even entice him, or pressure him, until he agreed.

Euthanasia meant "good death," but there was nothing good about the fate she had in mind for him.

His sister had wanted him to die because she thought money was being wasted. He could understand that—and he believed that she genuinely wanted him to die in peace. Cheng Xin, on the other hand, wanted him to suffer in eternity. Tianming was terrified of space. Like everyone who studied spaceflight for a living, he understood space's sinister nature better than the general public. Hell was not on Earth, but in heaven.

Cheng Xin wanted a part of him, the part that carried his soul, to wander forever in that frigid, endless, lightless abyss.

Actually, that would be the best outcome.

If the Trisolarans were to really capture his brain as Cheng Xin wished, then his true nightmare would begin. Aliens who shared nothing with humanity would attach sensors to his brain and begin tests involving the senses. They would be most interested in the sensation of pain, of course, and so, by turn, he would experience hunger, thirst, whipping, burning, suffocation, electric shocks, medieval torture techniques, death by a thousand cuts. . . .

Then they would search his memory to identify what forms of suffering he feared the most. They would discover a torture technique he had once read in a history book—first, the victim was whipped until not an inch of his skin remained intact; then the victim's body was tightly wrapped in bandages; and after the victim had stopped bleeding, the bandages would be torn off, ripping open all the wounds at once—then send signals replicating such torture into his brain. The victim in his history book couldn't live for long in those conditions, but Tianming's brain would not be able to die. The most that could happen was that his brain could shut down from shock. In the eyes of Trisolarans, it would resemble a computer locking up. They'd just restart his brain and run another experiment, driven by curiosity, or merely the desire for entertainment. . . .

He would have no escape. Without hands or body, he would have no way to commit suicide. His brain would resemble a battery, recharged again and again with pain.

There would be no end.

He howled with laughter.

Cheng Xin opened the door. "Tianming, what's wrong?"

He choked off his laugh and turned still as a corpse.

"Tianming, on behalf of the UN-PDC Strategic Intelligence Agency, I ask you whether you're willing to shoulder your responsibility as a member of the human race and accept this mission. This is entirely voluntary. You are free to say no."

He gazed at her face, at her solemn but eager expression. She was fighting for humanity, for Earth. . . . But what was wrong with the scene all around him? The light of the setting sun coming through the window fell against the wall like a pool of blood; the lonesome oak tree outside the window appeared as skeletal arms rising out of the grave. . . .

The hint of a smile—an agonized, melancholic smile—appeared at the corners of his mouth. Gradually, the smile spread to the rest of his face.

"Of course. I accept," he said.

Crisis Era, Years 5—7
The Staircase Program

Mikhail Vadimov died. While crossing the Harlem River on I-95, his car slammed through the guardrails on the Alexander Hamilton Bridge and plunged into the water below. It took more than a day before the car could be retrieved. An autopsy revealed that Vadimov had been suffering from leukemia; the accident was the result of retinal hemorrhages.

Cheng Xin mourned Vadimov, who had cared for her like a big brother and helped her adjust to life in a foreign country. She missed his generosity most of all. Though Cheng Xin had attracted notice with her intelligence and seemed to shine brighter than Vadimov—despite the fact that she was supposed to be his aide—he had never shown any jealousy. He had always encouraged her to display her brilliance on bigger and bigger stages.

Within the PIA, there were two types of reaction to Vadimov's death. Most of the technical staff, like Cheng Xin, grieved for their boss. The intelligence specialists, on the other hand, appeared more displeased by the fact that Vadimov's body had not been retrieved in time, rendering his brain unusable.

Gradually, a suspicion grew in Cheng Xin's mind. It seemed like too much of a coincidence. She shuddered the first time the idea surfaced in her mind—it was too frightening, too despicable to be endured.

She consulted medical specialists and learned that it was possible to intentionally induce leukemia. All you had to do was to place the victim in an environment with sufficient radiation. But getting the timing and dosage right was no trivial matter. Too little would not induce the illness in time, but too much would kill the victim with radiation sickness, possibly damaging the brain. Timing-wise, based on the advanced state of Vadimov's illness, the scheme against him would have to have begun right around the time the PDC started to promote euthanasia laws around the world. If there was a killer, he was extremely skilled.

Secretly, Cheng Xin swept Vadimov's office and apartment with a Geiger counter, but discovered nothing unusual. She saw the picture of Vadimov's family he kept under his pillow: His wife was a ballerina eleven years younger than him, and their little daughter . . . Cheng Xin wiped her eyes.

Vadimov had once told Cheng Xin that, superstitiously, he never left family photos on desks or nightstands. Doing so seemed to him to expose them to danger. He kept the pictures hidden and only took them out when he wanted to look at them.

Every time Cheng Xin thought of Vadimov, she also thought of Yun Tianming. Tianming and six other candidates had been moved to a secret base near PIA Headquarters to undergo a final series of tests, after which one of them would be picked.

Since meeting Tianming back in China, Cheng Xin's heart had grown heavier over time, until she sank into a depression. She recalled the first time they met. It was just after the start of their first semester in college, and all the aerospace engineering students took turns introducing themselves. She saw Tianming sitting by himself in a corner. From the moment she saw him, she understood his vulnerability and loneliness. She had met other boys who were isolated and forlorn, but she had never felt like this: as though she had stolen into his heart and could see his secrets.

Cheng Xin liked confident, optimistic boys, boys who were like sunlight, warming themselves as well as the girls with them. Tianming was the very opposite of her type. But she always had a desire to take care of him. In their interactions she was careful, fearful of hurting him, even if unintentionally. She had never been so protective of other boys.

When her friend had come to New York and Tianming's name came up, Cheng Xin discovered that although she had tucked him away in a distant corner of her memory, his image was surprisingly clear when she recalled him.

One night, Cheng Xin had another nightmare. She was again at her star, but the red sea algae had turned black. Then the star collapsed into a black hole, a lightless absence in the universe. Around the black hole, a tiny, glowing object moved. Trapped by the gravity of the black hole, the object would never be able to escape: It was a frozen brain.

Cheng Xin woke up and looked at the glow of New York's lights against her curtain. She understood what she had done.

From one perspective, she had simply passed along the PIA's request; he could have said no. She had recommended him because she was trying to protect the Earth and its civilization, and his life had almost reached its end—had she not arrived in time, he would be dead. In a way, she had saved him!

She had done nothing that she ought to be ashamed of, nothing that should trouble her conscience.

But she also understood that this was how someone could sell their mother to a whorehouse.

Cheng Xin thought about hibernation. The technology was mature enough that some people—mostly terminally ill patients seeking a cure in the future—had already entered the long sleep. Tianming had a chance. Given his social status, it would be hard for him to afford hibernation, but she could help him. It was a possibility, an opportunity that she had taken from him.

The next day, Cheng Xin went to see Wade.

As usual, Wade stared at his lit cigar in his office. She rarely saw him perform the tasks that she associated with conventional administration: making phone calls, reading documents, attending meetings, and so forth. She didn't know when, if ever, Wade did these things. All she could see was him sitting, deep in thought, always deep in thought.

Cheng Xin explained that she thought Candidate #5 was unsuitable. She wanted to withdraw her recommendation and ask that the man be removed from consideration.

"Why? He has scored the best in our tests."

Wade's comment stunned Cheng Xin and chilled her heart. One of the first tests they conducted was to put each candidate under a special form of general anesthesia that caused the person to lose feeling in all parts of the body and sensory organs but remain conscious. The experience was intended to simulate the conditions of a brain existing independent of the body. Then the examiners assessed the candidate's psychological ability to adapt to alien conditions. Of course, since the test designers knew nothing about conditions within the Trisolaran Fleet, they had to fill out their simulation with guesses. Overall, the test was quite harsh.

"But he has only an undergraduate degree," Cheng Xin said.

"You certainly have more degrees," said Wade. "But if we used your brain for this mission, it would, without a doubt, be one of the worst brains we could have chosen."

"He's a loner! I've never seen anyone so withdrawn. He doesn't have any ability to adjust and adapt to the conditions around him."

"That is precisely Candidate #5's best quality! You're talking about human society. Someone who feels comfortable with this environment has also learned to rely on it. Once one is cut off from the rest of humanity and finds oneself in a strange environment, one is very likely to suffer a fatal breakdown. You're a perfect example of what I'm talking about."

Cheng Xin had to admit that Wade's logic was sound. She probably would suffer a breakdown from the simulation alone.

She certainly knew that she had no clout to get the top administrator of the PIA to give up on a candidate for the Staircase Program. But she didn't want to give up. She steeled herself. She would say whatever was necessary to save Tianming.

"He's made no meaningful attachments in life. He has no sense of responsibility to humanity, or love." After saying this, Cheng Xin wondered if there was some truth to it.

"Oh, there is definitely something on Earth he's attached to."

Wade's gaze remained on the cigar, but Cheng Xin could feel his attention being deflected from the cigar's lit tip onto her, carrying with it some of the flame's heat. To her relief, Wade abruptly changed the subject.

"Another excellent quality of Candidate #5 is his creativity. This makes up for his lack of technical knowledge. Did you know that an idea of his made one of your classmates into a billionaire?"

Cheng Xin had indeed seen this in Tianming's background file—so she did know someone really rich, after all. But she didn't believe for a minute that Hu Wen was the one who had given her the star. The very idea was ridiculous. If he liked her, he would buy her a fancy car or a diamond necklace, not a star.

"I had thought none of the candidates were anywhere near being suitable, and I was running out of ideas. But you've reaffirmed my faith in #5. Thank you."

Wade finally lifted his eyes to look at Cheng Xin with his cold, predatory smile. As before, he seemed to take pleasure in her despair and pain.

But Cheng Xin didn't lose all hope.

She was attending the Oath of Allegiance Ceremony for Staircase Program candidates. According to the Space Convention, as amended post-Crisis, any person using resources of the Earth to leave the Solar System for economic development, emigration, scientific research, or other purposes must first take an oath pledging loyalty to humanity. Everyone had thought this provision would not be invoked until far in the future.

The ceremony took place in the UN General Assembly Hall. Unlike the session announcing the Wallfacer Project a few months ago, this ceremony was closed to the public. Besides the seven Staircase Program candidates, the only attendees were Secretary General Say, the PDC rotating chair, and a few observers—including Cheng Xin and other members of the PIA working on the Staircase Program—who filled the first two rows of seats.

The ceremony didn't take long. In turn, each candidate put his or her hand on the UN flag held up by Secretary General Say and recited the required oath to be "loyal to the human race for all time, and to never perform any act that harms humanity's well-being."

Four candidates were lined up before Yun Tianming—two Americans, a Russian, and a British man—and two more stood behind him: another American, and another Chinese. All the candidates looked sickly, and two had to use wheelchairs. But all looked to be in good spirits—not unlike oil lamps giving off a final burst of light before burning out.

Cheng Xin looked at Tianming. Since the last time she had seen him, he looked thinner and more pallid, but appeared very calm. He didn't look back in her direction.

The first four candidates' oaths went off without a hitch. One of the Americans, a physicist in his fifties with pancreatic cancer, struggled up from his wheelchair and climbed onto the rostrum by himself. The candidates' voices echoed in the empty hall, frail but full of dedication. The only interruption in the routine was the British man asking whether he would be allowed to take his oath on a Bible. His request was granted.

It was Tianming's turn. Though Cheng Xin was an atheist, at that moment she wished she could grab the Bible from that man and pray to it: *Tianming, please take the oath, please! I know you're a responsible man. You'll be faithful to the human race. Like Wade said, there are things here that you cannot bear to part with. . . .*

She watched as Tianming mounted the dais, watched as he walked in front of Secretary General Say, and then squeezed her eyes shut.

She didn't hear him repeat the oath.

Tianming picked up the blue UN flag from Say and lightly draped it on the lectern next to him.

"I will not take the oath. In this world, I feel like a stranger. I've never experienced much joy or happiness, and didn't receive much love. Of course, these can all be attributed to my faults—"

His tone was placid, as though he was reviewing his own life. Cheng Xin, sitting below the dais, began to tremble as though waiting for an apocalyptic judgment.

"—but I will not take this oath. I do not affirm any responsibility to the human race."

"Then why have you agreed to be in the Staircase Program?" asked Say. Her voice was gentle, as were her eyes on Tianming.

"I want to see another world. As for whether I'll be faithful to humanity, it will depend on what kind of civilization I see among the Trisolarans."

Say nodded. "Your oath is entirely voluntary. You may go. Next candidate, please."

Cheng Xin shook as though she had fallen into an ice cellar. She bit her bottom lip and forced herself not to cry.

Tianming had passed the final test.

Wade, who was sitting in the front row, turned around to look at Cheng Xin. He took delight in even more despair and pain. His eyes seemed to speak to Cheng Xin.

Now you see what he's made of.

But . . . what if he's telling the truth?

If even we believe him, the enemy will believe him, too.

Wade turned back to the rostrum, then seemed to remember something vital, and glanced back at Cheng Xin again.

This is a fun game, isn't it?

Tianming's unexpected refusal seemed to change the atmosphere in the hall. The last candidate, a forty-three-year-old HIV-positive American NASA engineer named Joyner, also refused to take the oath. She explained that she had not wanted to be here, but she had felt compelled to come because she believed that if she refused, her friends and family would despise her and leave her to die alone. No one knew if she was telling the truth or if Tianming had inspired her.

The next night, Joyner's condition suddenly deteriorated. An infection that turned into pneumonia caused her to stop breathing, and she died before dawn. The medical staff did not have enough time to remove her brain for flash freezing, and it was unusable.

Tianming was chosen to carry out the mission of the Staircase Program.

The moment had arrived. Cheng Xin was informed that Tianming's condition had suddenly deteriorated. They needed to remove his brain right away. The procedure would be conducted at Westchester Medical Center.

Cheng Xin hesitated outside the hospital. She didn't dare enter, but she couldn't bear to leave. All she could do was to suffer. Wade, who had come with her, walked ahead toward the hospital entrance alone. He stopped, turned around, and admired her pain. Then, satisfied, he delivered the final blow.

"Oh, I have another surprise for you: He gave you the star."

Cheng Xin stood frozen. Everything seemed to transform around her. What she had seen before were mere shadows; only now did life's true colors reveal themselves. The tidal wave of emotion made her stumble, as if the ground had disappeared.

She rushed into the hospital and dashed through the long, winding hallways until two guards outside the neurosurgery area stopped her. She struggled against them, but they held fast. She fumbled for her ID, waved it at them, and then continued her mad run toward the operating room. The crowd outside, surprised, parted for her. She slammed through the doors with glowing red lights over them.

She was too late.

A group of men and women in white coats turned around. The body had already been removed from the room. In the middle was a workbench, on top of which sat a cylindrical stainless steel insulating container, about a meter tall. It had just been sealed, and the white fog produced by the liquid helium still hadn't completely dissipated. Slowly, the white fog rolled down the surface of the container, flowed across the workbench, cascaded over the edge like a miniature waterfall, and pooled on the floor, where it finally broke apart. In the fog, the container appeared otherworldly.

Cheng Xin threw herself at the workbench. Her motion broke up the white fog, and she felt herself enveloped in a pocket of cold air that dissipated in a moment. It was as if she had briefly touched what she was seeking before losing it to another time, another place, forever.

Prostrate in front of the container of liquid helium, Cheng Xin sobbed. Her sorrow filled the operating room, overflowed the hospital building, flooded New York City. Above her, the sorrow became a lake, then an ocean. At its bottom, she felt close to drowning.

She didn't know how much time passed before she felt the hand placed against her shoulders. Maybe the hand had been there for a long time, and maybe the owner of the hand had been speaking for a long time, as well.

"There is hope." It was the voice of an old man, gentle and slow. "There is hope."

Still wracked by sobs, Cheng Xin could not catch her breath, but what the voice said next got her attention.

"Think! If they can revive that brain, what would be the ideal container for it?"

The voice did not offer empty platitudes, but a concrete idea.

She lifted her head, and through tear-blurred eyes, she recognized the white-haired old man: the world's foremost brain surgeon, affiliated with Harvard Medical School. He had been the lead surgeon during the operation.

"It would be the body that had carried this brain in the first place. Every cell in the brain contains all the genetic information necessary to reconstruct his body. They could clone him and implant the brain, and in this way, he would be whole again."

Cheng Xin stared at the stainless steel container. Tears rolled down her face, but she didn't care. Then she recovered and stunned everyone: "What is he going to eat?"

She sprinted out of the room, in as much of a rush as when she had barged in.

The next day, Cheng Xin returned to Wade's office and deposited an envelope on his desk. She looked as pale as some terminally ill patients.

"I request that these seeds be included in the Staircase capsule."

Wade opened the envelope and emptied its contents onto the desk: more than a dozen small packets. He ticked through them with interest: "Wheat, corn, potatoes, and these are . . . some vegetables, right? Hmmm, is this chili pepper?"

Cheng Xin nodded. "One of his favorites."

Wade put all the packets back into the envelope and pushed it across the desk. "No."

"Why? These weigh only eighteen grams in total."

"We must make every effort to remove even point one eight grams of excess mass."

"Just pretend his brain is eighteen grams heavier!"

"But it's *not*, is it? Adding this weight would lead to a slower final cruising speed for the spacecraft, and delay the encounter with the Trisolaran Fleet by many years." That cold smirk again appeared on Wade's face. "Besides, he's just a brain now—no mouth, no stomach. What would be the point? Don't believe that fairy tale about cloning. They'll just put the brain in a nice incubator and keep it alive."

Cheng Xin wanted to rip the cigar out of Wade's hand and put it out against his face. But she controlled herself. "I will bypass you and make the request to those with more authority."

"It won't work. Then?"

"Then I'll resign."

"I won't allow it. You're still useful to the PIA."

Cheng Xin laughed bitterly. "You can't stop me. You've never been my real boss."

"You will not do anything I don't allow."

Cheng Xin turned around and started to walk away.

"The Staircase Program needs to send someone who knows Yun Tianming to the future."

Cheng Xin stopped.

"However, that person must be a member of the PIA and under my command. Are you interested? Or do you want to hand in your resignation now?"

Cheng Xin continued walking, but her stride slowed down. Finally, she stopped a second time. Wade's voice came again. "You'd better be sure about your choice this time."

"I agree to go to the future," Cheng Xin said. She leaned against the door-frame for support. She didn't turn around.

The only time Cheng Xin got to see the Staircase spacecraft was when its radiation sail unfolded in orbit. The giant sail, twenty-five square kilometers in area, briefly reflected sunlight onto the Earth. Cheng Xin was already in Shanghai, and she saw an orange-red glowing spot appear in the pitch-black sky, gradually fading. Five minutes later, it was gone, like an eye that material-ized out of nowhere to look at the Earth and then slowly shut its eyelid. The craft's journey as it accelerated out of the Solar System was not visible to the naked eye.

Cheng Xin was comforted by the fact that the seeds did accompany Tianming—not her seeds, exactly, but seeds that had been carefully selected by the space agricultural department.

The giant sail's mass was 9.3 kilograms. Four five-hundred-kilometer cables connected it to the space capsule, whose diameter was only forty-five centi-meters. A layer of ablative material covered the capsule, making its launch mass 850 grams. After the acceleration leg, the capsule mass would be reduced to 510 grams.

The acceleration leg stretched from the Earth to the orbit of Jupiter. A total of 1,004 nuclear bombs were distributed along the route, two-thirds of which were fission bombs, the rest fusion. They were like a row of mines that the

Staircase craft triggered as it passed by. Numerous probes were also distributed along the route to monitor the craft's heading and speed and coordinate minute adjustments to the positions of the remaining bombs. Like the pulses of a heart, successive nuclear detonations lit up the space behind the sail with blinding glows, and a storm of radiation propelled this feather forward. By the time the spacecraft approached Jupiter's orbit and the 997th nuclear bomb exploded, monitoring probes showed that it had achieved 1 percent of light-speed.

That was when the accident occurred. Analysis of the frequency spectrum of the light reflected from the radiation sail showed that the sail had begun to curl, possibly because one of the towing cables had broken. However, the 998th nuclear bomb detonated before adjustments could be made, and the craft deviated from the projected course. As the sail continued to curl, its radar profile rapidly shrank, and it disappeared from the monitoring system. Without precise parameters for its trajectory, it would never be found again.

As time passed, the spacecraft's trajectory would deviate farther and farther from the projection. Hopes that it would intercept the Trisolaran Fleet diminished. Based on its approximate final heading, it should pass by another star in six thousand years and depart the Milky Way in five million years.

At least the Staircase Program was a half success. For the first time, a man-made object had been accelerated to quasi-relativistic speeds.

There was no real reason to send Cheng Xin to the future anymore, but the PIA still asked her to enter suspended animation. Her mission now was to act as a liaison to the Staircase Program in the future. If this pioneering effort was to be helpful to humanity's spaceflight efforts in two centuries, someone who understood it deeply had to be there to explain the dead data and interpret the mute documents. Of course, perhaps the real reason for sending her was only one of vanity, a wish that the Staircase Program would not be forgotten by the future. Other large contemporary engineering projects had made similar efforts to send liaisons to the future for similar reasons.

If the future wished to pass judgment on our struggles, then at least it was now possible to send someone to the future to explain the misunderstandings brought about by the passage of time.

As Cheng Xin's consciousness faded in the cold, she held on to a ray of comfort: Like Tianming, she would drift through an endless abyss for centuries.

PART II

Deterrence Era, Year 12
Bronze Age

It was now possible to see the Earth with the naked eye from the view window of *Bronze Age*. As the ship decelerated, those who weren't on duty came to the open space at the stern to observe the Earth through the wide portholes.

At this distance, the Earth still resembled a star, but it was possible to see a pale blue in its glow. The final deceleration stage had begun, and as the stellar drive came online, the crew, who had been floating in zero gravity, drifted toward the portholes like leaves falling in autumn, and finally landed against the broad sheets of glass. The artificial gravity generated by deceleration gradually increased until it reached 1G. The portholes now formed the floor, and the people lying down felt the weight like the embrace of Mother Earth ahead of them. Excitement echoed around the chamber.

"We're home!"

"Can you believe it?"

"I'll get to see my kids again."

"We can have kids!"

When *Bronze Age* left the Solar System, the law had dictated that no one could be born on the ship unless someone died.

"She said she'd wait for me."

"If you'll have her! You're now a hero of the human race; you'll have a flock of pretty girls after you."

"Oh, I haven't seen flocks of birds in *ages*!"

"Doesn't everything we've been through seem like a dream?"

"I feel like I'm dreaming now."

"I'm utterly terrified of space."

"Me too. I'm retiring as soon as we get back. I'm going to buy a farm and spend the rest of my life on solid ground."

It had been fourteen years since the complete destruction of the Earth's combined fleet. The survivors, after engaging in separate internecine battles of darkness, cut off all contact with the home planet. However, for a year and a half thereafter, *Bronze Age* continued to receive transmissions from Earth, most of which were surface radio communications, but which also included some transmissions intended for space.

And then, at the beginning of November in Year 208 of the Crisis Era, all radio transmissions from Earth ceased. Every frequency fell silent, as though the Earth was a lamp that had been suddenly shut off.

Excerpt from *A Past Outside of Time*
Nyctohylophobia

When humanity finally learned that the universe was a dark forest in which everyone hunted everyone else, the child who had once cried out for contact by the bright campfire put out the fire and shivered in the darkness. Even a spark terrified him.

During the first few days, even mobile phone use was forbidden, and antennas around the world were forcibly shut down. Such a move, which would have once caused riots in the streets, was widely supported by the populace.

Gradually, as reason was restored, so were the mobile networks, but severe restrictions regarding electromagnetic radiation were put in place. All radio communications had to operate at minimum power, and any violators risked being tried for crimes against humanity.

Most people surely understood that these reactions were excessive and meaningless. The peak of the Earth's projection of electromagnetic signals into space had occurred during the age of analog signals, when television and radio transmission towers operated at high power levels. But as digital communication became prevalent, most information was transmitted via wires and optical cables, and even radio transmissions for digital signals required far less power than analog signals. The amount of electromagnetic radiation spilling into space from the Earth had fallen so much that some pre-Crisis scholars had fretted that the Earth would become impossible to discover by friendly aliens.

Electromagnetic waves are, moreover, the most primitive and least power-efficient method of transmitting information in the universe. Radio waves attenuate and degrade rapidly in the vastness of space, and most electromagnetic signals spilling from the Earth could not be received beyond two light-years.

Only something like the transmission by Ye Wenjie, which relied on the power of the sun as an antenna, could be intercepted by listeners among the stars.

As humanity's technology advanced, two far more efficient methods of signaling became available: neutrinos and gravitational waves. The latter was the main method of deterrence that humanity later deployed against Trisolaris.

The dark forest theory had a profound impact on human civilization. That child sitting by the ashes of the campfire turned from optimism to isolation and paranoia, a loner in the universe.

Deterrence Era, Year 12
Bronze Age

Most of the crew aboard *Bronze Age* attributed the sudden cessation of all signals from the Earth to the complete conquest of the Solar System by Trisolaris. *Bronze Age* accelerated and headed for a star with terrestrial planets twenty-six light-years away.

But ten days later, *Bronze Age* received a radio transmission from Fleet Command. The transmission had been sent simultaneously to *Bronze Age* and *Blue Space*, which was at the other end of the Solar System. The transmission gave a brief account of what had happened on Earth and notified them of the successful creation of a deterrence system to defend against Trisolaris. The two ships were ordered to return to Earth immediately. Moreover, Earth had taken great risks to send out this message to the lost ships; it would not be repeated.

At first, *Bronze Age* dared not trust this message—wasn't it possible that it was a trap set by those who had conquered the Solar System? The warship stopped accelerating and repeatedly queried Earth for confirmation. No reply ever came, as Earth maintained radio silence.

Just as *Bronze Age* was about to begin accelerating away from home again, the unimaginable happened: A sophon unfolded into low dimensions on the ship, establishing a quantum communication channel with Earth. Finally, the crew received confirmation of all that had occurred.

The crew found that, as some of the only survivors of the holocaust suffered by the combined space forces of Earth, they were now heroes of the human race. The whole world awaited their return with bated breath. Fleet Command awarded all members of the crew with the highest military honors.

Bronze Age began its return voyage. It was currently in outer space, about twenty-three hundred AU from the Earth, far beyond the Kuiper Belt but still some distance from the Oort Cloud. As it was cruising near maximum speed, deceleration consumed most of its fusion fuel. Its journey toward the Earth had to be conducted at a low cruising speed, and took eleven years.

As they finally neared Earth, a small white dot appeared ahead of them and quickly grew. It was *Gravity*, the warship that had been dispatched to welcome *Bronze Age*.

Gravity was the first stellar-class warship built after the Doomsday Battle. Deterrence-Era spaceships were no longer constructed along fixed body plans. Rather, most large spaceships were constructed out of multiple modules that could be assembled into various configurations. But *Gravity* was an exception. It was a white cylinder, so regular that it seemed unreal, like a basic shape dropped into space by mathematical modeling software, a platonic ideal rather than reality.

If the crew of *Bronze Age* had seen the gravitational wave antennas on the Earth, they would have recognized *Gravity* as an almost perfect replica of them. Indeed, the entire hull of *Gravity* was a large gravitational wave antenna. Like its twins on the Earth's surface, the ship was capable of broadcasting gravitational wave messages toward all corners of the universe at a moment's notice. These gravitational wave antennas on Earth and in space comprised humanity's dark forest deterrence system against Trisolaris.

After another day of coasting, *Bronze Age*, escorted by *Gravity*, entered geosynchronous orbit and slowly sailed into the orbital spaceport. *Bronze Age*'s crew could see dense crowds filling the broad expanse of the habitat sector of the spaceport like the opening ceremony of the Olympics or the Hajj in Mecca. The warship drifted through a colorful snowstorm of bouquets. The crew looked through the crowd for their loved ones. Everyone seemed to have tears in their eyes, crying out in joy.

With a final tremor, *Bronze Age* came to a complete stop. The captain gave a status report to Fleet Command and declared his intent to leave a skeleton crew behind on the ship. Fleet Command replied that the priority was to quickly reunite all members of the crew with their loved ones. There was no need to leave anyone behind on the ship. Another captain from the fleet boarded the ship with a small duty team who greeted everyone they encountered with tearful embraces.

It was unclear from the duty team's uniforms which of the three space fleets they belonged to, but they explained to those aboard the ship that the new Solar System Fleet was a single, unified force, and all those who had been part of the Doomsday Battle—including all the men and women aboard *Bronze Age*—would be key figures in the new fleet.

"In our lifetimes, we will conquer Trisolaris and open up a second solar system for human colonization!" the fleet captain said.

Someone replied that they found space too terrifying and they would rather remain on the Earth. The fleet captain said that was perfectly acceptable. As heroes of humanity, they were free to choose their own paths in life. However, after a bit of R&R, they might change their minds. He, for one, hoped to see this famed warship in action again. .

The crew of *Bronze Age* began to disembark. Everyone entered the habitable region of the spaceport through a long passageway. Open space stretched around the crew. In contrast to the air on the ship, the air here smelled fresh and sweet, like after a rainstorm. Against the background of the spinning blue globe that was the Earth, the joyous shouts of the welcoming crowd filled the expansive area.

Per a request from the fleet captain, the captain of *Bronze Age* conducted a roll call. At the fleet captain's insistence, the roll call was repeated, to confirm that every member of the crew had disembarked and was present and accounted for.

Then there was silence.

Although the celebrating crowd around them continued to dance and wave their arms, they made no sound. All that anyone from *Bronze Age* could hear was the fleet captain's voice. His face still bore a kind smile, but in that eerie silence, his voice sounded as sharp as the edge of a sword.

"You're hereby informed that you have been dishonorably discharged. You are no longer members of the Solar System Fleet. But the stain you have brought upon the fleet can never be erased! You will never see your loved ones again, because they have no wish to see you. Your parents are ashamed of you, and most of your spouses have long ago divorced you. Even though society has not discriminated against your children, they spent the past decade growing up in the shadow of your disgrace. They despise you!

"You are hereby transferred to Fleet International's justice system."

The fleet captain left with his team. Simultaneously, the celebratory crowd disappeared and was replaced by darkness. A few roving spotlights revealed the ranks of fully armed military police surrounding the crew of *Bronze Age*. Standing on platforms around the broad square, they aimed their guns at the crew.

Some members of the crew turned around and saw that the bouquets of flowers floating around *Bronze Age* were real, not holographic mirages. But now they made the warship seem like a giant coffin about to be buried.

Power to the magnetic boots worn by the crew was cut off, and they floated up in free fall, like a bunch of helpless target dummies.

A cold voice spoke to them from somewhere. "All armed crew members must immediately relinquish your weapons. If you do not cooperate, we cannot guarantee your safety. You're under arrest for murder in the first degree and crimes against humanity."

Deterrence Era, Year 13
Trial

▬

The *Bronze Age* case was tried by a Solar System Fleet court-martial. Although Fleet International's main facilities were located near the orbit of Mars, the asteroid belt, and the orbit of Jupiter, due to the intense interest in the case from Earth International, the trial was held at the fleet base in geosynchronous orbit.

To accommodate the numerous observers from Earth, the base spun to generate artificial gravity. Outside the broad windows of the courtroom, blue Earth, bright Sun, and the silvery brilliance of the stars appeared in succession, a cosmic metaphor for the contest of values. The trial lasted a month under these shifting lights and shadows. Excerpts from the trial transcript follow.

Neil Scott, male, 45, captain, commanding officer of *Bronze Age*

JUDGE: Let's return to the events leading up to the decision to attack *Quantum*.

SCOTT: I repeat: The attack was my decision and I gave the order. I didn't discuss it ahead of time with any other officer aboard *Bronze Age*.

JUDGE: You've been consistently trying to claim all responsibility. However, this is not, in fact, a wise course of action for either you or those you're trying to protect.

PROSECUTION: We have already confirmed that a vote by the full crew was taken prior to the attack.

SCOTT: As I've explained, of the one thousand seven hundred and seventy-five crew members, only fifty-nine supported an attack. The vote was not the cause or basis for my decision to attack.

JUDGE: Can you produce a list of those fifty-nine names?

SCOTT: The vote was conducted anonymously over the ship's internal network. You can examine the cruise and battle logs to confirm this.

PROSECUTION: More lies. We have ample evidence that the vote was not anonymous. Moreover, the result was nothing like your description. You falsified the logs afterwards.

JUDGE: We need you to produce the true record of the vote.

SCOTT: I don't have what you want. The result I recited is the truth.

JUDGE: Mr. Neil Scott, let me remind you: If you continue to obstruct this tribunal's investigation, you will harm the innocent members of your crew. Some members did vote against the attack, but without the evidence that only you can provide, we cannot exonerate them, and must declare all officers, noncommissioned officers, and enlisted men and women of *Bronze Age* guilty as charged.

SCOTT: What are you talking about? Are you a real judge? Is this a real court of law? What about the presumption of innocence?

JUDGE: The presumption of innocence does not apply to crimes against humanity. This is a principle of international law established at the start of the Crisis Era. It's intended to ensure that traitors against humankind do not escape punishment.

SCOTT: We're not traitors against humanity! Where were you when we fought for Earth?

PROSECUTION: You are absolutely traitors! While the ETO from two centuries ago only betrayed the interests of humanity, today, you betray our most basic moral principles, a far worse crime.

SCOTT: *[silence]*

JUDGE: I want you to understand the consequences of fabricating evidence. At the commencement of this trial, you read a statement on behalf of all the accused expressing your remorse over the deaths of the one thousand eight hundred and forty-seven men and women aboard *Quantum*. It is now time to show that remorse.

SCOTT: *[after a long silence]* All right. I will produce the true results. You can recover the vote tally from an encrypted entry in the logs aboard *Bronze Age*.

PROSECUTION: We will work on recovering those immediately. Can you give me an estimate of how many voted to attack *Quantum*?

SCOTT: One thousand six hundred and seventy. That's ninety-four percent of the crew.

JUDGE: Order! Order in the court! I must remind members of the public to maintain silence during the proceedings.

SCOTT: But it wouldn't have mattered. Even if less than fifty percent had voted yes, I would have attacked anyway. The final decision was mine.

PROSECUTION: Nice try. But *Bronze Age* was not like the newer ships at the other end of the Solar System, such as *Natural Selection*. Your ship's AI systems were primitive. Without the cooperation of those under your command, you could not have carried out the attack alone.

Sebastian Schneider, male, 31, lieutenant commander, in charge of targeting systems and attack patterns aboard *Bronze Age*

PROSECUTION: Other than the captain, you're the only officer with the system authorization to prevent or terminate an attack.

SCHNEIDER: Correct.

JUDGE: And you didn't.

SCHNEIDER: I did not.

JUDGE: What went through your mind at that time?

SCHNEIDER: At that moment—not the moment of the attack, but the moment when I realized that *Bronze Age* would never return home, when the ship would be my entire world—I changed. There was no process; I was simply transformed from head to toe. It was like the legendary mental seal.

JUDGE: Do you really think that's a possibility? That your ship was equipped with mental seals?

SCHNEIDER: Of course not. I was talking metaphorically. Space itself is a kind of mental seal. . . . In that moment, I gave up my individual self. My existence would be meaningful only if the collective survived. . . . I can't explain it better than that. I don't expect you to understand, Your Honor. Even if you boarded *Bronze Age* and sailed twenty thousand AU from the Solar System, or even farther, you still wouldn't understand.

JUDGE: Why?

SCHNEIDER: Because you'd know that you could come back! Your soul would have remained on Earth. Only if the space behind the ship turned into a bottomless abyss—only if the Sun, the Earth, and everything else were swallowed by emptiness—would you have a chance of understanding the transformation that I went through.

I'm from California. In 1967, under the old calendar, a high school teacher in my hometown, Ron Jones, did something interesting—please don't interrupt me. Thank you.

In order to help his students understand Nazism and totalitarianism, he tried to create a simulation of a totalitarian society with his students. It took only five days for him to succeed and his class to become a miniature fascist state. Every student willingly gave up the self and freedom, became one with the supreme collective, and pursued the collective's goals with religious zeal. In the end, this teaching experiment that began as a harmless game almost spun out of control. The Germans made a film based on Jones's experiment, and Jones himself wrote a book about it: *The Third Wave*. When those of us aboard *Bronze Age* found out that we were doomed to wander space forever, we formed a totalitarian state as well. Do you know how long it took?

Five minutes.

That's right. Five minutes into the all-hands meeting, the fundamental values of this totalitarian society had received the support of the vast majority of the crew. So, let me tell you, when humans are lost in space, it takes only five minutes to reach totalitarianism.

Boris Rovinski, male, 36, commander, executive officer of *Bronze Age*

JUDGE: You led the first boarding party onto *Quantum* after the attack?

ROVINSKI: Yes.

JUDGE: Were there any survivors?

ROVINSKI: None.

JUDGE: Can you describe the scene?

ROVINSKI: The individuals aboard died from the infrasonic waves generated by *Quantum*'s hull as it was struck by the electromagnetic pulses of the H-bomb detonation. The bodies were well preserved, showing no external signs of damage.

JUDGE: What did you do with the bodies?

ROVINSKI: We built a monument to them, like *Blue Space* did.

JUDGE: You mean, you left the bodies in the monument?

ROVINSKI: No. I doubt that the monument built by *Blue Space* had any bodies in it, either.

JUDGE: You haven't answered my question. I asked what you did with the bodies.

ROVINSKI: We refilled the food stores on *Bronze Age* with them.

JUDGE: All of them?

ROVINSKI: All of them.

JUDGE: Who made the decision to turn the bodies into food?

ROVINSKI: I . . . really can't remember. It seemed a completely natural thing to do at the time. I was responsible for logistics and support aboard the ship, and I directed the storage and distribution of the bodies.

JUDGE: How were the bodies consumed?

ROVINSKI: Nothing special was done. They were mixed up with the vegetables and meats in the bio-recycling system and then cooked.

JUDGE: Who ate this food?

ROVINSKI: Everyone. Everyone onboard *Bronze Age* had to eat in one of the four mess halls, and there was only one source of food.

JUDGE: Did they know what they were eating?

ROVINSKI: Of course.

JUDGE: How did they react?

ROVINSKI: I'm sure a few were uncomfortable with it. But there was no protest. Oh, I do recall eating in the officer's mess hall once and hearing someone say, "Thank you, Carol Joiner."

JUDGE: What did he mean?

ROVINSKI: Carol Joiner was the communications officer aboard *Quantum*. He was eating a part of her.

JUDGE: How could he know that?

ROVINSKI: We were all fitted with a tracking and identification capsule about the size of a grain of rice. It was implanted under the skin of the left arm. Sometimes the cooking process didn't remove it. I'm sure he just found it on his plate and used his communicator to read it.

JUDGE: Order! Order in the courtroom! Please remove those who have fainted. Mr. Rovinski, surely you must have understood that you were violating the most fundamental laws that make us human?

ROVINSKI: We were constrained by other morals that you don't understand. During the Doomsday Battle, *Bronze Age* had to exceed its designed acceleration parameters. The power systems were overloaded, and the life support systems lost power for almost two hours, leading to massive damage throughout. The repairs had to be conducted slowly. Meanwhile, the hibernation systems were also affected, and only about five hundred people could be accommodated. Since more than one thousand people had to eat, if we didn't introduce additional food sources, half of the population would have starved to death.

Even without these constraints, considering the interminable voyage that lay in front of us, to abandon so much precious protein in space would have been truly unconscionable. . . .

I'm not trying to defend myself, and I'm not trying to defend anyone else on *Bronze Age*. Now that I've recovered the thinking patterns of humans anchored to the Earth, it is very difficult for me to speak these words. Very difficult.

Final statement made by Captain Neil Scott

I don't have much to say except a warning.

Life reached an evolutionary milestone when it climbed onto land from the ocean, but those first fish that climbed onto land ceased to be fish.

Similarly, when humans truly enter space and are freed from the Earth, they cease to be human. So, to all of you I say this: When you think about heading into outer space without looking back, please reconsider. The cost you must pay is far greater than you could imagine.

In the end, Captain Neil Scott and six other senior officers were convicted of murder and crimes against humanity and sentenced to life imprisonment. Of the remaining 1,768 members of the crew, only 138 were declared innocent. The rest received sentences ranging from twenty to three hundred years.

The Fleet International prison was located in the asteroid belt, between the orbits of Mars and Jupiter. Thus, the prisoners had to leave Earth again. Although *Bronze Age* had reached geosynchronous orbit, the prisoners were doomed never to travel the last thirty thousand kilometers of their 350-billion-kilometer voyage home.

As the prisoner transport ship accelerated, they once again drifted and fell against the portholes at the stern, like fallen leaves doomed to never reach the root of the tree. They looked outward as the blue globe that had haunted their dreams shrank and, once again, became just another star.

Before departing the fleet base, former Commander Rovinski, former Lieutenant Commander Schneider, and about a dozen other officers returned under guard to *Bronze Age* for the last time to assist with some details of the handover of the ship to her new crew.

For more than a decade, this ship had been their entire world. They had carefully decorated the inside with holograms of grasslands, forests, and oceans; cultivated real gardens; and built fishing ponds and water fountains, turning the ship into a real home. But now, all that was gone. All traces of their existence on the ship had been wiped away. *Bronze Age* was once again just a cold stellar warship.

Everyone they encountered in the halls looked at them coldly or simply ignored them. When they saluted, they made sure their eyes did not waver, to make it clear to the prisoners that the salute was for the military police escorting them only.

Schneider was brought to a spherical cabin to discuss technical details of the ship's targeting system with three officers. The three officers treated Schneider like a computer. They asked him questions in an emotionless voice and waited for his answers. There was not a hint of politeness, and not a single wasted word.

It took only an hour to complete the session. Schneider tapped the floating control interface a few times, as though closing some windows out of habit. All of a sudden, he kicked the spherical wall of the cabin hard, and propelled himself to the other end of the chamber. Simultaneously, the walls shifted and divided the cabin into two halves. The three officers and the military policeman were trapped in one half, and Schneider was alone in the other.

Schneider brought up a floating window. He tapped on it, his fingers a blur. It was the control interface for the communications system. Schneider brought the ship's high-powered interstellar communications antenna online.

A faint *pop*. A small hole appeared in the cabin wall, and the cabin was filled with white smoke. The barrel of the military policeman's gun poked through the hole and aimed at Schneider.

"This is your last warning. Stop what you're doing immediately and open the door."

"*Blue Space*, this is *Bronze Age*." Schneider's voice was quiet. He knew how far his message could travel had nothing to do with how loudly he spoke.

A laser beam shot through Schneider's chest. Red steam from vaporized blood erupted from the hole. Surrounded by a red fog made of his own blood, Schneider croaked out his last words:

"Don't come back. This is no longer your home!"

Blue Space had always responded to Earth's entreaties with more hesitation and suspicion than *Bronze Age* had, so they had only been decelerating slowly.

Thus, by the time they received *Bronze Age*'s warning, they were still heading away from the Solar System.

After Schneider's warning, *Blue Space* instantly shifted from decelerating to accelerating full speed ahead.

When Earth received the intelligence report from the sophons of Trisolaris, the two civilizations had a shared enemy for the first time in history.

Earth and Trisolaris were comforted by the fact that *Blue Space* didn't currently possess the ability to engage in dark forest deterrence against the two worlds. Even if it tried to broadcast the locations of the two solar systems to the universe at full power, it would be almost impossible for anyone to hear it. To reach Barnard's Star, the nearest star that *Blue Space* could use as a superantenna to repeat Ye Wenjie's feat, would take three hundred years. However, it hadn't shifted its course toward Barnard's Star. Instead, it was still heading toward NH558J2, which it wouldn't reach for two thousand more years.

Gravity, as the only Solar System ship capable of interstellar flight, immediately began to pursue *Blue Space*. Trisolaris brought up the idea of sending a speedy droplet—formally, it was called a strong-interaction space probe—to pursue and destroy *Blue Space*. But Earth unequivocally refused. From humanity's perspective, *Blue Space* should be dealt with as a matter of internal affairs. The Doomsday Battle was humanity's greatest wound, and after more than a decade, the pain had not lessened one whit. Permitting another droplet attack on humans was absolutely politically unacceptable. Even though the crew of *Blue Space* had become aliens in the minds of most people, only humanity should bring them to justice.

Out of consideration for the ample time that remained before *Blue Space* could become a threat, Trisolaris acquiesced. However, Trisolaris emphasized that, since *Gravity* possessed the ability to broadcast via gravitational waves, its security was a matter of life and death for Trisolaris. Therefore, droplets would be sent as escorts, but would also ensure an overwhelming advantage against *Blue Space*.

Thus, *Gravity* cruised in formation with two droplets a few thousand meters away. The contrast between the sizes of the two ship types couldn't be greater. If one pulled back far enough to see the entirety of *Gravity*, the droplets would be invisible. And if one pulled close enough to a droplet to observe it, its smooth surface would clearly reflect an image of *Gravity*.

Gravity was built about a decade after *Blue Space*. Other than the gravitational wave antenna, it was not significantly more advanced. Its propulsion systems, for example, were only slightly more powerful than *Blue Space*'s.

Gravity's confidence in the success of their hunt was due to their overwhelming advantage in fuel reserves.

Even so, based on the ships' current velocities and accelerations, it would take fifty years for *Gravity* to catch *Blue Space*.

Deterrence Era, Year 61
The Swordholder

———

Cheng Xin gazed up at her star from the top of a giant tree. It was why she had been awakened.

During the brief life of the Stars Our Destination Project, a total of fifteen individuals were granted ownership of seventeen stars. Other than Cheng Xin, the other fourteen owners were lost to history, and no legal heirs could be located. The Great Ravine acted like a giant sieve, and too many did not make it through. Now, Cheng Xin was the only one who held legal title to a star.

Though humanity still hadn't begun to reach for any star beyond the Solar System, the rapid pace of technological progress meant that stars within three hundred light-years of the Earth were no longer of mere symbolic value. DX3906, Cheng Xin's star, turned out to have planets after all. Of the two planets discovered so far, one seemed very similar to Earth based on its mass, orbit, and a spectrum analysis of its atmosphere. As a result, its value rose to stratospheric heights. To everyone's surprise, they discovered that this star already had an owner.

The UN and the Solar System Fleet wanted to reclaim DX3906, but this couldn't be done legally unless the owner agreed to transfer the title. Thus Cheng Xin was awakened from her slumber after 264 years of hibernation.

The first thing she found out after emerging from hibernation was this: As she had expected, there was no news whatsoever about the Staircase Program. The Trisolarans had not intercepted the probe, and they had no idea of its whereabouts. The Staircase Program had been forgotten by history, and Tianming's brain was lost in the vastness of space. But this man, this man who had merged into nothingness, had left a real, solid world for his beloved, a world composed of a star and two planets.

A Ph.D. in astronomy named 艾 AA[3] had discovered the planets around DX3906. As part of her dissertation, AA had developed a new technique that used one star as a gravitational lens through which to observe another.

To Cheng Xin, AA resembled a vivacious bird fluttering around her nonstop. AA told Cheng Xin that she was familiar with people like her, who had come from the past—known as "Common Era people" after the old calendar—since her own dissertation advisor was a physicist from back then. Her knowledge of Common Era people was why she had been appointed as Cheng Xin's liaison from the UN Space Development Agency as her first job after her doctorate.

The request from the UN and the fleet to sell the star back to them put Cheng Xin in an awkward position. She felt guilty possessing a whole world, but the idea of selling a gift that had been given to her out of pure love made her ill. She suggested that she could give up all claim of ownership over DX3906 and keep the deed only as a memento, but she was told that was unacceptable. By law, the authorities could not accept such valuable real estate without compensating the original owner, so they insisted on buying it. Cheng Xin refused.

After much reflection, she came up with a new proposal: She would sell the two planets, but retain ownership of the star. At the same time, she would sign a covenant with the UN and the fleet granting humanity the right to use the energy produced by the star. The legal experts eventually concluded that this proposal was acceptable.

AA told Cheng Xin that since she was only selling the planets, the amount of compensation offered by the UN was much lower. But it was still an astronomical sum, and she would need to form a company to manage it properly.

"Would you like me to help you run this company?" AA asked.

Cheng Xin agreed, and AA immediately called the UN Space Development Agency to resign.

"I'm working for you now," she said, "so let me speak for a minute about your interests. Are you nuts?! Of all the choices available to you, you picked the *worst*! You could have sold the star along with the planets, and you would have become one of the richest people in the universe! Alternatively, you could have refused to sell, and kept the entire solar system for yourself. The law's protection of private property is absolute, and no one could have taken it away

---

[3] *Translator's Note*: This is a name written in a mix of Chinese characters and English letters. The "艾" is the surname and is pronounced "Ai."

from you. And then you could have entered hibernation and woken up only when it's possible to fly to DX3906. Then you could go there! All that space! The ocean, the continents . . . you can do whatever you want, of course, but you should take me with you—"

"I've already made my decision," Cheng Xin said. "There's almost three centuries separating us. I don't expect us to understand each other right away."

"Fine." AA sighed. "But you should reevaluate your conception of duty and conscience. Duty drove you to give up the planets, and conscience made you keep the star, but duty again made you give up the star's energy output. You're one of those people from the past, like my dissertation advisor, torn by conflict between two ideals. But, in our age, conscience and duty are not ideals: an excess of either is seen as a mental illness called social-pressure personality disorder. You should seek treatment."

Even with the glow from the lights of the city below, Cheng Xin easily found DX3906. Compared to the twenty-first century, the air was far clearer. She turned from the night sky to the reality around her: She and AA stood like two ants on top of a glowing Christmas tree, and all around them stood a forest of Christmas trees. Buildings full of lights hung from branches like leaves. But this giant city was built on top of the earth, not below it. Thanks to the peace of the Deterrence Era, humanity's second cave-dwelling phase had come to an end.

They walked along the bough toward the tip. Each branch of the tree was a busy avenue full of floating translucent windows filled with information. They made the street look like a varicolored river. From time to time, a window or two left the traffic in the road and followed them for a while, and drifted back into the current when AA and Cheng Xin showed no interest. All the buildings on this branch-street hung below. Since this was the highest branch, the starry sky was right above them. If they had been walking along one of the lower branches, they would be surrounded by the bright buildings hanging from the branch above, and they would have felt like tiny insects flying through a dream forest, in which every leaf and fruit sparkled and dazzled.

Cheng Xin looked at the pedestrians along the street: a woman, two women, a group of women, another woman, three women—all of them were women, all beautiful. Dressed in pretty, luminous clothes, they seemed like the nymphs of this magical forest. Once in a while, they passed some older individuals, also women, their beauty undiminished by age. As they reached the end of the branch and surveyed the sea of lights below them, Cheng Xin asked the question that had been puzzling her for days. "What happened to the men?" In the few days since she had been awakened, she had not seen a single man.

"What do you mean? They're everywhere." AA pointed at the people around them. "Over there: See the man leaning against the balustrade? And there are three over there. And two walking toward us."

Cheng Xin stared. The individuals AA indicated had smooth, lovely faces; long hair that draped over their shoulders; slender, soft bodies—as if their bones were made of bananas. Their movements were graceful and gentle, and their voices, carried to her by the breeze, were sweet and tender. . . . Back in her century, these people would have been considered ultra-feminine.

Understanding dawned on her after a moment. The trend had been obvious even earlier. The decade of the 1980s was probably the last time when masculinity, as traditionally defined, was considered an ideal. After that, society and fashion preferred men who displayed traditionally feminine qualities. She recalled the Asian male pop stars of her own time who she had thought looked like pretty girls at first glance. The Great Ravine interrupted this tendency in the evolution of human society, but half a century of peace and ease brought about by the Deterrence Era accelerated the trend.

"It's true that Common Era people usually have trouble telling men and women apart at first," AA said. "But I'll teach you a trick. Pay attention to the way they look at you. A classical beauty like you is very attractive to them."

Cheng Xin looked at her, a bit flustered.

"No, no!" AA laughed. "I really am a woman, and I don't like you that way. But, honestly, I can't see what's attractive about the men of your era. Rude, savage, dirty—it's like they hadn't fully evolved. You'll adjust to and enjoy this age of beauty."

Close to three centuries ago, when Cheng Xin had been preparing for hibernation, she had imagined all kinds of difficulties she would face in the future, but this was something she was unprepared for. She imagined what it would be like to live the rest of her life in this feminine world . . . and her mood turned melancholic. She looked up and searched for her star.

"You're thinking of him again, aren't you?" AA grabbed her by the shoulders. "Even if he hadn't gone into space and had spent the rest of his life with you, the grandchildren of your grandchildren would be dead by now. This is a new age; a new life. Forget about the past!"

Cheng Xin tried to think as AA suggested and forced herself to return to the present. She had only been here for a few days, and had just grasped the broadest outline of the history of the past three centuries. The strategic balance between the humans and the Trisolarans as a result of dark forest deterrence had shocked her the most.

A thought popped into her mind. *A world dedicated to femininity . . . but what does that mean for deterrence?*

Cheng Xin and AA walked back along the bough. Again, a few informational windows drifted along with them, and this time, one drew Cheng Xin's attention. The window showed a man, clearly a man from the past: haggard, gaunt, messy hair, standing next to a black tombstone. The man and the tombstone were in shadows, but his eyes seemed to glow brightly with the reflected light of a distant dawn. A line of text appeared on the bottom of the screen:

Back during his time, a killer would be sentenced to death.

Cheng Xin thought the man's face looked familiar, but before she could look more closely, the image had disappeared. In his place appeared a middle-aged woman—well, at least Cheng Xin thought she was a woman. Wearing formal, non-glowing clothes that reminded Cheng Xin of a politician's, she was in the middle of giving a speech. The text earlier had been a part of the subtitles for her speech.

The window seemed to notice Cheng Xin's interest. It expanded and began to play the audio accompanying the video. The politician's voice was lovely and sweet, as though the words were strung together by strands of blown sugar. But the content of the speech was terrifying.

"Why the death penalty? Answer: because he killed. But that is only one correct answer.

"Another correct answer would be: because he killed too few. Killing one person was murder; killing a few or dozens was more murder; so killing thousands or tens of thousands ought to be punished by putting the murderer to death a thousand times. What about more than that? A few hundred thousand? The death penalty, right? Yet, those of you who know some history are starting to hesitate.

"What if he killed millions? I can guarantee you such a person would not be considered a murderer. Indeed, such a person may not even be thought to have broken any law. If you don't believe me, just study history! Anyone who has killed millions is deemed a 'great' man, a hero.

"And if that person destroyed a whole world and killed every life on it—he would be hailed as a savior!"

"They're talking about Luo Ji," said AA. "They want to put him on trial."

"Why?"

"It's complicated. But basically, it's because of that world, the world whose location he broadcast to the universe, causing it to be destroyed. We don't know if there was life on that world—it's a possibility. So they're charging him with suspected mundicide, the most serious crime under our laws."

"Hey, you must be Cheng Xin!"

The voice shocked Cheng Xin. It had come from the floating window in front of her. The politician in it gazed at Cheng Xin, joy and surprise on her face, as though she were seeing an old friend. "You're the woman who owns that faraway world! Like a ray of hope, you've brought the beauty of your time to us. As the only human being ever to possess an entire world, you will also save this world. All of us have faith in you. Oh, sorry, I should introduce myself—"

AA kicked the window and shut it off. Cheng Xin was utterly amazed by the technology level of this age. She had no idea how her own image had been transmitted to the speaker, and no idea how the speaker was then able to pick her out of the billions who were watching her speech.

AA rushed in front of Cheng Xin and walked backwards as they talked. "Would you have destroyed a world to create this form of deterrence? And, more importantly, if the enemy weren't deterred, would you press the button to ensure the destruction of two worlds?"

"This is a meaningless question. I would never put myself in that position."

AA stopped and grabbed Cheng Xin by the shoulders. She stared into her eyes. "Really? You wouldn't?"

"Of course not. Being put in such a position is the most terrifying fate I can think of. Far worse than death."

She couldn't understand why AA seemed so earnest, but AA nodded. "That puts me at ease. . . . Why don't we talk more tomorrow? You're tired and should get more rest. It takes a week to completely recover from hibernation."

The next morning, Cheng Xin got a call from AA.

AA showed up on the screen looking excited. "I'm going to surprise you and take you somewhere cool. Come on up. The car is at the top of the tree."

Cheng Xin went up and saw a flying car with its door open. She got in but didn't see AA. The door slid shut noiselessly and the seat molded itself around her, holding her tight like a hand. Gently, the car took off, merging into the streaming traffic of the forest-city.

It was still early, and shafts of sunlight, almost parallel to the ground, flickered through the car as it passed through the forest. Gradually, the giant trees thinned out and, finally, disappeared. Under the blue sky, Cheng Xin saw only grassland and woodland, an intoxicating green mosaic.

After the start of the Deterrence Era, most heavy industries had moved into orbit, and the Earth's natural ecology recovered. The surface of the Earth now looked more like it did in pre–Industrial Revolution times. Due to a drop in population and further industrialization of food production, much of the arable land was allowed to lie fallow and return to nature. The Earth was transforming into a giant park.

This beautiful world seemed unreal to Cheng Xin. Though awakened from hibernation, she felt as though she were in a dream.

Half an hour later, the car landed and the door slid open automatically. Cheng Xin got out, and the car rose into the air and left. After the turbulence from the propellers subsided, silence reigned over everything, pierced by occasional birdsong from far away. Cheng Xin looked around and found herself in the midst of a group of abandoned buildings. They looked like residential buildings from the Common Era. The bottom half of every building was covered in ivy.

The sight of the past covered by the green life of a new era gave Cheng Xin the sense of reality that she had been missing.

She called for AA, but a man's voice responded. "Hello."

She turned and saw a man standing on an ivy-covered second-story balcony. He wasn't like the soft, beautiful men of this time, but like the men of the past. Cheng Xin seemed to be dreaming again, a continuation of her nightmare from the Common Era.

It was Thomas Wade. He wore a black leather jacket, but he looked a bit older. Perhaps he had gone into hibernation after Cheng Xin, or perhaps he had awakened before her, or both.

Cheng Xin's eyes were focused on Wade's right hand. The hand, covered by a black leather glove, held an old Common-Era gun that was pointing at Cheng Xin.

"The bullet in here was designed to be shot underwater," said Wade. "It's supposed to last a long time. But it's been more than two hundred and seventy years. Who knows if it will work?" That familiar smile, the one he wore when he was taking delight in the despair of others, appeared on his face.

A flash. An explosion. Cheng Xin felt a hard punch against her left shoulder and the force slammed her against the broken wall behind her. The thick ivy muffled much of the noise from the gunshot. Distant birds continued to chitter.

"I can't use a modern gun," said Wade. "Every shot is automatically recorded in the public security databases now." His tone was as serene as it had been when he used to discuss routine tasks with her.

"Why?" Cheng Xin didn't feel pain. Her left shoulder felt numb, as if it didn't belong to her.

"I want to be the Swordholder. You are my competitor, and you're going to win. I don't harbor any ill will toward you. Whether you believe me or not, I feel terrible at this moment."

"Did you kill Vadimov?" she asked. Blood seeped from the corner of her mouth.

"Yes. The Staircase Program needed him. And now, my new plan does not need you. Both of you are very good, but you're in the way. I have to advance, advance without regard for consequences."

Another shot. The bullet went through the left side of Cheng Xin's abdomen. She still didn't feel pain, but the spreading numbness made her unable to keep standing. She slid down against the wall, leaving a bright trail of blood on the ivy behind her.

Wade pulled the trigger again. Finally, the passage of nearly three centuries caught up with the gun, and it made no sound. Wade racked the slide to clear the dud out of the chamber. Once again, he pointed the gun at Cheng Xin.

His right arm exploded. A puff of white smoke rose into the air, and Wade's right forearm was gone. Burnt bits of bone and flesh splattered into the green leaves around him, but the gun, undamaged, fell to the foot of the building. Wade didn't move. He took a look at the stump of his right arm and then looked up. A police car was diving toward him.

As the police car approached the ground, several armed police officers jumped out and landed in the thick grass waving in the turbulence thrown up by the propellers. They looked like slender, nimble women.

The last one to jump out of the car was AA. Cheng Xin's vision was blurring, but she could see AA's tearful face and hear her sobbing explanation.

". . . faked my call . . ."

A fierce wave of pain seized her, and she lost consciousness.

When Cheng Xin woke up, she found herself in a flying car. A film clung to her and wrapped her tightly. She couldn't feel pain, couldn't even feel the presence of her body. Her consciousness began to fade again. In a faint voice that no one but herself could hear, she asked, "What is a Swordholder?"

Excerpt from *A Past Outside of Time*
The Ghost of the Wallfacers:
The Swordholder

Without a doubt, Luo Ji's creation of dark forest deterrence against Trisolaris was a great achievement, but the Wallfacer Project that led to it was judged a ridiculous, childish act. Humanity, like a child entering society for the first time, had lashed out at the sinister universe with terror and confusion. Once Luo Ji had transferred control of the deterrence system to the UN and the Solar System Fleet, everyone thought the Wallfacer Project, a legendary bit of history, was over.

People turned their attention to deterrence itself, and a new field of study was born: deterrence game theory.

The main elements of deterrence are these: the deterrer and the deteree (in dark forest deterrence, humanity and Trisolaris); the threat (broadcasting the location of Trisolaris so as to ensure the destruction of both worlds); the controller (the person or organization holding the broadcast switch); and the goal (forcing Trisolaris to abandon its invasion plan and to share technology with humanity).

When the deterrent is the complete destruction of both the deterrer and the deteree, the system is said to be in a state of ultimate deterrence.

Compared to other types of deterrence, ultimate deterrence is distinguished by the fact that, should deterrence fail, carrying out the threat would be of no benefit to the deterrer.

Thus, the key to the success of ultimate deterrence is the belief by the deteree that the threat will almost certainly be carried out if the deteree thwarts the deterrer's goals. This probability, or degree of deterrence, is an important parameter in deterrence game theory. The degree of deterrence must exceed 80 percent for the deterrer to succeed.

But people soon discovered a discouraging fact: If the authority to carry out the threat in dark forest deterrence is held by humanity as a whole, then the degree of deterrence is close to zero.

Asking humanity to take an action that would destroy two worlds is difficult: The decision would violate deeply held moral principles and values. The particular conditions of dark forest deterrence made the task even harder. Should deterrence fail, humanity would survive for at least one more generation. In a sense, everyone alive would be unaffected. But in the event of deterrence failing, carrying out the threat and broadcasting would mean that destruction could come at any moment, a far worse result than not carrying out the threat. Thus, if deterrence failed, the reaction of humankind as a whole could be easily predicted.

But an individual's reaction could not be predicted.

The success of dark forest deterrence was founded on the unpredictability of Luo Ji as an individual. If deterrence failed, his actions would be guided by his own personality and psychology. Even if he acted rationally, his own interests might not match humanity's interests perfectly. At the beginning of the Deterrence Era, both worlds carefully analyzed Luo Ji's personality and built up detailed mathematical models. Human and Trisolaran deterrence game theorists reached remarkably similar conclusions: Depending on his mental state at the moment deterrence failed, Luo Ji's degree of deterrence hovered between 91.9 percent and 98.4 percent. Trisolaris would not gamble with such odds.

Of course, such careful analysis wasn't possible immediately after the creation of dark forest deterrence. But humanity quickly reached this conclusion intuitively, and the UN and the Solar System Fleet handed the authority to activate the deterrence system back to Luo Ji like a hot potato. The entire process from Luo Ji turning over the authority to getting it back took a total of eighteen hours. Yet that would have been long enough for droplets to destroy the ring of nuclear bombs surrounding the Sun and deprive humanity of the ability to broadcast their locations. The Trisolarans' failure to do so was widely considered their greatest strategic blunder during the war, and humanity, covered in cold sweat, let out a held breath.

Since then, the power to activate the dark forest deterrence system had always been vested in Luo Ji. His hand first held the detonation switch for the circumsolar ring of nuclear bombs, and then the switch for the gravitational wave broadcast.

Dark forest deterrence hung over two worlds like the Sword of Damocles, and Luo Ji was the single hair from a horse's tail that held up the sword. Thus, he came to be called the Swordholder.

The Wallfacer Project did not fade into history after all. Humanity could not escape the Wallfacers' ghost.

Although the Wallfacer Project was an unprecedented anomaly in the history of humankind, both dark forest deterrence and the Swordholder had precursors. The mutual assured destruction practiced by NATO and the Warsaw Pact during the Cold War was an example of ultimate deterrence. In 1974, The Soviet Union initiated the Perimeter System (Russian Система «Периметр»), or "Dead Hand." This was intended to guarantee that the Soviet Union possessed a viable second-strike capability in the event that an American-led first strike eliminated the Soviet government and high-level military command centers. The system relied on a monitoring system that gathered evidence of nuclear explosions within the Soviet Union; all the data was transmitted to a central computer that interpreted the data and decided whether to launch the Soviet Union's nuclear arsenal.

The heart of the system was a secret control chamber hidden deep underground. If the system determined that a counterstrike must be launched, an operator on duty would initiate it.

In 2009, an officer who had been on duty in the room decades earlier told a reporter that at the time, he was a twenty-five-year-old junior lieutenant, freshly graduated from Frunze Military Academy. If the system determined that a strike was necessary, he was the last check before the complete destruction of the world. At that moment, all of the Soviet Union and Eastern Europe would likely be a sea of flames, and all of his loved ones above ground almost certainly dead. If he pushed the button, North America would also turn into hell on Earth in half an hour, and the following nuclear winter would doom all of humanity. He would hold the fate of human civilization in his hand.

Later, he was asked this question many times: If that moment had really arrived, would you have pushed the button?

The first Swordholder in history answered: *I don't know.*

Humanity hoped that dark forest deterrence would have a happy ending, like the mutually assured destruction of the twentieth century.

Time passed in this strange balance. Deterrence had been in effect for sixty years, and Luo Ji, who was now over a hundred, still held the switch to initiate the broadcast. His image among the populace had also gradually changed.

Hawks who wished to take the hard line against Trisolaris did not like him. Near the beginning of the Deterrence Era, they advocated imposing more severe conditions on the Trisolarans, with the goal of completely disarming Trisolaris. Some of their proposals were absurd. For instance, one idea was the "naked resettlement" program, which would have demanded that all Triso-larans dehydrate and allow themselves to be transported by cargo ships to the Oort Cloud, where they would be picked up by human spaceships and brought to the Solar System to be stored in dehydratories on Mars or the moon. There-after, if the Trisolarans satisfied certain conditions, they would be rehydrated in small batches.

The doves, similarly, did not like Luo Ji. Their primary concern was whether the star 187J3X1, whose location had been broadcast by Luo Ji, had possessed planets that harbored life and civilization. No astronomer from the two worlds could definitively answer this question: It was impossible to prove the affirma-tive or the negative. But it was certain that Luo Ji could be suspected of having committed mundicide. The doves believed that in order for humanity and Trisolaris to peacefully coexist, the foundation must be universal "human" rights—in other words, the recognition that all civilized beings in the universe had inviolable, fundamental rights. To make such an ideal into reality, Luo Ji must be tried.

Luo Ji ignored them all. He held the switch to the gravitational wave broad-cast system and silently stood at the Swordholder post for half a century.

Humanity came to realize that all policies with respect to the Trisolarans had to take the Swordholder into account. Without his approval, no human policy had any effect on Trisolaris. Thus, the Swordholder became a powerful dictator, much like the Wallfacers had.

As time passed, Luo Ji slowly came to be seen as an irrational monster and a mundicidal despot.

People realized that the Deterrence Era was a strange time. On the one hand, human society had reached unprecedented heights of civilization: Human rights and democracy reigned supreme everywhere. On the other hand, the entire system existed within the shadow of a dictator. Experts believed that although science and technology usually contributed to the elimination of totalitarianism, when crises threatened the existence of civilization, science and technology could also give birth to new totalitarianism. In traditional to-talitarian states, the dictator could only enact his control through other people, which led to low efficiency and uncertainty. Thus, there had never been a 100 percent effective totalitarian society in human history. But technology pro-vided the possibility for such a super-totalitarianism, and both the Wallfacers and the Swordholder were concerning examples. The combination of super-technology and a supercrisis could throw humankind back into the dark ages.

But most people also agreed that deterrence remained necessary. After the sophons unblocked the progress of human technology and the Trisolarans began transferring their knowledge to humans, human science had advanced by leaps and bounds. However, compared to Trisolaris, Earth was still behind by at least two or three technology ages. Decommissioning the deterrence system was to be considered only when the two worlds were approximately equal in technology.

There was one more choice: turning over control of the deterrence system to artificial intelligence. This was a choice that had been evaluated seriously, and much effort was expended in researching its feasibility. Its biggest advantage was a very high degree of deterrence. But ultimately, it wasn't adopted. Handing over the fate of two worlds to machines was a terrifying idea. Experiments showed that AIs tended not to make correct decisions when faced with the complex conditions of deterrence—unsurprising, since correct judgment required more than logical reasoning. Moreover, changing from a dictatorship-by-man to a dictatorship-by-machine wouldn't have made people feel any better, and was politically worse. Finally, sophons could interfere with AI reasoning. Though no example of such interference had been discovered, the mere possibility made the choice inconceivable.

A compromise was to change the Swordholder. Even without the above considerations, Luo Ji was a centenarian. His thinking and psychological state were becoming more unreliable, and people were growing uneasy that the fate of both worlds rested in his hands.

Deterrence Era, Year 61
The Swordholder

Cheng Xin's recovery proceeded apace. The doctors told her that even if all ten seven-millimeter bullets in the gun had struck her, and even if her heart had been shattered, modern medicine was capable of reviving her and fixing her up good as new—though it would have been a different matter if her brain had been hit.

The police told her that the last murder case in the world had occurred twenty-eight years ago, and this city hadn't had a murder case in almost forty years. The police were out of practice when it came to the prevention and detection of murder, and that was why Wade had almost succeeded. Another candidate for the Swordholder position had warned the police. But Wade's competitor had presented no proof, only a suspicion of Wade's intent based on a sensitivity that this era lacked. The police, dubious of the accusation, wasted a lot of time. Only after discovering that Wade had faked a call from AA did they take action.

Many people came to visit Cheng Xin at the hospital: officials from the government, the UN, and the Solar System Fleet; members of the public; and, of course, AA and her friends. By now, Cheng Xin could easily tell the sexes apart, and she was growing used to modern men's completely feminized appearance, perceiving in them an elegance that the men of her era lacked. Still, they were not attractive to her.

The world no longer seemed so strange, and Cheng Xin yearned to know it better, but she was stuck in her hospital room.

One day, AA came and played a holographic movie for her. The movie, named A *Fairy Tale of Yangtze*, had won Best Picture at that year's Oscars. It

was based on a song composed in *busuanzi* verse form by the Song Dynasty
poet Li Zhiyi:

> *You live at one end of the Yangtze, and I the other.*
> *I think of you each day, beloved, though we cannot meet.*
> *We drink from the same river. . . .*

The film was set in some unspecified ancient golden age, and told the story
of a pair of lovers, one who lived at the source of the Yangtze, and the other at
its mouth. The pair was kept apart for the entire film; they never got to see
each other, not even in an imaginary scene. But their love was portrayed with
utter sorrow and pathos. The cinematography was also wonderful: The elegance and refinement of the lower Yangtze Delta and the vigor and strength
of the Tibetan Plateau contrasted and complemented each other, forming an
intoxicating mix for Cheng Xin. The film lacked the heavy-handedness of the
commercial films of her own era. Instead, the story flowed as naturally as the
Yangtze itself, and absorbed Cheng Xin effortlessly.

I'm at one end of the River of Time, Cheng Xin thought, *but the other end is
now empty. . . .*

The movie stimulated Cheng Xin's interest in the culture of her new era.
Once she recovered enough to walk, AA brought her to art shows and concerts.
Cheng Xin could clearly remember going to Factory 798[4] and the Shanghai
Biennale to see strange pieces of contemporary "art," and it was hard for her to
imagine how much art had evolved in the three centuries she was asleep. But
the paintings she saw at the art show were all realistic—beautiful colors enliv-
ened with vitality and feeling. She felt each painting was like a heart, beating
gently between the beauty of nature and human nature. As for the music, she
thought everything she heard sounded like classical symphonies, reminding
her of the Yangtze in the movie: imposing and forceful, but also calm and
soothing. She stared at the flowing river until it seemed that the water had
ceased moving, and it was she that was moving toward the source, a long, long
way. . . .

The art and culture of this age were nothing like what she had imagined,
but it wasn't simply a matter of a return to classical style, either. It was more of

---

[4] *Translator's Note*: A famous artistic community in Beijing housed in abandoned military factory buildings.
Artists began to congregate there in the 1990s.

a spiraling sublimation of post-postmodernism, built upon a new aesthetic foundation. For instance, A *Fairy Tale of Yangtze* contained profound metaphors for the universe and space and time. But Cheng Xin was most impressed by the disappearance of the gloomy despair and bizarre noise so prevalent in the postmodern culture and art of the twenty-first century. In their place was an unprecedented warm serenity and optimism.

"I love your era," said Cheng Xin. "I'm surprised."

"You'd be even more surprised if you knew the artists behind these films, paintings, and music. They're all Trisolarans from four light-years away." AA laughed uproariously as she observed Cheng Xin's stunned gape.

Excerpt from *A Past Outside of Time*
Cultural Reflection

After the creation of deterrence, the World Academy of Sciences—an international organization at the same level as the UN—was founded to receive and digest the scientific and technical information transmitted to Earth from Trisolaris.

People first predicted that Trisolaris would only provide knowledge to Earth in sporadic, disconnected fragments after much pressure, and sprinkle deliberate falsehoods and misleading ideas into what little they chose to share, so the scientists of Earth would have to sift through them carefully for nuggets of truth. But Trisolaris defied those expectations. Within a brief period of time, they systematically transmitted an enormous amount of knowledge. The treasure trove mainly consisted of basic scientific information, including mathematics, physics, cosmology, molecular biology of Trisolaran life forms, and so on. Every subject was a complete system.

There was so much knowledge, in fact, that it completely overwhelmed the scientific community on Earth. Trisolaris then provided ongoing guidance for the study and absorption of this knowledge. For a while, the whole world resembled a giant university. After the sophons ended their interference with the particle accelerators, Earth scientists were able to experimentally verify the core ideas of Trisolaran physics, giving humanity confidence in the veracity of these revelations. The Trisolarans even complained multiple times that humanity was absorbing the new knowledge too slowly. The aliens seemed eager for Earth to catch up to Trisolaris in scientific understanding—at least in the basic sciences.

Faced with such a puzzling response, humans came up with multiple explanations. The most plausible theory posited that the Trisolarans understood the advantage of the accelerating pace of human scientific development and wanted to gain access to new knowledge through us. Earth was treated as a knowledge battery: After it was charged fully with Trisolaran knowledge, it would provide more power.

The Trisolarans explained their own actions this way: Their generous gift of knowledge was done out of respect for Earth civilization. They claimed that Trisolaris had received even more benefits from Earth. Human culture gave Trisolaris new eyes, allowed Trisolarans to see deeper meanings in life and civilization and appreciate the beauty of nature and human nature in ways they had not understood. Human culture was widely disseminated on Trisolaris, and was rapidly and profoundly transforming Trisolaran society, leading to multiple revolutions in half a century and changing the social structure and political system on Trisolaris to be more similar to Earth's. Human values were accepted and respected in that distant world, and all Trisolarans were in love with human culture.

At the beginning, humans were skeptical of these claims, but the incredible wave of cultural reflection that followed seemed to prove them true.

After the tenth year of the Deterrence Era, besides additional scientific information, Trisolaris began to transmit cultural and artistic products done in imitation of human models: films, novels, poetry, music, paintings, and so on. Surprisingly, the imitations were not at all awkward or childish; right away, the Trisolarans produced sophisticated, high-quality art. Scholars called this phenomenon cultural reflection. Human civilization now possessed a mirror in the universe, through which humanity gained a new understanding of itself through a novel perspective. In the following ten years, Trisolaran reflection culture became popular on Earth, and began to displace the decadent native human culture that had lost its vitality. Reflection culture became the new source for scholars seeking new cultural and aesthetic ideas.

These days, without being explicitly told, it was very hard to tell if a film or novel was authored by a human or a Trisolaran. The characters in Trisolaran artistic creations were all human, and they were set on Earth, with no trace of alienness. This seemed a powerful confirmation of the acceptance of Earth culture by Trisolaris. At the same time, Trisolaris itself remained shrouded in mystery, with almost no details about the world itself being transmitted. The Trisolarans explained this by saying that their own crude native culture was not ready to be shown to humans. Given the vast gap in biology and natural environment between the two worlds, such displays might erect unexpected barriers in the valuable exchange that was already taking place.

Humanity was glad to see everything developing in a positive direction. A ray of sunlight lit up this corner of the dark forest.

Deterrence Era, Year 61
The Swordholder

On the day of Cheng Xin's discharge, AA told her that Sophon wanted to meet her.

Cheng Xin understood that AA wasn't referring to the subatomic particles endowed with intelligence sent by Trisolaris, but to a woman, a robot woman developed by the most advanced human AI and bionics technology. She was controlled by the sophons and acted as the Trisolaran ambassador to Earth. Her appearance facilitated a more natural interchange between the two worlds than having sophons manifest themselves by unfolding in lower dimensions.

Sophon lived on a giant tree at the edge of the city. Viewed from the flying car, the leaves on the tree were sparse, as though it were late autumn. Sophon lived on the branch at the top, where a single leaf hung, an elegant dwelling made of bamboo and surrounded by a white cloud. The day was cloudless, and it was clear that Sophon's house generated the white mist.

Cheng Xin and AA walked along the branch until they reached the tip. The road was lined with smooth pebbles, and they saw lush lawns on both sides. They descended a spiraling staircase to reach the door of the house itself, where Sophon welcomed them. The gorgeous Japanese kimono on her petite figure resembled a layer of blooming flowers, but when Cheng Xin saw her face, the flowers seemed to lose color. Cheng Xin could not imagine a more perfect beauty, a beauty animated by a lively soul. She smiled, and it was as though a breeze stirred a pond in spring and the gentle sunlight broke into a thousand softly undulating fragments. Slowly, Sophon bowed to them, and Cheng Xin felt her entire figure illustrated the Chinese character 柔, or *soft*, in both shape and meaning.

"Welcome, welcome! I wanted to pay a visit to your honored abode, but then

I wouldn't be able to properly entertain you with the Way of Tea. Please accept my humble apologies. I am so delighted to see you." Sophon bowed again. Her voice was as gentle and soft as her body, barely audible, but it possessed an irresistible charm, as if all other voices had to pause and step aside when she spoke.

The pair followed Sophon into the yard. The tiny white flowers in her bun quivered, and she turned around to smile at them from time to time. Cheng Xin had completely forgotten that she was an alien invader, that she was controlled by a powerful world four light-years away. All she saw was a lovely woman, distinguished by her overwhelming femininity, like a concentrated pigment pellet that could turn a whole lake pink.

Bamboo groves lined both sides of the trail through the yard. A white fog hung among the bamboo, which reached about waist-high and undulated. They crossed a little wooden bridge over a trickling spring, and Sophon stepped to the side, bowed, and showed them into the parlor. The parlor was decorated in a pure Eastern style, full of sunlight and wide openings in the four walls so that the space resembled a pavilion. They could see the blue sky and white clouds outside. The clouds were generated by the house itself and dissipated into tendrils. A small *ukiyo-e* Japanese woodblock print hung on the wall, along with a fan decorated with a Chinese-brush-painting landscape. The whole place exuded an air of simple elegance.

Sophon waited until Cheng Xin and AA were sitting cross-legged on the tatami mats, then sat herself down gracefully. Methodically, she laid out the implements for the tea ceremony in front of her.

"You're going to have to be patient," AA whispered in Cheng Xin's ear. "It'll be two hours before you get to drink any tea."

Sophon retrieved a spotless white cloth from her kimono and began wiping the equally spotless implements. First, she carefully, slowly wiped each and every tea scoop, delicate spoons with long handles carved from single pieces of bamboo. Then she wiped each and every white porcelain and yellow copper tea bowl. With a bamboo ladle, she transferred the clear spring water from a ceramic container to a teapot and placed it above a refined copper brazier to boil. Then she scooped powdered green tea from the tea caddy into the tea bowls, brushing them with a bamboo tea whisk in a circular motion. . . .

She performed each step in a deliberate, slow manner, even repeating some of the steps. Just wiping the tea ceremony implements took nearly twenty minutes. Clearly, Sophon executed these actions not for their results, but for their ceremonial significance.

But Cheng Xin didn't feel bored. Sophon's graceful, gentle movements had a hypnotic, mesmerizing effect on her. From time to time, a light breeze wafted through the room, and Sophon's pale arms seemed to move not of their own accord, but to drift with the breeze. Her hands, smooth as jade, seemed to be caressing not implements for making tea, but something softer, lighter, more cloudlike . . . like *time*. Yes, she was caressing time. Time turned malleable and meandered slowly, like the fog that drifted through the bamboo groves. This was another time. Here, the history of blood and fire had disappeared, and the world of everyday concerns retreated somewhere far away. All that was left were clouds, the bamboo grove, and the fragrance of tea. They had achieved *wa kei sei jaku*—harmony, respect, purity, and tranquility, the four principles of the Way of Tea.

After an unknown amount of time, the tea was ready. Following another series of complicated ceremonial procedures, Sophon finally handed the bowls of tea to Cheng Xin and AA. Cheng Xin took a sip of the lush, green drink. A fragrant, bitter sensation suffused her body, and her mind seemed to clear.

"When all of us women are together, the world is so beautiful." Sophon's voice was still slow and mild, barely audible. "But our world is also very fragile. All of us women must take care to protect it." Then she bowed deeply, and her voice grew excited. "Thank you for your care in advance! Thank you!"

Cheng Xin understood very well what was meant but not said, as well as the true significance of the tea ceremony.

The next meeting pulled Cheng Xin back into the complex reality around her.

The day after Cheng Xin visited Sophon, six Common Era men came to see her. These were the candidates competing to succeed Luo Ji in the Swordholder position. They were between thirty-four and sixty-eight years old. Compared to the beginning of the Deterrence Era, fewer Common Era individuals were emerging from hibernation, but they still formed a stratum of society on their own. All of them had some difficulty reintegrating into modern society. Most men from the Common Era tried to, consciously or otherwise, feminize their appearance and personality to adjust to the new feminine society. But the six men in front of Cheng Xin all stubbornly held on to their outdated masculine appearance and personality. If Cheng Xin had met them a few days ago, she would have found them comforting, but now, she felt only a sense of oppression.

She could see no sunlight in their eyes; their expressions appeared as masks that disguised their true feelings. Cheng Xin felt that she was facing a city wall built from six cold, hard rocks. The wall, roughened and toughened by the passing years, chilled her with its heaviness, and seemed to hint at death and bloodshed.

Cheng Xin first thanked the candidate who had warned the police. In this she was sincere—he had saved her life, after all. The forty-eight-year-old man was named Bi Yunfeng, and he had once been a designer for the world's largest particle collider. Like Cheng Xin, he was sent as a liaison to the future in the hope that the particle collider would be restarted once humankind broke through the lock placed on them by the sophons. Unfortunately, none of the particle accelerators built during his time had survived to the Deterrence Era.

"I hope I haven't made a mistake," he said. Perhaps he was trying to be funny, but Cheng Xin and the others didn't laugh.

"We're here to persuade you to not compete for the Swordholder position." Another man got right to the point. His name was Cao Bin, and he was thirty-four, the youngest of the candidates. At the start of the Trisolar Crisis, he had been a physicist, a colleague of the famous Ding Yi. After the truth of the sophons' lock on fundamental research was revealed, he was disappointed by the thought that physics had turned into a mathematical game divorced from experimental basis, and entered hibernation to wait for the lock to be released.

"If I do declare my candidacy, do you think I will win?" asked Cheng Xin. She had been pondering this question nonstop since her return from Sophon's home. She could barely sleep.

"If you do, it's almost certain that you will win," Ivan Antonov said. The handsome Russian was the next youngest of the candidates, at forty-three years old. He had an impressive résumé: Once the youngest vice-admiral in the Russian Navy, he later became the deputy commander of the Baltic Fleet. He had entered hibernation because of a terminal illness.

"Do I possess a lot of deterrent force?" asked Cheng Xin, smiling.

"You are not without qualifications. You once served in the PIA. During the last few centuries, that agency has actively gathered an enormous amount of intelligence about Trisolaris. Before the Doomsday Battle, it had even warned the human fleets about the imminent droplet attack, though the warning was ignored. Nowadays, the PIA is seen as a legendary organization, and this will give you points. In addition, you're the only human to possess another world, which makes you able to save this world. . . . Never mind that the leap in logic is suspect; that's how the public thinks—"

"Let me get to the point," a bald man interrupted Antonov. He was named A. J. Hopkins—or at least that's what he called himself. His identity had been completely lost by the time he emerged from hibernation, and he refused to divulge any information about himself, not even bothering to make it up. This made it difficult for him to become a citizen of the new world—though his mysterious past also helped make him a competitive candidate. He and Antonov were considered to possess the most deterrent force. "In the eyes of the public, the ideal Swordholder looks like this: He should terrify the Trisolarans without terrifying the people of Earth. Since such a combination cannot exist, the people will lean toward someone who doesn't terrify them. You don't frighten them because you're a woman, and a woman who seems angelic in their eyes, at that. These sissies are more naïve than even the children of our time; all they can see are superficial qualities. . . . Look, they all think everything is developing wonderfully, and we are on the cusp of achieving universal peace and love. Deterrence is no longer so important, so they want someone with a gentler hand holding the sword."

"Isn't it true, though?" Cheng Xin asked. Hopkins's contemptuous tone annoyed her.

The six men didn't answer her, but they exchanged glances with each other. Their gazes now looked even darker and colder. Standing in their midst, Cheng Xin felt as if she were on the bottom of a well. She shivered.

"Child, you're not suited to be the Swordholder." At sixty-eight, the speaker was the oldest of the candidates. Before hibernation, he had been South Korea's vice minister of foreign affairs. "You have no political experience, you are young, you lack the judgment to evaluate situations correctly, and you don't possess the requisite psychological qualities to be the Swordholder. All you have is kindness and a sense of responsibility."

The last candidate, an experienced attorney, now spoke up. "I don't think you really want to be the Swordholder. You must know what kind of sacrifices are required."

This last speech silenced Cheng Xin. She had just learned what Luo Ji had endured during the Deterrence Era.

After the six candidates departed, AA said to Cheng Xin, "I don't think what the Swordholder goes through can be called living. It's worse than being in hell. Why would these Common Era men want that?"

"To be able to determine the fate of all of humanity and another race with a single finger is very attractive to some men from that era. Some devote their entire lives to pursue such power. They become obsessed with it."

"Um, are you obsessed, too?"

Cheng Xin said nothing. Things were no longer simple.

"It's hard to imagine a man so dark, so crazy, so perverted." AA meant Wade.

"He's not the most dangerous."

This was true. Wade did not hide his viciousness deeply. The layers and layers of disguises that people of the Common Era wore to hide their real intentions and feelings were unimaginable to AA and contemporary humans. Who knew what was hidden behind the cold, expressionless masks worn by the six men? Who knew whether one of them might be another Ye Wenjie or Zhang Beihai? More terrifyingly, whether all of them were?

The beautiful world revealed its fragility to Cheng Xin, like a lovely soap bubble floating through a bramble bush: A single touch was enough to destroy everything.

A week later, Cheng Xin came to the UN Headquarters to attend the handover ceremony for the two planets in the DX3906 system.

Afterwards, the PDC chair spoke with her. On behalf of the UN and the Solar System Fleet, he asked her to declare her candidacy for the Swordholder. He explained that there was uncertainty about the six existing candidates. For any of them to be elected would lead to mass panic, as a considerable portion of the population believed each of the candidates to be a tremendous danger and threat. The consequences of electing any of them were unpredictable. In addition, all of the candidates distrusted Trisolaris and exhibited aggressive tendencies toward it. If one of them were elected, the second Swordholder might collaborate with the hardliners on Earth and in Fleet International to impose harsher policies toward Trisolaris and demand more concessions from them. Such a move might terminate the developing peace and scientific and cultural exchange between the two worlds, leading to disaster. . . .

But Cheng Xin could prevent all of this.

After humanity ended its second cave-dwelling stage, the UN Headquarters moved back to its old address. Cheng Xin was familiar with it: The exterior of the Secretariat Building looked the same as three centuries ago, and even the sculptures on the plaza in front were perfectly preserved, as was the lawn. Cheng Xin stood and recalled that tumultuous night 270 years ago: the announcement of the Wallfacer Project; Luo Ji's shooting; the chaotic crowd under the swaying spotlights; her hair blowing about in the turbulence from the helicopters; the ambulance departing with flashing red lights and shrill sirens . . . everything was as clear as yesterday. Wade stood with his back against the lights of New York City, and uttered the line that had transformed her life: "We'll send only a brain."

Without that statement, everything that was happening now would have nothing to do with her. She would be a common woman and would have died more than two centuries ago. Everything about her would have disappeared without a trace upstream in time's long river. If she had been fortunate, her tenth-generation descendants would now be waiting for the selection of the second Swordholder.

But she was alive. She faced the crowd on the plaza. A hologram of her image floated above them like a colorful cloud. A young mother came up to Cheng Xin and handed her baby, only a few months old, to her. The baby giggled at her, and she held him close, touching her face to his smooth baby cheeks. Her heart melted, and she felt as if she were holding a whole world, a new world as lovely and fragile as the baby in her arms.

"Look, she's like Saint Mary, the mother of Jesus!" the young mother called out to the crowd. She turned back to Cheng Xin and put her hands together. Tears flowed from her eyes. "Oh, beautiful, kind Madonna, protect this world! Do not let those bloodthirsty and savage men destroy all the beauty here."

The crowd cried out in joy. The baby in Cheng Xin's arms, startled, began to cry. She held the baby tighter.

Do I have another choice?

The answer came to her, brooking no doubt.

No. None at all.

There were three reasons.

First, being declared a savior was just like being pushed under the guillotine: There was no choice involved. This had happened to Luo Ji, and now it was happening to her.

Second, the young mother and the soft, warm bundle in Cheng Xin's arms made her realize something. She understood for the first time her own feelings toward this new world: maternal instinct. She had never experienced such a feeling during the Common Era. Subconsciously, she saw everyone in the new world as her child, and she could not bear to see them come to harm. Before, she had mistakenly thought of it as a sense of responsibility. But, no, maternal instinct was not subject to rationalization; she could not escape it.

The third fact stood in front of her like an unscalable wall. Even if the first two reasons did not exist, this wall would remain: Yun Tianming.

This situation was a hell, a bottomless abyss, the same as the abyss Yun

Tianming had plunged into for her sake. She could not back off now. She had to accept karma. It was her turn.

Cheng Xin's childhood had been full of her mother's love, but only her mother's love. She had asked her mother where her father was. Unlike some other single mothers, her mother responded calmly. She said she didn't know, and then, after a sigh, added that she wished she did. Cheng Xin had also asked her where she had come from, and her mother had told her she was found.

This wasn't a lie. Cheng Xin really had been found. Her mother had never married, but one night, while on a date with her boyfriend at the time, she saw a three-month-old baby abandoned on a park bench, along with a bottle of milk, a thousand yuan, and a slip of paper with the baby girl's birthday. Her mother and the boyfriend had intended to bring the baby to the police, who would have turned the baby over to the city's civil affairs department, who would have sent her to an orphanage.

Instead, her mother decided that she wanted to bring the baby home and go to the police in the morning. Perhaps it was the experience of being a mother for a night, or some other reason, but the next morning, she found that she couldn't send the child away. Every time she thought of parting from the young life, her heart ached, and so she decided to become the child's mother.

The boyfriend left her because of this. During the following decade, she dated four or five other men, but all of them ended up leaving her because of Cheng Xin. Later, Cheng Xin found out that none of the men had explicitly objected to her mother's decision to keep her, but if any of them ever showed a trace of impatience or lack of understanding, her mother broke up with him. She refused to let any harm come to Cheng Xin.

When she was little, Cheng Xin never thought her family was incomplete. Instead, she thought it just the way it should be: a small world made up of mother and daughter. The small world possessed so much love and joy that she even suspected that adding a father would be extraneous. Later, she did miss having a father's love—at first, only a vague sensation, but later a growing ache. And that was when her mother did find a father for her, a very kind man full of love and a sense of responsibility. He fell in love with Cheng Xin's mother in large part because of how much she loved Cheng Xin. And so a second sun appeared in Cheng Xin's life. She felt that her small world really was complete, and so her parents did not have another child.

Later, Cheng Xin left her parents to go to college. After that, her life was like a runaway horse that carried her farther and farther until, finally, not only did she have to part from them in space, but also time—she had to be sent to the future.

That night when she left her parents for the last time would be carved in her mind forever. She had lied to her parents and said that she'd be back the next day—she couldn't bear to say good-bye, and so she had to leave without saying anything. But they seemed to know the truth.

Her mother had held her hand and said, "My darling, the three of us are together because of love. . . ."

Cheng Xin spent that night standing in front of her parents' window. In her mind, the night breeze and the twinkling stars and everything else repeated her mother's last words.

Three centuries later, she was finally ready to do something for love.

"I will be a candidate for the Swordholder," she said to the young mother.

Deterrence Era, Year 62
Gravity, in the Vicinity of the Oort Cloud

———

Gravity had been pursuing *Blue Space* for half a century.

It finally approached its target. Only three AU separated the hunter and the hunted. Compared to the 1.5 light-years that the two ships had traversed, this was mere inches.

A decade ago, *Gravity* had passed through the Oort Cloud. This region, about one light-year from the sun at the edge of the Solar System, was the birthplace of comets. *Blue Space* and *Gravity* were the first human spaceships to cross this border. The region didn't feel anything like a cloud, though. Once in a while, a frozen ball of dirt and ice—a tailless comet—passed tens of thousands or hundreds of thousands of kilometers away, invisible to the naked eye.

Once *Gravity* left the Oort Cloud behind, the ship entered true outer space. From here, the sun appeared as just another star behind the ship. It lost its reality and became like an illusion. In every direction, all one could see was a bottomless abyss, and the only objects whose existence could be ascertained by the senses were the droplets flying in formation with *Gravity*. The droplets flanked the ship at a distance of about five kilometers, just visible to the naked eye. Those aboard *Gravity* liked to gaze at the droplets with telescopes as a source of comfort in the endless emptiness. Observing the droplets was, in a sense, just looking at themselves. The mirrorlike surface of the droplets reflected an image of *Gravity*. The dimensions were a bit distorted, but due to the perfect smoothness of the surface, the image was particularly clear. With sufficient magnification on their telescopes, the observers could even pick out the porthole, and themselves in it, in the reflection.

Most of the one hundred-plus officers and crew aboard *Gravity* didn't experience this solitude because they had spent the majority of the past fifty years in hibernation. During routine cruising, only about five to ten crew members needed to be on duty. As the crew rotated through hibernation, each person was usually on duty for three to five years.

The entire pursuit was a complex game of acceleration between *Gravity* and *Blue Space*. First of all, *Blue Space* couldn't just accelerate continuously, as doing so would cost it precious fuel and ultimately deprive it of mobility. Even if it managed to escape *Gravity*, it would be committing suicide in the endless empty desert of outer space if it exhausted its fuel. Although *Gravity* had more fuel onboard than *Blue Space*, it had constraints of its own. Since it needed to be prepared for a return voyage, its fuel reserves had to be divided into four equal parts: the acceleration away from the Solar System; the deceleration before its destination; the acceleration toward the Solar System; and the deceleration before arriving at the Earth. Thus, the portion available for acceleration during the pursuit amounted to only one-quarter of the fuel. Based on calculations of *Blue Space*'s previous maneuvers and intelligence gathered by the sophons, *Gravity* had an accurate idea of *Blue Space*'s fuel reserves, but the latter had no information about the former's stores. Thus, in this game, *Gravity* knew all the cards held by *Blue Space*, while *Blue Space* struggled in ignorance. During pursuit, *Gravity* consistently maintained a speed higher than *Blue Space*, but neither ship approached their maximum velocities. Moreover, twenty-five years after the start of the chase, *Blue Space* stopped accelerating, perhaps because it had used up all the fuel it dared.

During the half century of the hunt, *Gravity* repeatedly hailed *Blue Space*, explaining that running was meaningless. Even if the crew of *Blue Space* somehow escaped the hunters from Earth, the droplets would catch up and destroy them. But if they returned to Earth, they would receive a fair trial. They had the option to greatly shorten the pursuit by surrendering. But *Blue Space* ignored these entreaties.

A year previously, when *Gravity* and *Blue Space* were thirty AU apart, something not entirely unexpected occurred: *Gravity* and the two accompanying droplets entered a region of space where the sophons lost their quantum ties to home, terminating real-time communications with Earth. *Gravity* had to communicate with Earth through only neutrinos and radio. Transmissions from *Gravity* now took a year and three months to reach the Earth, and the ship had to wait an equally long time to receive a reply.

Excerpt from *A Past Outside of Time*
More Indirect Evidence for the Dark
Forest: Sophon-Blind Regions

Near the beginning of the Crisis Era, as Trisolaris sent sophons toward the Earth, it also launched six sophons at near-lightspeed to explore other regions of the galaxy.

All of these sophons soon entered blind regions and lost contact with home. The longest-lasting one managed to get seven light-years away. Additional sophons launched later met with the same fate. The closest blind region, only about 1.3 light-years from Earth, was the one encountered by the sophons that accompanied *Gravity*.

Once the quantum entanglement between sophons was broken, it could not be restored. Any sophon entering a blind region was lost forever.

Trisolaris remained mystified by the kind of interference the sophons received: Perhaps it was a natural phenomenon, or perhaps it was "man"-made. Scientists from both Trisolaris and Earth leaned toward the latter explanation.

Before being blinded, the sophons were able to explore only two nearby stars with planets. Neither system exhibited signs of life or civilization. But Earth and Trisolaris both came to the conclusion that their desolation was precisely why the sophons were allowed to approach.

Thus, even deep into the Deterrence Era, the universe at large remained hidden from the two worlds by a mysterious veil. The existence of these blind regions seemed to provide indirect proof for the dark forest nature of the universe: Something was preventing the cosmos from becoming transparent.

Deterrence Era, Year 62
Gravity, in the Vicinity of the Oort Cloud

Losing the sophons was not fatal to *Gravity*'s mission, though it did make the job much harder. Before, the sophons could enter *Blue Space* at will and report on everything that was going on; now *Blue Space* appeared to *Gravity* as a sealed box. Moreover, the droplets lost real-time communications with Trisolaris and had to rely on the onboard AI. This led to unpredictable results.

The captain of *Gravity* decided that he could no longer afford to wait. He ordered *Gravity* to accelerate further.

As *Gravity* approached, *Blue Space* hailed the hunters for the first time, proposing a plan: *Blue Space* would load two-thirds of the crew—including the main suspects—onto pinnaces and send the pinnaces to *Gravity* if the remainder of the crew was allowed to continue their voyage into deep space aboard *Blue Space*. This way, a vanguard and seed for the human race would be preserved in space, keeping alive the hope for further exploration.

Gravity vehemently denied this request. The entire crew of *Blue Space* was suspected of murder, and all had to be tried. Space had transformed them until they were no longer members of the human race. Under no circumstances could they be allowed to "represent" humanity in space exploration.

Blue Space apparently realized the futility of running and of resisting. If only a human spaceship pursued them, then they at least stood a chance if they fought. But the two droplets changed the strategic calculus. Before them, *Blue Space* was nothing but a paper target, and there was no chance of escape. When the two ships were only fifteen AU apart, *Blue Space* announced its surrender and began to decelerate at maximum power. The distance between the two ships shrank rapidly, and it seemed that the long hunt was at last coming to an end.

Gravity's crew emerged from hibernation and readied the ship for combat. The vessel, once silent and deserted, was once again filled with people.

Those who had been awakened faced the prospect of both a target nearly at hand and the loss of real-time communications with Earth. This loss did not pull them spiritually closer to the crew of *Blue Space.* To the contrary, like a child who was separated from her parents, the crew distrusted the parentless wild children even more. Everyone wished to capture *Blue Space* as quickly as possible and return home. Even though both crews were in the cold vastness of space, voyaging in the same direction at approximately the same speed, the natures of their voyages were completely different. *Gravity* had a spiritual anchor, while *Blue Space* was adrift.

In the ninety-eighth hour after the crew's emergence from hibernation, Dr. West, *Gravity*'s psychiatrist, received his first patient. This visit from Commander Devon surprised the doctor. According to his records, Devon had the highest stability score of anyone aboard. Devon was in charge of the military police aboard *Gravity,* and it would be his responsibility to disarm *Blue Space* and arrest the crew once it was caught. *Gravity*'s male crew members belonged to the last generation from Earth who still looked masculine, and Devon had the most masculine appearance among them. He was sometimes even mistaken for a Common Era man. He had often spoken out in favor of taking a hard line toward the suspects, suggesting that the death penalty ought to be revived.

"Doctor, I know that you'll keep my confidence," Devon said carefully. His tone was in marked contrast to his usual hard-edged style. "I know that what I'm about to say will sound funny."

"Commander, in my professional capacity, I wouldn't laugh at anyone."

"Yesterday, at approximately stellar time 436950, I left Conference Room Four and followed Passageway Seventeen back to my cabin. As I approached the Intelligence Center, a sublieutenant came toward me—or, at least, a man dressed in the uniform of a Space Force sublieutenant. At that time, except for crew members on duty, everyone should have been asleep. But I didn't think it was so strange to meet someone in the passageway. Except . . ." Devon shook his head and his eyes lost focus, as though trying to recall a dream.

"What was wrong?"

"The man and I passed by each other. He saluted me, and I glanced at him. . . ."

Devon stopped again, and the doctor nodded for him to continue.

"He was . . . he was the commander of the marines from *Blue Space*, Lieutenant Commander Park Ui-gun."

"You mean *Blue Space*, our prey?" West's tone was calm, betraying no hint of surprise.

Devon didn't answer the question. "Doctor, you know that as part of my duties, I've been monitoring the interior of *Blue Space* through the real-time images transmitted by the sophons. I know the crew of that ship better than I know the crew here. I know what Lieutenant Commander Park Ui-gun looks like."

"Maybe it was someone from our ship who looks like him."

"No, there's no one—I know everyone onboard. Also . . . after the salute, he passed by me without any expression. I stood there, stunned. But by the time I turned around, the passageway was empty."

"When did you wake up from hibernation?"

"Three years ago. I needed to keep an eye on the activities onboard our target. Before that, I was also among those aboard who had stayed out of hibernation the longest."

"Then you must have experienced the moment when we entered the sophons' blind region."

"Of course."

"Before that, you spent so much of your time watching those aboard *Blue Space* that I think you probably felt as though you were on *Blue Space* rather than *Gravity*."

"Yes, Doctor. I did often feel that way."

"And then, the surveillance images were cut off. You couldn't see anything over there anymore. And you were tired. . . . Commander, it's simple. Trust me: This is normal. I suggest you get more rest. We have plenty of people now to do the work that needs to be done."

"Doctor, I'm a survivor of the Doomsday Battle. After my ship exploded, I was curled up in a life pod the size of your desk, drifting in the vicinity of Neptune's orbit. By the time I was rescued, I was close to death, but my mind was still sound, and I never suffered any delusions. . . . I believe what I saw." Devon got up and walked away. He turned around at the cabin door. "If I meet that bastard again—doesn't matter where—I'm going to kill him."

Some time after that, an accident happened in Ecological Area #3—a nutrient tube ruptured. The tube was made of carbon fiber, and as it wasn't subject to pressure, the probability of a malfunction was very low. Ecological Engineer Ivantsov passed through the aeroponically grown plants, as dense as a rainforest, and saw that others had already shut off the valve leading to the ruptured tube and were cleaning up the yellow nutrient broth.

Ivantsov stopped dead when he saw the ruptured tube.

"This . . . is caused by a micrometeoroid!"

Someone laughed. Ivantsov was an experienced and prudent engineer, and that made his outburst even funnier. All the ecological areas were buried in the center of the ship. Ecological Area #3 was tens of meters away from the nearest section of the exterior hull.

"I worked more than a decade in external maintenance and I know what a micrometeoroid strike looks like! Look, you can see the typical signs of high-temperature ablation around the edges of the rupture."

Ivantsov closely examined the inside of the tube; then he asked a technician to cut off a ring of material around the rupture and magnify it. The chatter died down as everyone stared at the 1000x image. There were tiny black particles, a few microns in diameter, embedded in the wall of the tube. The particles twinkled like unfriendly eyes in the magnified image. They all knew what they were looking at. The meteoroid must have been about one hundred microns in diameter. It had shattered as it went through the tube, its broken pieces winding up embedded in the wall opposite the breach.

As one, they looked up.

The ceiling above the ruptured tube looked smooth and undamaged. Furthermore, above the ceiling, tens, maybe hundreds more bulkheads of various thicknesses separated this place from space. An impact-breach in any of these bulkheads would have triggered a high-level alert.

But the micrometeoroid had to have come from space. Based on the condition of the rupture, the micrometeoroid had struck the tube at a relative velocity of thirty thousand meters per second. It would have been impossible to accelerate the projectile to such speed from within the ship, much less from within the ecological area.

"It's like a ghost," a sublieutenant named Ike muttered, and left. His choice of words was meaningful: About ten hours earlier, he had seen another, bigger ghost.

Ike had been trying to fall asleep in his cabin when he saw a round opening appear in the wall opposite his bed. It was about a meter across, and occupied the space where a Hawaiian landscape had hung. It was true that many of the bulkheads on the ship could shift and transform so that doors could appear anywhere, but a circular opening like this was impossible. Moreover, the cabin walls of mid-level officers were made of metal and could not deform this way. A closer examination by Ike revealed that the edge of the opening was perfectly smooth and reflective, like a mirror.

Although the hole was strange, Ike was rather pleased by it. Sublieutenant Vera lived next door.

Verenskaya was the AI system engineer aboard *Gravity*. Ike had been trying to get the Russian beauty to go out with him, but she hadn't shown any interest. Ike still remembered his latest attempt two days ago.

He and Verenskaya had just gotten off duty. As usual, they walked back to the officers' quarters together, and as they reached Verenskaya's cabin, Ike tried to invite himself in. Verenskaya blocked her door.

"Come on, sweetheart," Ike said. "Let me in for a visit. It's not very neighborly to never invite me over. They'll think I'm not a real man."

Verenskaya looked askance at Ike. "Any real men on this ship would be too worried about our mission to think about getting into the pants of every woman around them."

"What's there to worry? After we catch those murderers, there will be no more danger. Happy times will be here!"

"They're not murderers! Without deterrence, *Blue Space* would be humankind's only hope. Yet we're now hunting them down, allied with the enemies of the human race. Don't you feel ashamed?"

"Um . . . baby, if you feel this way . . . how did you . . ."

"How did I get to join this mission? Is that what you want to say? Why don't you go to the psychiatrist and the captain to report me? They'll put me in forced hibernation and kick me out of the fleet after we return. That's just my wish!" Verenskaya slammed the door in his face.

However, now Ike had a perfect excuse to enter Verenskaya's cabin. He unbuckled his weightlessness belt and sat up in his bed, but stopped when he saw that the bottom half of the round opening made the top of the cabinet against the wall disappear as well. The edge of what remained of the cabinet was also perfectly smooth and reflective, like the edge of the opening itself. It was as if some invisible knife had cut through the cabinet and everything inside, including the stacks of folded clothes. The mirrorlike surface of the cross-section ran up against the edge of the round opening, and the whole reflective surface looked like a portion of the inside of a sphere.

Ike pushed against the bed and lifted off in the weightlessness. Looking through the opening, he almost screamed in fright. *This must be a nightmare!*

Through the hole, he could see that a part of Verenskaya's bed, pushed up against the cabin wall, had also disappeared. Verenskaya's lower legs had been cut off. Although the cross section of the bed and the legs were also smooth and reflective, as though covered by a layer of mercury, he could see Verenskaya's muscles and bones through it. But Verenskaya seemed all right. She was still in deep sleep, and her firm breasts slowly moved up and down as she breathed. Normally, Ike would have admired such a sight, but right now he only felt a supernatural fright. When he calmed down and looked closer, he saw that the cross-section of Verenskaya's legs and bed also formed a spherical surface that matched the round opening.

He was looking at a bubble-shaped space about a meter in diameter, which erased everything within its path.

Ike picked up a violin bow from the nightstand, and, with a trembling hand, poked it into the bubble. The part of the bow extended inside the bubble disappeared, but the bow hair remained taut. He pulled the bow back and saw that it was undamaged. But he was still glad that he hadn't tried to go through the hole—who knew if he would emerge from the other side unharmed?

Ike forced himself to be calm and tried to think of the most rational explanation for the eerie sight. Then he made what he thought was a wise decision: He put on his sleep cap and lay back down on the bed. He buckled his weightlessness belt back on and set the sleep cap for half an hour.

He woke up after half an hour, and the bubble was still there.

So he set the sleep cap for an hour. When he woke up this time, the bubble and the hole in the wall were gone. The Hawaiian landscape was back on the wall and everything was as it was before the incident.

But Ike was worried about Verenskaya. He dashed out of his cabin and stopped in front of Verenskaya's door. Instead of ringing the doorbell, he pounded on the door. His mind was filled with the terrifying vision of Verenskaya, close to death, lying on the bed with her legs cut off.

It took a while before the door opened, and a not-completely-awake Verenskaya demanded to know what he wanted.

"I came to see if you are . . . all right." Ike's gaze shifted down, and he saw that Verenskaya's beautiful legs were perfect below the hem of her nightgown.

"Idiot!" Verenskaya slammed the door shut.

After returning to his cabin, Ike put his sleep cap on and set it for eight hours. As for what he had seen, the only wise thing to do was to shut up and say nothing. Due to *Gravity*'s special mission, the crew's psychological state—especially that of the officers—was subject to constant monitoring. There was a special psychological monitoring corps aboard, comprising more than a dozen crew members out of the full complement of just over a hundred. Some crew members had wondered whether *Gravity* was a stellar ship or a psychiatric hospital. And then there was also the annoying civilian psychiatrist West, who thought of everything in terms of mental disorders and illnesses and blockages, until one could come to the conclusion that he would subject a clogged toilet to psychiatric analysis. The mental screening process onboard *Gravity* was extremely strict, and even slight mental disorders would result in the sufferer being forced into hibernation. Ike was terrified of missing the upcoming historical encounter between the two ships. If that happened, when the ship returned to Earth in half a century, the girls back home would not see him as a hero.

But Ike did feel a slight diminution in his dislike for the psych corps and Dr. West. He had always thought of them as making mountains out of molehills, but he had never imagined that people could suffer such realistic delusions.

Compared to Ike's minor delusion, Petty Officer Liu Xiaoming's supernatural encounter would be considered quite spectacular.

Liu was performing a routine exterior hull inspection. This involved piloting a small pinnace at a certain distance from *Gravity* and examining the hull for any abnormalities, such as evidence of meteor strikes. This was an ancient, outdated practice no longer strictly necessary and rarely performed. The ship was full of sensors that monitored the hull continuously; any problems would be detected right away. Also, the operation could only be done when *Gravity* was coasting instead of accelerating or decelerating. As the ship approached *Blue Space*, frequent acceleration and deceleration was necessary for adjustments. This was one of those rare windows when the ship was coasting again, and Petty Officer Liu was ordered to take advantage of the opportunity.

Liu piloted the pinnace out of the bay in the middle of the ship and smoothly glided away from *Gravity* until he was at a distance where he could see the whole ship. The giant hull was bathed in the light from the galaxy. Unlike when most of the crew was in hibernation, light spilled from all the portholes, making *Gravity* seem even more magnificent.

But Liu noticed something incredible: *Gravity* was shaped like a perfect cylinder, however, right now, its tail ended in an inclined plane! The ship was also much shorter than it should be—about 20 percent shorter, to be exact. A giant, invisible knife had cut off *Gravity*'s tail.

Liu shut his eyes, then opened them a few seconds later. The tail was still missing. He felt chilled to the bone. The giant ship before him was an organic whole. If the tail were suddenly gone, the power distribution systems would suffer a catastrophic failure, and the ship would shortly explode. But nothing of the sort was happening. The ship cruised along without trouble, as though suspended in space. No alerts of any kind came from his earpiece or were shown on his screens.

He pressed the switch for the intercom and got ready to give a report, but shut off the channel before saying anything. He recalled the words of an old spacer who had been at the Doomsday Battle: "Your intuition is unreliable in space. If you must act based on intuition, count from one to one hundred first. At least count from one to ten."

He closed his eyes and began to count. When he got to ten, he opened his eyes. The tail was still missing. He closed his eyes and continued to count, his breath coming faster now, but he struggled to remember his training, and forced himself to calm down. He opened his eyes when he reached thirty, and this time he saw the complete *Gravity*. He closed his eyes again, sighed, and waited until his heartbeat slowed down.

He piloted the pinnace to the stern of the ship, where he could see the three giant nozzles of the fusion drive. The engine wasn't on, and the fusion reactor was kept at minimal power so that the nozzles only showed a faint red glow, reminding him of the clouds back on Earth at dusk.

Petty Officer Liu was glad that he hadn't made a report. An officer might get therapy, but an NCO like himself would be forced into hibernation. Like Ike, Liu Xiaoming didn't want to return to Earth a useless man.

Dr. West went to find Guan Yifan, a civilian scholar who worked in the observatory at the stern. Guan had a midship cabin assigned to him as living quarters, but he rarely went there. Most of the time, he remained in the observatory and asked the service robots to bring his meals. The crew referred to him as "the hermit at the stern."

The observatory was a tiny spherical cabin where Guan lived and worked. His appearance was disheveled, with an unshaven face and long hair, but he still looked relatively youthful. When West saw Guan, he was floating in the middle of the cabin, looking restless: sweaty forehead, anxious eyes, his hand pulling at his collar as if he was unable to catch his breath.

"I already told you on the phone: I'm working and don't have time for a visit."

"It's precisely because your call betrayed signs of mental disorder that I came to see you."

"I'm not a member of the space force. As long as I'm no danger to the ship or the crew, you have no power over me."

"Fine. I'll leave." West turned around. "I just don't believe that someone with claustrophobia can work in here without trouble."

Guan called out for West to stop, but West ignored him. As he expected, Guan chased after him and stopped him. "How did you know that? I am indeed . . . claustrophobic. I feel like I'm being packed into a narrow tube, or sometimes squeezed between two iron plates until I'm flat as a sheet. . . ."

"Not surprising. Look at where you are." The doctor indicated the cabin—it resembled a tiny egg nestled in a nest of crisscrossing cables and pipes. "You research phenomena at the largest scale, but you stay in the smallest space. And how long have you been here? It's been four years since your last hibernation, hasn't it?"

"I'm not complaining. *Gravity*'s mission is bringing fugitives to justice, not scientific exploration. I'm grateful to have this space at all. . . . Look, my claustrophobia has nothing to do with this."

"Why don't we take a walk on Plaza One? It will help."

The doctor pulled Guan Yifan along, and the two drifted toward the bow of the ship. If the ship were accelerating, going from the stern of the ship to the bow would be equivalent to climbing up a one-kilometer well, but in the weightlessness of coasting, the trip was a lot easier. Plaza #1 was located at the bow of the cylindrical ship, under a semispherical, transparent dome. Standing there was like standing in space itself. Compared to the holographic projections of the star field on the walls of spherical cabins, this place induced an even stronger sense of the "desubstantiation effect."

"Desubstantiation effect" was a concept from astronautic psychology. Humans on Earth were surrounded by objects, and the image of the world in their subconscious was thus material and substantial. But in deep space, away from the Solar System, the stars were only distant points of light and the galaxy was nothing more than a luminous mist. To the senses and the mind, the world lost its materiality, and empty space dominated. A space voyager's subconscious image of the world thus became desubstantiated. This mental model was the baseline in astronautic psychology. Mentally, the ship became the only material entity in the universe. At sub-light speeds, the motion of the ship was undetectable, and the universe turned into one boundless, empty exhibition hall. Here, the stars were illusions, and the ship was the only object on display. This mental model brought with it a profound sense of loneliness, and it could cause the voyager to have subconscious delusions of being a "superobserver" toward the lone "object on display." This feeling of being completely exposed could lead to passivity and anxiety.

Thus, many of the negative psychological effects of deep-space flight were due to the extreme openness of the external environment. In West's extensive professional experience, it was extremely rare to develop claustrophobia the way Guan Yifan did. Even stranger to West was the fact that Guan did not seem relieved by the vast, open sky of Plaza #1; the restlessness caused by claustrophobia seemed to abate not one whit. This tended to support Guan's assertion that his claustrophobia had nothing to do with the narrow confines of his observatory. West grew even more interested in his case.

"Don't you feel better?"

"No, not at all. I feel trapped. Here, everything is so . . . enclosed."

Guan glanced at the starry sky and then focused his gaze in the direction *Gravity* was heading. The doctor knew he was looking for *Blue Space*. The two ships were now only one hundred thousand kilometers apart, and coasting at approximately the same speed. At the scale of deep space, the two ships were practically flying in close formation. The leadership of both ships was in the process of negotiating the technical details of their docking. But *Blue Space* was still too far away to be seen with the naked eye. The droplets were invisible as well. Based on the agreement made with Trisolaris half a century ago, the droplets had shifted to a position about three hundred thousand kilometers from both *Gravity* and *Blue Space*. The two ships and the droplets formed a narrow isosceles triangle.

Guan Yifan turned his gaze back to West. "Last night, I had a dream. I went somewhere, somewhere *really* open, open in a way that you can't even imagine. After I woke up, reality felt very enclosed and narrow, and that was how I came to be claustrophobic. It's like . . . if, as soon as you were born, you were locked inside a small box, you wouldn't care because that was all you've known. But once you've been let out and they put you back in, it feels completely different."

"Tell me more about this place in your dream."

Guan gave the doctor a mysterious smile. "I will describe it to the other sci-entists on the ship, maybe even the scientists on *Blue Space*. But I won't tell you. I don't have anything against you, Doctor, but I can't stand the attitude shared by everyone in your profession: If you think someone has a mental disorder, you treat everything he says as merely the delusion of a diseased mind."

"But you just told me it was a dream."

Guan shook his head, struggling to remember. "I don't know if it was a dream; I don't know if I was awake. Sometimes, you can think you're waking from a dream, only to find yourself still dreaming; other times, you're awake, but it seems like you're dreaming."

"The second situation is extremely rare. If you experienced that, then it was almost certainly a symptom of some mental disorder. Oh, sorry, now you're unhappy with me again."

"No, no. I think we're actually very similar. We both have our targets of ob-servation. You observe the deranged, and I observe the universe. Like you, I also have some criteria for evaluating whether the observed objects are sound: harmony and beauty, in the mathematical sense."

"Of course the objects you observe are sound."

"But you're wrong, Doctor." Guan pointed at the glowing Milky Way, but his gaze remained on West, as though showing him some monster that had suddenly appeared out of nowhere. "Out there is a patient who may be men-tally sound, but whose body suffers from paraplegia!"

"Why?"

Guan curled up and hugged his knees. The movement caused his body to slowly rotate in place. The magnificent Milky Way revolved around him, and he saw himself as the center of the universe.

"Because of the speed of light. The known universe is about sixteen billion light-years across, and it's still expanding. But the speed of light is only three hundred thousand kilometers per second, a snail's pace. This means that light can never go from one end of the universe to the other. Since nothing can move faster than the speed of light, it follows that no information and motive force can go from one end of the universe to the other. If the universe were a person, his neural signals couldn't cover his entire body; his brain would not know of the existence of his limbs, and his limbs would not know of the exis-tence of the brain. Isn't that paraplegia? The image in my mind is even worse: The universe is but a corpse puffing up."

"Interesting, Dr. Guan, very interesting!"

"Other than the speed of light, three hundred thousand kilometers per second, there's another three-based symptom."

"What do you mean?"

"The three dimensions. In string theory, excepting time, the universe has ten dimensions. But only three are accessible at the macroscopic scale, and those three form our world. All the others are folded up in the quantum realm."

"I think string theory provides an explanation."

"Some think that it is only when two strings encounter each other and some qualities are canceled out that the dimensions are unfolded into the macroscopic, and dimensions above three will never have such chances for encountering each other. . . . I don't think much of this explanation. It is not mathematically beautiful. Like I said, this is the universe's three and three hundred thousand syndrome."

"What do you propose as the cause?"

Guan laughed uproariously and put his arm around the doctor's shoulders. "Great question! I don't think anyone has thought this far. I'm sure there's a root cause, and it might be the most horrifying truth that science is capable of revealing. But . . . Doctor, who do you think I am? I'm nothing more than a tiny observer curled up in the tail of a spaceship, and only an assistant researcher at that." He released West's shoulders, and, facing the galaxy, let out a long sigh. "I've been in hibernation the longest of anyone aboard. When we left Earth, I was only twenty-six, and even now I'm only thirty-one. But in my eyes, the universe has already transformed from a source of beauty and faith into a bloating corpse. I feel old. The stars no longer hold any attraction for me. I want to go home."

Unlike Guan Yifan, West had been awake for much of the voyage. He always believed that to maintain the mental health of others, he needed to keep his own emotions under control. But something seemed to buffet his heart now, and as he reviewed his own half century of travels, his eyes moistened. "My friend, I'm old, too."

As if in response to their conversation, the battle alert klaxons blared, sounding like the entire sky full of stars was screaming. Warning information scrolled on floating windows that appeared above the plaza. The overlapping windows sprang up one after another and quickly covered the Milky Way like colorful clouds.

"Droplet attack!" West said to the confused Guan Yifan. "They're both accelerating. One is headed for *Blue Space*, the other for us!"

Guan looked around, instinctively searching for something to grab on to in case the ship accelerated. But there was nothing around. In the end, he held on to the doctor.

West held his hands. "There won't be enough time for any evasive maneuvers. We have only a few seconds left."

After a brief panic, both felt an unexpected sense of relief. They were glad that death would arrive so quickly that there wasn't even time to be terrified. Perhaps their discussion about the universe was the best preparation for death.

They both thought of the same thing, but Guan spoke it aloud first. "Looks like neither of us needs to worry about our patients anymore."

The high-speed elevator continued to descend, and the increasing layers of earth above seemed to put all their weight on Cheng Xin's heart.

Half a year ago, a joint session of the UN and the Solar System Fleet had elected Cheng Xin to succeed Luo Ji as the Swordholder and given her authority to control the gravitational wave deterrence system. She had received almost twice as many votes as the next candidate. She was now proceeding to the Deterrence Center in the Gobi Desert, where the deterrence authority handover ceremony was to take place.

The Deterrence Center was the deepest man-made structure ever, about forty-five kilometers beneath the surface. This location was already below the crust, past the Mohorovičić discontinuity, in the mantle of the Earth. The pressure and temperature here were both far higher than in the crust, and the stratum around her was made up mostly of solid, hard peridotite.

The elevator took almost twenty minutes to reach its terminus. Cheng Xin stepped out of the elevator and saw a black steel door. White text on the door gave the formal name for the Deterrence Center: Gravitational Wave Universal Broadcast System Control Station Zero. The insignias of the UN and the Solar System Fleet were embossed on the door.

This ultra-deep structure was quite complex. It possessed its own independent air circulation system and was not directly connected with the atmosphere above the surface—otherwise, the high air pressure generated by a depth of forty-five kilometers would cause great discomfort to the occupant. It was also equipped with a powerful cooling system to withstand the high temperature of the mantle, nearly five hundred degrees Celsius.

All Cheng Xin could see, however, was emptiness. The lobby's walls could all apparently act as electronic displays, but they showed nothing but whiteness, as though the building wasn't in use yet. Half a century ago, when the Deterrence Center was designed, Luo Ji had been consulted, but he had only provided one piece of input:

As simple as a tomb.

The handover ceremony was a solemn occasion, but the bulk of it had been held on the surface forty-five kilometers above. There, all the leaders of Earth International and Fleet International, representing all of humanity, had gathered, and they watched as Cheng Xin entered the elevator. Only two people would oversee the final handover: the PDC chair and the chief of staff for the Solar System Fleet, representing the two institutions directly operating the deterrence system.

The PDC chair pointed at the empty lobby and explained to Cheng Xin that they would redecorate the place based on her ideas. If she wanted, she could have a lawn, plants, a fountain, and so forth. She could also choose to have a holographic simulation of scenes from the surface.

"We don't want you to live like him," said the chief of staff. Perhaps because of his military uniform, Cheng Xin saw in him traces of men of the past, and his words warmed her slightly. But the heavy weight on her heart, as heavy as the forty-five kilometers of earth above her, did not lessen.

Excerpt from *A Past Outside of Time*
The Choice of the Swordholder:
Ten Minutes Between Existence and Annihilation

———

The first dark forest deterrence system consisted of more than three thousand nuclear bombs wrapped in an oil film substance deployed in orbit around the sun. After detonation, the film would cause the sun to flicker and broadcast the location of Trisolaris to the universe. Although the system was grand, it was extremely unstable. After the droplets stopped blockading electromagnetic radiation from the sun, a transmission system based on using the sun as a superantenna was immediately put in place to supplement the nuclear bomb deterrence system.

Both of these systems relied on electromagnetic radiation, including visible light, as the broadcast medium. We now know that this is the most primitive technique for interstellar communication, equivalent to smoke signals in space. Since electromagnetic waves decay and become distorted rapidly, the broadcast range is limited.

At the time of the founding of deterrence, humankind already had a basic grasp of the technology for detecting gravitational waves and neutrinos, but they lacked the ability to modulate and transmit. These were the very first technologies humans demanded from Trisolaris. Compared to quantum communications, these technologies were still primitive, since both gravitational waves and neutrinos were limited by the speed of light, but they were a whole level above electromagnetic waves.

Both of these means of transmission decayed relatively slowly and had very long broadcast ranges. Neutrinos, in particular, interacted with almost nothing else. Theoretically, a modulated beam of neutrinos could transmit information to the other end of the universe, and the accompanying decay and distortion would not affect the decoding of the information. But while neutrinos must be focused in a particular direction, gravitational waves were omnidirectional, thus gravitational waves became the main method of establishing dark forest deterrence.

The fundamental principle of gravitational wave transmission relied on the vibration of a long string of extremely dense matter. The ideal transmission antenna would involve a large number of black holes connected together to form a chain that generated gravitational waves as it vibrated. But even Trisolaris didn't possess such a level of technology, and humankind had to resort to constructing the vibrating string out of degenerate matter. The extremely dense degenerate matter packed an enormous mass into strings mere nanometers in diameter. A single string took up only a minuscule portion of the giant antenna, the bulk of which consisted of support and protection for the ultradense string. Thus, the total mass of the antenna wasn't extraordinarily large.

The degenerate matter forming the vibrating string was naturally found in white dwarves and neutron stars. Under typical conditions, this substance naturally decayed and turned into regular matter over time. Man-made vibrating strings typically had a half-life of around fifty years, beyond which the antennas lost their effectiveness. Thus, every half century, the antennas needed to be refreshed with new ones.

During the earliest stage of gravitational wave deterrence, the main strategic concern was with ensuring deterrence power. Plans were made to build a hundred broadcasting stations scattered around the continents. But gravitational wave communication suffered from a flaw: The transmission equipment could not be miniaturized. The complex, gigantic antennas were extremely costly to manufacture, and in the end only twenty-three gravitational transmitters were built. But the focus on ensuring deterrence finally faded, due to another event.

During the Deterrence Era, the ETO gradually disappeared, but another kind of extremist organization sprang up. They believed in the cause of human supremacy, and advocated for the complete annihilation of Trisolaris. The "Sons of the Earth" was one of the largest of these organizations. In Year 6 of the Deterrence Era, more than three hundred "Sons of the Earth" attacked a gravitational wave broadcasting station located on Antarctica with the aim of seizing the transmitter. Equipped with advanced weapons such as mini-infrasonic nuclear bombs, and aided by members who had infiltrated the broadcasting station ahead of time, the attackers nearly succeeded. If the defending troops stationed at the site hadn't destroyed the antenna in time, the consequences would have been disastrous.

This incident terrified both worlds. People began to realize the great danger posed by gravitational wave transmitters. Simultaneously, Trisolaris pressured Earth until gravitational wave transmission technology was strictly controlled, and the twenty-three broadcasting stations were cut down to four. Three of the stations were terrestrial, located in Asia, North America, and Europe, and the last one was the spaceship *Gravity*.

All the transmitters relied on an active trigger, because the dead hand trigger technique used in the circumsolar nuclear bomb system was no longer necessary. Luo Ji had established deterrence by himself, but now, if the Swordholder were killed, others would be able to take over.

Initially, the gigantic gravitational wave antennas had to be built on the surface. As technology advanced, in Year 12 of the Deterrence Era, the three terrestrial antennas and their support systems moved deep underground. Everyone understood, however, that burying the transmitters and the control center beneath the Earth's surface primarily guarded against a threat originating from humankind itself, but was meaningless against an attack by Trisolaris. For droplets constructed from strong-interaction material, tens of kilometers of rock were not much different from mere liquid, barely able to impede their progress.

After Earth established deterrence, the Trisolar invasion fleet veered away, as verified through observation. With that threat diminished, most people turned their focus to the whereabouts of the ten droplets that had already reached the Solar System. Trisolaris insisted that four of the droplets remain in the Solar System, justifying the decision by arguing that the gravitational wave transmitters could be seized by extremist factions within humankind, and Trisolaris should have the power to take steps to protect both worlds in the event of such an occurrence. Reluctantly, the Earth agreed, but required the four droplets to stay beyond the Kuiper Belt. Moreover, each droplet had to be accompanied by a human probe, so that the droplets' locations and orbits were known at all times. Thus, in the event of a droplet attack, the Earth would have about fifty hours of advance warning. Of these four droplets, two eventually followed *Gravity* to hunt *Blue Space*, and only two remained in the vicinity of the Kuiper Belt.

No one knew where the other six droplets had gone.

Trisolaris claimed that the six droplets had left the Solar System to rejoin the Trisolaran Fleet, but no one on Earth believed this.

Trisolarans were no longer creatures of transparent thought. During the past two centuries, they had learned a great deal about strategic thinking—lies, ruses, and tricks. This was perhaps the greatest benefit they gained from study-ing human culture.

Most people were convinced that the six droplets were hidden somewhere in the Solar System. But because the droplets were tiny, fast, and invisible to radar, they were extremely difficult to locate and track. Even by spreading oil films or using other advanced detection techniques, humans could only reli-ably detect droplets if they approached within 1/10 AU of the Earth, or fifteen million kilometers. Outside this sphere, the droplets were free to roam unde-tected.

At maximum speed, a droplet could cross fifteen million kilometers in ten minutes.

This was all the time the Swordholder would have to make a decision if dark forest deterrence broke down.

Deterrence Era, Year 62
November 28, 4:00 P.M. to 4:17 P.M.:
Deterrence Center

With a deep rumble, the meter-thick heavy steel door opened and Cheng Xin and the others walked into the heart of the dark forest deterrence system.

More emptiness and openness greeted Cheng Xin. This was a semicircular hall, with the curved wall facing her. The surface was translucent, resembling ice. The floor and ceiling were pure white. Cheng Xin's first thought was that she stood in front of an empty, iris-less eye, exuding a desolate sense of loss.

Then she saw Luo Ji.

Luo Ji sat cross-legged on the ground in the middle of the white hall, facing the curved wall. His long hair and beard, combed neatly, were also white, almost merging with the white wall. The whiteness everywhere contrasted strongly with his black Zhongshan suit.[5] Sitting there, he appeared as a stable upside-down T, a lonely anchor on a beach, immobile under the winds of time howling overhead and before the roaring waves of the ages, steadfastly waiting for a departed ship that would never return. In his right hand, he held a red ribbon, the hilt of his sword: the switch for the gravitational wave broadcast. His presence gave the empty eye of this room an iris. Though he was but a black dot, the desolate sense of loss was relieved, giving the eye a soul. Luo Ji sat facing the wall so that his own eyes were invisible, and he did not react to his visitors.

It was said that Master Batuo, the founder of Shaolin Monastery, had meditated in front of a wall for ten years until his shadow was carved into the stone. If so, Luo Ji could have inscribed his own shadow into this wall five times.

[5] *Translator's Note:* This style of Chinese tunic suit is usually known in the West as the "Mao suit." I've chosen to use a literal translation of the Chinese term to avoid unintended connotations. Sun Zhongshan (or Sun Yat-Sen) was the founder of the Republic of China, the predecessor state to the People's Republic of China on the mainland.

The PDC chair stopped Cheng Xin and the fleet chief of staff. "Still ten minutes until the handover," he whispered.

In the last ten minutes of his fifty-four-year career as the Swordholder, Luo Ji remained steadfast.

At the beginning of the Deterrence Era, Luo Ji had enjoyed a brief period of happiness. He had been reunited with his wife, Zhuang Yan, and daughter, Xia Xia, and relived the joy of two centuries ago. But within two years, Zhuang Yan took the child and left Luo Ji. There were many stories told about her reasons. A popular version went like this: While Luo Ji remained a savior in the eyes of the public, his image had already transformed in the minds of those he loved most. Gradually, Zhuang Yan had come to realize that she was living with a man who had already annihilated one world and held the fate of two more in his hand. He was a strange monster who terrified her, and so she left with their child. Another popular story said that Luo Ji left them, instead, so that they could live a normal life. No one knew where Zhuang Yan and their child had gone—they were probably still alive, living tranquil, ordinary lives somewhere.

His family had left him at the time when gravitational wave transmitters took over the task of deterrence from the circumsolar ring of nuclear bombs. Thereafter, Luo Ji embarked on his long career as the Swordholder.

In this cosmic arena, Luo Ji faced not the fancy moves of Chinese sword fighting, resembling dance more than war; nor the flourishes of Western sword fighting, designed to show off the wielder's skill; but the fatal blows of Japanese *kenjutsu*. Real Japanese sword fights often ended after a very brief struggle lasting no more than half a second to two seconds. By the time the swords had clashed but once, one side had already fallen in a pool of blood. But before this moment, the opponents stared at each other like statues, sometimes for as long as ten minutes. During this contest, the swordsman's weapon wasn't held by the hands, but by his heart. The heart-sword, transformed through the eyes into the gaze, stabbed into the depths of the enemy's soul. The real winner was determined during this process: In the silence suspended between the two swordsmen, the blades of their spirits parried and stabbed as soundless claps of thunder. Before a single blow was struck, victory, defeat, life, and death had already been decided.

Luo Ji stared at the white wall with just such an intense glare, aimed at a world four light-years away. He knew that the sophons could show his gaze to the enemy, and his gaze was endowed with the chill of the underworld and the heaviness of the rocks above him, endowed with the determination to sacrifice everything. The gaze made the enemy's heart palpitate and forced them to give up any ill-considered impulse.

There was always an end to the gaze of the swordsmen, a final moment of truth in the contest. For Luo Ji, one participant in this universal contest, the moment when the sword was swung for the first and last time might never arrive.

But it could also happen in the next second.

In this manner, Luo Ji and Trisolaris stared at each other for fifty-four years. Luo Ji had changed from a carefree, irresponsible man into a true Wall-facer, who faced his wall for more than half a century; the protector of Earth civilization who, for five decades, was ready to deal the fatal blow at a moment's notice.

Throughout this time, Luo Ji had remained silent, not uttering a single word. As a matter of fact, after a person ceased to speak for ten or fifteen years, he lost his powers of speech. He might still be able to understand language, but he would not be able to speak. Luo Ji certainly could no longer speak; everything he had to say, he put into his gaze against the wall. He had turned himself into a deterrence machine, a mine ready to explode on contact at each and every moment during the long years of the past half century, maintaining the precarious balance of terror between two worlds.

"It is time to hand over the final authority for the gravitational wave universal broadcast system." The PDC chair broke the silence solemnly.

Luo Ji did not move from his pose. The fleet chief of staff walked over, intending to help him get up, but Luo lifted a hand to stop him. Cheng Xin noticed that the motion of his arm was strong, energetic, without a hint of the hesitation one might expect in a centenarian. Then, Luo Ji stood up by himself, his posture steady. Cheng Xin was surprised to see that Luo Ji did not push against the ground with his hands as he uncrossed his legs and stood up. Even most young men couldn't perform such a motion effortlessly.

"Mr. Luo, this is Cheng Xin, your successor. Please pass the switch to her."

Luo Ji stood tall and straight. He looked at the white wall, which he had stared at for more than half a century, for a few more seconds. Then he bowed slightly.

He was paying his respects to his enemy. To have stared at each other across an abyss of four light-years for half a century had bonded them by a link of destiny.

Then he turned to face Cheng Xin. The old and new Swordholders stood apart, silently. Their eyes met for only a moment, but in that moment, Cheng Xin felt a sharp ray of light sweeping across the dark night of her soul. In that gaze, she felt as light and thin as a sheet of paper, even transparent. She could not imagine what kind of enlightenment the old man in front of her had achieved after fifty-four years of facing the wall. She imagined his thoughts precipitating, becoming as dense and heavy as the crust above them or as ethereal as the blue sky above that. She had no way to know, not until and unless she herself had walked the same path. Other than a bottomless profundity, she could not read his gaze.

With both hands, Luo Ji handed over the switch. With both hands, Cheng Xin accepted this heaviest object in the history of the Earth. And so, the fulcrum upon which two worlds rested moved from a 101-year-old man to a 29-year-old woman.

The switch retained the warmth from Luo Ji's hand. It really did resemble the hilt of a sword. It had four buttons, three on the side and one at the end. To prevent accidental activation, the buttons required some strength to press, and they had to be pressed in a certain order.

Luo Ji backed up two steps and nodded at the three people in front of him. With steady, strong strides, he walked toward the door.

Cheng Xin noticed that, throughout the entire process, no one offered a word of thanks to Luo Ji for his fifty-four years of service. She didn't know if the PDC chair or the fleet chief of staff meant to say something, but she could not recall any of the rehearsals for the ceremony including plans for thanking the old Swordholder.

Humankind did not feel grateful to Luo Ji.

In the lobby, a few black-suited men stopped Luo Ji. One of them said, "Mr. Luo, on behalf of the Prosecution for the International Tribunal, we inform you that you have been accused of suspected mundicide. You are under arrest and will be investigated."

Luo Ji did not even spare them a glance as he continued to walk toward the elevator. The prosecutors stepped aside instinctively. Perhaps Luo Ji did not even notice them. The sharp light in his eyes had been extinguished, and in its place was a tranquility like the glow of a sunset. His three-century-long mission was finally over, and the heavy load of responsibility was off his shoulders. From now on, even if the feminized humankind saw him as a devil and a monster, they all had to admit that his victory was unsurpassed in the entire history of civilization.

The steel door had remained open, and Cheng Xin heard the words spoken in the lobby. She felt an impulse to rush over and thank Luo Ji but stopped herself. Dejectedly, she watched him disappear into the elevator.

The PDC chair and the fleet chief of staff left as well, saying nothing.

With a deep rumble, the steel door closed. Cheng Xin felt her previous life seep out of the narrowing crack in the door like water escaping from a funnel. When the door shut completely, a new Cheng Xin was born.

She looked at the red switch in her hand. It was already a part of her. She and it would be inseparable from now on. Even when she slept, she had to keep it by her pillow.

The white, semicircular hall was deathly silent, as though time was sealed in here and no longer flowed. It really did resemble a tomb. But this would be her entire world from now on. She decided that she had to give life to this place. She didn't want to be like Luo Ji. She wasn't a warrior, a duelist; she was a woman, and she needed to live here for a long time—perhaps a decade, perhaps half a century. Indeed, she had been preparing for this mission her whole life. Now that she stood at the starting point of her long journey, she felt calm.

But fate had other ideas. Her career as the Swordholder, a career she had been preparing for since her birth, lasted only fifteen minutes from the moment she accepted the red switch.

The Final Ten Minutes of the Deterrence Era, Year 62 November 28, 4:17:34 P.M. to 4:27:58 P.M.: Deterrence Center

———

The white wall turned bloody red, as though the hellish magma behind it had burned through. Highest alert. A line of white text appeared against the red background, each character a terrifying scream.

> Incoming strong-interaction space probes detected.
> Total number: 6.
> One is headed toward the L1 Lagrangian point between the Earth and the Sun.
> The other 5 are headed for the Earth in a 1-2-2 formation.
> Speed: 25,000 km/s. Estimated arrival time at the surface: 10 minutes.

Five floating numbers appeared next to Cheng Xin, glowing with a green light. These were holographic buttons: Pressing any of them would bring up a corresponding floating window displaying more detailed information gathered from the advance warning system sweeping the region of space within fifteen million kilometers out from the Earth. The Solar System Fleet General Staff analyzed the data and passed it on to the Swordholder.

Later, Earth would learn that the six droplets had been hiding just outside the fifteen-million-kilometer advance-warning zone. Three of them had relied on solar interference from the Sun to avoid detection, and the other three had disguised themselves in the orbiting space trash scattered in this region. Most of the space trash consisted of spent fuel from the early fusion reactors. Even without these measures, it would have been nearly impossible for the Earth to discover them outside the advance-warning zone because people had always assumed that the droplets were hiding in the asteroid belt, farther away.

The thunderclap that Luo Ji had been waiting for for half a century arrived within five minutes of his departure, and struck Cheng Xin.

Cheng Xin didn't bother pressing any of the holographic buttons. She didn't need any more information.

Right away, she understood the profundity of her error. In the depths of her subconscious, the vision she had held of the mission of the Swordholder had always been utterly, completely wrong. To be sure, she had always planned for the worst, or at least made an effort to do so. Guided by specialists from the PDC and the fleet, she had studied the deterrence system in detail and discussed various possible scenarios with strategists. She had imagined scenarios even worse than the current one.

But she had also committed a fatal error, an error that she did not and could not have realized. The error, however, was also the very reason she had been elected to be the second Swordholder.

In her subconscious, she had never truly accepted that the events facing her now were possible.

Average distance of incoming formation of strong-interaction space probes: approximately 14 million kilometers. The closest one is at 13.5 million kilometers. Estimated arrival time at the surface: nine minutes.

In Cheng Xin's subconscious, she was a protector, not a destroyer; she was a woman, not a warrior. She was willing to use the rest of her life to maintain the balance between the two worlds, until the Earth grew stronger and stronger with Trisolaran science, until Trisolaris grew more and more civilized with Earth culture, until one day, a voice told her: *Put down that red switch and return to the surface. The world no longer needs dark forest deterrence, no longer needs a Swordholder.*

When she faced that distant world as the Swordholder, Cheng Xin, unlike Luo Ji, did not feel this was a life-or-death contest. She thought of it as a game of chess. She would sit tranquilly before the chessboard, thinking of all the openings, anticipating the opponent's attacks, and devising her own responses. She was ready to spend her life playing this game.

But her opponents hadn't bothered to move any pieces on the board. Instead, they had simply lifted the chessboard and smashed it at her head.

The moment Cheng Xin accepted the red switch from Luo Ji, the six droplets had begun accelerating at maximum power toward the Earth. The enemy did not waste a single second.

> Average distance of incoming formation of strong-interaction space
> probes: approximately 13 million kilometers. The closest one is at 12
> million kilometers. Estimated arrival time at the surface: eight min-
> utes.

Blankness.

> Average distance of incoming formation of strong-interaction space
> probes: approximately 11.5 million kilometers. The closest one is at
> 10.5 million kilometers. Estimated arrival time at the surface: seven
> minutes.

Blankness, nothing but blankness. In addition to the white hall and the
white letters, everything else around her had also turned a blank white. Cheng
Xin seemed to be suspended in a milky universe, just like a bubble of milk
sixteen billion light-years across. In this vast blankness, she found nothing to
hold on to.

> Average distance of incoming formation of strong-interaction space
> probes: approximately 10 million kilometers. The closest one is at
> 9 million kilometers. Estimated arrival time at the surface: six minutes.

What was she supposed to do?

> Average distance of incoming formation of strong-interaction space
> probes: approximately 9 million kilometers. The closest one is at
> 7.5 million kilometers. Estimated arrival time at the surface: five
> minutes.

The blankness began to dissipate. The forty-five-kilometer-thick crust above
her reasserted its presence: sedimentary time. The lowest stratum, or the layer
immediately above the Deterrence Center, had probably been deposited four
billion years ago. The Earth had been born only five hundred million years
before that. The turbid ocean was in its infancy, and nonstop flashes of lightning struck its surface; the Sun was a fuzzy ball of light in a haze-veiled sky,
casting a crimson reflection over the sea. At short intervals, other bright balls
of light streaked across the sky, crashing into the sea and trailing long tails of
fire; these meteor strikes caused tsunamis that propelled gigantic waves to

smash onto continents still laced with rivers of lava, raising clouds of vapor generated by fire and water that dimmed the Sun. . . .

In contrast to this hellish but magnificent sight, the turbid water brewed a microscopic tale. Here, organic molecules were born from lightning flashes and cosmic rays, and they collided, fused, broke apart again—a long-lasting game played with building blocks for five hundred million years. Finally, a chain of organic molecules, trembling, split into two strands. The strands attracted other molecules around them until two identical copies of the original were made, and these split apart again and replicated themselves. . . . In this game of building blocks, the probability of producing such a self-replicating chain of organic molecules was so minuscule that it was as if a tornado had picked up a pile of metallic trash and deposited it as a fully-assembled Mercedes-Benz.

But it happened, and so, a breathtaking history of 3.5 billion years had begun.

Average distance of incoming formation of strong-interaction space probes: approximately 7.5 million kilometers. The closest one is at 6 million kilometers. Estimated arrival time at the surface: four minutes.

The Archean Eon was followed by the Proterozoic Eon, each billions of years; then the Paleozoic: the Cambrian's seventy million years, the Ordovician's sixty million years, the Silurian's forty million years, the Devonian's fifty million years, the Carboniferous's sixty-five million years, and the Permian's fifty-five million years; then the Mesozoic: the Triassic's thirty-five million years, the Jurassic's fifty-eight million years, and the Cretaceous's seventy million years; then the Cenozoic: the Tertiary's 64.5 million years and the Quaternary's 2.5 million years.

Then humanity appeared. Compared to the eons before, mankind's history was but the blink of an eye. Dynasties and eras exploded like fireworks; the bone club tossed into the air by an ape turned into a spaceship. Finally, this 3.5-billion-year-long road full of trials and tribulations stopped in front of a tiny human individual, a single person out of the one hundred billion people who had ever lived on the Earth, holding a red switch.

Average distance of incoming formation of strong-interaction space probes: approximately 6 million kilometers. The closest one is at 4.5 million kilometers. Estimated arrival time at the surface: three minutes.

Four billion years were layered on top of Cheng Xin, suffocating her. Her subconscious tried to reach the surface, to catch a breath above it. In her subconscious, the surface was teeming with life, the most prominent form being the giant reptiles, including dinosaurs. Densely, they packed the ground, all the way to the horizon. Among the dinosaurs, between their legs and under their bellies, were the mammals, including humans. Still lower, under and between countless pairs of feet, were surging black currents of water: innumerable trilobites and ants. . . . In the sky, hundreds of billions of birds formed a dark, swirling vortex that blotted out the firmament, and giant pterodactyls could be seen among them from time to time. . . .

Everything was deathly quiet. The eyes were the most terrifying: the eyes of dinosaurs; the eyes of trilobites and ants; the eyes of birds and butterflies; the eyes of bacteria. . . . The humans alone possessed one hundred billion pairs of eyes, equal to the number of stars in the Milky Way. Among them were the eyes of ordinary men and women, and the eyes of Da Vinci, Shakespeare, and Einstein.

> Average distance of incoming formation of strong-interaction space probes: approximately 4.5 million kilometers. The closest one is at three million kilometers. Estimated arrival time at the surface: two minutes.
> Two of the probes are headed for Asia, two others for North America. The last one is aimed at Europe.

Pressing the switch would end the progress of 3.5 billion years. Everything would disappear in the eternal night of the universe, as though none of it had ever existed.

That baby seemed to be back in her arms: soft, cuddly, warm, his face moist, smiling sweetly, calling her *mama*.

> Average distance of incoming formation of strong-interaction space probes: approximately 3 million kilometers. The closest one is at 1.5 million kilometers, and it is rapidly decelerating. Estimated arrival time at the surface: one minute and thirty seconds.

"No—" Cheng Xin screamed, and threw the switch away. She watched it slide across the ground, as though watching a devil.

Strong-interaction space probes approaching lunar orbit and continuing to decelerate. Extending their trajectories suggests that their
targets are the gravitational wave broadcasting stations in North
America, Europe, and Asia, and Gravitational Wave Universal Broadcast System Control Station Zero. Estimated impact on the surface:
thirty seconds.

Like a strand of spider silk, these final moments stretched out endlessly. But
Cheng Xin did not vacillate; she had already made up her mind. This wasn't
a decision born of thought, but buried deep in her genes. These genes could
be traced to four billion years ago, when the decision was first made. The subsequent billions of years only strengthened it. Right or wrong, she knew she
had no other choice.

It was good that release was at hand.

A great jolt tumbled her to the ground: The droplets had penetrated the
crust. She felt as though the solid rocks around her had vanished, and the Deterrence Center was on top of a giant drumhead. She closed her eyes and
imagined the sight of a droplet passing through the crust like a fish swimming
through water, waiting for the arrival at cosmic velocity of the perfectly smooth
devil that would turn her and everything around her into molten lava.

But the quaking stopped after a few violent beats, like a drummer punctu-
ating the end of the piece.

The red light on the screen faded, replaced by the white background from
before. The room seemed brighter and more open. A few lines of black text
appeared:

North American gravitational wave transmitter destroyed.
European gravitational wave transmitter destroyed.
Asian gravitational wave transmitter destroyed.
Solar radio-amplification function suppressed on all bands.

Silence once again reigned over everything, except the faint sound of water
trickling somewhere. A pipe had burst during the quake.

Cheng Xin understood that the droplet attack on the Asian gravitational
wave transmitter had caused the earthquake. That antenna was about twenty
kilometers from here and was also deeply buried.

The droplets had not even bothered attacking the Swordholder.

The black text disappeared. After some moments of blankness, a last screen of text faded in:

Gravitational wave universal broadcast system cannot be recovered. Dark forest deterrence has been terminated.

Post-Deterrence Era, First Hour
A Lost World

Cheng Xin rode the elevator to the surface. Exiting the elevator station, she saw the plaza where the deterrence handover ceremony had taken place an hour ago. All the attendees had left, and the place was empty save for the long shadows cast by the flagpoles. The flags of the UN and the Solar System Fleet hung from the two tallest poles, and behind them were the flags of the various nations. The flags continued to flap tranquilly in the light breeze. Beyond them was the endless Gobi Desert. A few twittering birds landed in a stand of tamarisk nearby. In the distance, she could see the rolling Qilian Mountains, the snow cover on a few peaks giving them a silvery highlight.

Everything seemed the same, but this world no longer belonged to humans.

Cheng Xin didn't know what to do. No one had contacted her after the end of deterrence. The Swordholder no longer existed, just like deterrence.

She walked forward aimlessly. When she exited the gates of the compound, two guards saluted her. She was terrified of facing people, but she saw nothing but curiosity in their eyes—they didn't yet know what had happened. Regulations permitted the Swordholder to come onto the surface for brief intervals, and they must have thought she had come up to investigate the quake. Cheng Xin saw a few military officers standing next to a flying transport parked by the gate. They weren't even looking at her, merely in the direction she had come from. One of them pointed in that direction.

She turned around and saw the mushroom cloud on the horizon. Formed by the earth and dust thrown up from deep underground, it was very thick, appearing almost solid. It looked so out of place in the serene scene that it resembled a bad Photoshop job. A closer examination led Cheng Xin to imagine it as an ugly bust showing a strange expression in the setting sun. That was where the droplet had penetrated the Earth.

Someone called her name. She turned and saw 艾 AA running toward her. Dressed in a white jacket, her hair waving in the wind, she panted and told Cheng Xin that she had come to see her, but the sentries wouldn't let her in.

"I've brought some flowers for your new place," she said, pointing at her parked car. Then she turned to the mushroom cloud. "Is that a volcano? Did that cause the earthquake just now?"

Cheng Xin wanted to pull AA into her arms and cry, but she controlled herself. She wanted to delay the moment when this happy girl found out the truth, wanted to let the reverberations of the good times that had just ended linger a bit longer.

Excerpt from *A Past Outside of Time* Reflections on the Failure of Dark Forest Deterrence

The most important factor in the failure of deterrence was, of course, electing the wrong Swordholder. This is a topic that will be addressed elsewhere in a dedicated chapter. For now, let's focus on the technical weaknesses in the system design that contributed to the failure.

After the failure, most people immediately pointed to the small number of gravitational wave transmitters as a cause, and blamed people from the early Deterrence Era for dismantling nineteen of the twenty-three completed transmitters. But this reaction represented a failure to grasp the substance of the problem. From data gathered during the droplet attack, a droplet needed slightly more than ten seconds on average to penetrate the crust and destroy a transmitter. Even if the planned one hundred transmitters had been completed and deployed, it wouldn't have taken long for droplets to destroy the entire system.

The key was that the system *could* be destroyed. Humankind had had a chance to build an indestructible gravitational wave universal broadcast system, but hadn't taken it.

The problem wasn't the number of transmitters, but where they were deployed.

Imagine if the twenty-three transmitters had not been built on or below the surface, but in space—that is, twenty-three spaceships like *Gravity*. Normally, the ships would have been scattered around the Solar System. Even if the droplets had conducted a surprise attack, it would have been difficult for them to destroy all of them. One or more of the ships would have time to escape into deep space.

This would have greatly increased the degree of deterrence for the whole system, in a way that would not have been dependent on the Swordholder. The Trisolarans would have known that they controlled insufficient forces within the Solar System to completely destroy the deterrence system, and would have behaved with far more restraint.

Regrettably, there was only one *Gravity*.

There were two reasons that more ships with transmitters weren't built: First, there was the "Sons of the Earth" attack on the transmitter in Antarctica. Spaceships were deemed even more vulnerable to threats from extremist humans than underground stations. Second, it was a matter of economics. Since gravitational wave antennas were immense, they had to serve as the hull of the ship itself. Thus, the antenna had to be constructed out of materials that met the requirements of spaceflight, which increased costs many times. *Gravity* itself cost almost the equivalent of the twenty-three ground-based transmitters added together. Moreover, the hull of the ship itself could not be refreshed; when the vibrating string made of degenerate matter that ran the length of the ship reached its fifty-year half-life limit, a completely new gravitational wave ship had to be built.

But the deeper root cause could only be found in the minds of humankind. Never explicitly stated, and perhaps not even consciously understood, a gravitational wave ship was too powerful—so powerful that it terrified its creator. If something—a droplet attack or something else—forced such ships to depart for deep space, and they could never return to the Solar System due to the presence of enemy threats, they would turn into copies of *Blue Space* and *Bronze Age*, or something even more horrific. Each gravitational wave ship, with its no-longer-human crew, would also possess the power to broadcast to the universe (though limited by the half-life of the vibrating string), thus controlling the fate of humanity. A frightful instability would be permanently scattered among the stars.

At its root, this fear was a fear of dark forest deterrence itself. This was characteristic of ultimate deterrence: The deterrer and the deteree shared the same terror of deterrence itself.

Post-Deterrence Era, First Hour
A Lost World

Cheng Xin walked toward the officers and asked them to take her to the site of the eruption. A lieutenant colonel in charge of security for the compound immediately dispatched two cars: one to take her, the other to carry a few guards for security. Cheng Xin asked AA to stay and wait for her, but AA insisted on coming and got into the car.

The flying cars hovered barely above the ground and headed to the mushroom cloud at a low speed. AA asked the driver what was wrong, but he didn't know. The volcano had erupted twice, a few minutes apart. He thought it might be the first time in recorded history that a volcano had erupted within China's borders.

He couldn't have imagined that the "volcano" had once hidden the strategic fulcrum for the world: the gravitational wave antenna. The first eruption was caused by the impact of the droplet penetrating the crust. After destroying the antenna, it retraced its path and emerged from the ground, causing a second eruption. The eruptions were due to the droplet releasing its tremendous kinetic energy in the ground, not an outburst of material from the mantle, so they were very brief. The extremely high velocity of the droplet meant that it could not be observed by the naked eye as it penetrated or emerged from the ground.

Small smoking pits dotted the Gobi as it passed beneath the car: mini-impact craters from the lava and heated rocks that had been thrown up by the eruption. As they proceeded, the pits grew denser, and a thick layer of smoke hovered over the Gobi, revealing burning stands of tamarisk here and there. Though few people lived out here they occasionally saw old buildings collapsed by the quake. The whole scene resembled a battlefield where the fighting had just finished.

The cloud had dissipated a bit by now and no longer looked like a mushroom—it was more like a head of unkempt hair whose tips were colored crimson by the setting sun. A security line stopped the cars as they approached, and they had to land. But Cheng Xin persisted, and the sentries let her through. The soldiers didn't know that the world had already fallen, and they still respected Cheng Xin's authority as the Swordholder. They did, however, stop AA, and no matter how she screamed and struggled, they would not let her pass.

The steady wind had already driven most of the dust away, but the smoke broke the light of the setting sun into a series of flickering shadows. Cheng Xin walked about a hundred meters through the shadows until she reached the edge of a giant crater. Shaped like a funnel, the crater was forty or fifty meters deep at the center. Thick clouds of white smoke still poured out of it, and the bottom of the crater gave off a dim red molten glow: a pool of lava.

Forty-five kilometers below, the gravitational wave antenna, a cylinder with a length of fifteen hundred meters and a diameter of fifty meters suspended in an underground cave with magnetic levitation, had been smashed into smithereens and swallowed by the red-hot lava.

This should have been her fate. It would have been the best ending for a Swordholder who had given up the power to deter.

The red glow at the bottom of the crater attracted Cheng Xin. Just one more step, and she would achieve the release that she desired. As waves of heat buffeted her face, she stared at the dim red pool, mesmerized, until peals of laughter from behind her shook her out of her musing.

She turned around. In the flickering sunlight filtered by the smoke, a slender figure approached her. She didn't recognize the newcomer until she was very close: Sophon.

Other than the pale, lovely face, the robot looked completely different from the last time Cheng Xin had seen her. She was dressed in desert camouflage, and her hair, once tied up in a neat bun decorated with flowers, had been cut in a short and efficient style. Around her neck was the black scarf of a ninja, and on her back was strapped a long katana. She looked valiant and heroic, but the extreme femininity that she exuded had not vanished completely: Her postures and movements were still soft and gentle like water, but now they were also suffused with a glamorous air of killing and death, like a pliant but fatal noose. Even the heat spilling from the crater could not dispel the chill she brought.

"You acted just as we anticipated," Sophon said, sneering. "Don't be too hard on yourself. The fact is that humankind chose you, and they chose this result. Out of all the members of the human race, you're the only innocent."

Cheng Xin's heart jumped. She didn't feel comforted, but she had to admit that this lovely devil had a power that penetrated her soul.

Cheng Xin saw AA approach. She had apparently found out or guessed what had really happened. AA's eyes burned with fury as she stared at Sophon; she picked up a rock from the ground with both hands and smashed the back of Sophon's skull with it. But Sophon turned around and brushed the rock away like a mosquito. AA cursed at Sophon using every profane word she could think of, and went for another rock. Sophon unsheathed the katana on her back, easily pushing off the pleading Cheng Xin with her other hand, and twirled the katana. It sliced through the air, faster than the blades of an electric fan, whining loudly. When she stopped, strands of AA's hair drifted down around her head. AA stood frozen in place, terrified, her shoulders hunched.

Cheng Xin remembered that she had seen Sophon's katana in that eastern leaf-house shrouded in fog and cloud. Back then, it, and two shorter swords, had rested on a refined wooden stand next to the tea table, looking more decorative than deadly.

"Why?" Cheng Xin muttered, as if asking herself.

"Because the universe is not a fairy tale."

Rationally, Cheng Xin understood that, had the balance maintained by deterrence continued, the brighter future belonged to humankind, not Trisolaris. But in her subconscious, the universe remained a fairy tale, a fairy tale about love. Her biggest mistake was not looking at the problem from the perspective of the enemy.

From Sophon's gaze, Cheng Xin finally understood why she had been kept alive.

As the gravitational wave broadcast system had been destroyed and the sun's ability to amplify radio waves had been suppressed, a living Cheng Xin posed no threat. On the other hand, in the unlikely event that humans still possessed some other method of broadcasting to the universe unknown to Trisolaris, eliminating the Swordholder might cause others to activate the broadcast. As long as the Swordholder was alive, however, the probability of that happening was virtually nil: Others would have a reason and excuse to shirk their responsibility.

Instead of the deterrer, Cheng Xin had been turned into a safety shield. The enemy had seen through her completely.

She was a fairy tale.

"Don't celebrate too early," AA said to Sophon, having recovered some of her courage. "We still have the spaceship *Gravity*."

Sophon returned the katana to its sheath on her back in a single, smooth motion. "Foolish girl, *Gravity* has been destroyed. It happened an hour ago, when the handover occurred a light-year away. I regret that I can't show you the wreckage because the sophons are in a blind zone."

The Trisolarans had been planning and preparing for this moment for a long time. The exact time for the handover had been determined five months ago, before the sophons accompanying *Gravity* had entered the blind zone. The two droplets with *Gravity* had already received the order to destroy the ship at the moment of the handover.

"I'm leaving," said Sophon. "Please convey to Dr. Luo Ji the deepest respect of all of Trisolaris. He was a powerful deterrer, a great warrior. Oh, and if you get the chance, also give Mr. Thomas Wade our regrets."

Cheng Xin looked up, surprised.

"In our personality studies, your degree of deterrence hovered around ten percent, like a worm wriggling on the ground. Luo Ji's degree of deterrence was always around ninety percent, like a fearsome cobra poised to strike. But Wade—" Sophon gazed at the setting sun behind the smoke, only a sliver of which now was above ground. Terror glinted from her eyes. She shook her head vigorously, as though trying to chase away a mirage in her mind. "He had no curve at all. No matter what the other environmental parameters were, his degree of deterrence stayed at one hundred percent! What a devil! If he had become the Swordholder, none of this would have been possible. This peace would have had to last. We've already waited sixty-two years, but we'd have had to keep on waiting, maybe for fifty more years, or even longer. And then Trisolaris would face an Earth equal to us in technology and power. We'd have to compromise. . . . However, we knew that humanity would choose you."

Sophon walked away, taking large strides. She paused some distance away and turned around, calling out to the silent Cheng Xin and AA. "Get ready to go to Australia, you pitiful bugs."

Post-Deterrence Era, Day 60
A Lost World

On the thirty-eighth day after the end of deterrence, the Ringier-Fitzroy observation station at the outer rim of the asteroid belt discovered 415 new trails in the interstellar dust cloud near the Trisolaran star system. Apparently, Trisolaris had sent a second fleet toward the Solar System.

This second fleet had left Trisolaris five years ago, and passed through the dust cloud four years ago. This had been a huge risk on Trisolaris's part—if they couldn't destroy humanity's dark forest deterrence system within five years, the discovery of this fleet might have led to the activation of the deterrence broadcast. This meant that as long ago as five years, Trisolaris already had sensed the shifting mood toward dark forest deterrence among humanity and correctly predicted the kind of second Swordholder that would be elected.

History seemed to have been reset; a new cycle had begun.

The end of deterrence once again cast the future of humankind into darkness, but, just like in the first crisis over two centuries earlier, people did not connect this darkness with their individual fates. Based on analysis of the trails, the Second Trisolaran Fleet's velocity wasn't so different from that of the First Trisolaran Fleet. Even if they could accelerate more, the fleet wouldn't arrive at the Solar System for at least two or three centuries. Everyone alive would be able to live out the remainder of their lives in peace. After the lessons taught by the Great Ravine, modern men and women would never again sacrifice the present for the future.

But this time, humanity wasn't so fortunate.

Three days after the Second Trisolaran Fleet left the interstellar cloud, the observation system detected 415 trails in the second interstellar cloud. These trails couldn't belong to a different fleet. The First Trisolaran Fleet had taken five years to go from the first dust cloud to the second, while the Second Triso-laran Fleet had taken only six days.

The Trisolarans had achieved lightspeed.

Analysis of the trails in the second interstellar dust cloud confirmed that they continued to extend through the cloud at lightspeed. At such high veloci-ties, the trails left by the ships' impacts became particularly prominent.

Timing wise, it appeared that the fleet had entered lightspeed as soon as it exited the first dust cloud; there didn't appear to be a stage during which it accelerated.

If that was true, then the Second Trisolaran Fleet should have already or almost reached the Solar System. Using midsized telescopes, it was possible to see a patch of 415 bright lights about six thousand AU from the Earth. These were the lights generated by deceleration. Apparently the ships' propulsion systems were conventional. The fleet's velocity was now only 15 percent of the speed of light. This was evidently the fastest speed that still permitted safe de-celeration before arriving at the Solar System. Based on the observed velocity and deceleration, the Second Trisolaran Fleet would arrive at the edge of the Solar System in one year.

This was a bit puzzling. It appeared as if the Trisolar ships were capable of entering and dropping out of lightspeed within an extremely short period of time, but they chose not to do so too close to the Trisolaran star system or the Solar System. After the fleet had left Trisolaris, the ships accelerated under conventional power for an entire year, until they were about six thousand AU from home, before entering lightspeed. Similarly, they dropped out of lightspeed at the same distance from the Solar System and switched to conventional deceleration. This distance could be covered in a month at lightspeed, but the fleet chose to spend a year traversing it. The cruise of the Second Trisolaran Fleet would thus take two years longer than it would if the entire voyage were conducted at lightspeed.

Only one explanation for this curious decision came to mind: It was moti-vated by a desire not to harm either solar system during the process of entering and dropping out of lightspeed. The safe radius appeared to be two hundred times the distance from the Sun to Neptune. This suggested that the power generated by the drives was two orders of magnitude greater than a star, which seemed unimaginable.

Excerpt from *A Past Outside of Time*
Technology Explosion on Trisolaris

———

Exactly when the rate of Trisolaran technological progress had shifted from constant to explosive was a mystery. Some scholars believed that the acceleration began before the Crisis Era; others believed that the forward leap didn't happen until the Deterrence Era. There was, however, general consensus on the causes for the technology explosion.

First, Earth civilization had a tremendous impact on Trisolaran civilization— on this point, at least, the Trisolarans likely didn't lie. Since the arrival of the first sophon, the massive inflow of human culture profoundly changed Trisolaris, and some human values resonated with the Trisolarans. Trisolaran society broke down the barriers to scientific progress imposed by the extreme totalitarian political system that had been adopted as a reaction to the chaotic eras, encouraged freedom of thought, and began to respect the individual. These changes might have triggered ideological transformation movements akin to the Renaissance in that distant world, leading to leaps in scientific and technological progress. This must have been a glorious period in Trisolaran history, but the specific details were unknown.

A second possibility was only a guess: The exploratory sophon missions sent in other directions in the universe were not fruitless, as the Trisolarans claimed. Before being blinded, they might have found at least one other civilized world. If so, Trisolarans might have not only received technological knowledge from this other civilization, but also important information about the condition of the dark forest in the universe. If so, Trisolaris far surpassed the Earth in every domain of knowledge.

Post-Deterrence Era, Day 60
A Lost World

For the first time since the end of deterrence, Sophon appeared. Still dressed in camouflage and wearing the katana on her back, she announced to the world that the Second Trisolaran Fleet would arrive in four years to complete the total conquest of the Solar System.

Trisolaran policy toward humanity had changed since the first crisis. Sophon announced that Trisolaris no longer intended to exterminate human civilization, but would create reservations for humans within the Solar System—specifically, they would let humanity live in Australia and on one-third of the surface of Mars. This preserved the basic living space needed for human civilization.

To prepare for the Trisolaran conquest in four years, Sophon declared that humanity must immediately begin to resettle. To accomplish the so-called "defanging" of humanity, and to prevent the reappearance of dark forest deterrence or similar threats in the future, humanity must be completely disarmed and resettle "naked." No heavy equipment or facilities would be permitted in the reservations, and the resettlement must be completed within one year.

Human habitats on Mars and in space could accommodate about three million individuals at most; thus, the main destination for resettlement was Australia.

But most people still held on to the illusion that they would have at least a generation of tranquil life. After Sophon's speech, no country responded, and no one actually emigrated.

Five days after this historical "Reservation Proclamation," one of the five droplets cruising within the Earth's atmosphere attacked three large cities in Asia, Europe, and North America. The purpose of the attacks wasn't to destroy the cities, but to instill terror. The droplet passed straight through the giant forests of these cities, colliding with all hanging buildings that happened to be in the way. The struck buildings burned and then fell several hundred meters, like overripe fruits. Over three hundred thousand people died in the worst disaster since the Doomsday Battle.

People finally understood that, to the droplets, the human world was as fragile as eggs under a poised rock. Cities and large-scale facilities were defenseless. If the Trisolarans wanted, they could lay waste to every city, until the surface of the Earth was one large ruin.

As a matter of fact, humans had been working toward overcoming this disadvantage. Humans understood early on that only strong-interaction materials (SIM) could be used to defend against droplets. Before the termination of deterrence, research facilities on Earth and in the fleet could already produce small quantities of such material in laboratories, though large-scale manufacturing and utilization would not be possible for years. If humanity had had another ten years, production of large amounts of SIM would have been a reality. Although the propulsion systems of the droplets would still have been far beyond human capabilities, at least conventional missiles could have been made out of SIM to destroy the droplets by sheer numerical advantage. Alternatively, SIM could have been used to construct defensive screens. Even if the droplets had dared to attack these shields, they would have become one-time-use shells.

Alas, none of these visions would ever come true now.

Sophon made another speech, in which she explained that Trisolaris had changed its policy of extermination of humanity out of love and respect for human civilization. It was inevitable that resettlement of humanity to Australia would cause them to suffer somewhat for a period of time, but it would last only three to four years. After the arrival of the Trisolaran Fleet, the conquerors were capable of helping the four billion people in Australia live comfortably. Also, the conquerors would assist humanity in constructing additional habitats on Mars and in space. Five years after the arrival of the Trisolaran Fleet, humanity could begin to migrate in large numbers to Mars and space, a process projected to take fifteen years. By then, humanity would possess adequate living space, and the two civilizations would begin a life of peaceful coexistence.

But all of this depended on the successful accomplishment of the initial resettlement to Australia. If the relocation effort did not commence immediately, the droplets would continue to attack the cities. After the expiration of the one-year period, any humans found outside the reservations would be exterminated as invaders on Trisolaran territory. Of course, if humans left the cities and scattered across the continents, the five droplets alone would not be enough to locate and kill every single individual. But the Second Trisolaran Fleet arriving in four years would no doubt be able to.

"The glorious and resplendent civilization of Earth earned humanity this one chance at survival," said Sophon. "Please treasure it."

Thus began the Great Resettlement of all of humanity to Australia.

Post-Deterrence Era, Year 2
Australia

▬▬▬

Cheng Xin stood in front of Elder Fraisse's house and surveyed the Great Victoria Desert shimmering in the heat. Simple, just-completed shelter-houses were packed densely, as far as the eye could see. Under the noonday sun, the plywood and sheet-metal constructions seemed both brand-new and fragile, like origami toys scattered across the sand.

When James Cook had discovered Australia five centuries ago, he could never have imagined that, one day, all of humanity would be gathered on this empty, vast continent.

Cheng Xin and 艾AA had come to Australia with the earliest wave of forced migrants. Cheng Xin could have gone to a big city like Canberra or Sydney for a relatively comfortable life, but she had insisted on living as an ordinary migrant and gone to the interior resettlement zone in the deserts near Warburton, where conditions were the roughest. She was touched that AA, who could also have gone to a big city, insisted on accompanying her.

Life in the resettlement zone was difficult. Near the beginning, when few people were there, it was still tolerable. The harassment by other people was far harder to bear than the material deprivations. At first, Cheng Xin and AA had a shelter-house all to themselves. But as additional migrants came, more people were packed into the shelter-house, until eight women in total shared it. The other six women had all been born during the paradise-like Deterrence Era. Here, for the first time in their lives, they encountered rationing of water and food, dead walls that did not come alive with information, rooms with no air-conditioning, public toilets and showers, bunk beds. . . . This was a society of absolute equality: Money had no use here, and everyone received exactly the same ration. They had only ever seen such austerity in historical films, and life in the resettlement zones felt like hell. Naturally, Cheng Xin became the target of their fury. Unprovoked, they would curse at her and accuse her of being a waste of space—after all, she had not been able to deter Trisolaris. Her worst sin had been giving up as soon as she received the warning: Had she activated the gravitational wave broadcast, the Trisolarans would have run away in terror, and at least humanity would enjoy a few more decades of happiness. Even if the broadcast led to the immediate destruction of the Earth, it would be better than the current conditions.

At the beginning, the abuse was merely verbal, but it soon turned physical, and they began to snatch Cheng Xin's rations away from her. AA did all she could to protect her friend. She fought the other women, sometimes several times a day. Once, she grabbed the meanest one by the hair and slammed her head against a bedpost until blood covered her face. Thereafter, they left her and Cheng Xin alone.

But the enmity directed at Cheng Xin wasn't limited to their roommates: The migrants in the shelter-houses nearby also came to harass her. Sometimes they threw stones at Cheng Xin's shelter-house; sometimes a mob surrounded the shelter-house and shouted curses at her.

Cheng Xin bore all the abuse with equanimity. Indeed, the abuse even comforted her. As the failed Swordholder, she felt she deserved worse.

This persisted until an old man named Fraisse came and invited her and AA to move into his place. Fraisse was an Aboriginal man, over eighty years of age but still hale and hearty, with a white beard on his black face. As a native, he had been temporarily allowed to keep his own house. During the Common Era, he had been in charge of an organization for Aboriginal cultural preservation, and he had gone into hibernation at the beginning of the Crisis Era in order to continue his task in the future. When he awoke, he saw that his prediction had come true: The Australian Aboriginals and their culture were close to disappearing.

Fraisse's house, built back in the twenty-first century, was old but solid and had a nice copse of trees nearby. Once they moved there, Cheng Xin and AA's lives became much more stable. More importantly, the old man provided them with spiritual tranquility. He did not share the popular searing anger and bone-deep hatred toward the Trisolarans; indeed, he rarely talked about the crisis at all. All he said was, "Whatever people do, the gods remember."

True. Even *people* still remembered whatever people did. Five centuries ago, civilized men of Earth—most of whom had actually been criminals in Europe—stepped onto this continent and shot the Aboriginal peoples in the woods for sport. Later, even when they recognized that their quarries were men and women, not beasts, the slaughter continued. The Aboriginal peoples had lived in this vast land for tens of thousands of years. By the time the white men arrived, the native population was more than a half million, but that number soon diminished to thirty thousand refugees who had to escape to the desolate western deserts to survive. . . .

When Sophon proclaimed the establishment of "reservations," people paid attention. It brought to mind the tragic fate of the native peoples of North America, another faraway continent where the arrival of civilized men of Earth brought sorrow.

When she first arrived at Fraisse's, AA was curious about everything in the old house. It resembled a museum of Aboriginal culture. Everywhere there were rock and bark paintings, musical instruments made of wooden slats and hollow logs, woven grass skirts, boomerangs, spears, and other such objects. AA was most interested in a few pots of paint made of white clay and red and yellow ocher. She knew right away what they were for, and, dipping a finger into the pots, started to paint her own face. Then she began dancing in imitation of tribal dancers she had seen somewhere, making fearsome noises as she danced.

"This would have terrified those bitches living with us," she said.

Fraisse laughed and shook his head. He explained that AA wasn't imitating the Aboriginal peoples of Australia, but the Māori of New Zealand. Outsiders sometimes confused the two, but the Aboriginal peoples of Australia were gentle, while the Māori were fierce warriors. And, even so, she wasn't imitating the Māori dance correctly, and had failed to capture their spirit. Fraisse then painted his own face into an impressive mask and took off his shirt, revealing a dark chest and powerful muscles that seemed incongruous with his advanced age. He picked up a taiaha from the corner of the house and began to dance a real war haka.

Cheng Xin and AA were mesmerized. Fraisse's kind everyday demeanor disappeared, and he transformed into a threatening, awe-inspiring demon. His whole body seemed suffused with magnificent force. Every cry and foot stomp made the glass window panes quake in their frames, and the two women trembled. But it was his eyes that shocked them the most: Murderous chill and searing rage spewed from those wide-open orbs, combining the forces of typhoons and thunder in Oceania. His powerful gaze seemed to project earth-shattering shouts: "Do not run away! I will kill you! I will eat you!"

The haka over, Fraisse went back to his usual kind self. "For a Māori warrior, the key is to hold the enemy's gaze. He must defeat the enemy first with his eyes, then kill him with the taiaha." He came back and stood in front of Cheng Xin. "Child, you failed to hold the enemy's gaze." Then he patted her gently on the shoulder. "But, it's not your fault. Really not your fault."

The next day, Cheng Xin did something that surprised even herself: She went to see Wade.

Wade was sealing up the windows of a shelter-house with composite boards so that it could be used as a warehouse. One of his sleeves was empty. In this age, it would have been easy for him to acquire a prosthesis indistinguishable from the real thing, but for some reason, he had refused.

Two other prisoners—clearly also Common Era men—whistled at Cheng Xin. But once they realized who Cheng Xin had come to see, they shut up and went back to their work without looking up.

As Cheng Xin approached Wade, she was a bit surprised to see that while he was serving his sentence in harsh conditions, he looked much better groomed than the last time they met. He was clean-shaven and his hair was combed neatly. Prisoners in this age no longer wore uniforms, but his white shirt was the cleanest here, even more so than the shirts worn by the guards. Holding a few nails between his lips, he took them out one at a time with his left hand and pounded them into the composite boards with precise, forceful blows from the hammer. He glanced at Cheng Xin without changing his indifferent expression and went on working.

Cheng Xin knew right away that he had not given up. His ambitions, ideals, treachery, and whatever else was hidden in his heart, unknown to her—he had given up none of it.

Cheng Xin extended a hand to Wade. He glanced at her again, put down the hammer, spat out the nails, and deposited them in her hand. Then she handed him the nails one by one as he pounded them in, until they were all gone.

"Leave," he said. He grabbed another handful of nails from the tool chest. He didn't hand them over to Cheng Xin and didn't put them in his mouth. Instead, he placed them on the ground next to his feet.

"I . . . I just . . ." Cheng Xin didn't know what to say.

"I'm telling you to leave Australia." Wade's lips barely moved as he whispered. His gaze remained on the composite board. Anyone a little distance away would think he was concentrating on his work. "Hurry, before the resettlement is complete."

Like he had many times three centuries ago, Wade had managed to stun Cheng Xin with a single sentence. Each time it was as if he had tossed her a knotted ball of string that she must untangle layer by layer before she could understand the complex meaning hidden within. But this time, Wade's words made her shiver. She didn't even have the courage to begin to untangle his riddle.

"Go." Wade didn't give her a chance to ask questions. Then he turned to her and once again revealed his special smirk, like a crack in a frozen-over pond. "*Now* I'm telling you to get out of this house."

On the way back to Warburton, Cheng Xin saw the densely packed shelter-houses stretching to the horizon, saw the busy crowd laboring in the cracks between the shelter-houses. Suddenly, she felt her vision shift, as though she were watching everything from somewhere outside the world, and everything she saw turned into a writhing nest of ants. A nameless terror gripped her and the bright Australian sunlight seemed as cold as rain in winter.

Three months after the start of the Great Resettlement, more than a billion people had been relocated to Australia. Simultaneously, the governments of the nations of the world began to relocate to large Australian cities. The UN moved its headquarters to Sydney. Each government directed the resettlement of its own citizens, with the UN Resettlement Commission coordinating the efforts. In their new land, the migrants gathered into districts based on their nation of origin, and Australia became a miniature replica of the whole Earth. Other than the names of the largest cities, old place names were abandoned. Now "New York," "Tokyo," and "Shanghai" were nothing more than refugee camps full of basic shelter-houses.

No one had any experience in dealing with resettlement at such a large scale, either in the national governments or the UN, and many difficulties and dangers soon surfaced.

First, there was the problem of shelter. Leaders soon realized that even if all the construction materials in the world were shipped to Australia, and per capita space were limited to the dimensions of a bed, not even one-fifth of the final total population would have a roof over their heads. By the time five hundred million migrants were in Australia, there was no more material for building shelter-houses. They had to resort to erecting large tents, each of which was the size of a stadium and capable of housing more than ten thousand. But under such poor living and sanitation conditions, epidemics were a constant threat.

There was also the shortage of food. The agricultural factories in Australia were far from sufficient to satisfy the needs of the population, and it was necessary to transport food from across the world. As the population on the continent increased, the distribution of food became more complex and subject to more delays.

But the greatest danger was the prospect of loss of social order. In the resettlement zones, the hyper-information society disappeared. Newcomers poked the walls, bedside stands, or even their own clothes until they realized that everything was dead, un-networked. Even basic communications could not be guaranteed. People could obtain news about the world only through very limited channels. For a population used to a super-networked world full of information, it was as if they had all gone blind. Modern governments lost all their techniques for mass communication and leadership, and were ignorant of how to maintain order in a massively overcrowded society.

Simultaneously, resettlement was also proceeding in space.

At the end of the Deterrence Era, about 1.5 million people were living in space. About half a million spacers belonged to Earth International, living in space stations and space cities orbiting the Earth and bases on the moon. The rest belonged to the Solar System Fleet and were distributed between bases on Mars and around Jupiter, as well as warships patrolling the Solar System.

The spacers who belonged to Earth International mostly lived below the orbit of the moon. They had no choice but to return to the Earth and migrate to Australia.

The rest moved to the Martian base, which Trisolaris had designated as the second human reservation.

After the Doomsday Battle, the Solar System Fleet had never returned to its former size. Even at the end of the Deterrence Era, the fleet had barely more than one hundred stellar-class warships. Though technology had continued to improve, the maximum speed of the ships never increased, as fusion propulsion had already been pushed to the limit. The overwhelming advantage the Trisolar ships held was not only their ability to reach lightspeed, but, more terrifyingly, their ability to leap into lightspeed without a prolonged process of acceleration. In order to reach even 15 percent of lightspeed, human ships had to accelerate for a year, taking into account fuel consumption rates and the need to reserve fuel for the return voyage. Compared to Trisolaran ships, Earth ships were slow as snails.

When deterrence was dismantled, the stellar-class warships of the Solar System Fleet had a chance to escape into deep space. If the hundred-plus ships had sped away from the Solar System in different directions at maximum power, the eight droplets in the Solar System could not have caught them all. But not a single ship chose to do so; all obeyed Sophon and returned to Mars orbit. The reason for their obedience was simple: Resettlement on Mars was not like settling in Australia on Earth. Within the sealed habitat of the Martian base, a population of one million could maintain a comfortable, civilized existence. The base had been designed to accommodate the long-term needs of such a population. This was, without a doubt, superior to wandering deep space for the rest of their lives.

Trisolaris remained very wary of the humans on Mars. The two droplets recalled from the Kuiper Belt spent most of their time patrolling the space above the Martian city. Unlike the resettlement process on the surface of the Earth, although the Solar System Fleet had essentially been disarmed, people living on Mars still had access to modern technology—required for maintaining the habitability of the city. But the people living on Mars dared not engage in any adventures such as building a gravitational wave transmitter. The sophons certainly would have detected a large-scale venture like that, and people hadn't forgotten the terror of the Doomsday Battle. The Martian base was as fragile as an eggshell, and the depressurization caused by a single droplet impact would have meant complete disaster.

The space resettlement process was completed in three months. Other than the Martian base, there was no more human presence in space in the Solar System, save for empty cities and ships drifting in orbit around the Earth, Mars, Jupiter, and through the asteroid belt. They seemed to form a silent, metallic graveyard, where humankind's glory and dreams were buried.

From the safety of Fraisse's house, Cheng Xin could only find out the situation in the larger world through TV. One day, she saw a live broadcast from a food distribution center. The holographic broadcast made her feel as if she were right there. The technology required ultra-broadband connections and was reserved for extremely important news these days. Most news was broadcast via simple 2-D.

The distribution center was located in Carnegie, on the edge of the desert. A gigantic tent appeared in the holographic display, like a broken half of an egg dropped in the desert with people spilling out of it like albumen. The crowd was rushing out because a new shipment of food had just arrived. Two flying transports, small but powerful, dangled a huge cube of packed food in nets.

After the first transport gently set down its cargo, the crowd surged like a flood from a burst dam and quickly overwhelmed the food pile. The security barrier formed by a few dozen soldiers collapsed at once, and the few food distribution workers climbed back into the hovering transport in terror. The pile of food disappeared into the crowd like a snowball thrown into muddy waters.

The lens zoomed in. People were now snatching food from those who had grabbed it from the pile. The bags of food, like rice grains in a swarm of ants, were quickly torn apart, and the mob fought over whatever tumbled out. The second transport deposited another pile in an empty space a bit farther away. This time, there were no soldiers to provide security at all, and the distribution workers didn't dare get out of the plane. The crowd swarmed this new pile like iron shavings toward a magnet and quickly covered it.

A figure in green, slender and supple, leapt out of the transport and gracefully landed on the food pile about a dozen meters below. The crowd stopped. They saw that the figure standing atop it was Sophon. She was still dressed in camouflage, and the black scarf around her neck flapped in the hot wind, highlighting her pale face.

"Form a line!" Sophon shouted.

The lens zoomed in again. Sophon's beautiful eyes glared at the crowd. Her voice was very loud and could be heard over the rumbling of the transport engines. But the crowd below only paused briefly before resuming their agitated motion. Those closest to the pile began to cut through the netting to get at the food bags inside. The crowd became more frenzied, and a few daring ones began to climb up the pile, ignoring Sophon.

"You useless things! Why aren't you out here keeping order?" Sophon lifted her face and shouted at the transport. In the open door of the transport stood a few shocked officials from the UN Resettlement Commission. "Where are your armies? Your police? What about the weapons we allowed you to bring here? Where is your *responsibility*?"

The chair of the Resettlement Commission stood at the door of the transport. He held on to the doorframe with one hand for support, and waved his other hand at Sophon, shaking his head helplessly.

Sophon unsheathed her katana. Moving faster than the eye could see, she swung it three times and sliced three of the men climbing up the pile into six pieces. The three killing strokes were exactly the same: beginning at the left shoulder and ending at the right hip. The six pieces fell, and the viscera spilled out midair to land with a shower of blood among the rest of the people. Amidst screams of terror, she leapt from the pile and landed with her sword swinging, quickly killing more than a dozen individuals around her. The refugees shied away from her as though a drop of detergent had been deposited into the oil film over a dirty bowl, quickly clearing out a space around her. The bodies left behind in that empty space were also split from the left shoulder to the right hip, a method that guaranteed the maximum spilling of organs and blood.

Faced with so much gore and blood, many fainted. As Sophon walked forward, people hurried to back away. An invisible force field seemed to surround her, repelling the mob and keeping the space around her clear. She stopped after a few steps and the crowd froze.

"Form a line," Sophon said. Her voice was soft.

The chaotic mob quickly organized itself into a long, winding line, as though the people were enacting an array-sorting algorithm. The line extended to the gigantic tent and wound around it.

Sophon jumped back onto the pile and pointed at the line with her bloody katana. "The era for humanity's degenerate freedom is over. If you want to survive here, you must relearn collectivism and retrieve the dignity of your race!"

Cheng Xin couldn't sleep that night. Noiselessly, she stepped out of her room.

The hour was late, and she could see a flickering light on the steps of the porch: Fraisse was smoking. On his knees lay a didgeridoo, an Aboriginal instrument made from a thick, hollowed-out branch about a meter long. Every night, he played it for a while. The sound made by the didgeridoo was a deep, rich, rumbling whine, not like music, but more akin to the snores of the ground itself. Every night, AA and Cheng Xin fell asleep listening to it.

Cheng Xin sat down next to Fraisse. She liked being with the old man. His transcendence in the face of a miserable reality soothed the pain of her broken heart. He never watched TV and seemed to pay no attention to the events of the outside world. At night, he rarely returned to his room, but fell asleep leaning against the doorframe, waking up when the rising sun warmed his body. He did so even on stormy nights, saying that it was more comfortable than sleeping in a bed. Once, he said that if the government bastards ever came to take away his house, he would not move to the resettlement zones; instead, he would go into the woods and build himself a shelter out of woven grass. AA said that with his advanced age, such a plan was not realistic, but he countered that if his ancestors could live that way, then so could he. As early as the fourth ice age, his ancestors had crossed the Pacific from Asia in canoes. That had been forty thousand years ago, when Greece and Egypt didn't even exist as ideas. Back in the twenty-first century, he had been a wealthy doctor, with his own clinic in Melbourne. After emerging from hibernation in the Deterrence Era, he had also lived the comfortable life of a modern man. But when the Great Resettlement began, something in his body seemed to awaken. He felt himself becoming a creature of the earth and the forest and realized that very few things were truly necessary for life. Sleeping in the open was fine— very comfortable, in fact.

Fraisse said he didn't know what kind of portent this was.

Cheng Xin gazed at the resettlement zone in the distance. This late at night, the lights were sparse, and the endless rows of shelter-houses gave off a rarely-seen tranquility. A strange feeling seized her, as though she were seeing another age of immigration, the Australia of five centuries ago. The people sleeping in those houses were rough cowboys and ranchers, and she could even smell the fragrance of hay and the odor of horse excrement. Cheng Xin told Fraisse of the odd sensation.

"It wasn't so crowded back then," said Fraisse. "They say that if a white man wanted to buy land from another white man, he needed only to pay the price of a box of whiskey, and then he would ride out with the sunrise and return at sunset. The area he circumnavigated would belong to him."

Cheng Xin's past impressions of Australia had come from that old film of the same name. In the film, the hero and heroine crossed the spectacular landscape of north Australia on a cattle drive. However, the film wasn't set during Australia's age of immigration, but during the Second World War—still the recent past when she was a young woman, but now ancient history. She felt a pang of sorrow as she realized that Hugh Jackman and Nicole Kidman had both been dead for probably over two centuries. Then she thought about how Wade had resembled the movie's hero as he labored in the shelter-house.

Thinking of Wade, she repeated to Fraisse what the man had told her. She had been meaning to tell him, but had worried about disturbing his transcendent state of mind.

"I know the man," Fraisse said. "Child, I can tell you that you should listen to him. But leaving Australia is impossible. Don't worry about it. It's useless to ponder what cannot be done."

It was true. Leaving Australia now would be very difficult. Not only did the droplets keep watch, but Sophon had recruited her own naval force of humans.

Any aircraft or surface ship leaving Australia that was found to harbor resettled individuals would be attacked immediately. In addition, as Sophon's deadline approached, few wanted to attempt to return to their home countries. Though conditions in Australia were harsh, staying here was better than going back to certain death. A few cases of small-scale smuggling happened here and there, but Cheng Xin was a public figure, and such a path was closed to her.

Cheng Xin did not concern herself with these details. No matter what happened, she wasn't going to leave.

Fraisse seemed to want to change the topic, but Cheng Xin's silence in the darkness demanded more from him. "I'm an orthopedist. You probably know that when a bone is broken, it heals stronger because a knot forms around the fracture. The body, when given an opportunity to make up for an absence, may do so excessively, and recover to the point where it has more of that quality than those who had never suffered such inadequacy." He pointed up at the sky. "Compared to humans, the Trisolarans once lacked something. Do you think they also overcompensated? To what extent? No one knows."

Cheng Xin was stunned by the idea. But Fraisse was not interested in continuing the discussion. He looked up at the star-studded sky and began reciting poetry in a low voice. The poems spoke of dreams of long ago, of broken trust and shattered weapons, of the deaths of peoples and ways of life.

Cheng Xin was moved the same way she had been when Fraisse played the didgeridoo.

"That's the work of Jack Davis, an Aboriginal poet of the twentieth century."

The elder leaned against the doorframe and, after a few minutes, began to snore. Cheng Xin remained sitting under the stars—which did not deviate one whit from their usual course despite the upheaval in the world below—until dawn arrived in the east.

Six months after the commencement of the Great Resettlement, half of the world's population, or 2.1 billion people, had moved to Australia.

Buried crises began to come to the forefront. The Canberra Massacre, seven months after the commencement of resettlement, was just the beginning of a string of nightmares.

Sophon had demanded that humans resettle "naked." During the Deterrence Era, hardliners on Earth had also proposed a similar policy to deal with the eventual migration of Trisolarans to the Solar System. Other than construction materials and parts needed to build new agricultural factories, as well as medical equipment and other life necessities, the resettled population was not permitted to bring any heavy equipment for military or civilian use. The military forces dispatched by the various nations to the resettlement zones were only allowed the light weapons needed to maintain order. Humankind was to be completely disarmed.

But the Australian government was exempt—it was allowed to keep everything, including all the hardware for its army, navy, and air force. Thus, this country that had been on the periphery of international affairs since its birth became the hegemon of the world.

No one could find fault with the behavior of the Australian government near the beginning of the process. The government and all Australians made every effort to help with the influx of migrants. But as the flood of refugees from around the world poured into Australia, attitudes in this country—which was once the only state to possess an entire continent—changed. Native Australians complained bitterly, and they elected a new government that took a hard-line position against the newcomers. Those in the new government quickly discovered that their advantage over the rest of the world was comparable to the advantage Trisolaris held over the Earth. Late-arriving migrants were resettled in the desolate interior, whereas rich, desirable locations such as coastal New South Wales were "reserved territories" for Australians only. Canberra and Sydney were classified as "reserved cities," where immigration was similarly prohibited. The only large city in which migrants were permitted to settle was Melbourne. The Australian government also turned dictatorial toward the rest of the world, treating itself as superior to the UN and other national governments.

Although newcomers were not allowed to settle in New South Wales, it was impossible to prevent them from going there as tourists. Many migrants swarmed to Sydney in order to assuage their intense longing for city life—even if they couldn't stay, wandering the streets of Sydney homeless felt better than living in the resettlement zones. Here, at least, they felt they were still in civilized society. Sydney soon became overcrowded, and the Australian government decided to forcibly remove all migrants and bar them from visiting there. The police and army clashed with refugees who tarried in the city, and there were casualties.

The Sydney Incident set off the pent-up rage of the resettled population against the Australian government, and more than one hundred million people entered New South Wales, heading for Sydney. Facing a sea of rioting humanity, the Australian Army abandoned their positions. Tens of millions flooded

Sydney and looted it in the same manner a swarm of ants devours a fresh corpse, leaving behind only a bare skeleton. Sydney was left in flames and lawless, transformed into a forest of terror. Life there, for those who remained, became worse than in the resettlement zones.

Thereafter, the mob of refugees shifted their target to Canberra, about two hundred kilometers away. Since Canberra was the Australian capital, about half of the world's national governments had relocated there as well. Even the UN had just moved there from Sydney. To keep these governments safe, the army had no choice but to fire on the mob. More than half a million people were killed, most of whom didn't die at the hands of the Australian Army, but due to hunger, thirst, and the panicked stampede of a hundred million people. During the chaos that lasted more than ten days, tens of millions were completely cut off from food and potable water.

The society of resettled populations transformed in profound ways. People realized that, on this crowded, hungry continent, democracy was more terrifying than despotism. Everyone yearned for order and a strong government. The existing social order broke down. All the people cared about was that the government would bring them food, water, and enough space for a bed; nothing else mattered. Gradually, the society of the resettled succumbed to the seduction of totalitarianism, like the surface of a lake caught in a cold spell. Sophon's words after she killed those people at the food distribution center—"The era for humanity's degenerate freedom is over"—became a common slogan, and discarded dregs from the history of ideas, including fascism, crawled out of their tombs to the surface and became mainstream. The power of religions also recovered, and people gathered into different faiths and churches. Thus, theocracy, a zombie even more ancient than totalitarianism, reanimated itself.

War was the inevitable result of totalitarian politics. Conflicts between nations became more frequent. At first, the conflicts were over food and water, but they soon evolved to planned contests over living space. After the Canberra Massacre, the Australian armed forces became a powerful deterrent force within Resettlement International. At the request of the UN, the Australian Army began to maintain international order by force. Without them, an intra-Australia version of a world war would have erupted—and just as someone had predicted during the twentieth century, this one would be fought with sticks and stones. By this time, the armies of the various nations—Australia excepted—couldn't even manage to equip their personnel with mêlée weapons. The most common weapons were sticks made out of metal frames used for construction, and even ancient swords from museums were put into service again.

In those dark days, countless people woke up in the mornings incredulous that this was their reality. Within half a year, human society had regressed so far that one foot was already in the Middle Ages.

The only thing that prevented individuals and society as a whole from total collapse was the approaching Second Trisolaran Fleet. By now, the fleet had crossed the Kuiper Belt. On clear nights, it was even sometimes possible to see the flames of the decelerating ships with the naked eye. Upon those 415 dim lights now hung the hope of all of humanity. All recalled Sophon's promise and dreamed that the arrival of the fleet would bring a comfortable, serene life for everyone on this continent. A demon of the past transformed into an angel of salvation, and their only spiritual support. People prayed for their advent.

As the resettlement process continued, cities on continents outside of Australia fell dark one by one, turning into empty, silent shells. It was like a luxurious restaurant turning out the lights after the last diner had left.

By the ninth month of the Great Resettlement, 3.4 billion people lived in Australia. As living conditions continued to deteriorate, the resettlement process had to be halted temporarily. The droplets again attacked cities outside of Australia, and Sophon renewed her threat: Upon the expiration of the one-year period, the extermination of all humans outside of the reservations would begin immediately. Australia now resembled a prison cart heading down a road to a place it would never return from: The cage was already close to bursting from the number of captives aboard, but seven hundred million more still had to be packed in.

Sophon gave some thought to the difficulties posed by further immigration and proposed a solution: New Zealand and other nearby islands could be used as a buffer zone. Her suggestion worked, and during the next two and a half months, 630 million more refugees were moved into Australia via the buffer zone.

Finally, three days before the expiration of the deadline, the last three million refugees left New Zealand on boats and planes and headed for Australia.

The Great Resettlement was complete.

At this point, Australia held the vast majority of the human population: 4.16 billion people. Outside of Australia, there were about eight million more individuals. These were divided into three parts: one million on the Martian base, five million in the Earth Security Force, and about two million in the Earth Resistance Movement. A small number of individuals who couldn't be resettled for various reasons were scattered around the world, but their exact number was unknown.

Sophon had recruited the Earth Security Force to monitor the resettlement process. She promised those who joined that they would not have to migrate to Australia and could eventually live freely in the Trisolaris-conquered territories of the Earth. Many volunteered eagerly, and, according to the final tally, more than a billion people applied online. Of these, twenty million were offered interviews, and, in the end, five million were accepted into the ESF. These fortunate few paid no attention to the spittle and looks of disdain thrown their way by other humans—they knew that many of those who spat at them had submitted applications as well.

Some compared the Earth Security Force to the Earth-Trisolaris Organization from three centuries ago, but the two organizations were fundamentally different. The ETO was formed by warriors of faith, but the ESF recruits merely wanted to avoid resettlement and live in comfort.

The ESF was divided into three corps: Asian, European, and North American. They inherited all the military hardware the national armies were forced to leave behind during the resettlement. At the beginning of the process, the ESF behaved with some restraint, only following Sophon's orders to supervise the progress of emigration in various countries and protect the basic infrastructure in cities and regions from looting and sabotage. But as difficulties in Australia intensified, the resettlement failed to progress at a rate satisfactory to Sophon. Due to her constant demands and threats, the ESF became more crazed, and resorted to large-scale violence to enforce the resettlement. During this time, the ESF killed almost a million people. Finally, after the clock ran out on the resettlement period, Sophon gave the order to exterminate all humans outside of the reservations. The ESF now turned into demons. Riding flying cars and armed with laser sniper rifles, they soared over empty cities and fields like falcons and swooped down to kill anyone they saw.

In contrast, the Earth Resistance Movement represented the best of humanity, refined from the furnace of this disaster. This movement consisted of so many loose local branches that the exact number couldn't be verified. In total, an estimated one and a half to two million individuals participated. Hidden in remote mountains and deep tunnels beneath the cities, they waged guerrilla war against the ESF and waited for a chance to fight the final war against the Trisolaran invaders after their anticipated arrival in four years. Compared to all other resistance movements in human history, the Earth Resistance Movement doubtless made the greatest sacrifice. Because Sophon and the droplets assisted the ESF, every mission by the Earth Resistance Movement was akin to suicide. The conditions under which they fought also prevented them from pooling their forces, which made it possible for the ESF to eliminate them one cell at a time.

The composition of the Earth Resistance Movement was complex, and included individuals from all strata of society. A large portion were people from the Common Era. The six other candidates for the Swordholder position were all commanders in the resistance. At the end of the resettlement period, three of them had died in action: only Bi Yunfeng, the particle accelerator engineer, Cao Bing, the physicist, and Ivan Antonov, the former Russian vice-admiral, were left.

Every member of the resistance understood that they were engaged in a hopeless war. The moment the Second Trisolaran Fleet arrived would mark their complete annihilation. Hungry, dressed in rags, and hidden in caves in the mountains and sewers beneath cities, these warriors fought for the human race's final shred of dignity. Their existence was the only bright spot in this, the darkest period of humankind's history.

A series of booming rumbles awoke Cheng Xin at dawn. She hadn't slept well during the night due to the constant noise of newly arrived refugees outside. But she realized that it was no longer thunderstorm season, and, after the rumblings it grew quiet outside. She shivered, rolled out of bed, threw on her clothes, and came outside. She almost tripped over the sleeping figure of Fraisse at the door. He glanced up at her with sleepy eyes and then leaned back against the doorframe to continue his interrupted slumber.

It was barely light outside. Many people stood around anxiously looking toward the east and muttering amongst themselves. Cheng Xin followed the direction of their eyes and saw a thick column of black smoke on the horizon, as though the pale dawn had been ripped apart.

Cheng Xin eventually managed to learn from the others that, about an hour ago, the ESF had begun a series of aerial raids in Australia. Their main targets seemed to be electrical systems, harbors, and large-scale transportation equipment. The column of smoke came from a destroyed nuclear fusion power plant about five kilometers away. People looked up in fear and saw five white contrails extending across the blue-black sky: ESF bombers.

Cheng Xin went back into the house. AA was up as well and turned on the TV. But Cheng Xin didn't watch—she didn't need any more information. For almost a year now, she had been constantly praying that this moment would never come. Her nerves had turned extremely sensitive, and the slightest hint would lead her to the right conclusion. Even as she had been awakened by the rumbling noises, she already knew what had happened.

Wade was right, again.

Cheng Xin found that she was prepared for this moment. Without thinking, she knew what she had to do. Telling AA that she needed to visit the city government, she took a bike—the most convenient mode of transportation in the resettlement zones. She also brought some food and water, knowing that she very likely would not be able to accomplish her task and would have to be on the road for a long time.

She wound through the crowded streets, heading for the city government. The various nations had transplanted their own administrative systems to the resettlement zones, and Cheng Xin's zone was composed of people resettled from a midsized city in northwestern China. The city government was located in a large tent about two kilometers away, and she could see the tent's white tip.

A large number of refugees had flooded in during the last two weeks in the final push of the resettlement process. There was no time to distribute them to zones that corresponded to their origins, so they were stashed wherever there was room. Cheng Xin's zone was thus filled with people from other cities, regions, provinces, and even non-Chinese. The seven hundred million refugees shoved into Australia during the last two months made the already-crowded resettlement zones even more unbearable.

On both sides of the road, possessions were piled everywhere. The new arrivals had nowhere to live and slept in the open. The earlier explosions had awakened them, and now they looked anxiously in the direction of the column of smoke. The dawn light cast a dim blue glow over everything, making the faces around her even paler. Once again, Cheng Xin experienced the eerie feeling of looking down upon an ant colony. As she pressed between the pale faces, her subconscious mind despaired that the sun would never rise again.

A wave of nausea and weakness seized her. She squeezed the brakes, stopped by the side of the road, and retched, bringing tears to her eyes. She dry heaved until her stomach settled. She heard a child crying nearby, and looking up, saw a mother huddled in a bunch of rags hugging her baby. Haggard, hair disheveled, she didn't move as the child clutched at her, but continued to gaze woodenly toward the east. The dawn lit her eyes, which reflected only loss and numbness.

Cheng Xin thought of another mother, pretty, healthy, and full of life, handing her baby to Cheng Xin in front of the UN building . . . where were she and her child now?

As she approached the tent housing the city government, Cheng Xin was forced to get off her bike and squeeze through the dense crowd. This place was always crowded, but now, even more people had gathered to find out what had happened. Cheng Xin had to explain who she was to the sentry line blocking the entrance before being allowed through. The officer didn't know her and had to scan her ID card. When he confirmed her identity, his stare seared itself into Cheng Xin's memory.

Why did we pick you back then?

The inside of the city government tent brought back memories of the hyper-information age. Numerous holographic windows floated around the vast space, hovering over various officials and clerks. Many of them had apparently been up all night and looked exhausted, but they were still very busy. A large number of departments were packed in and jostled for space, reminding Cheng Xin of the trading floor on Wall Street back in the Common Era. The workers tapped or wrote inside the windows hovering in front of them, and then the windows automatically floated over to the next worker in the process. These glowing windows were like ghosts of an age that had just ended, and here was their final gathering place.

In a tiny office formed from composite partitions, Cheng Xin saw the mayor. He was very young, and his feminized, handsome face looked as exhausted as the others. He also looked a bit dazed and adrift, as though the load he had been given was beyond the ability of his fragile generation to bear. A very large information window appeared on one of the walls, showing an image of some city. Most of the buildings in the window looked old and conventional, with only a few tree-buildings sprinkled among them—evidently this was a mid-sized city. Cheng Xin noticed that the image wasn't static: Flying cars crossed the air from time to time, and it seemed to also be early morning there. Cheng Xin realized that the display simulated the view out of an office window, so perhaps this was where the mayor had once lived and worked before the Great Resettlement.

He looked at Cheng Xin, and his eyes also seemed to say *Why did we pick you?* Still, he remained polite, and asked Cheng Xin how he could help her.

"I need to contact Sophon," she said.

The mayor shook his head, but her unexpected request had chased away some of his exhaustion. He looked serious. "That's not possible. First, this department is too low level to directly establish contact with her. Even the provincial government doesn't have such authority. No one knows where on Earth she is now. Also, communication with the outside world is extremely difficult now. We've just been cut off from the provincial government, and we're about to lose electricity here."

"Can you send me to Canberra?"

"I can't provide an aircraft, but I can dispatch a ground vehicle. However, that may end up being even slower than walking. Ms. Cheng, I strongly urge you to stay put. There's chaos everywhere right now, and it's very dangerous. The cities are being bombed—believe it or not, it's relatively peaceful here."

Since there was no wireless power system, flying cars were not usable in the resettlement zones. Only self-powered aircraft and ground vehicles were available, but the roads had become impassable.

As soon as Cheng Xin left the city government, she heard another explosion. A new column of smoke rose in another direction, and the crowd turned from merely anxious to genuinely agitated. She pushed her way through and found her bike. She would have to ride more than fifty kilometers to reach the provincial government and try to contact Sophon from there. If that didn't work, she'd try to get to Canberra.

No matter what, she would not give up.

The crowd quieted as an immense information window appeared over the city government, almost as wide as the tent itself. This was used only when the government needed to broadcast extremely important news. Since the electric voltage wasn't stable, the window flickered, but against the dim sky of early dawn, it showed images very clearly.

In the window was Canberra's Parliament House. Though it was completed in 1988, people still referred to it as the "new" Parliament House. From a distance, the building appeared as a bunker nestled against a hill, and on top of it was possibly the world's tallest flag mast. The mast, over eighty meters in height, was further elevated by four gigantic steel beams. They were meant to symbolize stability, but they now resembled the frame of a large tent. The UN flag flew from the building: The UN had moved its headquarters here after the Sydney Riots.

Cheng Xin felt a giant fist close around her heart. She knew that the day of the Last Judgment had arrived.

The view shifted to inside the House of Representatives, which was filled by all the leaders of Earth International and Fleet International. Sophon had called for an emergency session of the UN General Assembly.

Sophon stood at the dispatch box, still dressed in camouflage and a black scarf, but without the katana. There was no trace on her face of the glamorous cruelty that everyone had grown used to in the past year; instead, she appeared radiant in her beauty. She bowed to the assembled leaders of humanity, and Cheng Xin saw again the gentle hostess practicing the Way of Tea whom she had met two years ago.

"The Great Resettlement is over!" Sophon bowed again. "Thank you! I'm grateful to all of you. This is a tremendous accomplishment, comparable to the walk out of Africa by your ancestors tens of thousands of years ago. A new era for our two civilizations has begun!"

Everyone in the House of Representatives turned their head anxiously as something exploded outside. The four lighting beams hanging from the ceiling swayed, and all the shadows along with them, as though the building was about to collapse. But Sophon continued speaking: "Before the magnificent Trisolaran Fleet arrives to bring you a happy new life, everyone must endure a difficult period lasting three months. I hope humanity will perform as well as it did during the Great Resettlement.

"I proclaim now the complete severance of the Australian Reservation from the outside world. Seven strong-interaction space probes and the Earth Security Force will enforce an absolute blockade. Anyone attempting to leave Australia will be treated as an invader of Trisolaris and be exterminated without mercy!

"The defanging of Earth must proceed. During the next three months, the reservation must be kept in a state of subsistence agriculture. The use of any modern technology, including electricity, is strictly prohibited. As everyone present can see, the Earth Security Force is in the process of systematically eliminating all electricity-generating equipment in Australia."

People around Cheng Xin looked at each other in disbelief, hoping that someone else could help explain what Sophon had just said.

"This is genocide!" someone in the House of Representatives cried out. The shadows continued to sway, like corpses dangling from nooses.

It was indeed genocide.

The prospect of keeping 4.2 billion people alive in Australia was difficult, but not unimaginable. Even after the Great Resettlement, the population density in Australia was only fifty people per square kilometer, lower than the population density of pre-Resettlement Japan.

But the plan had been premised on highly efficient agricultural factories. During the resettlement process, large numbers of agricultural factories had been relocated to Australia, and many of them had been reassembled and put in operation. In these factories, genetically modified crops grew at rates orders of magnitude above traditional crops, but natural lighting was insufficient to power such growth, so ultrabright artificial lights had to be used. This required massive amounts of electricity.

Without electricity, the crops in the growth tanks of the factories, dependent on ultraviolet or X-ray light for photosynthesis, would rot in a couple of days.

The existing food reserve was enough to maintain 4.2 billion people only for one month.

"I don't understand your reaction," Sophon said to the man who had yelled *genocide*. Her confusion appeared genuine.

"What about food? Where are we going to get *food*?" someone else shouted. They were no longer terrified of Sophon. All that was left was despair.

Sophon scanned the hall, meeting the eyes of everyone present. "Food? Everyone, look around: You are surrounded by food, living food."

Her tone was serene, as though reminding humanity of a storehouse they had forgotten.

No one said anything. The long-planned process of annihilation had reached its final step. It was too late for words.

Sophon continued. "The coming struggle for survival will eliminate most of humanity. By the time the fleet arrives in three months, there should be about thirty to fifty million people left on this continent. These final victors will begin a free and civilized life in the reservation. The fire of Earth civilization will not go out, but it will continue in a reduced form, like the eternal flame at a tomb."

The Australian House of Representatives was modeled on the British House of Commons. The high seats of the public galleries were to the sides, and the benches for the Members of Parliament—where the leaders of the world now sat—were down in the pit in the middle. Those sitting there now felt as if they were in a tomb that was about to be filled in.

"Mere existence is already the result of incredible luck. Such was the case on Earth in the past, and such has always been the case in this cruel universe.

But at some point, humanity began to develop the illusion that they're *entitled* to life, that life can be taken for granted. This is the fundamental reason for your defeat. The flag of evolution will be raised once again on this world, and you will now fight for your survival. I hope everyone present will be among the fifty million survivors at the end. I hope that you will eat food, and not be eaten by food."

"Ahhhhhhh—" A woman in the crowd near Cheng Xin screamed, slicing apart the silence like a sharp blade. But a deathlike hush immediately swallowed her scream.

Cheng Xin felt the sky and earth tumble around her. She didn't realize she had fallen down. All she saw was the sky pushing the government tent and the holographic window away, filling her entire field of view, then the ground touched her back, as though it had stood up behind her. The dawn sky appeared as a dim ocean, and the crimson clouds, lit by the rising sun, floated over it in bloody patches. Then a black spot appeared in her vision, spreading quickly, like a sheet of paper set aflame by the candle underneath, until murky shadows covered everything.

She recovered from the loss of consciousness quickly. Her hands found the ground—soft sand—and, pushing off it, she sat up. She grabbed her left arm with her right hand to be sure that she was okay. But the world had disappeared. All was enveloped in gloom. Cheng Xin opened her eyes wide, but she could see nothing but more darkness. She had gone blind.

Noises assaulted her; she could not tell which were real and which were illusions: footsteps like a tide, screams, sobs, and indistinct, eerie cries like a gale passing through a dead forest.

Someone running crashed into her, and she fell. She struggled to sit up. Darkness, only darkness remained before her eyes, thick as pitch. She turned to face what she thought of as the east, but even in her mind she couldn't see the rising sun. What rose there instead was a gigantic dark wheel, scattering black light across the world.

In this endless obscurity she seemed to see a pair of eyes. The black eyes melted into the murk, but she could feel their presence, could feel their gaze. Were these the eyes of Yun Tianming? She had fallen into the abyss, where she ought to meet him. She heard Tianming call her name. She tried to push the hallucinatory voice out of her mind, but it persisted. Finally, she was certain that the voice came from reality, as it was a feminized male voice that could only be from this era.

"Are you Dr. Cheng Xin?"

She nodded. Or, rather, felt herself nod. Her body seemed to move on its own.

"What happened to your eyes? Can you not see?"

"Who are you?"

"I'm the commander of a special team in the Earth Security Force. Sophon sent us to retrieve you from Australia."

"Where are you taking me?"

"Anywhere you want. She'll take care of you. Of course, she said that you have to be willing to go."

Cheng Xin noticed another sound. She thought it was another hallucination at first: the rumbling of a helicopter. Although humanity had learned antigravity technology, it consumed too much energy for practical use. Aircraft still mostly relied on traditional propellers. She felt gusts of wind, proof that a helicopter was hovering nearby.

"Can I talk to Sophon?"

An object was pushed into her hand—a mobile phone. She put the phone next to her ear and heard Sophon's voice.

"Hello, Swordholder."

"I've been looking for you."

"Why? Do you still think of yourself as the savior of the world?"

Cheng Xin shook her head slowly. "No. I've never thought of myself that way. I just want to save two people. Please?"

"Which two?"

"艾 AA and Fraisse."

"Ah, your chattering friend and that old Aboriginal? You wanted to find me just for this?"

Cheng Xin was surprised. Sophon had met AA, but how did she know who Fraisse was?

"Yes. Have the people you sent bring them away from Australia so that they can live freely."

"That's easy. What about you?"

"You don't need to be concerned about me."

"Can't you see what's happening?"

"I can't. I can't see a thing."

"You mean you've gone blind? Haven't you been eating properly?"

Cheng Xin, AA, and Fraisse had always been provided adequate rations during the last year, and Fraisse's house had never been taken away by the government. And once she and AA had moved in, no one had harassed her. Cheng Xin had always thought it was because the local government was protecting her, but now she realized that it was because Sophon had kept watch over her.

Cheng Xin understood that it was a group of aliens that controlled Sophon from four light-years away, but she, like other humans, always thought of Sophon as an individual, a woman. This woman, who was in the process of slaughtering 4.2 billion people, cared about her welfare.

"If you remain there, you'll be eaten by the others."

"I know." Cheng Xin's voice was calm.

Is that a sigh? "All right. A sophon will stay near you. If you change your mind or need some help, just speak. I'll hear you."

Cheng Xin said nothing. Not even thank you.

Someone grabbed her by the arm—the Earth Security Force commander. "I've been given the order to retrieve those two. It's best that you leave with us, Dr. Cheng. This place will turn into hell on Earth in no time."

Cheng Xin shook her head. "You know where they are? Good. Please go. Thank you."

She listened for the helicopter. The blindness seemed to make her hearing especially acute, like a third eye. She heard the helicopter take off and then land about two kilometers away. A few minutes later, it lifted off again, and gradually flew away.

Cheng Xin closed her eyes, satisfied. Whether she kept them open or not, there was only darkness. Finally, her broken heart had found some peace, bathed in a pool of blood. The impenetrable shadows now became a kind of protection. Outside the darkness was more terror. What had manifested there made even coldness itself shiver, even darkness itself stumble.

The frenzy around her intensified: sounds of running, clashing, guns firing, cursing, screaming, dying, crying . . . *Have they already started to eat people? It shouldn't happen so fast.* Cheng Xin believed that even in a month, when there would be no more food, most people would still refuse to eat other people.

That's why most people will die.

It was not important whether the fifty million that survived would still be considered human, or become something else. As a concept, "humanity" would disappear.

A single line could now encompass all of human history: We walked out of Africa; we walked for seventy thousand years; we came into Australia.

In Australia, humanity returned to its origin. But there would be no new voyage. This was the end.

A baby cried nearby. Cheng Xin wanted to wrap her arms around that new life. She recalled the baby she had held in front of the UN building: soft, warm, such a sweet smile. Maternal instinct broke Cheng Xin's heart. She was afraid that the baby would go hungry.

The Final Ten Minutes of the Deterrence Era, Year 62 November 28, 4:17:34 P.M. to 4:27:58 P.M.: *Gravity* and *Blue Space*, Deep Space

When the klaxons announced the droplet attack, only one man aboard *Gravity* felt a sense of relief: James Hunter, the oldest on the crew. He was seventy-eight, and everyone called him Old Hunter.

Half a century ago, at Fleet Command in Jupiter's orbit, a twenty-seven-year-old Hunter had received his mission from the chief of staff.

"You will be the culinary controller aboard *Gravity*."

This position was just a glorified name for the ship's cook. But since AI programming did most of the cooking on a warship, the culinary controller was responsible only for operating the system. This meant, for the most part, inputting the menu for each meal and choosing the staples. Most culinary controllers were petty officers, but Hunter had just been promoted to the rank of captain; in fact, he was the youngest captain in the fleet. But Hunter wasn't surprised. He knew what he was really supposed to do.

"Your real mission is to guard the gravitational wave transmitter. If the senior officers aboard *Gravity* lose control of the ship, you must destroy the transmitter. In unexpected situations, you may use whatever means you deem necessary to accomplish your goal."

Gravity's gravitational wave broadcasting system included the antenna and the controller. The antenna was the ship's hull, impossible to destroy, but disabling the controller was enough to stop transmission. Given the materials available on *Gravity* and *Blue Space*, it would be impossible to assemble a new controller.

Hunter knew that men similar to himself had served on nuclear submarines in ancient times. Back then, in the ballistic missile submarine fleets of both the Soviet Union and NATO, there were seamen and low-ranked officers serving in humble posts who also had such missions. If anyone had come close to seizing control of a submarine and the missiles it carried, these men would have emerged, unexpectedly, to take drastic action to stop such plots.

"You must pay attention to everything happening on the ship. Your mission requires you to monitor the situation during every duty cycle. Thus, you cannot hibernate."

"I don't know if I can live until I'm a hundred."

"You only need to live until you're eighty. By then, the degenerate matter vibrating string in the ship will have reached its half-life, *Gravity*'s gravitational wave transmission system will fail, and you'll have completed your mission. Thus, you just need to stay out of hibernation for the voyage out, but may return asleep. However, the mission will essentially require you to devote the rest of your life to it. You have the right to refuse."

"I accept."

The chief of staff asked a question that commanders in past eras would not have bothered with. "Why?"

"During the Doomsday Battle, I was a PIA intelligence analyst stationed aboard *Newton*. Before the droplet destroyed my ship, I escaped in a life pod. Though it was the smallest kind of life pod, it was capable of holding five. At the time, a group of my crewmates were headed toward me, and I was alone in my pod. But I released it—"

"I know about that. The court-martial results are unequivocal. You did nothing wrong. Ten seconds after jettisoning your life pod, the ship exploded. You had no time to wait for anyone else."

"Yes. But . . . I still feel it would have been better if I had stayed with *Newton*."

"I understand how our failures haunt us with survivor's guilt. But this time, you have a chance to save billions."

The two were silent for a while. Outside the window of the space station, the Great Red Spot of Jupiter stared at them like a gigantic eye.

"Before I explain to you the details of your task, I want you to understand one thing: Your highest priority is preventing the system from falling into the wrong hands. When you cannot ascertain the degree of risk with confidence, you should err on the side of destroying the transmission system—even if you should turn out to be mistaken. When you do decide to act, don't worry about collateral damage. If necessary, destroying the entire ship would be acceptable."

Hunter was in the first duty cycle when *Gravity* left Earth. During those five years, he regularly took a certain kind of small blue pills. At the end of the duty cycle, when he was scheduled to go into hibernation, a physical revealed that he had cerebrovascular coagulation disorder, which was also called "no-hibernation disease." Patients with this rare condition suffered no ill effects in daily life, but could not enter hibernation because the awakening process would cause massive brain damage. It was the only medical condition discovered so far that could prevent someone from going into hibernation. When the diagnosis was confirmed, everyone around Hunter looked at him as though they were at his funeral.

Thus, throughout the whole voyage, Hunter had remained awake. Every time someone emerged from hibernation, they saw he had aged more. He told all the newly awakened the interesting things that had happened in the dozen or so years that had passed while they slept. The lowly cook became the most beloved figure on the ship, and he was popular with officers and enlisted men alike. Gradually, he turned into a symbol of the long voyage of *Gravity*. No one suspected that this easygoing, generous man held the same rank as the captain and was also the only man other than the captain with the authority and ability to destroy the ship in the event of a crisis.

During the first thirty years of the journey, Hunter had several girlfriends. In this matter he held an advantage others did not possess: He could date women in different duty cycles, one after the other. But after a few decades, as Hunter became Old Hunter, the women, still young, treated him as only a friend with interesting stories.

During this half century, the only woman Old Hunter ever truly loved was Reiko Akihara. But most of that time, more than ten million AU separated them. This was because Sublieutenant Akihara was aboard *Blue Space*, where she was a navigator.

The hunt for *Blue Space* was the only undertaking where Earth and Trisolaris truly shared the same goal, because this lone ship heading into deep space was a threat to both worlds. During the Earth's attempt to lure back the two ships that had survived the dark battles, *Blue Space* had learned the dark forest nature of the universe. If *Blue Space* someday mastered the ability to broadcast to the universe, the consequences would be unimaginable. The hunt thus received the total cooperation of Trisolaris. Before entering the blind region, the sophons had provided *Gravity* with a real-time, continuous view of the interior of the prey.

Over the decades, Hunter was promoted from petty officer second class to petty officer first class, and then, as a special promotion, became a commissioned officer. Starting as an ensign, he was promoted all the way up to lieutenant. But even at the end, he never had the formal authorization to view the live feed of the interior of *Blue Space* transmitted by the sophons. However, he did possess the backdoor codes to all the ship's systems, and he often viewed a palm-sized version of the video feed in his own cabin.

He saw that *Blue Space* was a completely different society from *Gravity*. It was militaristic, authoritarian, and governed by strict codes of discipline. Everyone devoted their spiritual energy to the collective. The first time he saw Reiko was two years after the start of the chase. He was instantly smitten by this East Asian beauty. He would watch her for hours every day, and sometimes even thought he knew her life better than he knew his own. But a year later, Reiko went into hibernation, and the next time she woke up for duty was thirty years later. She was still young, but Hunter was already near sixty.

On Christmas Eve, after a wild party, he returned to his cabin and brought up the live feed from *Blue Space*. The view began with a diagram of the complex overall structure of the ship. He tapped the location of the navigation center, and the view zoomed in to show Reiko on duty. She was looking at a large holographic star map, on which a bright red line traced the course of *Blue Space*. Behind it was a white line that almost coincided with the red line, indicating the path taken by *Gravity*. Hunter noticed that the white line deviated slightly from *Gravity*'s true course. Right now, the two ships were still a few thousand AU apart. At this distance, it was difficult to track a target as small as a spaceship with certainty. The white line probably only indicated their best guess, although the estimate of the distance between the two ships was pretty accurate.

Hunter zoomed in some more. Reiko suddenly turned to face him, and, with a smile that made his heart clench, said, "Merry Christmas!" Hunter knew that Reiko wasn't talking to him, but to all those hunting her ship. She was aware that she was being watched by sophons, though she couldn't see her pursuers. Regardless, this was one of the happiest moments of Hunter's life.

Because the crew aboard *Blue Space* was large, Reiko's duty cycle didn't last long. One year later, she entered hibernation again. Hunter looked forward to the day he would meet Reiko face-to-face, when *Gravity* finally caught up to *Blue Space*. Sadly, he knew that he would be almost eighty by the time that happened. He hoped he would get to tell her he loved her and then watch as she was taken away for trial.

For half a century, Hunter faithfully carried out his mission. He remained alert for any unusual conditions aboard the ship, preparing in his mind action plans for various crises. But the mission didn't really put too much pressure on him. He knew that another form of insurance, utterly reliable, accompanied

Gravity. Like many others, he often watched the droplets cruising at a distance from the portholes. But the droplets, in his eyes, held another meaning. If anything unusual occurred on *Gravity*, especially if there were signs of a mutiny or illegal attempts to seize control of the gravitational wave transmission system, he knew that the droplets would destroy this ship. They could move far faster than he—a droplet could accelerate from a few thousand meters away and reach a target in no more than five seconds.

Now, Hunter's mission was almost over. The degenerate matter vibrating string at the heart of the gravitational wave antenna, less than ten nanometers in diameter but running the entire length of the fifteen-hundred-meter hull, had almost reached its half-life. In another two months, the density of the string would fall below the minimum threshold for gravitational wave transmissions, and the system would fail completely. *Gravity* would turn from a broadcast station that posed a threat to two worlds to an ordinary stellar spaceship, and Hunter's work would be done. He would reveal his true identity at that time. He was curious whether he would face admiration or condemnation from his crewmates. In any case, he would stop taking those blue pills, and his cerebro-vascular coagulation disorder would disappear. He would enter hibernation and awaken on the Earth to live out the rest of his days in a new era. But he would hibernate only after seeing Reiko, which should happen soon.

But then the sophons fell blind. During the voyage, he had imagined hundreds of possible crises, and this was one of the worst possibilities. The loss of the sophons meant that the droplets and Trisolaris no longer knew everything happening aboard *Gravity*. If the unexpected happened, the droplets could not react in time. This made the situation far more dangerous, and Hunter felt the weight on his shoulders increase tenfold, as though he had only started his mission.

Hunter now paid even closer attention to happenings on the ship. The entire crew of *Gravity* had been awakened from hibernation, and that made monitoring difficult. But Hunter was the only member of the crew everyone was familiar with, and he was popular and had an abundance of social connections. Moreover, his easygoing manner and his insignificant post meant that most were not on guard in his presence. The enlisted men and junior officers, especially, told him things they wouldn't dare say to senior officers or the psych corps. This allowed Hunter to have a full grasp of the situation.

After the sophons were blinded, strange things began to happen all over the ship: An ecological area in the middle of the ship was struck by a micromete-oroid; more than one person claimed to have seen openings suddenly appear in bulkheads, accompanied by the disappearance of certain objects that reappeared later, undamaged. . . .

Out of all these oddities, the experience of Commander Devon, head of the MP, made the deepest impression on Hunter. Devon was one of the senior officers on the ship. Normally Hunter did not interact with them much. But when he saw Devon seek out the psychiatrist—whom most people on the ship avoided—he grew alert. Over a bottle of vintage whiskey, he finally got Devon to spill the story of his strange encounter.

To be sure, other than the micrometeoroid strike, the most reasonable explanation for all the strange goings-on was that the crew was suffering from hallucinations. The loss of the sophons might have, in some unknown way, triggered a kind of mass mental disorder—at least that was how Dr. West and the psych corps explained it. Hunter's duty did not allow him to accept this explanation easily; but other than hallucinations or a mass mental disorder, the strange stories told by the crew seemed impossible. However, Hunter's mission was to respond to impossibilities that somehow became possible.

Despite the massive antenna, the controller unit for the gravitational wave transmitter took up little space. Situated in a small spherical cabin at the stern, the controller was completely independent and not connected to the other parts of the ship. The spherical cabin was like a reinforced safe. No one aboard *Gravity* had the codes for entry, not even the captain. Only the Swordholder on Earth could activate the gravitational wave broadcast—in such an event, a beam of neutrinos would be transmitted to *Gravity* and switch on the transmitter. Right now, such a signal would take a year to arrive from the Earth.

But if *Gravity* were hijacked, the safety measures around the spherical cabin would not last long.

Hunter's watch had a special button. When pressed, it would trigger a heat bomb inside the spherical cabin, which would vaporize everything inside. His job was very simple: No matter what the crisis, as soon as he judged the risk to be in excess of a certain threshold, he would press the button and destroy the controller, rendering the gravitational wave transmitter inoperable.

In a sense, Hunter was an "Anti-Swordholder."

Hunter didn't put all his trust in the button on his watch and the heat bomb in the cabin, which he had never laid eyes on. Ideally, he wanted to keep watch outside the control cabin day and night, but of course that would draw suspicion, and his hidden identity was his biggest advantage. Still, he wanted to be as close to the control cabin as possible, so he tried to regularly visit the astronomical observatory, also located at the stern. Since the entire crew was out of hibernation, Hunter had assistants to take care of his culinary duties, which gave him plenty of time to himself. In addition, as Dr. Guan Yifan was the only civilian scientist aboard and thus not subject to military discipline, no one thought it strange that Hunter often went to Guan to share the liquor that he was able to obtain due to his position. Dr. Guan, in turn, enjoyed the drinks, and lectured Hunter on the "universe's three and three hundred thousand syndrome." Soon, Hunter spent most of his time in the observatory, separated from the gravitational wave transmission controller by only a short corridor about twenty meters long.

Hunter was on his way to the observatory again when he passed Guan Yifan and Dr. West heading for the bow of the ship. He decided that he would take a peek at the control cabin. When he was about ten meters away, the klaxons for the droplet attack started blaring. Due to his rank, the information window appearing before him displayed very few details, but he knew that the droplets were, at this time, farther away from the ship than when they had flown in formation. He had about ten to twenty seconds until impact.

During these final moments, Old Hunter felt only relief and joy. No matter what happened next, he would have completed his mission. He looked forward not to death, but to his victory.

This was why, half a minute later, when the klaxons stopped, Hunter became the only one aboard who felt no relief from his extreme terror. The cessation of the alarm indicated, for him, great danger: In a situation of great uncertainty, the gravitational wave transmitter was still intact. Without hesitation, he pressed the button on his watch.

Nothing happened. Even though the control cabin was tightly sealed, he should have been able to feel the tremors from the detonation. A line of text appeared on his wristwatch display:

Failure: The self-destruct module has been dismantled.

Hunter wasn't even surprised. He had already intuitively anticipated that the worst had happened. He had been but a few seconds from relief, but the relief would never come.

Neither droplet struck their respective targets. Both brushed by *Gravity* or *Blue Space* at extremely close range—only a few tens of meters.

Three minutes after the attack alert was lifted, Joseph Morovich, captain of

Gravity, finally managed to gather his senior staff at the combat center, in the middle of which was a giant situation map. No stars were shown against the dark expanse of space, only the positions of the two ships and the attack trajectories of the droplets. The two long white trails appeared as straight lines, but the data indicated they were parabolas with very low curvature. As the two droplets accelerated toward their targets in the simulation, their headings began to drift. The changes were small, but cumulatively, they resulted in the droplets barely missing their targets. Many of the senior officers had participated in the Doomsday Battle, and their memory of the sharp turns the droplets were capable of executing while moving at extremely high velocities still brought heart-stopping terror. However, the trajectories on the display were completely different: It was as though some outside force perpendicular to the attack vectors of the droplets had steadily pushed them out of the way.

"Replay the recording," the captain ordered. "Visible light range."

The stars and the galaxy appeared. This was no longer a computer simulation. In one corner, flickering numbers showed the passage of time. Everyone relived the terror of a few minutes ago, when all they could do was wait for death because evasive maneuvers and defensive shots were all meaningless. Soon, the numbers stopped changing. The droplets had already swept past the ships, but because they were moving so fast, no one could see them.

The display shifted to slow-motion replay of the high-speed recording. Since the complete recording, over ten seconds long, would take a long time to play through, only the last few seconds were shown. The officers saw a droplet pass in front of the camera like a faint meteor across the sea of stars in the background. The recording was played again, and froze when the droplet was in the middle of the screen. The image zoomed in until the droplet took up most of the display.

Half a century of cruising in formation with the droplets made everyone familiar with their appearance, and what they saw now shocked them. The droplet on the display was still shaped like a teardrop, but its surface was no longer a perfectly smooth mirror. Instead, it was dim and coppery yellow, as though full of rust. It was as if a magician's spell of eternal youth had failed, and the marks left by three centuries of spaceflight had all appeared at once. Instead of a shining spirit, the droplet had turned into an ancient artillery shell drifting through space. Communications with the Earth during the last few years had given these officers some basic insight into the principles of strong-interaction materials. They knew that the surface of a droplet was held in a force field generated by mechanisms inside. This force field counteracted the electromagnetic force between particles, allowing the strong nuclear force to spill out. Without the force field, strong-interaction material reverted to ordinary metal.

The droplets had died.

Next, they reviewed the post-attack data. The simulation showed that after the droplet brushed by *Gravity*, the mysterious perpendicular force making small heading changes vanished, and the droplet coasted along its final vector. But this only lasted a few seconds. Thereafter, the droplet began to decelerate. The combat analysis computer concluded that the force decelerating the droplet was equal in magnitude to the force that had changed its heading. The obvious conclusion was that the source of the force had shifted from pushing at the side of the droplet to pushing from the front.

Since the recording was made by high-magnification telescopic lens, it was possible to see the back of the departing droplet. The droplet turned ninety degrees so that it was perpendicular to its own direction of motion and continued to coast. Then it began to decelerate. The next scene seemed to be taken from a fairy tale—good thing Dr. West was also present, or else he would again declare the others to be suffering from hallucinations. A triangular object, about twice as long as the droplet, appeared in front of it. The staff immediately recognized it as a shuttle from *Blue Space*! In order to increase its propulsive power, multiple small fusion drives were attached to the hull of the shuttle. Although the nozzles of the drives all pointed away from the camera, it was still possible to see the glow they made as they operated under maximum output. The shuttle was pushing against the droplet to slow it down. And it was easy to deduce that it was also the source of the force that caused the droplets to deviate from their attack vectors.

After the shuttle's appearance, two human figures wearing space suits appeared on the other side of the droplet—the side closest to the camera. The deceleration caused the figures to stick to the surface of the droplet; one of them held some kind of instrument in his hands and appeared to be analyzing the droplet. In the past, droplets had seemed almost divine in the eyes of humankind, not belonging to this world and not approachable. The only people who had ever come close to touching a droplet had been vaporized in the Doomsday Battle. But now, the droplet had lost all its mystery. Without its mirrorlike sheen, it seemed ordinary, broken-down, older and less advanced than the shuttle and the astronauts—some antique or piece of trash collected by the latter. A few seconds later, the shuttle and the astronauts disappeared, and the dead droplet was once again alone in space. But it continued to decelerate, indicating that the shuttle was still there pushing against it, only now invisible.

"They know how to disable the droplets!" someone cried out.

Captain Morovich could think of only one thing. Like Hunter a few minutes ago, he didn't hesitate to push the button on his watch. The error message appeared in a red information window that appeared midair:

Failure: The self-destruct module has been dismantled.

The captain dashed out of the combat center and headed for the stern. The other officers followed.

The first person from *Gravity* to arrive at the gravitational wave transmission control room was Old Hunter. Though he had no authorization to enter the cabin, he wanted to try to break the link between the controller and the antenna. This would at least temporarily disable the transmission system until he figured out how to destroy the controller itself.

But someone was already there, examining the control cabin.

Hunter took out his sidearm and aimed it at the man. He wore the uniform of a sublieutenant on *Gravity*, not the uniform dating from the Doomsday Battle that Hunter expected to see—the man had stolen it. Hunter recognized him from the back. "I knew Commander Devon was right."

Lieutenant Commander Park Ui-gun, head of the marines on *Blue Space*, turned around. He looked no older than thirty, but his face showed that he had endured experiences that no one aboard *Gravity* could imagine. He was slightly surprised. Perhaps he didn't expect anyone here so soon; perhaps he didn't expect to see Hunter. Yet, he remained calm. With both hands half raised, he said, "Please let me explain—"

Old Hunter wasn't interested in an explanation. He didn't want to know how this man had boarded *Gravity*, and didn't even want to know if he was a man or a ghost. Whatever the facts, the situation was too dangerous. All he wanted was to destroy the transmission controller unit. It was his only goal in life, and this man from *Blue Space* stood in the way. He squeezed the trigger.

The bullet struck Park in the chest, and the impact threw him against the cabin door. Hunter's gun was loaded with special bullets designed for use inside the ship: They wouldn't damage the bulkheads or other equipment, but they

also weren't as deadly as laser beams. Some blood oozed out of the wound, but Park managed to stay erect in the weightlessness and reached into his bloody uniform for his own weapon. Hunter shot again, and there was a fresh wound in Park's chest. More blood oozed out, floating in the gravity-less air. Finally, Hunter took aim at Park's head, but he didn't get a chance for the third shot.

This was the scene that greeted Captain Morovich and the other officers when they arrived: Hunter's gun was floating far away from him. The old cook's body was stiff, his open eyes showing only white, his limbs twitching. Blood erupted forth from his mouth like a fountain, coagulating into spheres of various sizes drifting around him in a cloud. In the middle of the bloody, translucent spheres was a dark red object about the size of a fist, dragging two tubes behind it like tails.

Rhythmically, it pulsed in midair, and with every pulse, more blood was squeezed out of its two tubular tails. The object propelled itself forward like a crimson jellyfish swimming through the air.

It was Hunter's heart.

During the struggle a few moments earlier, Hunter had slammed his right hand against his chest, and then, desperately, torn open his clothes. Thus, his bare chest lay revealed, and everyone could see that the skin was perfect, with not a single scratch.

"He can be saved if we get him into surgery right away," Sublieutenant Park said with some difficulty, his voice very hoarse. Blood continued to spill from the two wounds in his chest. "Good thing that doctors don't need to open his chest to reattach his heart anymore. . . . Don't move! It's as easy for them to pluck out your heart or brain as it is for you to pick an apple dangling from a branch in front of you. *Gravity* has been captured."

Fully armed marines rushed in from another corridor. Most of them wore the dark blue lightweight space suits dating from before the Doomsday Battle—apparently they were all from *Blue Space*. All the marines were equipped with powerful laser assault rifles.

Captain Morovich nodded at his officers. Without speaking, they tossed their weapons away. *Blue Space* had ten times more people than *Gravity*, and just their detachment of marines numbered more than a hundred. They could easily control *Gravity*.

There was nothing beyond belief anymore. *Blue Space* had turned into a supernatural warship wielding magic. The crew of *Gravity* again experienced the shock they had last suffered during the Doomsday Battle.

More than fourteen hundred people floated in the middle of *Blue Space*'s spherical great hall. The largest portion, over twelve hundred, belonged to the crew of *Blue Space*. Sixty years ago, the officers and enlisted men of this ship had also lined up here to accept Zhang Beihai's command, and most of them were still here. Since only a few individuals needed to be awake and on duty for regular cruising, the crew had aged only three to five years on average. They hadn't experienced the bulk of the intervening years, and the searing flames of the dark battles and the cold funerals held in space remained fresh in their minds. The remainder belonged to the one-hundred-strong crew of *Gravity*. The two crews—one large, one small, wearing distinct uniforms and suspicious of each other—gathered into two clusters far apart from each other.

Before the two crews, the senior officers of the two ships were mixed together. Captain Chu Yan of *Blue Space* drew the most attention. He was forty-three, but looked younger, and he was the model of the scholarly military officer. Refined and calm in his speech and mannerisms, he even gave off a hint of shyness. But on Earth, Chu Yan was already a figure of legend. During the dark battles, he was the one who had given the order to turn the interior of *Blue Space* into a vacuum, thereby preventing the crew from death in the infrasonic nuclear bomb attack. Even now, public opinion on Earth remained divided as to whether *Blue Space*'s actions during the dark battle should be classified as self-defense or murder. After the founding of dark forest deterrence, he was the one who had resisted the heavy pressure of majority opinion aboard and delayed *Blue Space*'s return, thus giving the ship sufficient time to escape after the warning from *Bronze Age*. There were many other rumors concerning Chu Yan. For instance, when *Natural Selection* had chosen to defect and escape the Doomsday Battle, he was the only captain to ask to give chase. Some claimed that he had a different purpose in mind, wanting to hijack *Blue Space* and escape along with *Natural Selection*. Of course, those were just rumors.

"Almost everyone from the two ships is gathered here," said Chu Yan. "Although much still divides us, we prefer to think of everyone as belonging to the same world, formed from *Blue Space* and *Gravity*. Before we plan the future of our world together, we need to take care of an urgent matter."

A large holographic display window appeared midair, showing somewhere in space where the stars were sparse. In the middle of the region was a faint white fog, and the fog was etched with several hundred straight parallel lines,

"Then you're just seeking revenge!" an officer fror

"Vengeance against Trisolaris *is* our right. They
they've committed. In war, it is right and just to des
deduction is correct, humankind's gravitational w;
been destroyed, and the Earth is now under occup
the genocide of the human race is underway.

"Activating the universal broadcast would give th
If the location of the Solar System is revealed, it w
value to Trisolaris because it could be destroyed at ;
force the Trisolarans to leave the Solar System, and th
have to turn away. We may be able to save the hun
annihilation. To give them more time, our broadcas
cation of Trisolaris."

"That's the same as revealing the Solar System! I

"We all know that, but hopefully this will give th
and allow more humans to escape. Whether they w
them."

"You're talking about destroying two worlds!" saic
one of them is our mother. This decision is the La
made so lightly."

"I agree."

A holographic rectangular red button about a me
the two existing information windows. Below it was

Chu Yan continued. "As I said earlier: together, v
in this world is an ordinary person, but fate has put (
ing the last judgment about two worlds. This deci
single person or even a few persons shouldn't mak
sion of the whole world through a referendum. All ;
location of Trisolaris to the universe, please press tl
or abstaining, do nothing.

"Right now, the total number of people aboar(
including all present and those on duty, is one th
fifteen. If the ayes reach or exceed two-thirds of th
four, the universal broadcast will begin immediatel
activate the broadcast and let the antenna decay ar

"Begin."

Chu Yan turned and pressed the giant red button
flashed, and the number below it turned from 0 to 1.

like brush bristles. The white lines had clearly been enhanced and stood out
in the image. In the past two centuries, these "brushes" had become very familiar to people, and some brands even used them in their logos.

"These trails were observed eight days ago in the stellar dust cloud near
Trisolaris. Please pay attention to the video."

Everyone stared at the image, and the trails could be seen to grow in the fog.

"How many times have you sped up the video?" an officer from *Gravity*
asked.

"It's not sped up at all."

The crowd grew agitated, like a forest struck by a sudden rainstorm.

"By a rough estimate . . . these ships are moving at close to the speed of
light," Captain Morovich of *Gravity* said. His voice was very tranquil. He had
experienced too many incredible sights in the last two days.

"That's right. The Second Trisolaran Fleet is heading for Earth at lightspeed, and should arrive in four years." Chu Yan looked at *Gravity*'s crew with
caring eyes, as though sorry that he had to deliver this news. "After you left,
the Earth sank into a dream of universal peace and prosperity, and completely
misjudged the situation. Trisolaris has been waiting patiently, and now they've
finally seized their chance."

"How do we know this is authentic?" someone from *Gravity* called out.

"I can attest to it!" said Guan Yifan. Among the small gathering in front of
the crews, he was the only one not in a military uniform. "My observatory had
also detected the same trails. However, since I was focused on large-scale cosmological observations, I didn't pay much attention to them. But I've gone
back and retrieved the recorded data. The Solar System, the Trisolaran system,
and our ships form a scalene triangle. The side between the Solar System and
the Trisolaran system is the longest. The side between the Solar System and us
is the shortest. The side going from the Trisolaran system to us is in between.
In other words, we are closer to the Trisolaran system than the Solar System is
to the Trisolaran system. About forty days from now, the Earth will also detect
the trails we're seeing."

Chu Yan took over. "We believe that something has already taken place on
the Earth. More specifically, it happened about five hours ago, when the droplets attacked our two ships. Based on information provided by *Gravity*, that was
the scheduled time for the Swordholder to transfer his authority to his successor. This was the opportunity Trisolaris had been waiting for for half a century.
The two droplets had clearly been given orders before entering the blind zone.
This was a long-planned, coordinated attack.

"I must conclude that the peace brought by dark
breached. There are only two possibilities: The g
broadcast has been initiated, or it hasn't."

Chu Yan tapped in the air and brought up C
holographic display. This picture of the new Swoi
obtained from *Gravity*. Cheng Xin stood in front of t
holding a baby. Her picture had been blown up tc
bristles, and the contrast between the two image
basic color scheme of space was black and silver—
cold light of the stars. But Cheng Xin resembled a
warm, golden glow bathed her and the baby, givin
ing of being close to the sun, a sensation that they ha

"We believe the latter scenario is true," Chu Yai

"How did they pick such a person to be Swordh
Space asked.

Captain Morovich answered. "It's been sixty yea
fifty for us. Everything on Earth has changed. Dete
cradle, and as humanity napped inside, it regresse

"Don't you know that there are no more men
Gravity shouted.

"Humans on Earth lost the ability to maintain d
Yan said. "We had planned to capture *Gravity* a
deterrence. But we've just found out that due to deca
to broadcast gravitational waves will only last two
this has been an incredible blow to all of us. We ha
diately activate the universal broadcast."

The crowd erupted. Next to the view of cold sp
trails of the Trisolaran Fleet, Cheng Xin gazed at
images portrayed their two choices.

"Are you really willing to commit mundicide
manded.

Chu Yan maintained his serenity against the ch
rovich, he spoke to the crowd. "For us, initiating th
Neither the Earth nor Trisolaris can catch us now.

Everyone understood this. The sophons were
home, and the droplets had been destroyed. Earth ar
to trace them. In the vast, deep space beyond the C
ships operating at lightspeed would never be able t

of *Blue Space* pressed the buttons in quick succession. The tally went up to 3.
Then the other senior officers of *Blue Space*, followed by the junior officers
and enlisted men, filed past the red button in a long line, pressing the button
again and again.

As the red button flashed, the tally crept up. These were the final beats of
the heart of history, the final steps taken toward the terminal point.

When the number reached 795, Guan Yifan pressed the button. He was the
first person from *Gravity* to support the broadcast. After him, several more
officers and enlisted men from *Gravity* also pressed the button.

Finally, the number reached 943, and a large line of text appeared above
the button:

The next affirmative vote will activate the universal broadcast.

The next person to vote was an enlisted man. Many others were lined up
behind him. He placed his hand above the button, but didn't push. He waited
until the ensign behind him put his hand on his, and then more hands joined
theirs in a thick stack.

"Please wait," Captain Morovich said. He drifted over and, as everyone
watched, placed his hand atop the pile.

Then dozens of hands moved together, and the button flashed one more
time.

Three hundred fifteen years had passed since that morning in the twentieth century when Ye Wenjie had pushed another red button.

The gravitational wave broadcast began. Everyone present felt a strong
tremor. The feeling seemed to come not from without, but from within each
body, as though every person had become a vibrating string. This instrument
of death played for only twelve seconds before stopping, and then everything
was silent.

Outside the ship, the thin membrane of space-time rippled with the gravitational waves, like a placid lake surface disturbed by a night breeze. The judgment of death for both worlds spread across the cosmos at the speed of light.

"It's possible to detect the warped points using the naked eye," Chu Yan said. "But the best way is to monitor the electromagnetic radiation. The emission from these points is very faint, but it has a distinct spectral signature. The regular sensors on our ships can detect and locate them. Typically, a volume of space as large as a ship in this region contains one to two warped points, but we once found twelve at once. Look, right now there are three."

Chu Yan, Morovich, and Guan Yifan were floating through a long corridor on *Blue Space*. In front of them drifted an information window showing a map of the interior of the ship. Three red dots flashed on the map, and the three of them were approaching one of these dots now.

"Right there!" Guan pointed straight ahead.

In the bulkhead in front of them was a circular hole about a meter in diameter. The edge was smooth, mirrorlike. Through the hole they could see tubes of various thicknesses. Several tubes had entire sections missing in the middle. In two of the thicker tubes, they could see liquid flowing. The liquid seemed to flow from one section, disappear, and then reappear in the corresponding section of the tube on the other side. The missing sections were of different lengths, but overall seemed to describe a spherical space. Based on the shape of the missing sections, part of the invisible bubble protruded into the corridor. Morovich and Guan carefully avoided it.

Chu Yan carelessly extended a hand into the invisible bubble, and half of his arm disappeared. Standing to the side, Guan Yifan saw a clear cross section of his cut-off arm, like the cross sections of Vera's legs that had been seen by Sublieutenant Ike aboard the *Gravity*. Chu Yan pulled his arm back and showed the astonished Morovich and Guan that it was unharmed. Then he encouraged them to try it. The two carefully reached into the invisible bubble. They watched their hands, and then arms, vanish, but they felt nothing.

"Let's go in," said Chu Yan. Then he jumped into the bubble, as though diving into a pool. Morovich and Guan watched in consternation as Captain Chu disappeared from head to toe. The cross section of his body on the surface of the invisible bubble rapidly changed shape, and the mirrorlike edge of the hole threw reflections onto the surrounding bulkheads like ripples.

As Morovich and Guan stared at each other, two hands and forearms emerged from the bubble and remained suspended in midair. Each hand grabbed hold of one of theirs, and they were pulled into fourth-dimensional space.

All who had experienced it agree that the sensation of being in four-dimensional space was indescribable. They would even say that it was the only thing encountered by humanity thus far that absolutely could not be captured by language.

People usually resorted to this analogy: Imagine a race of flat beings living inside a two-dimensional picture. No matter how rich or colorful the picture was, the flat people could only see the profile of the world around them. In their eyes, everything consisted of line segments of various lengths. Only when such a two-dimensional being was taken up out of the picture into three-dimensional space and looking down on the world could he see the entirety of the image.

This analogy simply expressed in some more detail the indescribability of experiencing four-dimensional space.

A person looking back upon the three-dimensional world from four-dimensional space for the first time realized this right away: He had never *seen* the world while he was in it. If the three-dimensional world were likened to a picture, all he had seen before was just a narrow view from the side: a line. Only from four-dimensional space could he see the picture as a whole. He would describe it this way: Nothing blocked whatever was placed behind it. Even the interiors of sealed spaces were laid open. This seemed a simple change, but when the world was displayed this way, the visual effect was utterly stunning. When all barriers and concealments were stripped away, and everything was exposed, the amount of information entering the viewer's eyes was hundreds of millions times greater than when he was in three-dimensional space. The brain could not even process so much information right away.

In Morovich and Guan's eyes, *Blue Space* was a magnificent, immense painting that had just been unrolled. They could see all the way to the stern, and all the way to the bow; they could see the inside of every cabin and every sealed container in the ship; they could see the liquid flowing through the maze of tubes, and the fiery ball of fusion in the reactor at the stern. . . . Of course, the rules of perspective remained in operation, and objects far away appeared indistinct, but everything was *visible*.

Given this description, those who had never experienced four-dimensional space might get the wrong impression that they were seeing everything "through" the hull. But no, they were not seeing "through" anything. Everything was laid out in the open, just like when we look at a circle drawn on a piece of paper, we can see the inside of the circle without looking "through" anything. This kind of openness extended to every level, and the hardest part was describing how it applied to solid objects. One could see the interior of solids, such as the bulkheads or a piece of metal or a rock—one could see all the cross sections at once! Morovich and Guan were drowning in a sea of information—all the details of the universe were gathered around them and fighting for their attention in vivid colors.

Morovich and Guan had to learn to deal with an entirely novel visual phenomenon: unlimited details. In three-dimensional space, the human visual system dealt with limited details. No matter how complicated the environment or the object, the visible elements were limited. Given enough time, it was always possible to take in most of the details one by one. But when one viewed the three-dimensional world from four-dimensional space, all concealed and hidden details were revealed simultaneously, since three-dimensional objects were laid open at every level. Take a sealed container as an example: One could see not only what was inside, but also the interiors of the objects inside. This boundless disclosure and exposure led to the unlimited details on display.

Everything in the ship lay exposed before Morovich and Guan, but even when observing some specific object, such as a cup or a pen, they saw infinite details, and the information received by their visual systems was incalculable. Even a lifetime would not be enough to take in the shape of any one of these objects in four-dimensional space. When an object was revealed at all levels in four-dimensional space, it created in the viewer a vertigo-inducing sensation of depth, like a set of Russian nesting dolls that went on without end. Bounded in a nutshell but counting oneself a king of infinite space was no longer merely a metaphor.

Morovich and Guan looked at each other, then looked at Chu Yan to the side. They saw bodies revealed at every level with the details displayed in parallel: They could see bones, organs, the marrow inside the bones, the blood flowing through the ventricles and atria of the heart, the openings and closings of the mitral and tricuspid valves. When gazing at each other, they could see clearly the interior structure of the lenses of the eyes. . . .

The phrase "in parallel" might also lead to misunderstanding. The physical locations of the parts of the body had not been shifted around: The skin still enclosed the organs and the bones, and the familiar shape of each person in three-dimensional space persisted—but it was now merely one detail among an infinity of details, visible at the same time, in parallel.

"Be careful of where you move your hands," Chu Yan said. "You might poke an internal organ—yours or someone else's—by mistake. But as long as you don't use too much force, even contact won't be a big deal. You'll feel a bit of pain or nausea, and of course there's the risk of infections. Also, don't touch or move things unless you know exactly what they are. Everything on the ship is now naked: You might be touching a live wire or heated steam, or even integrated circuits, and cause system malfunctions. Overall, you're like gods in the three-dimensional world, but you have to get used to being in four-dimensional space before you can use your powers effectively."

Morovich and Guan quickly learned how to avoid touching inner organs. By moving in a certain direction, they could grasp someone's hand instead of the bones inside the hand. To touch the bones or organs required exertion in *another* direction—a direction that didn't exist in three-dimensional space.

Next, Morovich and Guan discovered something else that excited them: They could see the stars in every direction. They could see the bright glow of the Milky Way extending through the universal eternal night. They knew that they were still inside the ship—none of them wore space suits, and all breathed the air on the ship—but in the fourth dimension, they were exposed to space. All three veteran spacers had performed countless spacewalks, but they had never felt so utterly intimate with space. During spacewalks, they were at least enclosed by space suits, but now, nothing stood between space and them. The ship that revealed infinite details did not shield them from space. In the fourth dimension, the ship lay in parallel with all of space.

The brain that had been adapted from birth to sense and feel three-dimensional space could not handle the infinite information generated by countless details, and initially, information overload threatened to shut down processing. But the brain soon grew used to the four-dimensional environment, and without conscious thought it learned to ignore most details, leaving only the frames around objects.

After the initial vertigo, Morovich and Guan experienced another, even greater shock. Once their attention was no longer completely absorbed by the inexhaustible details of the environment around them, they sensed space itself, or sensed the fourth dimension. Later, people would call this feeling "high-dimensional spatial sense." For those who had experienced it, high-dimensional spatial sense was hard to convey in words. They often tried to explain it this way: Concepts like "vastness" or "boundlessness" in three-dimensional space were replicated an infinite number of times in four-dimensional space in a direction that did not exist in three-dimensional space. They often resorted to the analogy of two mirrors facing each other: In either mirror one could see a boundless multitude of replicated mirrors, a hall of mirrors that extended into infinity. In this analogy, each mirror in the hall was a three-dimensional space. In other words, the vastness that one experienced in three-dimensional space was but a cross-section of the vastness of four-dimensional space. The difficulty of describing high-dimensional spatial sense lay in the fact that for observers situated in four-dimensional space, the space they could see was empty and uniform, but there was a *depth* to it that could not be captured by language. This *depth* was not a matter of distance: It was bound up in every point in space. Guan Yifan's exclamation later became a classic quote:

"A bottomless abyss exists in every inch."

The experience of high-dimensional spatial sense was a spiritual baptism. In one moment, concepts like *freedom, openness, profundity,* and *infinity* all gained brand-new meanings.

Chu Yan said, "We should return. The warped points remain stable for only a brief period of time before drifting away or disappearing. To find a new warped point requires moving in four-dimensional space. That's a dangerous undertaking for novices like you."

"How does one find a warped point in four-dimensional space?" Morovich asked.

"Simple. A warped point is usually spherical. Light is refracted inside the sphere, and objects inside are distorted, causing a visual break in the image of the objects. Of course, this is just an optical effect in four-dimensional space, not a real change in the shapes of the objects. Look over there—"

Chu Yan pointed in the direction they had come from. Morovich and Guan saw those tubes again, which now also lay open so that all the liquids flowing through them could be seen clearly. Inside the spherical region, the tubes were curved and distorted, and the sphere appeared like a drop of dew hanging on a spiderweb. This was different from how the region had appeared in three-dimensional space. There, the warped point didn't refract light, and so appeared completely invisible. Its presence could only be made known via the disappearance of objects that had entered four-dimensional space inside the bubble.

"If you come here again, you must wear space suits. Novices can't always tell locations accurately, and finding a new warped point for the return trip might result in landing outside the ship in three-dimensional space."

Chu Yan indicated that the other two should follow, and entered the dewdrop-like bubble. In an instant they were back inside the three-dimensional world, back in the corridor inside the ship, in exactly the place where, ten minutes ago, they had entered four-dimensional space. In fact, they had never left—the space they were in had just gained an extra dimension. The round opening in the bulkhead was still there, and they could still see the "broken" tubes inside.

But to Morovich and Guan, the world no longer seemed familiar. They now experienced the three-dimensional world as narrow and smothering. Guan dealt with it slightly better—he had at least experienced four-dimensional space once before, in a semiconscious state. But Morovich was feeling claustrophobic, as though he was being suffocated.

"This is normal. You'll get used to it after a few times." Chu Yan laughed. "The two of you now know what real vastness means. Even if you put on space suits and go take a walk in space now, you'll feel confined."

"How did all this happen?" Morovich tore open his collar and gasped.

"We entered a region of space where space has four dimensions. That's it. We call this region a four-dimensional fragment."

"But we're in three-dimensional space now!"

"Four-dimensional space contains three-dimensional space, just as three-dimensional space contains two-dimensional space. To make another analogy: We're located inside a three-dimensional sheet of paper in four-dimensional space."

"Let me propose a model," said Guan excitedly. "The entirety of our three-dimensional space is a large, thin sheet of paper, sixteen billion light-years across. Somewhere on this sheet of paper is a tiny, four-dimensional soap bubble."

"Perfect, Dr. Guan!" Chu Yan clapped Guan's shoulder, making him tumble in weightlessness. "I've been trying to come up with a good analogy, and you hit it in one try. This is why we need a cosmologist! You're exactly right. We were on this three-dimensional sheet of paper, crawling over the surface. Then we came into the soap bubble. From a warped point, we can manage to leave the surface of the paper and entered the space inside the bubble."

"Though we were in four-dimensional space just now, our bodies remained three-dimensional," Morovich said.

"That's right. We were flat, three-dimensional people drifting in four-dimensional space. It's not clear how our bodies are able to survive in four-dimensional space, given that the physical laws are likely different. There are many such mysteries."

"What exactly are warped points?"

"The three-dimensional sheet of paper is not completely flat everywhere. Some places are warped, reaching into the fourth dimension. That's what a warped point is: a tunnel from lower dimensions into higher dimensions. We can get into four-dimensional space by jumping into them."

"Are there many warped points?"

"Oh yes. They're everywhere. *Blue Space* was able to discover their secret earlier because we have more people aboard, and so there were many more opportunities to encounter warped points. *Gravity*, besides having fewer people, also had a much stricter psychological monitoring regime—even those who encountered warped points dared not discuss them."

"Are all warped points this small?"

"No. Some are much bigger. There's one mystery we've never been able to solve: We once observed that the rear third of *Gravity* had warped into four-dimensional space, and stayed there for several minutes. How could you have not noticed anything odd?"

"Well, the last third of the ship usually had no crew. Oh, wait, he was there." Morovich turned to Guan Yifan. "You must have experienced that. I think I heard about it from Dr. West."

"I was only half awake. Later, that idiot convinced me that I was only hallucinating."

"It's not possible to look into the fourth dimension from three-dimensional space. But it *is* possible to be in four-dimensional space and see everything happening in three-dimensional space and to affect things in it. We were able to lay an ambush against the droplets from four-dimensional space. No matter how powerful the strong-interaction probes were, they were still three-dimensional objects. In a sense, three-dimensionality is synonymous with fragility. Viewed from four-dimensional space, it was an unrolled painting, defenseless. We approached it from the fourth dimension, and, without understanding its principles of operation, sabotaged its internal mechanisms—completely exposed—at random.

"Is Trisolaris aware of the existence of the four-dimensional fragment?"

"We think not."

"The soap bubble—uh, four-dimensional fragment—how big is it?"

"Talking about the size of four-dimensional space from three-dimensional space is kind of meaningless. We can only discuss how big the projection of the fragment is in three dimensions. Based on preliminary investigation, we think the three-dimensional projection is spherical. If that's true, based on the data collected so far, its radius is between forty to fifty AU."

"About the size of the Solar System."

The round opening in the bulkhead next to the three of them began to move slowly and to shrink. When it was just over ten meters from them, the opening disappeared completely. But the information window floating near them indicated that two more warped points had appeared aboard *Blue Space*.

"How could a four-dimensional fragment appear in three-dimensional space?" Guan Yifan muttered to himself.

"No one knows. Doctor, this is your puzzle to solve."

After the discovery of the four-dimensional fragment, *Blue Space* had explored and studied the space inside extensively. The addition of *Gravity* brought more advanced equipment and techniques, so the crews could conduct more comprehensive and in-depth exploration.

In three-dimensional space, this region appeared very empty and showed no irregularities. Much of the exploration had to be conducted in four-dimensional space. Since releasing probes into four-dimensional space was no trivial matter, most of the research was conducted by inserting a telescope into the fragment through a warped point. Manipulating a three-dimensional instrument in four dimensions required some practice, and a period of adjustment, but once the scientists got the hang of it, they immediately made shocking discoveries.

Through the telescope, they discovered a ring-shaped object. Since it was impossible to determine its distance from the ship, it was also impossible to estimate its size. The best guess was that its three-dimensional diameter was between eighty to one hundred kilometers, and the band of the ring was about twenty kilometers thick. The whole thing resembled a giant wedding band spinning in space. Complex patterns resembling circuitry could be discerned on the surface of the band. Based on the evidence, it seemed reasonable to conclude that the ring had been constructed by intelligent beings.

This was the first time humanity had observed another civilization outside of the Earth and Trisolaris.

But the most shocking thing was that the "Ring" was sealed. It existed in four-dimensional space, but didn't reveal its interior as a three-dimensional object would have. Since its inside was concealed, that meant it was a true four-dimensional object. This was also the first true four-dimensional object detected by humanity since entering four-dimensional space.

People initially feared an attack, but the surface of the Ring showed no signs of any activity. They also detected no emission of any electromagnetic, neutrino, or gravitational wave signals. Other than a slow, stately revolving motion, the Ring showed no acceleration. The working theory was that this was a ruin, perhaps a long-abandoned space city or spaceship.

Further observations revealed more unknown objects in the depths of four-dimensional space. They were all sealed four-dimensional objects of different sizes and shapes, and many seemed to be artifacts fashioned by intelligence: pyramids, crosses, polyhedral frames, and so on. Other objects were irregular forms composed from simpler shapes, also clearly not natural. More than a dozen of these objects had shapes that could be discerned by telescope, though farther away were many more objects that appeared only as point sources. In total, about a hundred such objects were found. Like the Ring, none of them showed signs of activity, and they emitted no detectable signals.

Guan Yifan proposed to Captain Chu the plan of piloting a pinnace to the Ring and studying it up close. If possible, he wanted to enter the Ring. The captain denied this proposal unequivocally. Navigating through four-dimensional space was fraught with risks. To precisely fix one's location required four coordinates, but equipment brought from three-dimensional space could only determine three coordinates. This meant three-dimensional explorers could not determine the location of any object in four-dimensional space with precision. An explorer could not ascertain the location or distance of the Ring using instrumentation or visual observation, so it would be possible to collide with the Ring at any moment.

Similarly, locating a warped point to return to three-dimensional space would be very difficult. Since the coordinate in one of the four directions could not be determined, when a warped point was found, all that was known was its direction, not its distance from the observer. The crew of the pinnace could use a warped point to return to three-dimensional space and, to their surprise, find themselves far away from *Blue Space*.

Finally, most of the radio waves linking *Blue Space* and the pinnace would spill into the fourth dimension, leading to far faster decay of signal strength and causing communication difficulties.

After that, *Blue Space* and *Gravity* suffered six micrometeoroid strikes in one day. A 140-nanometer micrometeoroid struck and completely destroyed the magnetic levitation controller of *Blue Space*'s fusion reactor core. This was a key system aboard the ship. The fusion reactor core could reach temperatures as high as a million degrees, which would vaporize any material it came in contact with. A magnetic field kept it centered within the reaction chamber. If the controller failed, the superheated reactor core could escape from the magnetic field and instantly destroy the ship. Fortunately, the backup unit kicked in immediately and shut off the reactor—which was operating at minimal power—and averted catastrophe.

As the two ships sailed deeper into the four-dimensional fragment, the density of micrometeoroid strikes increased, and even larger meteoroids, visible to the naked eye, passed near the ships. Their velocity relative to the ships was several times the third cosmic velocity. In three-dimensional space, the critical parts of the ships were wrapped in layers of protection, but here, they lay exposed to the fourth dimension, completely defenseless.

Chu Yan decided that the two ships should retreat from the four-dimensional fragment. The fragment as a whole was moving away from the Solar System, heading in the same direction as the ships' course; thus, although *Blue Space* and *Gravity* were sailing away from the Solar System at a high speed, their velocity relative to the fragment was small, and they had only slowly caught up to the fragment. They weren't deep within the fragment and should be able to decelerate and leave it easily.

Guan Yifan raged against this decision. "The greatest mystery in the universe is right in front of us. The answers to all our cosmological questions may be found here. How can we leave?"

"Are you talking about the three and three hundred thousand syndrome? The fragment did remind me of it."

"Even if you focus only on the practical, we can probably recover unimaginable knowledge and artifacts from that ring-shaped ruin."

"Such gains are only meaningful if we survive this ordeal. Right now, both of our ships could be annihilated any moment."

Guan sighed and shook his head. "Fine. But before you leave, let me ride a pinnace to explore the Ring. Give me a chance. You spoke of survival, but perhaps our future survival depends on what I can discover here!"

"We can consider sending a drone."

"In a four-dimensional world, only a live observer can understand what is seen. You know this better than I."

———

After a brief discussion, the senior staff of both ships approved Guan's proposal. Guan Yifan, Lieutenant Zhuo Wen, and Dr. West made up the exploratory team. Lieutenant Zhuo was the science officer aboard *Blue Space* and had comparatively extensive experience navigating in four dimensions. Dr. West, on the other hand, simply insisted that he come; the request was ultimately approved because he had studied Trisolaran language before the voyage.

Prior to this, the longest voyage in four-dimensional space had been the attack on the droplets and *Gravity*. During the attack, a pinnace had sailed through four-dimensional space to approach *Gravity*, and then three people, including Lieutenant Commander Park Ui-gun, had entered *Gravity* via a warped point to reconnoiter. Thereafter, more than sixty marines had boarded *Gravity* in three separate waves. The attack on the droplets had relied on smaller shuttles. But this voyage of discovery to the Ring would be far longer.

The pinnace entered four-dimensional space from a warped point between the two ships. At the tail of the pinnace, the small fusion reactor's core turned from dim red to a faint blue as its power level increased. This flame, together with the balls of fire in the reactors of the two larger ships, illuminated this world of infinity times infinity. *Blue Space* and *Gravity* quickly receded, and as the pinnace sailed deeper into four-dimensional space, the high-dimensional spatial sensation intensified. Although Dr. West had already been to four-dimensional space twice, he exclaimed, "How grand is the spirit that can grasp such a world!"

Lieutenant Zhuo piloted the pinnace using voice commands or by moving the cursor with his gaze—it was a good idea to avoid using hands and risking contact with some sensitive piece of equipment that now lay exposed in four dimensions. To the naked eye, the Ring was still but a barely visible dot, but Zhuo cautiously kept the pinnace flying at a very low speed. Due to the extra unmeasurable dimension, visual judgments of distance were completely unreliable. The Ring might be as far away as an astronomical unit or as close as the pinnace's bow.

After three hours, the pinnace had already exceeded the previous record of distance sailed from the ships in four-dimensional space. The Ring remained but a dot. Lieutenant Zhuo grew even more cautious and was prepared to decelerate at full power and to change the heading at a moment's notice. Guan Yifan grew impatient and asked Zhuo to fly faster. Just then, West cried out in surprise.

The Ring turned into a real ring—it just happened. One moment, it was still a dot; the next moment, it was a ring the size of a coin. There was no gradual process of change at all.

"You've got to remember that we're basically blind in the fourth dimension," Lieutenant Zhuo said. He decreased their speed again.

Two more hours passed. If they were still in three-dimensional space, they would have sailed about two hundred thousand kilometers.

All of a sudden, the coin-sized Ring turned into a gigantic structure. Lieutenant Zhuo banked sharply and barely managed to avoid collision. The pinnace passed through the Ring like an arch in space. The pinnace decelerated, turned around, and came to a stop a short distance from the Ring.

This was the first time humans had come close to a four-dimensional object. Similar to high-dimensional spatial sense, they felt the magnificence of high-dimensional materiality. The Ring was completely sealed, and they could not look inside the band, but they could feel an immense sense of depth and of containment. What they were seeing wasn't just a Ring, but an infinity of Rings all stacked together in concealment. This sensation of four-dimensionality impressed itself upon the soul, and gave the observers the experience of seeing the mountain contained in a mustard seed described in Buddhist parables.

From up close, the surface of the Ring appeared very different from images taken by the telescope. Instead of a golden yellow light, it gave off a dark copper glow. Those faint etched lines that had looked like circuitry were really lines left by micrometeoroids striking its surface. There was still no evidence of any activity, and it didn't emit light or other radiation. Looking at the ancient surface of the Ring, all three felt a sense of familiarity. They recalled the destroyed droplets, and then tried to imagine the immense four-dimensional Ring with a mirrorlike smooth surface—it would have been a breathtaking sight.

Following the preestablished plan, Lieutenant Zhuo transmitted a message to the Ring via medium-frequency radio waves. This was a simple bitmap, a bit array that could be interpreted as six lines of dots that formed a sequence of prime numbers: 2, 3, 5, 7, 11, 13.

They weren't expecting any answers, but an answer arrived immediately, so fast that they couldn't believe their eyes. The information window hovering in the middle of the pinnace cabin displayed a simple bitmap similar to the one they had sent. It also consisted of six lines portraying the next six prime numbers: 17, 19, 23, 29, 31, 37.

The original plan had intended the hailing message as an experiment; there

was no preparation for how to develop further communications. While the
three in the pinnace debated what to do, the Ring sent a second bitmap to
the pinnace: 1, 3, 5, 7, 11, 13, 1, 4, 2, 1, 5, 9.

Then a third bitmap: 1, 3, 5, 7, 11, 13, 16, 6, 10, 10, 4, 7.

A fourth: 1, 3, 5, 7, 11, 13, 19, 5, 1, 15, 4, 8.

A fifth: 1, 3, 5, 7, 11, 13, 7, 2, 16, 4, 1, 14.

The bitmaps came one after another. The first six numbers in each consisted of the six prime numbers sent by the pinnace as a greeting. As for the
next six numbers in each series, both Lieutenant Zhuo and Dr. West turned to
Guan Yifan, the scientist. The cosmologist stared at the scrolling numbers in
the floating window and shrugged.

"I can't see any pattern."

"Then let's suppose that there is no pattern." West pointed at the window.
"The first six numbers were sent by us, so it's possible that they mean 'you.'
The next six numbers in the transmissions show no recognizable pattern, so
maybe they mean 'all'—'everything about you.'"

"They—or it—want to know everything about us?"

"Or at least a linguistic sample. It wants to decode it, study it, and then communicate with us further."

"Then we should send it the Rosetta System."

"We have to ask for authorization."

The Rosetta System was a database developed to teach Earth languages to
Trisolarans. The database included about two million characters' worth of documents concerning the natural and human histories of Earth with numerous
videos and images. There was also software to draw connections between the
linguistic symbols and the images so that an alien civilization could decode
and study Earth languages.

The mother ship authorized the request from the exploration team. But the
pinnace didn't have the Rosetta System in its onboard computer memory, and
due to the extremely tenuous communication link between the pinnace and
the mother ship, it was impossible to transmit such a large volume of data. The
only solution was to have the mother ship beam the information directly at the
Ring. This couldn't be done via radio, but luckily, *Gravity* was equipped with
a neutrino communication system. They weren't sure if the Ring could receive
neutrino signals, however.

Three minutes after *Gravity* transmitted the Rosetta System via a neutrino
beam to the Ring, the pinnace received a new series of bitmaps from the Ring.

The first one was a perfect square of sixty-four dots arranged eight by eight; the second bitmap was missing one dot in a corner, leaving sixty-three; the third bitmap was missing two, leaving sixty-two. . . .

"It's a countdown, or a progress bar," said West. "I think this is to show that it has received the Rosetta System and is in the process of decoding it. We should wait."

"Why sixty-four dots?"

"It's a reasonably big number if you're in base two. It's like how we use one hundred for lots of things in base ten."

Lieutenant Zhuo and Guan were both glad to have West with them. The psychologist did seem to have some skills when it came to establishing communications with unknown intelligences.

When the countdown reached fifty-seven, something exciting happened: The next number didn't come in the form of a bitmap of dots. The Ring transmitted the Arabic number 56.

"Wow, fast learner," Guan said.

The number kept on decreasing by one every ten seconds or so. A few minutes later, the number reached 0. The last message consisted of four Chinese characters:

I am a tomb.

The Rosetta System was written in a language that mixed English with Chinese. It would make sense that the Ring would use the same language to communicate with them. It just happened that this message consisted entirely of Chinese characters. Guan Yifan typed a question into the floating window, and began the conversation between humanity and the Ring.

Whose tomb is this?
The tomb of those who created it.
Is this a spaceship?
It used to be a spaceship. But now it's dead, and so it's a tomb.
Who are you? Who is conversing with us?
I am the tomb. It is the tomb speaking to you. I'm dead.
You mean you're a ship whose crew died? In other words, you're the
    control system for the ship?

(There was no reply to this.)

We can see many other objects in this region of space. Are they also
    tombs?
Most of them are tombs. The others will be tombs soon. I don't know
    them all.
Are you from far away? Or have you always been here?
I'm from far away; they're also from far away, from different places
    far away.
Where?

(There was no answer.)

Did you build this four-dimensional fragment?
You told me that you came from the sea. Did you build the sea?
Are you saying that for you, or at least for your creators, this four-
    dimensional space is like the sea for us?
More like a puddle. The sea has gone dry.
Why are so many ships, or tombs, gathered in such a small space?
When the sea is drying, the fish have to gather into a puddle. The
    puddle is also drying, and all the fish are going to disappear.
Are all the fish here?
The fish responsible for drying the sea are not here.
We're sorry. What you said is really hard to understand.
The fish who dried the sea went onto land before they did this. They
    moved from one dark forest to another dark forest.

The last sentence was like a thunderclap. The three inside the pinnace
cabin and everyone in the distant two mother ships hearing the exchange via
a faint link all shuddered.

Dark forest . . . what do you mean?
The same thing you mean.
Are you going to attack us?
I'm a tomb; I'm dead; I won't attack anyone. There is no dark forest state
    between spaces of different dimensions. The lower-dimensional
    space cannot threaten the higher-dimensional space, and the re-
    sources of the lower-dimensional space are of no use to the higher-
    dimensional space. But the dark forest exists everywhere between
    those sharing the same dimensions.

Can you give us any suggestions?

Leave this puddle immediately. You are thin pictures. You're fragile. If
    you stay in the puddle, you'll turn into tombs in no time. . . . Wait,
    there seem to be fish on your pinnace.

Guan sat there, stunned for a few seconds, and then realized that the pinnace really did have some fish. He always carried an ecological sphere with
him, about the size of a fist. Inside the glass sphere was water, a tiny fish, and
some seaweed; together, everything formed a carefully designed miniature enclosed ecosystem. This was Guan's favorite possession, so he had taken it with
him on this adventure. If he couldn't return, this would have accompanied
him into the afterlife.

I like fish. Can I have it?

How do we give it to you?

Toss it over.

The three put on the helmets for their space suits and opened the pinnace's
hatch. Guan lifted the ecological sphere to his eyes. Carefully, since he was in
four-dimensional space, he held the sphere by its three-dimensional edge, and
gave it a final glance. From this four-dimensional perspective, every detail in
the sphere was revealed, and this tiny world of life seemed even more rich,
varied, and colorful. Guan swung his arm and tossed the sphere in the direction of the Ring. He watched as the small, transparent sphere disappeared in
space. Then he closed the hatch and continued the conversation.

Is this the only puddle in the universe?

There was no answer. After that, the Ring remained silent and responded
no more to attempts at communication.

Gravity informed them that more micrometeoroids had struck *Blue Space*.
An increasing number of drifting objects, including some small-scale four-
dimensional objects, possibly debris from ships or other artifacts, surrounded
both ships. Captain Chu ordered their immediate return. The plan to board
the Ring had to be scrapped.

Since they now knew their distance from the mother ship, the return trip
could be covered twice as fast. In two hours, they were back in the vicinity of
Blue Space, and successfully located a warped point to return home.

The explorers were treated as heroes and given a celebratory welcome—even if their discoveries appeared to yield no practical applications for the future of the two ships.

Captain Chu asked, "Dr. Guan, what do you think is the answer to the last question you asked the Ring?"

"I go back to the analogy I made before. The probability that we managed to stumble into the only soap bubble with a diameter of forty to fifty astronomical units on the surface of a sheet of paper sixteen billion light-years across is so minuscule that it might as well be zero. I'm certain that there are other soap bubbles, probably many more."

"Do you think we'll encounter more in the future?"

"I think there's an even more interesting question: Have we encountered them before? Think about the Earth: It's been careening through space for several billion years. Is it not possible that it had entered a four-dimensional fragment in the past?"

"That would have been an astonishing sight. I find it hard to imagine that humanity had experienced it. . . . But I wonder if dinosaurs could have located warped points . . ."

"Why are there bubbles at all? Why are there so many four-dimensional fragments in three-dimensional space?"

"It's a great mystery."

"Captain, I think it's likely a dark secret."

Blue Space and *Gravity* began to back out of the fragment. As the ships accelerated, gravity pulled them toward the ships' sterns. Guan Yifan and the science officers from both ships tried to cram as much research about the fragment as possible into the next few days and spent almost all their time in four-dimensional space. This was only in part due to the requirements of their research—they also found the confinement and claustrophobia of being in three-dimensional space unbearable.

On the fifth day after beginning acceleration, all those in four-dimensional space found themselves back in three-dimensional space in a flash without having passed through a warped point. The electromagnetic sensors on the two ships indicated that there were no more warped points aboard either ship.

Blue Space and *Gravity* were outside the fragment.

This surprised them. Based on their calculations, they should still be cruising through the fragment for another twenty hours. Their early exit was probably due to one of two reasons: one, the fragment had sped up in a direction opposite to the ships' current heading. Two, the fragment was shrinking. The crews believed reason number two was more likely. Other than the data, they also remembered the answer from the Ring:

> When the sea is drying, the fish have to gather into a puddle. The puddle is also drying, and all the fish are going to disappear.

The two ships stopped accelerating and began to decelerate at full power. Finally, they stopped at the vicinity of the boundary of the four-dimensional fragment, where it was safe.

The edge of the four-dimensional fragment was invisible. The space before them was empty, placid like the surface of a deep pool. The sea of stars that was the Milky Way shone brightly, giving no hint that a great secret was hidden close by.

But soon they did notice a strange and spectacular sight: From time to time, luminous lines appeared in the space before them. Those lines were very thin, and very straight on first appearance. They seemed to have no thickness to the naked eye, and stretched in length between five thousand and thirty thousand kilometers. The lines appeared suddenly. At first, they gave off a blue glow. Then the color gradually shifted to red, and the straight lines curved and broke into many pieces, until they finally vanished. Observation showed that these lines manifested at the edge of the fragment, as though a giant pen constantly marked out the boundary.

They launched an unmanned probe toward the region of space where the lines appeared, and by luck, the probe managed to observe one of the lines when it flashed into existence at close range. The probe was about a hundred kilometers away, rushing toward the line at full speed. By the time it arrived, the line had curled, broken up, and disappeared. The probe detected massive quantities of hydrogen and helium in the vicinity, and also some dust from heavy elements, mainly iron and silicon.

After analyzing the data, Guan and the science officers concluded that the lines were created by four-dimensional matter entering three-dimensional space. As the fragment shrank, four-dimensional matter dropped into three-dimensional space and decayed instantly. Although these bits of matter took up very little volume in four-dimensional space, their decay into three dimensions flattened the fourth dimension, causing their volume to increase greatly and expand into the form of straight lines. By their calculations, a few tens of grams of four-dimensional matter could form a line stretching almost ten thousand kilometers in three dimensions.

Based on the rate at which the boundary of the fragment was receding, in twenty days or so, the Ring would also enter three-dimensional space. The two ships decided to wait to observe such a wonder of the universe—they had plenty of time, after all. Using the glowing decay-lines as markers, the two ships cautiously proceeded, maintaining the same speed as the receding edge of the fragment.

During the next dozen or so days, Guan Yifan was absorbed in deep thought and calculations, and the science officers engaged in vigorous debates. Finally, they reached the consensus that, based on current theoretical physics, they could not do too much theoretical analysis of the four-dimensional fragment. But the theories that had been developed in the past three centuries could at least make some predictions that were confirmed by observations: A higher dimension existing in macro form decayed toward lower dimensions as inevitably as water fell over a cliff. The decay of four-dimensional space into three dimensions was the root cause of the fragment's shrinking.

But the lost dimension wasn't truly lost: It simply curled up from the macroscopic to the microscopic and became one of the seven dimensions folded up within the quantum realm.

They could again see the Ring with the naked eye. The existence of this self-declared tomb would soon end in three-dimensional space.

Both *Blue Space* and *Gravity* stopped advancing and backed off three hundred thousand kilometers. As the Ring entered three-dimensional space, the decay process would release tremendous amounts of energy—this was why the lines that appeared earlier had given off so much light.

Twenty-two days later, the edge of the fragment receded past the Ring. The moment the Ring entered three-dimensional space, the universe seemed to be cut in half. The cut surface glowed with a blinding light, as though a star had been pulled into a line in an instant. From the spaceships it was impossible to see the end points, but it was as if God had held a T-square against the plan for the universe and sketched a line straight across from left to right. Careful observation by instruments revealed that the line was close to one AU in length, or about 130 million kilometers, almost long enough to connect the Earth with the Sun. In contrast to other lines that had been observed, this one had a thickness that was visible even from several hundred thousand kilometers away. The light emitted by the line turned from a hot bluish-white to a merely warm red, and then gradually dimmed. The line itself also became twisted and loose, breaking into a belt of dust. It no longer glowed by itself, but seemed suffused with the light of the stars, a serene silver. Observers from both ships shared a strange impression: The dust belt resembled the Milky Way in the background. What had happened seemed to be the flash of a giant camera that took a picture of the galaxy. Afterwards, the photograph slowly developed in space.

Guan felt a trace of sorrow in the face of such a majestic sight. He was thinking of the ecological sphere he had given to the Ring. It wasn't able to enjoy the gift for long. As it decayed into three-dimensional space, the Ring's internal four-dimensional structures were annihilated instantaneously. Those other dead or dying ships within the fragment would not be able to escape a similar fate in the end. In this vast universe, they could only persist for a time in the tiny four-dimensional corner.

A vast and dark secret.

Blue Space and *Gravity* sent out many probes to the dust belt. Other than scientific investigation, they also wanted to see if they could gather some useful resources. The Ring had decayed into common elements in three-dimensional space: mostly hydrogen and helium. These could be collected as fuel for nuclear fusion. However, since these elements existed mostly in the form of gas in the dust belt, they dissipated quickly, and in the end very little was collected. There were also some heavy elements, however, and they were able to gather some useful metals.

The two ships now had to consider their own future. A temporary council formed of the crews of both *Blue Space* and *Gravity* announced that everyone could pick between continuing the journey with the two ships or returning to the Solar System.

An independent hibernation ark would be constructed and powered by one of the seven fusion reactors on the two ships. Anyone wishing to go home would board this ark and return to the Solar System after a voyage of thirty-five years. The two ships would inform the Earth of the hibernation ark's course via a neutrino transmission so that the Earth could dispatch ships to meet it upon arrival. In order to prevent Trisolaris from locating *Blue Space* and *Gravity* based on this transmission, the neutrino transmission would only be made after the hibernation ark had already been on its way for some time. If the Earth could send out ships to assist the ark with deceleration before its arrival, more of the ark's fuel could be spent for acceleration and shorten the voyage to between ten and twenty years.

Assuming the Earth and the Solar System still existed by then.

Only about two hundred people chose to return. The rest didn't want to go back to that world doomed to destruction; they would rather stay with *Blue Space* and *Gravity* and continue into the unknown depths of space.

A month later, the hibernation ark and the two ships both embarked on their new voyages. The hibernation ark headed for the Solar System, while *Blue Space* and *Gravity* planned to divert around the four-dimensional fragment and then aim for a new target star system.

The luminous glow from the fusion reactors lit up the already sparse dust belt and cast it in a golden-red hue, like a warm sunset on Earth. Everyone, whether homeward bound or heading far away, felt hot tears filling their eyes. The beautiful space sunset quickly faded, and the eternal night fell over everything.

The two seeds of human civilization continued to drift into the depths of the starry sea. Whatever fate held in store for them, at least they were starting again.

PART III

Broadcast Era, Year 7
Cheng Xin

艾 AA told Cheng Xin that her eyes were even prettier and brighter than before, and perhaps she wasn't lying. Cheng Xin had been mildly myopic before, but now she saw everything with extreme clarity, as though the world had been given a fresh coat of paint.

Six years had passed since their return from Australia, but the trials of the Great Resettlement and the intervening years seemed to have left no mark on AA. She was like a fresh, resilient plant that allowed the hardships of the past to roll off her smooth leaves. During these six years, Cheng Xin's company had developed rapidly under AA's management and become one of the prominent players in near-orbit space construction. But AA didn't look like a powerful CEO; instead, she retained the look of a lively, fun young woman. Of course, that was not unusual in this age.

The six years hadn't touched Cheng Xin either—she had spent them in hibernation. After their return from Australia, her blindness had been examined and diagnosed. It had started out as psychosomatic—the result of extreme emotional distress—but later developed into a detached retina followed by necrosis. The recommended treatment was to produce cloned retinas suitable for transplant out of stem cells developed from her DNA, but the process would take five years. Cheng Xin spending five years in complete darkness in her extremely depressed state would have led to total breakdown, and so the doctors allowed her to hibernate.

The world had indeed been refreshed. After receiving news of the gravitational wave universal broadcast, the whole world celebrated. *Blue Space* and *Gravity* became salvation ships out of myths, and the two crews became superheroes worshipped by all. The charge that *Blue Space* had committed suspected murder during the dark battles was withdrawn, and replaced with the affirmation that it had acted in justified self-defense after being attacked. Simultaneously, members of the Earth Resistance Movement who had persisted in a hopeless struggle during the Great Resettlement were also hailed as heroes. When those resistance fighters dressed in rags appeared before the public, everyone felt hot tears in their eyes. *Blue Space, Gravity,* and the Resistance became symbols of the grandness of the human spirit, and countless worshippers seemed to think that they themselves had also always possessed such spirit.

Retaliation against the Earth Security Force followed. Objectively speaking, the good done by the ESF far exceeded that done by the Resistance. The ESF had been able to protect the big cities and other basic infrastructure. Although they had done so for the benefit of Trisolaran civilization, their efforts allowed the world to recover economically after the Great Resettlement with minimal delay. During the post-resettlement evacuation of Australia, Australia almost plunged into total chaos multiple times due to the lack of food and electricity, and it was the ESF that maintained order and kept supplies flowing, making it possible to complete the evacuation in four months. During that extraordinary, tumultuous time, if this well-equipped armed force had not been present, the results would have been unimaginably tragic. But none of these accomplishments were taken into account by the tribunals sitting in judgment over them. All ESF members were tried, and half were convicted of crimes against humanity. During the Great Resettlement, many nations revived capital punishment, and this persisted even after the return from Australia. During these five years, many former ESF members were executed, even though many among the cheering crowd had also submitted applications to the ESF.

Eventually, peace returned, and people began to rebuild their lives. As the cities and industrial infrastructure remained intact, recovery was rapid. Within two years, the cities had eliminated the scars from the chaotic times and recovered their pre-resettlement prosperity. Everyone resolved to enjoy life.

This tranquility was premised on this fact: When Luo Ji had conducted his dark forest experiment, 157 years had passed between when he first broadcast the coordinates of 187J3X1 to the universe and when that star was destroyed. That was equivalent to the life span of a modern human. To be sure, birthrates declined to their lowest levels in recorded history because no one wanted to bring a child into a world doomed to die. But most believed that they would be able to live out the rest of their days in peace and happiness.

The gravitational wave broadcast was far stronger than the Sun-amplified radio broadcast employed by Luo Ji, but humanity soon found refuge in a new way to comfort themselves: questioning the validity of dark forest theory itself.

Excerpt from *A Past Outside of Time*
Delusions of Cosmic Persecution: The Last Attempt to Invalidate Dark Forest Theory

For sixty-some years—the entirety of the Deterrence Era—dark forest theory formed the backdrop to human history. But scholars had always questioned it, and until the start of the Broadcast Era, there had never been any scientific proof for its validity. The existing few pieces of evidence all lacked rigorous scientific foundation.

The first piece of evidence: Luo Ji's dark forest experiment that led to the destruction of 187J3X1 and its planetary system. The supposition that the system had been destroyed by some extraterrestrial intelligence had always been controversial. The astronomical community had always voiced the loudest objections. There were two main views: One camp believed that the object observed striking the star at lightspeed was insufficient to destroy the star. The death of 187J3X1 was thus likely the result of a natural supernova. Since there was incomplete predestruction data for this star, it was impossible to say definitively whether the star possessed the requisite conditions for going supernova. Considering the long time that elapsed between Luo Ji's broadcast and the star's explosion, there was a high probability that the event was indeed natural. A second camp conceded that a lightspeed object did kill the star, but the "photoid" might very well be a natural phenomenon in the galaxy. Although to date no second photoid had been detected, there had been observations of massive objects being accelerated to extremely high speeds by naturally occurring forces. For instance, a supermassive black hole near the center of the galaxy was perfectly capable of accelerating some small object to near the speed of light. In fact, the center of the galaxy might produce a large number of such projectiles, but due to their small size, they were rarely seen.

The second piece of evidence: the terror Trisolaris showed for dark forest deterrence. This was, to date, the most convincing proof for dark forest theory, but humanity knew nothing of the Trisolarans' own process of derivation and the evidence they relied on; so, scientifically speaking, it was insufficient to constitute direct proof. It was possible that Trisolaris submitted to a state of deterrence balance with humanity for some other unknown reason, and finally gave up the conquest of the Solar System. Many hypotheses were proposed to explain this unknown reason, and although none were absolutely convincing, none could be conclusively disproven, either. Some scholars proposed a new theory of "delusions of cosmic persecution," which argued that the Trisolarans also had no proof of the validity of dark forest theory. However, due to the extremely harsh environment they had evolved in, the Trisolarans suffered a mass persecution complex against cosmic society. This persecution delusion was similar to Medieval religions on the Earth, and was merely a faith held by a majority of Trisolarans.

The third piece of evidence: the confirmation of dark forest theory given by the four-dimensional Ring. Clearly, the Ring had obtained the words "dark forest" from the Rosetta System, specifically the section discussing human history. This phrase appeared often in historical records dating from the Deterrence Era, and it was not surprising that the Ring would use it. However, in the dialogue between the Ring and the exploration team, the section where the concept was invoked was very brief and its exact meaning ambiguous. It was not enough to conclude that the Ring really understood the meaning of the words it used.

Since the Deterrence Era, the study of dark forest theory had developed into its own subject. Other than theoretical research, scholars also conducted large numbers of astronomical observations and built numerous mathematical models. But for most scholars, the theory remained a hypothesis that could be neither confirmed nor disproven. Dark forest theory's true believers were the politicians and the public, and members of the public mostly chose to believe or disbelieve based on their own situations. After the commencement of the Broadcast Era, more and more people leaned toward treating dark forest theory as merely a delusion of cosmic persecution.

Broadcast Era, Year 7
Cheng Xin

After the dust settled, humanity turned its attention from the universal broadcast to reflecting on the end of the Deterrence Era. A veritable flood of accusations and denunciations against the Swordholder began to appear. If Cheng Xin had activated the broadcast at the start of the droplet attack, then, at a minimum, the disaster of the Great Resettlement could have been avoided. Most of the negative public opinion, however, was concentrated on the process of choosing the Swordholder.

The election had been a complicated process—public opinion had turned into political pressure exerted on the UN and Fleet International. The public vigorously debated who was ultimately responsible, but almost no one suggested that it was the result dictated by the herd mentality of all involved. Public opinion was relatively forgiving to Cheng Xin herself. Her positive public image provided some measure of protection, and her suffering as an ordinary person during the Great Resettlement gained her some sympathy. Most people tended to think she was also a victim.

Overall, the Swordholder's decision to capitulate made history take a long detour, but didn't change its overall direction. In the end, the universal broadcast had been initiated, and so the debate over that period of history eventually subsided. Cheng Xin gradually faded from the public consciousness. After all, the most important thing was to enjoy life.

But for Cheng Xin, life had turned into an endless torture. Although her eyes could see again, her heart remained in darkness, sunken in a sea of depression. Although her internal pain was no longer searing and heart-rending, there also was no end in sight. Suffering and depression seemed to suffuse every cell in her body, and she could no longer recall the presence of sunlight in her life. She spoke to no one, did not seek out news about the outside world, and paid no attention even to her growing company. Although AA cared about Cheng Xin, she was busy and could spend little time with Cheng Xin. Fraisse was the only one who provided the support Cheng Xin needed.

During the dark period at the end of the Great Resettlement, Fraisse and AA had been taken out of Australia together. He lived in Shanghai for a while but didn't wait for the evacuation to complete before returning to his house near Warburton. After Australia returned to normalcy, he donated his house to the government to be used as an Aboriginal cultural museum. He, on the other hand, went into the woods and built a small tent, and really took up the primitive life of his ancestors. Though he lived in the open, his physical health seemed to improve. The only modern convenience he possessed was a mobile phone, which he used to call Cheng Xin a few times a day.

These conversations consisted of a few simple sentences:

"Child, the sun is rising here."

"Child, the sunset is lovely here."

"Child, I spent the day picking up debris from the shelter-houses. I'd like to see the desert return to how it was before."

"Child, it's raining. Do you remember the smell of humid air in the desert?"

There was a two-hour time difference between Australia and China, and gradually, Cheng Xin grew used to the daily rhythms of Fraisse's life. Every time she heard the old man's voice, she imagined herself also living in that distant forest surrounded by desert, sheltered under a tranquility that kept the rest of the world at bay.

One night, the telephone roused Cheng Xin from her slumber. She saw that the caller was Fraisse. It was 1:14 A.M. in China, and 3:14 in Australia. Fraisse knew that Cheng Xin suffered from severe insomnia, and without a sleep-aid machine, she could only manage two to three hours of rest a night. Unless it was an emergency, he would never be disturbing her at a time like this.

He sounded anxious. "Child, go out and look up in the sky."

Cheng Xin could already tell something unusual was happening. In her uneasy sleep, she had been gripped by a nightmare. The dream was a familiar one: A gigantic tomb stood in the middle of a plain covered by the darkness of night. A bluish glow spilled from within the tomb and illuminated the ground nearby. . . .

Just that kind of blue light could be seen outside.

She went onto the balcony and saw a blue star in the sky, brighter than all the other stars. Its fixed position distinguished it from the man-made structures orbiting in near-Earth orbit. It was a star outside the Solar System. Its brightness was still intensifying, and even overpowered the lights of the city around her, casting shadows against the ground. About two minutes later, the brightness reached a peak and was brighter even than a full moon. It was no longer possible to look at it directly, and the color of the light shifted to a harsh white, illuminating the city as though it were daytime.

Cheng Xin recognized the star. For almost three centuries, humans had looked at it more than at any other spot in the heavens.

Someone screamed in the leaf-building nearby, and there was the sound of something crashing to the floor.

The star now began to fade. From white it gradually dimmed to red, and about half an hour later, it went out.

Cheng Xin hadn't brought the phone with her, but the floating communication window had followed her. She could still hear Fraisse's voice, which had recovered its usual serenity and transcendence. "Child, don't be afraid. What will happen, will happen."

A lovely dream had ended: Dark forest theory had received its final confirmation with the annihilation of Trisolaris.

Excerpt from *A Past Outside of Time*
A New Model for the Dark Forest

Trisolaris was shattered three years and ten months after the start of the Broadcast Era. No one had expected the attack to come so soon after the gravitational wave broadcast.

Since Trisolaris had always been under intense surveillance, plenty of data was captured concerning its extinction. The attack on the Trisolaran system was identical to the attack on Luo Ji's 187J3X1: A small object traveling near the speed of light struck one of the three stars in the system and destroyed it through its relativistically amplified mass. At the time, Trisolaris had just started to revolve around the star, and the stellar explosion annihilated the planet.

When it made the gravitational wave broadcast, *Gravity* was about three light-years from Trisolaris. Taking into account the lightspeed propagation of gravitational waves, the photoid must have been launched from a point that was even closer to Trisolaris than *Gravity*—and the launch must have been practically instantaneous after receiving the coordinates. Observations confirmed this: The trail of the photoid traversing the interstellar dust cloud near Trisolaris was clearly recorded, but there were no other solar systems within this zone of space—the only conclusion was that the photoid had been launched from a spacecraft.

The old model for dark forest theory had always assumed planetary systems around stars as the foundation. People simply assumed that attacks on systems whose coordinates had been exposed must come from other planetary systems. But once the possibility of attacks from spacecraft entered the scene, the situation became far more complex. While the locations of stars were relatively well known, humans had no information at all concerning spacecraft made by other intelligences—save for the Trisolaran Fleet. How many extraterrestrial spaceships were there? How densely were they deployed in space? How fast did they fly? What were their headings? There were no answers to these questions.

The possible sources of dark forest attacks could no longer be predicted, and the attacks might come much faster than previously imagined. Other than the surviving stars of the Trisolaran system, the nearest star was six light-years from the Solar System. But the ghostlike alien spaceships could be, at that moment, passing next to the Sun. Death, once only a figure on the horizon, now loomed before our eyes.

Broadcast Era, Year 7
Sophon

For the first time, humanity witnessed the extinction of a civilization, and realized such a fate might befall Earth at any moment. The threat of Trisolaris, a crisis that had lasted close to three centuries, dissipated overnight, yet what took its place was an even crueler universe.

However, the anticipated mass hysteria did not occur. Faced with the catastrophe four light-years away, human society became strangely quiet. Everyone seemed to be waiting, but at a loss as to what they were waiting for.

Ever since the Great Ravine, although history had taken multiple big turns, humanity, as a whole, had always lived in a society that was highly democratic, with ample welfare. For two centuries, the human race had held on to a subconscious consensus: No matter how bad things got, *someone* would step in to take care of them. This faith had almost collapsed during the disastrous Great Resettlement, but on that darkest of mornings six years ago, a miracle had nonetheless taken place.

They were waiting for another miracle.

On the third day after witnessing the destruction of Trisolaris, Sophon invited Cheng Xin and Luo Ji to tea. She said that she had no ulterior motives. They were old friends, after all, and she missed them.

The UN and Fleet International were intensely interested in the meeting. The expectant, lost attitude prevalent in society posed a terrible danger. Human society was as fragile as a sand castle on the beach, prone to collapse with a passing gale. The leaders wanted the two former Swordholders to gather some information from Sophon that would reassure the people. In an emergency session of the PDC convened for this purpose, someone even hinted to Cheng

Xin and Luo Ji that even if they couldn't get such intelligence from Sophon, perhaps it was acceptable to manufacture some.

After the universal broadcast of six years ago, Sophon had retreated from public life. Once in a while, she might appear in public, but only to serve as an expressionless speaking tube for Trisolaris. She had remained in that elegant dwelling hanging from a tree branch, though most of the time she was probably in standby mode.

Cheng Xin met Luo Ji on the bough leading to Sophon's house. Luo Ji had spent the Great Resettlement with the Resistance. Although he did not directly participate or lead any operations, he remained the spiritual center of the resistance fighters. The Earth Security Force and the droplets had made every effort to seek him out and kill him, but somehow, he had managed to evade them. Not even the sophons could locate him.

To Cheng Xin's eyes, Luo Ji appeared to have retained his upright, cold demeanor. Other than the fact that his hair and beard appeared even whiter in the breeze, the past seven years seemed to have left no mark on him. But then, without speaking, he smiled at her, and the gesture made her feel warm. Luo Ji reminded Cheng Xin of Fraisse. Though the two were completely different, they both brought with them some mountainlike strength from the Common Era, and gave Cheng Xin the sense that they could be relied on in this strange new time. Wade, the Common Era man who was as evil and vicious as a wolf and who had almost killed her, also had it—so she found herself relying even on him. It was an odd feeling.

Sophon welcomed them in front of her house. Once again, she was dressed in a splendid kimono, and she wore fresh flowers in her bun. That vicious ninja dressed in camouflage had disappeared completely, and she was once again a woman who resembled a bubbling spring nestled among flowers.

"Welcome, welcome! I wanted to pay a visit to your honored abode, but then I wouldn't be able to properly entertain you with the Way of Tea. Please accept my humble apologies. I am so delighted to see you." Sophon bowed to them, and her words were as gentle and soft as the first time Cheng Xin had met her. She led the two through the bamboo grove in her yard, across the little wooden bridge over the trickling spring, and into the pavilionlike parlor. Then the three sat down on tatami mats, and Sophon began to set out the implements for the Way of Tea. Time passed tranquilly, and clouds rolled and unfurled across the blue sky outside.

A complex mix of feelings flooded Cheng Xin's heart as she watched Sophon's graceful movements.

Yes, she (or they?) could have succeeded in wiping them out, and had al-most succeeded several times. But each time, humanity had snatched victory from the jaws of defeat through tenaciousness, cunning, and luck. After a three-century-long march, all Sophon had managed was to see her home an-nihilated in a sea of flames.

Sophon had known of the destruction of Trisolaris four years ago. Three days earlier, after the light from the explosion had reached the Earth, she had given a brief speech to the public. She recounted the death of Trisolaris in simple words, and made no denunciation or judgment of the cause—the grav-itational wave broadcast initiated by two human ships. Many suspected that four years ago, when Trisolaris had been wiped out, those who had controlled her from four light-years away had perished in the fiery flames, but her current controllers were more likely on the spaceships of the Trisolaran Fleet. During the speech, Sophon's tone and expression had been calm. This wasn't the same as the woodenness she had shown when she had merely acted as a speaking tube, but a manifestation of her controllers' soul and spirit, a dignity and no-bility in the face of annihilation that humanity could not hope to equal. People now felt an unprecedented awe toward this civilization that had lost its home world.

The limited information provided by Sophon and the Earth's own observa-tions drew a rough picture of Trisolaris's destruction.

At the time of the catastrophe, Trisolaris was in a stable era, orbiting around one of the three stars in the system at a distance of about 0.6 AU. The photoid struck the star and tore a hole through the photosphere and the convection zone. The hole was about fifty thousand kilometers in diameter, wide enough for four Earths laid side by side. Whether as a result of a deliberate choice by the attacker or coincidence, the photoid struck the star at a point along the line where the star intersected Trisolaris's ecliptic plane. Viewed from the surface of Trisolaris, an extremely bright spot appeared on the surface of the sun. Like a furnace with its door open, the powerful radiation generated by the core of the sun shot through the hole; passed through the convection zone, the photosphere, and the chromosphere; and struck the planet directly. All life out-doors on the hemisphere exposed to the radiation was burnt to a crisp within a few seconds.

Next, material from the core of the sun erupted from the hole, forming a fifty-thousand-kilometer-thick fiery plume. The spewed material was tens of millions of degrees in temperature, and while some of the material fell back onto the surface of the sun under the influence of gravity, the remainder reached escape velocity and shot into space. Viewed from Trisolaris, a brilliant tree of fire grew from the surface of the sun. About four hours later, the ejected solar material reached 0.6 AU from the surface of the sun, and the tip of the flaming tree intersected the orbit of Trisolaris. After another two hours, the orbiting planet reached the tip of the fire tree and continued to pass through the ejected solar material for about thirty minutes. During this time, the planet might as well be moving through the interior of the sun—even after the journey through space, the spewed material was still at a blazing temperature of tens of thousands of degrees. By the time Trisolaris emerged from the fire tree, it glowed with a dim red light. The entire surface had liquefied, and an ocean of lava covered the planet. Behind the planet was a long white trail through space—steam from the boiled-off ocean. The solar wind stretched the trail out, making the planet appear as a long-tailed comet.

All signs of life on Trisolaris had been cleansed away, but only the fuse of the catastrophe had been lit.

The ejected solar material caused drag against the planet. After passing through the material, Trisolaris slowed down, and its orbit fell lower toward the star. The fire tree acted like a claw extended from the sun, pulling Trisolaris down with each revolution. After about ten more revolutions, Trisolaris would fall into the sun itself, and the cosmic football game played between three suns would come to its end. But this sun wouldn't survive long enough to see itself emerge as the victor.

The solar eruption also lowered the pressure inside the sun, temporarily slowing down the fusion within the core. The sun dimmed rapidly until it was but a hazy outline. The giant fiery tree growing from the surface, in contrast, appeared even more striking, more brilliant, like a sharp scratch made against the inky black film of the universe. The diminished fusion meant that the core radiation no longer exerted sufficient pressure against the weight of the solar shell, and the sun began to collapse. The dim shell fell into the core, triggering a final explosion.

This was the sight witnessed by humankind three days ago on Earth.

The solar explosion destroyed everything within the planetary system: The vast majority of spaceships and space habitats trying to escape were vaporized. Only a few extremely fortunate ships that happened to be behind the two other suns, which acted as shields, were safe.

Thereafter, the remaining two suns formed a stable double-star system, but no life would witness the regular sunrises and sunsets. The cinders of the exploded star and the incinerated Trisolaris formed two vast accretion discs around the two suns, like two gray graveyards.

"How many escaped?" Cheng Xin asked softly.

"Counting the Trisolaran Fleets far from home, no more than one-thousandth of the entire population." Sophon's reply was even softer than Cheng Xin's query. She was focused on the Way of Tea, and did not raise her head.

Cheng Xin had much more to say, words from one woman to another, but she was a member of the human race, and the chasm that now divided her from Sophon could not be crossed. She resorted to the questions the leaders had wanted her to ask. The conversation that followed would come to be known as the Conversation of the Way of Tea, which would profoundly change the subsequent progress of history.

"How much longer do we have?" Cheng Xin asked.

"We can't tell. The attack could come at any moment. But probabilistically, you should have a bit more time: maybe as long as one to two centuries, like your last experiment." Sophon glanced at Luo Ji and then sat up straight, her face expressionless.

"But—"

"Trisolaris was in a different situation from the Solar System. First, the broadcast only included the coordinates of Trisolaris. To discover the existence of Earth based on this requires examining the record of communications between the two worlds from three centuries ago. That will definitely happen, but it will take time. More important, from a distance, the Trisolaran system appears far more dangerous than the Solar System."

Cheng Xin looked at Luo Ji in shock, but the latter showed no reaction. She asked, "Why?"

Sophon shook her head determinedly. "We can never explain this to you."

Cheng Xin returned to the planned questions. "The two attacks we've seen both used photoids striking the stars. Is this a common attack method? Will the future attack on the Solar System be similar?"

"Dark forest attacks all share two qualities: one, they're casual; two, they're economical."

"Elaborate, please."

"These attacks are not part of some interstellar war, but a matter of conveniently eliminating possible threats. By 'casual,' what I mean is that the only basis for the attack is the exposure of the target's location. There will be no reconnaissance or exploration conducted against the target beforehand. For a supercivilization, such exploration is more expensive than a blind strike. By 'economical,' what I mean is that the attack will employ the least expensive method: using a small, worthless projectile to trigger the destructive potential already present in the target star system."

"The energy within the stars."

Sophon nodded. "That is what we've seen so far."

"Any possible defenses?"

Sophon smiled and shook her head. She spoke patiently, as though to a naïve child. "The whole universe is in darkness, but we remain lit. We're a tiny bird tied to a branch in the dark forest, with a spotlight trained on us. The attack could come from any direction, at any time."

"But based on the two attacks we've seen, there may be a way to engage in passive defenses. Even some Trisolaran ships survived in the home star system behind the other suns."

"Please believe me. Humankind has no chance of surviving a strike. Your only choice is to try to escape."

"Become refugees among the stars? But we cannot manage to get even one-thousandth of our population away."

"That's still better than complete annihilation."

Not by our values, Cheng Xin thought, though she said nothing.

"Let's talk no more of this. Please don't ask more questions. I've told you everything I can. I asked my friends here for tea." Sophon bowed to the two, and then presented two bowls of green tea.

Cheng Xin had many more questions on her list. She was anxious as she accepted the tea, but she knew that asking more questions would be useless.

Luo Ji, who had said nothing so far, seemed relaxed. He appeared familiar with the Way of Tea, and holding up his bowl in the palm of his left hand, he rotated it three times with his right hand before taking a drink. He drank slowly, letting time pass in silence, not finishing until the clouds outside the window were colored a golden yellow by the setting sun. He set down the bowl slowly, and said his first words. "May I ask some questions, then?"

Luo Ji's respect among the Trisolarans had been shown through Sophon's attitude. Cheng Xin noticed right away that while Sophon was gentle and friendly with her, she was awed by Luo Ji. Whenever she faced Luo Ji, her eyes revealed her feelings, and she always sat farther away from Luo Ji than Cheng Xin, and bowed to him slower and deeper.

In response to Luo Ji's question, Sophon bowed again. "Please wait." She lowered her eyes and sat still, as though deep in thought. Cheng Xin knew that several light-years away, on the ships of the Trisolaran Fleet, Sophon's controllers were engaged in an urgent debate. About two minutes later, she opened her eyes.

"Honored Luo Ji, you may ask one question. I can only affirm, deny, or tell you I don't know."

Luo Ji set down the tea bowl again. But Sophon raised her hand, asking him to wait. "This is a gesture of respect from our world to you. My answer will be true, even if the answer could cause harm to Trisolarans. But you have only one question, and my answer must be from those three choices. Please consider it carefully before you speak."

Cheng Xin gazed at Luo Ji anxiously, but the latter didn't pause at all. In a decisive tone, he said, "I've considered it. Here's my question: If Trisolaris showed certain signs of being dangerous when observed from a distance, does there exist some sign that can be shown to the universe to indicate that a civilization is harmless and will not threaten anyone else, thus avoiding a dark forest strike? Can Earth civilization broadcast such a 'safety notice,' if you will, to the universe?"

Sophon did not answer for a long time. Again, she sat still, pondering with her eyes lowered. Cheng Xin felt time flow more slowly than ever. With every passing second, her hope diminished, and she was certain that Sophon's answer was going to be *no* or *I don't know*. But abruptly, Sophon looked up at Luo Ji with clear eyes—before then, she had never even dared to meet his gaze directly—and answered without any doubt:

"Yes."

"How?" Cheng Xin couldn't help herself.

Sophon looked away from Luo Ji, shook her head, and refilled their tea bowls. "I can tell you nothing more. Really. I can never tell you anything again."

The Conversation of the Way of Tea gave the tiniest bit of hope for the expectant mass of humanity: It was possible to broadcast a safety notice to the cosmos to avoid dark forest strikes.

After the conversation between Sophon, Cheng Xin, and Luo Ji was publicized, everyone began to ponder the problem of how to broadcast a safety notice. Countless proposals flooded in, sent by sources as august as the World Academy of Sciences and as humble as elementary schools. It was perhaps the first time in the history of humanity that the entire species focused their mental energy on the same practical problem.

The more they thought about it, the more the safety notice turned into a riddle.

All the proposals could be divided into two broad categories: the declaratory camp and the self-mutilation camp.

The declaratory camp's basic conception, as can be intuited from the name, was a broadcast to the universe proclaiming the harmlessness of Earth civilization. Their main efforts were directed at how to express such a message. But in the eyes of most, their premise seemed foolish. No matter how well crafted the message, who in this heartless universe would believe it? The fundamental requirement for a safety notice was that the countless civilizations in the universe would trust it.

The self-mutilation camp represented the majority view. They theorized that the safety notice had to represent the truth, which implied that the notice required both "talking" and "doing." And of the two, "doing" was the key. Humanity had to pay a price for living in the dark forest and transform Earth civilization into a truly safe civilization—in other words, Earth civilization had to mutilate itself to eliminate its potential to threaten others.

Most of the self-mutilation plans focused on technology and advocated humanity to retreat from the space age and the information age and found a low-technology society—perhaps a society reliant on electricity and the internal combustion engine, such as at the end of the nineteenth century, or even an agrarian society. Considering the rapid decline in global population, these plans were feasible. In that case, the safety notice would be nothing more than an announcement that the Earth possessed a low level of technology.

More extreme ideas emerging from the self-mutilation camp proposed intellectual disablement. Using drugs or other neuromanipulation techniques, humans could lower their own intelligence. Moreover, such lowered intelligence could be fixed via genetic manipulation in future generations. As a result, a low-technology society would result naturally. Most people were revolted by the notion, but it remained in wide circulation. According to the proponents, the safety notice was equivalent to public disclosure of humanity's low intelligence.

There were other ideas as well. For instance, the self-deterrence camp advocated building a system that, once activated, would be beyond human control. The system would monitor humanity for any behavior incongruent with its self-proclaimed safe nature and initiate the destruction of the world upon detection.

This was a feast for the imagination. Countless plans competed for attention: some subtle, some strange, yet others as sinister and terrifying as cults.

But none of these plans captured the essence of the safety notice.

As Sophon pointed out, a key characteristic of dark forest strikes was their casual nature. The attacker did not bother to conduct close-range surveillance of the target. All these plans engaged in performance art with no audience. No matter how faithful the act, no one would see it except the performer. Even under the most optimistic conditions—suppose some civilizations, like doting parents, cared to observe Earth civilization up close, perhaps even devoting long-term monitoring equipment to the Solar System similar to the sophons, they would still make up only a minuscule portion of the large number of civilizations in the universe. In the eyes of the vast majority of civilizations, the sun was but a dim dot many, many light-years away, showing no distinguishing details at all. This was the fundamental mathematical reality of the cosmic dark forest.

Once, when humankind had been far more naïve, some scientists had believed that it was possible to detect the presence of distant civilizations by astronomical observation: for instance, the absorption spectral signatures of oxygen, carbon dioxide, and water vapor in exoplanetary atmospheres, or electromagnetic emissions. They even came up with whimsical notions like searching for signs of Dyson spheres. But we found ourselves in a universe in which every civilization endeavored to hide itself. If no signs of intelligence could be detected in a solar system from far away, it was possible that it really was desolate, but it was also possible that the civilization there had truly matured.

A safety notice was in reality a universal broadcast as well, and it had to ensure that all listeners would trust its message.

Take a distant star, a barely visible dot. Anyone casually glancing at it would say: Oh, that star is safe; that star will not threaten us. That was what a cosmic safety notice had to accomplish.

Utterly impossible.

Another mystery that no one seemed able to solve: Why wouldn't Sophon tell humanity how to broadcast such a safety notice?

It was understandable that the survivors of Trisolaran civilization would no longer transfer technology to humanity. After the gravitational wave broadcast, both worlds faced enmity from the entire galaxy, even the entire universe. They were no longer each other's greatest threats, and the Trisolarans had no time to spare for the Earth. As the Trisolaran Fleet sailed farther away, the connection between the two civilizations grew ever more tenuous. But there was one fact that neither Trisolarans nor humankind could forget: Everything that had happened started with Trisolaris. They were the ones who had initiated the invasion of the Solar System; who had attempted, but failed, to commit genocide. If the Earth managed to make great leaps in technology, revenge was inevitable. Humans were likely to come after whatever new home the surviving Trisolarans found among the stars, and they might complete their revenge before the Earth was destroyed in a dark forest strike.

But a safety notice was different: If such a notice could make the whole universe believe the Earth was harmless, then, by definition, the Earth would be harmless toward the Trisolarans. Wasn't this just what they wanted?

Broadcast Era, Year 7
Sophon

Although there were no clues for how to send out a true safety notice, and any serious research only confirmed the impossibility of such an endeavor, the public's yearning for the notice could not be stopped. Although most people understood that none of the existing proposals would work, attempts to implement them never ceased.

A European NGO tried to build an extremely powerful antenna that would take advantage of the Sun's amplification ability to broadcast their draft version of such a notice. The police stopped them in time. The six droplets in the Solar System had left six years ago, and there were no more blocks on the Sun's amplification function, but such a transmission would have been extremely dangerous and exposed the Earth's location even sooner.

Another organization named Green Saviors had several million members. They advocated humanity's return to an agrarian existence, thereby proclaiming their safety to the universe. About twenty thousand of their members moved to Australia. On this sparsely populated continent where the Great Resettlement was but a memory, they planned to create a model society. The agrarian lives of these Green Saviors were continuously broadcast to the rest of the world. In this age, it was no longer possible to find traditional farming implements, and so the tools they used had to be custom-made with funds from their sponsors. There wasn't much arable land in Australia, and all of it was devoted to high-end, expensive foods, and so the settlers had to open up new land in desolate areas designated by the government.

It took only one week before these pioneers stopped collective farming. It wasn't because the Green Saviors were lazy—their enthusiasm alone could have sustained them through some period of diligence—rather, it was because the bodies of modern humans had changed considerably from the past. They were more flexible and agile compared to past generations, but were no longer adapted to boring, repetitious physical labor. And opening up wastelands, even in agrarian times, was an extremely physically demanding task. After the leaders of the Green Saviors suitably expressed their respect for their farming ancestors, the movement dissolved, and the idea of a model agrarian society was abandoned.

Perverted ideas about the safety notice also led to vicious acts of terrorism. Some "anti-intellect" organizations were formed to put into practice the proposal to lower human intelligence. One of these planned to add large quantities of "neural suppressors" to the water supply of New York City, which would have caused permanent brain damage. Fortunately, the plot was uncovered in time and no harm was done, though NYC's water supply was out of commission for a few hours. Of course, without exception, these "anti-intellect" organizations wanted to maintain the intelligence of their own members, arguing that they had the responsibility to be the last of the intelligent people so that they could complete the creation of a society of low-intelligence humans and direct its operation.

Faced with the omnipresent threat of death and the lure of a different state of existence, religion once again took center stage in social life.

Historically, the discovery of the dark forest state of the universe was a giant blow to most major religions, especially Christianity. In fact, the damage to religion was evident even early on during the Crisis Era. When Trisolaran civilization was discovered, Christians had to wrestle with the fact that the aliens were not in the Garden of Eden, and God never mentioned them in Genesis. For more than a century, churches and theologians struggled to complete a new interpretation of the Bible and of accepted doctrines—and just when they had almost succeeded in patching up the faith, the monster that was the dark forest appeared. People had to accept the knowledge that many, many intelligent civilizations existed in the universe, and if each civilization had an Adam and an Eve, then the population of Eden must have been about the same as the current population of Earth.

But during the disastrous Great Resettlement, religions revived themselves. A new belief now became popular: In the past seventy years, humanity twice came to the brink of utter annihilation, but each time, they escaped miraculously. The two miracles, the creation of dark forest deterrence and the initiation of the universal gravitational wave broadcast, shared many characteristics: They both happened under the direction of a small number of individuals; their occurrence depended on a series of improbable coincidences (such as the fact that *Gravity, Blue Space,* and the droplets all entered the four-dimensional fragment simultaneously) . . . All these were clearly signs from some deity. At the time of both crises, the faithful had engaged in mass prayer sessions in public. It was precisely such fervent demonstrations of faith that finally led to divine salvation—though just which god was responsible was a topic of endless debate.

And so the Earth turned into a giant church, a planet of prayer. Everyone prayed with unprecedented faith for another act of salvation. The Vatican led numerous globe-wide Masses, and people prayed everywhere in small groups or individually. Before meals and sleep, they all prayed for the same thing: *Lord, please give us a hint; guide us to express our goodwill to the stars; let the cosmos know that we're harmless.*

A cosmopolitan space church was built in near-Earth orbit. Though it was called a church, there was no physical building other than a gigantic cross. The two beams making up the cross were twenty kilometers and forty kilometers long, respectively, and glowed so bright that the cross was visible from the Earth at night. The faithful would drift below it in space suits in worship, and as many as tens of thousands sometimes participated. Drifting along with them were countless giant candles capable of burning in vacuum, and the candles competed with the stars in brilliance. Viewed from the surface, the candles and the worshipping congregation seemed like a cloud of glowing space dust. And each night, innumerable individuals on the surface prayed to the cross among the stars.

Even Trisolaran civilization became the object of worship. Historically, Trisolaran civilization's image changed continuously in the eyes of humankind. At the beginning of the Crisis Era, they were powerful, evil alien invaders, but were also deified by the ETO. Later, Trisolaris gradually changed from devils and gods to *people.* With the creation of dark forest deterrence, Trisolaris's position in the eyes of humanity reached its nadir, and Trisolarans became uncivilized savages living at the pleasure of humankind. After deterrence failed, the Trisolarans revealed themselves to be genocidal conquerors. However, after the universal broadcast was initiated—and especially after the destruction of Trisolaris—Trisolarans turned into victims who deserved sympathy from humans, fellow refugees in the same boat.

After finding out about the concept of a safety notice, humans initially reacted to the news unanimously: a vociferous demand that Sophon divulge the method to broadcast a safety notice accompanied by the warning that she not commit mundicide by withholding such information. Yet soon people realized that rage and denunciations were useless against a civilization that had mastered technology far beyond humanity's knowledge and was moving farther and farther away in interstellar space. It would be far better to ask nicely, which then turned into begging. Gradually, as humans begged and begged in a cultural environment of waxing religiosity, the image of the Trisolarans transformed again. Since they possessed the secret of broadcasting the safety notice, they were angels of salvation sent by God. The only reason that humanity had not yet received such salvation was due to insufficient expression of their faith. And so the pleas directed at Sophon turned into prayers, and the Trisolarans once again became gods. Sophon's abode became a holy place, and every day, large numbers of the faithful gathered below the giant tree. At its peak, the congregation was a group several times larger than that of pilgrims in Mecca, forming an endless sea. Sophon's house hung in the air about four hundred meters above the crowd. From the surface it appeared tiny, hidden from time to time by the cloud it generated. Occasionally, Sophon would appear—the crowd couldn't see any details, but they could see her kimono as a tiny flower in the cloud. These moments were few and far between, and they became sacred. Adherents of every faith in the crowd expressed their piety in various ways: some prayed more fervently, some cheered, some cried and poured out their hearts, some knelt, some threw themselves down and touched their foreheads to the ground. On these occasions, Sophon bowed slightly to the mass of humanity below and then quietly retreated into her house.

"Even if salvation were to arrive now, it would be meaningless," said Bi Yunfeng. "We have no shred of dignity left." He had once been one of the candidates for the Swordholder position, as well as the commander of the Earth Resistance Movement's branch in Asia.

There were still many sensible people like him pursuing in-depth research on the safety notice in all areas of study. The explorers worked tirelessly, trying to find a method built on a solid scientific foundation. But all avenues of research seemed to lead to one inescapable conclusion: If there really were a way to release a safety notice, it would require a brand-new kind of technology. The technology must far exceed the current level of science on Earth and was unknown to humankind.

Like a moody child, human society's attitude toward *Blue Space*, which had already vanished in the depths of space, transformed again. From an angel of salvation, this ship again turned into a ship of darkness, a ship of devils. It had hijacked *Gravity* and cast a sinful spell of destruction on two worlds. Its crimes were unforgivable. It was Satan in the flesh. Sophon's worshippers also pleaded for the Trisolaran Fleet to find and destroy the two ships, to safeguard justice and the dignity of the Lord. As with their other prayers, Sophon did not respond.

Simultaneously, Cheng Xin's image in the public consciousness slowly changed as well. She was no longer a Swordholder unqualified for the position; she was again a great woman. People dug up an ancient story, Ivan Turgenev's "Threshold," and used it to describe her. Like the young Russian girl in that story, Cheng Xin had stepped over the threshold that no others dared to approach. Then, at the crucial moment, she had shouldered an unimaginable burden and accepted the endless humiliation that would be her lot in the days to come by refusing to send out the signal of death to the cosmos. People did not linger on the consequences of her failure to deter; instead, they focused on her love for humanity, the love that had caused so much pain that she had gone blind.

At a deeper level, the public's feeling for Cheng Xin was a reaction to her subconscious maternal love. In this family-less age, mother's love was a rare thing. The welfare state that seemed like heaven satiated the children's need for the love of a mother. But now, humanity was exposed to the cruel, cold universe, where Death's scythe may fall at a moment's notice. The baby that was human civilization had been abandoned in a sinister, terrifying dark forest; it cried, hoping for a mother's touch. Cheng Xin was the perfect target for this yearning, mother's love incarnate. As the public's feelings for Cheng Xin gradually melded with the thickening atmosphere of religiosity, her image as the Saint Mary of a new era once again gained prominence.

For Cheng Xin, this cut off the last of her will to live.

Life had long ago become a burden and torture for Cheng Xin. She had chosen to remain alive because she didn't want to avoid what she needed to bear—her continued existence was the fairest punishment for her great error, and she accepted it. But now, she had turned into a dangerous cultural symbol. The growing cult centered on her was adding to the fog that already trapped a lost humanity. To vanish forever would be her last act of responsibility.

Cheng Xin found the decision to be easy—effortless, really. She was like someone who had long ago planned to go on a long journey: finally, she had been relieved of her daily grind, and she was ready to pack lightly and set off.

She took out a tiny bottle: the medication for short-term hibernation. There was only one capsule left inside. It was the same drug she had used to hibernate for six years, but without an external cardiopulmonary bypass system to maintain life, it was fatal.

Cheng Xin's mind was as transparent and empty as space: there was no memory, no sensation. The surface of her consciousness was smooth as a mirror, the setting sun of her life reflected in it, as natural as any dusk. . . . It was right and proper. If a world could turn to dust in the snap of a finger, then the end of a person's life should be as placid and indifferent as a dewdrop rolling off the end of a blade of grass.

Just as Cheng Xin picked up the capsule in her hand, her phone rang. It was Fraisse.

"Child, the moon is very lovely tonight. I just saw a kangaroo. I guess the refugees hadn't eaten them all."

Fraisse never used the video function of his phone, as though he thought his words would be more vivid than any image. Although she knew he couldn't see her, Cheng Xin smiled. "That's wonderful, Fraisse. Thank you."

"Child, everything is going to get better." Fraisse hung up.

He shouldn't have noticed anything different. Their conversations were all this brief.

艾 AA had come that morning as well, excitedly telling Cheng Xin that her company had won the bid on another large project: building an even bigger cross in geosynchronous orbit.

Cheng Xin realized that she still had two friends. In this brief, nightmarish period of history, she had only these two real friends. If she ended her life now, how would they feel? Her transparent, empty heart tightened and cramped up, as though squeezed by numerous hands. The placid surface of the lake in her mind shattered, and the reflected sunlight burned like fire. Seven years ago, she hadn't been able to press that red button in front of all of humanity; now, thinking of her two friends, she could not swallow this capsule that would bring her relief. She saw again her boundless weakness. She was nothing.

A moment ago, the river in front of her had been frozen solid, and she could have easily walked to the other shore. But now, the surface had melted, and she would have to wade through the black, icy water. This was going to be a long process of torture, but she trusted herself to walk to the other shore. Perhaps she would hesitate and struggle until the next morning, but she would swallow that capsule in the end. She had no other choice.

The phone rang again. It was Sophon. She invited Cheng Xin and Luo Ji to tea again. She was going to tell them good-bye for the last time.

Slowly, Cheng Xin put the capsule back in the bottle. She would make this appointment. This meant she had enough time to wade across the river of pain.

———

The next morning, Cheng Xin and Luo Ji returned to Sophon's aerial abode. They saw a gigantic crowd gathered a few hundred meters below it. Sophon had announced to the world last night that she was going to leave, and the crowd of worshippers was several times larger than typical. Instead of the usual prayers and pleas, the congregation was silent, as though waiting for something.

In front of the door to her house, Sophon welcomed them the same way.

This time, the Way of Tea was conducted in silence. They all knew that everything that needed to be said between the two worlds had already been said.

Cheng Xin and Luo Ji could both feel the presence of the people below. The expectant crowd was like a giant noise-absorbing carpet that deepened the silence in the parlor. It was almost oppressive, as if the clouds outside the window had grown more solid. But Sophon's movements remained gentle and graceful, making no noise even when the implements came in contact with porcelain. Sophon seemed to be using her grace and elegance to counteract the heavy air. More than an hour passed, but Cheng Xin and Luo Ji did not feel the flow of time.

Sophon presented a bowl of tea to Luo Ji with both hands. "I'm leaving. I hope the two of you will take care and be well." Then she presented Cheng Xin with her bowl. "The universe is grand, but life is grander. Perhaps fate will direct us to meet again."

Cheng Xin sipped the tea quietly. She closed her eyes to concentrate on the taste. The clear bitterness seemed to suffuse her body, as though she had drunk cold starlight. She drank slowly, but finally, she was done.

Cheng Xin and Luo Ji got up to say farewell for the last time. Sophon accompanied them all the way up onto the branch. They saw that the white clouds generated by Sophon's house had disappeared for the first time in memory. Below them, the sea of expectant people still waited in silence.

"Before we say good-bye, I'm going to finish my last mission. It's a message." Sophon bowed deeply to both of them. Then she straightened up and looked at Cheng Xin.

"Yun Tianming would like to see you."

Excerpt from *A Past Outside of Time*
The Long Staircase

———

Near the beginning of the Crisis Era, before the Great Ravine had extinguished humanity's enthusiasm, the nations of the Earth had banded together and accomplished a series of great deeds for the defense of the Solar System. These gigantic engineering projects had all reached or breached the limits of the most advanced technology of the time. Some of them, such as the space elevator, the test of the stellar-class nuclear bombs on Mercury, the breakthroughs in controlled nuclear fusion, and so on, had been recorded by history. These projects built a solid foundation for the technological leap after the Great Ravine.

But the Staircase Project wasn't one of them; it had been forgotten even before the Great Ravine. In the eyes of historians, the Staircase Project was a typical result of the ill-thought-out impulsiveness that marked the beginning of the Crisis Era, a hastily conducted, poorly planned adventure. In addition to the complete failure to accomplish its objectives, it left nothing of technological value. The space technology that eventually developed took a completely different direction.

No one could have predicted that nearly three centuries later, the Staircase Project would bring a ray of hope to an Earth mired in despair.

It would probably forever remain a mystery how the Trisolarans managed to intercept and capture the probe carrying Yun Tianming's brain.

One of the cables holding the sail to the Staircase probe had broken near the orbit of Jupiter. The craft had deviated from its planned path, and the Earth, deprived of its flight parameters, lost it to the endless depths of space. If the Trisolarans had been able to intercept it later, they must have had its flight parameters after the cable broke; otherwise, even the advanced Trisolaran technology would have been incapable of locating such a small object in the vastness of space outside the Solar System. The most likely explanation was that the sophons had followed the Staircase Project probe, at least through its acceleration leg, to gather its final flight parameters. But it seemed unlikely that the sophons had followed the craft for the remainder of its long journey. The craft had passed through the Kuiper Belt and the Oort Cloud. In these regions, it could have decelerated or been pushed off course by interstellar dust. It appeared that none of these things happened, because Trisolarans wouldn't have been able to get updated parameters. Thus, the successful interception of the probe required some measure of luck.

It was virtually certain that a ship from the First Trisolaran Fleet was responsible for capturing the probe—most likely the one ship that had never decelerated. At the time, it had been sent way ahead of the rest of the fleet so that it could arrive in the Solar System a century and a half before the other ships—but, due to its extremely high velocity, it couldn't have decelerated in time, and would have had to pass straight through the Solar System. The goal of this ship was still a mystery. After the creation of dark forest deterrence, this ship, along with the rest of the First Trisolaran Fleet, had turned away from the Solar System. The Earth had never ascertained its precise flight parameters, but if it had turned in the same general direction as the rest of the First Fleet, then it was possible that it encountered the Staircase probe. Of course, even so, the two crafts were still at great distances from each other; without precise parameters for the probe's trajectory, the Trisolaran ship couldn't have located it.

A rough estimate—the only estimate possible given the lack of more information—would place the moment of interception between thirty and fifty years ago, but not before the Deterrence Era.

It was understandable that the Trisolaran Fleet would attempt to capture the Staircase probe. Until the very end, direct contact between the Trisolarans and humans was limited to the droplets. They would have been interested in a live human specimen.

Yun Tianming was now aboard the First Trisolaran Fleet. Most of the ships in the fleet were headed in the direction of Sirius. His exact condition was unknown: Perhaps his brain was kept alive by itself; or perhaps it had been implanted in a cloned body. But people were far more interested in a different question:

Was Yun Tianming still working for the interests of humanity?

This was a reasonable worry. The fact that Yun Tianming's request to see Cheng Xin had been approved showed that he had already integrated into Trisolaran society, and perhaps even possessed some social status there.

The next question was even more troubling: Had he participated in recent history? Did the events of the past century between the two worlds have anything to do with him?

Still, Yun Tianming had appeared at the exact moment when Earth civilization seemed to be bereft of hope. When the news became public, people's first reaction was that their prayers had been answered: The angel of salvation had finally arrived.

Broadcast Era, Year 7
Yun Tianming

━━━━━

Viewed through the portholes in the elevator, Cheng Xin's entire world consisted of an eighty-centimeter-thick guide rail. The guide rail extended endlessly both above and below her, shrinking into invisibility in each direction. She had been riding for an hour already and was more than a thousand kilometers above sea level, outside the atmosphere. The Earth below her was in the shadow of night, and the continents were mere hazy outlines with no substance. The space above her was inky blackness, and the terminal station, thirty thousand kilometers away, was invisible. One felt as though the guide rail pointed to a road from which there was no return.

Although she was an aerospace engineer from the Common Era, Cheng Xin had never been in space until this day, three centuries later. It no longer required special training to ride any space vehicles, but in consideration for her lack of experience, the technical support staff suggested that she ascend in the space elevator. Since the entirety of the ride was conducted at the same speed, there would be no hypergravity. And the gravity inside the elevator car now wasn't noticeably lower—gravity would diminish gradually, until she achieved complete weightlessness at the terminal station in geosynchronous orbit. At this altitude, one would experience weightlessness only when orbiting the Earth, not when going up in a space elevator. Occasionally, Cheng Xin saw tiny dots sweep past in the distance—probably from satellites coasting at first cosmic velocity.

The guide rail's surface was very smooth, and it was almost impossible to see motion. The elevator car seemed to be sitting still on the rail. In reality, her velocity was fifteen hundred kilometers per hour, equivalent to a supersonic jet. Reaching geosynchronous orbit would take about twenty hours, which made this a very slow journey in the context of space. Cheng Xin recalled a conversation during college where Tianming had pointed out that in principle, it was perfectly possible to achieve spaceflight at low speeds. As long as one maintained an ever-upward speed, one could go into space going as slow as a car or even walking. One could even walk up to the orbit of the moon in this manner, though it would be impossible to step onto the moon—by then, the relative velocity of the moon with respect to the climber would be more than three thousand kilometers per hour, and if one were to attempt to remain at rest with respect to the moon, the result would once again be high-speed astronautics. Cheng Xin clearly recalled that he had said at the end that it would be an amazing sight to be in the vicinity of the moon's orbit and watch the gigantic satellite sweep overhead. She was now experiencing the low-speed spaceflight he had imagined.

The elevator car was shaped like a capsule, but divided into four decks. She was in the top deck, and those who accompanied her were in the lower three decks. No one came up to bother her. She was in the luxurious business-class cabin, like a room in a five-star hotel. There was a comfortable bed and a shower, but the suite was small, about the size of a college dorm room.

She was always thinking about her time in college these days, thinking about Tianming.

At this altitude, the Earth's umbral cone was narrower, and the Sun thus became visible. Everything outside was submerged in the powerful, bright light, and the portholes automatically adjusted to decrease their transparency. Cheng Xin lay on the sofa and watched the guide rail above her through the porthole overhead. The endless straight line seemed to descend directly from the Milky Way. She wanted to see signs of motion against the guide rail, or at least to imagine it. The sight was hypnotic, and eventually she fell asleep.

She heard someone call her name softly, a man's voice. She saw that she was in a college dorm sleeping in the bottom bunk of a bunk bed. But the room was otherwise empty. A streak of light moved across the wall, like streetlights inside a moving car. She looked outside the window and saw that, behind the familiar Chinese parasol tree, the Sun swept across the sky rapidly, rising and setting every few seconds. Even when the Sun was up, however, the sky behind it remained inky black, and the stars shone along with the Sun. The voice continued to call her name. She wanted to get up to look around, but found her body floating up from the bed. Books, cups, her notebook computer, and other objects floated around her. . . .

Cheng Xin woke up with a start, and found herself truly floating in air, hovering a small distance above the sofa. She reached out to pull herself back onto the sofa, but inadvertently pushed herself away. She rose until she was next to the porthole in the ceiling, where she turned around weightlessly and pushed against the glass, successfully sending herself back to the sofa. Everything looked the same in the cabin, except that the weightlessness released some of the settled dust motes, and they sparkled in the sunlight.

She saw that an official from the PDC had come up from the cabin below. It was probably he who had been calling her name earlier. He stared at her, astonished. "Dr. Cheng, I understand this is the first time you've been in space?" he asked. After Cheng Xin nodded, he smiled and shook his head. "But you look like an old spacer."

Cheng Xin herself felt surprised as well. This first experience of weightlessness did not cause her discomfort or anxiety. She felt relaxed, and there was no dizziness or nausea. It was as if she naturally belonged here, belonged to space.

"We're almost there," the official said, pointing up.

Cheng Xin looked up. She saw the guide rail again, but now she could tell they were moving by its surface—a sign that they were slowing down. At the end of the rail, the geosynchronous terminal station was coming into view. It was formed of multiple concentric rings connected together by five radial spokes. The original terminal station was just a small part in the center. The concentric rings were later additions, with the outer rings being newer. The entire structure slowly rotated in place.

Cheng Xin also saw other space buildings appear around her. The dense cluster of buildings in this region was the result of engineers taking advantage of proximity to the space elevator terminal station for transportation of construction materials. The buildings were of different shapes and appeared from the distance as a bunch of intricate toys—only when one swept past at close range could their immensity be felt. Cheng Xin knew that one of these housed the headquarters of the Halo Group, her space construction company. AA was working in it right now, but she couldn't tell which building it was.

The elevator car passed through a massive frame. The dense struts in the frame made the sunlight flicker. By the time the car emerged from the other end of the frame, the terminal station took up most of the view, and the Milky Way twinkled only from the space between the concentric rings. The immense structure pressed down, and as the car entered the station, everything dimmed as though the car was entering a tunnel. A few minutes later, bright lights illuminated the outside: The car was in the terminal hall. The hall spun around the car, and for the first time Cheng Xin felt dizzy. But as the car detached from the guide rail, it was clamped by the platform. After a slight jolt, the car began to spin along with the station, and everything around her seemed to be still again.

Cheng Xin, accompanied by four others, emerged into the circular hall from the car. As their car was the only one at the platform, the hall seemed very empty. Cheng Xin felt a sense of familiarity right away: Although information windows floated everywhere, the main structure of the hall was built from metallic materials that were rare in this age, mainly stainless steel and lead alloys. She could see the marks left by the passage of years everywhere, and she felt herself situated in an old train station instead of in space. The elevator she had ridden was the first space elevator ever built, and this terminal station, completed in Year 15 of the Crisis Era, had been in continuous operation for more than two centuries, even through the Great Ravine. Cheng Xin noticed the guardrails crisscrossing the hall, installed to help people move around in weightlessness. The guardrails were mainly made of stainless steel, though some were made from copper. Observing their surfaces, bearing the marks of countless hands through more than two centuries of service, Cheng Xin was reminded of the deep ruts left in front of ancient city doors.

The rails were leftovers from an earlier age, since everyone now relied on individual tiny thrusters which could be worn on the belt or over the shoulders. They generated enough thrust to propel people around in weightlessness, controlled by a handheld remote. Cheng Xin's companions tried to give her a first lesson in space—how to use the weightless thrusters. But Cheng Xin preferred to navigate around by grabbing on to the guardrails. As they arrived at the exit to the main hall, Cheng Xin paused to admire a few propaganda posters on the wall. These were ancient, and most of them dealt with the construction of the Solar System defense system. In one of the posters, a soldier's figure filled most of the image. He was dressed in a uniform unfamiliar to Cheng Xin, and his fiery eyes stared at the viewer. Below him was a line of large text: *The Earth needs you!* Next to it was an even larger poster in which people of all races and nationalities stood, arms linked, to form a dense wall. Behind them, the blue flag of the UN took up most of the picture. The text on the poster read: *Let us build a new Great Wall for the Solar System with our flesh!* Although Cheng Xin was interested in the posters, they didn't feel familiar. They seemed to harken back to an older style, reminding people of an age before she had even been born.

"These were from the beginning of the Great Ravine," one of the PDC officials traveling with her said.

That had been a brief, despotic age, when the whole world had been militarized before everything, from faith to life, collapsed. . . . But why had these posters been kept until now? To remember, or to forget?

Cheng Xin and the others exited the main hall into a long corridor, whose cross section was also circular. The corridor extended ahead of her for some distance, and she couldn't see to the end. She knew that this was one of the five radial spokes of the station. At first, they moved in total weightlessness, but soon, "gravity" appeared, in the form of centrifugal force. At first, the force was very weak, but it was enough to induce a sense of up and down: the corridor suddenly turned into a deep well, and instead of floating, they were falling. Cheng Xin felt dizzy, but many guardrails protruded from the wall of the "well." If she felt she was falling too fast, she could decelerate by grabbing on to one of the rails.

They passed the intersection between the spoke and the first ring. Cheng Xin looked to the right and left, and saw that the ground rose up on both sides, as though she were at the bottom of a valley. Over the entrances to the ring on both sides were red-glowing signs: *First Ring, Gravity 0.15G*. The wall of the curved corridor of the ring was punctuated by multiple doors, which opened and closed from time to time. Cheng Xin saw many pedestrians. They stood on the floor of the ring due to the microgravity, but they still moved by leaping ahead with the aid of the weightless thrusters.

After passing through the first ring, the weight increased further, and free-falling was no longer safe. Escalators appeared on the wall of the "well," one going up and one going down. Cheng Xin observed the passengers riding up and saw that they were dressed casually, indistinguishable from Earth dwellers. The wall of the well had many information windows of different sizes, and more than a few of them were broadcasting the image of Cheng Xin stepping onto the space elevator more than twenty hours ago. But at the moment, Cheng Xin's four escorts surrounded her, and she was also wearing her wide-framed sunglasses. No one recognized her.

As they descended, they passed through seven more concentric rings. As the diameter of each successive ring grew, the curvature of the corridors to the sides became less noticeable. Cheng Xin felt as though she was passing through strata of history. Each ring used different construction material from the rings before it, and looked newer. Each ring's method of construction and decorative style formed a time capsule of an age: the repressive militaristic uniformity of the Great Ravine; the optimism and romanticism of the latter half of the Crisis Era; the hedonistic freedom and indolence of the Deterrence Era. Before the fourth ring, the cabins in the rings were integrated into the structure of the rings, but starting with the fifth ring, the rings only provided construction spaces, and the buildings in the rings were planned and constructed later as additional fixtures, showing a rich variety of styles. As Cheng Xin descended through the rings, signs of this being a space station gradually faded, and the environment resembled daily life on the surface more. By the time they reached the eighth ring, the outermost ring of the station, the construction style and scenery were indistinguishable from a small city on the surface. The corridor looked like a bustling pedestrian promenade. Add to that the standard gravity of 1G, and Cheng Xin could almost forget that she was in space, thirty-four thousand kilometers above the Earth.

But the city scene soon disappeared, as a small motor vehicle brought them to a place where they could see space again. The entrance to the flat hall was marked with "Port A225," and a few dozen small spacecraft of various designs parked on the smooth, plazalike floor. One side of the hall was completely open to space and the stars spinning around the station. Not too far away from them, a bright light started to glow, illuminating the whole port. Gradually, the light turned from orange to pure blue, and the spaceship that had turned on its engines lifted off the floor, accelerated, and shot into space from the open side of the port. Cheng Xin was witnessing a technological miracle that had become commonplace for others, but she couldn't figure out how it was possible to maintain atmosphere and pressure in space without the area being completely enclosed.

They passed by the rows of spacecraft until they arrived at a small open space at the end of the port. There, a small spaceship—a dinghy, really—sat by itself. Next to it stood a group of people who had apparently been waiting for her. The Milky Way slowly swept by the open side of the port, and its light cast long shadows from the dinghy and those standing next to it, turning the open space into a giant clock, over which the roving shadows acted as hands.

The group next to the dinghy consisted of the special team convened by the PDC and the fleet for this encounter. Cheng Xin knew most of the members—they had attended the Swordholder handover ceremony seven years ago. The two team heads were the rotating chair of the PDC and the chief of staff for the fleet. The rotating chair was new, but the fleet chief was the same person as before. These seven years, the longest in the history of the human race had left indelible marks on their faces. No one said anything as they silently shook hands and silently remembered.

Cheng Xin examined the dinghy before her. Short-range spacecraft now came in a variety of shapes, but the streamlined profile popular in the imagination of past generations was absent. This dinghy had the most common shape: a sphere. It was so regular that Cheng Xin couldn't even tell where the thruster was. The dinghy was about the size of an old medium-sized bus. It had only a serial number and no name. This common vehicle was going to carry her to the meeting with Yun Tianming.

The meeting was to take place at the point where the Earth's and the Sun's gravities balanced each other: a Lagrangian point about 1.5 million kilometers away. The sophons would facilitate the meeting with their real-time link with the First Trisolaran Fleet. There would be both voice and video.

Why conduct the meeting in space? In an age where neutrino communication was possible, being in space wasn't much more isolated than being on the surface of the Earth. Sophon had explained the request as symbolic: The meeting should occur in an isolated environment to show that it was independent of both worlds. The Lagrangian point was chosen to allow Cheng Xin's position to be relatively stable. Also, it was the long-held custom among Trisolarans to conduct meetings at points of balance between celestial bodies.

That much Cheng Xin already knew, but now she was told something much more important.

The fleet chief brought Cheng Xin into the dinghy. There wasn't much room inside, just enough for four people. As soon as the two of them sat down, half of the spherical hull—the part facing them—became transparent, so that they seemed to be sitting inside the helmet of a gigantic space suit. This type of dinghy was chosen in part for its open field of view.

Modern spacecraft no longer had physical controls—the controls were holographic projections—thus, the interior of the hull was completely empty. If a Common Era person came here for the first time, he or she would think this was an empty shell with nothing inside. But Cheng Xin immediately noticed three unusual objects, clearly new additions. These were three circles attached to the hull above the transparent part, colored green, yellow, and red, reminding her of traffic lights from the past. The fleet chief explained:

"These three lights are controlled by Sophon. Your meeting will be monitored throughout by the Trisolarans. As long as they believe the contents of your conversation are acceptable, the green light will stay on. If they wish to warn you about topics verging on the unacceptable, the yellow light will be lit."

The fleet chief paused, and only after a long while, as though he had to prepare himself, did he explain the red light.

"If they think you're being given information you may not receive, the red light will be lit."

He turned around and pointed to the nontransparent part of the hull. Cheng Xin saw a small metallic attachment resembling a weight used on an ancient balance.

"This bomb is controlled by Sophon. It will detonate three seconds after the red light turns on."

"What will be destroyed?" Cheng Xin asked. She wasn't thinking of herself.

"Just our side of the meeting. You don't need to worry about Tianming's safety. Sophon has made it clear that even if the red light is lit, only this dinghy will explode; Tianming will not be harmed in any way.

"The red light may be lit during your conversation. However, even if the meeting completes successfully, the Trisolarans may decide, upon review of the conversation record, to turn on the red light. I'm going to tell you the most important part now—" The fleet chief paused again.

Cheng Xin's gaze remained placid. She nodded at him, encouraging him to continue.

"You must remember that the lights will not be used as a traffic light. They may not warn you before deciding that you've stepped over the line. The green light may change to a red light immediately, without going through the yellow light."

"All right. I understand." Cheng Xin's voice was soft, like a passing breeze.

"Other than the contents of the conversation, Sophon may also light the red light if she discovers recording equipment on the dinghy or some means of transmitting your conversation outside the dinghy. You may rest easy on this point. We've examined this dinghy repeatedly for recording devices, and we've eliminated all communications equipment. The navigation system isn't even capable of keeping a log. Your entire journey will be directed by the shipboard AI system, which will not communicate with the outside world prior to your return. Dr. Cheng, please think through what I've said to be sure you understand the implications."

"If I don't return, then you get nothing."

"I'm glad you see. This is what we want to emphasize. Do as they say, and only talk about private matters between the two of you. Do not mention other topics, not even through hints or metaphors. At all times, remember that if you don't return, Earth gets absolutely nothing."

"But if I do as you say and return, Earth will still get nothing. That is not what I want."

The fleet chief looked at Cheng Xin, but not directly, only at her reflection on the transparent hull. Her image was superimposed against the universe, and her lovely eyes serenely reflected the stars. He seemed to see her as the center of the universe, the stars revolving around her. Once again, he forced himself to not dissuade her from taking a risk.

Instead, he pointed behind him. "This is a miniature hydrogen bomb. Under the old measurement system you're familiar with, its yield is about five kilotons. If . . . it really has to happen, everything will end in a flash. You will not feel it."

Cheng Xin smiled at the fleet chief. "Thank you. I understand."

Five hours later, the dinghy began its journey. The hypergravity of 3G pressed Cheng Xin against the seat—this was the limit on the acceleration an individual without special training could bear. In a window that showed what was behind her, she saw the immense hull of the terminal station reflecting the fire from her dinghy's drive. The tiny dinghy appeared as a spark flying out of a furnace, but the terminal station rapidly shrank, and soon turned into a tiny dot. Only the Earth itself, still imposing, took up half the sky.

The special team had told Cheng Xin again and again that the flight itself would be routine, no more special than the airplane rides she used to take. The distance between the terminal station and the Lagrangian point was about 1.5 million kilometers, or one hundredth of an astronomical unit. This was considered an extremely short spaceflight, and the craft she rode in was well suited for such brief trips. Cheng Xin recalled that three centuries ago, one of the things that had lured her into aerospace engineering was a great accomplishment by humankind during the twentieth century: fifteen men had managed to step onto the moon. Their voyage had only been a fifth as long as the journey she was about to undertake.

Ten minutes later, Cheng Xin got to see a sunrise in space. The Sun slowly rose over the curved edge of the Earth. From such distance, the waves over the Pacific were invisible, and the ocean was like a mirror reflecting sunlight. The clouds appeared as soapy foam over the mirror. From this vantage point, the Sun appeared much smaller than the Earth, like a shining golden egg being birthed by this dark blue world. By the time the Sun had completely emerged from the curved horizon, the side of the Earth facing the Sun turned into a giant crescent. The crescent was so bright that the rest of the Earth merged into dark shadow, and the Sun and the crescent seemed to form a giant symbol hovering in space. Cheng Xin thought of the mark as symbolizing rebirth.

She knew that this could very well be her last sunrise. In the upcoming meeting, even if she and Tianming faithfully followed the rules around their conversation, there was a possibility that the distant Trisolarans would not permit her to live, and she wasn't interested in following the rules at all. But she thought everything was perfect; she had no regrets.

As the dinghy progressed, the lit portion of the Earth expanded. Cheng Xin saw the outlines of the continents, and easily picked out Australia. It resembled a dry leaf floating in the Pacific. The continent was emerging from the shadow, and the terminator was right in the middle of the continent. It was morning in Warburton, and she thought of the desert sunrise seen by Fraisse from the edge of the wood.

Her dinghy swept over the Earth. By the time the curved horizon had finally disappeared over the edge of the viewport, acceleration stopped. As the hypergravity disappeared, Cheng Xin felt as though a pair of arms hugging her tightly had relaxed. The dinghy coasted toward the Sun, and the light from the Sun overwhelmed all the stars. The transparent hull adjusted and dimmed until the Sun was a disc whose brightness was no longer blinding. Cheng Xin reached out to adjust it even more, until the Sun resembled the full moon. She still had six more hours to travel. She drifted in weightlessness, drifted in the moonlight-like sun.

Five hours later, the dinghy turned 180 degrees and the engine came to life for deceleration. As the dinghy turned, Cheng Xin saw the Sun gradually move away, and then the stars and the Milky Way swept past her vision like a long scroll. By the time the dinghy stopped, the Earth was once again at the center of her view. It now looked about as big as the moon from the surface of the Earth, and the immensity it had displayed a few hours ago was gone. Now it looked fragile, like a fetus floating in blue amniotic fluid about to emerge from the warm womb and be exposed to the frigidity and darkness of space.

With the engine turned on, gravity returned to embrace Cheng Xin. The deceleration lasted about half an hour before the drive started to pulse for precision position maneuvers. Finally, gravity disappeared again, and every-thing became quiet.

This was the Lagrangian point. Here, the dinghy was a satellite of the Sun, orbiting in synch with the Earth.

Cheng Xin glanced at her watch. The voyage had been planned very well. She still had ten minutes before the meeting. The space around her was empty, and she struggled to empty her mind as well. She was preparing herself for the task of memorization: The only thing that could retain anything from the meeting was her brain. She had to turn herself into an emotionless audio and video recorder so that during the next two hours she could remember as much as possible of what she saw and heard.

She imagined the corner of space she happened to be in. Here, the Sun's gravity overcame the Earth's, reaching balance, so this place held an extra measure of emptiness compared to other spots in space. She was in this empti-ness of zero, a lonely, independent presence that had no connections to any other part of the cosmos. . . . In this way, she managed to drive her complicated emotions out of her consciousness, until she achieved the blank, transcendent state she wanted.

Not too far ahead of the dinghy, a sophon began to unfold into lower-dimensional space. Cheng Xin saw a sphere about three or four meters in diameter appear a few meters in front of the dinghy. The sphere blocked the Earth and took up most of her view. The surface of the sphere was perfectly reflective, and Cheng Xin could clearly see the reflection of her dinghy and herself. She wasn't sure if the sophon had been lurking inside the dinghy or if it had just arrived.

The reflection on the surface of the sphere disappeared as the sphere turned translucent, like a ball of ice. At times, Cheng Xin thought it resembled a hole dug in space. Next, countless snowflake-like bright spots floated up from deep within the sphere, forming a flickering pattern on the surface. Cheng Xin rec-ognized that this was just white noise, like the random snow seen on a televi-sion screen when there was no reception.

The white noise lasted about three minutes, and then a scene from several light-years away took its place. It was crystal clear, with no signs of distortion or interference.

Cheng Xin had entertained countless guesses as to what she would see. Maybe she would only have voice and text; maybe she would see a brain float-ing in nutrient fluid; maybe she would see Yun Tianming whole. Though she believed that this last possibility was practically impossible, she tried to imagine the environment Tianming would be living in. She thought of innumerable scenarios, but none was like what she actually saw.

A golden field of wheat bathed in sunlight.

The field was about a tenth of an acre. The crop looked to be doing well, and it was time for the harvest. The soil appeared a bit eerie: pure black, and the particles sparkled in the sunlight like innumerable stars. A common shovel was stuck into the black soil next to the field of wheat. It looked perfectly ordinary, and even the handle appeared to be made of wood. A straw hat woven from wheat stalks hung from the top of the shovel—it looked old and well used, and loose stalks stuck out of the worn rim. Behind the wheat field was another field planted with something green, probably vegetables. A breeze passed through, and the wheat rippled.

Above this dark-soiled scene was an alien sky—a dome, to be exact, formed of a knotty mess of intertwined pipes, some thick, some thin, all of which were leaden gray in color. Among the thousands of pipes, two or three glowed red. The light from them was very bright, making them appear as incandescent filaments. The exposed portions of these pipes illuminated the fields and apparently provided the source of energy for the crops. Each illuminated pipe only shone briefly before dimming, to be replaced by another pipe that lit up elsewhere. At each moment, two or three pipes were on. The shifting lights caused the shadows in the field to shift constantly as well, as though the sun were weaving in and out of clouds.

Cheng Xin was taken aback by the chaotic arrangement of the pipes. It wasn't the result of carelessness; on the contrary, to create this kind of utter chaos required great effort and design. The arrangement seemed to find even the hint of a pattern to be taboo. This suggested an aesthetic utterly at odds with human values: Patterns were ugly, but the lack of order was beautiful. Those glowing pipes gave the entire knotty mess a kind of liveliness, like sunlight glanced through clouds. Cheng Xin even wondered whether the arrangement was meant to be an artistic representation of the sun and clouds. But the next moment, she felt the arrangement evoking a giant model of the human brain, and the flickering, glowing pipes represented the formation of each neural feedback loop. . . .

Rationally, she had to reject these fantasies. A far more likely explanation was that the entire system was nothing more than a heat dissipation device, and the farm fields below only took advantage of the lights as a side effect. Going by appearance alone, and without understanding its operation, Cheng Xin intuited that the system showed a kind of engineering ideal that could not be understood by humanity. She felt mystified, but also mesmerized.

A man walked toward her from deep within the wheat field. *Tianming.*

He wore a silver jacket, made out of some kind of reflective film. It looked as old as his straw hat, but was otherwise unremarkable. Cheng Xin couldn't see his pants due to all the wheat, but they were likely made of the same material. As he came closer, Cheng Xin got a better look at his face. He looked young, about the same age as when they had parted three centuries ago. But his physique looked more fit, and his face was tanned. He wasn't gazing in Cheng Xin's direction; instead, he pulled off an ear of wheat, rubbed it in his fingers, blew away the husk, and then tossed the grains into his mouth. He emerged from the field still chewing. Just when Cheng Xin wondered whether Tianming knew she was there, he looked up, smiled, and waved at her.

"Hello, Cheng Xin!" he said. In his eyes was pure joy, a very natural kind of joy, like a farm boy working in the fields greeting a girl from the same village who had come back from the city. The three centuries that had passed did not seem to matter, and neither did the several light-years separating them. They had always been together. Cheng Xin had never imagined this. Tianming's gaze caressed her like a gentle pair of hands, and her high-strung nerves relaxed slightly.

The green light above the viewport came on.

"Hello!" Cheng Xin said. A wave of emotion that had traversed three centuries surged deep within her consciousness, like a volcano preparing to erupt. But she decisively blocked off all emotional outlets, and silently repeated to herself: *Memorize, just memorize, memorize everything.* "Can you see me?"

"Yes." Tianming smiled and nodded, and tossed another grain of wheat into his mouth.

"What are you doing?"

Tianming seemed taken aback by the question. He waved at the field. "Farming."

"For yourself?"

"Of course. How else would I get to eat?"

The Tianming in Cheng Xin's memory looked different. During the Staircase Project, he was a haggard, weak, terminal patient; before then, he was a solitary, alienated college student. But though the Tianming of the past had sealed his heart to the outside world, he had also exposed his state in life—it was possible to tell, at a glance, what his basic story was. The Tianming of the present revealed only maturity. One couldn't read his story at all, though he certainly had stories, stories that probably offered more twists, strange events, and spectacular sights than ten *Odysseys*. Three centuries of drifting alone in the depths of space, an unimaginable life among aliens, the countless tribulations and trials endured in body and spirit—none of these had left any mark on his body. All that was left was maturity, a sunlit maturity, like the swaying stalks of golden wheat behind him.

Tianming was a victor in life.

"Thank you for the seeds you sent," Tianming said. His tone was sincere. "I planted them all. Generation after generation, they've done well. I couldn't get the cucumbers to grow though—they're tough."

Cheng Xin chewed over Tianming's words. *How does he know that I sent him the seeds? Did they tell him? Or . . .*

"I thought you would have to grow them using aeroculture and aquaculture. I never thought there would be soil on a spaceship."

Tianming bent down and picked up a handful of black soil, letting the particles seep out from between his fingers. The soil sparkled as it fell. "This is made from meteoroids. Soil like this—"

The green light went off and the yellow light went on.

Apparently, Tianming could see the warning as well. He stopped, smiled, and raised a hand. The expression and gesture were clearly intended for those listening in. The yellow light went off and the green light went on again.

"How long has it been?" Cheng Xin asked. She deliberately asked an ambiguous question that could be interpreted many ways: how long he'd been planting; or how long his brain had been implanted in a cloned body; or how long ago the Staircase probe had been captured; or something else. She wanted to leave him plenty of room to pass on information.

"A long time."

Tianming's answer was even more ambiguous. He looked as calm as before, but the yellow light must have terrified him. He didn't want Cheng Xin to be hurt.

"At first I knew nothing about farming," said Tianming. "I wanted to learn by watching others. But, as you know, there are no real farmers anymore, so I had to figure it out myself. I learned slowly, so it's a good thing that I don't eat much."

Cheng Xin's earlier guess had been confirmed. What Tianming was really saying was very clear: If the Earth still had real farmers, he would have been able to observe them. In other words, he could see the information gathered

by the sophons on Earth! This at least showed that Tianming had a close relationship with Trisolaran society.

"The wheat looks really good. Is it time for the harvest?"

"Yes. This has been a good year."

"A good year?"

"Oh, if the engines are operating at high power, then I have a good year,
otherwise—"

The yellow light came on.

Another guess had been confirmed. The mess of pipes in the ceiling really
was some kind of cooling system for the engines. Their light came from the
antimatter propulsion system on the ship.

"All right, let's talk about something else." Cheng Xin smiled. "You want to
know what I've been up to? After you left—"

"I know everything. I've always been with you."

Tianming's tone was steady and calm, but Cheng Xin's heart quaked. Yes,
he had always been with her, observing her life through the sophons. He must
have seen how she had become the Swordholder, how she had thrown away
that red switch in the last moments of the Deterrence Era, how she had endured in Australia, how she had lost her sight from extreme pain, until, finally,
how she had picked up that tiny capsule. . . . He had gone through all these
trials with her. It was easy to imagine that when he had seen her struggle
through her hell from several light-years away, he must have suffered even
more pain. If she had known earlier that this man who loved her had crossed
the light-years to keep watch over her, she would have been comforted. But
Cheng Xin had thought Tianming lost forever in the vastness of space, and
most of the time, she had never believed that he still existed.

"If I had known . . ." Cheng Xin muttered, as if to herself.

"You couldn't have." Tianming shook his head.

The emotions Cheng Xin had pushed deep down surged again. She forced
herself to not cry.

"Then . . . what about your experience? Can you tell me anything?" Cheng
Xin asked. This was a naked attempt at gathering intelligence. But she had to
take a step.

"Hmmm, let me think . . ." Tianming pondered.

The yellow light came up. Tianming hadn't even said anything. This was a
serious warning.

Tianming shook his head resolutely. "I can't tell you anything. Absolutely
nothing."

Cheng Xin said nothing. She knew that as far as her mission was concerned, she had done all she could. All she could do now was to wait and see what Tianming wanted to do.

"We can't talk like this," said Tianming, and sighed. Then, with his eyes, he said more: *for your sake.*

Yes, it was too dangerous. The yellow light had gone on three times already.

Cheng Xin sighed in her heart. Tianming had given up. Her mission would be unfulfilled. But there was no other choice. She understood.

Once they had set aside the mission, this space that contained them, a few light-years across, became their secret world. Indeed, between the two of them, they needed no language; their eyes were able to say everything they needed. Now that she was no longer so focused on the mission, Cheng Xin could feel even more meaning in Tianming's gaze. She was brought back to her college days, when Tianming had looked at her often in this way. He had been discreet, but her girlish instincts had felt him. Now, his gaze was infused with his maturity, and the sunlight crossed light-years to submerge her in warmth and happiness.

Cheng Xin wanted this silence to last forever, but Tianming spoke again. "Cheng Xin, do you remember how we used to spend our time when we were little?"

Cheng Xin shook her head. The question was unexpected and incomprehensible. *When we were little?* But she successfully hid her surprise.

"So many nights, we'd call each other and chat before going to bed. We made up stories and told them to each other. You always made up better stories. How many stories did we tell each other? At least a hundred?"

"Yes, I think so. A lot." Cheng Xin used to be unable to lie, but she was surprised to find herself performing well.

"Do you remember any of those stories?"

"Not many. I've moved far away from childhood."

"But it's not so far away from me. During these years, I've told those stories—yours and mine—again and again."

"To yourself?"

"No, not to myself. I came here, and I felt the need to give this world something. But what? After much thinking, I decided that I could bring childhood to this world, and so I told them our stories. The children here love them. I even put out a collection, *Fairy Tales from Earth*, which was very popular. This book belongs to both of us—I didn't plagiarize you; all the stories you told me still have your name in the byline. So you're a famous author here."

Based on the still very limited knowledge humans had of the Trisolarans, sex among them involved the two partners melding their bodies into one. Thereafter, the combined body would split into three to five new lives. These were their descendants, and the "children" referred to by Tianming. But these individuals inherited part of their parents' memories, and were relatively mature at birth, which differentiated them from human children. Trisolarans really didn't have childhood. Both Trisolaran and human scholars believed that this biological difference was one of the root causes of the great differences between their cultures and societies.

Cheng Xin became anxious again. She knew now that Tianming had not given up, and the key moment was here. She had to do something, but she had to be very, very careful. Smiling, she said, "Although we can't talk about anything else, surely we can talk about those stories. Those belong only to us."

"The stories I made up or the ones you made up?"

"Tell the ones I made up. Bring me back to my childhood." Cheng Xin did not hesitate at all. Even she was surprised at how quickly she had caught on to Tianming's plan.

"All right. Then let's not talk about anything else. Just the stories. Your stories." Tianming spread his hands and looked up, clearly addressing those monitoring the conversation. His meaning was clear: *You shouldn't object to this, right? Everything is safe.* Then he turned to Cheng Xin. "We have about an hour. Which story? Hmmm . . . how about 'The New Royal Painter'?"

And so, Tianming began to tell the story. His voice was deep and soothing, as though he was chanting an ancient song. Cheng Xin tried hard to memorize, but she was gradually absorbed by the story. Much time passed as Tianming spun his fairy tale. He told three stories, all connected to each other: "The New Royal Painter," "The Glutton's Sea," and "Prince Deep Water." After he finished the last story, the sophon put up a countdown, indicating that they had only one minute left.

The moment of parting was at hand.

Cheng Xin awakened from the dream of the fairy tales. Something struck her heart hard, and it was almost unbearable. She said, "The universe is grand, but life is grander. We're certain to meet again." Only when she was done did she realize she had almost repeated Sophon's farewell.

"Then let's pick a spot to meet, somewhere other than the Earth, somewhere in the Milky Way."

"How about at the star you gave me? Our star." Cheng Xin didn't even need to think.

"All right. At our star!"

As they gazed at each other across the light-years, the countdown reached zero, and the image disappeared, returning to the snow of white noise. Then the unfolded sophon turned purely reflective again.

The green light went off. Now none of the lights were on. Cheng Xin understood that she was now on the precipice of death. On a ship in the First Trisolaran Fleet several light-years away, the conversation between her and Tianming was being replayed and examined. The red light of death could go on at any moment, and there would be no warning yellow light.

Against the unfolded spherical surface of the sophon, Cheng Xin saw the reflection of her own dinghy and herself. The half of her dinghy facing the sophon was completely transparent, like an intricate locket dangling from a necklace, and she herself was a picture placed in the locket. She was dressed in a snow-white lightweight space suit, and she appeared pure, youthful, beautiful. She was surprised by her own eyes: clear, placid, showing nothing of the surging waves inside her. She felt comforted as she imagined this lovely locket hanging on Tianming's heart.

After an unknown amount of time had passed, the sophon disappeared. The red light did not come on. The space outside looked the same as before: The blue Earth appeared again in the distance, and behind it the Sun. They were witness to all.

She felt hypergravity again. The dinghy's thruster was accelerating, and she was going home.

During the few hours of the return voyage, Cheng Xin adjusted the dinghy's hull so that it was completely solid. She sealed herself in and turned herself into a memorization machine. Again and again, she repeated Tianming's words and his stories. The acceleration stopped; the dinghy coasted; the thruster turned around; the dinghy decelerated—she didn't notice any of it. Finally, after a series of tremors, the door opened, and the terminal station port's light spilled in.

Two of the officials who had accompanied her to the station met her. Their faces were impassive. After a simple greeting, they brought Cheng Xin across the port to a sealed door.

"Dr. Cheng, you need to rest. Don't dwell on the past. We never held much hope that you'd get anything of use," the PDC official said. And then he gestured for Cheng Xin to enter the sealed door that had just opened.

Cheng Xin had thought this was the exit to the port, but she found herself in an extremely small room. All the walls were made of some dark metal. After the door closed behind her, she couldn't even see the seams. This was not a place of rest. It was simply furnished, with a small desk and a chair. On top of the desk was a microphone. Microphones were rarely seen in this age, and only used for high-fidelity recording. The air in the room had an acrid smell, almost sulfuric, and her skin felt itchy—the air was clearly heavy with static electricity.

The room was filled with people: All the members of the special team were here. As soon as the two officials who had received her entered, their expressions changed. They now looked as anxious and concerned as the rest.

"This is a blind zone for the sophons," someone said to Cheng Xin. Only then did she realize that humans had finally achieved the technology to shield themselves from the ever-present listeners, though it was only possible within extremely confined spaces like this one.

The fleet chief said, "Please recite the entirety of your conversation. Don't omit any details that you can recall. Every word may be important."

Then the members of the special team left the room one by one. The last to depart was an engineer who explained to Cheng Xin that the walls of the sophon-free room were all electrified, and she should be careful to not touch them.

Only Cheng Xin was left. She sat down at the desk and began to record everything she could remember. An hour and ten minutes later, she was done. She drank a bit of water and milk, took a brief break, and began to record a second time, then a third. When she was ready to record for the fourth time, she was asked to recount the events backwards, with the latest events first. The fifth recording was done under the guidance of a team of psychologists. They used some drug to keep her in a semi-hypnotized state, and she didn't even know what she said. Before she knew it, more than six hours had passed.

After she had finished the last recounting, the special team filled the room again. They embraced Cheng Xin and shook her hand. Hot tears flowed, and they told her she had accomplished a heroic deed. But Cheng Xin remained numb, like a memorization machine.

Only when she had returned to the comfortable cabin in the space elevator did the memorization machine in her brain shut off. She became a person again. Extreme exhaustion and waves of emotion overwhelmed her, and as she faced the approaching blue sphere of the Earth, she began to cry. Only one voice echoed in her mind:

Our star. Our star . . .

At that moment, on the surface more than thirty thousand kilometers below, Sophon's house went up in flames. The robot that had been Sophon's avatar was burnt up as well. Before this, she had proclaimed to the world that all the sophons in the Solar System would be withdrawn.

People only half-believed Sophon. It was likely that only the robot was gone, but a few sophons remained on the Earth and in the Solar System. But it was also possible that she was telling the truth. Sophons were precious resources. What remained of Trisolaran civilization was in a fleet of spaceships, and they wouldn't be able to construct any new sophons for a long, long time. Besides, keeping watch over the Solar System and the Earth no longer had much meaning. If the fleet entered a blind region for the sophons, they might lose the sophons in the Solar System forever.

If the last situation occurred, then the Trisolarans and humanity would lose all contact, and once again become cosmic strangers. A three-century-long history of warfare and resentment would turn into so much ephemera in the universe. Even if they were to meet again because of fate—as Sophon had predicted—it would be in the distant future. But neither world knew if they had a future.

Broadcast Era, Year 7
Yun Tianming's Fairy Tales

The first meeting of the Intelligence Decipherment Committee (IDC) was also conducted in a sophon-free room. Although most people now favored the view that the sophons were gone, and the Solar System and the Earth were now "clean," they still took this precaution. Their main concern was that if the sophons were still present, they might endanger Yun Tianming.

The conversation between Tianming and Cheng Xin was publicized, but the real intelligence given by Tianming, the content of the three fairy tales, was kept in absolute secrecy. For a transparent, modern society, keeping such important information secret was a difficult task for both the UN and Fleet International. But the nations of the world soon reached consensus on this point: If the fairy tales were revealed, the world would be swept up by the enthusiasm of trying to decipher them, thereby exposing Tianming. The safety of Tianming wasn't just important for him individually, he, to date, the only person embedded in an alien society. His position was irreplaceable for humanity's future survival.

The secret decipherment of Tianming's message was another sign of the UN's authority and operational capabilities; it was another step on the way to a world government.

This sophon-free room was larger than the one Cheng Xin had used on the terminal station, though it wasn't by any means spacious for a conference room. The force field necessary to keep sophons out could enclose only a limited volume.

About thirty people were in attendance. Other than Cheng Xin, two other Common Era individuals were also present: the particle-accelerator engineer

Bi Yunfeng and the physicist Cao Bin—both former candidates for the Sword-holder position.

Everyone wore high-voltage protective suits because the metallic walls of the sophon-free room were electrified. In particular, everyone was required to wear protective gloves, lest someone tap a wall out of habit, in an attempt to summon an information window. No electronics could function within the force field, thus the room had no information windows at all. To help the force field stay evenly distributed, equipment within the room was reduced to a minimum. Only chairs were provided, and there was no table. Since the protective suits were requisitioned from electrical engineers, the meeting within the metallic room resembled an ancient pre-shift gathering on a factory floor.

No one complained about the crowded, rough conditions, or the acrid smell in the air and the tingling on the skin brought about by the electrified air. After living for nearly three centuries under the constant surveillance of the sophons, being free of the alien voyeurs brought a sudden, fresh sense of relief. The ability to shield space from sophons had been developed soon after the Great Resettlement. It was rumored that those who had entered the very first sophon-free room came down with something called "screen syndrome": They talked incessantly as if they were drunk, and bared all their secrets to their companions. A reporter described the condition this way: "In this narrow slice of heaven, the people opened their hearts. Our gazes were no longer veiled."

The IDC was a combined effort by Fleet International and the UN PDC to decipher Yun Tianming's message. It oversaw the work of twenty-five working groups focusing on different subjects and areas of expertise. The attendees at this meeting were not experts or scientists, but the IDC committee members, who were also the leaders of the working groups.

The IDC chair first thanked Yun Tianming and Cheng Xin on behalf of Fleet International and the UN. He called Tianming the bravest warrior in the history of the human race. He was the first human to successfully survive in an alien world. Alone, deep in the heart of the enemy, situated in an unimaginable environment, he fought on and brought hope to an Earth in crisis. Cheng Xin, on the other hand, had successfully retrieved the intelligence from Tianming through a combination of wits and guts.

In a soft voice, Cheng Xin requested a chance to speak. She stood up and surveyed all those present. "All this is the result of the Staircase Project. This endeavor cannot be separated from a particular man. Three centuries ago, his steadfastness, decisive leadership, and peerless creativity allowed the Staircase Project to overcome multiple difficulties and become reality. The man I'm talking about is Thomas Wade, chief of the PDC Strategic Intelligence Agency. I think we should thank him as well."

The conference room sank into silence. No one seconded Cheng Xin's suggestion. For most people, Wade was the very symbol of the darkness in Common Era human nature, the very antithesis of the lovely woman—who had almost been killed by Wade—standing in front of them. They shivered just thinking about him.

The chair—he happened to also be the PIA's current chief, a successor to Wade's position, though they were divided by three centuries—said nothing in response to Cheng Xin's proposal. He simply continued down the agenda for the meeting. "The committee has established a basic principle and hope for the decipherment process. We believe the message is unlikely to contain any concrete technical information, but will more likely point out the correct direction for research. It may contain the guide to the correct theoretical framework for unknown technologies such as lightspeed spaceflight or the cosmic safety notice. If we can get that far, it will bring tremendous hope to humanity.

"In total, we gathered two pieces of intelligence: the conversation between Dr. Cheng and Yun Tianming, and the three stories he told. Preliminary analysis points to the important information being hidden entirely within the three stories. We won't be paying much attention to the conversation in the future, but I will summarize what we've gleaned from it here.

"First, we know that in order to send this message, Yun Tianming had to do a lot of preparatory work. He created over a hundred fairy tales, and mixed in three containing secret intelligence. He told these stories and published them over a long period of time to familiarize the Trisolarans with them—no easy task. If the Trisolarans hadn't discovered the secrets contained within them during that process, they'll likely continue to treat these stories as harmless in the future. But even so, he tried to place yet another layer of protection around the stories."

The chair turned to Cheng Xin. "I want to ask a question. Did you really know each other as kids, as Tianming said?"

Cheng Xin shook her head. "No. We met only in college. He and I did come from the same city, but we didn't go to the same primary or secondary schools."

"That bastard! His lie could have killed Cheng Xin!" yelled AA, who was sitting next to Cheng Xin. The others gave her angry looks. She wasn't a member of the IDC, and was allowed to attend only at Cheng Xin's insistence as her assistant. AA had once been an accomplished astronomer, but because her CV wasn't very long, the others looked down on her. They all thought Cheng Xin ought to have someone more qualified to be her technical aide, and even Cheng Xin herself sometimes forgot that AA was a scientist.

A PIA officer said, "He didn't take a great risk with the lie. Their childhoods predated the Crisis Era, before the sophons had even arrived on the Earth. And back then they couldn't have been targets of sophon surveillance."

"But they could check records from the Common Era."

"It's not so easy to get records of two children from before the Crisis Era. Even if they somehow managed to check the household registration records or school records and found out that they hadn't gone to the same elementary school or middle school, they still couldn't rule out the possibility that they did know each other. And there's something else you aren't thinking of." The PIA officer didn't bother hiding his contempt for AA's lack of professional experience. "Tianming could direct the sophons. He must have checked the records already."

The chair continued. "The risk had to be taken. By attributing the three stories to Cheng Xin, he further convinced the enemy that these tales were innocuous. During the hour it took to tell the stories, the yellow light never came on. We also found out that by the time Tianming finished telling the last story, the deadline set by Sophon had already elapsed. The Trisolarans had, as a gesture of compassion, extended the encounter by six minutes so that Tianming could finish his story. This confirms that they really thought the stories harmless. Tianming credited her for a specific reason: to show us that the three stories contained important intelligence.

"There's not much else that we could get out of the conversation. We do all agree that Tianming's final words are very important." The chair waved his right hand in the air out of habit, in an attempt to invoke an information window. After noticing that there was no response, he went on awkwardly. "'Then let's pick a spot to meet, somewhere other than the Earth, somewhere in the Milky Way.' He meant two things by this: One, he was hinting that he would never be able to return to the Solar System. Two—" The chair paused, and waved his hand again, as if trying to dispel something. "It's not important. Let's just go on."

The air in the room grew heavier. Everyone knew what the chair was going to say: *Yun Tianming had very little faith that the Earth would survive.*

A document with a blue cover was distributed to the attendees. In this age, it was very rare to see paper documents. There was only a serial number, no title.

"The document can only be read in here. Do not bring it outside this room, and do not record it in any way. For most of you, this will be your first time reading it. Let's begin."

The room quieted. Everyone started to read these three fairy tales that might save human civilization.

The First Tale of Yun Tianming
"The New Royal Painter"

━━━━━

A long time ago, there was a kingdom called the Storyless Kingdom.

This kingdom had no stories. For a kingdom, not having any stories was a good thing. The people of such a kingdom were the happiest. Stories meant twists and catastrophes.

The Storyless Kingdom had a wise king, a kind queen, a group of just, capable ministers, and hardworking, honest common people. Life in the kingdom was as placid as a mirror: Yesterday was like today, and today is like tomorrow; last year was like this year, and this year is like next year. There were never any stories.

Until the princes and the princess grew up.

The king had two sons: Prince Deep Water and Prince Ice Sand. He also had a daughter: Princess Dewdrop.

As a child, Prince Deep Water had gone to Tomb Island in the middle of the Glutton's Sea and never returned. As for why, that's a story for later.

Prince Ice Sand grew up by the side of the king and queen, and they worried about him a great deal. The child was smart, but from a young age, he showed a cruel streak. He directed the servants to collect small animals from outside the palace, and he pretended he was the emperor of the animals. His "subjects" were his slaves, and if they disobeyed him even a little, he ordered them beheaded. Often, at the end of one of his play sessions, all the animals were dead, and he stood in a pool of blood, laughing hysterically. . . .

As he grew older, the prince became more restrained. He was a man of few words, and his gaze was somber. But the king knew that the wolf had only hidden his teeth, and in Prince Ice Sand's heart was a hibernating poisonous snake, waiting for the right moment to emerge. Ultimately, the king decided to not make him the crown prince, instead designating Princess Dewdrop the heir apparent. The Storyless Kingdom would eventually have a queen regnant.

If the good character the king and queen passed on to their children was a fixed quantity, then Princess Dewdrop must have inherited the portion Prince Ice Sand lacked. She was smart, kind, and beautiful beyond measure. When she walked about during the day, the sun dimmed its light, shamed by the comparison; when she took a stroll at night, the moon opened its eyes wide to get a better look; when she spoke, the birds stopped twittering to listen; and when she traipsed over barren ground, flowers bloomed. The people loved the thought of having her as their queen, and the ministers were certain to dedicate themselves to helping her. Even Prince Ice Sand voiced no objections, though his gaze became even more somber and cold.

And so, story came to the Storyless Kingdom.

The king made his announcement about the new plan of succession on his sixtieth birthday. On that night, the kingdom celebrated: Fireworks turned the sky into a splendid garden, and the brilliant lights everywhere transformed the palace into a crystalline, magical place. There was laughter and joyful conversation everywhere, and wine flowed like rivers. . . .

Everyone was happy, and even Prince Ice Sand's cold heart seemed to have melted. Contrary to his typical moody silence, he humbly wished his father a happy birthday, and expressed his desire that the king live as long as the sun, bathing the kingdom with his light. He also declared his support for the king's decision, saying that Dewdrop really was better suited to be the monarch than he. He congratulated his little sister and said he hoped that she would learn more of the skills for ruling a kingdom from their father so that she could discharge her future duties well. His sincerity and generosity moved everyone present.

"My son, I'm greatly pleased to see you like this," the king said, and caressed the prince's head. "I want it to be like this moment, always."

A minister suggested that a large painting of the scene should be made and hung in the palace to help remember this night.

The king shook his head. "The royal painter is old. The world is shrouded by a fog in his eyes, and his hands tremble so much that he can no longer capture the joy in our faces."

"I was just about to get to that." Prince Ice Sand bowed deeply. "Father, allow me to present you with a new painter."

The prince turned and nodded, and the new painter came in. He was an older boy, about fourteen or fifteen years of age. Wrapped in a friar's gray hooded mantle, he resembled a terrified mouse among the bejeweled guests standing in the splendor of the palace. As he approached, he huddled and compressed his already-thin body to be even smaller, as though he were trying to avoid invisible brambles all around him.

The king was a bit disappointed by the sight. "He's so young! Does he have enough skill?"

The prince bowed again. "Father, this is Needle-Eye, from He'ershingenmosiken. He's the best student of the great painter Master Ethereal. He began studying with the master at the age of five, and after ten years, has learned everything the great man can teach him. He is as sensitive to the colors and shapes of the world as we are to a red-hot branding iron. This sensitivity is then fixed and expressed by his paintbrush. Other than Master Ethereal himself, there is none with such skill in the world." The prince turned to Needle-Eye. "As the royal painter, you may look at the king directly without a breach in etiquette."

Needle-Eye looked up at the king, and then lowered his eyes again.

The king was surprised. "Child, your gaze is as piercing as a sword unsheathed next to a roaring fire. It's at odds with your youth."

Needle-Eye spoke for the first time. "Your Majesty, dread sovereign, please excuse a lowly painter if he has given offense. My eyes are a painter's eyes. A painter must paint first in the heart. I have already drawn in my heart an image of you, and of your dignity and wisdom. These I will transfer to the painting."

"You may also look at the queen," the prince said.

Needle-Eye looked at the queen, then lowered his eyes. "Your Majesty, most honored queen, please forgive a lowly painter's breach of decorum. I have already drawn in my heart an image of you, and of your nobility and elegance. These I will transfer to the painting."

"Look at the princess, the future queen regnant. You must paint her as well."

Needle-Eye took even less time to look at the princess. After the briefest of glances, he lowered his head and said, "Your Royal Highness, beloved princess of the people, please condone my lapse in courtly habits. Your beauty pains me like the midday sun, and I will, for the first time, feel the inadequacy of my paintbrush. But I have already drawn in my heart an image of you, and of your nonpareil loveliness. These I will transfer to the painting."

Then the prince asked Needle-Eye to look at each minister. He did, resting his gaze only briefly on each face. He lowered his eyes. "Your Honors, please excuse a lowly painter's offenses. I have already drawn in my heart an image of you, and of your talents and intellects. These I will transfer to the painting."

The celebration continued, and Prince Ice Sand pulled Needle-Eye into a corner. In a whisper, he asked, "Have you memorized all of them?"

Needle-Eye kept his head low, his face entirely hidden within the shadow of his hood. The cape appeared empty, containing only shadows and no substance. "Yes, my king."

"Everything?"

"Everything, my king. I can now paint a picture of each strand of hair on their bodies and head, and it will be an exact replica of the original."

The celebration ended after midnight. The lights in the palace went out, one after another. It was the darkest hour before dawn: The moon had already set, and dark clouds, like a curtain, veiled the sky from west to east. The earth was submerged in ink. A chill wind blew through, and birds shivered in their nests, while terrified flowers folded their petals together.

Like ghosts, two horses emerged from the palace and sped west. The riders were Needle-Eye and Prince Ice Sand. They came to an underground bunker a few miles from the palace. It seemed sunken into the deepest sea of night: dank, gloomy, like the belly of a cold-blooded beast in deep slumber. Their two shadows swayed and flickered in torchlight, and their bodies were but two dark spots at the end of the long shadows. Needle-Eye took a scroll out of a canvas bag and unrolled it: a painting, about as long as a man was tall. It was the portrait of an old man. White hair and beard surrounded his face like silver flames, and his piercing gaze was very similar to Needle-Eye's, though endowed with more depth. The portrait showed off the skill of the painter— lifelike, with every detail captured.

"My king, this is—was—my teacher, Master Ethereal."

The prince nodded. "Excellent. It was a smart decision to paint him first."

"Yes, I had to, so that he would not paint me first." With great care, Needle-Eye hung the portrait on the damp wall. "All right, now I can get to work on the new pictures for you."

From a corner of the bunker, Needle-Eye retrieved a roll of something snowy white. "My king, this is a section of the trunk of a snow-wave tree of He'ershingenmosiken. When the tree reaches a hundred years of age, the trunk can be unrolled like paper—the perfect medium for painting. My magic is only effective when I paint on snow-wave paper." He placed the roll on a stone table, unrolled a section, and pressed it under an obsidian slab. Then he took a sharp knife and cut the paper against the edge of the slab. When he lifted off the slab, the section of cut paper was pressed flat against the table. The pure white surface seemed to glow by itself.

The painter retrieved his implements from the canvas bag and laid them out. "My king, look at these brushes, made from the ear tufts of the wolves found in He'ershingenmosiken. The paints are also from there: The red is made from the blood of giant bats; the black is the ink of squids caught in the deep sea; the blue and the yellow are extracted from meteorites. . . . All the paints must be mixed with the tears of a species of giant bird called the moon-blanket bird—"

"Just get on with it," the prince said.

"Of course, of course. Who should I paint first?"

"The king."

Needle-Eye picked up his brush. He worked casually, a dab here, a streak there. Gradually, various colors appeared on the paper, but no shape could be discerned. It was as if the paper had been laid out in a multicolored rain, and drops of all hues continuously fell onto the paper. Over time, the paper was filled with colors—a chaotic swirl, like a garden trampled by rampaging horses. The brush continued to glide through this maze of colors, as though the paint-er's hand no longer guided it, but it was leading the painter's hand. Puzzled, the prince watched from the side. He wanted to ask questions, but the move-ments of the colors emerging and gathering had a hypnotic effect, and he was mesmerized.

Then, in a moment, as though a rippling surface suddenly froze, all the random spots connected to each other, and all the colors had meaning. Shapes appeared, and quickly turned crystal clear.

The prince saw a portrait of the king. The king was dressed like he had been earlier at the palace: a golden crown on his head and a magnificent ceremonial robe draped over his body. But the expression on his face was different: There was no longer dignity and wisdom in his eyes. Instead, a complex mixture of emotions could be detected: awakening from a dream, confusion, shock, sorrow . . . and behind them all was a terror that couldn't be fully expressed, as though his closest companion was attacking him with a sword.

"The portrait of the king is finished," said Needle-Eye.

"Very good." The prince nodded at the portrait. The torches reflected in his irises, as though his soul burned in deep wells.

Miles away in the palace, the king disappeared from his bedchamber. In his bed, held up by posts carved into the shapes of four gods, the blankets still retained his body heat, and the sheets still retained the impression of his weight. But of his body, there was no trace.

The prince picked up the finished painting and threw it on the floor. "I will have this mounted and framed and hang it on the wall here. I'll come here from time to time to look at it. Paint the queen next."

Needle-Eye flattened another sheet of snow-wave paper with the obsidian slab, and began to paint the queen's portrait. This time, the prince did not stand to the side to observe, but paced around in the bunker. The empty space echoed with his repetitive footsteps. This time, the painting was done in only half the time it took to do the first.

"My king, the portrait of the queen is finished."

"Very good."

In the palace, the queen disappeared from her bedchamber. In her bed, held up by posts carved into the shapes of four angels, the blankets still retained her body heat, and the sheets still retained the impression of her weight. But of her body, there was no trace.

In the garden outside the palace, a hound seemed to detect something and barked loudly a few times. But the sounds were instantaneously swallowed up by the boundless darkness, and it fell silent in fear. Trembling as it shrank into seclusion, it melded with the night.

"Is the princess next?" asked Needle-Eye.

"No, paint the ministers first. They are more dangerous. Of course, paint only those ministers who are loyal to my father. Do you remember them?"

"Of course, I remember everything. I can paint a picture of each strand of hair on their bodies and head—"

"Just do it. Hurry. You must finish before sunrise."

"That will not be a problem, my king. Before dawn, I will paint a portrait of each minister loyal to the old king, and the princess."

Needle-Eye flattened several sheets of snow-wave paper and began to paint like mad. Every time he finished a portrait, the subject disappeared from his or her bed. As the night flew by, the enemies of Prince Ice Sand turned one by one into pictures on the wall of the bunker.

Princess Dewdrop was awakened by insistent, loud knocks. No one had ever dared to knock on her door like this before. She got up and came to the door, which had just been opened by Auntie Wide.

Auntie Wide had been Dewdrop's wet nurse, and then cared for her as she grew up. The princess felt closer to her than even her own mother, the queen. Auntie Wide stared at the captain of the palace guards outside the door, whose armor still gave off the chill air of the night.

"Have you gone mad? How dare you wake the princess! She hasn't been sleeping well the last few nights."

The captain ignored Auntie Wide. He bowed slightly to Dewdrop. "Princess, someone wants to see you." Then he stepped aside, revealing an old man.

The old man's white hair and beard surrounded his face like silver flames. His gaze was both sharp and deep. This was the man who had been in the first portrait shown to the prince by Needle-Eye. His face and cape were caked with grime, his boots were covered in mud, and he carried a large canvas bag on his back; clearly, he had been on a long journey.

But, oddly, he was holding up an umbrella. Stranger still was the fashion in which he held it: The umbrella spun nonstop in his hand. A closer examination of the umbrella revealed his reason: The pole and the canopy were both pure black, and at the tip of each rib was a small sphere made of some translucent, weighty stone. The stretchers for the ribs within the umbrella were all broken and could not hold the canopy up. Only by spinning the umbrella continuously to make the stones fly up could the canopy be kept open.

"How can you allow random strangers in here? And such a strange old man at that," said Auntie Wide.

"The sentries stopped him, of course, but he said"—the captain of the guards gave an anxious look to the princess—"that the king is already gone."

"What are you talking about? You *are* mad!" Auntie Wide shouted.

But the princess said nothing. Her hands clutched at the front of her nightgown.

"But the king really has disappeared, as has the queen. My men said that both bedchambers were empty."

The princess cried out and held on to Auntie Wide for support.

The old man spoke. "Your Royal Highness, please let me explain."

"Master, please come in," the princess said. Then she turned to the captain. "Guard this door."

Still spinning the umbrella, the old man bowed to the princess, as though respecting her for her calmness in the face of a crisis.

"Why are you spinning that umbrella like some clown?" Auntie Wide asked.

"I must keep this umbrella open lest I disappear like the king and the queen."

"Then come in with the umbrella," the princess said. Auntie Wide opened the door more so that the old man could come in with the spinning umbrella.

Once inside, the man set down the canvas bag on his back and let out an exhausted sigh. But the umbrella never stopped moving in his hand, and the small stone balls along the rim of the canopy flickered in the candlelight, casting bright spots along the walls like racing stars.

"I am Ethereal, a painter from He'ershingenmosiken. The new royal painter, Needle-Eye, is—was—my student."

"I've met him," said the princess.

"Did he look at you?" Ethereal asked, anxious.

"Yes, of course."

"Terrible news, Princess. Terrible!" Ethereal sighed. "He is a devil. With his devilish art, he paints people into pictures."

"That's a lot of wasted breath," said Auntie Wide. "Isn't the job of a painter to paint people into pictures?"

"You misunderstand me," said Ethereal. "After he paints a portrait, the subject is gone. A live person turns into a dead picture."

"Then we must dispatch men to kill him right away."

The captain poked his head into the room. "I've sent all the guards. We can't find him. I wanted to find the minister of war and ask him to mobilize the capital garrison. But Master Ethereal said that the minister of war is probably already gone as well."

Ethereal shook his head. "More soldiers won't be of any use. Prince Ice Sand and Needle-Eye are certainly no longer anywhere near the palace. Needle-Eye could be painting anywhere in the world and still kill everyone here."

"Did you say Prince Ice Sand?" asked Auntie Wide.

"Yes. The prince wants to wield Needle-Eye as a weapon and eliminate the king and all those loyal to him, so that he can become the king."

Ethereal saw that the princess, Auntie Wide, and the captain of the guards were not surprised by this revelation.

"We have to worry about the matter at hand! Needle-Eye could be painting the princess any second—he might already be doing it right now." Auntie Wide wrapped her arms around the princess, as if she could keep her safe.

Ethereal continued. "Only I can stop Needle-Eye. He's already painted me, but this umbrella can ensure that I don't disappear. If I paint him, he'll be gone."

"Then start painting!" said Auntie Wide. "I'll hold up the umbrella for you."

Ethereal shook his head again. "No. The magic only works if I paint on snow-wave paper. But the paper I have with me hasn't been flattened, and cannot be used for painting."

Auntie Wide opened the master painter's canvas bag and retrieved a section of a snow-wave tree. The bark had already been peeled off, revealing the paper roll underneath. Auntie Wide and the princess unrolled a section, and the white paper seemed to brighten the room. They tried to flatten the paper on the floor, but no matter how much they pressed, as soon as they let go, the paper rolled back up.

The painter said, "It won't work. Only a slate made from the obsidian of He'ershingenmosiken can flatten snow-wave paper. That type of obsidian is very rare, and I only had one slab, which Needle-Eye stole from me."

"There's really nothing else that will flatten this?"

"No. Only the obsidian from He'ershingenmosiken will do the job. I was hoping to get the obsidian slab back from Needle-Eye."

"He'ershingenmosiken? Obsidian?" Auntie Wide slapped her forehead. "I have an iron that I use for pressing the princess's best formal gowns. It was made in He'ershingenmosiken, and it's obsidian!"

"That might work!"

Auntie Wide dashed out of the room and returned soon with a shiny black iron. She and the princess once again unrolled a section of the snow-wave scroll, and she pressed the iron against a corner for a few seconds. She lifted the iron, and the corner remained flat.

"Hold the umbrella for me, please, and I'll flatten the paper," Ethereal said to Auntie Wide. As he handed the umbrella over, he said, "Keep it spinning! If it ever falls closed, I'll disappear." He watched until Auntie Wide was spinning the umbrella overhead to his satisfaction. Then he squatted and began to flatten the paper, one small section at a time.

"Can't you fix the stretchers for the ribs?" asked the princess as she stared at the spinning umbrella.

"The umbrella did have stretchers." The painter continued to press the paper as he answered. "This umbrella has an unusual history. In the past, other painters of He'ershingenmosiken also had Needle-Eye's and my skill. Besides people, they were also able to capture animals and plants. One day, an abyss dragon came to our land. The dragon was black in color, and it could fly as well as swim in the deep sea. Three painters painted it, but it continued to fly and swim. Then, the painters pooled their money and hired a magic warrior, who finally managed to slay the dragon with a fire sword. The struggle was so fierce that the ocean near He'ershingenmosiken boiled. Most of the abyss dragon's body was burnt to charcoal, but I was able to collect some body parts out of the ashes to make this umbrella. The canopy is made from the dragon's wing membranes, and the pole, handle, and ribs were all made from the dragon's bones. The stones you see at the tips of the ribs were taken from the ashes of the dragon's kidneys. The umbrella has the power to protect the user from being painted into a picture.

"Later, the stretchers broke, and I tried to repair it with bamboo stretchers, but found the umbrella's magic disappeared. I took the bamboo out, and the magic returned. Then I tried to hold the canopy up with my hand, and that didn't work either. Apparently, no foreign material of any kind could be used in the umbrella. But I don't have any more dragon bones, and this is the only way to keep the umbrella open. . . ."

The clock in the corner of the room sounded. Ethereal looked up and saw it was almost sunrise. He looked down and saw that only about a palm's width of the snow-wave paper lay flat on the floor, not enough for a painting. He dropped the iron and sighed.

"There's no time. It will take too long for me to paint my portrait of Needle-Eye, but he could be done with his painting of the princess at any moment. You two." He pointed at Auntie Wide and the captain. "Has Needle-Eye seen you?"

"I'm sure he hasn't seen me," said Auntie Wide.

"I saw him from a distance when he came into the palace," said the captain. "But I'm sure he didn't see me."

"Good." Ethereal stood up. "Please accompany the princess to the Glutton's Sea, and find Prince Deep Water on Tomb Island."

"But . . . even if we get to the Glutton's Sea, we can't get onto Tomb Island. You know that the sea has—"

"Cross that bridge when you get to it. This is the only way. By dawn, all the ministers loyal to the king will have been painted into pictures, and Prince Ice Sand will have control of the capital garrison and the palace guards. He will seize the throne, and only Prince Deep Water can stop him."

"If Prince Deep Water returns to the palace, won't Needle-Eye paint him into a picture as well?" asked the princess.

"Don't worry. Needle-Eye will not be able to paint Prince Deep Water. The prince is the only person in the kingdom who cannot be painted by Needle-Eye.

Luckily, I only taught Needle-Eye how to paint in the Western style, but never taught him Eastern painting."

The princess and the other two weren't sure what the master painter was talking about, but Ethereal didn't elaborate. He went on. "You must bring Deep Water back to the palace and kill Needle-Eye. Then you must find the painting of the princess and burn it. It's the only way to keep her safe."

"What if we can find the paintings of the king and the queen—"

"Your Royal Highness, it's too late. They're gone. They're now only paintings. If you find them, don't burn them. Keep them for memory."

Grief crushed Princess Dewdrop, and she fell to the floor sobbing.

"Princess, now is not the time for sorrow. If you want to avenge your father and mother, you had better be on your way." The old master turned to Auntie Wide and the captain. "Remember, until you locate and destroy the princess's portrait, you must keep the umbrella open over her. She can't be without its protection, not even for a second." He took the umbrella from Auntie Wide's hands, and kept spinning it. "Don't spin it too slowly, because it will fall closed; but don't spin it too fast, because the umbrella is old, and it may fall apart. The umbrella is alive, in a sense. If you spin it too slow, it will cry out like a bird. Listen—" He slowed down the spinning until the stones at the rim of the canopy began to droop, and the umbrella emitted a nightingale-like sound. The slower he spun it, the louder the noise. The old master sped up the spinning. "If you spin it too fast, it will ring like a bell. Like this—" The old master spun the umbrella even faster, and the umbrella began to sound like a wind chime, but faster and louder. "All right. Now protect the princess." He handed the umbrella back to Auntie Wide.

"Master Ethereal, let's leave together," Princess Dewdrop said, looking up with tear-filled eyes.

"No. The dragon umbrella is only able to protect one person. If two individuals who have been painted by Needle-Eye try to use it together, they'll both die a terrible death: Half of each person will be painted into the picture, and the other half will remain under the umbrella. . . . Now raise the umbrella over the princess and go! Each moment you delay increases the danger. Needle-Eye may finish the picture any moment now!"

Auntie Wide kept spinning the umbrella over the old master. She looked at the princess, then back to the painter, hesitating.

"I taught that vile spawn how to paint. Death is what I deserve. What are you waiting for? Do you want to see the princess disappear before your eyes?"

Auntie Wide shivered. She moved the umbrella over the princess.

The old painter stroked his beard and smiled. "It's all right. I've painted all my life. To be turned into a painting is not a bad way to go. I trust my student's technique. The portrait will be excellent. . . ."

As he spoke, his body slowly became transparent, then faded away like a wisp of fog.

Princess Dewdrop stared at the empty space where the painter had been and muttered, "Let's go. To the Glutton's Sea."

Auntie Wide said to the captain, "Can you keep the umbrella up for a while? I need to go pack."

The captain took over. "Hurry! Prince Ice Sand's men are everywhere. We'll have trouble getting away after daylight."

"But I have to pack! The princess has never been away. I've got to take her traveling cloak and boots, and lots of clothes, and her water, and . . . also the bath soap from He'ershingenmosiken—she can't sleep if she doesn't bathe with it. . . ." Auntie Wide continued to mutter as she left.

Half an hour later, by the faint glow of dawn, a light carriage left the palace from a side door. The captain drove. In the carriage were the princess and Auntie Wide, who held up the spinning umbrella. They were all dressed as commoners, and the carriage soon disappeared in the fog.

In that distant underground bunker, Needle-Eye had just completed the portrait of Princess Dewdrop.

"This is the most beautiful portrait I've ever painted," he said to Prince Ice Sand.

The Second Tale of Yun Tianming
"The Glutton's Sea"

Once they were outside the palace, the captain drove the horses as fast as they would go. All three were anxious. In the brightening darkness, they felt danger looming in every shadowy copse and field they passed. After the sky brightened even more, the carriage came to the top of a hill, where the captain stopped so they could look back along the road. The kingdom spread out below the hill, and the road was like a straight line that divided the world in half. At the end of the line was the palace, looking like a pile of toy blocks forgotten on the horizon. No one was chasing after them; apparently Prince Ice Sand thought the princess no longer existed because she had been captured by Needle-Eye's brush.

They continued in a more relaxed manner. As the sky continued to brighten and illuminate everything around them, the world resembled a picture being painted. At first, there were only vague outlines and hazy colors; later, the outlines became more defined, the colors richer and more vivid. The moment just before the sun rose was when the painting became complete.

The princess, who had always lived in the palace, had never seen such large patches of vibrant colors: the green of forests, grassland, and fields, the bright red and brilliant yellow of wildflowers, the silver of the sky reflected in lakes and ponds, the snowy white of flocks of sheep . . . As the sun rose, it was as if the painter of this world-picture scattered a handful of gold dust boldly over the surface of the painting.

"It's so lovely outside," said the princess. "It's as if we're already in the picture."

"That's true," said Auntie Wide, spinning the umbrella. "But you're alive in *this* picture. In the other picture, you're already dead."

The princess was reminded of her departed parents. She forced herself to not cry. She understood that she was no longer a young girl, but a queen with duties she had to bear.

They talked about Prince Deep Water.

"Why was he exiled to Tomb Island?" asked the princess.

"They say he's a monster," said the captain.

"Prince Deep Water is no monster!" said Auntie Wide.

"They say he's a giant."

"He's no giant. I held him when he was a baby. I know."

"When we get to the sea, you'll see. Many others have seen him. He really is a giant."

"Even if he's a giant, he's still the prince," said the princess. "Why was he exiled to the island?"

"He wasn't exiled. When he was little, he took a boat to Tomb Island to fish. But that was when the glutton fish appeared in the sea. He couldn't come back, so he had to grow up on the island."

Now that it was light out, the road gradually filled with more pedestrians and carriages. Since the princess had rarely set foot outside the palace in the past, people did not recognize her. She was also wearing a veil so that only her eyes showed, but anyone who saw her still exclaimed at her beauty. The people also admired the handsome young carriage driver and chuckled at the sight of the silly old mother holding up the umbrella for her pretty daughter—and what a strange way to keep the umbrella up! It was a bright, sunny day, and everyone thought it was a parasol.

It was noon, and the captain shot two hares with his bow. The three ate by the side of the road in an open space between some trees. Princess Dewdrop caressed the soft grass next to her, inhaled the fragrance of herbs and wild-flowers, watched the sunlight dappling the ground, and listened to the birds singing in the woods and some distant shepherd playing his flute—she was curious and delighted by this new world.

But Auntie Wide sighed. "Oh, Princess, I'm so sorry you have to be away from the palace, suffering."

"I think being outside is better than being in the palace."

"Silly girl, how can out here be better than the palace? You don't know what it's like out here. Right now, it's spring. But in winter, it's cold, and in summer, it's hot. There are gales, and rainstorms, and all kinds of different people out here—"

"I never knew anything about the outside before. In the palace, I studied music, painting, poetry, mathematics, and two languages that no one speaks anymore. But no one told me what was outside. How am I supposed to govern this kingdom?"

"Princess, your ministers will help you."

"The ministers who would have helped me have all been painted into pictures. . . . I still think the outside is better."

A day's journey lay between the palace and the sea. But the princess's party avoided the major roads and towns, so they didn't reach the sea until midnight.

Dewdrop had never seen such a wide, open sky full of stars, and for the first time she felt how *dark* and *silent* the night could be. The torch on the carriage could only illuminate a small patch around her, and the world beyond was black velvet. The horses' hoofbeats seemed loud enough to shake the stars from the sky. The princess pulled on the captain's arm and asked him to stop.

"Listen! What is that? It sounds like a giant breathing."

"It's the sound of the sea, Princess."

They went on a bit farther, and the princess could see vague shapes on both sides—giant bananas?

"What are these?"

The captain stopped, hopped down, and took the torch close to one of the objects. "Princess, you should recognize these."

"Boats?"

"Yes, boats."

"Why are the boats . . . on land?"

"Because the sea has glutton fish."

The light from the captain's torch revealed a long-abandoned boat. The sand buried half of it, and the exposed part seemed like the skeleton of some beast.

"Look over there!" The princess pointed ahead. "A big white snake!"

"Don't be scared, Princess. That's not a snake, but the surf. We've reached the sea."

The princess and Auntie Wide, who kept the umbrella over her, climbed down from the carriage. She had only seen the sea in pictures before, and those painted seas were blue waves under a blue sky. But the sea she saw now was a black ocean at night, filled with the grandness and mystery of starlight, like another sky in liquid form. The princess advanced toward the sea, as if compelled by some force. The captain and Auntie Wide stopped her.

"It's dangerous to get too close," said the captain.

"I don't think the water is very deep. Will I drown?"

"The glutton fish will tear you apart and eat you!" said Auntie Wide.

The captain picked up a loose plank lying nearby and walked ahead, tossing it into the sea. The plank bobbed over the water a few times before a black shadow surfaced and headed for it. Since most of the shadowy creature was underwater, it was hard to tell how large it was. The scales on its body flickered in the torchlight. Then, three or four more shadows surfaced and also swam for the plank. The shadows fought over the plank, and as the water splashed, the sound of sharp teeth sawing through and crunching the wood could be heard. In a few moments, the shadows and the plank all disappeared.

"They could make short work of even a large ship," said the captain.

"Where's Tomb Island?" asked Auntie Wide.

"In that direction." The captain pointed at the horizon. "But we can't see it now. We'll have to wait until daylight."

They camped on the beach. Auntie Wide handed the spinning umbrella to the captain and retrieved a small wooden basin from the carriage.

"Princess, I'm afraid you won't be able to bathe tonight. But at least you can wash your face."

The captain handed the umbrella back to Auntie Wide and took the basin to go find water. His figure disappeared in the night.

"What a good young man." Auntie Wide yawned.

The captain returned with a basin full of fresh water. Auntie Wide took out the princess's bath soap and touched it to the water. With a pop, the surface of the water became full of foam, and some of the foam spilled out the sides.

The captain stared at the soap foam. He turned to Auntie Wide. "May I see the soap?"

Auntie Wide carefully handed over the pure white bath soap. "Hold on tight! It's lighter than a feather. If you let go, it will float away."

The captain hefted the soap; it seemed to have no weight at all, like holding a white shadow. "This really is from He'ershingenmosiken! I'm amazed we still have any."

"I think only two bars are left in the entire palace—no, the entire kingdom. I saved one from years back for the princess. Anything from He'ershingenmosiken is superior, but fewer and fewer of these objects are left." Auntie Wide took back the bath soap and carefully packed it away.

As she watched the white foam, the princess recalled her life in the palace for the first time since the start of the journey. Every night, in her elegant, ornate bathing suite, the bathing pool was covered by foam just like this. In the light of the various lamps, the bubbles sometimes looked pure white like a cloud pulled from the sky, sometimes iridescent, like a pile of jewels. As she soaked among the bubbles, she felt her body turn soft as noodles, felt herself melt *into* the bubbles. It felt so comfortable that she didn't want to move anymore, so that the servant girls had to lift her out, dry her, and then carry her to the bed to sleep. The wonderful feeling lasted until the next morning.

After the princess washed her face with the He'ershingenmosiken bath soap, her face felt relaxed and soft, but her body remained tired and stiff. After a quick supper, she lay down on the beach—she tried lying on a blanket first, then realized that it was more comfortable to sleep on the sand directly. The sand retained some of the heat of the day, and made her feel as though she were being held in a warm, giant palm. The rhythmic surf was like a lullaby, and she soon fell asleep.

After an unknown amount of time, Princess Dewdrop was awakened by a ringing bell. The sound came from the black umbrella spinning overhead. Auntie Wide was asleep next to her, and the umbrella-spinner was the captain of the guards. The torches had already been extinguished, and night covered all like black velvet. The captain appeared as a cutout against the starry sky, and only his armor reflected the starlight, while his hair swayed with the wind. The umbrella spun steadily in his hand, a tiny dome that blocked out half the sky. She couldn't see his eyes, but could feel them and innumerable twinkling stars gazing at her.

"Sorry, Princess. I spun a bit too fast," whispered the captain.

"What time is it?"

"After midnight."

"We seem to be farther away from the sea."

"It's low tide. Tomorrow morning, the water will come back."

"Have you been taking turns with the umbrella?"

"Yes. Auntie Wide did it for the whole day. I'll relieve her by doing it a bit longer tonight."

"But you drove all day. Let me do it. You get some rest."

Princess Dewdrop was a bit surprised by her own words. As far as she could remember, this was the first time she had ever thought about the needs of others.

"No, Princess. Your hands are smooth and delicate; spinning the umbrella will give you blisters. Let me keep on doing this."

"What is your name?"

Though they'd traveled together for a whole day, she hadn't thought to ask for his name until now. Before, she would have thought this perfectly normal. But now she felt a bit guilty.

"I'm called Long-Sail."

"Sail?" The princess looked around. They were camped by the side of a large boat on the beach, which shielded them from the wind. Unlike the other boats stranded on the beach, this one still had its mast, like a sword pointing at the stars. "Isn't a sail the cloth hung on the long stick?"

"Yes. That's called a mast. The sail hangs from it so that the wind can push the boat."

"Sails are so white on the sea. Very pretty."

"Only in pictures. Real sails are not so white."

"I believe you are from He'ershingenmosiken?"

"That's right. My father was an architect in He'ershingenmosiken. He brought our whole family here when I was little."

"Do you ever think about going home—I mean, to He'ershingenmosiken?"

"Not really. I was so young when I left that I don't remember much of it. And even if I do remember, it's useless. I can never leave the Storyless Kingdom."

The waves crashed against the beach some distance away, as though repeating Long-Sail's words again and again: *can never leave; can never leave* . . .

"Tell me some stories about the outside world. I don't know anything," said the princess.

"You don't need to know. You are the princess of the Storyless Kingdom, and it's natural that the kingdom has no stories for you. As a matter of fact, no one outside the palace tells their children any stories either. But my parents were different. They were from He'ershingenmosiken, and so they did tell me some stories."

"My father told me that long ago, the Storyless Kingdom had stories, too."

"That's true. . . . Princess, do you know that the kingdom is surrounded by the sea? The palace is at the center of the kingdom. No matter which direction you pick, you'll end up eventually at the shore. The Storyless Kingdom is a big island."

"Of course. I knew that."

"In the past, the sea around the kingdom wasn't called the Glutton's Sea. Back then, there were no glutton fish, and ships plied the waters freely.

Every day, countless ships passed between the Storyless Kingdom and He'ershingenmosiken—well, back then, this was called the Storyful Kingdom, and life was very different."

"Oh?"

"Life was full of stories, and filled with changes and surprises. There were several big bustling cities in the kingdom, and the palace wasn't surrounded by forests and fields, but by a flourishing capital. Everywhere in the cities you could find the valuable goods and the singular tools and utensils of He'ershingenmosiken. And the goods of the Storyless Kingdom—oh, I mean the Storyful Kingdom—flowed to He'ershingenmosiken over the sea without cease. People's lives were unpredictable, like riding a fast horse through the mountains: One moment you'd be atop a peak, and the next moment you'd have fallen into a ravine. There was opportunity and danger: A poor person could become rich overnight, and a wealthy person could also lose everything in a moment. Upon awakening, no one knew what was going to happen that day, or who they were going to meet. Life was stimulating and astonishing.

"But one day, a merchant ship from He'ershingenmosiken brought a stock of rare small fish in cast-iron barrels. The fish was only about as long as a finger, black in color, and looked perfectly ordinary. The merchant performed for the public in the markets: He stuck a sword into the iron barrel, and after an ear-piercing series of grinding noises, pulled the sword out to show that it had been bitten into a saw. The fish were called glutton fish, a freshwater species found in dark pools deep in the caves of He'ershingenmosiken.

"The glutton fish sold very well in the kingdom. Although the fish's teeth were tiny, they were as hard as diamonds and could be used as drill heads. Their fins were also very sharp, and could be made into arrowheads or small knives. Thus, more and more glutton fish were shipped from He'ershingenmosiken to this kingdom. Once, a typhoon caused one of these transport ships to capsize near the coast, and more than twenty barrels of glutton fish were lost at sea.

"It turned out that the glutton fish thrived in the ocean, and grew to be as long as a man, far larger than their freshwater form. Also, they bred quickly, and their population exploded. They began to eat everything that floated on the surface. Ships and boats that weren't dragged onto the shore in time were chewed into pieces. When glutton fish surrounded a ship, they chewed huge holes through the bottom. But the ship didn't even have time to sink before it was chewed into nothing, as though it had melted. The schools of glutton fish swam around the kingdom and quickly formed a barrier in the sea.

"And so the glutton fish laid siege to the Storyful Kingdom, and the shore became a land of death. There were no more ships and sails, and the kingdom was sealed off, with all connections to He'ershingenmosiken and the larger world cut off. It reverted to a self-sufficient agrarian land. The bustling cities disappeared and turned into small towns and ranches. Life became calm and dull, with no more changes, no more stimulation and surprises. Yesterday was like today, and today is like tomorrow. The people gradually grew used to this and stopped yearning for a different life. Their memories of the past, like the exotic goods from He'ershingenmosiken, grew fewer with each passing day. People even deliberately tried to forget the past, and also the present. All in all, they no longer wanted stories, so they patterned their life into a storyless one. And so the Storyful Kingdom became the Storyless Kingdom."

Princess Dewdrop was mesmerized by the story. Only long after Long-Sail had stopped did she ask, "Are there still glutton fish everywhere in the sea?"

"No. They live only around the coast of the Storyless Kingdom. Those with good eyes can sometimes see distant seabirds floating on the surface of the ocean hunting for food. There are no glutton fish there. The ocean is immense and boundless."

"So, there are other places in the world in addition to the Storyless Kingdom and He'ershingenmosiken?"

"Princess, do you really think the world consists of only these two places?"

"That's what the royal tutor taught me when I was little."

"He doesn't even believe that lie himself. The world is very, very large. The ocean has no edge, and holds innumerable islands. Some are smaller than the kingdom, others larger. There are even continents."

"What are continents?"

"Land that is as vast as the sea. Even on a fast horse, you wouldn't be able to go from one end to the other after many months."

"As large as all that?" The princess sighed. Then, abruptly, she asked, "Can you see me?"

"I can only see your eyes. There are stars in them."

"Then you must be able to see my yearning. I want to ride a sailboat across the sea, and go to faraway places."

"Impossible. We can never leave the Storyless Kingdom, Princess, never ever. . . . If you're afraid of the dark, let's light the torches."

"All right."

The torches were lit. Princess Dewdrop looked at Captain Long-Sail, but noticed that he was looking elsewhere.

"What are you looking at?" the princess asked softly.

"There, Princess—look over there."

Long-Sail was pointing at a small clump of grass in the sand. A few small droplets glistened in the torchlight on the grass blades.

"Those are called dewdrops," said Long-Sail.

"Ah, like me. Do they look like me?"

"They do. You're all beautiful, like crystals."

"When it's daytime, they'll be even prettier in the sun."

The captain sighed deeply. He did it without making any noise, but the princess felt it.

"What's wrong?"

"Dewdrops will evaporate and disappear in the sun."

The princess nodded. Her eyes dimmed. "Then they're even more like me. If this umbrella closes, I will disappear. I will be the dewdrop in the sun."

"I will not let you disappear."

"You and I both know that we cannot get to Tomb Island, and we can't bring Prince Deep Water back."

"If so, I'll just hold the umbrella up for you forever."

The Third Tale of Yun Tianming
"Prince Deep Water"

The next time Princess Dewdrop awakened, it was light out. The sea had turned from black to blue, but the princess still thought it looked completely different from pictures she had seen. The vastness that had been hidden by night now lay bare. Under the morning sun, the surface of the sea was completely empty. But in the princess's imagination, the glutton fish didn't cause this emptiness; rather, the sea was empty for her, just as her suites in the palace were empty, waiting for her. The yearning she had spoken of to Long-Sail during the night now became more intense. She imagined a white sail belonging to her appearing on the sea, drifting away with the wind until it disappeared.

Auntie Wide now held the umbrella up for her. The captain called for them from the beach ahead. When they came to his side, he pointed to the ocean. "Look, that's Tomb Island."

What the princess saw first wasn't the island, but the giant standing on the island. It was clearly Prince Deep Water. He stood on the island like a lonesome mountain: his skin bronzed by the sun, his muscles rippling and bulging like folds of rock, his hair drifting in the wind like trees near the peak. He looked like Ice Sand, but wasn't gloomy or dismal; rather, his gaze and expression all gave the viewer the feeling that he was open like the sea. The sun hadn't completely risen yet, but the giant's head was already bathed in the golden light, as though he were on fire. He shaded his eyes with a huge hand, and for a moment, the princess thought her gaze met his, and she cried out:

"Big brother! I'm Dewdrop, your little sister! I'm your baby sister Dewdrop! We're here!"

The giant gave no indication that he heard. His gaze swept past where they stood and moved elsewhere. Then he put his hand down, shook his head thoughtfully, and turned away.

"Why isn't he paying attention to us?" asked the anxious princess.

"Who would notice three ants in the distance?" The captain turned to Auntie Wide. "I told you Prince Deep Water is a giant."

"But when I held him he really was just a tiny baby! How did he get so big? But it's a good thing he's a giant. No one can stop him. He can punish those evildoers and retrieve the princess's portrait."

"We still have to let him know what's happened first," said the captain.

"We must go over there! Let's go to Tomb Island!" The princess clutched at Long-Sail.

"We can't. In all these years, no one has been able to get on Tomb Island. And no one there can come here."

"Is there really no way?" Tears escaped the princess's eyes. "We came here to look for him! You must know what to do."

Watching the tearful princess, Long-Sail seemed helpless. "I really don't know of a way. Coming here was the right decision, because you had to get away from the palace—otherwise you'd just be waiting to die. But I knew from the start that we wouldn't be able to get to Tomb Island. Maybe . . . we can send him a message by messenger pigeon."

"Great idea! Let's go find a messenger pigeon right away."

"But what good would it do? Even if he got the message, he still wouldn't be able to come here. He might be a giant, but even he would be torn apart by the glutton fish in the sea. . . . Let's have breakfast before we decide what to do. I'll go prepare."

"Oh no, my basin!" Auntie Wide cried out. It was high tide, and the rising waves had reached the wooden basin the princess had used the night before to wash her face. The basin had already floated some distance into the sea. It was upside down, and the soapy water inside had thrown white foam across a patch of the sea. They could see a few glutton fish swimming toward the basin, their sharp fins cutting through the surface like knives. The basin was going to turn into woodchips in their teeth in a second.

But something incredible happened: The glutton fish didn't get to the basin. As soon as they reached the foam, they stopped swimming and floated to the surface. The fierce fish seemed to lose their drive, and became listless. A few slowly swung their tails back and forth—not to swim, but to display their relaxation. Others even decided to float with their white bellies up.

The three observed the sight in silence, stunned. Then the princess said, "I . . . think I know how they feel. You're so comfortable in the foam that it's like you've gone boneless. They don't want to move."

Auntie Wide said, "The bath soap from He'ershingenmosiken really is wonderful. Too bad there are only two bars left."

"Even in He'ershingenmosiken, this kind of soap is very precious," said Captain Long-Sail. "Do you know how it is made? There's a magical forest in He'ershingenmosiken made up of thousand-year-old bubble trees, all very tall. Normally, there's nothing special about the bubble trees, but whenever there's a strong wind, soap bubbles come out of the trees. The stronger the wind, the more bubbles emerge. The He'ershingenmosiken bath soap is made from those bubbles, but collecting the bubbles is no easy matter. The bubbles drift very fast in the wind, and since they are transparent, it's very hard to see them. Only if someone were running as fast as the bubbles, such that they're at rest relative to the bubbles, would they be able to see them. This is possible only by riding the fastest horses, of which there are no more than ten in all of He'ershingenmosiken. Whenever the bubble trees begin to blow bubbles, the soap-makers ride these horses to chase after the wind and try to collect the bubbles with a thin gauze net. The bubbles come in different sizes, but even the largest bubble, once it's in the net, will burst and end up smaller than the eye could see. Hundreds of thousands of such bubbles have to be collected—sometimes millions—to make one bar of soap.

"But once the soap is in the water, each bubble from the bubble tree turns into millions of new bubbles. This is why this kind of bath soap generates so much foam. The bubbles have no weight, which is why pure, authentic He'ershingenmosiken bath soap also has no weight. It's the lightest substance in the world, but extremely precious. The bars that Auntie Wide has were probably given as gifts by the He'ershingenmosiken ambassador at the king's coronation. After that—"

Long-Sail abruptly stopped talking and stared at the sea, deep in thought. The few glutton fish continued to float lazily in the white foam. In front of them was the wooden basin, undamaged.

"I think there may be a way to get to Tomb Island!" Long-Sail pointed to the basin. "What if that's a little boat?"

"Absolutely not!" said Auntie Wide. "How can the princess take such a risk?"

"I wasn't talking about the princess."

The princess could tell by his determined gaze that the captain had already made up his mind.

"If you go alone, how can you make Prince Deep Water believe you?" The princess's excited face was flushed. "I'll go, too. I have to!"

"Even if you get to the island, how can you prove you are who you say you are?" The captain looked meaningfully at the commoner's garb on the princess.

Auntie Wide said nothing. She knew there was a way.

"My brother and I can prove our relationship by testing our blood," said the princess.

"Even so, the princess cannot go. It's too frightening!" But Auntie Wide's tone was no longer so nonnegotiable.

"Do you think I'm going to be safe staying here?" The princess pointed to the spinning black umbrella in Auntie Wide's hand. "We'll attract too much attention, and Ice Sand is going to follow us here. If I remain here, Ice Sand's army will catch me even if I don't end up in a painting. I'll be safer on Tomb Island."

And so they decided to go for it.

The captain found the smallest boat on the beach and used the horses to drag it to where the waves could just lick it. He couldn't find a working sail, but was able to retrieve a pair of old oars from other ships. He had the princess and Auntie Wide, who held the umbrella, board the boat first. Then he skewered the bar of He'ershingenmosiken bath soap with his sword and handed the sword to the princess.

"As soon as the boat is in the water, stick the soap in."

The princess nodded.

He pushed the boat into the sea and waded until the water had risen to his waist before jumping into the boat himself. He rowed with all his strength, and the boat headed for Tomb Island.

The black fins of the glutton fish began to appear around them and to approach. The princess sat at the stern, and submerged the soap on the sword into the water. Foam instantly swelled out of the sea until the bubbles were as high as a man before spreading out in the wake of the ship. As the glutton fish swam into the bubbles, they began to drift, as though they were enjoying the incomparable sensation of cozying up on a soft, white, plush blanket. This was the first time the princess had been able to get such a close look at the glutton fish: Except for their white bellies, they were entirely black, like machines made of steel and iron—and now they were lazy and docile in the foam.

The boat proceeded over the serene sea, dragging a long foamy wake like a wisp of cloud fallen to the sea. Innumerable glutton fish approached from both sides and swam into the foam like pilgrims congregating at a river of clouds. Once in a while, a few glutton fish approached from the front of the boat and managed to get a few bites in on the bottom—one even managed to bite off a chunk of the oar in the captain's hand. But soon, even these fish were lured away by the foam behind the boat, and not much damage was done. As the princess took in the pure white cloud-river of bubbles behind the boat and the intoxicated multitude of glutton fish, she was reminded of Heaven as described by the priests.

The shore receded and the boat approached Tomb Island.

Auntie Wide cried out, "Look! Prince Deep Water seems to be growing shorter."

The princess looked. Auntie Wide was right. The prince was still a giant, but he was clearly smaller than he had been when seen from the shore. He still stood with his back to them and looked out in another direction.

The princess pulled her gaze back to Long-Sail, who was propelling the boat. He looked even more the embodiment of strength: his muscles bulging everywhere, the two oars in his hands swinging rhythmically like a pair of wings, pushing the boat ahead steadily. The man seemed born for the sea; his movements were freer and more confident than when he had been on land.

"The prince sees us!" Auntie Wide called out. On Tomb Island, Prince Deep Water turned in their direction. One of his hands pointed at them, and his eyes gave a look of surprise. His mouth moved as though shouting something. It was no wonder that he was surprised. Theirs was the only boat on this sea of death, the farther back it was from the boat, the wider the foamy wake grew. From his vantage point, the sea seemed to suddenly be inhabited by a long-tailed comet.

They soon realized that the prince wasn't shouting at them. A few normal-sized individuals appeared at the prince's feet. At this distance, the men looked tiny, and their faces couldn't be clearly seen. But they were all looking in the direction of the boat, and a few waved.

Tomb Island had once been uninhabited. Twenty years ago, when Deep Water had gone to the island for fishing, he had brought with him a palace guardian, a royal tutor, and a few guards and servants. As soon as they came onto the island, schools of glutton fish came into the nearby shallows and sealed off the way home.

The princess and the others noticed that the prince looked shorter still. The closer they approached the island, the shorter the prince grew.

The boat was almost at the island. They could see eight or so normal-height people, most of them dressed in rough clothing made of canvas. like the prince himself. Two of them wore ceremonial robes from the palace, though they were very old and worn. Most also had swords. They ran onto the beach, leaving the prince behind them. By now he looked only about twice as tall as the others, no longer a giant.

The captain rowed harder and the boat dashed forward. The waves pushed the boat like a giant's hands, and the hull jolted as the bottom came to rest against the sand, almost toppling the princess out. The people onshore hesitated, apparently worried about the glutton fish, but four of them did come forward into the water to help stabilize the boat and support the princess as she disembarked.

"Careful! The princess has to be under the umbrella," Auntie Wide shouted. She was now very skilled with the umbrella, and managed to keep it spinning above the princess even with only one hand.

The welcoming party did not bother to disguise their surprise. They looked from the spinning black umbrella to the wake of the ship: The white foam from the He'ershingenmosiken bath soap and the countless floating glutton fish formed a speckled path of black and white across the sea, connecting the kingdom with Tomb Island.

Prince Deep Water came forward. Now he looked no taller than an ordinary man—in fact, he was shorter than two of his followers. He smiled at the newcomers like a kindhearted fisherman, but the princess could see shades of their father in his movements. With eyes full of hot tears, she called out, "Brother! I'm your sister, Dewdrop."

"You do look like my sister." The prince smiled and held out his arms for her. But a few of his guards stopped the princess and separated the newcomers from the prince. Some had unsheathed their swords and watched the captain with suspicion. Long-Sail ignored them, but he picked up the sword the princess had dropped to examine it. In order to put the prince's jittery guards at ease, he held the sword by the tip. He saw that the trip to Tomb Island had consumed only about one-third of the He'ershingenmosiken bath soap skewered on the sword.

"You must prove the princess's identity," an old man said. His uniform, though worn and patched, was still neat. His face showed the trials of many years, but his beard was neatly trimmed. Even on this desolate island, he had clearly tried to maintain the dignity of his position as an official of the palace.

"Don't you recognize me?" Auntie Wide said. "You're Guardian Shaded-Forest, and that, over there, is Royal Tutor Open-Field."

Both of them nodded. Open-Field said, "Auntie Wide, you're looking hale and hearty, despite the years."

"And you two have aged, as well." Auntie Wide wiped her eyes with her free hand.

Guardian Shaded-Forest kept his expression grim. "It's been twenty years, and we have no idea what has happened back home. We must request that the princess prove her identity." He turned to the princess. "Are you willing to have your blood tested?"

The princess nodded.

"I don't think this is necessary," said the prince. "I know she's my sister."

"Your Royal Highness," said the guardian. "This must be done."

Someone brought over two tiny daggers and handed one each to Guardian Shaded-Forest and Royal Tutor Open-Field. Unlike the rusty swords worn by the prince's men, these daggers still gleamed like new. The princess held out a hand, and Shaded-Forest lightly pricked her index finger with the dagger and picked up a drop of blood with the tip of the dagger. Open-Field did the same with the prince. Then Shaded-Forest took both daggers and carefully touched the drops of blood together. The red blood instantly turned blue.

"She is indeed Princess Dewdrop," the guardian said solemnly. Then, together with the royal tutor, they both bowed to the princess. The prince's other followers also knelt on one knee. Then they stood up and backed away, giving the royal siblings a chance to embrace.

"I held you when you were little," said the prince. "Back then, you were only about this big."

A sobbing princess told the prince all that had happened in the Storyless Kingdom. The prince held her hand and listened without interrupting. His face, marked by the tribulations of twenty years, but still youthful, remained calm and steady throughout.

Everyone gathered around the prince and the princess to listen to the story, but Captain Long-Sail engaged in some odd antics. He ran some distance away on the beach to look at the prince, and then came back, before dashing away again. Finally, Aunt Wide pulled him aside.

"I told you: Prince Deep Water is not a giant," whispered Auntie Wide.

"He *is* and he *isn't*," whispered the captain. "When you look at a regular person, the farther away he is, the smaller he appears in our eyes, right? But the prince is not like this. No matter how far away he is, he looks the same size in our eyes. This is why from far away he appears to be a giant."

Auntie Wide nodded. "I've noticed the same thing."

After the princess finished her story, Prince Deep Water simply said, "Let's go back."

They took two boats. The prince joined the princess's party on the small boat; the other eight took a larger boat, the same one that had carried the prince and his followers to Tomb Island twenty years ago. The larger boat leaked, but was safe enough for a short trip. They took care to retrace the wake of the princess's boat. Although the foam had dissipated somewhat, the glutton fish remained adrift without moving much. Once in a while, one of the boats or oars would strike a floating glutton fish, but the fish only wriggled lazily out of the way without a more strenuous response. The big boat's sail was still somewhat functional, and so it sailed in front, opening up a path through the floating schools of glutton fish for the small boat.

"I think it's best if you dip the soap back into the sea for insurance. What if they wake up?" Auntie Wide nervously surveyed the drifting mass of glutton fish.

"They've remained awake—they're not moving much because they're too comfortable. We don't have much of the soap left, and I don't want to waste any. I won't be bathing with it in the future, either."

Someone in the big boat ahead called out, "The army!"

A detachment of cavalry appeared on the shores of the kingdom. They rushed onto the beach like a dark tide. The armor and weapons of the mounted warriors gleamed in the sun.

"Keep on going," said Prince Deep Water.

"They're here to kill us!" Blood drained from the princess's face.

"Don't be afraid," said the prince, and lightly patted her hand.

Dewdrop looked at her older brother. She knew now that he was even better suited to the throne than she.

As the wind was at their backs, the return trip took much less time despite the floating glutton fish bumping into the boats along the way. As both boats came onto the beach, the cavalry surrounded them like a solid wall. Both the princess and Auntie Wide were terrified, but Captain Long-Sail, who was more experienced, relaxed a bit. He saw that the soldiers all kept their swords sheathed and their lances vertical. More important, he noticed the eyes of the men: They wore heavy armor so that only their eyes were visible, but the eyes were focused beyond the fugitives at the foamy path over the sea filled with glutton fish. Long-Sail saw only awe in those eyes.

An officer dismounted and jogged over to the beached boats. The people on the boats disembarked, and the prince's followers unsheathed their swords and stepped between the officer and the prince and princess.

"This is Prince Deep Water and Princess Dewdrop. Watch your words and acts!" Guardian Shaded-Forest shouted at the officer.

The officer knelt down on one knee and bowed his head. "We know. But our orders are to pursue and kill the princess."

"Princess Dewdrop is the heir to the throne by law! But Ice Sand is a traitor, guilty of regicide and patricide! How can you follow his orders?"

"We know this as well, which is why we will not carry out this order. But Prince Ice Sand ascended to the throne yesterday afternoon. We . . . are uncertain whose orders we should obey."

Shaded-Forest was about to say more, but Prince Deep Water stepped forward and stopped him. The prince turned to the officer. "Why don't the princess and I return to the palace with you? We'll confront Ice Sand there and resolve this once and for all."

The newly crowned King Ice Sand was celebrating in the most luxurious hall in the palace with those ministers who had sworn fealty to him, when messengers arrived to report that Prince Deep Water and Princess Dewdrop were speeding toward the palace at the head of an army. They would arrive in an hour. The hall instantly became silent.

"Deep Water? How did he cross the sea? Did he grow wings?" Ice Sand muttered to himself, but his face didn't show the terror and surprise evident on others'. "Don't worry. The army will not obey those two, unless I'm dead. . . . Needle-Eye!"

Needle-Eye emerged from the shadows. He was still dressed in his gray cloak, and appeared even frailer than before.

"Take snow-wave paper and your brushes and ride toward Deep Water. When you see him, paint him. It will be easy. You won't need to get too close. As soon as he appears over the horizon, you'll get a good look at him."

"Yes, my king." Needle-Eye departed noiselessly like a rat.

"As for Dewdrop, what can a mere girl do? I'll tear that umbrella away from her." Ice Sand lifted his flagon.

The celebratory feast ended in a subdued atmosphere. The ministers left with worried expressions, and only Ice Sand remained in the empty hall.

After an unknown amount of time, Ice Sand saw Needle-Eye return. Ice

Sand's heart sped up—it wasn't because Needle-Eye's hands were empty, and it wasn't because of Needle-Eye's appearance: He looked as sensitive and careful as before. Rather, it was because Ice Sand heard Needle-Eye's footsteps. Before, the painter had always moved in complete silence, like a squirrel gliding across the floor, but now, Ice Sand heard the echoes of his loud steps, like a heartbeat that couldn't be suppressed.

"I saw Prince Deep Water," said Needle-Eye, his eyes lowered. "But I couldn't paint him."

"Did he have wings?" Ice Sand's voice was chilly.

"Even if he did, I could still capture him. I could paint each feather in his wing and make it lifelike. But, my king, the truth is more frightening than if he had sprouted wings: He does not obey the laws of perspective."

"What is perspective?"

"The principles of perspective dictate that objects farther away appear smaller than those up close. I am a painter trained in Western traditions, and Western painting follows the rules of perspective. I cannot paint him."

"Are there schools of painting that do not follow the rules of perspective?"

"Indeed. My king, look at those Eastern paintings." Needle-Eye pointed to a brush-painting landscape scroll hanging on one of the walls in the hall. The scroll showed an elegant, ethereal landscape where the negative space, the emptiness, resembled water and fog. The style contrasted sharply with the colorful, solid oil paintings nearby. "You can tell that the scroll does not obey the laws of perspective. But I never studied Eastern painting. Master Ethereal refused to teach me—perhaps he had foreseen today."

"You may leave." Ice Sand's face was impassive.

"Of course. Deep Water will arrive at the palace soon. He will kill me, and he will kill you. But I won't wait helplessly for death. I will take my own life by painting a masterpiece with it." Needle-Eye left, again moving noiselessly.

Ice Sand summoned his guards. "Bring me my sword."

Dense hoofbeats came into the hall from the outside: at first barely audible, then growing to resemble a thunderstorm. The sounds abruptly ceased right outside the palace.

Ice Sand stood up and exited the hall with his sword. He saw that Deep Water was ascending the stairs in front of the palace, and Dewdrop was behind him, with Auntie Wide next to her, holding up the umbrella. In the plaza below the stairs, the army stood in dense array. The soldiers waited quietly, not clearly showing their support for either side. When Ice Sand saw Deep Water for the first time, he seemed twice as tall as an ordinary man. But as he came closer, he seemed to shrink to a more normal size.

Ice Sand's thoughts returned in a flash to his childhood more than twenty years ago. He had known that the glutton fish were amassing around Tomb Island, but he nonetheless lured Deep Water to go fishing there. Back then, their father had been in the grip of some disease, and he told Deep Water that Tomb Island was the home to a special kind of fish whose liver oil could cure the king's illness. Deep Water, normally so careful, believed him, and, as Ice Sand had wanted, left without coming back. That had always been one of Ice Sand's proudest plots, and no one in the kingdom knew the truth.

Ice Sand's thoughts returned to the present. Deep Water was now on the dais at the top of the stairs, before the door to the palace. He looked as tall as a regular person.

"My brother," said Ice Sand. "I'm glad to see you and Dewdrop. But you must understand that this is my kingdom, and I am the king. You must immediately pledge fealty to me."

One of Deep Water's hands was on the grip of his rusty sword, and the other hand pointed at Ice Sand. "You have committed unforgivable crimes."

Ice Sand chuckled. "Needle-Eye may not be able to paint you, but I can pierce your heart." He unsheathed his sword.

Ice Sand and Deep Water were equally skilled swordsmen, but since Deep Water didn't obey the laws of perspective, it was very hard for Ice Sand to judge accurately how far away his opponent was. The fight quickly came to an end when Deep Water's sword stabbed through Ice Sand's chest. Ice Sand tumbled down the stairs and left a long trail of blood on the stone steps.

The army cheered and declared their fealty to Prince Deep Water and Princess Dewdrop.

While Deep Water and Ice Sand struggled, Captain Long-Sail had been searching for Needle-Eye in the palace. Someone informed him that the painter had gone to his own studio, which was in a distant corner of the palace. The captain saw that only one sentry stood at the door. He had served under Long-Sail.

"He came here an hour ago," said the sentry. "He's been inside since."

The captain broke down the door and stepped in.

The studio was windowless. The candles on the two silver candelabras had mostly burnt out, and the studio was as dim as an underground bunker. The place was empty.

But Long-Sail saw a painting on the easel. It had just been completed, and the paint wasn't even dry: a self-portrait of Needle-Eye. The painting truly was a masterpiece. It was like a window to another world, and Needle-Eye stood there gazing at this world. Although an uplifted corner of the snow-white paper showed that this was but a painting, the captain felt compelled to avoid the piercing gaze of the man in the painting.

Long-Sail looked around and saw other portraits hanging on the wall: the king, the queen, and the ministers loyal to them. He saw the painting of Princess Dewdrop, and the beautiful princess in the painting seemed to make this dim studio as bright as heaven. The eyes in the picture seized his soul, and he felt himself growing intoxicated. But in the end, Long-Sail came to his senses. He took down the painting, tossed away the frame, and lit the rolled-up scroll with one of the candles.

Just as the flames consumed the painting, the door to the studio opened and the real Princess Dewdrop came in. She was still dressed in the garb of a commoner, and she held up the spinning black umbrella by herself.

"Where's Auntie Wide?"

"I told her to stay outside; I have some things I want to say . . . just to you."

"Your portrait is gone." Long-Sail pointed to the still-glowing ashes on the ground. "You don't need the umbrella anymore."

The princess slowed down the spinning, and the umbrella began to cry like a nightingale. As the canopy fell, the cries grew louder and faster, until they resembled the screams of jackdaws—the final warning before the advent of Death. Then the umbrella closed and the stone spheres at the rim collided together in a series of sharp snaps.

The princess was unharmed.

The captain looked at the princess and let out a long sigh of relief. He turned to the ashes. "It's too bad. The portrait was lovely, and I would have liked you to see it. But I dared not delay . . . it was really, really beautiful."

"Prettier than me?"

"It was you."

The princess retrieved the two bars of He'ershingenmosiken bath soap. She let go, and the weightless, white bars floated in the air like feathers.

"I'm going to leave the kingdom and sail the seas. Will you come with me?" asked the princess.

"What? But Prince Deep Water already announced that your coronation is tomorrow. He pledged to aid you with all his heart."

The princess shook her head. "My brother is more suited to be king than I. And if he hadn't been imprisoned on Tomb Island, he ought to have inherited the throne. When he's the king, he can stand somewhere high in the palace, and the entire kingdom can see him. But I don't want to be a queen. I like the outside more than the palace. I don't want to live the rest of my life in the Storyless Kingdom. I want to go where there are stories."

"That life is full of danger and hardship."

"I'm not afraid." The princess's eyes glowed with the spark of life in the candlelight. Long-Sail felt everything around him growing brighter again.

"I'm not afraid, either. Princess, I will follow you to the end of the sea, to the end of the world."

"Then we'll be the last two to leave the kingdom." The princess reached out and grabbed the two floating bars of soap.

"We'll take a sailboat."

"Yes, with snow-white sails."

The next morning, on a beach somewhere in the kingdom, people saw a white sail appear in the sea. Behind the sail was a long wake of cloudlike foam. It headed away from the kingdom by the light of the rising sun.

Thereafter, no one in the kingdom knew what happened to Princess Dewdrop and Long-Sail. As a matter of fact, the kingdom never received any information of the outside world. The princess had taken away the last bars of He'ershingenmosiken bath soap, and no one could break through the barriers formed by the schools of glutton fish. But no one complained. The people were used to their serene lives. After this story, there were never any other stories in the Storyless Kingdom.

But sometimes, late at night, some would tell stories that were not stories: imagined lives of Princess Dewdrop and Long-Sail. Everyone imagined different things, but all agreed that they journeyed to many exotic, mysterious kingdoms, including continents as vast as the sea. They lived ever after in wandering and trekking, and no matter where they went, they were happily together.

Broadcast Era, Year 7
Yun Tianming's Fairy Tales

In the sophon-free room, those who had finished reading began to talk amongst themselves, though most were still absorbed in the world of the Storyless Kingdom, the sea, the princess and the princes. Some remained deep in thought; some stared at the document, as though hoping to glean more meaning from the cover.

"That princess is a lot like you," said AA to Cheng Xin.

"Try to focus on the serious business here . . . and am I really that delicate?! I would have held up the umbrella myself." Cheng Xin was the only one who didn't bother reading the document. The stories were seared into her memory. She had, of course, wondered many times if Princess Dewdrop was modeled in some measure on herself. But the captain of the guards didn't resemble Yun Tianming.

Does he think I'm going to sail away somehow? With another man?

Once the chair noticed that everyone present had finished reading, he asked for opinions—mainly suggested directions for next steps to be taken by the various working groups under the IDC.

The committee member representing the literary analysis group asked to speak first. This group had been a last-minute addition, composed mainly of writers and scholars of Common Era literature. It was thought that there might be a minuscule chance—unlikely though it was—that they could be of use.

The speaker was a writer of children's stories. "I know that from now on, my group is unlikely to make any useful contributions. But I wanted to say a few words first." He lifted the blue-covered document. "I'm sorry to say that I don't believe this message can ever be deciphered."

"Why do you say that?" asked the chair.

"To be clear, we're trying to ascertain the strategic direction of humanity's struggles for the future. If this message really exists, no matter what it is, it must have a concrete meaning. We can't take vague, ambiguous information and turn it into strategic directions. But vagueness and ambiguity are at the heart of literary expression. Out of security considerations, I'm sure the true meaning behind these three stories is buried very deeply, and this makes the interpretations even more vague and ambiguous. The difficulty we are facing isn't that we can't get anything useful out of these three stories, but that there are too many plausible interpretations, and we can't be certain of any of them.

"Let me say something else that's not directly relevant here. As a writer, I want to express my respect for the author. As fairy tales, these are very good."

The next day, the IDC's work of deciphering Yun Tianming's message began in earnest. Very soon, everyone came to appreciate the warning by the children's story writer.

The three tales of Yun Tianming were rich in metaphors and symbolism; every detail could be interpreted in multiple ways, and each interpretation could find some support, but it was impossible to tell which one was the message intended by the author, and thus it was impossible to take any interpretation as strategic intelligence.

For instance, the idea of painting people into pictures was, by consensus, a rather obvious metaphor. But experts in different fields could not agree on a single interpretation. Some believed that the paintings were a reference to the digitization trend in the modern world, and thus this detail in the story suggested that humans should also be digitized as a way to avoid dark forest strikes. Scholars who held this view also noted that those who had been painted into the paintings were no longer able to harm those in the real world, and so digitizing humanity was perhaps a way to promulgate the cosmic safety notice.

But another camp held that the paintings were intended to suggest special dimensions. The real world and the world of the paintings were of different dimensionalities, and when a person was painted, that person disappeared from three-dimensional space. This brought to mind the experiences of *Blue Space* and *Gravity* in the four-dimensional fragment, and so perhaps Tianming had intended to suggest that humanity could use four-dimensional space as a refuge, or broadcast the cosmic safety notice in some manner through four-dimensional space. Some scholars pointed to Prince Deep Water's violations of the rules of perspective as further evidence that the author meant four-dimensional space.

As another example, what was the meaning of the glutton fish? Some focused on their large numbers, their habit of remaining hidden, and their fierce, aggressive tendency, and reached the conclusion that they symbolized cosmic civilization as a whole in the dark forest state. The soap that allowed the glutton fish to feel so comfortable as to forget to attack represented some unknown principles behind the cosmic safety notice. Others, however, reached the opposite conclusion: They believed that the glutton fish represented intelligent machines that must be built by humankind. These machines would be small in size and capable of self-replication. Once released into space, the machines would use the matter found in the Kuiper Belt or the Oort Cloud to self-replicate in large numbers until they formed an intelligent barrier around the Solar System. The barrier could have multiple functions, e.g., intercepting photoids headed for the Sun, or altering the appearance of the Solar System from a distance in a manner that would achieve the goal of a cosmic safety notice.

This explanation, dubbed the Shoaling Interpretation, was given more attention than other competing interpretations. Compared to the other hypotheses, the Shoaling Interpretation offered a relatively clear technical framework and became one of the first interpretations to be treated as an in-depth research topic by the World Academy of Sciences. But the IDC never put too much hope in the Shoaling Interpretation—although the idea seemed technically feasible, further study revealed that it would take tens of thousands of years for the self-replicating "shoals of fish" to form a barrier around the Solar System. Moreover, the limited functionality of AI machines meant that the protective and safety notice functions of the barrier were at best impractical visions. Ultimately, the Shoaling Interpretation had to be abandoned.

Countless competing interpretations were also offered for the spinning umbrella, the mysterious snow-wave paper and obsidian slab, the He'ershingenmosiken bath soap . . .

Just like the writer of children's literature had said, all these explanations seemed justifiable, but it was impossible to ascertain which one was really meant.

It was not the case, however, that all the contents of the three stories were so vague and ambiguous. The IDC experts were certain that at least one detail in the story offered a concrete piece of intelligence, and was perhaps the key to unlocking the secrets of Yun Tianming's message.

They referred to the strange place name in the stories: *He'ershingenmosiken*.

Tianming had told Cheng Xin his stories in Chinese. People noticed that most of the place names and names of the characters had clear meanings in Chinese: the Storyless Kingdom, the Glutton's Sea, Tomb Island, Princess Dewdrop, Prince Ice Sand, Prince Deep Water, Needle-Eye, Master Ethereal, Captain Long-Sail, Auntie Wide, etc. However, mixed in was also this other name that appeared to be a phonetic transcription of the name of a foreign place. Not only was it strange phonetically for Chinese, it was also really long. The name also appeared repeatedly in the story in a way that clearly suggested something out of the ordinary: Needle-Eye and Master Ethereal had come from He'ershingenmosiken; the snow-wave paper they used also came from He'ershingenmosiken; the obsidian slab and iron used for pressing the paper were also of He'ershingenmosiken; Captain Long-Sail had been born in He'ershingenmosiken; the bath soap of He'ershingenmosiken; the glutton fish of He'ershingenmosiken. . . . The author seemed to be repeatedly emphasizing the importance of this name, but there was no detailed description of He'ershingenmosiken at all. Was it another large island like the Storyless Kingdom? A continent? An archipelago?

Experts weren't even sure what language the name came from. When Yun Tianming had left on the Staircase probe, his English proficiency wasn't great, and he didn't know a third language—but it was possible that he had learned another language later. The name didn't resemble English, and it wasn't even clear if the name belonged to some Romance language. Of course the name couldn't be Trisolaran, since the Trisolaran language wasn't spoken or expressed by sounds.

Scholars tried to spell the name in all the world's known languages, to seek help from all fields, to search for it on the web and in all kinds of specialized databases, but nothing came of these efforts. Before this name, the most brilliant minds of humanity in various fields of study stood helpless.

The leaders of the various teams asked Cheng Xin: Was she sure she had remembered the pronunciation of the name correctly? Cheng Xin was unequivocal: She had noticed right away how strange the name sounded, and paid special attention to memorize it correctly. The name also appeared repeatedly in the story, and it was impossible that she had gotten it wrong.

The IDC's analysis made no progress. Such difficulties were not entirely unexpected: If humans could easily decipher Yun Tianming's stories for strategic intelligence, then so could the Trisolarans. The real intelligence information must be hidden deep. The experts in the various teams were exhausted, and the static electricity and acrid odor in the sophon-free room made them irritable. Each team was divided into multiple factions who argued over competing interpretations without reaching consensus.

As the decipherment effort reached an impasse, doubts began to creep into the hearts of those in the IDC. Did the three stories really contain meaningful strategic intelligence? The suspicion was mainly directed at Yun Tianming himself. After all, he had only an undergraduate degree dating back to the Common Era, which meant that he had less knowledge than a contemporary middle school student. In his pre-mission life, he had mostly worked on routine, entry-level tasks, without any experience in conducting advanced scientific research or reasoning about novel fundamental scientific theories. Of course, after he was captured and cloned, he had plenty of opportunity for study, but the experts were doubtful whether he could understand the supertechnology of the Trisolarans, especially the basic theories that supported such technology.

Even worse, as the days went on, some unavoidable complexities began to creep into the IDC. At first, everyone strove to solve the riddle for the future of humanity as a whole. But later, various political forces and interest groups began to make themselves felt: Fleet International, the UN, the various nation states, multinational corporations, religions, and so on. All of these groups tried to interpret the stories according to their own political aims and self-interest, and treated the work of interpretation as just another opportunity to disseminate propaganda about their brand of politics. The stories turned into empty baskets capable of carrying any goods. The work of the IDC changed, and the debates between the various factions became politicized and utilitarian, which lowered morale.

But the lack of progress by the IDC also had a positive effect: It forced people to give up the illusion of a miracle. In actuality, the public had long ago stopped believing in the miracle, since they didn't even know of the existence of Yun Tianming's message. The political pressure exerted by the populace forced Fleet International and the UN to shift their attention from Yun Tianming's message to searching for ways to preserve Earth civilization based on known technologies.

Viewed at the scale of the cosmos, the destruction of Trisolaris had occurred right next door, giving humans a chance to observe in detail the complete process of the extinction of a star and to gather massive amounts of data. Since the star that was destroyed was very similar to the Sun in terms of mass and position in the main sequence, humanity could potentially create a precise mathematical model of the catastrophic failure of the Sun in the event of a dark forest strike. As a matter of fact, this research had begun in earnest as soon as those on Earth had witnessed the end of Trisolaris. The direct result of research in this direction was the Bunker Project, which took the place of Yun Tianming's message as the focus of international attention.

Excerpt from *A Past Outside of Time*
The Bunker Project: An Ark for Earth Civilization

I. Projected timeframe from exposure of Earth's coordinates to dark forest strike against the planet: optimistic scenario, one hundred to one hundred fifty years. Average scenario: fifty to eighty years. Pessimistic scenario: ten to thirty years. Plans for the survival of the human race used seventy years as a benchmark.

II. Total number of individuals who would need to be saved: Based on the rate of decrease in world population, the number would be six hundred to eight hundred million in seventy years.

III. Projected course of the anticipated dark forest strike: Using data from the destruction of Trisolaris's star, a mathematical model of the explosion of what would happen to the Sun if struck in the same way was constructed. Simulations based on the model showed that if the Sun were struck by a photoid, all terrestrial planets within the orbit of Mars would be destroyed. Immediately after the strike, Mercury and Venus would be vaporized. The Earth would retain some of its mass and keep a spherical form, but a five-hundred-kilometer surface layer, including all of the crust and part of the mantle, would be stripped away. Mars would lose a layer about one hundred kilometers thick. Later, all the remaining terrestrial planets would lose velocity due to the material released by the solar explosion and crash into the surviving core of the Sun.

The model indicated that the destructive force of the solar explosion—including radiation and impact from solar material—would be inversely proportional to the square of the distance from the Sun. That is, the destructive force would diminish rapidly for objects far enough from the Sun. This would allow the Jovian planets to survive the explosion.

During the initial phase of the strike, the surface of Jupiter would be greatly disturbed, but its overall structure would be undamaged, including its satellites. The surfaces of Saturn, Uranus, and Neptune would also be disturbed without deeper damage. The dissipating ejected solar material would slow the orbits of the planets down to some degree, but later, as the solar material formed into a spiraling nebula, the angular velocity of its spin would match that of the Jovian planets and not degrade the orbits of those planets further.

The four gas giants, Jupiter, Saturn, Uranus, and Neptune, would survive a dark forest strike relatively unscathed. This prediction was the fundamental premise for the Bunker Project.

IV. **Abandoned plans for the survival of the human race**

1. Stellar Escape Plan: technically impossible. Humanity could not gain large-scale stellar navigation capabilities within the timeframe required. No more than one-thousandth of the overall population could fit into stellar escape arks. Moreover, it was highly unlikely that such arks would be able to locate and reach habitable exoplanets prior to fuel exhaustion and permanent breakdowns in long-term life support and ecological cycling systems.

As any plan along these lines could ensure the survival of only an extremely small portion of the total population, it violated the fundamental values and moral principles of the human race. Politically, it was also unfeasible, as it could lead to massive social upheaval and the total collapse of society.

2. Long-distance Avoidance Plan: extremely low feasibility. This plan would involve constructing a human habitat at sufficient distance from the Sun to avoid its explosive destructive power. Based on the model and projected development of engineering techniques for hardening space cities in the foreseeable future, the minimum safe distance would be sixty AU from the Sun, which is beyond the Kuiper Belt. At that distance, few resources would be available in space for constructing a space city. Similarly, the lack of resources meant that even if such a city were built, it would be almost impossible to maintain for human occupation.

V. **The Bunker Project:** the four gas giants could be used as barriers to avoid the solar explosion from a dark forest strike. In the shade of the four planets, away from the sun, sufficient space habitats would be constructed to house the entirety of the human population. These space cities would be located next to the planets, but would not be their satellites. Instead, they would orbit the Sun in synchrony with the planets, staying within their shadows. The plan called for a total of fifty space cities, each of which was capable of housing about fifteen million individuals. Specifically, twenty cities would be shielded by Jupiter, twenty by Saturn, six by Uranus, and four by Neptune.

VI. **Technical challenges facing the Bunker Project:** The technology required by this plan had all been mastered by humanity. Fleet International possessed extensive experience constructing space cities, and there was already a sizable base around Jupiter. There were some technical challenges that could be overcome within the required timeframe, such as how to regulate the positions of the space cities. Since the space cities would not be satellites of the gas giants, but would have to stay in close proximity of the planets, they would fall toward the planets, unless propulsion systems were installed to counteract gravity and maintain their distance from them. Initially, the plan called for the space cities to be positioned at the L2 Lagrangian points, such that the space cities' orbital periods would match their respective gas giants' without needing to expend much energy. However, it was later discovered that the L2 Lagrangian points would be too far away from the gas giants to provide sufficient protection.

VII. **The survival of the human race in the Solar System after a dark forest strike:** After the destruction of the Sun, the space cities would rely on nuclear fusion as their energy source. By then, the Solar System would appear as a spiral nebula, and the scattered solar material would provide an inexhaustible supply of easily collectable fusion material. It should also be possible to gather more fusion fuel from the remaining core of the Sun, sufficient to ensure humanity's long-term energy needs. Every space city could be equipped with its own artificial sun that would generate an amount of energy equivalent to the amount that had reached the surface of the Earth before the strike. From an energy efficiency point of view, the energy supply available to humans would actually be orders of magnitude higher than the pre-strike period because the space cities would consume fusion fuel at only one-billion-billionth the rate of the Sun. In that sense, the extinction of the Sun would be an improvement, because it would stop the extremely wasteful consumption of fusion material in the Solar System.

Once the nebula had stabilized somewhat after the dark forest strike, all the space cities could leave their barrier planets and find more suitable locations within the Solar System. It might be advisable for them to depart from the ecliptic plane so that they could avoid disturbance from the nebula while being able to dip into it for resources. Since the solar explosion would destroy the terrestrial planets, the mineral resources of the Solar System would be scattered in the nebula, making them easier to collect. This would make it possible for more space cities to be constructed. The only projected resource limitation on the number of space cities was water, but there was a 160-kilometer-deep ocean covering Europa, providing a source of water greater in volume than the Earth's oceans, and capable of supplying a thousand space cities with individual populations ranging from ten to twenty million. More water could also be obtained from the nebula itself.

Thus, the post-strike Solar System nebula was capable of supporting over ten billion people in comfort, leaving human civilization plenty of room for development.

VIII. Impact on international relations from the Bunker Project: It was an unprecedented plan for the entire human race to construct a new world. The greatest barrier standing in its way wasn't technical, but a matter of international politics. The public was worried that the Bunker Project would exhaust the Earth's resources and reverse global progress in social welfare, politics, and economics, perhaps even leading to a second Great Ravine. But Fleet International and the UN were in agreement that such danger could be avoided. The Bunker Project was to be engineered entirely with resources from the Solar System outside the Earth, mainly from the satellites of the four Jovian planets and the rings of Saturn, Uranus, and Neptune. There should be no drain on Earth resources or its economy. In fact, once development of space resources reached a certain stage, the project might even enhance the Earth's economy.

IX. Overall program for the Bunker Project: It would take twenty years to build the industrial infrastructure for extracting and exploiting resources from the gas giants, and sixty years to construct the space cities. The two stages would overlap by ten years.

X. The possibility of a second dark forest strike: The results of the first dark forest strike should convince most distant observers that the

Solar System was lifeless. Simultaneously, as a result of the destruction of the Sun, the Solar System would no longer contain an energy source capable of supporting an economical attack from a distance. Thus, the possibility of a second dark forest strike seemed minute. The conditions of 187J3X1 after its destruction also provided support for this view.

Broadcast Era, Year 7
Yun Tianming's Fairy Tales

As preparations for the Bunker Project got underway, Yun Tianming faded from the public consciousness. The IDC continued to work on deciphering the message, but it was only treated as one of the PDC's many projects. The hope for retrieving important strategic intelligence from the stories diminished daily. Some members of the IDC even connected the Bunker Project with Yun Tianming's fairy tales and came up with several interpretations that pointed to that as the right plan. For instance, the umbrella was naturally read as a hint at some defensive structure. Someone pointed out that the stone spheres at the rim of the canopy could symbolize the Jovian planets, but there were only four planets within the Solar System capable of acting as barriers. Tianming's stories did not mention the number of ribs in the canopy, but, rationally, four ribs for an umbrella seemed rather low. Of course, not many people really believed this interpretation, but in some sense, Tianming's stories had now acquired a status akin to the Bible. Without realizing it, people were no longer searching for real strategic intelligence, but reassurance that they were already on the right course.

Then came the unexpected breakthrough in interpreting the stories.

One day, 艾 AA came to see Cheng Xin. She had long ceased to accompany Cheng Xin to the IDC meetings, but devoted all her energy to the pursuit of involving the Halo Group in the Bunker Project. Building a new world outside the orbit of Jupiter represented a limitless opportunity for a space construction company. And wasn't it fortuitous that the company was named the Halo

Group when the "halos" of the Jovian planets would provide much of the re-sources for constructing the space cities?

"I want a bar of bath soap," said AA.

Cheng Xin ignored her. Her eyes didn't leave the e-book in front of her, and she asked AA a question about fusion physics. After her awakening, she had devoted herself to the study of modern science. Common Era spaceflight tech-nologies had all disappeared by this point, and even a tiny shuttlecraft now relied on nuclear fusion propulsion. Cheng Xin had to begin with basic phys-ics, but she made rapid progress. As a matter of fact, the gap of years didn't impose too high a barrier in her studies: Most of the shifts in fundamental theory had occurred only after the start of the Deterrence Era. With some dili-gence, most scientists and engineers from the Common Era could once again adapt to their chosen professions.

AA turned off Cheng Xin's book. "Give me bath soap!"

"I don't have any. You understand that actual bath soap doesn't have the magic of those fairy tales, right?" What Cheng Xin really meant was for AA to stop acting so childish.

"I know. But I like bubbles. I want to take a bubble bath like the princess!"

Modern baths had nothing to do with bubbles. Soap and other similar toi-letries had disappeared more than a century ago. Contemporary bathing prac-tices involved two methods: supersonic waves and cleaning agents. Cleaning agents were nanorobots invisible to the naked eye. One could use them with or without water. They cleaned skin and other surfaces instantaneously.

Cheng Xin had to go with AA to shop for bath soap. Whenever she had been depressed in the past, AA often dragged her out like this to cheer her up.

Faced with the giant forest that was the city, they pondered their choices and decided in the end that the most likely place to find bath soap was a mu-seum. They succeeded in their quest in a city history museum's exhibit hall dedicated to the daily necessities of Common Era life: home appliances, cloth-ing, furniture, etc. These objects were well preserved, and some even looked brand new. Mentally, Cheng Xin couldn't accept that these were artifacts from centuries ago; to her, they seemed to be from just yesterday. Although so much had happened since she was first awakened, this new age still felt like a dream to her. Her spirit had stubbornly been living in the past.

The bath soap was in a display case along with other cleaning products such as laundry detergent. Cheng Xin stared at the translucent bar and saw the fa-miliar eagle logo carved into the soap: product of the Nice Group. It was pure white, just like the soap in the story.

The museum director initially claimed that the bath soap was a precious artifact and not for sale, but then he proceeded to name an outrageous price.

"That's enough money to build a small factory for cleaning products," said Cheng Xin to AA.

"So? I've been working for you for years as the CEO. You should give me a present. And who knows? Maybe it will appreciate in value in the future."

And so they bought the bath soap. Cheng Xin had suggested that if AA really wanted a bubble bath, then it would be better to buy the bottle of bubble bath liquid. But AA insisted on the soap because the princess used soap. After the bar of bath soap was carefully retrieved from the display case, Cheng Xin held it and noticed that, despite the passage of more than two centuries, the soap still gave off a faint fragrance.

After returning home, AA ripped off the packaging and went into the bathroom with the soap. Then came the sound of the tub being filled.

Cheng Xin knocked on the door. "I suggest you don't bathe with it. The soap is alkaline. Since you've never used it, your skin might be damaged."

AA didn't respond. A long time later, after the water stopped, the bathroom door opened. Cheng Xin saw that AA was still dressed. Waving a white sheet of paper at Cheng Xin, AA asked, "Do you know how to make an origami boat?"

"I suppose this is also a lost art?" asked Cheng Xin as she took the paper.

"Obviously. We hardly see paper now."

Cheng Xin sat down and began to fold. Her thoughts returned to that drizzly afternoon in college. She and Tianming sat by the reservoir and watched as the tiny paper boat she made drifted away on the water covered by mist and rain. Then she thought about the white sail at the end of Tianming's stories. . . .

AA picked up the canopied paper boat and admired it. Then she indicated that Cheng Xin should follow her into the bathroom. With a pocketknife, she cut off a tiny corner from the bar of soap, poked a hole in the stern of the boat, and stuck the soap fragment into the hole. After giving Cheng Xin a mysterious smile, she deposited the boat into the calm water in the bathtub.

The boat began to move by itself, sailing from one edge of the tub to the other.

Cheng Xin understood right away. As the soap dissolved in the water, it lowered the surface tension of the water behind the boat. But as the tension in the water in front of the boat remained unchanged, it pulled the boat forward.

A bolt of lightning seemed to illuminate Cheng Xin's thoughts. In her eyes, the serene surface of the water in the tub turned into the darkness of space, and the white paper boat sailed across this endless sea at the speed of light. . . .

Then Cheng Xin remembered something else: Tianming's safety.

The string of her thought stopped vibrating immediately, as though a hand had been placed against it. Cheng Xin forced herself to look away from the boat, maintaining, as much as possible, a look of boredom and disinterest. The boat had now reached the other edge of the tub and stopped. She picked it out of the tub, shook off the water, and dropped it on the washstand. She almost tossed the boat into the toilet to flush it away, but thought that might appear excessive. She made up her mind, however, to not put the boat in water again.

Danger.

Though Cheng Xin also leaned to the view that no sophons were present in the Solar System, it was better to be cautious.

Cheng Xin and AA locked gazes. They each saw in the eyes of the other the same thing: the excitement of enlightenment dancing within. Cheng Xin looked away. "I don't have time to waste on silly games. If you want a bubble bath, go for it." She left the bathroom.

AA followed. They poured themselves two glasses of wine and began to chat about random topics. First, they discussed the future of the Halo Group in the Bunker Project. Then they recalled their college lives in different centuries. Then they talked about life in the present. AA asked Cheng Xin why she had not found a man she liked after living in the new age for so long, and Cheng Xin replied that she couldn't live a regular life, not yet. Then she pointed out that AA's problem was that she dated too many men—of course she was welcome to bring her boyfriends to visit Cheng Xin, but it was best to bring only one at a time. They also discussed the fashions and tastes of the women of their respective eras, their similarities and differences. . . .

Language was merely the vehicle through which they expressed their excitement. They dared not stop, lest the silence rob them of their hidden joy. Finally, in a break in the meandering conversation that would not be noticed by a listener, Cheng Xin said, "Curvature—"

She finished her sentence with her eyes: *propulsion?*

AA nodded. Her eyes said, *Yes, curvature propulsion!*

Space wasn't flat, but curved. If one imagined the universe as a large, thin membrane, the surface would be shaped like a bowl. The entire membrane might even be an enclosed bubble. Though at the local scale, the membrane seemed flat, the curvature of space was omnipresent.

During the Common Era, many ambitious ideas for spaceflight were proposed. One of them involved folding space. The idea was to imagine an increase in the curvature of space and fold it like a sheet of paper so that two spots tens of millions of light-years apart could touch each other. Strictly speaking, this wasn't a plan for spaceflight, but "space-dragging." It didn't involve navigating to the destination, but pulling the destination over to you by bending space.

Only God could have carried out such a plan—and once the limitations of basic theory were taken into account, perhaps not even God.

Later, there was a more moderate and localized proposal for taking advantage of curved space for navigation. Supposing a spaceship could somehow iron flat the space behind it and decrease its curvature, the more curved space in front of it would pull it forward. This was the idea of curvature propulsion.

Unlike folding space, curvature propulsion couldn't get a spaceship to its destination instantaneously, but it would be possible to drive it asymptotically to the speed of light.

Until Yun Tianming's message had been correctly interpreted, curvature propulsion remained a dream, like hundreds of other proposals for lightspeed spaceflight. No one knew whether it was possible at either a theory or practice level.

Broadcast Era, Year 7
Yun Tianming's Fairy Tales

A jubilant AA said to Cheng Xin, "Before the Deterrence Era, clothes with animated images were popular. Back then, everyone looked like blinking Christmas trees, but now, only children dress like that. Classical looks are in vogue again."

But AA's eyes were saying something else entirely. Her eyes dimmed. *This interpretation looks very good, but it's still impossible to be certain. We can never get confirmation.*

Cheng Xin said, "I'm most surprised that precious metals and gems no longer exist! Gold is now a common metal, and both of our drinking glasses are made of diamonds. . . . Did you know that where—er, when—I come from, owning a tiny diamond—like this big—would have been an unattainable dream for most girls."

Her eyes were saying, *No, AA, this time it's different. We can be sure.*

"Well, at least you had cheap aluminum. Before the invention of electrolysis, aluminum was a precious metal as well. I've heard that some kings even had crowns made of aluminum."

How can we be sure?

Cheng Xin couldn't express what she wanted with only her eyes. IDC had once offered to build her a sophon-free room in her apartment. That would have involved a large amount of noisy equipment, so she had turned them down. Now she regretted that decision.

"Snow-wave paper," she whispered.

AA's eyes lit up again. The flame of excitement burned even brighter than before.

"There's really nothing else that will flatten this?"

"No. Only the obsidian from He'ershingenmosiken will do the job. I was hoping to get the obsidian slab back from Needle-Eye."

The clock in the corner of the room sounded. Ethereal looked up and saw it was almost sunrise. He looked down and saw that only about a palm's width of the snow-wave paper lay flat on the floor, not enough for a painting. He dropped the iron and sighed.

A scroll was a rolled-up sheet of paper with curvature; a section was pulled out and ironed flat, decreasing the curvature.

This was clearly a hint for the difference in space in front of and behind a ship driven by curvature propulsion. It couldn't mean anything else.

"Let's go," said Cheng Xin as she got up.

"Yes," AA said. They needed to get to the nearest sophon-free room.

Two days later, the IDC chair announced at a committee meeting that the heads of all the working groups had unanimously endorsed the curvature propulsion interpretation.

Yun Tianming was telling the Earth that the Trisolaran ships used space curvature drives.

This was an extremely important piece of strategic intelligence. Out of all the possible paths for researching lightspeed spaceflight, curvature propulsion was confirmed to be feasible. Like a beacon in dark night, this indicated the right direction for further development of human spaceflight technology.

Equally important was the fact that the interpretation provided the model for how Tianming had hidden his message in the three stories. He employed two basic methods: dual-layer metaphors and two-dimensional metaphors.

The dual-layer metaphors in the stories did not directly point to the real meaning, but to something far simpler. The tenor of this first metaphor became the vehicle for a second metaphor, which pointed to the real intelligence. In the current example, the princess's boat, the He'ershingenmosiken soap, and the Glutton's Sea formed a metaphor for a paper boat driven by soap. The paper boat, in turn, pointed to curvature propulsion. Previous attempts at decipherment had failed largely due to people's habitual belief that the stories only involved a single layer of metaphors to hide the real message.

The two-dimensional metaphors were a technique used to resolve the ambiguities introduced by literary devices employed in conveying strategic intelligence. After a dual-layer metaphor, a single-layer supporting metaphor was added to confirm the meaning of the dual-layer metaphor. In the current example, the curved snow-wave paper and the ironing required to flatten it served as a metaphor for curved space, confirming the interpretation of the soap-driven boat. If one viewed the stories as a two-dimensional plane, the dual-layer metaphor only provided one coordinate; the supporting single-layer metaphor provided a second coordinate that fixed the interpretation on the plane. Thus, this single-layer metaphor was also called the bearing coordinate. Viewed by itself, the bearing coordinate seemed meaningless, but once combined with the dual-layer metaphor, it resolved the inherent ambiguities in literary language.

"A subtle and sophisticated system," a PIA specialist said admiringly.

All the committee members congratulated Cheng Xin and AA. AA, who had always been looked down on, saw her status greatly elevated among the committee members.

Cheng Xin's eyes moistened. She was thinking of Tianming, of the man who struggled alone in the long night of outer space and an eerie, sinister alien society. To convey his important message to the human race, he must have racked his brain until he had devised such a metaphorical system, and then spent ages in his lonely existence to create over a hundred fairy tales and carefully disguise the intelligence report in three of those stories. Three centuries ago, he had given Cheng Xin a star; now, he brought hope to the human race.

Thereafter, steady progress was made in deciphering the message. Other than the discovery of the metaphorical system, the effort was also aided by another guess that was commonly accepted, though unconfirmed: While the first part of the message to be successfully deciphered involved escape from the Solar System, the rest of the message likely had to do with the safety notice.

The interpreters soon realized that compared to the first bit of intelligence, the rest of the information hidden in the three stories was far more complex.

At the next IDC meeting, the chair produced a custom-made umbrella that looked just like the one in the fairy tales. The black umbrella had eight ribs, and at the end of each was a small stone sphere. In this era, umbrellas were no longer in common use. To avoid the rain, modern people used something called a rainshield, a device about the size of a flashlight that protected the user by blowing air up to form an invisible canopy. People certainly knew about umbrellas and saw them in movies, but few had experience with the real thing. Curious, they played with the chair's umbrella, and noticed that, just like in the stories, the canopy could be kept open by spinning. Spinning faster or slower resulted in corresponding alarm sounds.

"This is really tiring," someone complained as he spun the umbrella.

Everyone gained new respect for the princess's wet nurse, who'd managed to spin the umbrella nonstop for a whole day.

AA took over the umbrella. Her hands weren't as strong, and the canopy began to fall. They all heard the warning birdsong.

Cheng Xin had kept her eyes on the umbrella since the chair had opened it. Now she cried out to AA, "Don't stop!"

AA spun faster, and the birdsong stopped.

"Faster," said Cheng Xin.

AA put all her strength into spinning, and the wind chime began to play. Then Cheng Xin asked her to slow down, until the birdsong appeared. This went back and forth a few times.

"This is not an umbrella at all!" said Cheng Xin. "But I know what it is now."

Bi Yunfeng, who stood to the side, nodded. "Me too." Then he turned to Cao Bin. "Probably only the three of us can recognize this object."

"Yes," said an excited Cao. "But even in our time, this was rarely seen."

Some of the attendees looked at these three individuals from the past; others looked at the umbrella. All were puzzled, but also expectant.

"It's a centrifugal governor," said Cheng Xin. "For steam engines."

"What's that? Some kind of control circuit?"

Bi Yunfeng shook his head. "The world wasn't electrified back when this was invented."

Cao Bin explained. "This was a device from the eighteenth century for regulating the speed of a steam engine. It's made of two or four lever arms equipped with spherical masses at the ends and a central spindle with a sleeve—it looks just like this umbrella, except with fewer ribs. The steam engine's operation rotates the spindle. When it spins too fast, the metal balls lift the lever arms due to centrifugal force, which pulls up on the sleeve and reduces the aperture of the throttle valve connected to the sleeve, thereby reducing the fluid entering the cylinder and the engine's speed. Conversely, when it spins too slowly, the lever arms fall due to the weight of the metal balls—like an umbrella closing—and the sleeve is pushed down, increasing the aperture of the throttle valve and the speed of the engine. . . . This was one of the earliest industrial automatic control systems."

Thus was the first level of the dual-layer metaphor in the umbrella decoded. But unlike the soap-propelled boat, the centrifugal governor didn't seem to clearly point to anything. This second-layer metaphor could be interpreted in multiple ways, with two possibilities deemed most likely: negative-feedback automatic control and constant speed.

The interpreters began to look for the corresponding bearing coordinate for this dual-layer metaphor. Soon, they fixed on Prince Deep Water. The prince's height didn't change in the observers' eyes regardless of distance. This could also be interpreted in multiple ways, with two possibilities being most obvious: a method of information transmission where the signal strength did not decay due to distance, or a physical quantity that remained constant regardless of the frame of reference used.

Taken together with the metaphorical meanings of the umbrella, the true meaning instantly emerged: a constant speed that did not change with the frame of reference.

Clearly, it referred to the speed of light.

Unexpectedly, the interpreters found yet another bearing coordinate for the metaphor of the umbrella.

> The He'ershingenmosiken bath soap is made from those bubbles, but collecting the bubbles is no easy matter. The bubbles drift very fast in the wind. . . . Only if someone were running as fast as the bubbles, such that they're at rest relative to the bubbles, would they be able to see them. This is possible only by riding the fastest horses. . . . The soap-makers ride these horses to chase after the wind and try to collect the bubbles with a thin gauze net. . . . The bubbles have no weight, which is why pure, authentic He'ershingenmosiken soap also has no weight. It's the lightest substance in the world. . . .

The fastest; with no weight, or massless—this was a clear, single-layer metaphor for light.

Everything indicated that the umbrella stood in for light, but capturing the bubbles from the bubble tree had two possible interpretations: collecting the power of light or lowering the speed of light.

Most interpreters didn't think the first interpretation had much to do with humanity's strategic goals, so most of the focus was on the second interpretation.

Although they still couldn't tell the exact meaning of the message, the interpreters debated the second interpretation, concentrating on the connection between lowering the speed of light and the cosmic safety notice.

"Suppose that we could lower the speed of light in the Solar System. That is, within the Kuiper Belt or Neptune's orbit, we could produce an effect observable from a distance—at cosmic scales."

This thought excited everyone.

"Suppose we reduced the speed of light by ten percent within the Solar System—would that make a cosmic observer think we're safer?"

"Undoubtedly. If humans possessed lightspeed spaceships, it would take them longer to emerge from the Solar System. But it wouldn't mean *that* much."

"To really indicate to the universe that we're safe, a reduction by ten percent is insufficient. We may have to reduce the speed of light to ten percent of its original value, or maybe even one percent. Observers would see that we've surrounded ourselves in a buffer zone that made certain that our ships would take a long time to emerge from the Solar System. This should increase their feelings of safety."

"But by that reasoning, lowering the speed of light to one-tenth of one percent would be insufficient. Think about it: Even at three hundred kilometers per second, it still wouldn't take that long to get out of the Solar System. Also, if humans were capable of modifying a physical constant within a region of space with a radius of fifty astronomical units, then this would be tantamount to a declaration that humans possessed very advanced technology. Instead of a cosmic safety notice, it would be a cosmic danger warning!"

From the dual-layer metaphor of the umbrella and the bearing coordinates provided by Prince Deep Water and the bubble tree, the interpreters were able to ascertain the general tenor of their import, but not the specific strategic intelligence. The metaphor was no longer two-dimensional but three-dimensional. Some started to guess at the existence of yet another bearing coordinate, and the interpreters searched exhaustively through the stories, but they turned up nothing.

Just then, the mysterious name He'ershingenmosiken was finally deciphered.

———

A linguistic working group was added by the IDC specifically to deal with He'ershingenmosiken. A historical linguist and philologist, Palermo, had been added to the group because his expertise differed from the others'. Instead of focusing on one language family, he was familiar with the ancient languages of many linguistic families. But even Palermo could offer no insight on this strange name. That he succeeded was due to an unexpected stroke of good luck, and had little to do with his professional expertise.

One morning, after Palermo woke up, his girlfriend, a blond Scandinavian, asked him whether he'd ever been to her homeland.

"Norway? No, never."

"Then why were you mumbling those two place names in your dream?"

"What names?"

"Helseggen and Mosken."

The names sounded vaguely familiar to Palermo. Since his girlfriend had nothing to do with the IDC, it was a little eerie to hear those sounds coming from her. "You mean *He'ershingenmosiken*?"

"Yes, though you're running them together and not saying them quite right."

"I'm saying the name of a single place. It's a Chinese transliteration—so the sounds are approximate. If you break the syllables into arbitrary groups, they probably sound like the names of many places in different languages."

"But both of these places are in Norway."

"A coincidence, that's all."

"Let me tell you, the average Norwegian isn't likely to know those places either. They are ancient names, no longer used. I know of them only because my specialty is Norwegian history. Both are in Nordland County."

"My dear, that's still just a coincidence. You can break that string of syllables anywhere."

"Oh please, stop teasing! You must have known that Helseggen is the name of a mountain, and Mosken is a tiny island in the Loften archipelago."

"I really didn't. Look, there's a phenomenon in linguistics where a listener who doesn't know the language will arbitrarily divide a series of syllables into groupings almost subconsciously. That's what's happening here."

Palermo had encountered such arbitrary divisions numerous times during his work for the IDC, so he didn't take his girlfriend's "discovery" seriously. But what she said next changed everything.

"Fine, let me point out one more thing: Helseggen is located right next to the sea. You can see Mosken from the top—it's the closest isle to Helseggen!"

———————

Two days later, Cheng Xin stood on Mosken Island and looked over the sea at the craggy cliffs of Helseggen. The cliffs were black, and because the sky was overcast, the sea appeared black as well. Only a white line of surf appeared at the foot of the cliffs. Before coming here, Cheng Xin had heard that although this location was within the Arctic Circle, warm sea currents made the climate relatively mild. However, the wind coming off the sea still chilled her.

The steep, craggy Loften Islands were carved by glaciers, and formed a 160-kilometer-long barrier between the North Sea and deep Vestfjorden, like a wall that divided the Arctic Ocean from the Scandinavian Peninsula. The currents between the islands were strong and rapid. In the past, few people had inhabited the islands, and most were seasonal fishermen. Now that seafood mainly came from aquaculture, open-sea fishing had virtually disappeared. The islands had again grown desolate, and probably resembled how they had looked during the time of the Vikings.

Mosken was only a tiny isle in the archipelago, and Helseggen was a nameless mountain—these names had changed at the end of the Crisis Era.

Faced with the forlorn desolation at the world's end, Cheng Xin nonetheless felt serenity in her heart. Not long ago, she had thought her own life had reached its terminus, but now there were many reasons to continue living. She saw a sliver of blue revealed at the edge of the leaden sky, and the sun peeked out of the opening for a few minutes, instantaneously changing this cold world. It reminded her of a line from Tianming's stories: . . . *as if the painter of this world-picture scattered a handful of gold dust boldly over the surface of the painting.* This was her life now, hope hidden in despair, warmth felt through frost.

AA had come with her, as well as a few IDC experts, including Bi Yunfeng, Cao Bin, and Palermo the linguist.

Mosken's only inhabitant was an old man named Jason. He was more than eighty years of age and had come from the Common Era. His square face showed the marks left by the years and reminded Cheng Xin of Fraisse. When he was asked if there was anything special in the vicinity of Helseggen and Mosken, Jason pointed to the western edge of the island.

"Of course. Look there."

They saw a white lighthouse. Although it was only dusk, the lighthouse was already lit and blinked rhythmically.

"What's that for?" asked AA.

"Ha! Children these days . . ." Jason shook his head. "It's an ancient navigation aid. Back during the Common Era, I was an engineer responsible for designing lighthouses and beacon lights. As a matter of fact, many lighthouses remained in use until the Crisis Era, though they're all gone by now. I built this lighthouse here so that kids would know that such a thing existed once."

The IDC members were all interested in the lighthouse. It reminded them of the centrifugal governor for steam engines, another ancient technology that had disappeared. But a brief investigation showed that this couldn't be what they were looking for. The lighthouse had been constructed recently and utilized modern building materials that were strong and light. It had taken only half a month to complete. Jason was also certain that historically, Mosken did not have a lighthouse. Thus, based on timing alone, the lighthouse had nothing to do with Tianming's hidden message.

"Anything else interesting or special around here?" someone asked.

Jason shrugged at the cold sky and sea. "What could be here? I don't like this bleak and dreary place, but they wouldn't let me build a lighthouse anywhere else."

So everyone decided to go to Helseggen and take a look around. Just as they were about to get into the helicopter, AA suddenly had the idea to go over on Jason's tiny boat.

"Sure thing, but the waves are powerful today, child. You'll get seasick," Jason said.

AA pointed to the mountain across the strait. "This is a really short ride."

Jason shook his head. "I can't sail straight across. Not today. We have to go the long way around."

"Why?"

"The maelstrom, of course. It will swallow up any boat."

Cheng Xin's party looked at each other and then turned to Jason as one. Someone asked, "I thought you said there was nothing special here."

"The Moskstraumen is nothing special for us locals. It's just part of the sea. You can often see it there."

"Where?"

"Right there. You may not be able to see it, but you can hear it."

They quieted, and did hear a rumbling from the sea, like thousands of horses stampeding in the distance.

The helicopter could take them to investigate the maelstrom, but Cheng Xin wanted to go over on a boat, and the others agreed. Jason's boat, the only one available on the island, could seat five or six safely. Cheng Xin, AA, Bi Yunfeng, Cao Bin, and Palermo got onto the boat while the others took the helicopter.

The boat left Mosken Island, bumping over the waves. The wind over the open sea was stronger and colder, and salty spray struck their faces without cease. The surface of the sea was a dark gray, and appeared eerie and mysterious in the dimming light. The rumbling grew louder, but they still couldn't see the great whirlpool.

"Oh, I remember now!" Cao Bin shouted.

Cheng Xin also remembered. She had thought that perhaps Tianming had found out something new about this place through the sophons, but the real answer was far simpler.

"Edgar Allan Poe," said Cheng Xin.

"What? Who?" asked AA.

"A nineteenth-century writer."

Jason said, "Right. Poe wrote a story about Mosken—'A Descent into the Maelstrom.' I read it when I was younger. It's very exaggerated. I remember him writing that the surface of the whirlpool formed a forty-five-degree angle. That's absurd."

Written narrative literature had disappeared more than a century ago. "Literature" and "authors" still existed, but narratives were constructed with digital images. Classical written novels and stories were now treated as ancient artifacts. The Great Ravine had caused the loss of the works of many ancient writers, including Poe.

The rumbling grew even louder. "Where's the whirlpool?" someone asked.

Jason pointed at the sea surface. "The maelstrom is lower than the surface here. Look at that line: you have to cross it to see the Moskstraumen." The passengers saw a fluctuating band of waves whose frothy tips formed a long, white arc that extended into the distance.

"Then let's cross it!" Bi Yunfeng said.

Jason glared at him. "That's a line separating life from death. A boat that crosses cannot return."

"How long could a boat circle around the inside of the whirlpool before being pulled under?"

"Forty minutes to an hour."

"Then we should be fine. The helicopter will save us in time."

"But my boat—"

"We'll compensate you."

"Cheaper than a bar of soap," AA interjected. Jason didn't know what she was talking about.

Carefully, Jason aimed the boat at the band of waves and navigated through.

The boat swayed from side to side violently and then stabilized. Some invisible force seemed to seize it, and the boat began to glide along in the same direction as the waves as if riding on rails.

"The maelstrom has caught us," Jason cried out. "My God, this is the first time I've been this close!"

The Moskstraumen revealed itself below them as though they stood on top of a mountain. The monstrous funnel-shaped depression was about a kilometer in diameter. The slanting sides were indeed not as steep as the forty-five degrees mentioned by Poe, but they were at least thirty degrees. The surface of the vortex was smooth as a solid. Since the boat was only at the edge of the whirlpool, the spin wasn't very fast. But as they got closer to the center, the spin would become faster. At the tiny hole down in the center, the speed of the churning sea was highest, and the bone-shattering rumbling came from there. The rumbling expressed a mad power capable of grinding everything into pieces and sucking them out of existence.

"I refuse to believe we can't force our way out," said AA. She shouted at Jason, "Follow a straight line at maximum power!"

Jason did as she asked. The boat was electrically powered, and the quiet engine sounded like a mosquito in the rumbling of the whirlpool. The boat approached the wave band at the edge of the maelstrom and appeared to come close to leaving, but then lost momentum and turned away from the froth, like a tossed pebble that passed the apex of its trajectory. They tried a few more times, but each time, they slid back down farther into the maelstrom.

"Now you see: this is the gate of hell. No normal boat can return," said Jason.

By now, the boat was so deep down in the whirlpool that the frothy waves at the rim were no longer visible. Behind them was the mountain formed of seawater, and they could only see the slow-moving top of the mountain at the other side of the whirlpool. Everyone felt the terror of being at the mercy of an irresistible force. Only the helicopter hovering overhead gave them any measure of comfort.

"Let's have supper," said Jason. The sun had not yet set behind the clouds, but since it was the Arctic summer, it was already after 9 P.M. Jason took a large cod out of the hold and explained that it had been freshly caught. Then he took out three bottles of wine, placed the fish on a large iron platter, and poured a bottle of wine over the fish. With a lighter, he set the fish on fire, explaining that this was the local method of preparation. Five minutes later, he began to pull pieces off of the still-burning fish and eat them. The passengers imitated him, enjoying the fish, wine, and the magnificence of the maelstrom.

"Child, I recognize you," Jason said to Cheng Xin. "You were the Sword-holder. I'm sure you and your people came here for some important mission, but you must keep your cool. We can't avoid the apocalypse, so we must enjoy the present."

"I doubt you could keep your cool if that helicopter weren't there," said AA.

"Ha, kid, I would. I surely would. Back in the Common Era, I was only forty when I found out I had a terminal illness. But I wasn't afraid, and I never even planned to go into hibernation. It was only after I went into shock that the doctors put me into hibernation. By the time I woke up, it was already the Deterrence Era. I thought I had been given a new life, but that turned out to be just an illusion. Death only backed off a little ways to wait for me on the road ahead. . . .

"The night I finished building the lighthouse, I took my boat out to the sea to look at it from a distance. And all of a sudden I had a thought: Death is the only lighthouse that is always lit. No matter where you sail, ultimately, you must turn toward it. Everything fades in the world, but Death endures."

It had been twenty minutes since they entered the whirlpool, and the boat had slid about a third of the way down toward the bottom. The boat became more slanted, but due to centrifugal force, the passengers weren't sliding toward the portside. The wall of water filled their field of view, and they could no longer see the top, even on the other side of the whirlpool. Everyone avoided looking up at the sky because, in the maelstrom, the boat moved along with the spinning wall of water, and it was almost impossible to feel the motion—the boat seemed to adhere to the side of a watery basin. But if they looked up, the motion instantly became evident. The cloud-filled sky spun overhead faster and faster, making them dizzy. Since the centrifugal force was stronger lower in the vortex, the water wall below the boat became even smoother and felt more solid, like ice. The rumbling from the eye of the maelstrom overwhelmed every other sound, and conversation was no longer possible. The Sun in the west peeked out of cracks in the cloud cover, and a ray of golden light shone into the swirling vortex. But the light couldn't reach the maw at the bottom, and only illuminated a small part of the wall of water, making the bottom appear even more dark and menacing by contrast. Mist and fog swirled out of the eye at the center, forming a rainbow in the ray of sunlight that arced grandly across the rotating abyss.

"I remember Poe describing a rainbow in the maelstrom as well. I think it was even in moonlight. He called it a bridge between Time and Eternity." Jason was shouting, but no one could hear what he was saying.

The helicopter came to their rescue. Hovering about two or three meters above the boat, it dangled a rope ladder so that everyone in the boat could climb out. Then the empty boat drifted away and continued to circle the monstrous vortex. The unfinished cod on the boat still glowed with the remnants of a blue flame.

The helicopter hovered above the maw of the maelstrom, and as everyone looked down at the spinning funnel, they soon felt nauseated and dizzy. Someone entered directions into the navigation system for the helicopter to spin, matching the whirlpool's rotation below. This way, the whirlpool appeared still, but the world outside—sky, sea, and mountains—began to spin around them. The maelstrom seemed to become the center of the world, and the observer's nausea wasn't reduced in the slightest. AA vomited up all the fish she had eaten.

As she gazed at the whirlpool below, another whirlpool appeared in Cheng Xin's mind: It was made up of a hundred billion silver stars spinning in the sea that was the universe, taking 250 million years to complete one rotation—it was the Milky Way. The Earth was not even as big as a mote of dust in this whirlpool, and the Moskstraumen was but another mote of dust on the Earth-dust.

Half an hour later, the boat fell into the eye and disappeared abruptly. Amidst the unchanging rumbling, they seemed to detect the sound of the boat being ground apart.

The helicopter dropped Jason off at Mosken, and Cheng Xin promised to compensate him with a new boat as soon as possible. Then they said farewell and the helicopter headed for Oslo, the nearest city with a sophon-free room.

Everyone remained deep in thought through the voyage, not even conversing with their eyes.

The Moskstraumen's meaning was so obvious that no thought was required.

But the question remained: What did lowering the speed of light have to do with black holes? What did black holes have to do with the cosmic safety notice?

A black hole couldn't change the speed of light; all it could do was to change the wavelength.

Lowering the speed of light in vacuum to one-tenth, one-hundredth, or even one-thousandth of its natural speed would mean thirty thousand kilometers per second, three thousand kilometers per second, and three hundred kilometers per second, respectively. It was hard to tell how black holes would be involved.

There was a threshold here that had to be crossed—hard to do for normal patterns of thinking, but not so for this group, among the most brilliant minds humanity had to offer. Cao Bin, in particular, was good at unconventional ideas. As a physicist who had crossed three centuries, he knew something else: Back during the Common Era, a research group had successfully reduced the speed of light through a medium in a lab to seventeen meters per second, slower than someone riding a bike. Of course, this was not the same as lowering the speed of light through vacuum, but at least it made what he imagined next seem not so crazy.

What if the speed of light were reduced even further, to thirty kilometers per second? Would that involve black holes? It still seemed essentially the same process as before . . . wait!

"Sixteen point seven!" Cao Bin shouted. The fire in his eyes quickly set the other eyes around him ablaze.

The third cosmic velocity of the Solar System was 16.7 kilometers per second. A spacecraft from the Earth could not leave the Solar System without exceeding this limit.

It was the same with light.

If the speed of light through vacuum in the Solar System were reduced to below 16.7 kilometers per second, light would no longer be able to escape the gravity of the Sun, and the Solar System would become a black hole. This was an inescapable consequence of the derivation of the Schwarzschild radius of an object, even if the object was the Solar System. More precisely, the necessary speed limit would be even lower if a larger Schwarzschild radius were desired.

Since nothing could exceed the speed of light, if light couldn't leave the Solar System's event horizon, nothing else could either. The Solar System would be hermetically sealed off from the rest of the universe.

And therefore completely safe—as far as the rest of the universe was concerned.

How would a distant observer see the Solar System black hole created by lowering the speed of light? There were two possibilities: for technologically primitive observers, the Solar System would simply disappear; and, for technologically advanced observers, they should be able to detect the black hole, but instantly understand that the system was safe.

Take a distant star, a barely visible dot. Anyone casually glancing at it would say: Oh, that star is safe; that star will not threaten us.

This was the cosmic safety notice. The impossible was possible, after all.

The interpreters thought of the Glutton's Sea, thought of the Storyless

Kingdom sealed off from the rest of the universe by the sea. This additional bearing coordinate really wasn't necessary—they already understood.

Later, people would call a black hole formed by lowering the speed of light a "black domain." Compared to black holes where the speed of light was unaltered, a reduced-lightspeed black hole had a much larger Schwarzschild radius. The interior was not a space-time singularity, but a fairly open region.

The helicopter continued above the clouds. It was now after 11 P.M., and the sun slowly set in the west, leaving only a slice visible. In the golden light of the midnight sun, everyone tried to imagine life in a world where light moved just below 16.7 kilometers per second, tried to imagine the creeping light of such a sunset.

By now, most of the puzzle pieces in Yun Tianming's stories had fallen into place. But one piece remained: the paintings of Needle-Eye. The interpreters couldn't figure out the dual-layer metaphor or find any bearing coordinates. Some thought that the paintings might be another bearing coordinate for the Moskstraumen, symbolizing the event horizon of the black domain. They reasoned that from an outside observer's perspective, anything entering the black domain would be forever fixed at the event horizon, which resembled being painted into a picture. But most interpreters disagreed. The meaning of the Moskstraumen was very clear, and Tianming had used the Glutton's Sea to act as a bearing coordinate. There was no need for another.

Ultimately, this last piece of the puzzle could not be deciphered. Like the missing arms of *Venus de Milo*, the paintings of Needle-Eye remained mysterious. But as this detail formed the foundation for all three stories and described an elegant ruthlessness, an exquisite cruelty, and a beautiful death, it must have hinted at a great secret of life and death.

Excerpt from *A Past Outside of Time*
Three Paths of Survival for Earth Civilization

━━━━━

I. The Bunker Project: This was the plan with the most hope for success, because it was based entirely on known technologies and involved no theoretical unknowns. In some sense, the Bunker Project could be viewed as a natural continuation of the development of the human race. Even without the threat of a dark forest strike, it was time for humanity to begin colonizing the rest of the Solar System. The Bunker Project just made the effort more focused and the goals clearer.

This was also a plan devised entirely by the Earth itself; it had not been described in the message from Yun Tianming.

II. The Black Domain Plan: This involved transforming the Solar System into a reduced-lightspeed black hole to broadcast a cosmic safety notice. Out of all the choices, this was the most technically challenging. Within a region of space fifty AU (or 7.5 billion kilometers) in radius, a physical constant had to be altered. This was dubbed God's Engineering Project. The theoretical unknowns were immense.

But if the Black Domain Plan were to succeed, it would provide the most protection for Earth civilization. Setting aside its effect as a cosmic safety notice, the black domain itself would act as a highly effective protective barrier. Any external missile, such as a photoid, would be traveling at a very high velocity to produce the necessary destructive power, and would thus enter the black domain with a speed far in excess of the modified speed of light inside. Under the theory of relativity, such an object would have to proceed at the (new, low) speed of light as soon as it crossed the barrier, and its excess kinetic energy would be converted to mass. The first part of the object entering the black domain would suddenly slow down and acquire a much larger mass, while the rest of the object, still moving at the unaltered speed of light, would run into the first part, thereby destroying the entire missile with the impact. Calculations showed that even objects made of strong-interaction materials such as droplets would be completely shattered at the boundary of the black domain. Thus, a black domain was also dubbed "the cosmic safe."

There was yet another advantage to the Black Domain Plan: Out of all three choices, it was the only plan that allowed humanity to continue to live on the familiar surface of the Earth and avoid an exile in space.

But Earth civilization would pay a heavy price. The Solar System would be completely divided from the rest of the universe, equivalent to humanity shrinking their universe from 16 billion light-years across to one hundred AU. Moreover, it was impossible to know what life in such a world would be like. It was certain that electronic and quantum computers would have to operate at extremely low speeds, so humanity might regress to a low-technology society. This would be an even more absolute seal than the technology seal imposed by the sophons. Besides being a cosmic safety notice, the Black Domain Plan was also a form of technological self-mutilation. Humans would never be able to escape from this reduced-lightspeed trap.

III. Lightspeed Spaceflight Plan: Although the theoretical foundation for curvature propulsion was unknown, it was clearly easier than the Black Domain Plan.

Lightspeed spaceflight could not, however, provide any security for Earth civilization. It was only good for escape into the stars. Of all three plans, this involved the most unknowns. Even if it succeeded, members of the human race who escaped into the vast emptiness of space faced unpredictable dangers. Also, the dangers of escapism meant that the plan faced numerous political barriers and traps.

Yet a portion of humanity was certain to be obsessed with lightspeed spaceflight for reasons other than survival.

For people of the Broadcast Era, the only smart choice was to carry out all three plans simultaneously.

Broadcast Era, Year 8
Fate's Choice

Cheng Xin came to the headquarters of the Halo Group.

This was her first time here. She had never participated in its operation because, subconsciously, she never thought of the enormous wealth as truly hers, or Yun Tianming's. They possessed that star, but the wealth generated by the star belonged to society.

But now, perhaps, the Halo Group could help her realize her dream.

The corporate headquarters occupied an entire giant tree. Interestingly, all the buildings on the tree were transparent. Moreover, as the refractive index in the construction material was close to that of the air, all internal structures were visible. One could see employees moving inside as well as countless information windows. The hanging buildings resembled transparent ant farms with colorful ants milling about inside.

Inside the large conference room at the tip of the tree, Cheng Xin got to meet most of the high-level executives of the Halo Group. They were all young, smart, and vivacious. Most of them had never met Cheng Xin before, and they did not disguise their awe and adoration.

After the meeting, when only Cheng Xin and AA remained in the large, empty room, they began to talk about the future of the company. The message from Yun Tianming and the deciphering progress remained secrets from the public. To protect Tianming, Fleet International and the UN planned to release the results gradually to the public and to make them appear as the fruits of research on Earth. Some deliberate false research results would also be mixed in to further conceal the real origin of the information.

Cheng Xin had gotten used to the transparent floor and no longer felt so acrophobic. A few large information windows drifted in the conference room, displaying live video feeds from a few of the Halo Group's construction projects in Earth orbit, one of which was the giant cross in geosynchronous orbit. After Tianming's reappearance, the public's hopes for a miracle gradually faded, and with the initiation of the Bunker Project, the religious fervor dimmed. The church stopped investing in the giant cross, and it was abandoned. Now it was in the process of being dismantled so that only a giant "1" remained—a rather meaningful sight.

"I don't like 'black domain,'" said AA. "It would be more appropriate to call it 'black tomb,' a tomb we dig for ourselves."

Cheng Xin looked at the city below through the transparent floor. "I don't think of it that way. During the era I was from, the Earth was completely separated from the rest of the universe. Everyone lived on the surface, and very rarely did they glance up at the stars. People had lived that way for five thousand years, and you can't just say that wasn't a good life. Even now, the Solar System is basically separated from the rest of the universe. The only people who are in deep space are the thousand or so people on those two spaceships."

"But I feel that if we separate ourselves from the stars, dreams will die."

"Not at all. In ancient times there was happiness and joy as well, and they had no fewer dreams than we. Also, even inside a black domain, we would still see the stars, only . . . who knows what that would look like. . . . Personally, I don't like 'black domain' either."

"I know you don't."

"I like lightspeed ships."

"We all like lightspeed ships. The Halo Group should build lightspeed ships!"

"I thought you weren't going to agree," Cheng Xin said. "This requires heavy investment in basic research."

"You think I'm just a capitalist? Well, you're not wrong. I am, and so are the members of the board of directors. We want to maximize profits. But that doesn't conflict with lightspeed spaceships. Politically, the government will devote the most resources into the Bunker Project and the black domain, but lightspeed ships will be left to entrepreneurs. . . . We should put our efforts into the Bunker Project, and then use some of the profits to research lightspeed ships."

"Here's my thinking, AA: Curvature propulsion and the black domain probably share some fundamental theories. We can wait for the government and the World Academy of Sciences to complete that part of the research, then develop it toward curvature propulsion."

"All right. We should start a Halo Group Academy of Sciences, too, and re-cruit scientists. Many of them have dreamed about lightspeed spaceflight, but they can't find such opportunities in national or international projects—"

AA was interrupted by a sudden surge of new information windows. Windows of all sizes appeared in every direction like a colorful avalanche, quickly burying the few original information windows showing feeds from the Halo Group's projects. A "window avalanche" like this usually indicated the sudden occurrence of some important event, but the flood of information often caused people to be overwhelmed, unable to find out what actually happened. Such was the case with AA and Cheng Xin. They saw that most of the windows were filled with complex text and animated figures, and only those windows that showed pure images could be taken in at a glance. In one of the windows, Cheng Xin saw a few faces looking upwards, then the lens zoomed in until a frightened pair of eyes filled the frame, accompanied by a cacophony of screams. . . .

A new window came to the forefront showing AA's secretary. She stared at AA and Cheng Xin, her face full of terror and shock.

"A warning! An attack!" she shouted.

"Any specifics?" AA asked.

"They activated the first observation unit in the Solar System advance warn-ing system and found a photoid right away!"

"In what direction? How far?"

"I don't know. I don't know anything. All I know—"

"Is this an official warning?" Cheng Xin asked calmly.

"I don't think so. But it's in all the media. I'm sure it's real! Let's get to the spaceport and run for our lives!" The secretary disappeared from the window.

Cheng Xin and AA passed through the dense congeries of information windows and arrived at the transparent wall of the conference room. They saw that panic had already seized the city below them. A massive increase in the number of flying cars outside resulted in chaos, and every vehicle tried to force itself through the jam at high speed. One of the cars struck a giant tree build-ing and erupted into a fireball. Soon, fire and columns of smoke appeared in two other locations in the city. . . .

AA picked out a few information windows and perused them carefully. Cheng Xin, on the other hand, tried to get in touch with the members of the IDC. Most of their phones were busy, and Cheng Xin managed to talk to only two committee members. One of them, like AA and Cheng Xin, knew noth-ing. The other, a PDC official, told Cheng Xin that he could confirm that

Observation Unit #1 in the Solar System advance warning system had noticed some significant anomaly, but he didn't know the specifics. He also confirmed that Fleet International and the UN had not issued a formal dark forest strike alarm, but he wasn't optimistic.

"There are two possibilities for why no alarm has been issued: One, nothing has happened. Two, the photoid is too close and an alarm would be useless."

AA was only able to obtain one piece of specific information from her reading: The photoid was coming along the ecliptic plane. There were conflicting reports concerning its exact direction and distance from the Sun, and estimates of when the photoid would strike the sun diverged wildly: Some claimed that the world had another month; others said only a few hours.

"We should go to *Halo*," AA said.

"Is there enough time?"

Halo was a corporate spaceship that belonged to the Halo Group. Right now, it was parked at the company's geosynchronous base. If the alarm was real, their only hope now was to ride the ship to Jupiter and hide out behind the gas giant before the photoid struck. As Jupiter was in opposition, and therefore as close to the Earth as it could be, it would take twenty-five to thirty days for the ship to fly from the Earth to Jupiter, which was just under the upper end of the range of estimates for when the photoid would strike. But this estimate seemed highly unreliable: The advance warning system was still being constructed, and couldn't have given such an early alert.

"We have to do something instead of waiting here to die!" AA said. She dragged Cheng Xin out of the conference room and onto the parking lot at the top of the tree. They ducked into a flying car, but AA seemed to remember something and got out again. A few minutes later, she returned with an oblong object that resembled a violin case. She opened the case, took out what was inside, and carried it with her into the car, leaving the case behind.

Cheng Xin looked at what was in AA's hand and recognized the implement: a rifle, though adapted to shoot laser bolts instead of bullets.

"Why are you bringing this?" Cheng Xin asked.

"The spaceport is sure to be filled with people—who knows what's going to happen?" AA tossed the rifle onto the backseat and started the flying car.

Every city had a spaceport to service various small space vessels—rather like ancient airports.

The flying car merged into a mighty aerial stream of traffic. All the countless cars in the stream, like a swarm of locusts, were headed for the spaceport.

They cast a flowing shadow along the ground, as though the city's blood was seeping out.

Ahead, a dozen or so white lines rose into the blue sky, trails left by spaceships. They rose straight up and then turned east and disappeared in the depths of the firmament. New white lines continuously shot up from the ground and extended into air, each line headed by a fireball that was brighter even than the sun: the flame from the fusion drives of the ships.

On an information window inside the car, Cheng Xin saw a live video feed taken from near-Earth orbit. Countless rising white lines appeared against the tan background of the continent and extended upward. They grew more numerous, denser, as though the Earth was growing white hair. The fireballs at the ends of the white lines were like fireflies drifting into space. This was the greatest collective escape into space in human history.

Their car arrived above the spaceport. About a hundred spacecraft were arrayed below, and more were being moved out of the giant hangar in the distance. Space planes had long since fallen out of use, and modern shuttles all took off vertically. Unlike the oddly shaped spacecraft Cheng Xin had seen at the port in the space elevator terminal station, these shuttles all had streamlined profiles, with three or four tail fins. They were now erected helter-skelter in the parking lot of the spaceport, like a forest of steel.

AA had called ahead to the hangar to move one of the Halo Group's shuttles onto the lot. She quickly picked out the shuttle from the air and landed their car next to it.

Cheng Xin looked at the shuttles around her. They were of different sizes: The smaller ones were only about a few meters tall, looking like giant versions of artillery shells. It was hard to imagine that such tiny crafts could escape the Earth's gravity well. There were also larger vessels, some as big as ancient airliners. The Halo Group's shuttle was medium-small in size, about ten meters tall, covered with a reflective metallic surface reminiscent of the droplets. The shuttle was parked on a wheeled launch frame so that it could be dragged to the launch point at a moment's notice. They would ride this shuttle to reach *Halo* in orbit.

A loud rumbling came from the launch area, strangely reminding Cheng Xin of the noise made by the Moskstraumen. The ground quaked and her legs felt numb. A great bright glow appeared in the launch area, and a shuttle rose into the air on a ball of flame, adding yet another column of smoke to the sky. A great billowing cloud of white fog flowed toward them, bringing with it a strange burning smell. The fog wasn't generated by the engine of the shuttle, but by the boiled water from the coolant pool below the launch pad. As the launch area and the ships disappeared in the sweltering, muggy steam, people became even more agitated and anxious.

AA and Cheng Xin climbed up a slender set of stairs to board the shuttle. As the fog dissipated, Cheng Xin saw a crowd of children gathered not too far away. They appeared to be elementary school students under the age of ten, dressed in their school uniforms. A young teacher stood with them. Her long hair was buffeted by gusts of wind and she looked around helplessly.

"Can we wait a bit?" Cheng Xin asked.

AA looked over at the children and understood what Cheng Xin wanted. "All right. Go. We have to wait for our turn to get to the launch pad. It will be a while."

In principle, shuttles could take off from any flat part of the ground. However, to prevent ground damage from the ultrahigh-temperature plasma generated by the fusion drive, the shuttles used a launch pad. The launch pad was equipped with a coolant pool and diversion channels to safely redirect the plasma.

The teacher saw Cheng Xin walking over, and came up and grabbed her. "This shuttle is yours, isn't it? Please, please save the children." Her bangs stuck to her forehead, and tears and condensed fog wetted her face. She stared at Cheng Xin intently, as if hoping to seize her with her gaze. The children came over as well, and looked expectantly at Cheng Xin. "They're here for space camp, and they were scheduled to go up in orbit. But after the alert was issued, they refused to take us and sent others up in our place."

"Where's your ship?" AA asked as she walked over.

"It's gone. Please, please!"

"Let's bring them," Cheng Xin said to AA.

AA looked at Cheng Xin for a few seconds. *There are billions of people on the Earth. Do you think you can save them all?*

Cheng Xin's gaze did not waver.

AA shook her head. "We can only bring three more."

"But our shuttle's capacity is eighteen!"

"*Halo* can only seat five under maximum acceleration because it's equipped with only five deep-sea-state capsules. Anyone not in a deep-sea state is going to be crushed into a meat pie."

The answer surprised Cheng Xin. The deep-sea acceleration fluid was only necessary for stellar spaceships. But she had always thought *Halo* was a planetary ship and wasn't capable of voyaging beyond the Solar System.

"All right. Then bring three!" The teacher let go of Cheng Xin and grabbed on to AA, terrified of losing this one chance.

"You pick three, then," said AA.

The teacher let go of AA and stared at her, even more terrified than before. "How am I supposed to pick? How . . ." She looked around, not daring to meet the eyes of the children. She looked to be in utter pain, as if the gazes of the children burned her.

"Fine. I'll pick," AA said. She turned to the children and smiled. "Everyone, listen up. I'm going to ask three questions. Whoever gives the right answers first gets to come with us." She ignored the stunned looks from the teacher and Cheng Xin, and held up a finger. "First question: Say we have a light which is off. After one minute, it blinks. Half a minute later, it blinks again. Fifteen seconds later, it blinks a third time. It keeps on going like this, blinking at intervals that are half of the immediately preceding interval. I want to know how many times it will have blinked by the two-minute mark."

"A hundred!" one of the children blurted out.

AA shook her head. "Wrong."

"A thousand!"

"No. Think carefully."

After a long pause, a timid voice spoke up. The speaker was a gentle and quiet little girl and it was hard to hear her with all the noise. "An infinite number of times."

"Come here," AA said, pointing at the little girl. When she walked over, AA guided her to stand behind herself. "Second question: Say we have a rope whose thickness is uneven. To burn it from one end to the other takes an hour. How do you use this rope to track the passage of fifteen minutes? Remember, the thickness is uneven!"

This time, no child spoke up in a hurry, and they all fell into deep thought. Soon, a boy raised his hand. "Fold the rope end to end, and then burn it from both ends at the same time."

AA nodded. "Come over." She pulled the boy behind her to stand with the girl. "Third question: eighty-two, fifty, twenty-six. What's the next number?"

"Ten!" a girl shouted.

AA gave her a thumb up. "Well done. Come over." Then she nodded at Cheng Xin, took the three children, and headed for the shuttle.

Cheng Xin followed them to the stairs for boarding the shuttle. She looked back. The remaining children and their teacher looked at her as if at a sun that would never rise again. Tears blurred the scene in front of her, and as she climbed up, she could still feel the gazes of despair behind her, like ten thousand arrows piercing her heart. She had felt like this before, during the last moments of her brief career as the Swordholder, and also in Australia when Sophon had announced the plan for exterminating the human race. It was a pain worse than death.

The cabin inside the shuttle was spacious; eighteen seats were arranged in two columns. Since the cabin was vertical, like a well, everyone had to climb a ladder to get to the seats. Cheng Xin experienced the same feeling she had when inside the spherical spacecraft she took to meet Tianming—the shuttle seemed to be a shell only, and she couldn't see where there was space for the engine and the control systems. She thought back to the chemical rockets of the Common Era, each as big as a skyscraper, but the effective payload was only a tiny capsule near the top.

She couldn't see any control surfaces inside the shuttle, and only a few information windows drifted by. The shuttle's AI seemed to recognize AA. As soon as she entered, the windows gathered around her. They moved with her while she went around securing the children's and Cheng Xin's seat belts.

"Don't look at me like that. I gave them a chance. Competition is necessary for survival," AA whispered to Cheng Xin.

"Auntie, are they going to die on the surface?" the boy asked.

"Everyone is going to die. It's just a matter of when." AA sat down next to Cheng Xin. She didn't buckle her seat belt, but continued to examine the information windows. "Damn it. There are still twenty-nine launches ahead of us."

The spaceport had a total of eight launch pads. After each launch, the pad had to cool for ten minutes before the next use because the coolant pools needed to be replenished with fresh water.

The wait shouldn't have mattered much to their survival. The flight to Jupiter would take a month. If the dark forest strike happened before they arrived, it really made no difference if they were on the ground or in space. However, the problem now was that any delay might cause them to not be able to take off at all.

Society had already descended into pandemonium. Driven by the instinct for survival, the more than ten million inhabitants of the city swarmed toward the spaceport. The shuttles, like passenger aircraft during ancient times, could only carry away a small number of people in a short period of time. Possessing a private space vessel was like owning a private airplane, an unattainable dream for most of the population. Even with the space elevator, no more than one percent of the population could reach near-Earth orbit within a week. Those who could finally make the voyage to Jupiter would be one-tenth of that one percent.

There were no portholes on the shuttle, but a few information windows showed the scene outside. They saw dark masses flooding into the parking area. Crowds surrounded every vessel, screaming with their fists raised, hoping to squeeze onto one of them. At the same time, outside the spaceport, some flying cars that had landed took off again. The cars were all empty, and their owners piloted them by remote control in an attempt to stop any more space launches. More and more flying cars gathered in the air, forming a dark, hovering barrier above the launch pads. Very soon, no one would be able to leave.

Cheng Xin minimized the information window and turned around to comfort the three children seated behind her. AA screamed. Cheng Xin turned around and saw a window that had been maximized to fill the entire cabin. In the window, a blinding fireball had appeared in the forest of shuttles.

Someone had begun to launch while surrounded by people in the parking lot!

The plasma emitted by the nuclear fusion drive was tens of times hotter than the emissions of ancient chemical rockets. When launched from a flat surface, the plasma would melt the crust instantaneously and spill out in every direction. No one could survive within a thirty-meter radius. The video feed in the window showed many black dots scattering from the fireball. One of the dots struck a nearby shuttle and left a black mark: a burnt-up body. Several other shuttles around the one that took off toppled, probably because their launch frames had been melted.

The crowd quieted. They looked up and saw the shuttle that had probably killed dozens of people lifting off from the parking lot, rumbling, dragging its white trail until it was high in the air, then turning east. They seemed unable to believe their eyes. A few seconds later, yet another shuttle took off from the parking lot, even closer to them. The rumbling, flames, and waves of superheated air threw the stunned crowd into complete panic. Then a third, a fourth . . . the shuttles in the parking lot took off one after another. Amidst the fiery balls of flame, burnt remains of bodies flew through the air, turning the parking lot into a crematorium.

AA watched the horrifying scene and bit her bottom lip. Then she waved the window away and began to type on another small window.

"What are you doing?" Cheng Xin asked.

"We're taking off."

"No."

"Look." AA tossed another small window at Cheng Xin, which showed the few shuttles around them. A cooling loop was located just above the tail nozzle of each vehicle. The loops were used to dissipate the heat from the fusion reactors. Cheng Xin saw that the loops of all the surrounding shuttles had begun to glow with a dim red light, indicating that their reactors had been turned on in preparation for liftoff.

"We'd better launch before they do," said AA. If any of these shuttles took off, the plasma would probably melt the launch frames of the rest of the shuttles, causing them to topple onto the molten ground.

"No. Stop." Cheng Xin's voice was calm, but unwavering. She had experienced even worse catastrophes, and she would face this one with serenity.

"Why?" AA's voice was equally calm.

"Because there are people around."

AA stopped typing and turned to face Cheng Xin. "Soon, you, me, the crowd, and the Earth itself will all turn into tiny fragments. Can you tell which ones are honorable and which ones despicable in that mess?"

"Our values still hold, at least for now. I'm the president of the Halo Group. This shuttle belongs to the Halo Group, and you're the company's employee. I have the authority to make this decision."

AA stared at Cheng Xin for a few moments, then she nodded and closed the control window. She also turned off all the other information windows, thus isolating the cabin from the mad, noisy world outside.

"Thank you," said Cheng Xin.

AA said nothing. But then she jumped up, as if suddenly remembering something. She picked up the laser rifle from one of the empty seats and climbed down the ladder. "Keep your seat belts on. The shuttle might fall over any moment."

"What are you going to do?" Cheng Xin asked.

"If we can't leave, they can't leave either. Fuck them."

AA opened the cabin door, went out, and immediately closed the door and locked it to prevent anyone from trying to force their way in. Then she climbed down the stairs and began to shoot at the tail fin of the nearest shuttle. Smoke rose up from the tail fin, leaving behind a tiny hole about the size of a finger. That was enough. The self-monitoring system within the shuttle would discover the damage to the tail fin and the AI would refuse to initiate the launch sequence. This was a safety measure that couldn't be overridden by those inside. The cooling ring around the shuttle began to fade, indicating a reactor shutdown. AA turned around in a circle and shot a hole through the tail fins of each of the eight shuttles around them. As the crowd was in total panic, no one noticed what she was doing amidst the waves of heat and smoke and dust.

The door of one of the other shuttles opened, and an elegantly dressed woman climbed down. She walked around the tail of the shuttle and soon discovered the hole. She began to cry hysterically, then rolled around on the ground. She tried to head-butt the launch frame, but no one paid any attention to her. All the crowd cared about was the door to her shuttle, which had been left open. They surged up the stairs and tried to squeeze into the shuttle that could no longer fly.

AA climbed back up the stairs and pushed Cheng Xin, who had poked her head out, back in. Then she followed and shut the door behind her. She began to vomit.

"It smells like . . . barbeque out there," AA finally said after the heaves subsided.

"Are we going to die?" asked one of the girls, poking her head into the aisle from the seat above them.

"We're going to witness a magnificent sight of the cosmos," AA said, a mysterious expression on her face.

"What sight?"

"It's the most impressive thing ever. The Sun is going to turn into a giant firework."

"And then?"

"Then . . . nothing. What can there be when there's nothing?" AA climbed up and patted the three children on their heads in turn. She wasn't going to lie to them. If they could answer her questions, surely they were smart enough to understand the situation.

Again, AA and Cheng Xin sat down next to each other. Cheng Xin put a hand over AA's hand. "I'm sorry."

AA smiled back. It was a smile Cheng Xin was familiar with. In her eyes, AA had always seemed young, less worn down by the darkness of the world that Cheng Xin had experienced. She felt more mature in front of AA, but also powerless.

"Don't worry about it. It's all just busywork anyway. In the end, the result is going to be the same. At least now we can relax." AA exhaled.

If *Halo* really were a stellar ship, then it would be able to get to Jupiter much faster than she had expected. Although the distance between the Earth and

Jupiter wasn't long enough for it to reach maximum acceleration, the whole journey should take only about two weeks.

AA seemed to sense what Cheng Xin was thinking. "Even if the advance warning system had been completely operational, we'd get at most a day's warning. . . . But now that I've thought about it some, I think it's likely a false alarm."

Cheng Xin wasn't sure if that was why AA had submitted to her authority earlier so easily.

AA's theory was quickly proven. The PDC official who was also a member of the IDC called Cheng Xin to let her know that Fleet International and the UN had issued a joint statement that the alarm was false. No signs of a dark forest strike had been detected. AA opened a few information windows, and most of them were broadcasting the announcement from Fleet International and the UN. Outside, the unauthorized launches had ceased. It was still chaotic, but at least the situation wouldn't deteriorate further.

Once the outside had calmed down a bit, Cheng Xin and AA exited the shuttle. The scene that greeted them was like a battlefield. Burnt bodies lay everywhere, charcoal-black, a few still on fire. Many of the shuttles lay on the ground while others leaned against each other. In total, nine shuttles had taken off from the parking lot, and their trails were still clearly visible in the sky, like sliced-open wounds. The crowd was no longer frantic. Some sat on the still-hot ground, some stood in place, stunned, some wandered around aimlessly— and everyone seemed uncertain whether they were experiencing reality or a nightmare. The police had arrived to maintain order, and rescue operations were underway.

"The next warning may be real," AA said to Cheng Xin. "You should come with me to the back of Jupiter. The Halo Group will build a space city for the Bunker Project."

Instead of answering her, Cheng Xin asked, "What is going on with *Halo*?"

"We're not talking about the original ship with that name, but a new miniature stellar spaceship. It can seat twenty during planetary voyages, and five for stellar flight. The board of directors agreed to build it for you, and you can use it as a mobile office at Jupiter."

The difference between a planetary spaceship and a stellar spaceship was like the difference between a ferryboat with a single oar plying a river and an oceangoing container ship with a tonnage measured in tens of thousands. Of course, in spaceships, the difference wasn't merely a matter of volume—there were small stellar spaceships, too. Compared to planetary ships, stellar ships had more advanced propulsion systems, were equipped with ecological cycling systems, and every subsystem had three or four backups. If Cheng Xin really rode the new *Halo* into the shadow of Jupiter, the ship would be able to maintain her for the rest of her life, no matter what happened.

Cheng Xin shook her head. "You should go. Take *Halo*. I don't participate in the day-to-day operations of the company, and it's fine for me to stay on the Earth."

"You just don't want to be one of the few to survive."

"I'm here with billions of people. No matter what happens, if it happens to several billion at the same time, it won't be frightening."

"I'm worried about you," AA said, and grabbed Cheng Xin by both shoulders. "I'm not worried that you'll die along with a few billion others, but that you'll experience things worse than death."

"I've been through that already."

"If you continue to pursue the dream of lightspeed spaceflight, you'll encounter more such experiences. Can you really endure them?"

The false alarm was the largest social disturbance since the Great Resettlement. Although brief in duration and limited in the damage caused, it left an indelible mark in the psyche of the world.

Most of the thousands of spaceports across the world had shuttles that took off while surrounded by crowds, and more than ten thousand people died in the flames of fusion drives. Armed conflicts also took place at the base stations of space elevators. Unlike at the spaceports, the fights at the space elevators involved nations. Some countries attempted to occupy the international elevator's base station in tropical waters, and only the timely confirmation that the attack alarm was false prevented full-scale warfare. In orbits around Earth, and even on Mars, groups of people fought over spaceships.

In addition to the degenerates who were willing to kill to ensure their own survival, the public discovered something else that disgusted them during the course of the false alarm: tens of small stellar spaceships and near-stellar spaceships were discovered to be in secret construction in geosynchronous orbit and on the dark side of the moon. Near-stellar spaceships possessed the ecological cycling systems of stellar ships, but were only equipped with propulsion systems for interplanetary flight. Some of these luxurious yachts belonged to large companies, and others to extremely wealthy individuals. All the crafts were small, and could only maintain a few people with their ecological cycling systems. They had only one purpose: long-term seclusion behind the giant planets.

The advance warning system that was still being constructed could only provide a warning window of about twenty-four hours. If a dark forest strike really arrived, there wasn't enough time for any spacecraft to go from the Earth to Jupiter, the nearest barrier planet. In actuality, the Earth dangled over a sea of death. Rationally, everyone understood this, and the ugly fights that broke out during the false alarm were nothing more than meaningless mass madness driven by a survival instinct that overwhelmed rational thinking. Currently, about fifty thousand individuals resided at Jupiter—most of them were space force personnel at the Jupiter base, along with some staff doing preparatory work for the Bunker Project. They had plenty of justification for being at Jupiter, and the public did not begrudge them their place. But once these secret stellar ships were completed, their wealthy owners would be able to hide in the shadow of Jupiter indefinitely.

Legally—at least right now—there was no international or national prohibition against the construction of stellar ships by organizations or individuals, and hiding out behind the gas giants wasn't the same as Escapism. However, the inequality here was seen as the greatest in human history: inequality before death.

Historically, inequality mainly manifested itself in areas like economics or social status, but death basically treated everyone the same. To be sure, such equality wasn't absolute: For instance, access to medical care wasn't evenly distributed; the wealthy fared better in natural disasters than the poor; soldiers and civilians had different rates of survival in war; and so on. But never before had a situation like this presented itself: less than one-ten-thousandth of the population could go into safe hiding, leaving billions on Earth to die.

Even in ancient times, such manifest inequality would have been intolerable, let alone now.

This led directly to international skepticism about the plan for lightspeed ships.

Although spaceships hiding permanently behind Jupiter or Saturn could survive a dark forest strike, life on those ships would not be enviable. No matter how comfortable the ecological cycling systems made the shipboard environment, the occupants would be living in the cold, desolate regions of the outer Solar System in isolation. But as observations of the Second Trisolaran Fleet revealed, spacecraft powered by curvature propulsion could achieve lightspeed almost instantaneously. A lightspeed ship could go from the Earth to Jupiter in less than an hour, and the advance warning system would be more than sufficient. Powerful and wealthy individuals who possessed lightspeed ships could thus live in comfort on the Earth and then escape at the last minute, without regard for the billions left behind. This was a prospect society simply could not tolerate. The terrifying sights from the false alarm remained fresh in the public's mind, and most people agreed that the appearance of lightspeed ships would lead to worldwide chaos. Thus, the plan for developing lightspeed ships faced unprecedented resistance.

The false alarm was the result of the explosive amplifying effects of a hyper-information society when fed sensitive news. Its source was an anomaly detected by the first observation unit of the advance warning system. The anomaly was real, though it had nothing to do with photoids.

Excerpt from *A Past Outside of Time*
Space Sentries: The Solar System Advance Warning System

The Earth had observed photoids only twice in the past: the destruction of 187J3X1 and of the Trisolaran system. Knowledge about the phenomenon was thus limited. All that was known was that a photoid moved at close to the speed of light, but there was no data concerning its volume, rest mass, or relativistic mass as it approached the speed of light. A photoid was certainly the most primitive weapon capable of attacking a star, since it relied only on the enormous kinetic energy generated by its high relativistic mass to damage the target. Once a civilization possessed the technology to accelerate an object to near the speed of light, a "bullet" with very little mass possessed immense destructive power. This was indeed "economical."

The most valuable data concerning photoids was obtained right before the annihilation of the Trisolaran system. Scientists were able to make an important discovery: Due to a photoid's ultrahigh velocity, powerful radiation ranging from visible light to gamma rays was emitted as it collided with the few atoms scattered in space and interstellar dust. The radiation had distinctive characteristics. Since the photoids were extremely small, direct observation of them was impossible. But the characteristic radiation could be detected.

At first blush, it seemed impossible to give advance warning for photoids, because they moved at close to the speed of light. This meant that they moved almost as fast as the radiation they generated, and reached their target almost simultaneously. In other words, the observer was outside the event's light cone.

But reality was a bit more complicated. Any object with rest mass could not achieve lightspeed. Although a photoid's speed approached lightspeed, it was still slightly slower than true lightspeed. This difference meant that the radiation from the photoid moved just a bit faster than the photoid itself. If the photoid had to travel a long distance, this difference was magnified. Also, a photoid's trajectory to the target wasn't an absolute straight line. Since it wasn't massless, it couldn't avoid the gravitational attractions of nearby celestial bodies, and its path typically ended up being slightly curved. The curvature was much greater than the curvature of light through the same gravitational field. For the photoid to strike the target, its trajectory had to take this effect into account. This meant that the path traveled by the photoid was longer than the path taken by its radiation.

For these two reasons, the radiation from the photoid would reach the Solar System before the photoid itself. The twenty-four-hour estimated warning period was calculated based on the maximum distance at which photoid emissions could be observed. By the time the radiation reached the Earth, the photoid itself would still be about 180 AU away.

But that was merely the ideal scenario. If the photoid were launched from a nearby spaceship, there would be almost no warning—like what had happened to Trisolaris.

Thirty-five observation units were planned for the Solar System advance warning system. These would monitor the sky in every direction for photoid emissions.

Broadcast Era, Year 8
Fate's Choice

Two days before the false alarm; Observation Unit #1

Observation Unit #1 was in fact just the Ringier-Fitzroy Station from the end of the Crisis Era. More than seventy years ago, it was this observation station that had first discovered the strong-interaction space probes—the droplets. The station was still located on the outer edge of the asteroid belt, but all its equipment had been updated. Take the visible light telescope, for instance: The lenses were even bigger, and the first lens's diameter had increased from twelve hundred meters to two thousand meters, big enough for a small town to fit on it. These gigantic lenses were made from materials taken directly from the asteroid belt. The first one was a medium-sized lens five hundred meters in diameter. After that was finished, it was used to focus sunlight on asteroids so that the melted rock could be made into pure glass and then formed into additional lenses. In total, six lenses floated in a ten-kilometer-long column in space, far apart from each other. The observation station itself was located at the end of the column of lenses, and could only hold a crew of two.

The crew was still made up of a scientist and a military officer. The officer was responsible for monitoring photoid emissions, while the scientist conducted astronomical and cosmological research. Thus, the tradition of fighting for observation time begun three centuries ago by General Fitzroy and Dr. Ringier continued.

After this, the largest telescope in history, had completed its shakedown tests and successfully taken its first image—a star forty-seven light-years away—Widnall, the astronomer on the crew, was as excited as if he'd just had a son. Laymen did not understand that previous telescopes could only amplify the luminosity of stars outside the Solar System, not reveal any shapes. No matter how powerful the telescopes were, the stars always showed up as tiny point sources, only incrementally brighter than images taken by lesser telescopes. But now, in the view of this ultrapowerful telescope, a star showed up as a disk for the first time. Though it was small, like a Ping-Pong ball seen from tens of meters away, and one couldn't see any details in the disk, this was still an epochal moment in the history of the ancient science of visible-light astronomy.

"The cataracts have been removed from the eyes of astronomy!" said Widnall dramatically, wiping his eyes.

But Sublieutenant Vasilenko wasn't impressed. "I think you need to remember our role here: We are sentries. In the old days, we'd be perched atop a wooden watchtower on the frontier, a desolate desert or snowfield around us. Standing erect in the frigid breeze, we'd be gazing in the direction of the enemy. As soon as we saw tanks coming up the horizon, or men on horses, we'd make a call or light smoke signals to inform the homeland that the enemy invasion had begun. . . . You need to get into that mental space. Don't think of yourself as being in an observatory."

Widnall's eyes temporarily left the terminal showing the image from the telescope and looked out the porthole of the station. He could see a few irregularly shaped rocks drifting at some distance: fragments of asteroids left from the glass-making operation. They spun slowly in the cold sunlight and seemed to emphasize the desolation of space. The scene did seem to evoke a sense of the "mental space" the sublieutenant described.

Widnall said, "If we really discover a photoid, it would be better to not issue a warning at all. It's useless, anyway. To die suddenly without even knowing what hit you is actually a rather fortunate fate. But you'd rather torture a few billion people for twenty-four hours. I think that's akin to a crime against humanity."

"By that logic, you and I would be the most unfortunate people in the world since we would know about our fate the longest."

The observation station received new orders from Fleet Command to adjust the telescope and observe the remnants of the Trisolaran system. Widnall didn't argue with Vasilenko this time, because he was very interested in that ruined world as well.

The floating lenses began to move around and adjust their positions, the plasma thrusters at the rims of the lenses emitting blue flames. Only now did the lenses in the distance reveal themselves, the blue flames marking out the overall shape of the telescope. The ten-kilometer-long group of lenses slowly turned, stopping when the telescope was pointed in the direction of the Trisolaran system. Then the lenses shifted up and down the axis to focus. Finally, most of the flames went out, with only a few fireflies flickering now and then as the lenses engaged in precision focus adjustments.

In the unprocessed view of the telescope, the Trisolaran system looked very ordinary, just a small patch of white against the background of space, like a feather. But after the image had been processed and magnified, it appeared as a magnificent nebula that took up the entire screen. It had been seven years since the explosion of the star, so what they were seeing now was the scene three years after the explosion. Under the influence of gravity and the exploded star's angular momentum, the nebula had turned from sharp radiating rays into a soft blur of clouds, which was then flattened by the centrifugal force of the spin into a spiral. Above the nebula, the two remaining stars could be seen. One of them showed up as a disk, while the other one, more distant, remained a point of light distinguished only by its motion against the background stars.

The two stars that survived the catastrophe achieved the dream of generations on Trisolaris and formed a stable double-star system, but no life would enjoy their light, as the entire system was now uninhabitable. It was now apparent that the dark forest strike had destroyed only one star out of the three, not only because of economics, but also to achieve a more sinister goal: As long as the system still retained one or two stars, the material in the nebula would be constantly absorbed by the stars, generating powerful radiation in the process. The Trisolaran system was now a radiation furnace, a domain of death for life and civilization. It was the powerful radiation that caused the nebula itself to glow and appear so clear and bright on the telescope.

"I'm reminded of the clouds viewed from atop Mount Emei," said Vasilenko. "That's a mountain in China. Viewing the moon from the peak is an exquisite sight. The night I was there, the peak floated in a boundless sea of clouds, turned pure silver by the moon above. It looked a lot like this."

Seeing this silvery graveyard more than forty trillion kilometers away made Widnall wax philosophical. "From a scientific perspective, 'destroy' isn't really accurate. Nothing has disappeared. All the matter that used to be there is still there, and so is all the angular momentum. It's only the arrangement of matter that has changed, like a deck of cards being reshuffled. But life is like a straight flush: Once you shuffle, it's gone."

Widnall examined the image some more and made an important discovery.

"What is *that*?!" He pointed at a spot in the image some distance from the nebula. By scale, it was about thirty AU from the nebula center.

Vasilenko stared at the spot. He lacked the trained eye of an astronomer, and couldn't see anything unusual at first. But eventually, he saw a vague circular outline against the pitch-black background, like a soap bubble in space.

"It's very large. The diameter is about . . . ten astronomical units. Is it dust?"

"Absolutely not. Dust doesn't look anything like that."

"You've never seen it before?"

"No one could have seen it. Whatever it is, it's transparent, with a very faint border. The largest telescopes in the past wouldn't have been able to detect it."

Widnall zoomed out a bit to get a better sense of the position of the strange new object with respect to the double stars, and to try to observe the spin of the nebula. On the screen, the nebula again turned into a small patch of white against the black abyss of space.

About six thousand AU from the Trisolaran system, he found another "soap bubble." This one was much bigger than the first, with a diameter of about fifty AU, spacious enough to contain the Trisolaran system or the Solar System.

"My God!" Vasilenko cried out. "Do you know where that is?"

Widnall stared at the screen for a while and said, tentatively, "That's where the Second Trisolaran Fleet went into lightspeed, isn't it?"

"Exactly."

"You're certain?"

"My old job was to observe this part of space. I know it better than the palm of my hand."

The conclusion was inescapable: Ships using curvature propulsion left behind trails as they accelerated to lightspeed. The trails apparently did not fade with time, but expanded and altered the nature of the space around them.

The first, smaller bubble was inside the Trisolaran system. There were several possible explanations for its existence. Perhaps the Trisolarans did not know initially that curvature propulsion would leave behind such trails, and the bubble was an accident created during engine tests or test flights; or perhaps they did know about the trails, but left them within the star system by mistake. But it was certain that they wanted to avoid purposefully leaving such trails. Eleven years ago, the Second Trisolaran Fleet had cruised for a full year using conventional means, and only when they were six thousand AU from their home world did they engage the curvature engines to enter lightspeed. The purpose was to start the trails as far from the home world as possible, though by that time it was already too late.

At the time, the behavior of the Second Trisolaran Fleet had puzzled people. The most convincing explanation was that they were trying to avoid ill effects on the home world caused by 415 ships entering lightspeed. However, it was clear now that they were trying to avoid exposing the location of Trisolaris by the trails of curvature propulsion. The Second Trisolaran Fleet had exited lightspeed when it was still six thousand AU from the Solar System for the same reason.

Widnall and Vasilenko stared at each other, and they could each see the terror building in the other's eyes. They had reached the same conclusion.

"We have to report this right away," said Widnall.

"But it's not time yet for our scheduled report. A report now would be treated as an alarm."

"This *is* an alarm! We have to tell people not to expose us."

"That's a bit of a stretch. We've just begun researching lightspeed ships. It would be impressive if we managed to build one in half a century."

"But what if an initial test generates such a trail? Maybe they're already conducting such trials somewhere in the Solar System!"

And so this information was transmitted to Fleet Command with an alarm-level neutrino beam, then passed on to the PDC. There, it was leaked and mistaken as a photoid attack alarm, which caused the global panic two days later.

The curvature trails were left behind when ships entered lightspeed, just as a rocket launching from the ground left burn marks on the launch pad. Once the ship was at lightspeed, it continued to coast by inertia, and left no more trails. It was a reasonable conjecture that dropping out of lightspeed would leave behind similar marks. It was still unknown how long such trails would persist in space. A guess was that the trails represented some kind of distortion in space due to curvature propulsion, and might last a long time—maybe even forever.

It was reasonable to conclude that Sophon had claimed Trisolaris appeared more dangerous than the Solar System when observed from a distance because of the ten-AU-diameter curvature propulsion trail left behind within the Trisolaran system, which is what caused the dark forest strike against Trisolaris to come so quickly. The trail and the broadcast of Trisolaris's location mutually provided confirmation and made the danger value of the Trisolaran system skyrocket.

During the following month, Observation Unit #1 discovered six more curvature propulsion trails in different parts of space. All of these were approximately spherical, though their sizes varied widely, ranging from fifteen to two hundred AU. One of these bubbles was only six thousand AU from the Solar System, apparently the mark left by the Second Trisolaran Fleet as it dropped out of lightspeed. The directions and distances of the other trails, however, seemed to indicate that they had nothing to do with the Second Trisolaran Fleet. It appeared that curvature propulsion trails were common in the universe.

After *Blue Space* and *Gravity*'s discovery inside the four-dimensional space fragment, this provided yet more direct evidence that large numbers of highly intelligent civilizations existed in the cosmos.

One of the trails was only 1.4 light-years from the Sun, close to the Oort Cloud. A spaceship had apparently lingered there and then left by entering lightspeed. No one knew when this had happened.

The discovery of the curvature propulsion trail finally eliminated lightspeed space flight, already facing mounting skepticism, from consideration as a viable plan. Fleet International and the UN quickly enacted legislation prohibiting any further research and development of curvature propulsion, and the nation states followed suit. This was the most severe legal restriction against a technology since the nuclear nonproliferation treaties of three centuries ago.

Humanity now had only two choices left: the Bunker Project and the Black Domain Plan.

Superficially, research and development of lightspeed spaceflight died for obvious reasons: to avoid advance exposure of the existence of Earth civilization by the trails generated from curvature propulsion, and to prevent increasing the Solar System's danger value in the eyes of observers elsewhere in the cosmos, either of which might have led to an earlier dark forest strike. But there were deeper reasons, too.

From the Common Era to the end of the Crisis Era, humanity looked at the stars with hope. But the first few steps they took toward the stars resulted in failure and pain. The tragic Doomsday Battle revealed the extent of humanity's fragility in the cosmos, and the internecine warfare of the Battle of Darkness had injured the human spirit in equal measure. Later events, such as the judgment of *Bronze Age* and the hijacking of *Gravity* by *Blue Space*, resulting in the universal broadcast, all deepened these wounds and elevated the pain to the level of philosophy.

As a matter of fact, most of the general public was relatively uninvested in the quest for lightspeed spaceships. They believed that even if such ships could be built within their lifetimes, they would have no chance of making use of them.

They cared far more about the Bunker Project, which seemed the most practical path to survival. To be sure, they also cared for the Black Domain Plan, because three centuries of horror had infused them with a strong desire for a serene life, and the Black Domain Plan promised just such a life. Although people were disappointed at the prospect of being sealed off from the rest of the universe, the Solar System itself was large enough that the disappointment was tolerable. The reason they were more interested in the Bunker Project than the Black Domain Plan was because even laypeople could see the extreme technical challenges of slowing down lightspeed, and generally agreed that it was unlikely for mere Man to complete God's Engineering Project.

On the other hand, both staunch opponents and fervent supporters of lightspeed spaceships belonged to the elite classes of society.

The faction in support of researching lightspeed spaceflight believed that the ultimate security of the human race required expansion into the Milky Way and settlement among the stars. In this unfeeling cosmos, only outward-facing civilizations had a chance of survival, and isolationism ultimately led to annihilation. Those who held such views generally did not oppose the Bunker Project, but passionately despised the Black Domain Plan, viewing it as an attempt to dig humankind's own grave. Even though they conceded that a black domain would guarantee the long-term survival of the human race, they saw such life as death for the civilization.

The faction opposed to researching lightspeed vessels felt this way for political reasons. They believed that human civilization had suffered many trials before reaching a nearly ideal democratic society, but once humanity headed for space, it would inevitably regress socially. Space was like a distorting mirror that magnified the dark side of humanity to the maximum. A line from one of the Bronze Age defendants, Sebastian Schneider, became their slogan:

> When humans are lost in space, it takes only five minutes to reach totalitarianism.

For a democratic, civilized Earth to scatter innumerable seeds of totalitarianism among the Milky Way was a prospect that these people found intolerable.

The child that was human civilization had opened the door to her home and glanced outside. The endless night terrified her so much that she shuddered against the expansive and profound darkness, and shut the door firmly.

Cheng Xin once again returned to the point in space where the Sun's and the Earth's gravities balanced each other out. A year had passed since the meeting with Yun Tianming, and she was far more relaxed for this trip. She was here as a volunteer for the Bunker Project simulation test.

Fleet International and the UN conducted this simulation jointly. Its goal was to test the effectiveness of the giant planets as barriers in the event of a solar explosion.

A supersized hydrogen bomb would play the role of the exploding sun. The power of nuclear bombs was no longer measured in TNT-equivalents, but this bomb's yield would be approximately three hundred megatons. In order to more realistically simulate the physical conditions of a solar explosion, the hydrogen bomb was wrapped in a thick shell to mimic the solar material that would be thrown off by the explosion. The eight planets were modeled with fragments of asteroids. Of these, the four asteroids modeling terrestrial planets were around ten meters in diameter; the ones modeling the gas giants were far bigger, each around one hundred meters in diameter. The eight fragments were positioned around the hydrogen bomb at distances that replicated the relative distances of the planets, so that the entire system resembled a miniature Solar System. "Mercury," which was closest, was about four kilometers from the "Sun," and "Neptune," which was farthest, was about three hundred kilometers away. The test was conducted at the Lagrangian point to minimize the effects of the Sun's and the planets' gravities so that the system could remain stable for some time.

Scientifically, this experiment wasn't really necessary. Computer modeling based on existing data was more than adequate to produce results that could be trusted. Even if physical tests had to be done, they could have taken place in a laboratory. Though the scale would have to be smaller, careful design would have yielded considerable precision. As a science experiment, this large-scale simulation in space was clumsy to the point of being idiotic.

But the experimenters who had envisioned, designed, and implemented the simulation understood that the ultimate goal of this trial wasn't science. It was actually an expensive propaganda effort to stabilize international faith in the Bunker Project. The trial had to be direct and visually impactful, so that it could be broadcast to the world.

After the total rejection of any further research into lightspeed spaceflight, conditions on Earth resembled the beginning of the Crisis Era. Back then, global defense against the Trisolaran invasion expended effort in two areas: one was the mainstream plan of constructing the Solar System's defenses, and the other was the Wallfacer Project. Now, humankind's mainstream survival plan was the Bunker Project, and the Black Domain Plan, like the Wallfacer Project, was a gamble filled with unknowns. The plans were carried out in parallel, but since only theoretical research was possible on black domains, limited resources were committed. The Bunker Project, on the other hand, extensively impacted all of human society, and great effort had to be expended to secure the public's support.

It would have been sufficient to leave monitoring equipment behind the rocky fragments, in order to test the shielding effects of the "gas giants," or perhaps animal subjects. But in order to ensure a sensational reaction, the organizers decided that live human subjects were necessary, and so a global effort was undertaken to recruit volunteers.

艾 AA was the one who suggested Cheng Xin send in an application. AA believed that this was an excellent opportunity to do some free marketing to burnish the Halo Group's public image in preparation for entry into the Bunker Project. She and Cheng Xin also both understood that the trial had been planned carefully. It might look unsettling, but there was basically no danger.

Cheng Xin's spacecraft stopped in the shadow of the fragment representing Jupiter. This irregular asteroid was shaped like a potato. It was about 110 meters long, with an average width of around seventy meters. Over a period of two months, the asteroid had been pushed from its home in the asteroid belt to here. During its voyage, some artistic engineer who had too much time on his hands had painted it with colorful bands similar to the ones on the real Jupiter, including the Great Red Spot. Overall, however, the painted asteroid did not resemble Jupiter, but some space monster with a Cyclopean red eye.

As on her last voyage, Cheng Xin's spacecraft flew against the brilliant sun, but once it entered the shadow of the asteroid, everything darkened immediately, because there was no air in space to scatter the sunlight. The Sun on the other side of the asteroid might as well not have existed. Cheng Xin felt she was at the foot of a cliff at midnight.

Even without the barrier of the asteroid, it would have been impossible to see the hydrogen bomb simulating the Sun fifty kilometers away. But in the other direction, she could see the simulated "Saturn." By scale, it was just about a hundred kilometers from the "Sun" and fifty kilometers from "Jupiter." It was about the same size as this asteroid fragment, and, illuminated by the real Sun, stood out against the backdrop of space so that Cheng Xin could just tell its shape. She could also see "Uranus" about two hundred kilometers away, though that was just a shiny dot, hard to tell apart from the stars. The rest of the "planets" were invisible.

Along with Cheng Xin's dinghy, about nineteen other space vessels were parked behind "Jupiter." Together, these simulated the twenty planned Jovian space cities. The spaceships were lined up in three rows behind the asteroid, and Cheng Xin was in the front-most row, about ten meters from the asteroid. More than a hundred volunteers were seated in the ships. Originally, AA had planned to come with Cheng Xin, but company business kept her away. Thus, Cheng Xin's dinghy might be the only one sheltered behind "Jupiter" with a lone passenger.

They could see the bright blue Earth about 1.5 million kilometers away. More than three billion people there were watching a live broadcast of the trial.

The countdown indicated that about ten minutes remained before the start of the detonation. The communications channels quieted. Abruptly, a man's voice spoke up.

"Hello. I'm next to you."

Cheng Xin shuddered as she recognized the voice. Her dinghy was at one end of the five vessels in the first row. Looking to her right, she saw a spherical dinghy very similar to the one she had ridden in a year ago parked right next to hers. Almost half the hull was transparent, and she could see five passengers inside. Thomas Wade was sitting on the side closest to her, and waved at her. Cheng Xin was able to recognize him right away because, unlike the other four passengers, he wasn't wearing a lightweight space suit; instead, he wore only his black leather jacket, as if to show his contempt for space. His sleeve remained empty, indicating that he still had not gotten a prosthetic hand.

"Let's dock so I can come over," Wade said. Without waiting for Cheng Xin to agree, he initiated the docking sequence. The dinghy he was in started its maneuvering thrusters and slowly approached Cheng Xin's dinghy. Reluctantly, Cheng Xin initiated the docking procedure as well. After a slight tremor, the two ships were connected, and both sets of cabin doors slid open noiselessly. As the pressure between the two ships equalized, Cheng Xin's ears popped.

Wade floated over. He couldn't have had much experience in space, but like Cheng Xin, he moved as though he was born to it. Though he had only one hand, his movements in weightlessness were steady and firm, as though gravity still worked on him. The interior of the cabin was dim. Sunlight, reflected from the Earth, was deflected again by the asteroid into the dinghy. In this obscure light, Cheng Xin looked Wade over and found him not much changed by the intervening eight years. He still looked pretty much the same as he had in Australia.

"What are you doing here?" Cheng Xin asked, trying to keep her voice cool. But she always seemed to have trouble maintaining her composure in front of this man. After what she had gone through the last few years, everything in her heart had been polished until it was as smooth as the asteroid in front of her, but Wade remained a singular sharp corner.

"I finished my sentence a month ago." Wade took half of a cigar from his jacket pocket—though he couldn't light it here. "It was reduced. A murderer, out in eleven years—I know that's not fair . . . to you."

"We all have to follow the law. There's nothing unfair about that."

"Follow the law in everything? Including lightspeed propulsion?"

Just like before, Wade got straight to the point without wasting any time. Cheng Xin didn't answer.

"Why do you want lightspeed ships?" Wade asked. He turned and stared at Cheng Xin brazenly.

"Because that is the only choice that makes humankind grand," Cheng Xin said. She met his gaze fearlessly.

Wade nodded and took the cigar out of his mouth. "Very good. You're grand."

Cheng Xin looked at him, her eyes asking the unspoken question.

"You know what is right, and you have the courage and sense of duty to do it. This makes you extraordinary."

"But?" Cheng Xin prompted.

"But, you don't have the skill or the will to complete this task. We share the same ideal. I also want to see lightspeed ships built."

"What are you trying to say?"

"Give it to me."

"Give what to you?"

"Everything you own. Your company, your wealth, your authority, your position—and if possible, your reputation and glory. I will use them all to build lightspeed ships, for your ideals, and for the grandness of the human spirit."

The thrusters of the dinghy came on again. Although the asteroid generated little gravity, it was still enough to make the dinghy fall toward it slowly. The thrusters pushed the dinghy away from the rock until it returned to its assigned location. The plasma nozzle illuminated the surface of the asteroid fragment, and the red spot painted on it looked like a suddenly opened eye. Cheng Xin's heart tensed, whether due to this eye or Wade's words. Wade stared back at the giant eye, his gaze sharp and cold, with a hint of mockery.

Cheng Xin said nothing. She couldn't think of anything to say.

"Don't make the same mistake a second time," Wade said. Each word struck Cheng Xin's heart like a heavy hammer.

It was time: The hydrogen bomb exploded. Without the obstruction of an atmosphere, nearly all of its energy was released in the form of radiation. In the live feed taken from about four hundred kilometers away, a fireball appeared next to the Sun. Soon, the brightness and size of the fireball exceeded the Sun itself, and the camera's filters quickly dimmed the light. If someone were to gaze at it directly from this distance, he or she would be blinded permanently. By the time the fireball reached maximum brightness, there was nothing in the camera's view but pure whiteness. The flame seemed ready to swallow the entire universe.

Sheltered in the shadow of the giant rock, Cheng Xin and Wade did not witness this sight. The live broadcast feed was shut off within the cabin, but they could see "Saturn" behind them increase in brightness abruptly. Next, the molten lava generated on the side of "Jupiter" facing the "Sun" flew around them. The lava glowed red as it dripped away from the edge of the asteroid, but after it flew some distance away, the reflected light from the nuclear detonation exceeded its inherent red glow, and the thin dribbles of lava turned into brilliant fireworks. The view from the dinghy resembled the view from the top of a silvery waterfall tumbling down toward the Earth. By now, the four smaller asteroid fragments simulating the terrestrial planets had been incinerated, and the four larger asteroid fragments simulating the gas giants behaved as four scoops of ice cream being heated on one side by a blowtorch. The side facing the detonation melted and turned into a smooth hemisphere, and every "planet" dripped a silvery tail of lava. More than ten seconds after the radiation reached "Jupiter," the simulated stellar material, consisting of pieces of the exploded shell of the hydrogen bomb, struck the massive asteroid fragment, causing it to quake and drift slowly away from the "Sun." The dinghy's thrusters activated and maintained distance from the fragment.

The fireball persisted for about thirty seconds before going out. Space seemed like a hall where the light had suddenly been shut off. The real Sun, about one AU away, appeared dim. As the fireball disappeared, the light emitted by the red-glowing half of the asteroid fragment became visible. Initially, the light was very bright, as though the rock were on fire, but the frigidity of space quickly chilled it to a dim red glow. The solidified lava at the rim of the fragment formed a circle of long stalactites.

The fifty spaceships sheltered behind the four giant asteroid fragments were unharmed.

The live feed arrived at the Earth five seconds later, and the world erupted into cheers. Hope for the future exploded everywhere like the hydrogen bomb. The goal of the Bunker Project simulation test had been achieved.

"Don't make the same mistake twice," Wade repeated, as though all that had just happened was nothing more than noise that had briefly interrupted their conversation.

Cheng Xin stared at the dinghy Wade had come from. The four men in space suits had been looking in this direction the entire time, oblivious to the magnificent sight that had just taken place. Cheng Xin knew that tens of thousands of people had volunteered for the test, and only famous or important people had been selected. Although Wade had just gotten out of prison, he already had powerful followers—those four men, at least—and the dinghy probably also belonged to him. Even eleven years ago, when he had competed for the Swordholder position, he had had many loyal followers, and even more supporters. It was rumored that he had founded a secret organization, which had perhaps survived. He was like a piece of nuclear fuel. Even when it was sealed up in a lead container, one could feel its power and threat.

"Let me think about it," said Cheng Xin.

"Of course you need to think about it." Wade nodded at Cheng Xin, then left noiselessly as he drifted back to his own ship. The cabin door closed, and the two ships separated.

In the direction of the Earth, the cooled lava bits drifted languidly against the starry background like a field of dust. Cheng Xin felt the tension in her heart give way, and she herself felt like a mote of dust drifting through the cosmos.

On the way back, when the dinghy was within three hundred thousand kilometers of the Earth so that there was essentially no delay in communications, Cheng Xin called AA and told her about the meeting with Wade.

"Do as he said," AA said without hesitation. "Give him everything he asked for."

"You . . ." Cheng Xin stared at AA in the information window, astonished. She had imagined AA would be the biggest obstacle.

"He's right. You don't have the capacity for this. The attempt will ruin you! But he can get it done. This bastard, devil, murderer, careerist, political hooligan, technophilic madman . . . he can get it done. He has the will and skill for this, so let him! It's hell, so step aside for him to jump in."

"What about you?"

AA smiled. "I would never work under him, of course. Ever since they proscribed lightspeed ships, I've grown afraid, too. I will take what I deserve and go do something I enjoy. I hope you do, too."

Two days later, in the transparent conference hall at the top of the Halo Group headquarters, Cheng Xin met with Wade.

"I can give you everything you want," Cheng Xin said.

"Then you'll go into hibernation," Wade said. "Because your presence may affect our task."

Cheng Xin nodded. "Yes. That is my plan."

"We'll awaken you on the day we achieve success, which will be your success as well. On that day, if lightspeed ships are still against the law, we'll accept all responsibility. If such ships are welcomed by the world, the honor will belong to you. . . . It will be at least half a century, or even longer. We'll be old, but you'll still be young."

"I have one condition."

"Speak."

"If this project ever has the potential to harm the human race, you must awaken me. The final decision is mine, and I have the right to take back all the authority I give you."

"I can't accept that."

"Then we have nothing to discuss. I'll give you nothing."

"Cheng Xin, you must know what path we'll be taking. Sometimes, one must—"

"Forget it. We'll go our separate ways."

Wade stared at Cheng Xin. In his eyes were feelings rarely seen in him: hesitation, even helplessness. It was as unexpected to see these things in him as it was to see water in fire. "Let me think about it."

He turned and walked over to one of the transparent walls and gazed at the metropolitan forest outside. On that night three centuries ago at the plaza in front of the UN, Cheng Xin had also seen the back of this black figure against the lights of New York City.

About two minutes later, Wade turned around. Still standing at the transparent wall, he looked at Cheng Xin from across the room. "All right. I accept."

Cheng Xin remembered that three centuries ago, after turning around, he had said, "We'll send only a brain." Those words had changed the course of history.

"I don't have many means to enforce our deal. I can only trust your promise."

That smile, like a crack in the ice, spread across Wade's face. "You are perfectly aware that if I break my promise, it will actually be a blessing for you. But unfortunately, I will keep my promise."

Wade walked back and straightened his leather jacket, which only caused more wrinkles to appear. He stood in front of Cheng Xin and solemnly said, "I promise that if, during the process of researching lightspeed spaceflight, we discover anything that may harm the human race, regardless of the form of the danger, we'll awaken you. You'll have the final say and can take back all of my authority."

After hearing about the meeting with Wade, AA said to Cheng Xin, "Then I'll need to go into hibernation with you. We have to be prepared to take back the Halo Group at a moment's notice."

"You believe he'll keep his promise?" asked Cheng Xin.

AA stared straight ahead, as though looking at a ghost Wade. "I do. I think the devil will do as he says. But just like he said, that's not necessarily a good thing for you. You could have saved yourself, Cheng Xin, but in the end, you didn't."

Ten days later, Thomas Wade became the president of the Halo Group and took over all operations.

Cheng Xin and AA entered hibernation. Their consciousnesses gradually faded in the cold. It felt as though they had been drifting for a long time in a river. Exhausted, they climbed onto the shore, stopped, and watched the river continue to flow before their eyes, watched as the familiar water flowed into the distance.

While they stepped briefly outside the river of time, the story of humanity went on.

PART IV

Bunker Era, Year 11
Bunker World

#37813, your hibernation is at an end. You have been in hibernation for 62 years, 8 months, 21 days, and 13 hours. Your remaining hibernation allotment is 238 years, 3 months, 9 days. This is Asia Hibernation Center #1, Bunker Era, Year 11, May 9, 2:17 P.M.

The small information window hovered in front of the just-awakened Cheng Xin for no more than a minute before disappearing. She looked at the smooth metallic ceiling. Out of habit, she stared at a certain spot in the ceiling. During the age she last entered hibernation, doing so would have caused the ceiling to recognize her gaze and bring up an information window. But the ceiling didn't respond. Although she still didn't have the strength to turn her head, she was able to see part of the room: All the walls were made of metal and there were no information windows. The air remained empty as well, with no holographic displays. The metal in the wall looked familiar: stainless steel or aluminum alloy, no decorations.

A nurse appeared in her field of view. She was very young and didn't look at Cheng Xin. Instead, the nurse busied herself around her bed, probably disconnecting the medical equipment attached to her body. Cheng Xin's body couldn't sense what the nurse was doing, but something about the nurse seemed familiar to her—her uniform. During the last age Cheng Xin was awake, people wore self-cleaning clothes that always looked brand new, but this nurse's white uniform showed signs of wear. Although it was still clean, she could see signs of it being old, signs of the passage of time.

The ceiling began to move. Cheng Xin's bed was being pushed out of the awakening room. She was astonished to find that the nurse was pushing the bed—the bed actually needed someone to push it to move.

The hallway was made of empty metallic walls as well. Other than some ceiling lights, there were no other decorations. The lights looked ordinary enough, and Cheng Xin saw that the frame around one of the lights was loose and dangled from the ceiling. Between the frame and the ceiling she saw . . . wires.

Cheng Xin struggled to recall the information window she had seen upon first awakening, but she couldn't be certain it had really been there. It now seemed a hallucination.

There were many pedestrians in the hallway, and no one paid attention to Cheng Xin. She concentrated on the clothes people wore. A few were medical personnel in white uniforms, and the rest wore simple, plain clothing that resembled work overalls. Cheng Xin had the impression that many people here seemed to be from the Common Era, but soon realized that she was wrong. The Common Era was a long time ago, and the human race had changed eras four times already. It was impossible for so many Common Era people to be around.

Her impression was due to the fact that she saw some men who looked like the men she was used to.

The men who had disappeared during the Deterrence Era had returned. This was another age capable of producing men.

Everyone seemed to be in a hurry. This seemed to be another swing of the pendulum: the leisure and comfort of the last age had disappeared, and it was once again a harried society. In this age, most people no longer belonged to the leisure class, but had to work for a living.

Cheng Xin's bed was pushed into a small room. "Number 37813 awakened without irregularities," the nurse called out. "She's in recovery room twenty-eight." Then the nurse left and closed the door. Cheng Xin noticed that she had to pull the door shut.

She was left alone in the room. For a long time, no one came to check on her, a situation in total contrast to the previous two awakenings she had experienced, when she had received a great deal of attention and care. She was certain of two things: First, in this age, hibernation and awakening were common events. Second, not many people knew that she had awakened.

After Cheng Xin recovered some motor control, she moved her head and saw the window. She remembered the world before she had gone into hibernation: The hibernation center had been a giant tree at the edge of the city, and she had been in one of the leaves near the top, from where she could see the grand city-forest. But now, outside this window, she could only see a few ordinary buildings erected on the ground, all of them the same shape and design. Based on the sunlight glinting off them, they were constructed of metal as well. The buildings gave her the feeling of having returned to the Common Era.

She suddenly wondered if she had just awakened from a long dream. The Deterrence Era, the Broadcast Era—they were all dreams. Although the memories were clear, they seemed too surreal, fantastic. Perhaps she had never leapt across time on three occasions, but had been in the Common Era all along?

A holographic display window appeared next to her bed, removing her doubts. The window contained only a few simple buttons that could be used to call for the doctor and the nurse. The place seemed very familiar with the hibernation recovery process: The window had appeared just as Cheng Xin recovered the ability to lift her hand. But it was only a small window; the hyperinformation society where information windows filled every surface was gone.

Unlike the previous two awakenings, Cheng Xin recovered very quickly. By the time it was dark out, she was already able to get out of bed and walk about a bit. She found that the center provided only the simplest services. A doctor came in once to give her a cursory examination and then left; she had to do everything else by herself. She had to bathe herself while she still felt weak all over. As for meals, if she hadn't asked for them through that tiny holographic display, she might never have gotten to eat. Cheng Xin wasn't annoyed by this lack of solicitousness, as she had never completely adjusted to that excessively generous era where every person's every need was taken care of. She was still a Common Era woman at heart, and she felt at home here.

The next morning, a visitor came to see her. She recognized Cao Bin right away. This physicist had once been the youngest Swordholder candidate, but now he was much older, and a few strands of white appeared in his hair. Cheng Xin was certain, though, that he had not aged by sixty-two years.

"Mr. Thomas Wade asked me to come and get you."

"What happened?" Cheng Xin's heart sank as she recalled the conditions for her awakening.

"We'll talk about it after we get there." Cao Bin paused, and then added, "I'll take you around this new world before then so that you can make the right decision based on facts."

Cheng Xin glanced at the undistinguished buildings outside the window; she didn't feel the world was new.

"What happened to you? You weren't awake these last sixty years," Cheng Xin asked.

"I went into hibernation at about the same time you did. Seventeen years later, the circumsolar particle accelerator was operational, and I was awakened to research basic theory. That took fifteen years. Later, the research work turned to technical applications, and I was no longer needed, so I went back into hibernation until two years ago."

"How's the curvature propulsion project going?"

"There have been some developments. . . . We'll talk about it later." Cao Bin clearly didn't relish the topic.

Cheng Xin looked outside again. A breeze passed by, and a small tree in front of the window rustled. A cloud seemed to pass overhead, and the glint given off by the metallic buildings dimmed. How could such a commonplace world have anything to do with lightspeed spaceships?

Cao Bin followed Cheng Xin's gaze and laughed. "You must feel the same as when I first awakened—rather disappointed in this era, aren't you? . . . If you are up to it, let's go outside and take a look."

Half an hour later, Cheng Xin, dressed in a white outfit appropriate for this era, came onto a balcony of the hibernation center with Cao Bin. The city spread out before her, and Cheng Xin was again struck by the feeling that time had flowed backwards. After she had awakened for the first time during the Deterrence Era, the impact of seeing the giant forest-city for the first time was indescribable. After that, she never thought she would again see a cityscape so familiar: The plan for the city was very regular, as though all the buildings had been erected at once. The buildings themselves were monotonous and uniform, as though designed solely for utility with no consideration for architectural aesthetics. All of them were rectangular with no surface decorations, and all sported the same metallic gray exterior—reminding her strangely of the aluminum lunch boxes of her youth. The buildings were neatly and densely arranged as far as she could see. At the horizon, the ground rose up like the side of a mountain, and the city extended onto the mountainside.

"Where is this?" Cheng Xin asked.

"Hmm, why is it overcast again? We can't see the other side." Cao Bin didn't answer her question, but shook his head at the sky in disappointment, as though the weather had something to do with Cheng Xin's understanding of this new world. But soon, she saw how strange the sky was.

The sun was below the clouds.

The clouds began to dissipate, revealing a large opening. Through the opening, Cheng Xin did not see a blue sky; instead, she saw . . . more ground.

The ground in the sky was studded with the buildings of a city very similar to the city around her, except she was now looking "down"—or "up"—at it. This must have been the "other side" Cao Bin referred to. Cheng Xin realized that the rising "mountainside" in the distance wasn't a mountain at all, but continued to rise until it connected with the "sky." The world was a giant cylinder, and she was standing on the inside of it.

"This is Space City Asia I, in the shadow of Jupiter," Cao Bin said.

The new world that had seemed so common a moment ago now stunned her. Cheng Xin felt that she had finally, truly awakened.

In the afternoon, Cao Bin brought Cheng Xin on a trip to the gateway terminal at the northern end of the city.

By custom, the central axis of the space city was treated as oriented north-south. They got on a bus outside the hibernation center—this was a real bus that moved along the ground; probably running on electricity, but it looked indistinguishable from an ancient city bus. The bus was crowded, and Cheng Xin and Cao Bin took the last two seats at the back so that additional passengers had to stand. Cheng Xin thought back to the last time she had taken a bus—even during the Common Era, she had long ceased riding crowded public transportation.

The bus moved slowly, so she could take in the view leisurely. Everything now held a new meaning for her. She saw swaths of buildings sweep past the window, interspersed with green parks and pools; she saw two schools with exercise yards painted in blue; she saw brown soil covering the ground on the sides of the road, looking no different from soil on Earth. Broad-leafed trees resembling Chinese parasol trees lined the road, and advertising billboards appeared from time to time—Cheng Xin didn't recognize most of the products or brands, but the style of the ads was familiar.

The main difference from a Common Era city was that the entire world seemed to be constructed out of metal. The buildings were metallic, and the inside of the bus seemed to be mostly metal as well. She saw no plastic, and no composites either.

Cheng Xin paid the most attention to the other passengers on the bus. Across the aisle sat two men, one of whom dozed with a black briefcase on his

lap, while the other wore yellow work overalls with black oil stains. Next to
the man's feet was a tool bag, and some instrument Cheng Xin did not recognize poked out of it: It resembled an ancient power drill, but was translucent.
The man's face showed the exhaustion and numbness of someone who performed physical labor. The last time Cheng Xin had seen such an expression
was on the faces of migrant laborers in Common Era cities. In front of her sat
a young couple. The man whispered something in the woman's ear, and the
woman giggled from time to time while spooning something pink out of a
paper cup—ice cream, since Cheng Xin picked up the sweet fragrance of
cream, no different from her memory of more than three centuries ago. Two
middle-aged women stood in the aisle—they were of a type familiar to Cheng
Xin: The drudgery of everyday life had ground away their glamour, and they
no longer took care with their appearance or were fashionable. Women like
that had disappeared during the Deterrence Era or the Broadcast Era. Back
then, women always had smooth, delicate skin, and no matter how old they
were, they looked beautiful and refined, appropriate for their age. Cheng Xin
eavesdropped on their conversation:

"You got it wrong. The morning market and the evening market have similar prices. Don't be lazy. Go to the wholesale market on the west side."

"They don't have enough, and they won't sell at wholesale prices anyway."

"You have to go later, after seven or so. The vegetable vendors will be gone,
and they'll sell at wholesale prices."

She overheard snippets of other conversations in the bus as well.

"The city government is different from the atmospheric system, much more
complicated. When you get there, pay attention to the office politics. Don't
get too close to anyone at first, but don't hold yourself apart either." . . . "It's
not right to charge separately for the heat; that should have been included in
the electric bill." . . . "If they had subbed for that fool earlier they wouldn't
have lost so badly." . . . "Don't be so disappointed. I've been here since the city
was built, and how much do you think I make every year?" . . . "That fish is no
longer fresh. Don't even think about steaming it." . . . "The other day, when
they had to make an orbital adjustment, Park Four's water spilled again and
flooded a large area." . . . "If she doesn't like him, he should just give up. All
that effort is just going to be wasted." . . . "That can't be authentic. I don't
even think it's a high-quality imitation. Are you kidding me? At that price?" . . .

Cheng Xin's heart felt warm and content. Ever since she had awakened for
the first time during the Deterrence Era, she had been searching for this feeling. She had thought she'd never find it. She absorbed the conversations

around her as though slaking a thirst, and didn't pay much attention to Cao Bin's narration of the city.

Space City Asia I was one of the earliest to be built as part of the Bunker Project. It was a regular cylinder that simulated gravity with the centrifugal force generated by spinning. With a length of thirty kilometers and a diameter of seven kilometers, its usable interior surface area was 659 square kilometers, about half the size of ancient Beijing. Once, about twenty million inhabitants had lived here, but after the completion of newer cities, the population had decreased to about nine million, so that it was no longer so crowded. . . .

Cheng Xin saw another sun appear in the sky before her. Cao Bin explained that there were a total of three artificial suns in the space city, all of them floating along the central axis, each separated by about ten kilometers. These produced energy by nuclear fusion, and brightened and dimmed on a twenty-four-hour cycle.

Cheng Xin felt a series of jolts. The bus was already at a stop, and the tremors seemed to originate from deep within the ground. She felt a force pushing against her back, but the bus remained unmoving. Outside the window, she could see the shadows cast by the trees and buildings suddenly shift to a new angle as the artificial suns abruptly shifted positions. But soon, the suns moved back into place. Cheng Xin saw that none of the passengers seemed surprised by this.

"The space city was adjusting its position," said Cao Bin.

The bus arrived at the last stop after about thirty minutes. After getting off the bus, she saw that the everyday scenes that had so intoxicated her disappeared. In front of her was an enormous wall whose immense size made her gasp. It was as though she was standing at the end of the world—and indeed, she *was*. This was the "northernmost" point in the city, a large circular disk eight kilometers in diameter. She couldn't see the entire disk from where she stood, but she could tell that the ground rose up on both sides of her. The top of the disk—the other side of the city—was about as high as the peak of Mount Everest. Many radial spokes converged from the rim of the disk to the center, four kilometers above. Each spoke was an elevator shaft, and the center was the space city's gateway.

Before entering the elevator, Cheng Xin cast a lingering glance back at this city that already seemed so familiar. From here, all three suns were visible in a row toward the other end of the city. It was dusk, and the suns dimmed, turning from a blinding orange-white to a gentle red, bathing the city in a warm golden glow. Cheng Xin saw a few girls in white school uniforms chatting and laughing on a lawn not too far away, their hair wafting in the breeze and drenched in the golden glow of the evening sun.

The interior of the elevator car was very spacious, like a large hall. The side facing the city was transparent, turning the car into an observation deck. Every seat was equipped with seat belts because, as the elevator rose, gravity quickly diminished. As they looked outside, the ground sank lower, while the "sky," another ground, grew clearer. By the time the elevator reached the center of the circle, gravity had completely disappeared, as well as the sensation of "up" and "down" when looking outside. Since this was the axis around which the city spun, the ground surrounded them in every direction. Here, the view of the city was at its most magnificent.

The three suns had dimmed to the level of moonlight, and their colors shifted to silver. Viewed from here, the three suns—or moons—were stacked on top of each other. All the clouds were concentrated in the gravity-free zone, forming an axis of white mist extending through the center of the city to the other end. The "southern" end, forty-five kilometers away, could be seen clearly. Cao Bin told Cheng Xin that that was where the city's thrusters were located. The lights of the city had just come on. In Cheng Xin's eyes, a sea of lights surrounded her and extended into the distance. She seemed to be looking down a giant well whose wall was covered with a brilliant carpet.

Cheng Xin casually locked her gaze on a certain spot in the city, and found the arrangement of buildings there very similar to the residential district of her home back in the Common Era. She imagined a certain ordinary apartment building in that area and a certain window on the second floor: Through blue curtains, a gentle light seeped, and behind the curtain, her mom and dad waited for her. . . .

She could not hold back her tears.

Ever since awakening for the first time during the Deterrence Era, Cheng Xin had never been able to integrate into the new eras, always feeling like a stranger from another time. But she could never have imagined that she would once again feel at home more than half a century later, here behind Jupiter, more than eight hundred million kilometers from the Earth. It was as if everything that she had been familiar with from more than three centuries ago had been picked up by a pair of invisible hands, rolled up like a giant painting, and then placed here as a new world slowly spinning around her.

Cheng Xin and Cao Bin entered a weightless corridor. This was a tube in which people moved by pulling themselves along handholds on cables. The passengers riding up from all the elevators along the rim gathered here to exit the city, and the corridor was filled with streaming crowds. A row of information windows appeared around the circular wall of the corridor, and the animated images in the windows were mostly news and ads. But the windows were few in number and neatly arranged, unlike the chaotic profusion of information windows in the previous era.

Cheng Xin had long since noticed that the overwhelming hyperinformation age had apparently ended. Information appeared in this world in a restrained, directed manner. Was this the result of changes in the Bunker World's political and economic systems?

Emerging from the corridor, Cheng Xin first noticed the stars spinning overhead. The spin was very rapid and made her dizzy. The view around her opened up dramatically. They were standing on a circular plaza with a diameter of eight kilometers "atop" the space city. This was the city's spaceport, and many spacecraft were parked here. Most of the vessels were shaped not too differently from those Cheng Xin had seen over sixty years ago, though these were generally smaller. Many were about the size of ancient automobiles. Cheng Xin noticed that the flames at the nozzles of the spaceships as they took off were far dimmer than what she remembered from more than half a century ago. The glow was a dark blue and no longer so blinding. This probably meant that the miniature fusion engines were much more efficient.

Cheng Xin saw an eye-catching red-glowing circle all around the exit, with a radius of about a hundred meters. She quickly understood its meaning: The space city was spinning, and, outside the circle, the centrifugal force became very strong. Moving outside the warning circle meant a dramatic increase in centrifugal force, and vessels parked out there had to be anchored, while pedestrians needed to wear magnetic shoes lest they be thrown out.

It was very cold here. Only when a nearby vessel took off did the engine's heat bring a brief feeling of warmth. Cheng Xin shuddered—not just from the cold, but because she realized that she was completely exposed to space! But the air around her and the air pressure were real, and she could feel cold breezes. It appeared that the technology to contain an atmosphere in a nonenclosed area had advanced even further, to the point where an atmosphere could be maintained in completely open space.

Cao Bin saw her shock and said, "Oh, right now we can only maintain an atmosphere about ten meters thick above 'ground.'" He hadn't been in this world for too long, either, but he was already jaded by the technology that seemed like magic to Cheng Xin. He wanted to show her far more impressive sights.

Against the background of the spinning stars, Cheng Xin saw the Bunker World.

From here, most of the space cities behind Jupiter could be seen. She saw twenty-two cities (including the one she stood on), and there were four more blocked by the city they stood on. All twenty-six cities (six more than planned) were hiding in the shadow of Jupiter. They were loosely lined up in four rows, and reminded Cheng Xin of the spaceships lined up behind the giant rock in space more than sixty years ago. To one side of Asia I was North America I and Oceania I, and to the other side was Asia III. Only about fifty kilometers separated Asia I from its neighbors on either side, and Cheng Xin could feel their immensity, like two planets. The next row of four cities was 150 kilometers away, and it was difficult to tell their size visually. The most distant space cities were about one thousand kilometers away, and looked like delicate toys from here.

Cheng Xin thought of the space cities as a school of tiny fish hovering in place behind a giant rock to avoid the torrents in the river.

North America I, closest to Asia I, was a pure sphere. It and the cylindrical Asia I represented the two extremes of space city design. Most of the other space cities were football-shaped, though the ratios of major to minor axes were different in each. A few other space cities took on unusual shapes: a wheel with spokes, a spindle, etc.

Behind the other three gas giants were three more space city clusters, consisting of a total of thirty-eight space cities. Twenty-six were behind Saturn, four behind Uranus, and eight more behind Neptune. Those space cities were in safer locations, though the environs were even more desolate.

One of the space cities in front suddenly emitted a blue light. It was as though a small blue sun appeared in space, casting long shadows of the people and spaceships on the plaza. Cao Bin told Cheng Xin that this was because the space city's thrusters had been activated to adjust its position. The space cities revolved around the Sun in parallel with Jupiter, just outside its orbit. Jupiter's gravity gradually pulled the cities closer, and the cities had to constantly adjust their positions with thrusters. This operation required a great deal of energy. Once, the suggestion had been floated to turn the cities into Jupiter's satellites that would only shift into new orbits around the Sun after the issuance of a dark forest strike warning. But until the advance warning system had been further refined and proven to be reliable, no space city wanted to take the risk.

"Lucky you! Now you get to see a sight that happens only once every three days." Cao Bin pointed into space. Cheng Xin saw a tiny white dot in the distance, gradually growing bigger. Soon, it was a white sphere as big as a Ping-Pong ball.

"Europa?"

"That's right. We're very close to its orbit right now. Watch your footing and don't be scared."

Cheng Xin tried to figure out what Cao meant. She had always thought of celestial bodies as moving slowly, almost imperceptibly—as they did in most Earth-based observations. But then she remembered that the space city was not a Jovian satellite but remained stationary relative to it. Europa, on the other hand, was a satellite that moved very fast. She remembered its speed was about fourteen kilometers per second. If the space city was very close to Europa's orbit, then . . .

The white sphere expanded rapidly—so fast that it seemed unreal. Europa soon took up most of the sky, and turned from a Ping-Pong ball into a giant planet. The sensation of "up" and "down" switched in an instant, and Cheng Xin felt as if Asia I were falling toward that white world. Next, the three-thousand-kilometer-diameter moon swept overhead so that for an instant, it took up the entire sky. The space city was skimming over the icy oceans of Europa, and Cheng Xin could clearly see the crisscrossing lines in that frozen landscape, like lines in a giant palm print. The air, disturbed by the passage of Europa, whipped around her, and Cheng Xin felt an invisible force dragging her from left to right—if she weren't wearing magnetic shoes, she was sure she'd be pulled off the ground. Whatever was nearby that hadn't been secured to the ground flew up, and a few cables attached to spaceships also drifted into the air. A terrifying rumbling came from below her—it was the immense frame of the space city reacting to the rapidly shifting gravity field of Europa. It took only about three minutes for Europa to hurtle past Asia I, and then it was on the other side of the city and began to shrink rapidly. The eight space cities in the two front-most rows all activated their thrusters to adjust their positions after the disturbance caused by Europa. Eight fireballs lit up the sky.

"How . . . how close was that?" Cheng Xin asked in an unsteady voice.

"The closest approach, like you experienced just now, was a hundred and fifty kilometers, basically brushing right by us. We don't really have a choice. Jupiter has thirteen moons, and it's impossible for the space cities to avoid them all. Europa's orbit is inclined only slightly from the equator, and so it's very close to these cities here. It's the main source of water for the Jovian cities, and we've built a lot of industry on it. But when the dark forest strike comes, all of it will have to be sacrificed. After the solar explosion, all of the Jovian moons' orbits will shift dramatically. Maneuvering the space cities to avoid them at that time will be a very complicated operation."

Cao Bin found the dinghy he had taken to come here. It was tiny, shaped and sized like an ancient automobile, capable of seating only two. Cheng Xin instinctively felt unsafe going into space in such a tiny vehicle, even though she knew her fear wasn't reasonable. Cao Bin told the AI to go to North America I, and the dinghy took off.

Cheng Xin saw the ground receding quickly, and the dinghy flew along at a tangent to the spinning city. Soon, the eight-kilometer-diameter plaza came into view, followed by the entirety of Asia I. Behind the cylinder was a vast expanse of dark yellow. Only when the edge of this yellow expanse appeared did Cheng Xin realize that she was looking at Jupiter. Here, in the shadow of the gas giant, everything was cold and dark, and the Sun seemed to not exist at all. Only the phosphorescence of the planet's liquid helium and hydrogen, diffused through the thick atmosphere, formed patches of hazy light roving about like eyeballs behind the closed eyelids of a dreamer. The immensity of Jupiter astonished Cheng Xin. From here, she could only see a small portion of its rim, and the rim's curvature was minuscule. The planet was a dark barrier that blocked out everything, and once again gave Cheng Xin the feeling of standing at a giant wall at the end of the world.

In the following three days, Cao Bin took Cheng Xin to visit four more space cities.

The first was North America I, the closest city to Asia I. The main advantage of its spherical construction was that a single artificial sun at the center was sufficient to illuminate the entire city, but the disadvantage of such a design was obvious as well: The gravity changed depending on one's latitude. The equator had the most gravity, which decreased as you went up in latitude. The polar regions were weightless. Inhabitants in the different regions had to adjust to life under various gravity conditions.

Unlike Asia I, small spacecraft could enter the city directly from the gateway at the north pole. Once the dinghy was inside, the entire world spun around it, and the dinghy had to match the city's spin before landing. Cheng Xin and Cao Bin rode a high-speed rail to go to low-latitude regions, and the train moved far faster than the bus in Asia I. Cheng Xin saw that the buildings here were denser and taller, looking like a metropolis. At the high-latitude, low-gravity regions especially, the buildings' heights were limited only by the volume of the sphere. Near the polar regions, some buildings were as tall as ten kilometers, looking like long thorns extending up from the ground toward the sun.

North America I had been completed early on. With a radius of twenty kilometers and twenty million inhabitants, it was the largest city by population. It acted as the prosperous commercial center for all the Jovian cities.

Here, Cheng Xin got to see a splendid sight that was absent from Asia I: the equatorial ring-ocean. As a matter of fact, most space cities had ring-oceans of various widths, and Asia I was rather unique in lacking one. In spherical or football-shaped cities, the equator was the lowest point in the city's simulated gravity, and all the city's water naturally collected there, forming a sparkling, undulating belt for the city. Standing on the shore, one could see the ocean rising on both sides and dividing the "sky" behind the sun. Cheng Xin and Cao Bin took a fast boat and navigated around the sea—a journey of some sixty kilometers. The water in the sea came from Europa, clear, cold, and reflecting rippling light onto the skyscrapers on both sides. The dikes along the edge of the sea closest to Jupiter were higher, to avoid the water spilling out when the city accelerated during position adjustments. Even so, when the city had to engage in unexpected maneuvers, small-scale flooding would occur from time to time.

Next, Cao Bin took Cheng Xin to Europe IV, which sported a typical football-shaped design. Its distinguishing characteristic was the lack of a common artificial sun. Every district had its own miniature fusion sun, and the tiny suns hovered about two hundred to three hundred meters high to provide illumination. The advantage of this approach was that the weightless axis could be more efficiently utilized. The axis of Europe IV was taken up by the longest—or tallest—building among all the space cities. It was forty kilometers long and connected the north and south poles of the football. Since the interior of the building was weightless, it was mainly used as a spaceport and commercial entertainment district.

Europe IV had the smallest population of all the cities, only 4.5 million. It was the wealthiest city of the Bunker World. The exquisite houses illuminated by miniature suns amazed Cheng Xin. Each house came with its own swimming pool, and a few had wide lawns. Tiny white sails dotted the serene equatorial sea, and people sat on the shore, fishing leisurely. She saw a yacht sail by slowly, and it looked as luxurious as any yacht on ancient Earth. There was a cocktail party being held aboard the yacht with live musicians. . . . She was astonished that such life could be transplanted into the shadow of Jupiter, eight hundred million kilometers from the Earth.

Pacific I, on the other hand, was the antithesis of Europe IV. This was the very first city completed by the Bunker Project, and like North America I, it was a sphere. Unlike all the other Jovian cities, it did orbit Jupiter as a satellite.

Millions of construction workers had lived in Pacific I during the early years of the Bunker Project. As the project progressed, it was used to warehouse construction materials. Later, as the numerous flaws of this early-phase experimental space city became apparent, it was abandoned. But, after the resettlement to the Bunker World had been completed, people began to live here again, and finally formed a city of their own, with a city government and police force. However, the authorities only maintained the most basic public infrastructure, and society was left basically to run on its own. Pacific I was the only city to which people were free to immigrate without a residential permit. Most of the population consisted of unemployed and homeless wanderers, poor people who had lost social security for various reasons, and bohemian artists. Later, it became the base for extremist political organizations.

Pacific I had no city thrusters, and there was no artificial sun inside. It also didn't spin, so the interior was completely weightless.

After entering the city, Cheng Xin saw a fairy-tale world. It was as if a broken-down but once prosperous city had lost gravity abruptly, so that everything floated in the air. Pacific I was a city in permanent night, and each building maintained illumination with a nuclear battery. Thus, the interior was filled with glowing, floating lights. Most of the buildings in the city were simple shacks built from abandoned construction materials. Since there was no "up" or "down," most of the shacks were cube-shaped, with windows (which also acted as doors) on all six sides. Some were shaped as spheres, which had the advantage of being more resilient, as the drifting buildings inevitably collided against each other.

There was no notion of land ownership in Pacific I because all the buildings drifted around with no permanent location. In principle, each resident had the right to use any space in the city. The city had a large number of homeless individuals who didn't even possess a shack. All of their possessions were kept in a large net sling to prevent them from scattering everywhere, and the owners drifted along with the net slings. Transportation within the city was simple: There were no cars or weightless cables or personal thrusters. The residents moved around by pushing and kicking off buildings and drifting. Since the buildings were densely packed inside the city, one could navigate anywhere that way, but this method of locomotion required great skill. As Cheng Xin observed the residents flitting around the dense clusters of floating buildings, she was reminded of gibbons swinging easily from branch to branch.

Cheng Xin and Cao Bin drifted close to a group of homeless men gathered around an open fire. Such a fire would have been prohibited in any other city. The fuel seemed to be some kind of flammable construction material. Due to the weightlessness, the flames did not rise up, but formed a ball of fire floating in place. The way they drank was also special. They tossed alcohol out of bottles, forming liquid spheres in the air. Then the men, dressed in rags and with unshaven faces, drifted along with them, capturing the spheres with their mouths and swallowing. One of the drunken men vomited, and the vomit rushing out of his mouth propelled him back, sending him tumbling in midair. . . .

Cheng Xin and Cao Bin came to a market. All the goods floated in the air, forming a heterogeneous mess illuminated by a few drifting lights, with customers and vendors drifting among the hovering objects. In this chaos, it seemed hard to tell what belonged to whom, but if a customer examined something closely, a vendor would drift over to haggle. The goods offered for sale included clothing, electronics, food and liquor, nuclear batteries of various capacities, small arms, and so on. There were also exotic antiques on sale. In one place, a few metallic fragments were offered at very high prices. The vendor claimed that it was debris gathered from the outer Solar System from warships destroyed during the Doomsday Battle—it was impossible to tell if he was telling the truth.

Cheng Xin was surprised to find a vendor who sold antique books. She flipped through a few—these books were not ancient for her. All the books drifted in a cloud, and many had their pages spread open like a flock of white-winged birds in the light. . . . Cheng Xin saw a small wooden box drift in front of her, marked as cigars. She caught it, and immediately a young boy kicked his way over and swore up and down that these were authentic ancient Havana cigars that had been preserved for close to two hundred years. Since they had dried out a bit, he was willing to let them go at a low price that she would not be able to find anywhere else in the Solar System. He even opened the box to let Cheng Xin see what she was getting. She agreed and bought them.

Cao Bin took Cheng Xin to the edge of the city—the inside face of the spherical hull. There were no buildings attached to the hull, and there was no soil—everything was left as bare as the day the city was constructed. It was impossible to tell the curvature in a small area, and they seemed to be standing on a large, flat plaza. Above them, the dense buildings of the city floated, and flickering lights projected onto the "plaza." Cheng Xin saw that the hull was marked with all kinds of graffiti, stretching as far as she could see. These pictures were vibrant, wild, unrestrained, wanton and full of energy. In the shifting, uncertain light, they seemed to come alive, as though they were dreams deposited from the city above.

Cao Bin didn't bring Cheng Xin deeper into the city. According to him, the center of the city was chaotic and rather violent. Gangs fought each other, and a few years ago, one of the gang fights had managed to rupture the hull, causing a massive decompression incident. Later, the gangs seemed to come to some kind of unspoken agreement, and settled their disputes in the center of the city, away from the hull.

Cao Bin also told Cheng Xin that the Federation Government had devoted enormous resources to build a social welfare system here in Pacific I. The six million or so inhabitants here were mostly unemployed, but at least they could get the basic necessities for life.

"What will happen here in the event of a dark forest strike?"

"Only annihilation. This city has no thrusters, and even if it did have them, it would be impossible to move it into the shadow of Jupiter and keep it there. Look—" He pointed to the drifting buildings. "If the city accelerated, everything would smash through the hull. Then the city would be like a bag with a hole in the bottom. If we receive a dark forest strike alert, the only thing that can be done is to evacuate the population to the other cities."

As they left the floating city in eternal night, Cheng Xin gazed at it through the porthole of the dinghy. This was a city of poverty and homelessness, but it also possessed its own rich life, like a weightless version of the famous Song Dynasty painting, *Along the River During the Qingming Festival.*

She understood that compared to the last era, the Bunker World was not at all an ideal society. The migration to the rim of the Solar System had caused some toxic social conditions, long eliminated by progress, to reemerge. This wasn't exactly regression, but a kind of spiraling ascent, a necessary condition for the exploration and settlement of new frontiers.

———

After they left Pacific I, Cao Bin brought Cheng Xin to see a few more space cities with unusual designs. One of them, fairly close to Pacific I, was a wheel with spokes, not unlike a larger version of the space elevator terminal station that Cheng Xin had visited more than sixty years ago.

Cheng Xin was a bit puzzled by the designs of the cities. As a matter of engineering, the wheel seemed ideal. It was far easier to construct than the large, hollow shells used by the other cities, and when completed, a wheel was stronger and better able to survive disasters, as well as being easier to expand.

Cao Bin's succinct reply to Cheng Xin's query was "world-sense."

"What?"

"The sensation of being inside a world. A space city has to have ample interior volume and wide-open views so that the residents can feel they are living inside a world. Although the usable interior surface area isn't too different from a hollow-shell design, in a wheel design, people always know that they are living inside a narrow tube or a series of such tubes."

There were some other cities with even stranger designs. Most of these were industrial or agricultural centers with no permanent residents. For instance, there was a city called Resource I. Its length was 120 kilometers, but the diameter was only three kilometers, like a thin stick. It did not spin around the long axis, but rather, tumbled about its center, end over end. The city's interior was divided into levels, and the gravity at each level differed dramatically. Only a few levels were suitable for living, while the rest were devoted to various industries adapted to the different gravities. According to Cao Bin, near Saturn and Uranus, there were cities formed by combining two or more stick-shaped cities into crosses or stars.

The earliest city clusters of the Bunker Project were built near Jupiter and Saturn. Later, as cities were built near Uranus and Neptune, some new city-design concepts emerged. The most important idea was city docking. In those two clusters at the edge of the Solar System, every city was equipped with one or more standardized docks so that cities could be interconnected. Docking multiplied the space available for inhabitants and created even better world-sense, greatly encouraging economic development. In addition, after docking, the atmospheres and ecological systems of the various cities merged, and that helped to stabilize their operation and maintenance.

Currently, most cities docked along their axis of spin. This way, after docking, the cities could continue to spin as before without changing the distribution of gravity. There were proposals for parallel or perpendicular docking as well, which would allow the combined cities to expand in multiple directions, as opposed to only along the axis of spin. But the spin of such combinations would dramatically change the interior distribution of gravity, and these proposals had not been tested so far.

The biggest combined city so far was located at Neptune, where four of the eight cities were docked together along their axis of spin, forming a two-hundred-kilometer-long combined city. When necessary—such as when a dark forest strike alert was issued—the combined city could be quickly taken apart to increase the mobility of each city. People hoped that, one day, all the cities in each cluster could be combined into one, so that humanity would live in four complete worlds.

In total, behind Jupiter, Saturn, Uranus, and Neptune, there were sixty-four large space cities and nearly a hundred medium and small cities, plus numerous space stations. Nine hundred million people lived in the Bunker World.

This was almost the entirety of the human race. Even before the arrival of the dark forest strike, Earth civilization had battened down the hatches.

Every space city was politically equivalent to a state. The four city clusters together formed the Solar System Federation, and the original UN had evolved into the Federation Government. Most of the Earth's major ancient civilizations had passed through a city-state stage—and now, city-states had reemerged at the rim of the Solar System.

The Earth was now barely inhabited. Only about five million people remained there. These were individuals who did not wish to leave their home and who had no fear of the prospect of Death at any moment. Many brave men and women living in the Bunker World also traveled to Earth as tourists, though each journey meant gambling with their lives. As time passed, the anticipated dark forest strike loomed larger, and people gradually adapted to life in the Bunker World. Their yearning for their homeland lessened as they busied themselves in their new homes, and fewer and fewer now visited the Earth. The public no longer cared much about news from the home world, and were only vaguely aware that Nature was enjoying a resurgence. Forests and grasslands covered every continent, and those who stayed behind had to carry guns to defend against wild beasts when they went out, but it was rumored that they lived like kings, each with a vast estate and personal forests and lakes. The entire Earth was now only a single city in the Solar System Federation.

Cheng Xin and Cao Bin's small dinghy was now at the outer edge of the Jovian cities. Before the immense, dark Jupiter, these cities appeared so small, so alone, like a few shacks at the foot of a gigantic cliff. From a distance, faint candlelight spilled out of them. Though tiny, they were the only hints of warmth, of home, in this endless frigidity and desolation, the goal of all weary travelers. Cheng Xin's mind churned up a short poem she had read in middle school, a composition by a long-forgotten Chinese poet of the Republican era:

> *The sun has set.*
> *Mountain, tree, rock, river—*
> *All the grand buildings are buried in shadows.*
> *People light their lamps with great interest,*
> *Delighting in all they can see,*
> *Hoping to find what they wish.*[6]

---

[6] *Translator's Note:* The poem is by Xu Yunuo (1894–1958), a modern Chinese poet most prominently associated with the May Fourth Movement.

Bunker Era, Year 11
Lightspeed II

▬▬▬

The final destination of Cheng Xin and Cao Bin was Halo City, a medium space city. Medium cities were space cities whose interior areas were below two hundred square kilometers but above fifty square kilometers. Typically, these cities were mixed within formations of large cities, but two of the medium cities, Halo City and Lightspeed II, were situated far from the Jovian city cluster, almost outside the protection of Jupiter's shadow.

Before arriving at Halo City, the dinghy passed by Lightspeed II. Cao Bin told Cheng Xin that Lightspeed II used to be a science city and was one of the two research centers studying how to lower the speed of light to achieve the black domain state, but it had been abandoned. Cheng Xin was very interested and wanted to stop for a visit. Reluctantly, Cao Bin turned the dinghy in that direction.

"Why don't we just take a look from the outside?" Cao Bin said. "It's best not to go in."

"Is it dangerous?"

"Yes."

"But we went inside Pacific I, which was also dangerous."

"It's not the same. There's no one inside Lightspeed II. It's a . . . ghost city. At least, that's what everyone says."

As the dinghy approached, Cheng Xin realized that the city really was in ruins. It didn't spin, and the exterior appeared broken and cracked. In some places, the skin of the city had been ripped open, revealing the structural frame underneath. As she surveyed the giant ruin illuminated by the search-lights of the dinghy, Cheng Xin felt awe as well as terror. She thought of the ruin as a beached whale. It had lain there for eons, until all that was left was cracked skin and bones, and life had long ago drained away. She seemed to be looking at something even older than the Acropolis of Athens, with even more secrets.

They slowly approached a large crack, several times as wide as the body of their dinghy. The beams in the structural frame were also bent and twisted, opening up a way to the interior. The beam of the searchlight shone in so that Cheng Xin could see the distant "ground," which was completely bare. After the dinghy descended a short distance into the interior of the space city, it stopped and swept the searchlight about them. Cheng Xin saw that the "ground" was bare in every direction. Not only were there no buildings, there wasn't anything at all to indicate that people had once lived here. The criss-crossing beams forming the frame for the city were visible on the "ground."

"Is it just an empty shell?" Cheng Xin asked.

"No."

Cao Bin looked at Cheng Xin for a few seconds, as if assessing her courage. Then he reached out and shut off the searchlights.

At first, all Cheng Xin could see was darkness. Starlight spilled in from the crack in front, as though she was gazing up at the sky through a broken roof. Eventually, her eyes adjusted to the dark, and she realized that the interior of the ruined space city wasn't entirely dark, but was illuminated with a faint, flickering blue light. Cheng Xin shivered. She forced herself to calm down and looked for the source. The blue glow came from the center of the interior of the space city.

The light source blinked without pattern, like a twitching eye. The empty ground was filled with strange shadows, like a desolate wasteland illuminated by flashes of lightning on the horizon at night.

"The light is caused by space dust falling into the black hole," Cao Bin said, pointing in the direction of the light source. He was trying to relieve some of Cheng Xin's terror.

"There's a black hole over there?"

"Yes. It's about . . . no more than five kilometers from here. A microscopic black hole with a Schwarzschild radius of twenty nanometers and a mass equivalent to Leda, the Jovian moon."

In this phosphorescent blue glow, Cao Bin told Cheng Xin the story of Lightspeed II and 高 Way.[7]

---

[7] *Translator's Note:* Like "艾 AA," "高 Way" is a mixed Chinese-English name ("高" is the surname and pronounced "Gao").

The research into lowering the speed of light through vacuum began at about the same time as the Bunker Project. As the Black Domain Plan was the second path for human survival, the international community devoted enormous resources to it, and the Bunker Project even built a large space city as a research center devoted to the subject—that would be Lightspeed I, located in the Saturn cluster. But sixty years of extensive research yielded no breakthroughs, and not even much advancement in theoretical foundation.

Lowering the speed of light through a medium wasn't particularly difficult. As early as 2008 C.E., researchers had succeeded in lowering the speed of light through a medium to an incredible seventeen meters per second in a laboratory setting. But this was fundamentally different from lowering the speed of light through vacuum. The former only required causing the atoms in the medium to absorb and re-emit the photons—light continued to travel at its usual speed between atoms. This wasn't useful for the Black Domain Plan.

The speed of light through vacuum was one of the fundamental constants of the universe. Altering it was equivalent to altering the laws of physics. Thus, lowering the speed of light required breakthroughs in fundamental physics—and considerable serendipity. After sixty years, the only substantive result of basic research was the creation of the circumsolar particle accelerator. This, in turn, led to the success of the largest project under the Black Domain Plan: the Black Hole Project.

Scientists had tried all kinds of extreme physical techniques in their efforts to alter the speed of light. Once, the strongest artificial magnetic field had been used. But the best way to influence light in vacuum was through a gravity field. Since it was extremely difficult to generate a local gravity field in a laboratory setting, the only path forward seemed to be a black hole. The circumsolar particle accelerator was capable of creating microscopic black holes.

The head of the Black Hole Project was 高 Way. Cao Bin had worked with him for a few years. He could not hide his complex feelings about the man as he described him to Cheng Xin.

"The man suffered from severe autism—no, I'm not talking about some kind of lonely genius choosing to isolate himself, but a real mental condition. He was extremely closed off and had trouble communicating with anyone, and he had never even touched a woman. His extraordinary professional success would only be possible in this age, but despite his accomplishments, most of his supervisors and colleagues thought of him as merely a high-powered intelligence battery. He was tortured by his illness and tried to change himself, and in this, he was different from other geniuses.

"Starting from, oh, I think the eighth year of the Broadcast Era, he dedicated himself to the theoretical study of lowering the speed of light. Over time, I think he began to develop a strange identification between the speed of light and his own personality—if he could change the speed of light, then it was the same as changing himself.

"But the speed of light through vacuum really was the most stable thing in the cosmos. Research into lowering the speed of light resembled torturing light without regard for consequences. People tried to do everything with light: strike it, twist it, break it, dissect it, stretch it, crush it, even destroy it—but the result was, at most, a change in its frequency in vacuum. But the speed of light remained unchanged, like an unscalable wall. After all these decades, theoreticians and experimenters alike were in despair. There was a saying: If there really were a Creator, the only thing He welded shut in all Creation was the speed of light.

"For 高 Way, the despair had yet another layer. By the time I went into hibernation, he was almost fifty. He had still never been with a woman, and he thought of his own fate as being as resistant as the speed of light; he became even more withdrawn and solitary.

"The Black Hole Project began in Year 1 of the Bunker Era and lasted eleven years. The planners did not invest much hope in it. Both theoretical calculations and astronomical observations had indicated that even black holes could not change the speed of light. These demons of the universe could only use their gravity fields to change the path of light and its frequency, not affecting the speed of light through vacuum one iota. However, to continue the research for the Black Domain Plan, it was necessary to create experimental conditions with superpowerful gravity fields, which depended on black holes. In addition, since a black domain is in essence a large-scale reduced-lightspeed black hole, perhaps close-range observation of a microscopic regular-lightspeed black hole would yield unexpected insights.

"The circumsolar particle accelerator was capable of producing microscopic black holes rapidly, but these tiny black holes also evaporated very quickly. To produce a stable black hole, a microscopic black hole was guided out of the accelerator as soon as it was produced, and then injected into Leda.

"Leda was Jupiter's smallest moon, with a mean radius of only eight kilometers. It was nothing more than a large rock. Before making the black hole, they had lowered the moon from its high orbit and turned it into a body orbiting the Sun in parallel with Jupiter, like the city cluster. However, unlike the city cluster, it was located at the Sun-Jupiter L2 Lagrangian point, which is where we are now. This allowed it to maintain a stable distance from Jupiter without having to constantly adjust its position. At the time, this was the most massive body humans had managed to move through space until then.

"After the microscopic black hole was injected into Leda, it began to absorb mass and rapidly grow. At the same time, the intense radiation generated by material falling into the black hole melted the surrounding rock. Soon, the eight-kilometer-radius Leda melted entirely, and the potato-shaped rock turned into a red-glowing ball of lava. The lava ball shrank slowly, but glowed brighter and brighter, until it finally disappeared with a blinding flash. Observation showed that other than a small amount of material ejected by the radiation, most of the mass of Leda had been absorbed by the black hole. The black hole remained stable, and its Schwarzschild radius, or event horizon radius, had grown from the size of a fundamental particle to twenty-one nanometers.

"They constructed a space city around the black hole—that's Lightspeed II. The black hole was suspended in the middle of the space city, which was empty, didn't spin, and whose interior was a vacuum connected to space. It was, in essence, a giant container for the black hole. Personnel and equipment could be brought into the city to study the black hole.

"The research continued for many years. This was the first time that humans could study a black hole specimen in laboratory conditions, and many discoveries were made that helped with the development of theoretical physics and fundamental cosmology. But none of these results helped with the task of lowering the speed of light in vacuum.

"Six years after the commencement of studies on the black hole specimen, 高 Way died. According to the official account of the World Academy of Sciences, he was accidentally 'sucked into the black hole' during an experiment.

"Anyone with some basic scientific background knows that the probability that Gao was 'sucked' into the black hole was practically nonexistent. The reason that black holes are traps from which even light cannot escape isn't because their overall gravitational power is overwhelming—though a large black hole formed by the collapse of a star does possess immense overall gravity—but due to the density of their gravitational fields. From a distance, the total gravity of a black hole is no different from the gravity of a quantity of normal matter of equivalent mass. If the Sun collapsed into a black hole, the Earth and the other planets would still continue on in their orbits without being sucked in. It's only when you got very close to the black hole that its gravity displayed strange behavior.

"Inside Lightspeed II, there was a protective net around the black hole with a radius of five thousand meters. Research personnel were forbidden to enter. Since the radius of Leda was originally only eight thousand meters, the black hole's gravity at this distance was not much greater than the gravity on the surface of the original Leda. It's not a very powerful pull—a person standing there was essentially weightless, and could easily escape using the thrusters on their space suit. Thus, Gao couldn't have been 'sucked' in.

"Ever since the stable black hole specimen was obtained, 高 Way was infatuated with it. After struggling against the speed of light for so many years and not being able to alter even a single one of the many digits in this constant that came close to three hundred thousand, Gao was agitated and filled with a sense of failure. As the constancy of the speed of light was one of the fundamental laws of nature, he had come to despise the laws of nature, as well as being afraid of them. But now, in front of his eyes, was something that had compressed Leda into twenty-one nanometers. Within its event horizon, in that space-time singularity, known laws of nature had no effect.

"高 Way often hung against the protective net and stared for hours at the black hole five kilometers away. He watched its luminescence—like we're doing now—and sometimes claimed that the black hole was talking to him, that he could decipher the message of its flickering light.

"No one saw the process of Gao's disappearance, and if there was a recording, it's never been released. He was one of the Black Hole Project's principal physicists, and he had the password to open the protective net. I'm certain that he went in and drifted toward the black hole until he was too close to return. . . . He probably wanted to get a close-up look at the object of his infatuation, or perhaps he wanted to enter into that singularity where the laws of nature no longer mattered, so that he could escape all this.

"What happened after 高 Way was sucked in was almost too strange to describe. Scientists observed the black hole via remote-controlled microscopes, and discovered that at the black hole's event horizon—that's the surface of that tiny sphere with a diameter of twenty-one nanometers—there was the figure of a person. It was 高 Way passing through the event horizon.

"Under general relativity, a distant observer would see a clock near the event horizon slow down, and the process of 高 Way falling toward the event horizon would also slow down and stretch into infinity.

"But within 高 Way's own frame of reference, he had already passed through the event horizon.

"Even more oddly, the figure's proportions were normal. Perhaps it was because the black hole was so small, but tidal forces did not seem to be at work. He had been compressed into the nanometer range, but space there was also extremely curved. More than one physicist believed that the body structure of 高 Way wasn't harmed at the event horizon. In other words, he's probably still alive at this moment.

"And thus the life insurance company refused to pay out, although 高 Way had passed through the event horizon in his frame of reference, and should now be dead. But the insurance contract was made within the frame of reference of our world, and from this perspective, it is impossible to prove that 高 Way is dead. It's not even possible to begin the settlement process. Insurance claims settlement can only occur after the conclusion of an accident, but as 高 Way is still falling toward the black hole, the accident isn't over, and will never be over.

"A woman then sued the World Academy of Sciences and demanded that the academy cease all further research on this black hole specimen. By that point, distant observation was unlikely to yield any further results. In order to be useful, future research would have to manipulate the black hole in some way, such as sending experimental objects into the black hole, which would generate massive amounts of radiation, and might disturb space-time in the vicinity of the event horizon. If 高 Way were still alive, these experiments might endanger his life. The woman didn't win her suit, but for a variety of reasons, research on this black hole stopped, and Lightspeed II was abandoned. Now we can only wait for this black hole to evaporate, which is estimated to take another half century.

"However, we now know that at least one woman did love 高 Way, though he never knew it. Later, that woman still came here regularly and tried to send radio or neutrino messages at the black hole. She even wrote her love in big letters and posted it against the protective net, hoping that the falling 高 Way could see it. But based on his own frame of reference, he had already passed through the event horizon into the singularity. . . . It's a complicated matter."

Cheng Xin stared at the blue phosphorescence far away in the darkness. She now knew that there was a man there, a man who was falling forever, at the event horizon where time stopped. Such a man was still alive when viewed from this world, but had already died in his own world. . . . So many strange fates, and so many unimaginable lives. . . .

Cheng Xin now felt the flickering black hole was really sending out a message, even more like someone blinking. She pulled her gaze back, feeling as empty in her heart as this ruin in space. Softly, she said to Cao Bin, "Let's go to Halo City."

Bunker Era, Year 11
Halo City

As they approached Halo City, Cheng Xin and Cao Bin's dinghy encountered the Federation Fleet's blockade line. More than twenty stellar-class warships surrounded Halo City, and the blockade had lasted two weeks already.

The stellar-class ships were immense, but next to the space city they appeared as tiny skiffs around a giant ocean liner. The Federation Fleet had sent the bulk of their ships to enforce this blockade of Halo City.

After the two Trisolaran Fleets had disappeared in the depths of space and the Trisolarans lost all contact with humankind, the extraterrestrial threats facing humanity took on an entirely new form. Fleet International, which had been formed to combat the Trisolaran invasion, lost its reason for existence and gradually diminished in relevance until it was finally dissolved. The Solar System Fleet that had belonged to Fleet International became the property of the Solar System Federation. This was the first time in human history where a unified world government controlled the majority of humanity's armed forces. Since it was no longer necessary to maintain a large space force, the fleet's size was drastically reduced. After the commencement of the Bunker Project, most of the then-extant hundred-plus stellar-class warships were converted for civilian use. After they were disarmed and their ecological cycling systems removed, they became interplanetary industrial transports for the Bunker Project. Only about thirty stellar-class warships remained in service. Over the last sixty-plus years, no new warships had been built because large warships were extremely expensive. It took the same amount of investment to build two or three stellar-class warships as it did to build a large space city. Moreover, there was no need for new warships. Most of the Federation Fleet's efforts were devoted to building the advance warning system.

The dinghy stopped advancing as it received the blockade order. A military patrol boat sailed toward it. It was very small, and from a distance Cheng Xin could only see the glow from its thrusters—its hull could be seen only once it got closer. When the patrol boat docked with the dinghy, Cheng Xin had a chance to look at the uniformed men inside it. Their military uniforms were very different from those of the last era and seemed to hearken to the styling of an earlier age. The uniforms had fewer space-based characteristics and looked more like the uniforms of old Earth-based armies.

The man who drifted over after the two vessels docked was middle-aged and dressed in a suit. Even in weightlessness, he moved gracefully and calmly, not appearing ill at ease at all in the cramped space that was meant only for two.

"Good day. I'm Blair, special envoy of the Federation president. I'm about to try, for the last time, to negotiate with Halo City's city government. I could have talked to you from my ship, but out of respect for Common Era customs, I decided to come here in person."

Cheng Xin noticed that even the politicians of this age had changed. The assertive and outspoken mannerisms of the last era had been replaced by prudence, restraint, and politeness.

"The Federation Government has announced a total blockade of Halo City, and no one is permitted to enter or leave. However, we know that the passenger here is Dr. Cheng Xin." The envoy nodded at her. "We give you permission to pass and will assist your entrance into Halo City. We hope that you will use your influence to persuade the city government to cease their deranged, illegal resistance, and prevent the situation from deteriorating further. I am expressing the wishes of the Federation president."

The special envoy waved his hand and opened up an information window. The Federation president appeared in the window. In the office behind him were the flags of the various cities of the Bunker World, none of which were familiar to Cheng Xin. Nation states had disappeared along with their flags. The president was an ordinary-looking man of Asian descent. His face looked tired, and after nodding a greeting at Cheng Xin, he said, "Envoy Blair is right. This is the will of the Federation Government. Mr. Wade said that the final decision rests with you, an assertion that we do not fully believe. But we wish you the best of success. I'm glad to see you still looking so young. Although, for this matter, perhaps you're too young."

After the president disappeared from the window, Blair said to Cheng Xin, "I know that you already have some understanding of the situation, but I'd still like to give you an overall explanation. I'll strive to be objective and fair."

Cheng Xin noticed that both the envoy and the president spoke only to her, ignoring Cao Bin's presence, indicating by this omission the deep enmity they felt toward him. As a matter of fact, Cao Bin had already explained the situation to her in detail, and the envoy's account wasn't too different.

After Thomas Wade took over the Halo Group, the company became a key contractor in the Bunker Project. Within eight years, it had grown tenfold and become one of the largest economic entities in the world. Wade himself was not an extraordinary entrepreneur; indeed, he was not even as skilled as 艾 AA at managing the company's operations. The company's growth was the result of the new management team he put in place. He personally did not participate in the running of the company and had little interest in it, but much of the profit generated by the company was taken by him and reinvested in the development of lightspeed spaceflight.

As soon as the Bunker Project began, the Halo Group constructed Halo City as a research center. The Sun-Jupiter L2 Lagrangian point was chosen as the ideal space to set up Halo City in order to eliminate the need for city thrusters and the consumption of resources for position maintenance. Halo City was the only space science city outside the jurisdiction of the Federation Government. While Halo City was being constructed, Wade also began the construction of the circumsolar particle accelerator, a project that was dubbed "The Great Wall of the Solar System" because it enclosed the Sun in a ring.

For half a century, the Halo Group devoted itself to basic research for lightspeed spaceflight. Ever since the Deterrence Era, large companies had often engaged in basic research. In the new economic system, basic research could generate enormous profits. Thus, the behavior of the Halo Group wasn't too unusual. The Halo Group's ultimate goal of constructing lightspeed spaceships was an open secret, but as long as it stuck to basic research, the Federation Government could not accuse it of violating the law. However, the government continued to be suspicious of the Halo Group, and investigated it multiple times. For half a century, the relationship between the company and the government was basically cordial. Since lightspeed ships and the Black Domain Plan called for much of the same basic research, the Halo Group and the World Academy of Sciences maintained a good collaborative working relationship. For instance, the Academy's Black Hole Project used the Halo Group's circumsolar particle accelerator to produce its black hole specimen.

However, six years ago, the Halo Group had suddenly announced its plan to develop curvature propulsion ships. Such open defiance caused an uproar in the international community. Thereafter, conflict between the Halo Group and the Federation Government never ceased. After multiple rounds of negotiations, the Halo Group promised that when the curvature propulsion drive was ready for trials, the testing site would be at least five hundred AU from the Sun so as to avoid exposing the location of Earth civilization with the trails. But the Federation Government felt that the very development of lightspeed ships was a gross violation of the laws and constitution of the Federation. The danger of lightspeed ships lay not only in the trails, but also in upsetting the new social stability in the Bunker World, a prospect that could not be tolerated. A resolution was passed to authorize the government takeover of Halo City and the circumsolar particle accelerator, and to put a complete stop to the Halo Group's theoretical research and technical development in curvature propulsion. Thereafter, the Halo Group's behavior would be subjected to close monitoring.

In response, the Halo Group declared independence from the Solar System Federation. Thus, the conflict between the Halo Group and the Federation escalated yet further.

The international community did not take the Halo Group's declaration of independence too seriously. As a matter of fact, after the commencement of the Bunker Era, conflicts between individual space cities and the Federation Government were not infrequent. For instance, two space cities in the distant city clusters near Uranus and Neptune, Africa II and Indian Ocean I, had declared independence in the past, but nothing had ultimately come of those efforts. Although the Federation Fleet was nowhere near the size it had been in the past, it was still an overwhelming force if applied against individual space cities. By law, space cities were not allowed to possess their own independent armed forces—they could only have limited national guards who had no capacity for space warfare at all. The economy of the Bunker World was also highly integrated such that no individual space city could survive a blockade longer than two months.

"On this point, I can't understand Wade either," said Cao Bin. "He's a man with foresight, and mindful of the big picture, and he never takes a step without having thought through the consequences. So why declare independence? It seems idiotic to provide the Federation Government with an excuse to take over Halo City by force."

The envoy had already left, and the dinghy, now occupied only by Cheng Xin and Cao Bin, continued on course to Halo City. A ring-shaped structure appeared in space ahead, and Cao Bin ordered the dinghy to approach it and decelerate. The smooth metallic surface of the ring reflected the stars as long streaks and distorted the image of the dinghy, bringing to mind the Ring that *Blue Space* and *Gravity* had encountered in four-dimensional space. The dinghy stopped and hovered next to the ring. Cheng Xin estimated that the ring's diameter was about two hundred meters across, and the band about fifty meters thick.

"You're looking at the circumsolar particle accelerator," Cao Bin said, his tone awed.

"It's . . . rather small."

"Oh, sorry; I wasn't clear. This is but one of the coils in the particle accelerator. There are thirty-two hundred coils like this, each about one point five million kilometers apart, forming a large circle around the Sun in the vicinity of Jupiter's orbit. Particles pass through the center of these coils, where they're accelerated by the force field generated by the coil toward the next coil, where they're accelerated again. . . . A particle might travel around the Sun multiple times during the process."

When Cao Bin had spoken to Cheng Xin about the circumsolar particle accelerator in the past, she had always pictured it as a giant doughnut hanging in space. But in reality, to build a solid "Great Wall" around the Sun, even within the orbit of Mercury, would have been an impossible feat approaching the level of God's Engineering Project. Cheng Xin finally realized that while an enclosed tubular ring was necessary for terrestrial particle accelerators to maintain vacuum, it was not necessary in the vacuum of space. The particles being accelerated could simply fly through space, being accelerated by one coil after another. Cheng Xin couldn't help turning to look past the coil for the next one.

"The next coil is one point five million kilometers away, four or five times the distance from the Earth to the moon. You can't see it," Cao Bin said. "This is a supercollider capable of accelerating a particle to the energy level of the big bang. Ships are not allowed anywhere near the orbit of the accelerator. A few years ago, a lost freighter drifted into the orbit by mistake and was hit by a beam of accelerated particles. The ultrahigh-energy particles struck the ship and produced high-energy secondary showers that vaporized the ship and its cargo of millions of tons of mineral ore in an instant."

Cao Bin also told Cheng Xin that the circumsolar particle accelerator's chief designer was Bi Yunfeng. Of the past sixty-plus years, he had spent thirty-five of them working on this project and hibernated for the rest. He had been awakened last year, but was much older than Cao Bin now.

"The old man's lucky, though. He had worked on a terrestrial accelerator back during the Common Era, and now, three centuries later, he got to build a circumsolar particle accelerator. I'd call that a successful career, wouldn't you? But he's a bit of an extremist, and a fanatic supporter of Halo City independence."

While the public and the politicians opposed lightspeed ships, many scientists supported the effort. Halo City became a holy site for scientists who yearned for lightspeed spaceflight and attracted many excellent researchers. Even scientists working within the Federation scientific establishment often collaborated with Halo City—openly or in secret. This caused Halo City to be on the cutting edge in many areas of basic research.

The dinghy left the coil and continued its voyage. Halo City was straight ahead. This space city was built along the rarely seen wheel plan. The structure provided strength but had little interior volume, lacking "world-sense." It was said that the inhabitants of Halo City did not need world-sense, because for them, the world was the entire universe.

The dinghy entered the axis of the giant wheel, where Cheng Xin and Cao Bin had to enter the city through an eight-kilometer spoke. This was one of the least convenient aspects of a wheel plan. Cheng Xin was reminded of her experience more than sixty years ago at the terminal station of the space elevator, and she thought about the great hall that reminded her of an old train station. But the feeling here was different. Halo City was more than ten times larger than that terminal station, and the interior was rather spacious and didn't look run-down.

On the escalator of the spoke, gravity gradually set in. By the time it reached 1G, they were in the city proper. The science city was made up of three parts: the Halo Academy of Sciences, the Halo Academy of Engineering, and the Control Center for the circumsolar particle accelerator. The city was in fact a ring-shaped tunnel thirty-some kilometers in length. Although it wasn't nearly as open or spacious as the large, hollow shells of other cities, one didn't feel claustrophobic, either.

Cheng Xin didn't see any motor vehicles in the city at first. Most residents got around on bicycles, many of which were parked on the side of the road for anyone to use. But a small convertible motor vehicle came to pick up Cheng Xin and Cao Bin.

Since the simulated gravity in the ring pulled toward the outer rim, the city was built along that surface. A holographic image of blue sky with white clouds was projected onto the inner rim, which made up some for the lack of world-sense. A flock of twittering birds flitted overhead, and Cheng Xin noticed that they were not holograms, but real. Here, Cheng Xin felt a sense of comfort that she had not experienced in the other space cities. There were plenty of trees and lawns everywhere. None of the buildings was very tall. Those belonging to the Academy of Sciences were painted white, while those belonging to the Academy of Engineering were painted blue, but each building was unique. The delicate buildings were half-hidden by the green plants, and made her feel as though she were on a college campus.

Cheng Xin saw an interesting sight on her drive. There was a ruin like an ancient Greek temple. On a stone platform stood a few broken Greek columns covered with climbing ivy. In the middle of the columns was a fountain shooting a column of limpid water merrily into the sunlight. A few casually dressed men and women were leaning against the columns or lying on the lawn next to the fountain, lazing about comfortably. They seemed not to care that the city was under siege by the Federation Fleet.

A few statues were scattered on the lawn next to the ruin. Cheng Xin's attention was drawn to one of the statues: A gauntleted hand was picking wreaths woven with stars out of a pool with a sword, and flowing water dripped from the wreaths continuously. This sight triggered something deep in Cheng Xin's memory, but she couldn't recall where exactly she had seen it before. She gazed at the statue from the motorcar until it disappeared.

The car stopped in front of a blue building. It was a laboratory marked with a sign: "Academy of Engineering, Basic Technology 021." Cheng Xin saw Wade and Bi Yunfeng on the lawn in front of the laboratory.

Wade had never entered hibernation since taking over the Halo Group, and was now 110 years old. He kept his hair and beard short, but both were now white as snow. He didn't use a cane, and his stride was steady, but his back was a bit bent, and one of his sleeves still hung empty. In the moment they locked gazes, Cheng Xin understood that time had not defeated this man. What was at his core had not been worn away by the passing years, but had only become more prominent—like a rock revealed after the snow and ice had melted away.

Bi Yunfeng should be much younger than Wade, but he looked older. He was very excited to see Cheng Xin and seemed eager to show her something.

"Hello, little girl," Wade said. "I'm now three times your age." His smile still couldn't make Cheng Xin warm, but it no longer felt as cold as ice water.

Cheng Xin faced these two old men with mixed feelings. They had struggled for their ideals for more than sixty years and were now near the end of their lives' journeys. She, on the other hand, had gone through so many trials after awakening for the first time during the Deterrence Era—but in reality, she had spent no more than four years out of hibernation. She was now 33, still a young woman in this era where average life expectancy was 150.

Cheng Xin greeted the two, and then no one wasted time by saying more. Wade led Cheng Xin into the laboratory with Bi Yunfeng and Cao Bin following. They entered a spacious, windowless hall. The familiar acrid odor of static told Cheng Xin they were in a sophon-free room. After more than sixty years, people still could not be sure that the sophons had left the Solar System, and maybe they'd never be sure. The hall must have been filled with instruments and equipment not long ago, but now all the lab equipment was scattered in a chaotic pile next to the walls, as though it had been moved away in a hurry to clear out the center. In the middle of the hall was a single machine. The surrounding chaos and the emptiness in the center displayed an irrepressible excitement, as though a team of treasure hunters had suddenly found a priceless artifact, tossed their tools to the side, and carefully moved their prize to the center of the open space.

The machine's complex structure reminded Cheng Xin of a tokamak from the Common Era, but miniaturized. The bulk of the machine consisted of a sphere bisected horizontally by a flat black metallic plane that extended several meters over the edge of the sphere. The plane, holding up the sphere at about waist-height, also served as a lab bench with sturdy legs. The surface of the bench was mostly empty save for a few tools and manipulators attached to telescoping arms.

The metal hemisphere below the bench was studded with tubes of various thicknesses, all aimed at the invisible center of the sphere, causing the machine to look like a naval mine studded with Hertz horns. Apparently, the arrangement was designed to concentrate some kind of energy at the center.

The hemisphere above the bench, in contrast, was made of transparent glass. The two hemispheres together formed a whole divided by the metal plane, contrasting simple transparency with complex opacity.

Looking down through the glass dome, Cheng Xin could see a small rectangular metallic platform whose sides measured only a few centimeters, about the size of a pack of cigarettes, and whose surface was smooth and reflective like a mirror. The platform under the glass dome was like a tiny, delicate stage; and the complicated mechanism below the plane the orchestra that would accompany the performance, though it was unimaginable what that performance would be.

"Let's allow a physical part of you to experience this grand moment," Wade said. Bi Yunfeng lifted the glass dome as Wade walked over to Cheng Xin and held up a pair of scissors. Cheng Xin tensed, but did not shy away. Carefully, assisted by a tool on the platform, Wade lifted a strand of her hair and cut off a small section at the end. He held the hair clipping with the tool, examined it, and concluded it was still too long. He cut the clipping in half so that the remaining piece was only about two or three millimeters long, almost invisible. Wade walked over to the side of the opened glass dome and carefully placed the hair on the smooth metal platform. Although Wade was over a hundred years of age and had only one hand, his movements were precise and steady, showing no tremors.

"Come, watch carefully," Wade said.

Cheng Xin leaned down to look through the glass dome. She could see her hair resting against the smooth stage. There was a red line down the middle of the stage, and the hair was on one side of it.

Wade nodded at Bi Yunfeng, who opened a control window in the air and activated the machine. Cheng Xin looked down and saw that a few tubes connected to the machine began to glow red, reminding her of the glimpse she had caught of the inside of the Trisolaran spaceship. She heard a rumbling but didn't feel any heat. She returned her gaze to the small platform and felt some invisible disturbance spread out from the platform, brushing across her face like a light breeze. She couldn't be sure it wasn't just an illusion.

She saw that her hair had moved to the other side of the red line, but she hadn't seen it move.

After another series of rumblings, the machine stopped.

"What did you see?" Wade asked.

"You spent half a century to move a three-millimeter section of hair two centimeters," said Cheng Xin.

"It was curvature propulsion," Wade said.

"If we used the same technique to continue to accelerate the hair, it would be moving at lightspeed in about ten meters," Bi Yunfeng said. "Of course we can't achieve this now, and we dare not try it here. If we did, this bit of hair, moving at lightspeed, would destroy Halo City."

Cheng Xin pondered the strand of hair that had been moved two centimeters by curving space. "You are saying that you've invented gunpowder and managed to make a firecracker, but the ultimate goal is to make a space rocket. A thousand years may separate those two achievements."

"Your analogy is flawed," Bi Yunfeng said. "We have invented the equation relating energy to mass, and we've discovered the principle of radioactivity.

The ultimate goal is to make the atom bomb. Only a few decades divide those two achievements."

"In fifty years, we should be able to construct curvature propulsion spaceships capable of lightspeed flight. This will require massive amounts of technical testing and development work. We have to lay our cards on the table now so that the government can back off and give us the environment necessary to carry out these tasks."

"But your current approach will make you lose everything."

"Everything depends on your decision," Wade said. "You must think that we're helpless against the power of that fleet out there. Not so." He gestured at the door. "Come in."

A group of forty or fifty armed men filed in and soon filled the hall. They were all young men dressed in black space camouflage, and their presence seemed to make the hall dimmer. They wore military-issue lightweight space suits that seemed no different from ordinary military uniforms, but they could enter space as soon as they put on helmets and life-support backpacks. Cheng Xin was astonished, however, to see the weapons they carried: rifles, from the Common Era. Perhaps they were newly made, but the design was ancient and entirely mechanical, with manual bolts and triggers. The ammunition they carried confirmed this: Everyone wore two crossed bandoliers filled with glistening yellow cartridges.

To see these men in this age was akin to seeing a group of men armed with bows and swords during the Common Era. This was not to say that the fighters did not appear visually intimidating. Cheng Xin felt the presence of the past not only because of their ancient weapons, but also their appearance. They displayed a trained esprit de corps: they were uniform not only in dress and equipment, but also in their spirit. The men appeared tough and strong, with muscles bulging beneath their thin space suits. The gazes and expressions on their bold, angular faces were very similar: an indifferent, metallic grimness that viewed life as cheap as grass.

"This is our city self-defense force." Wade waved at the assembled men. "They are all we have to protect Halo City and the ideal of the lightspeed ship. You can see almost all of them here—there are a few more outside, but the total is no more than a hundred. As for their equipment—" Wade took a rifle from one of the soldiers and pulled the bolt. "You can trust your eyes: ancient weapons constructed of modern materials. The bullets do not rely on gunpowder as the propellant and have much better range and precision compared to genuine ancient weapons. In space, these rifles can hit a ship from two thousand kilometers away, but fundamentally, they're primitive weapons. You must think this ridiculous, and I would, too, except for one thing." He returned the rifle to the soldier and pulled one of the cartridges from his bandolier. "As I said, the cartridges are basically of ancient design, but the bullets are new. So new, in fact, that they might as well come from the future. The bullet is a super-conducting container and the interior is a pure vacuum. A magnetic field suspends a small ball in the middle to prevent it from contacting the bullet's body. The ball is made of antimatter."

Bi Yunfeng's voice was filled with pride. "The circumsolar particle accelerator was not only used for basic research experiments, but also to produce antimatter. In the last four years, we've used it to make antimatter practically the entire time. We now possess fifteen thousand bullets of this design."

The primitive-seeming cartridge held in Wade's hand now caused Cheng Xin to suffer chills. She now worried about the reliability of the containment magnetic field within that superconducting bullet: a single malfunction would be enough to cause the complete destruction of Halo City in a brilliant flash. She looked at the golden bandoliers hanging over the chests of every soldier: These were the chains of the god of Death. A single bandolier possessed enough power to destroy the entire Bunker World.

Wade continued, "We don't even have to go into space to attack. We just have to wait until the fleet approaches the city. We can shoot dozens or even hundreds of bullets at each of the twenty or so ships—a single hit is enough to destroy it. Although the tactic is primitive, it's effective and flexible. A single soldier with a gun is a fighting unit capable of threatening an entire warship. Also, we have agents in other space cities with handguns." He returned the cartridge to the soldier's bandolier. "We don't want war. During the final negotiations, we'll show our weapons to the Federation envoy and explain our tactics. We hope the Federation Government will weigh the costs of war and abandon their threat against Halo City. We're not asking for much, only to build a research center several hundred AU from the Sun devoted to curvature propulsion testing."

"But if we go to war, can you guarantee victory?" Cao Bin asked. He had not spoken so far. Unlike Bi Yunfeng, he apparently was not in favor of war.

"No," Wade answered calmly. "But neither can they. We can only try."

As soon as Cheng Xin saw the antimatter bullet in Wade's hand, she knew what she must do. She wasn't too worried about the Federation Fleet—she believed that they'd come up with ways to deal with this tactic. Her mind was focused on only one thing:

Also, we have agents in other space cities with handguns.

If war were to erupt, any of the guerrilla fighters hidden in the other space cities could casually shoot one of the antimatter bullets at the ground and the explosion of matter-antimatter annihilation would instantaneously tear apart the thin shell of the city and incinerate everything within. Next, the spinning space city would break into fragments and millions would die.

Space cities were as fragile as eggs.

Wade had not explicitly said that he would attack the space cities, but he also hadn't said he wouldn't. She again saw Wade aiming a gun at her 133 years ago—an image which had been branded into her heart. She didn't know how cold a man would have to be to make such a decision, but the core of this man was the utter madness and coldness brought about by extreme rationality. She seemed to see again the young Wade from three centuries ago, screaming like a crazy beast: "Advance, advance without regard for consequences!"

Even if Wade did not want to attack the space cities, what if others on his force did?

As if confirming Cheng Xin's fear, a soldier spoke to her. "Dr. Cheng, please be assured that we will fight to the end."

Another soldier spoke up. "We are not fighting for you, for Mr. Wade, or this city." He pointed upwards, and fire seemed to light up his eyes. "Do you know what they're trying to take away from here? Not the city or lightspeed ships, but the entire universe outside the Solar System! There are billions and billions of new worlds out there, but they won't let us go; they want to lock us and our descendants in this prison, a prison fifty astronomical units in radius called the Solar System. We are fighting for freedom, for a chance to live as free men in the universe. Our cause is the same as every ancient struggle for freedom. We will fight to the very last. I speak for everyone in the self-defense force."

The other soldiers nodded at Cheng Xin, their eyes grim and cold.

In the years to come, Cheng Xin would recall the soldier's words countless times. But at this moment, they did not move her. She felt the world going dark, and she was mired in terror. She felt as though she was again standing in front of the UN headquarters, holding that baby from more than 130 years ago. She felt the baby in her arms was facing a flock of hungry wolves, and she had to protect the child at all costs.

"Will you keep your promise?" she asked Wade.

Wade nodded. "Of course. Why else would I ask you to come here?"

"Then stop all preparation for war and cease all resistance. Turn over all antimatter bullets to the Federation Government. Order those agents you've sent to the other cities to do the same immediately!"

The soldiers gazed at Cheng Xin, as if trying to burn her to a crisp with their eyes. The power differential between the two sides was overwhelming. She was faced with a cold machine of war. Every man carried more than a hundred hydrogen bombs, and, led by a strong, mad leader, they formed a powerful black wheel capable of crushing all resistance. She was nothing more than a blade of grass in front of this giant wheel, not able to even slow down its progress. But she had to do what she could.

However, things did not develop as she expected. The gazes of the soldiers moved away from her one by one, turning to Wade. The suffocating pressure seemed to let up gradually, but she still had trouble breathing. Wade continued to look at the curvature propulsion platform under the glass dome holding up Cheng Xin's hair as though gazing at a sacred altar. Cheng Xin could imagine that Wade had once gathered his warriors around this altar to prophesy war.

"Why don't you think about it some more?" Wade said.

"There's no need." Cheng Xin's voice was like iron. "I have made my final decision. Cease all resistance, and turn over all antimatter in Halo City."

Wade lifted his head and looked at Cheng Xin with rarely seen helplessness and pleading. He spoke slowly. "If we lose our human nature, we lose much, but if we lose our bestial nature, we lose everything."

"I choose human nature," Cheng Xin said, looking around at everyone. "I believe you all will, as well."

Bi Yunfeng was about to speak, but Wade stopped him. His eyes dimmed. Something had gone out in them, extinguished forever. The weight of years abruptly crushed him, and he appeared exhausted. He supported himself on the metal platform with his one hand and slowly sat down on a chair someone else brought over. Then he lifted his hand and pointed to the platform in front of him, keeping his eyes down. "Disarm. Leave all your ammunition here."

No one moved at first. But Cheng Xin felt something soften. That dark force was dissipating. The soldiers looked away from Wade and no longer focused on a single point. Finally, someone walked over and placed two bandoliers on the platform. Though his movements were gentle, the metallic sound made by the cartridges scraping against the platform caused Cheng Xin to shudder. The bandoliers lay still on the platform like two gold-colored snakes. A second man walked over and deposited his bandoliers, then more. The platform was soon covered by a golden pile. After all the cartridges had been collected, the metallic noises stopped, and everything became quiet again.

"Order all of our agents in the Bunker World to disarm and surrender to the Federation Government," Wade said. "The Halo City government will collaborate with the fleet to turn over the city. Do not take any drastic action."

"All right," someone answered. Deprived of their bandoliers, these men dressed in black space suits made the place even dimmer.

Wade gestured for the self-defense force to leave. They departed noiselessly, and the hall brightened as though a dark cloud had dissipated. Wade struggled to stand, walked around the pile of antimatter cartridges, and slowly opened the glass dome. He blew at the curvature propulsion platform and Cheng Xin's hair disappeared. He closed the dome, turned to Cheng Xin, and smiled. "You see, I've kept my promise, little girl."

After the Halo City Incident, the Federation Government did not immediately disclose the existence of antimatter weapons. The international community thought the event concluded as they had expected, and there wasn't much reaction. As the creator of the circumsolar particle accelerator, the Halo Group enjoyed great prestige internationally, and public opinion was mostly forgiving of them, suggesting that there was no reason to pursue anyone legally, and Halo City should be allowed to self-govern again as soon as possible. As long as the Halo Group promised to never again engage in any research and development of curvature propulsion and submitted to Federation monitoring, it should be allowed to go on with its business.

But one week later, Federation Fleet Command revealed to the world the captured antimatter bullets. The pile of golden Death stunned everyone.

The Halo Group was declared an illegal organization, and the Federation Government confiscated all its property and took over the circumsolar particle accelerator. The Federation Fleet declared a long-term occupation of Halo City, and the Academies of Science and Engineering were dissolved. More than three hundred people, including Wade, the other leaders of the Halo Group, and the city self-defense force, were arrested.

In the subsequent trial in Federation court, Thomas Wade was convicted of crimes against humanity, war crimes, and violations of the laws prohibiting research into curvature propulsion. The sentence was death.

Cheng Xin went to a detention center located near the Supreme Federation Court in Earth I, the Solar System Federation's capital, to see Wade one last time. They looked at each other through a transparent barrier and said nothing. Cheng Xin saw that this old man, 110 years old, was as placid as the puddle at the bottom of a well that was about to dry out. There would be no more ripples.

Cheng Xin passed the box of cigars she had bought in Pacific I through an opening in the barrier. Wade opened the box, took out three of the ten cigars, and pushed the box back through the opening.

"I won't be able to use the rest," he said.

"Tell me more about yourself. Your work, your life. I want to tell those who would come later about you," Cheng Xin said.

Wade shook his head. "I am but one of the countless who have died and will die. What is there to tell?"

Cheng Xin knew that what divided them wasn't just this transparent barrier, but also the deepest chasm in this world, a chasm that could never be bridged.

"Do you have anything to say to me?" Cheng Xin asked. She was surprised that she wanted to hear his answer.

"Thank you for the cigars."

It took a long while before Cheng Xin understood that this was what Wade wanted to say to her. His last words. All his words.

They sat in silence, neither looking at the other. Time turned into a stagnant pool that drowned them. Then, the tremors of the space city adjusting its position returned Cheng Xin to reality. She stood up slowly and softly said good-bye.

Once she was outside the detention center, Cheng Xin picked out one of the cigars and borrowed a light from one of the guards. She took her first puff of a cigar in her life. Oddly, she didn't cough. She watched the white smoke rise in the sunlight of the capital, watched it dissipate in her tear-filled vision like the three centuries she and Wade had lived through.

Three days later, a powerful laser vaporized Thomas Wade in one-ten-thousandth of a second.

Cheng Xin returned to Asia I's hibernation center and awakened 艾 AA. They returned to the Earth.

They rode *Halo* back. After the Halo Group had been dissolved and its property confiscated, the Federation Government returned a small portion of the company's vast wealth to Cheng Xin. The amount was about equal to the value of the Halo Group at the time Wade took over. It was still a large sum, though minuscule when compared to the total wealth of the vanished company. *Halo* was part of the property returned to Cheng Xin—though this was the third ship to bear that name. It was a small stellar yacht capable of seating up to three. The shipboard ecological cycling system was comfortable and refined, like a lovely small garden.

Cheng Xin and AA wandered over the barely inhabited continents of the Earth. They swept over endless forests, rode on trotting horses across grasslands, lingered over empty beaches. Most cities had become covered by forests and vines, leaving only small patches of civilization for the remaining residents. The total human population on the Earth was about what it was near the end of the Neolithic Age.

The longer they stayed on the Earth, the more all of civilization's history seemed a dream.

They returned to Australia. Only Canberra remained inhabited, and a tiny town government there called itself the Australian Federal Government. The Parliament House where Sophon had proclaimed the plan for the extermination of the human race was still there, but thick layers of vegetation sealed its doors, and vines climbed up the eighty-meter-tall flagpole. They found Fraisse's record in the government archives. He had lived until he was 150, but finally, time had defeated him. He had died more than ten years ago.

They went to Mosken Island. The lighthouse built by Jason was still there, but it was no longer lit. The region was completely uninhabited. They heard again the rumbling of the Mosskstraumen, but all they could see was the empty sea in the light of the setting Sun.

Their future was equally empty.

AA said, "Why don't we go to the world after the strike, the world after the Sun is gone? Only then will we find a life of serenity."

Cheng Xin also wanted to go to that time, but not for a life of serenity. She had stopped a catastrophic war and she was becoming the target of the worship of millions. She could no longer live in this era. She wanted to see Earth civilization survive the dark forest strike and prosper after—it was the only hope that could comfort her heart. She imagined life in that post-strike nebula. There, she would find true tranquility, maybe even happiness. That would be the last harbor of her life's voyage.

She was only thirty-three.

Cheng Xin and AA rode *Halo* back to the Jovian city cluster and once again entered hibernation in Asia I. The contracted-for time was two hundred years, but they included a provision in the contract stating they should be awakened if a dark forest strike occurred before then.

And then they slept. Dreamless.

PART V

Bunker Era, Year 67
Orion Arm of the Milky Way

Examining the data was Singer's job; judging the sincerity of the coordinates was Singer's joy.

Singer understood that what he did wasn't important—it just filled in the pieces. But it had to be done, and the task was enjoyable.

Speaking of enjoyment, when this seed had departed from the home world, that world was still a place full of joy. But later, as the home world began to war against the fringe world, joy diminished. By now, more than ten thousand grains of time had passed. There wasn't much joy to speak of on the home world or in this seed. The happiness of the past was recorded in classical songs, and singing those songs was another of the few joys left.

Singer sang one of these classical songs as he reviewed the data.

> *I see my love;*
> *I fly next to her;*
> *I present her with my gift,*
> *A small piece of solidified time.*
> *Lovely markings are carved into time*
> *As soft to the touch as the mud in shallow sea.*

Singer did not complain much. Survival required so much thought and mental energy.

Entropy increased in the universe, and order decreased. The process was like the boundless wings of the giant balance bird pressing down upon all of existence. But low-entropy entities were different. The low-entropy entities decreased their entropy and increased their order, like columns of phosphorescence rising over the inky-dark sea. This was meaning, the highest meaning, higher than enjoyment. To maintain this meaning, low-entropy entities had to continue to exist.

As for any meaning higher than that, it was pointless to think about. Thinking about the subject led nowhere and was dangerous. It was even more pointless to think about the apex of the tower of meaning—maybe there wasn't an apex at all.

Back to the coordinates. Many sets of coordinates flitted across space, like the matrix insects flitting across the sky of the home world. Picking up coordinates was the job of the main core, which swallowed all the messages passing through space: medium membrane, long membrane, light membrane, and maybe one day even short membrane. The main core remembered the positions of all the stars. By matching the received data against various map projections and position schema, it could pick out the coordinates of the messages' origin. It was said that the main core could match position schema from five hundred million time grains ago. Singer never tried anything like that—it would be meaningless. In that distant age, the low-entropy clusters in space were rare and far apart, and had not evolved the hiding gene and the cleansing gene. But now—

Hide yourself well; cleanse well.

Out of all the coordinates, only some were sincere. Believing in insincere coordinates meant cleansing empty worlds. This was wasteful. And there were other harms besides. These empty worlds might be useful in the future. It was incomprehensible why anyone would send out insincere coordinates—they would get what they deserved someday.

Sincere coordinates followed certain patterns. For instance, a mass cluster of coordinates was usually insincere. But these patterns were all only heuristics. Judging the sincerity of coordinates effectively required intuition. The main core on this seed was incapable of this task, and even the supercore back on the home world could not do it. This was one reason why low-entropy entities had no substitute.

Singer had this skill, this intuition, but it wasn't a gift or instinct; rather, it was something honed by the accumulated experience of tens of thousands of time grains. A set of coordinates seemed nothing more than a simple matrix in the eyes of the uninitiated, but to Singer, it was alive. Its every detail was expressive. For instance, how many reference points were taken? What was the method for marking the target star? And many other subtle details besides. The main core was able to provide some information, such as the historical records associated with this set of coordinates, the direction of the coordinate broadcast source, the broadcast time, and so forth. Together, these formed an organic whole, and what emerged in Singer's consciousness was a sense of the coordinate broadcaster himself. Singer's spirit crossed the chasm of space and time, resonated with the spirit of the broadcaster, and felt its terror and anxiety, along with other feelings unfamiliar to the home world, such as hatred, envy, greed, and so on. But for the most part, it was terror. Terror was what endowed a set of coordinates with sincerity. For all low-entropy entities, terror guaranteed existence.

Just then, Singer noticed a sincere set of coordinates near the course of the seed. The set of coordinates was broadcast by long membrane, and even Singer himself couldn't be sure what told him that the set of coordinates was sincere— intuition could not always be explained. He decided to cleanse it. He wasn't busy, and the task wasn't going to distract him from singing. Even if he got it wrong, it was not a big deal. Cleansing was not a precision task and didn't require absolute accuracy. It also wasn't urgent. He just had to get it done eventually. This was also why his position wasn't prestigious.

Singer took a mass dot out of the seed's magazine, then he turned to look for the star indicated by the set of coordinates. The main core guided his gaze, like a spear sweeping through the starry sky. Singer grasped the mass dot with a force field feeler and prepared to flick it. But then he saw the location indicated by the set of coordinates and the feeler relaxed.

Of the three stars, one was missing. There was a white cloud of dust in its place, like the feces of an abyss whale.

It's already been cleansed. Nothing more to do.

Singer put the mass dot back into storage.

That was fast.

He activated a main core process to trace the source of the mass dot that had killed that star. This was a hopeless task with almost zero chance of success, but required by established procedure. The process soon terminated, and like every other time, yielded no results.

Singer soon understood why the cleansing had happened so fast. He saw a slow fog in the vicinity of that destroyed world. The slow fog was about half a structure length away from that world. Seen by itself, it wasn't apparent where the fog had come from, but when connected with the broadcast coordinates, it was obvious that the fog belonged to that world. The slow fog showed that the world was dangerous, which was why the cleansing had come so quickly. It appeared that there were other low-entropy entities with even sharper intuition than he; but that wasn't strange. It was as the Elder said: *In the cosmos, no matter how fast you are, someone will be faster; no matter how slow you are, someone will be slower.*

Every set of broadcast coordinates would eventually be cleansed; it was just a matter of sooner versus later. One low-entropy entity might think this set of coordinates insincere, but on the millions upon millions of low-entropy worlds there were billions upon billions tasked with cleansing—someone would think it sincere. All low-entropy entities possessed the cleansing gene, and cleansing was an instinct. Also, cleansing was a very simple thing. The cosmos was full of sources of potential power—one just had to trigger them to complete the task. It required so very little, and didn't even delay singing.

If Singer were patient, all sincere coordinates would eventually be cleansed by other, unknown low-entropy entities. But this was not a good thing for either the home world or the seed. Since Singer had received the set of coordinates and even glanced at the world pointed to by the coordinates, Singer had a connection to that world. It would be naïve to think of this connection as unidirectional. Recall the great law of reversible discovery: If you could see a low-entropy world, then that low-entropy world could also see you—it was only a matter of time. Thus, waiting for others to complete cleansing was dangerous.

The next task was to put this now-useless set of coordinates into the data bank called the tomb. This was also required by established procedure. Of course, all other information having to do with the location needed to go into the data bank as well, just as personal effects were buried with the body, as was the custom on the home world.

Among the "personal effects" was something that piqued Singer's interest. It was a record of the dead world's three communications with another location using medium membrane. Medium membrane was the least efficient communication membrane, also called primitive membrane. Most communications preferred long membrane, though it was said that even short membrane could be used to convey messages. If true, that would make the communicators akin to gods. But Singer liked primitive membrane. He thought primitive membrane possessed a simple beauty, symbolizing an age full of joy. He often turned primitive membrane messages into songs. He thought they sounded pretty, even if he didn't understand them. Understanding them wasn't necessary, however; other than coordinates, primitive membrane messages didn't have much useful information. It was enough to enjoy the music.

But this time, Singer was able to understand some of the message, because some parts carried a self-decoding system! Although Singer was only able to understand a little, grasp an outline, it was enough for him to see an incredible history.

First, the other location had broadcast a message via primitive membrane. The low-entropy entities of that world clumsily plucked their star—Singer decided to call them the Star-Pluckers—like ancient bards of the home world plucking the strings of the rough country zither, to send out the message. It was this message that contained the self-decoding system.

Although the self-decoding system was primitive and clumsy, it was sufficient to allow Singer to see that a subsequent message sent out by the dead three-star world followed the same encoding scheme—apparently an answer to the first message sent by the Star-Pluckers! This was already nearly inconceivable, but after that, the Star-Pluckers responded again!

Interesting. Very interesting!

Singer had indeed heard of low-entropy worlds that possessed neither the hiding gene nor the hiding instinct, but this was the first time he had seen one. Of course, the three communications between these two would not reveal their absolute coordinates, but they did expose the distance between the two worlds. If the distance were fairly large, it wouldn't be a big deal either; but the distance was very short, only 416 structures—the two worlds were practically on top of each other. This meant that if one world's coordinates were exposed, the other would also be exposed—it was just a matter of time.

This was how the Star-Pluckers' coordinates were revealed.

Nine time grains after the first three communications, another record appeared: The Star-Pluckers plucked their star again to send out another broadcast . . . a set of coordinates! The main core was certain that it was a set of coordinates. Singer looked for the star indicated by the coordinates and saw that it had also been cleansed, about thirty-five time grains ago.

Singer thought that perhaps he had been wrong. The Star-Pluckers must have possessed the hiding gene. They obviously had the cleansing gene, so it was impossible that they didn't also possess the hiding gene. But like most co-ordinate broadcasters, they didn't have the ability to cleanse on their own.

Interesting. Very interesting.

Why did whoever cleansed the dead three-star world not also cleanse the world of the Star-Pluckers? Many possibilities. Perhaps they hadn't noticed these three communications—primitive membrane messages often didn't get much attention. But given the millions upon millions of worlds out there, *someone* would have noticed—Singer was just one who did. Even without

Singer, some other low-entropy entity would have noticed them; it was just a matter of time. Or perhaps they *had* noticed them, but decided that a low-entropy group that didn't possess the hiding gene wasn't much of a threat, and cleansing them was more trouble than it was worth.

But that would be a mistake, a terrible mistake! Broadly speaking, if low-entropy entities like these Star-Pluckers really didn't have the hiding gene, then they would not be afraid of exposing their own presence, and they would expand and attack without fear.

At least until they got killed.

However, as applied to this particular case, the situation was more complicated. The first three communications were followed nine time grains later by the coordinate broadcast. Then, sixty time grains after that, there was another long-membrane coordinate broadcast from somewhere else, pointing at the dead three-star world. The chain of events painted an uneasy picture, a picture that indicated danger. The cleansing against the dead three-star world had happened twelve time grains ago, so the Star-Pluckers must have realized that their own position had been revealed. Their only choice was to shroud themselves in slow fog so that they would appear perfectly safe and no one would bother them.

But they hadn't. Maybe they didn't have the ability? But more than sufficient time had passed from the time they could pluck their star to send out a primitive membrane message for them to possess this ability.

Perhaps they didn't want to shroud themselves.

If that was so, that made the Star-Pluckers very dangerous; far more dangerous than the dead world.

Hide yourself well; cleanse well.

Singer gazed at the world of the Star-Pluckers. It was an ordinary star that had at least a billion more time grains of life left. It possessed eight planets: four giant liquid planets and four solid ones. Singer's experience told him that the low-entropy entities who had sent out the primitive membrane broadcast lived on one of the solid planets.

Singer activated the process for the big eye—he rarely did this; he was exceeding his authority.

"What are you doing?" asked the seed's Elder. "The big eye is busy."

"I'd like to take a closer look at one of the low-entropy worlds."

"Your job doesn't require close-up examinations."

"I'm just curious."

"The big eye has to observe more important targets. There's no time for your curiosity. Go back to doing your job."

Singer didn't persist in his request. The cleansing agent had the lowest position on the seed. Everyone thought of him contemptuously, thought of his work as easy and trivial. But they forgot that coordinates that had been broadcast often indicated far more danger than the vast majority who kept themselves well hidden.

The only thing left was cleansing. Singer took a mass dot out of the magazine again, then realized that he couldn't use a mass dot to cleanse the Star-Pluckers. Their planetary system had a different structure than the dead world's system: it possessed blind corners. Using a mass dot might leave something behind, thereby wasting effort. He needed to use a dual-vector foil. However, Singer didn't have the authority to retrieve a dual-vector foil out of the magazine; he had to ask the Elder for approval.

"I need a dual-vector foil for cleansing."

"Permission granted," said the Elder.

The dual-vector foil drifted in front of Singer. It was sealed in its package, crystal clear. Although it was an ordinary object, Singer liked it a lot. He didn't like the expensive tools too much; they were too violent. He liked the unyielding tenderness displayed by the dual-vector foil, a kind of aesthetic that could turn death into a song.

Yet Singer felt a bit uneasy. "Why did you give it to me without so much as asking a question?"

"It's not like this is very costly."

"But if we make too much use of this—"

"It's being used everywhere in the cosmos."

"Yes, that is true. But in the past, we've always been restrained. Now—"

"Have you heard something?" The Elder began to riffle through Singer's thoughts, and Singer shuddered. Very quickly, the Elder found the rumor in Singer's mind. It wasn't a great sin—the rumor was an open secret on the seed.

It was a rumor about the war between the home world and the fringe world. Before, news about the war had been frequent, but then the reports stopped, indicating that the war wasn't going well, perhaps even heading into a crisis. But the home world couldn't coexist with the fringe world. The fringe world had to be destroyed, lest the home world be destroyed by it. If the war couldn't be won, then . . .

"Has the home world decided to transform into two dimensions?" Singer asked. Of course, the Elder already knew the question.

The Elder did not answer, which was also an answer.

If the rumor was true, then it was a great sorrow. Singer couldn't imagine such a life. On the tower of values, survival ranked above all. When survival was threatened, all low-entropy entities could only pick the lesser of two evils.

Singer removed these thoughts from his organ of cogitation. These were not thoughts he should have, and he was only going to be uselessly troubled by them. He tried to remember where he had stopped in his song. It took a while before he found his place. He continued to sing:

> Lovely markings are carved into time
> As soft to the touch as the mud in shallow sea.
> She covers her body with time,
> And pulls me along to fly to the edge of existence.
> This is a spiritual flight:
> In our eyes, the stars appear as ghosts;
> In the eyes of the stars, we appear as ghosts.

As he continued to sing, Singer picked up the dual-vector foil with a force field feeler and carelessly tossed it at the Star-Pluckers.

Bunker Era, Year 67
Halo

Cheng Xin awakened to find herself in weightlessness.

Hibernation wasn't like regular sleep. A hibernator didn't feel the passage of time. Throughout the entire process, one could only feel time during the hour spent entering hibernation and the hour emerging from it. No matter how much time passed during hibernation, subjectively, the hibernator only felt that he or she had slept no more than two hours. Thus, waking up always involved a sharp break, a feeling that the self had passed through a door in time and emerged into a new world.

Cheng Xin found herself in a white spherical space. She saw that 艾 AA was floating nearby, dressed in the same skintight hibernation suit. Her hair was wet and her limbs were spread out powerlessly; clearly, she had just been awakened as well. As their eyes met, Cheng Xin wanted to speak, but the numbness caused by the cold had still not left her, and she couldn't make any noise. AA shook her head, meaning that she was in the same state and didn't know anything.

Cheng Xin noticed that the space was filled with a golden light like the setting sun. The light came in through a circular window—a porthole. Outside the porthole, Cheng Xin could see only blurred streaks and swirling lines. The lines were arranged into parallel bands of blue and yellow, revealing a world covered by raging storms and torrents, clearly the surface of Jupiter. Cheng Xin saw that the surface of Jupiter looked much brighter than she remembered.

Strangely, the wide, raging cloud band in the middle reminded her of the Yellow River. She knew, of course, that an eddy in this "Yellow River" was big enough to contain the Earth. Against this background, Cheng Xin saw an object. The main body of the object was a long column whose sections were of different diameters. Three short cylinders were perpendicularly attached to the main column at different locations. The entire assembly slowly rotated around the axis of the column. Cheng Xin decided that she was looking at a combined space city formed from eight separate space cities docked together.

She discovered another amazing fact as well: The place they were in stayed at rest relative to the combined space city, but Jupiter was slowly moving in the background. Based on the brightness of Jupiter, they were now on the side facing the Sun, and she could see the shadow of the combined space city against the gaseous surface of Jupiter. After a while, the Jovian terminator appeared, dividing Jupiter's day from night, and she saw the monstrous eye that was the Great Red Spot drifting into view. Everything confirmed the fact that both the place they were in and the combined space city were not in Jupiter's shadow and did not orbit the Sun in parallel with Jupiter; instead, they were Jupiter's satellites and revolved around the gas giant.

"Where are we?" Cheng Xin asked. She was finally able to speak in a hoarse voice, but she still couldn't move her body.

AA shook her head again. "No idea. I think we're on a spaceship."

They continued to drift in the golden glow of Jupiter, like a dreamscape.

"You're on *Halo*."

The voice came from an information window that had just popped up next to them. In the window was an old man with a head full of white hair. Cheng Xin recognized him as Cao Bin. Based on his age, she realized that she had leapt across another long stretch of years. Cao Bin told her that it was now May 19 of Year 67 of the Bunker Era. She realized that fifty-six more years had passed since her last brief awakening.

She avoided life by staying outside of time, and she watched as others aged, seemingly in an instant. Her heart was filled with regret and guilt. She decided that no matter what happened from now on, this was her last hibernation.

Cao Bin told them that they were on the latest ship to bear the *Halo* name. It had been constructed only three years ago. After the Halo City Incident, more than half a century earlier, he and Bi Yunfeng had both been convicted, though both had served short sentences and then been released. Bi Yunfeng had died more than ten years earlier, and Cao Bin brought along his well wishes for her and AA. Cheng Xin's eyes moistened.

Cao Bin also told them that there were now fifty-two large space cities in the Jupiter cluster, most of which had been combined into bigger cities. What they could see was Jupiter Combination II. Since the advance warning system had been refined twenty years ago, all cities had decided to become Jovian satellites. Only after an alert was issued would the cities change orbit and go into hiding.

"Life in the cities is once again like being in paradise. It's too bad that you won't get to see it, because there's no time." Cao Bin paused. Cheng Xin and AA exchanged uneasy glances. They realized that he had been so loquacious until now because he was trying to delay this moment.

"Was there an attack alert?"

Cao Bin nodded. "Yes, there's been an alert. During the last half century, there were two false alarms, and each time, we almost awakened you. But this time it's real. Children—I'm already one hundred and twelve years of age, so I think I can call you that—the dark forest strike is finally here."

Cheng Xin's heart tensed. It wasn't because the attack had arrived— humanity had been preparing for this moment for more than a century. Rather, she sensed that something was wrong. She and AA had been awakened by contract. It would have taken at least four to five hours for them to recover to this stage, which meant that the alert had been issued some time ago. But outside the porthole, Jupiter Combination II had not disassembled nor changed its orbit, but continued to drift as a Jovian satellite, as though nothing had happened. They turned to Cao Bin: The centenarian's expression was too placid, as though hiding utter despair.

"Where are you now?" AA asked.

"I'm at the advance warning center," Cao Bin said, and pointed behind him.

Cheng Xin saw a hall behind him that looked like a control center. Information windows filled almost every bit of space. The windows drifted around the hall, but new windows kept on popping open before them, only to be covered in turn by still newer windows—like the flood after a burst dam. But the people in the hall seemed to be doing nothing. Half of them were in military uniforms, but they all either stood leaning against a desk or sat still. Everyone had dull eyes, and all had the same ominous calm expression that was on Cao Bin's face.

It shouldn't be like this.

This didn't look like a world hunkered down inside a bunker, certain it could survive the attack. It looked more like three centuries ago—no, four centuries ago now—when the Trisolar Crisis had first developed. Back then, at the offices of the PIA and the PDC, Cheng Xin had seen this kind of atmosphere and expression everywhere: despair against some superpowerful force in the universe, a kind of numbness and indifference that said *We give up.*

Most of the people in the control center were quiet, but a few whispered to each other with somber faces. Cheng Xin saw a man sitting numbly. A cup had fallen over on the table in front of him, and a blue liquid spilled off the table onto his pants, but he ignored it. On the other side, in front of a large information window that seemed to show some complicated, evolving situation, a man in military uniform embraced a woman dressed as a civilian. The woman's face seemed wet. . . .

"Why aren't we entering Jupiter's shadow?" AA pointed at the combined city outside the porthole.

"There's no point. The bunker is useless," Cao Bin said, lowering his eyes.

"How far is the photoid from the Sun?" Cheng Xin asked.

"There's no photoid."

"Then what have you found?"

Cao Bin gave a wretched laugh. "A slip of paper."

Bunker Era, Year 66
Outside the Solar System

A year before Cheng Xin's awakening, the advance warning system discovered an unknown flying object sweeping past the edge of the Oort Cloud at a speed close to lightspeed. At its closest approach, the object was only 1.3 light-years from the Sun. The object's volume was immense, and at its near-lightspeed velocity, the radiation generated by its impact with the scattered dust and atoms in space was intense. The advance warning system also observed the object making a small course change during flight to avoid a patch of interstellar dust, before resuming its previous course. It was most certainly an intelligent spaceship.

This was the first time that Solar System humans—as opposed to Galactic humans—had observed another extraterrestrial civilization besides the Trisolarans.

Due to lessons learned from the previous three false alarms, the Federation Government did not publicize this discovery. No more than a thousand people in the entire Bunker World knew about it. During the few days when the spaceship had been closest to the Solar System, these individuals lived in extreme anxiety and terror. In the few tens of space observation units comprising the advance warning system, in the advance warning center (a space city in the Jupiter cluster), in the battle center of Federation Fleet Command, and in the office of the president of the Solar System Federation, people held their breaths and watched the spaceship's course like a trembling school of fish hiding at the bottom of a pond, waiting for the trawler to pass overhead. These individuals' terror developed to absurd levels later: They refused to use radio communications, walked noiselessly, and spoke only in whispers. . . . In reality, everyone understood that these gestures were meaningless, not the least because what the advance warning system observed had happened a year and four months ago. By now, the spaceship was already gone.

After the extraterrestrial spaceship moved farther away, these individuals did not relax. The advance warning system discovered something else that was worrisome. The strange spaceship did not shoot a photoid at the Sun, but did launch something else. This object was also shot at the Sun at lightspeed, but it produced none of the emissions associated with photoids and was completely invisible electromagnetically. The advance warning system only managed to discover it through gravitational waves. The object continuously emitted weak gravitational waves whose strength and frequency remained constant. The waves clearly carried no message, and were probably the result of some physical characteristic of the projectile. When the advance warning system initially discovered these gravitational waves, the source was thought to be the extra-terrestrial spaceship. But they soon found that the source was separate from the spaceship, and it was approaching the Solar System at lightspeed.

Further analysis of the observation data revealed that the projectile wasn't aimed precisely at the Sun. According to its current trajectory, it would sweep past the Sun outside the orbit of Mars. If the intended target had been the Sun, this was a relatively gross error. This showed another way that the projectile was different from a photoid: The data gathered from the previous two photoid strikes all showed that after a photoid was launched, it followed a precise, straight trajectory to the target star (taking into account the motion of the star) and did not require any course correction. It could be surmised that a photoid was essentially a rock flying under inertia at lightspeed. Tracking the gravitational wave source showed that the projectile did not make any course corrections, apparently indicating that its target was not the Sun. This provided some comfort for everyone involved.

When the projectile was about 150 AU from the Sun, the gravitational waves it emitted began to rapidly decrease in frequency. The advance warning system discovered that this was due to its deceleration. Within a few days, the projectile's velocity went from lightspeed to one-thousandth of lightspeed, and continued to decrease. Such low speed meant that it wasn't enough to threaten the Sun, which provided further comfort. In addition, at this speed, human spacecraft could keep up with it. In other words, it was possible to send out ships to intercept it.

Revelation and *Alaska* departed the Neptune city cluster and flew in formation to investigate the unknown projectile.

Both ships were equipped with gravitational wave reception systems and could form a positioning network to determine the location of the transmission source with precision at close range. Since the Broadcast Era, more ships had been built that could transmit and receive gravitational waves. But the design concepts used in these ships were very different from earlier antenna ships. One of the main innovations was separating the gravitational wave antenna from the ship itself so that they formed two independent units. The antenna could then be combined with different ships, and could be replaced after it failed due to decay. *Revelation* and *Alaska* were only medium-sized ships, but they had about the same total volumes as large ships because the gravitational wave antennas made up a large portion of their structures. The two ships resembled helium-filled airships of the Common Era: They looked immense, but the effective payload was just the small gondola hanging below the gasbags.

Ten days after the two ships left port, General Vasilenko and 白 Ice,[8] dressed in lightweight space suits and magnetic shoes, took a stroll on the gravitational wave antenna of *Revelation*. They enjoyed doing this because there was much more space out here compared to the interior of the spaceship, and walking around the antenna made one feel like walking on solid earth. They were the leaders of the first exploratory team: Vasilenko was the commander while 白 Ice was in charge of technical matters.

Alexei Vasilenko had been an observer in the advance warning system during the Broadcast Era. Together with Widnall, he had discovered the trails of the Trisolaran lightspeed ships, which led to the first false alarm. After the incident, Sublieutenant Vasilenko was made one of the scapegoats and was dishonorably discharged. But he thought the punishment unjust and hoped that history would ultimately clear his name, and thus entered hibernation. As time passed, the discovery of the lightspeed trails grew in importance, and the damage from the first false alarm was gradually forgotten. Vasilenko awakened in Year 9 of the Bunker Era, was restored to his former rank, and by now had been promoted to vice admiral of the Solar Federation Space Force. However, he was close to eighty years of age. As he looked at 白 Ice strolling next to him, he

---

[8] *Translator's Note:* The surname "白" is pronounced "Bai."

thought how unfair life was: This man had been born eighty years before himself and came from the Crisis Era; yet, after hibernation, he was just over forty.

白 Ice's original name was Bai Aisi.[9] After awakening, he wanted to appear more integrated and not so behind the times, and chose a more common modern name that mixed English and Chinese elements. He had been a doctoral student under Ding Yi and had gone into hibernation near the end of the Crisis Era, awakening only twenty-two years ago. Usually, such a long leap across the years meant the hibernator would have trouble catching up to the new age, but theoretical physics was a special case. The sophon lock meant that Common Era physicists could still be considered professionally relevant during the Deterrence Era, and the creation of the circumsolar particle accelerator upended all the assumptions of fundamental theoretical physics, as though a deck of cards had been reshuffled.

Back during the Common Era, superstring theory had been thought of as advanced theory, the physics of the twenty-second century. The creation of the circumsolar particle accelerator allowed superstring theory to be confirmed via experiments. The result, however, was disastrous. Concepts that had to be rejected far outnumbered predictions that were confirmed. Many results that the Trisolarans had passed on were falsified. Based on the high level of technology the Trisolarans were later able to achieve, it was inconceivable that they had made such mistakes in fundamental theory. The only conclusion was that they had lied to humans even in the areas of basic theory.

白 Ice had proposed some theoretical models that were among the few confirmed by the circumsolar particle accelerator. By the time he awakened, physics had essentially been called back to the starting line. He quickly distinguished himself and won great honors, and after ten or so years, he was once again at the vanguard of the field.

"Look familiar?" Vasilenko gestured at everything around them.

"Indeed. But the self-confidence and arrogance of humanity are all gone," said 白 Ice.

This resonated with Vasilenko. He looked back along the ship's course. Neptune was only a tiny blue dot and the Sun a faint spot of light, incapable of even casting their shadows against the antenna surface. Where were the two thousand stellar-class warships that had formed a magnificent phalanx all those years ago? Now, there were just these two lonely ships with a complement of

---

[9] *Translator's Note:* This is the pinyin romanization of the original fully Chinese name: "白艾思."

no more than a hundred crew. *Alaska* was about a hundred thousand kilometers away but not visible to them. That ship wasn't only acting as the other end of the positioning network, but also held another exploratory team organized the same as the team aboard *Revelation*. Fleet Command called the team aboard *Alaska* the backup, indicating that the brass had made ample preparations for the risk and danger inherent in this expedition. Here, at the cold, desolate frontier of the Solar System, the antenna under their feet seemed a lonesome island in the universe. Vasilenko wanted to sigh, but thought better of it. He took something out of the pocket of his spacesuit and let it float between the two of them, spinning slowly.

"Check this out."

The object appeared to be a bone from some animal. In fact, it was a metallic machine component; the frigid light of the stars glinted against its smooth surface.

Vasilenko pointed at the spinning object. "About a hundred hours ago, we detected a patch of floating metallic debris next to the ship's course. A drone retrieved a few items, and this is one of them: a piece of the cooling system for a nuclear fusion reactor aboard a stellar-class warship from the end of the Crisis Era."

"It's from the Doomsday Battle?" asked an awed 白 Ice.

"Yes. We also found the armrest from a chair and a bulkhead fragment."

They had been passing through the vicinity of the ancient battlefield from nearly two centuries earlier. After the Bunker Project started, people often discovered remnants of ancient warships. Some were placed in museums while others were bought and sold through the black market. 白 Ice held the component and felt a chill pass through the glove of the space suit, straight into his marrow. He let it go, and the component continued to spin slowly, as though moved by some soul embedded within. 白 Ice moved his eyes away and gazed into the distance. All he could see was a bottomless, empty abyss. Two thousand warships and millions of dead bodies had been drifting in this patch of desolate space for nearly two centuries. The sacrificial blood of the dead had long ago sublimated from ice to gas and dissipated.

"The target of our exploration might be more dangerous than even the droplets this time," 白 Ice said.

"True. Back then, we already had some familiarity with the Trisolarans. But we know nothing about the world that created and sent this. . . . Dr. Bai, do you have any guesses as to what we will encounter?"

"Only a massive object can emit gravitational waves, so I guess that object must be large both in mass and volume, perhaps even a spaceship. . . . Well, in this business, the unexpected is to be expected."

The two ships of the expedition continued on their course for another week until the distance between them and the gravitational wave source was only about a million kilometers. The expedition decelerated until their velocity was zero, and began to accelerate toward the Sun. This way, by the time the projectile caught up to the expedition, they would fly in parallel. Most of the close-range exploration would be conducted by *Revelation*; *Alaska* would observe from a distance of about a hundred thousand kilometers.

The distance continued to shrink; the projectile was now only about ten thousand kilometers from *Revelation*. The gravitational wave emissions were very clear and could be used for precise positioning. But even from this distance, radar returned no echo and nothing could be seen in the visible light range. By the time the distance shrank to one thousand kilometers, they still couldn't see anything at the location of the gravitational wave source.

The crew of *Revelation* was close to panicking. Before departure, they had imagined all kinds of scenarios, but the idea of not being able to see their target when they were practically on top of it had never occurred to them. Vasilenko radioed the base at Neptune for instructions, and forty minutes later, received the order to approach the target until they were only 150 kilometers away.

Finally, the visible light detection systems noticed something: a small white dot at the gravitational wave source, visible even with a common telescope from the ship. *Revelation* sent out a drone to investigate. The drone flew at the target, the distance between them shrinking rapidly: five hundred kilometers, fifty kilometers, five hundred meters . . . Finally, the drone stopped five meters from the target. The clear holographic video it transmitted allowed the crew of both ships to see this extraterrestrial object that had been shot at the Sun.

A slip of paper.

There was really no better description. Formally, the object was called a rectangular membrane-like object: length: 8.5 cm; width: 5.2 cm; slightly bigger than a credit card. It was so thin that its thickness could not be measured. The surface was pure white, looking exactly like a slip of paper.

The members of the exploratory team were among the best officers and professionals in the world, and all had cool, rational minds. But instinct was more powerful. They had been prepared for giant, invasive objects. Some had guessed they would find a spaceship the size of Europa—a not unlikely possibility, given the strength of its gravitational wave emissions.

Faced with this paper slip—that was what they all called it—everyone heaved a sigh of relief. Rationally, they were still guarded. The object could certainly be a weapon that possessed enough power to destroy both spaceships. But it was impossible to believe that it could threaten the entire Solar System. By appearance, it was delicate, harmless, like a white feather floating in night air. People had long ceased to write letters on paper, but they were familiar with the concept from period films about the ancient world, and so the paper slip seemed almost romantic in their eyes.

Further investigation showed that the paper slip did not reflect electromagnetic radiation at any wavelength. The slip's white color wasn't reflected light, but light emitted by the object itself. All electromagnetic radiation, including visible light, simply passed through the slip, which was thus completely transparent. Images taken at close range showed the stars behind the slip, but due to interference from the white light it emitted and the dark background of space, it appeared as an opaque white from a distance. At least superficially, the object seemed harmless.

Maybe it really was a letter?

Since the drone had no appropriate collection tools, another drone with a mechanical arm and a sealable scoop had to be dispatched to capture the slip. As the open scoop extended toward the slip at the end of the mechanical arm, the hearts of everyone on the two ships hung in their throats.

This was another scene that seemed familiar.

The scoop closed around the slip and the arm pulled back.

But the slip remained where it was.

The attempt was repeated several more times with the same result. The drone operators aboard *Revelation* tried to maneuver the mechanical arm to touch the slip. The arm passed right through the slip, and neither appeared damaged. The arm felt no resistance, and the slip didn't change its position. Finally, the operator directed the drone to approach the paper slowly, in an attempt to push it. As the hull of the drone came into contact with the slip, the slip disappeared inside the drone, and as the drone continued to move forward, the slip emerged from the stern, unchanged. During the process when the slip was inside the drone, its internal systems detected no anomalies.

By now, the expedition members understood that the paper slip was no ordinary object. It was like an illusion that did not interact with anything in the physical world. It was also like a tiny cosmic reference plane that maintained its position, unmovable. No contact was capable of shifting its position—or, more accurately, its set trajectory.

白 Ice decided to go investigate in person. Vasilenko insisted on coming with him. Having both leaders of the first exploratory team go together was a controversial proposition, and they had to wait forty minutes to receive approval from the base at Neptune. Their request was reluctantly granted, as Vasilenko would not back down, and there was also a backup team.

The two headed for the paper slip in a pinnace. As *Revelation* and its immense gravitational wave antenna shrank in the distance, 白 Ice thought he was leaving the only support in the universe, and his heart became fearful.

"Your advisor, Dr. Ding, must have felt the same way years ago," Vasilenko said. He appeared perfectly calm.

白 Ice agreed with the sentiment in silence. He did feel spiritually connected to the Ding Yi of two centuries ago. Both of them headed for a great unknown, toward equally unknown fates.

"Don't worry. This time, we can trust our intuition." Vasilenko patted 白 Ice on the shoulder, but 白 Ice did not feel much comfort.

The pinnace was now next to the paper slip. After checking their space suits, they opened the pinnace's hatch so that they were exposed to space. They fine-tuned the pinnace's position until the paper slip hung half a meter above their heads. The tiny white plane was perfectly smooth, and through it they saw the stars behind, confirming that it really was a glowing, transparent object. The white light it emitted made the stars behind it appear a bit blurred.

They lifted themselves up in the pinnace until their eyes were lined up with the edge of the plane. Just like the camera had shown, the paper had no thickness. From the side, it completely disappeared. Vasilenko extended a hand toward the paper, but 白 Ice caught him.

"What are you doing?" 白 Ice asked severely. His eyes said the rest. *Think about what happened to my teacher.*

"If it really is a letter, perhaps the message won't be released until an intelligent body makes direct contact with it." Vasilenko brushed off 白 Ice's hand.

Vasilenko touched the paper with his gloved hand. His hand passed through the paper and was not damaged. Vasilenko received no mental message, either. He again moved his hand through the paper and stopped, allowing the small white plane to divide his hand into two parts. Still, he felt nothing. The paper showed an outline of the cross section of the hand where the hand penetrated it: clearly, the sheet hadn't been broken, but passed through the hand unharmed. Vasilenko pulled his hand back, and the slip hung still as before—or, more accurately, continued to move toward the Solar System at the rate of two hundred kilometers per second.

白 Ice also tried to touch the slip, then pulled his hand back. "It's like a projection from another universe that has nothing to do with ours."

Vasilenko had more practical concerns. "If nothing can affect it, then we have no way to bring it to the ship for further analysis."

白 Ice laughed. "That's a simple problem to solve. Have you forgotten the story told by Francis Bacon? 'If the mountain will not come to Muhammad, then Muhammad must go to the mountain.'"

And so, *Revelation* slowly sailed toward the paper slip, made contact, and then allowed it to enter the ship. Even more slowly, it adjusted its position until the slip hung in the middle of the laboratory cabin. The only way to move the slip during study was to move the ship itself. This odd way to manipulate the research subject posed some challenges near the beginning, but luckily, *Revelation* was originally designed to investigate small space objects in the Kuiper Belt and possessed excellent maneuverability. The gravitational wave antenna was equipped with twelve high-precision thrusters. After the ship's AI grew used to the necessary adjustments, the manipulation became quick and precise. If the world could not affect the slip in any way, the only solution was to let the world surround the slip and move about it.

Thus, an odd sight came to be: The slip was located in the center of *Revelation*, but the ship had no dynamical connection to the slip. The two simply happened to occupy the same space as both moved toward the Solar System at the same velocity.

Inside the spaceship, due to the stronger background light, the transparency of the slip became more obvious. It now no longer resembled a slip of paper, but some transparent film that only indicated its presence by the faint light it emitted. People continued to refer to it as a paper slip, however. When the ambient light was very strong, it was sometimes possible to lose sight of it, so the researchers had to dim the lights in the laboratory to see the slip better.

The first thing the researchers tried to do was to ascertain the slip's mass. The only applicable method was to measure the gravity it generated. However, even at the highest precision level, the gravity meter showed nothing, suggesting that the slip's mass was extremely small, perhaps even zero. Based on the latter possibility, some guessed that the object might be a photon or neutrino in macro form, but its geometric shape suggested that it was artificial.

No progress could be made on analysis of the slip because electromagnetic waves of all wavelengths passed through it without diffraction. Magnetic fields, no matter how strong, seemed to have no effect on it. The object appeared to have no internal structure.

Twenty hours later, the exploratory team still knew next to nothing about the slip. They were able to observe one thing, however: The intensity of the light and gravitational waves emitted by the slip was decreasing. This suggested that the light and gravitational waves it emitted were probably a form of evaporation. Since these two were the only indication of the existence of the slip, their disappearance would be the same as the disappearance of the slip itself.

The base informed the exploratory team that *Tomorrow*, a large science vessel, had left the Neptune city cluster and would meet the expedition in seven days' time. *Tomorrow* possessed more advanced investigative instruments, and could study the slip in more depth.

As they became more used to the slip, the crew on *Revelation* became less guarded and were no longer so careful about keeping a respectful distance from it. They knew that the object did not interact with the real world and emitted no harmful radiation. They touched it casually, allowing it to pass through their bodies. Someone even let the plane pass through his eyes and brain, asking a friend to take a picture of the sight.

白 Ice was enraged when he saw this. "Stop it! This is not some joke," he screamed. Having worked nonstop in the lab for more than twenty hours, he left the laboratory and returned to his own cabin.

白 Ice turned off the light in his cabin and tried to go to sleep. But in the darkness he felt uneasy; he imagined the paper slip would float into his cabin, glowing white, at any moment. So he turned on the light and drifted in the gentle light and memories.

One hundred and ninety-two years had passed since he said good-bye to his teacher for the last time.

It was dusk, and he and Ding Yi and he had come to the surface from the underground city and taken a car into the desert. Ding Yi liked to stroll and think in the desert, and even to hold his lectures there sometimes. His students hated the experience, but he explained his eccentric habit this way: "I like desolate places. Life is a distraction for physics."

The weather that day was good. There was no wind and no sandstorms, and the early spring air smelled fresh. The two of them, teacher and student, lay against a dune. The desert of Northern China was bathed in the light of the setting sun. Normally, Bai Aisi thought of these rolling dunes as a woman's body—possibly a comparison that had originated with Ding Yi himself—but now he thought of them as an exposed brain. In the golden dusk, the brain revealed its profusion of grooves and folds. He looked up at the sky. Today, the dusty air managed to let through a bit of long-missed blue, like a mind about to be enlightened.

Ding Yi said, "Aisi, I want to tell you a few things that you should not repeat to others. Even if I don't return, don't tell others. There's no special reason. I just don't want to be laughed at."

"Professor Ding, why not wait until you're back to tell me?"

Bai Aisi wasn't trying to comfort Ding Yi. He was sincere. He was still drunk with the ecstasy and vision of humanity's imminent great victory over the Trisolaran fleet, and he did not think Ding Yi's trip to the droplet would involve much danger.

"Answer a question first, please." Ding Yi ignored Bai Aisi's question and pointed at the desert lit by the westering sun. "Forget about the uncertainty principle for a minute and suppose everything is determinable. If you know the initial conditions, you can calculate and derive the conditions at any later point in time. Suppose an extraterrestrial scientist were given all data about the Earth several billion years ago. Do you think it could predict the existence of this desert solely through calculation?"

Bai Aisi pondered this. "No. This desert wasn't the result of the Earth's natural evolution, but the result of man-made forces. The behavior of civilizations can't be grasped through the laws of physics."

"Very good. Then why do we and our colleagues all want to try to explain the conditions of today's cosmos, and to predict its future, solely through deductions based on the laws of physics?"

Ding Yi's words surprised Bai Aisi. The man had never revealed such thoughts in the past.

Bai Aisi said, "I think that's beyond physics. The goal of physics is to discover the fundamental laws of nature. Although the man-made desertification of the Earth could not be calculated directly from physics, it still follows laws. Universal laws are constant."

"Heh heh heh heh." Ding Yi's laugh was not joyous at all. As he recalled it later, Bai Aisi thought it was the most sinister laughter he had ever heard. There was a hint of masochistic pleasure, an excitement at seeing everything falling into the abyss, an attempt to use joy as a cover for terror, until terror itself became an indulgence. "Your last sentence! I've often comforted myself this way. I've always forced myself to believe that there's at least one table at this banquet filled with dishes that remain fucking untouched. . . . I tell myself that again and again. And I'm going to say it one more time before I die."

Bai Aisi thought Ding Yi's mind was elsewhere and that he talked as if he were dreaming. He didn't know what to say.

Ding Yi continued, "At the beginning of the crisis, when the sophons were interfering with the particle accelerators, a few people committed suicide. At the time, I thought what they did made no sense. Theoreticians should be excited by such experimental data! But now I understand. Those people knew more than I did. Take Yang Dong, for instance. She knew much more than I did, and thought further. She probably knew things we don't even know now. Do you think only sophons create illusions? Do you think the only illusions exist in the particle accelerator terminals? Do you think the rest of the universe is as pure as a virgin, waiting for us to explore? Too bad that she left with everything she knew."

"If she had talked with you more back then, perhaps she wouldn't have chosen to go."

"Perhaps I would have gone with her."

Ding Yi dug a pit in the sand and watched as the sand on the rim flowed back in like a waterfall. "If I don't come back, everything in my room is yours. I know that you've always liked those Common Era things I brought."

"That's true, especially those tobacco pipes. . . . But I don't think I'll get them."

"I hope you're right. I also have some money—"

"Please, Professor!"

"I want you to use it to pay for hibernation. The longer the better—of course, that's assuming you want to. I have two goals in mind: One, I want you to go look at the endgame for me—the endgame for physics. Two . . . how do I say this? I don't want you to waste your life. After others have decided that physics actually exists, there will still be plenty of time for you to go do physics."

"That . . . seems like something Yang Dong would say."

"Maybe it's not nonsense."

Bai Aisi noticed that the pit Ding Yi had dug in the desert was rapidly expanding. They stood up and backed away as the pit continued to grow, getting deeper as well as wider. Soon, the bottom disappeared in shadows. Sand flooded into the pit in torrents, and soon, the diameter of the pit was close to a hundred meters, and a nearby dune was swallowed up. Bai Aisi ran toward the car and got into the driver's seat; Ding Yi followed into the passenger seat. Bai

Aisi noticed that the car was moving slowly toward the pit, dragged along by the sand underneath. He turned on the engine and the wheels began to turn, but the car continued to slide backwards.

Ding Yi laughed that sinister laugh again. "Heh heh heh heh . . ."

Bai Aisi turned the electric motor to the highest setting and the wheels spun madly, throwing up sand everywhere. But the car still moved toward the pit like a plate pulled along on a tablecloth.

"Niagara Falls! Heh heh heh heh . . ."

Bai Aisi looked back and saw a sight that made his blood curdle: The pit now took up his entire field of vision. The whole desert was swallowed up by it, and the world was like a giant pit whose bottom was an abyss. At the rim, flowing sand poured in and formed a spectacular yellow sandfall. Ding Yi wasn't exactly right in his description: The Niagara Falls were minuscule compared to this sandfall of terror. The sandfall extended from the near edge of the pit all the way to the far edge on the horizon, forming an immense sandfall ring. The sand torrents rumbled as if the world itself were coming apart. The car continued to slide toward the pit, faster and faster. Bai Aisi floored the accelerator and leaned his weight into it, but there was no effect.

"You fool. Do you really think we can escape?" Ding Yi said while still laughing sinisterly. "Escape velocity! Why don't you calculate the escape velocity? Are you thinking with your butt? Heh heh heh heh . . ."

The car tumbled over the rim and dropped in the sandfall. The sand raining down around them seemed to stop as everything plunged into the abyss. Bai Aisi screamed with utter terror, but he couldn't hear himself. All he heard was Ding Yi's wild laughter.

"Hahahahaha . . . There's no table untouched at the dinner party, and there's no virgin untouched in the universe . . . waheeheeheehee . . . wahahahaha . . ."

白 Ice woke from his nightmare and found himself covered in cold sweat. Around him, more droplets of sweat hung suspended in air. He floated for a while, his body stiff, and then dashed out of his cabin and headed for Vasilenko's cabin. It took a while before the door opened, as Vasilenko was also sleeping.

"General! Do not keep that thing, that thing they call a slip of paper, in the spaceship! No, I mean, don't allow *Revelation* to hover around it. We should leave immediately, and get as far away as possible!"

"What have you discovered?"

"Nothing. It's my intuition."

"You don't look so good. Exhaustion? I think you're worrying too much. That thing . . . I don't think it's anything. There's nothing inside. It should be harmless."

白 Ice grabbed Vasilenko by the shoulders and gazed into his eyes. "Don't be arrogant!"

"What?"

"Don't be arrogant. Weakness and ignorance are not barriers to survival, but arrogance is. Remember the droplet!"

白 Ice's last sentence had an effect. Vasilenko stared at him in silence for a few seconds, then nodded slowly. "All right, Dr. Bai, I'll listen to you. *Revelation* will depart from the slip and back off one thousand kilometers. We'll leave just a pinnace to monitor it. . . . Maybe two thousand kilometers?"

白 Ice let Vasilenko go and wiped his forehead. "You decide. I suggest, the farther the better. I will write a formal report as soon as possible and let Command know of my theories." Stumbling, he drifted away.

Revelation left the slip. It passed through the ship's hull and was reexposed to space. Since the background was dark again, it once again appeared to be an opaque white slip of paper. *Revelation* pulled away from the slip until the two were about two thousand kilometers apart, then continued to sail in parallel, waiting for the arrival of *Tomorrow*. A pinnace with a crew of two stayed about ten meters from the slip to monitor it continuously.

The gravitational waves emitted by the paper slip continued to diminish, and its light gradually dimmed.

On *Revelation*, 白 Ice shut himself in the laboratory. Around him, he set up more than a dozen information windows, all connected to the ship's quantum computer, which was carrying out massive computations. The windows were packed with equations, curves, and matrices. Surrounded by the windows, 白 Ice was anxious and irritable, like a trapped animal.

Fifty hours after the separation from *Revelation*, the gravitational wave emitted from the paper slip disappeared completely. The white light from it blinked twice and also went out. The slip of paper was gone.

"Has it evaporated?" Vasilenko asked.

"I don't think so. But we can't see it anymore." 白 Ice shook his head wearily and closed the information windows around him one by one.

After another hour during which no signs of the slip could be detected, Vasilenko ordered the pinnace to return to *Revelation*. But the two crew members on duty in the pinnace didn't acknowledge the order; the radio only transmitted a hurried conversation between them.

"Look out below! What's going on?"

"It's rising!"

"Don't touch it! Get out!!"

"My leg! Ahhh—"

After the scream, the monitoring terminal on *Revelation* showed one of the crew members leaving the pinnace and activating the thrusters on his space suit in an attempt to escape. They saw a bright light; the source was the bottom of the pinnace, which was melting! The pinnace looked like a scoop of ice cream dropped onto a scalding sheet of glass: The bottom was melting and spreading in every direction. The "glass" was invisible, and the plane's existence was indicated only by the spreading pool of melted pinnace material. The pool spread into an extremely thin sheet and emitted bewitching, colorful lights, like fireworks scattered through a sheet of glass.

The escaped crewman flew some distance but seemed to be pulled by gravity toward that plane marked by the melted pinnace. His feet touched the plane and immediately melted into a shiny puddle. The rest of his body also began to spread out on the plane, and he had time only for a scream that was abruptly cut off.

"All hands to hypergravitation seats! Full Ahead!"

As soon as he saw the escaping crewman's feet touch the invisible plane, Vasilenko gave the order. *Revelation* wasn't a stellar ship, so when it engaged in Full Ahead acceleration, the crew did not need to enter into the protective deep-sea state. But the hypergravity was enough to sink everyone deep into their seats. Since the order was given in such a hurry, a few couldn't get to their seats in time and fell to the stern of the ship with injuries. *Revelation*'s exhaust nozzles emitted a plasma stream several kilometers long that pierced the dark night of space. Far in the distance, where the pinnace was still melting, they could see the phosphorescent glow like will-o'-the-wisps in the wilderness.

From the zoomed-in view on the monitoring terminal, they could see that only the very top part of the pinnace was left, and that too soon disappeared into the brilliant plane. The body of the dead crewman was also diffused into the plane, showing up as a gigantic, man-shaped glow. His body had been transformed into a slice on the plane without thickness. Though large in area, it had no volume.

"We're not moving," the pilot of *Revelation* said. He had trouble talking through the hypergravity. "The ship isn't accelerating."

"What are you babbling about?" Vasilenko wanted to shout, but the hypergravity turned it into a whisper.

It really did seem as if the pilot should have been wrong. Everyone on the ship was pressed against their seat by hypergravity, which indicated that the ship was in the process of extreme acceleration. It was visually impossible for a passenger to tell whether the ship was moving in space because all celestial bodies that could act as reference points were too far away, so they couldn't see parallax in a short time frame. However, the ship's navigation system could detect even tiny amounts of motion and acceleration; it couldn't be wrong.

Revelation was under hypergravity, but had no acceleration. Some force had nailed it to this point in space.

"There *is* acceleration," said 白 Ice weakly. "But the space in this region is flowing in the opposite direction, thus canceling out our motion."

"The space is flowing? Where to?"

"There, of course."

白 Ice couldn't lift his hand, which was now too heavy. But everyone knew where he meant. *Revelation* sank into a deathlike silence. Normally, hypergravity made people feel safe, as though they were escaping from danger under the embrace of some protective power. But now it seemed as oppressive and suffocating as a tomb.

"Open a channel to Command," 白 Ice said. "There's no time, so we'll treat this as our formal report."

"Channel open."

"General, you once said, 'I don't think it's anything. There's nothing inside.' You were right. That slip really wasn't anything, and contained nothing. It's only space, just like the space around us, which isn't anything and contains nothing. But there's a difference: It's two-dimensional. It's not a block, but a slice. A slice without thickness."

"Hadn't it evaporated?"

"The protective field around it evaporated. The force field acted like packaging that separated the two-dimensional space from the three-dimensional space. But now the two are in direct contact. Do you remember what *Blue Space* and *Gravity* saw?"

No one answered, but they all remembered: the four-dimensional space falling into three dimensions, like a waterfall off a cliff.

"Just as four-dimensional space collapses into three dimensions, three-dimensional space can collapse into two dimensions, with one dimension folding and curling into the quantum realm. The area of that slice of two-dimensional space—it only has area—will rapidly expand, causing more space to collapse. . . . We're now in space that is falling toward two dimensions, and ultimately, the entire Solar System will follow. In other words, the Solar System will turn into a painting with no thickness."

"Can we escape it?"

"Escaping this is like rowing a boat above a waterfall. Unless we exceed a certain escape velocity, we'll tumble over the cliff. It's like tossing a pebble up from the ground: No matter how high you throw the rock, it will eventually fall back down. The entire Solar System is within the zone of collapse, and anyone trying to escape must reach escape velocity."

"What is the escape velocity?"

"I've computed it four separate times. Pretty sure I got it right."

"What is it?!"

Everyone aboard *Revelation* and *Alaska* held their breaths and listened to this final calculation as representatives of humanity.

白 Ice calmly announced his judgment. "Lightspeed."

The navigation system showed that *Revelation* was now moving in the opposite direction from its heading. It started by moving slowly toward the two-dimensional space, but gradually accelerated. The ship's drive was still powering Full Ahead. This would at least slow down the rate of the ship's fall and delay the inevitable.

On the plane two thousand kilometers away, the light emitted by the two-dimensionalized pinnace and crewmen had already gone out. Compared to collapsing from four dimensions to three, the fall from three dimensions to two gave off much less energy. Two two-dimensional structures were revealed clearly by the starlight. On the two-dimensionalized pinnace, it was possible to see the details of three-dimensional structures unfolded in two dimensions—the crew cabin, the fusion reactor, and so on—as well as the curled-up figure of the crewman in the cabin. In the figure of the other crewman, the bones and blood vessels could be clearly discerned, as well as all the body parts. During the process of falling into two dimensions, every point on a three-dimensional object was projected onto the plane in accordance with precise geometric principles, and so these two figures turned out to be the most complete and precise images of the original three-dimensional pinnace and people. All the internal structures were now laid out side by side in two dimensions with nothing hidden. The projection process, however, was very different from that used in engineering drawings, and so it was difficult to visually reimagine the shapes' original three-dimensional structure. The greatest difference from engineering drawings lay in the fact that the two-dimensional unfolding occurred at every scale: All the original three-dimensional structures and details were laid out in parallel in two dimensions, and the result replicated, in some measure, the effect of viewing the three-dimensional world from four-dimensional space. This closely resembled drawings of fractals: No matter how much you zoomed in on a part of the image, it would get no less complex. However, fractals were theoretical concepts—actual representations were inevitably limited by the resolution, and after zooming in a number of times, the images lost their fractal nature. The complexity of the two-dimensionalized three-dimensional objects, on the other hand, was real: The resolution was at the level of fundamental particles. On the monitoring terminal of *Revelation*, the eye could only see a limited resolution, but the complexity and number of details already made the viewers dizzy. This was the universe's most complicated image; staring at it for too long would drive one mad.

Of course, the pinnace and the crewmen no longer possessed any thickness.

It was unclear how large the plane had spread by now; only those two images indicated its presence.

Revelation slid faster toward the plane, toward that abyss whose thickness was zero.

"Everyone, don't be sad. No one will be able to escape from the Solar System, not even a bacteria or virus. All of us will become a part of this grand picture." 白 Ice now looked calm and stoic.

"Stop accelerating," said Vasilenko. "What difference does a few minutes make? Let's at least breathe easier at the end."

Revelation's engine shut off. The plasma column at the stern of the ship disappeared, and the ship drifted, powerless, in space. In reality, the ship was still accelerating toward the two-dimensional patch of space, but since the ship moved along with the surrounding space, those inside could not feel any gravity from acceleration. They enjoyed the weightlessness and took deep breaths.

"You know what I'm thinking of? Needle-Eye's pictures from Yun Tianming's fairy tales," 白 Ice said.

Only a few people aboard *Revelation* knew about Yun Tianming's secret message. Now, in a flash, they all understood the meaning of this detail in the stories. It was a simple metaphor, and there were no bearing coordinates because it was so direct. Yun must have thought he was taking a great risk to put such an obvious metaphor into his stories, yet he had to try because the message was so important.

He probably thought that with the knowledge of *Blue Space* and *Gravity*'s discoveries, humanity would understand the metaphor. Unfortunately, he had overestimated their ability to comprehend.

The inability to decipher this key piece of information led humanity to place all their hopes in the Bunker Project.

It was true that both dark forest strikes humans had witnessed involved photoids, but they ignored a salient fact: Those two target planetary systems were structured differently from the Solar System. The star known as 187J3X1 had three giant Jupiter-like planets, but they all orbited extremely close to their sun. Their average distance from the sun was but 3 percent of the distance from Jupiter to the Sun, even closer than Mercury's orbit. Since they almost brushed up against their sun, the solar explosion destroyed them completely, and they could not have been used as barriers. The Trisolaran system, on the other hand, had only one planet, Trisolaris.

The structure of the planetary system around a star was a characteristic observable from a distance. For a sufficiently advanced civilization, a quick glance was sufficient.

If humans could figure out the plan to use the gas giants as barriers, couldn't observers from such advanced civilizations do so, as well?

Weakness and ignorance are not barriers to survival, but arrogance is.

Revelation was now no more than a thousand kilometers from the plane; it fell faster and faster.

"Thank you, everyone, for doing your duty. Although we haven't been together long, we worked together well," Vasilenko said.

"I also thank every member of the human race," said 白 Ice. "Once, we lived together in the Solar System."

Revelation fell into the two-dimensional space. In a few seconds, it was flattened. Light akin to fireworks once again lit up the darkness of space. This was a vast two-dimensional image that could be clearly seen from *Alaska,* a hundred thousand kilometers away. It was possible to distinguish every individual on *Revelation*: They were laid out side by side, holding hands, every single cell in their body exposed to space in two dimensions.

They were the first to be painted into this grand painting of annihilation.

Bunker Era, Year 68
Pluto

———

"Let's head back to the Earth," Cheng Xin said softly. This was the first idea that floated up through the chaos and darkness of her jumbled thoughts.

"The Earth is not a bad place to wait for the end. A falling leaf seeks to return to the root. But we hope *Halo* will go to Pluto," Cao Bin said.

"Pluto?"

"Pluto is at its apogee, rather far from the two-dimensional space. The Federation Government is about to issue a formal attack alert to the world, and many ships will be headed there. Although the final result will be the same, at least there will be more time left."

"How much longer?"

"The entire Solar System within the Kuiper Belt will collapse into two dimensions in eight to ten days."

"That's not long enough to be worth worrying about. Let's go back to Earth," said AA.

"The Federation Government would like to ask you to do something."

"What can we possibly do now?"

"Not anything important. There's nothing important now. But someone came up with the idea that theoretically, there might exist image-processing software that could process a two-dimensionalized image of a three-dimensional object and re-create the three-dimensional object. We hope that in the distant future, some intelligent civilization might re-create a three-dimensional representation of our world from its two-dimensionalized image. Though it would be nothing more than a dead representation, at least human civilization would not be forgotten.

"The Earth Civilization Museum is on Pluto. A large portion of humanity's precious artifacts are stored there. The museum is buried under the surface, however, and we are concerned that during the process of falling into the plane, these artifacts would be mixed together with the strata of the crust and their structures would be damaged. We'd like to ask you to carry some of the artifacts away from Pluto on *Halo* and scatter them in space so that they can fall into two dimensions separately. This way, their structures would be preserved without harm in two dimensions. I guess this counts as a kind of rescue mission. . . . Of course, I admit that the idea is nearly science fiction, but doing something now is better than doing nothing.

"Also, Luo Ji is on Pluto. He wants to see you."

"Luo Ji? He's alive?!" AA cried out.

"Yes. He's almost two hundred."

"All right. Let's go to Pluto," Cheng Xin said. In the past, this would have been an extraordinary journey. But now, nothing mattered.

A pleasant male voice spoke up. "Do you wish to go to Pluto?"

"Who are you?" asked AA.

"I'm *Halo,* or *Halo*'s AI. Do you wish to go to Pluto?"

"Yes. What do we do?"

"You just have to confirm the request. There's no need to do anything. I will complete the voyage for you."

"Yes, we want to go to Pluto."

"Authorization confirmed. Processing. *Halo* will accelerate at 1G in three minutes. Please pay attention to the direction of gravity."

Cao Bin said, "Good. Better leave early. After the attack alert is issued, there might be total mayhem. Hopefully we'll get a chance to talk again." He closed the window link before AA and Cheng Xin could say good-bye. At this moment, AA, Cheng Xin, and *Halo* were not his top priorities.

Outside the porthole, they could see a few blue reflections appearing on the shell of the combined city—reflections of *Halo*'s nozzle lights. Cheng Xin and AA fell to one side of the spherical hall and felt their bodies grow heavier. The acceleration soon reached 1G. After the two of them—still weak from hibernation—struggled up and looked outside the porthole again, they saw the entirety of Jupiter. It was still immense, and shrinking at too slow a rate to be perceived.

The ship's AI led AA and Cheng Xin on a tour of the ship to familiarize them with it. Like its predecessor, this new *Halo* was still a small stellar yacht with a maximum capacity of four. Most of the space on the ship was taken up by the ecological cycling system. By conventional measures, the ecological cycling system was extremely redundant—a volume of space that would have supported forty was used to provide for only four. The system was divided into four identical subsystems, linked together and acting as each other's backups. If any of the four failed accidentally, the other three could bring it back to life. *Halo*'s other distinguishing characteristic was the ability to land directly on a medium-sized solid planet. This was a rare design choice among stellar ships— similar ships typically used shuttles to carry landing parties onto planets. Directly descending into a planet's deep gravity well required the ship to have a very strong hull, which greatly increased the cost. Moreover, the need for atmospheric flight required a streamlined profile, which was also very rare among stellar ships. All of these design features meant that if *Halo* could find another Earthlike planet in outer space, it could act as a habitable base for the crew on the surface of the planet for a considerable amount of time. Maybe it was these characteristics of *Halo* that led to it being chosen for the artifact-rescuing mission to Pluto.

There were numerous other unusual features on the yacht. For instance, it had six small courtyards, each about twenty to thirty square meters in size. Each courtyard automatically adjusted to the direction of gravity under acceleration, and, during coasting, spun independently within the ship to generate artificial gravity. Each courtyard displayed a different natural scene: a green lawn with a babbling brook running through the grass; a small copse with a spring in the middle; a beach with waves of clear water throwing up surf. . . . These scenes were small but exquisite, like a string of pearls made of the best parts of the Earth. On a small stellar spaceship, such a design was extremely luxurious.

Cheng Xin felt both distressed and sorry for *Halo*. Such a perfect little world was soon going to be turned into a slice without thickness. She tried to avoid thinking about those other grander things facing imminent destruction— annihilation covered the sky of her thoughts like a giant pair of black wings, and she dared not look directly up at it.

Two hours after departure, *Halo* received the formal dark forest attack alert issued by the Solar System Federation Government. The president, a beautiful woman who looked very young, made the announcement. She stood in front of the blue flag of the Federation and spoke without expression. Cheng Xin noticed that the blue flag resembled the ancient UN flag, though a diagram of the Sun replaced the diagram of the Earth. This most important document, marking the end of human history, was very short:

Five hours ago, the advance warning system confirmed that a dark forest strike has been initiated against our world.

The attack takes the form of a dimensional strike, which will collapse the space around the Solar System from three dimensions to two dimensions. The result will be the complete destruction of all life.

The process is estimated to take eight to ten days. At this moment, the collapse is ongoing and the rate and extent of collapse are rapidly growing.

We have confirmed that the escape velocity for the collapsing region is the speed of light.

An hour ago, the Federation Government and Parliament have passed a new resolution that repeals all laws regarding Escapism. However, the government wishes to remind all citizens that the escape velocity far exceeds the maximum velocity of all human space vehicles. The probability of a successful escape is zero.

The Federation Government, Parliament, the Supreme Court, and Federation Fleet will carry out their duties until the end.

AA and Cheng Xin didn't bother to watch more news. It was possible that, just like Cao Bin said, the Bunker World had approached paradise. They wanted to see what paradise looked like, but they didn't dare look. If everything was heading toward ruination, the more beautiful it all was, the more pain they would suffer. In any event, it was a paradise that was collapsing in the terror of death.

Halo stopped accelerating. Behind it, Jupiter became a small yellow dot. The next few days of the voyage were spent in the uninterrupted slumber produced by the sleep-aid machine. In this lonely voyage through the night before the end, just the unstoppable mad imaginings were enough to make anyone fall apart.

Halo's AI awakened AA and Cheng Xin from their dreamless sleep as the ship reached Pluto.

Out of the porthole and on the monitor they could see the entirety of Pluto. Their initial impression of the dwarf planet was one of darkness, like an eye that remained perpetually shut. This far from the Sun, the light was extremely dim. Only when *Halo* entered low orbit could they see the colors on the surface of the planet: Pluto's crust appeared to be made of patches of blue and black. The black was rocks—not necessarily black in color, but the light was too dim to tell otherwise. The blue was solidified nitrogen and methane. Two centuries ago, when Pluto had been near its perigee and inside Neptune's orbit, the surface would have looked completely different. The ice cover would have partially melted and produced a thin atmosphere. From the distance, it would have appeared a deep yellow.

Halo continued to descend. On Earth, this would have involved a soul-stirring atmospheric reentry, but *Halo* continued to fly through the silent vacuum, decelerating by the power of its own thrusters. On the blue-black ground below, an attention-grabbing line of white text appeared:

EARTH CIVILIZATION

The text was written in the modern script that mixed Latin and Chinese elements. After it, there were a few more lines of smaller text repeating the same thing in different scripts. Cheng Xin noticed that none of them said "museum." The yacht was still about one hundred kilometers above the surface, which meant that the text was gigantic. Cheng Xin couldn't make an exact estimate of the size of the characters, but she was certain that these were the largest written characters ever produced by humankind, each big enough to contain a city. By the time *Halo* was only about ten thousand meters above the surface, one of the large characters took up the entire field of view. Finally, *Halo* touched down on the broad landing field, which was the topmost dot in the Chinese character *qiu* (球), a part of the word *Earth*.

With the guidance of the ship's AI, Cheng Xin and AA put on light space suits and exited *Halo* onto the surface of Pluto. Given the frigid surroundings, the heating systems in their space suits were operating at maximum power. The landing field was empty, white, and seemed to phosphoresce in the starlight. The numerous burn marks left on the ground indicated that many spacecraft had once landed and taken off here, but *Halo* was the only ship here now.

During the Bunker Era, Pluto was akin to Antarctica on ancient Earth. No one lived here permanently, and few came to visit.

In the sky, a black sphere moved rapidly among the stars. It was large, but the surface was shrouded in darkness: Charon, Pluto's moon. Its mass was a tenth of Pluto's, and the two almost formed a double-planet system, revolving around a common center of mass.

Halo turned on its searchlights. Due to the lack of atmosphere, there wasn't a visible beam of light. It cast a circle of light on a distant rectangular object. This black monolith was the only protrusion above the white ground. It gave off an eerie sense of simplicity, as though it was an abstraction of the real world.

"That looks a bit familiar," Cheng Xin said.

"I don't know what it is, but I don't have a good feeling about it."

Cheng Xin and AA headed for the monolith. Pluto's gravity was only one-tenth of the Earth's, and so they proceeded by leaping. Along the way, they noticed a row of arrows pointing toward the monolith on the ground. Only when they reached the monolith did its immensity impress itself on their minds. When they looked up, it was as though a chunk had been taken out of the starry sky. They looked around and saw that there were rows of arrows coming from other directions, all pointing toward the monolith. At the foot of the monolith was another prominent protuberance: a metal wheel about a meter in diameter. To their surprise, they found the wheel to be hand-operated. Above the wheel was a diagram formed from white lines against the black surface of the monolith. Two curved arrows indicated the directions in which the wheel could be turned. Next to one of the arrows was a drawing of a half-open door, while the other bore a drawing of a shut door. Cheng Xin turned to survey the arrows on the ground pointing to the monolith. All the simple, clear, wordless instructions gave her a strange feeling, which AA voiced.

"These things . . . I don't think they're intended for humans."

They turned the wheel clockwise. The wheel was stiff, but eventually a door opened in the surface of the monolith. Some gas escaped, and the water vapor within quickly deposited into ice crystals that glinted in the searchlight. They entered the door and saw another door facing them, also operated by a wheel. This time, there were simple written instructions above the wheel, informing them that they were in an air lock and needed to close the first door before opening the second. This was unusual, since as early as the end of the Crisis Era, pressurized buildings could open their doors directly to vacuum without needing an air lock.

Cheng Xin and AA turned the wheel on the inside of the door they had entered to shut it. The searchlight was cut off. They were about to turn on the lights on their space suits to hold off the terror of darkness when they noticed a small lamp in the ceiling of the narrow air lock. This was the first sign they had seen of electricity. They began to turn the wheel to open the second door. Cheng Xin was certain that even if they hadn't closed the first door, they would still have been able to open the second. The only thing that prevented air from leaking was following the instructions. In this low-technology environment, there was no automatic mechanism to prevent errors.

The rush of air almost toppled them, and the rapidly warming temperature fogged their visors. But the space suits told them that the external air pressure and composition was breathable; they could open their helmets.

They saw a tunnel lit by a series of dim lamps heading into the earth. The dark walls of the tunnel swallowed up the dim light they emitted so that, between the cones of light, all was darkness. The floor of the tunnel was a smooth incline. Although the angle was steep, close to forty-five degrees, there were no stairs. This design was probably motivated by two considerations: There was no need for stairs in low gravity, or the path wasn't meant for humans.

"There's no elevator?" AA asked. She was frightened by the steep way down.

"An elevator might break down over time. This building was intended to last through geologic eons." The voice came from the other end of the tunnel, where an old man appeared. In the dim light, his long white hair and beard floated in the low gravity. They seemed to be giving off their own light.

"Are you Luo Ji?" AA shouted.

"Who else? Children, my legs don't work so well anymore, so forgive me for not coming up to meet you. Come on down by yourselves."

Cheng Xin and AA descended the incline in leaps. Due to the low gravity, this wasn't a very dangerous maneuver. As they approached the old man, they saw that he was indeed Luo Ji. He wore a long white *changshan*, a Chinese-style robe, and leaned against a cane. His back was slightly bowed, but his voice was hale and loud.

At the bottom of the incline, Cheng Xin bowed deeply. "Honored Elder, hello."

"Haha, there's no need for that." Luo Ji waved his hands. "We used to be . . . colleagues." He looked at Cheng Xin and in his eyes was a surprised delight that almost seemed incongruent with his age. "You're still so young. There was a time when I saw you only as the Swordholder, and then, gradually, you became a lovely young woman. Haha. . . ."

In Cheng Xin's and AA's eyes, Luo Ji had also changed. The stately Swordholder was gone. They didn't know that the cynical, playful Luo Ji in front of them now was a return to the Luo Ji from four centuries ago, before he had become a Wallfacer. That Luo Ji had returned, as if awakening from hibernation, but the passage of time had moderated him, and filled him with more transcendence.

"Do you know what has happened?" AA asked.

"Of course, child." He pointed behind him with his cane. "Those idiots all left on spaceships. They knew that they ultimately couldn't escape, but they still tried to run. Foolish."

He meant the other workers in the Earth Civilization Museum.

"You and I have both busied ourselves for nothing," said Luo Ji to Cheng Xin.

It took Cheng Xin a bit of time before she understood what he meant, but the flood of emotions and memories was interrupted by Luo Ji's next words. "Forget it. *Carpe diem* has always been the right path. Of course there's not much *diem* now for *carpe*, but we need not look for trouble. Let's go. You don't need to help support me. You haven't even learned how to walk properly around here yet."

Given Luo Ji's advanced age of two hundred, the difficulty of locomotion under such low gravity wasn't moving too slow, but too fast. The cane wasn't so much a support as a decelerator.

After a while, space opened up before them. Cheng Xin and AA realized that they were now in a much wider and bigger tunnel—a cavern, really. The ceiling was high above, but the space was still only lit by a dim row of lights. The cavern looked very long, and the other end was not visible.

"This is the main body of the museum," Luo Ji said.

"Where are the artifacts?"

"In the halls down at the other end. Those aren't so important. How long can they keep? Ten thousand years? A hundred thousand years? A million, at the most. Practically all of them will have turned to dust by then. But these—" Luo Ji pointed around them. "—were intended to be preserved for hundreds of millions of years. Why, do you still think this is a museum? No, no one visits here. This is not a place for visitors. All of this is but a tombstone—humankind's tombstone."

Cheng Xin looked around the empty, dim cavern and thought back to all she had seen. Indeed, everything was filled with hints of death.

"How did such an idea come up?" AA looked all around.

"You ask that because you're too young." Luo Ji pointed to Cheng Xin and himself. "During our time, people often planned for their own gravesites while they were still alive. Finding a graveyard for humanity isn't so easy, but erecting a tombstone is doable." He turned to Cheng Xin. "Do you remember Secretary General Say?"

Cheng Xin nodded. "Of course."

Four centuries ago, while she had worked for the PIA, Cheng Xin had met

Say, the UN secretary general, a few times at various meetings. The last time was at a PIA briefing. Wade was there, too. On a big screen, Cheng Xin had given Say a PowerPoint presentation about the Staircase Project. Say had sat there quietly and listened to the whole thing without asking any questions. Afterwards, Say walked next to Cheng Xin, leaned in, and whispered, "We need more people to think like you."

"She was a true visionary. I've thought of her often through the years. Could she really have died almost four hundred years ago?" Luo Ji leaned on the cane with both hands and sighed. "She was the one who thought of this first. She wanted to do something so that humanity would leave behind a legacy that could be preserved for a long time after our civilization was gone. She planned an unmanned ship filled with cultural artifacts and information about us, but it was deemed a form of Escapism, and the project halted with her death. Three centuries later, after the Bunker Project began, people remembered it. That was a time when people worried that the world was going to end any moment. The new Federation Government decided to build a tombstone at the same time that the Bunker Project was built, but it was officially referred to as the Earth Civilization Museum so as not to be seen as a sign of pessimism. I was named the chair of the tombstone committee.

"At first, we engaged in a large research project to study how to preserve information across geologic eons. The initial benchmark was a billion years. Ha! A billion. Those idiots thought that would be easy—after all, if we could build the Bunker World, how difficult could this be? But they soon realized that modern quantum storage devices, while capable of storing a whole library in a grain of rice, could only preserve the information without loss for about two thousand years. After that, decay would make it impossible to decode. As a matter of fact, that only applied to the highest-quality storage devices. Two-thirds of more common varieties failed within five hundred years. This suddenly transformed the project from a detached, contemplative matter into an interesting practical problem. Five hundred years was real—you and I came from only four hundred years ago, right? So the government stopped all work on the museum and directed us to study how to back up important data about the modern world so that it could be read in five hundred years, heh heh. . . . Eventually, a special institute had to be set up to tackle the problem so that the rest of us could focus on the museum, or tombstone.

"Scientists realized that in terms of data longevity, storage devices from our time were better. They found some USB flash drives and hard drives from the Common Era and some still had recoverable data! Experiments showed that if these devices were of high quality, information was safe on them for about five thousand years. The optical disks from our era were especially resilient. When made from special metal, they could reliably preserve data for a hundred thousand years. But none of these were a match for printed material. Special ink printed on composite paper could be read in two hundred thousand years. But that was the limit. Our conventional data storage techniques could preserve information for two hundred thousand years, but we needed to get to a billion!

"We informed the government that, given current technology, preserving ten gigabytes of images and one gigabyte of text—that was the basic information requirement for the museum—for one billion years was impossible. They wouldn't believe us, and we had to show them the evidence. Finally, they agreed to lower the requirement to one hundred million years.

"But this was still an extremely difficult task. We looked for information that had survived for such a long time. Patterns drawn on prehistoric pottery survived about ten thousand years. Cave paintings in Europe were from about forty thousand years ago. If you count the markings made on stones back when our ancestors, the hominids, made the first tools as information, then the earliest instances occurred during the Pliocene, two point five million years ago. And we did indeed find information left one hundred million years ago, though it wasn't left by humans: dinosaur footprints.

"The research continued, but there was no progress. The other specialists had obviously reached conclusions, but they didn't want to speak up. I told them, 'Don't worry about it. Whatever conclusions you've reached, no matter how bizarre or outrageous, we must accept them if there are no alternatives.' I promised them that there was nothing that could be more bizarre and outrageous than what I'd gone through, and I would not laugh at them. So they told me that, according to the most advanced theories and techniques in every field, based on extensive theoretical research and experimentation, through analysis and comparison of multiple proposals, they did find a way to preserve information for about one hundred million years. And they emphasized that this was the only method known to be practicable. Which is—" Luo Ji lifted the cane over his head, and as his white hair and beard danced in the air, he resembled Moses parting the Red Sea. Solemnly, he intoned, "—carving words into stone."

AA giggled. But Cheng Xin wasn't laughing. She was stunned.

"Carving words into stone." Luo Ji pointed at the walls of the cavern.

Cheng Xin walked to one of the walls. In the dim light, she saw that it was covered with dense, carved text, as well as images in relief. The wall was not the original rock, but seemed to have been infused with metal, or perhaps the surface had been coated with some durable titanium alloy or gold. Fundamentally, however, it was no different from carving words into stone. The carved text wasn't small: each character or letter was about a square centimeter. This was another feature intended to help with information longevity, as smaller text tended to be harder to preserve.

"Of course, this approach meant that the information storage capacity was greatly reduced, leaving us with less than one-ten-thousandth of the planned amount. But they had no choice but to accept this limitation," Luo Ji said.

"These lamps are really strange," said AA.

Cheng Xin looked at the lamp on the cave wall. First, she noticed its shape: an arm poking out of the wall holding a torch. She thought this was a familiar design, but clearly that wasn't what AA meant. The torch-shaped lamp seemed very clumsy. The size and structure resembled an ancient searchlight, but the light it emitted was very weak, about the same as an ancient twenty-watt incandescent light bulb. After passing through the thick lampshade, the light was not much brighter than a candle.

Luo Ji said, "Back that way is the machinery dedicated to providing electricity to this complex, like a power plant. This lamp is an amazing accomplishment. There's no filament or excitable gas inside, and I don't know what the luminous element is, but it can continue to glow for a hundred thousand years. The doors you came through should continue to be operable under normal conditions for five hundred thousand years. After that, the doors will deform and whoever wants to come in will have to break them down. By then, these lamps will have gone out more than four hundred thousand years earlier, and darkness will reign here. But that will be but the start of the journey of a hundred million years."

Cheng Xin took off a space suit glove and caressed the characters carved into the cold stone. Then she leaned against the cave wall and stared woodenly at the lamps. She realized where she had seen this design: the Panthéon in Paris. A hand holding a torch just like the one on Rousseau's tomb. The faint yellow lights before her now didn't seem to be electric, but like tiny flames about to go out.

"You are not very talkative," Luo Ji said. His voice was suffused with a solicitousness that Cheng Xin had long missed.

"She's always been like that," said AA.

"Ah, I used to love to talk, and then I forgot how. But now I've learned again. I can't stop chattering, like a kid. I hope I'm not bothering you?"

Cheng Xin struggled to smile. "Not at all. It's just that . . . looking at all this, I don't know what to say."

True. What was there to say? Civilization was like a mad dash that lasted five thousand years. Progress begot more progress; countless miracles gave birth to more miracles; humankind seemed to possess the power of gods; but in the end, the real power was wielded by time. Leaving behind a mark was tougher than creating a world. At the end of civilization, all they could do was the same thing they had done in the distant past, when humanity was but a babe:

Carving words into stone.

Cheng Xin examined the carvings on the wall carefully. They began with the relief carving of a man and a woman, perhaps an attempt to show future discoverers what humans looked like. But unlike the stiff bearing of the drawings of the man and woman on the metal plaque carried by the Pioneer probes during the Common Era, the two cave carvings were done with lively expressions and postures, evoking Adam and Eve.

Cheng Xin walked along the wall. After the man and the woman came some hieroglyphs and cuneiforms, probably copied from ancient artifacts—it was possible that some of them were not even intelligible to modern men and women, and if so, how would future extraterrestrial discoverers understand them? Going further, Cheng Xin saw Chinese poetry—or, at least, she could tell the carvings were poetry based on the arrangement of the characters. But she didn't recognize any of the characters; she could only tell they were in Great Seal Script.

"That's the *Classic of Poetry*, from a millennium before the time of Christ," Luo Ji said. "If you keep on walking, you'll see fragments of Classical Greek philosophy. To see letters and characters that you can read, you'll have to walk tens of meters."

Under the Greek letters, Cheng Xin saw another relief, which seemed to portray ancient scholars in simple robes debating in an agora surrounded by stone columns.

Cheng Xin had a strange idea. She turned back and looked near the beginning of the cave carvings, but didn't find what she was looking for.

"You are looking for a Rosetta Stone?" Luo Ji asked.

"Yes. Isn't there some system to help with interpretation?"

"Child, we're talking about carving in stone, not a computer. How can we possibly fit something like that here?"

AA looked at the cave wall and then stared at Luo Ji. "You're saying that we've carved things here that we don't even understand with the hope that someday, some extraterrestrial will be able to read them?"

True, to the extraterrestrial discoverers of the far future, the human classics left on the walls here would probably resemble Linear A, Cretan hieroglyphics, and other ancient scripts that no one could read. Perhaps there was no realistic hope that anyone would. By the time the builders of this monument truly understood the power of time, they no longer believed that a vanished civilization could really leave behind any marks that would last through geologic eons. As Luo Ji had said, this wasn't a museum.

A museum was built for visitors; a tombstone was built for the builders.

The three continued onward, and Luo Ji's cane tapped along the ground rhythmically.

"I often stroll around here thinking my own crazy thoughts." Luo Ji paused and pointed at a relief carving of an ancient soldier in armor and wielding a spear. "This is about the conquests of Alexander the Great. If he had kept on going a bit farther east, he would have encountered the Qin at the end of the Warring States Period—what would have happened then? And how would history have changed?" They walked some more, and he pointed at the cave wall again. By now, the characters carved on the wall had turned from Small Seal Script to Clerical Script. "Ah, we've reached the Han Dynasty. From here to later, China completed two unifications. Are a unified territory and a unified system of thought good things for civilization as a whole? The Han Dynasty ended up endorsing Confucianism above all, but if the multiplicity of schools of thinking during the Spring and Autumn Period had continued, what would have happened later? How would the present be different?" He waved his cane around in a circle. "At every moment in history, you can find endless missed opportunities."

"Like life," said Cheng Xin softly.

"Oh, no no no." Luo Ji shook his head vigorously. "At least not for me. I don't think I've missed anything, haha." He looked at Cheng Xin. "Child, do you think you've missed out? Then don't let opportunities go by again in the future."

"There's no future now," said AA coldly. She wondered if Luo Ji was suffering from dementia.

They reached the end of the cave. Turning around to survey this underground tombstone, Luo Ji sighed. "We had designed this place to last a hundred million years, but it won't even survive a hundred."

"Who knows? Perhaps a flat two-dimensional civilization will be able to see all this," said AA.

"Interesting! I hope you're right. . . . Look, this is where the artifacts are kept. We have a total of three halls."

Cheng Xin and AA saw space open up before them once more. The room they were in didn't resemble an exhibit hall so much as a warehouse. All the artifacts were placed in identical metal boxes, and each box was labeled in detail.

Luo Ji tapped one of the nearby boxes with his cane. "As I said, these are not so important. Most of these objects have longevities shorter than fifty thousand years, though some of the statues can survive up to a million years. But I suggest you not move the statues: Though the gravity makes them easy to move, they take up too much space. . . . All right, pick whatever you like."

AA looked around excitedly. "I suggest we take paintings. We can forget about old classics and ancient manuscripts—no one will understand those." She walked in front of one of the metal boxes and pushed what looked like a button on top, but the box didn't open by itself, and there were no instructions. Cheng Xin walked over and struggled to lift the cover open. AA took out an oil painting.

"I guess paintings take up a lot of space, too," said AA.

Luo Ji picked up a set of work overalls from on top of another box and retrieved a small knife and screwdriver from the pockets. "The frame takes up a lot of space. You can take it off."

AA picked up the screwdriver, but before she could get started on the painting, Cheng Xin cried out. "No!" The painting was Van Gogh's *Starry Night*.

Cheng Xin's surprise wasn't just because the painting was valuable. She had seen it once before. Four centuries ago, right after she had started working at the PIA, she had visited New York's Museum of Modern Art on a weekend and saw a few of Van Gogh's paintings. Van Gogh's representation of space had left a deep impression on her. In his subconscious, space seemed to have structure. Cheng Xin wasn't an expert in theoretical physics back then, but she knew that according to string theory, space, like material objects, was made up of many microscopic vibrating strings. Van Gogh had painted these strings: In his paintings, space—like mountains, wheat fields, houses, and trees—was filled with minute vibrations. *Starry Night* had left an indelible mark in her mind, and she was amazed to see it again four centuries later on Pluto.

"Get rid of the frame. That way, you can take more." Luo Ji waved his cane carelessly. "Do you think these objects are still worth a city's ransom? Now, even a city is worthless."

And so they pried away the frame that was perhaps five centuries old, but they kept the hard backing to avoid damaging the painting by bending the canvas. They continued to do the same to other oil paintings, and soon, empty frames littered the floor. Luo Ji came over and put his hand on a small painting.

"Would you leave this one for me?"

Cheng Xin and AA moved the painting aside and set it on top of a box next to the wall. They were surprised to see that it was the *Mona Lisa*.

Cheng Xin and AA continued to work at disassembling frames. AA whispered, "Clever old man. He kept the most expensive piece for himself."

"I don't think that's the reason."

"Maybe he once loved a girl named Mona Lisa?"

Luo Ji sat next to the *Mona Lisa* and caressed the ancient frame with one hand. He muttered, "I didn't know you were here. Otherwise I could have come to see you often."

Cheng Xin saw that he wasn't looking at the painting. His eyes stared ahead as if looking into the depths of time. Cheng Xin saw that his ancient eyes were filled with tears, and she wasn't sure if she was mistaken.

Inside the grand tomb under the surface of Pluto, lit by the dim lamps that could shine for a hundred thousand years, Mona Lisa's smile seemed to appear and disappear. The smile had puzzled humankind for nearly nine centuries, and it looked even more mysterious and eerie now, as though it meant everything and nothing, like the approaching Death.

Cheng Xin and AA carried the first batch of artifacts to the surface. Other than a dozen or so frameless paintings, they also carried two bronze ritual vessels from the Western Zhou Period and some ancient books. Under standard 1G gravity, they would not have been able to move all these, but with Pluto's weak gravity, it didn't require too much effort. Going through the air lock, they were careful to close the inner door first before opening the outer door, lest they and the artifacts be blown into the open by escaping air. As soon as they opened the outer door, the small amount of air inside the air lock turned into a flurry of ice crystals. Initially, they thought the ice crystals were illuminated by the searchlight on *Halo*, but after the flurry subsided, they realized that *Halo*'s searchlight had already shut off. Some source of light in space illuminated Pluto's surface, and *Halo* and the black monolith cast long shadows on the white ground. They looked up, and backed up two steps with shock.

A pair of giant eyes stared down at them from space.

Two glowing ovals hung in space, looking exactly like eyes. The "whites" were white or light yellow, and the "irises" were dark.

"That's Neptune, and the other one is Ura—oh, no, that's Saturn!" AA said.

Both gas giants had been two-dimensionalized. Uranus's orbit was outside Saturn's, but since Uranus was currently on the other side of the Sun, Saturn had fallen into the two-dimensional plane first. The giant planets ought to look like circles after collapsing, but due to the angle of view from Pluto, they appeared as ovals. The two-dimensional planets showed up as clear, concentric rings. Neptune consisted mainly of three rings: the outermost was blue, bright and vivid, like lashes and eye shadow—that was the atmosphere of hydrogen and helium. The middle ring was white—that was the twenty-thousand-kilometer mantle, which astronomers thought of as a water-ammonia ocean. The dark center was the core, formed of rocks and ice, with a mass equal to the entire Earth. Saturn's structure was similar, except it didn't have the outer blue ring.

Each large ring was composed of many smaller rings, full of detailed structures. As they examined the planets further, the two giant eyes now more resembled the rings of a newly felled tree. Around each two-dimensional planet were a dozen or so small circles—moons that had also been flattened. Around Saturn was another faint large circle—its rings. They could still find the Sun in the sky, a small disk emitting faint yellow light. Since the two planets were still on the other side of the sun, their area after collapsing into two dimensions was breathtaking.

Both planets had no thickness anymore.

In the light emitted by these two-dimensional planets, Cheng Xin and AA carried the artifacts across the white landing field toward *Halo*. The ship's smooth, streamlined body was like a funhouse mirror, and the reflections of the two-dimensional planets were stretched into long, flowing shapes. The yacht's profile naturally made people think of droplets, and evinced a comforting strength and lightness. On the way to Pluto, AA had told Cheng Xin that she thought *Halo*'s hull was probably made up in large part of strong-interaction materials.

As they approached, the door on the bottom of the ship slid open noiselessly. They carried the artifacts up the airstair and into the cabin, took off their helmets, and took a deep breath in their cozy little world. Relief filled their hearts—without consciously being aware of it, they already thought of the yacht as *home*.

Cheng Xin asked the ship's AI whether it had received any transmissions from Neptune and Saturn. As soon as she made the request, information windows flooded forth like a colorful avalanche that threatened to bury them. The scene reminded them of the first false alarm of 118 years ago. Back then, most of the information had come from media reports, but now, the news media seemed to have disappeared. Most of the information windows contained no discernible images at all—some were blurred, others shook, and most showed meaningless close-ups. But a few of the windows were filled with patches of gorgeous color which, as they flowed and shifted, revealed complex, detailed structures. They probably showed the two-dimensional universe.

AA asked the AI to filter the images. The AI asked them what kind of information they wanted. Cheng Xin asked for information about the space cities. The flood of windows cleared and was replaced by about a dozen others arranged in order. One of the windows enlarged and moved before the others. The AI explained that this had been taken twelve hours ago at Europe VI in the Neptune cluster. The city had once been part of a combined city that had separated after the strike alert.

The image was stable, and the field of view wide. The camera was probably at one end of the city, and almost the entire city could be seen.

Electricity had gone out in Europe VI, and only a few searchlight beams projected unsteady circles of light onto the city's far side. The three artificial fusion suns along the city's axis had all turned into silvery moons, giving out only illumination, but no heat. This was a standard football-shaped city, but the buildings inside the city were very different from what Cheng Xin had seen half a century ago. The Bunker World had prospered, and the buildings inside the city were no longer monotonous and uniform. They were much taller, and each had a unique design. The tips of some of the skyscrapers almost touched the axis of the city. Buildings in the shapes of trees reappeared as well, and they looked about as large as the ones that had been built on Earth, though the leaves hung more densely. It was possible to imagine the city's beauty and magnificence when lit up at night. But now, only cold moonlight illuminated it, and the tree-buildings cast wide shadows so that the rest of the city appeared as ruins nestled in the shade of a giant forest.

The city had stopped spinning and everything was weightless. Countless objects floated through the air—vehicles, miscellaneous goods, and even entire buildings.

A black belt of clouds appeared along the city's axis, connecting the two poles. The ship's AI outlined a rectangular region in the image and zoomed in, creating a new information window. Cheng Xin and AA were shocked to see that the black cloud was formed from people drifting in the middle of the city! Some of the weightless individuals had pulled together into a cluster; some had linked hands and formed a line; but most floated alone. Everyone wore helmets and clothes that covered all parts of their body—most likely space suits. Even during Cheng Xin's last time out of hibernation, it was hard to tell everyday clothes apart from space suits. Everyone seemed to have a pack for life-support systems—some wore it on their back, while others held it in their hands. But most people had their visors open, and it was possible to see a light breeze blowing through the city, indicating that the city still retained a breathable atmosphere. Many had congregated around the suns, perhaps hoping for more light as well as a bit of warmth, but the light emitted by the fusion suns was cold light. The silvery light shone through cracks in the people-cloud and turned into dappled shadows in the surrounding city.

According to the ship's AI, of the six million inhabitants of Europe VI, half had already left the city on space vehicles. Of the remaining three million, some had no way to get off the city, but most understood that any attempt at escape was hopeless. Even if some ships miraculously managed to escape the collapsing zone and reached outer space, most ships had no ecological cycling system to maintain life for long. Access to stellar ships that could survive indefinitely in outer space was still a privilege of the very few. These people chose to wait for the end in a place they were familiar with.

The transmission wasn't muted, but Cheng Xin couldn't hear anything. The people-cloud and the city were both eerily quiet. Everyone looked in one direction. That part of the city looked no different from any other, filled with crisscrossing streets and row upon row of buildings. Everyone waited. In the watery, cold moonlight, people's faces appeared as white as ghosts. The sight reminded Cheng Xin of the bloody dawn in Australia 126 years ago. Like then, Cheng Xin felt as though she were looking down upon an ant colony, and the black people-cloud looked just like a drifting swarm of ants.

Someone in the people-cloud screamed. A glowing dot appeared at a spot on the city's equator, the same spot where everyone had been gazing. It was like a small opening in the roof of a dark house letting in the sunlight.

That was where Europe VI first came into contact with two-dimensional space.

The light grew rapidly and turned into a glowing oval. The light it emitted was sliced into many shafts by the tall buildings all around, and illuminated the people-cloud on the city's axis. The space city now resembled a giant ship whose bottom had been breached, sinking in a flat sea. The plane of the two-dimensional space rose like water, and everything that came into contact with the surface instantaneously turned into two dimensions. Clusters of buildings were cut, and their two-dimensional images spread out on the plane. Since the city's cross section was but a small portion of the entire flattened city, most of the two-dimensionalized buildings had expanded beyond the oval marked by the city's hull. On the rising, expanding plane, gorgeous colors and complicated structures flashed by and zoomed away in every direction, as though the plane was a lens through which one could see colorful beasts running. Because the city still possessed air, they could hear the sound of the three-dimensional world falling into two dimensions: a crisp, piercing series of crunches, as though the buildings and the city itself were made of exquisitely carved glass and a giant roller was crushing everything.

As the plane continued to rise, the people-cloud began to spread out in the opposite direction, like a curtain being lifted by an invisible hand. The scene reminded Cheng Xin of a massive flock of millions of birds that she had seen once. The flock had seemed like a unified organism changing shape in the dusk sky.

Soon, the plane had swallowed one-third of the city, and it continued to flicker frantically as it rose irresistibly toward the axis. Some people had begun to fall into the plane by now. They either fell behind due to malfunctions in their space suit thrusters or they had given up on running. Like drops of colorful ink, they spread open on the plane in an instant, and each appeared as a unique figure in two dimensions. On one of the zoomed-in images shown by the AI, they saw a pair of lovers leaping into the plane while in an embrace. Even after the two had been flattened, it was possible to see the figures in an embrace lying side by side—their postures appeared odd, as though drawn by a clumsy child who did not understand the principles of perspective. Nearby there was a mother who lifted her baby overhead as she fell into the plane, all so that the baby would survive for an extra tenth of a second. The mother and child were also vividly portrayed in this giant painting. As the plane kept on rising, the rain of people falling on it became denser. Two-dimensional human figures flooded forth on the plane, most moving outside the boundary of the space city.

By the time the two-dimensional space approached the axis, most of the surviving population had landed against the city's far side. Half of the city was now gone, and as people looked "up" they could no longer see the familiar city on the other side, but only a chaotic, two-dimensional sky pressing down on the parts of Europe VI that remained in three dimensions. It was now no longer possible to escape from the main gateway at the north pole, so people congregated around the equator, where there were three emergency exits. The weightless crowd piled into mountains around the exits.

The two-dimensional space passed through the axis and swallowed up the three suns, but the light emitted by the two-dimensionalizing process made the world even brighter.

A low whistling sound began: The city was losing its air to space. The three emergency exits along the equator were wide open, each as large as a football field; outside them was the still-three-dimensional space.

The ship's AI pushed another information window to the front. This was a feed from space looking down at Europe VI. The two-dimensionalized portion of the space city spread across the invisible plane, making the rapidly sinking, still-three-dimensional portion look minuscule by comparison, like the back of a whale peering out of the vast ocean. Three clumps of black smoke rose out of the city and dissipated in space; the "smoke" was formed from the people blown out by the fierce winds of the decompressing space city. The lonely, three-dimensional island continued to sink and melt into the two-dimensional sea. In less than ten minutes, all of Europe VI had turned into a painting.

The painting of Europe VI was so vast that it was hard to estimate its exact area. It was a dead city, but perhaps it was more accurate to call it a 1:1 drawing of the city. The drawing reflected every detail of the city, down to every screw, every fiber, every mite, and even every bacterium. The precision of the drawing was at the level of the individual atom. Every atom in the original three-dimensional space was projected onto its corresponding place in two-dimensional space according to ironclad laws. The basic principles governing this drawing were that there could be no overlap and no hidden parts, and every single detail had to be laid out on the plane. Here, complexity was a substitute for grandeur. The drawing wasn't easy to interpret—it was possible to see the overall plan of the city and recognize some big structures, such as the giant trees, which still looked like trees even in two dimensions. But buildings looked very different after being flattened: it was almost impossible to deduce the original three-dimensional structure from the two-dimensional drawing by imagination alone. However, it was certain that image-processing software equipped with the right mathematical model would be able to.

In the information window, it was also possible to see two other flattened space cities in the distance. The cities appeared as perfectly flat continents drifting in dark space, gazing at each other across the plane. But the camera—perhaps located on a drone—was also falling toward the plane, and soon the two-dimensional Europe VI filled the screen.

Close to a million people had escaped Europe VI via the emergency exits; now, caught by the three-dimensional space around them collapsing into two dimensions, they fell toward the plane like a swarm of ants caught in a waterfall. A majestic rain of people fell onto the plane, and the two-dimensional human figures in the city multiplied. Flattened persons took up a lot of area—though still minuscule compared to the vast two-dimensional buildings—and resembled tiny, barely man-shaped marks in the immense picture.

More objects appeared in three-dimensional space in the information window: the skiffs and dinghies that had left Europe VI earlier. Their fusion reactors were operating at maximum capacity, but they still fell inexorably toward the plane. For a moment, Cheng Xin thought the blue flame of the fusion drives penetrated that depthless plane, but the plasma had simply been two-dimensionalized. In those areas, the two-dimensional buildings were distorted and twisted by the two-dimensional flames. Next, the skiffs and dinghies became part of the giant drawing. Obeying the no-overlapping principle, the two-dimensionalized city expanded to give these new objects space, and the whole image resembled spreading ripples on the surface of a pond.

The camera continued to fall toward the plane. Cheng Xin stared at the approaching two-dimensional city, hoping to find signs of movement in the city. But no, other than the distortion caused by the plasma flames earlier, everything in the flat city was still. Similarly, the two-dimensional bodies did not move at all, and gave no signs of being alive.

This was a dead world. A dead picture.

The camera moved still closer to the plane, falling toward a two-dimensional body. The body's limbs soon filled the whole image, and then came the complicated patterns of muscle fibers and blood vessels. Perhaps it was just an illusion, but Cheng Xin seemed to see red, two-dimensional blood flowing through two-dimensional blood vessels. In a flash, the picture was gone.

Cheng Xin and AA began their second trip to retrieve more artifacts. They both felt the mission was likely to be meaningless. After observing the two-dimensionalized cities, they understood that the process preserved most of the information from the three-dimensional world. Any information loss would be at the atomic level. Due to the nonoverlapping principle used in projection, the flattened Pluto's crust wouldn't be commingled with the artifacts in the museum, and so the information in the artifacts should be preserved. But since they had accepted this mission, they would finish it. Like Cao Bin said, doing something was better than doing nothing.

They exited *Halo* and saw the two flattened planets still suspended overhead, but now they were much dimmer. This made the new long, glowing belt that appeared below the planets even more noticeable. The light belt went from one end of the sky to the other, like a necklace formed from numerous individual glowing spots.

"Is that the asteroid belt?" Cheng Xin asked.

"Yes. Mars will be next," said AA.

"Mars is on this side of the Sun right now."

The two fell silent. Without looking at the flattened asteroid belt, they walked toward the black monolith.

The Earth was next.

In the great hall of the museum, they saw that Luo Ji had already prepped a bunch of additional artifacts for them. Many of them were Chinese-brush-painting scrolls. AA unrolled one of them: *Along the River During the Qing-ming Festival.*

Cheng Xin and AA no longer had the initial awe and delight of seeing such precious works of art—compared to the grandeur of the destruction in process outside, this was nothing more than an old painting. When future explorers arrived at the great painting that was the flattened Solar System, they would have trouble imagining that this twenty-four-centimeter-by-five-meter rectangle was once very special.

Cheng Xin and AA asked Luo Ji to come onto *Halo.* Luo Ji said he would like to see it, and went to look for a space suit.

As the three of them carried the artifacts out of the monolith, the sight of a flattening Earth greeted them.

The Earth was the first solid planet to collapse into two dimensions. Compared to Neptune and Saturn, the "tree rings" in the two-dimensionalized Earth were even more replete with fine details—the yellow mantle gradually shifted over to the deep red nickel-iron core—but the overall area was much smaller than the gas giants.

Unlike in their imagination, they couldn't see any hint of blue.

"What happened to our oceans?" Luo Ji asked.

"They should be near the outside . . . But two-dimensionalized water is transparent, so we can't see it," AA said.

The three carried the artifacts to *Halo* in silence. They couldn't feel the grief yet, like one didn't immediately feel the pain of a fresh wound cut by a sharp knife.

But the flattened Earth did show her own wonders. At her outermost rim, a white ring gradually appeared. At first it was barely visible, but soon it stood out sharply against the black backdrop of space. The white ring was pure, flaw-less, but seemed uneven in its makeup, like it was formed from countless small white grains.

"That's our ocean!" Cheng Xin said.

"The water froze in two-dimensional space," said AA. "It's cold there."

"Oh—" Luo Ji wanted to stroke his beard, but the visor got in the way of his hand.

The three carried the boxes of artifacts onto *Halo*. Luo Ji seemed familiar with the ship's layout, heading for the ship's hold without instruction from Cheng Xin or AA. The ship's AI also recognized him, and accepted his orders. After they secured the artifacts, the three returned to the yacht's living quarters. Luo Ji asked the AI for a cup of hot tea, and soon, a little robot that Cheng Xin and AA had never seen before brought it to him. Clearly, Luo Ji had some history with this ship that the two women did not know about. They were curious about the story, though more urgent matters had to be taken care of first.

Cheng Xin asked the AI to play some news from the Earth, but the AI said that it had received only a few transmissions from the planet, and the visual and audio content was essentially impossible to make sense of. They looked at the few open information windows and saw only blurred images taken by unmanned cameras. The AI added that it could provide the video taken by the spacecraft monitoring system near the Earth. A new, large window popped up and the flatted Earth filled the screen.

The three immediately thought the image looked unreal, even suspecting that the AI had synthesized the image to fool them.

"What in the world is this?" AA cried out.

"It's the Earth about seven hours ago. The camera is fifty astronomical units away, and angular magnification is four hundred and fifty times."

They looked more closely at the holographic video taken by the telescopic lens. The body of the flattened Earth appeared very clearly, and the "tree rings" were even denser than when observed with the naked eye. The collapse had probably already been completed, and the two-dimensional Earth was dimming. But what really shocked them was the frozen two-dimensional ocean—the white ring around the rim of the Earth. They could clearly make out the grains forming the ring: snowflakes! These were unimaginably large snowflakes, hexagonal in plan, but each with unique crystal branches—exquisite, lovely beyond words. To see snowflakes from fifty AU away was already extremely surreal, and these immense snowflakes were arranged side by side on the plane with no overlap, which further enhanced the feeling of unreality. They seemed to be purely artistic portrayals of snowflakes, powerfully decorative, turning the frozen two-dimensional sea into a piece of stage art.

"How big are the snowflakes?" AA asked.

"Most have diameters between four thousand and five thousand kilometers." The ship's AI, incapable of wonder, continued to speak in a serene tone.

"Bigger than the moon!" Cheng Xin said.

The AI opened a few other windows, and each showed a zoomed-in snow-flake. In these images, the sense of scale was lost, and they seemed to be tiny spirits under a magnifying lens, each snowflake ready to turn into a tiny droplet as soon as it touched down on a palm.

"Oh—" Luo Ji stroked his beard again, and this time, succeeded.

"How are they formed?" AA asked.

"I don't know," the AI said. "I can't find any information about the crystal-lization of water at astronomical scales."

In three-dimensional space, snowflakes formed in accordance with the laws of ice-crystal growth. Theoretically, these laws did not restrict the size of snow-flakes. The largest snowflake previously on record was thirty-eight centimeters in diameter.

No one knew the laws of ice crystal growth in two-dimensional space. What-ever they were, they permitted ice crystals in two dimensions to grow to five thousand kilometers.

"There's water on Neptune and Saturn, and ammonia can also form crys-tals. Why didn't we see large snowflakes there?" Cheng Xin asked.

The AI said it didn't know.

Luo Ji squinted his eyes and enjoyed the two-dimensional version of the Earth. "The ocean looks rather nice this way, don't you think? Only the Earth is worthy of such a lovely wreath."

"I really want to know what the forests look like, what the grasslands look like, what the ancient cities look like," Cheng Xin said slowly.

Grief finally struck them, and AA began to sob. Cheng Xin turned her eyes away from the snowflake ocean and made no sound as her eyes filled with tears. Luo Ji shook his head, sighed, and continued to sip his tea. Their grief was moderated to some extent by the thought that the two-dimensional space would also be their home in the end.

They would attain their eternal rest alongside Mother Earth on that plane.

The three decided to begin their third cargo trip. They exited *Halo*, gazed up at the sky, and saw the three two-dimensional planets. Neptune, Saturn, and the Earth had grown even larger, and the asteroid belt was wider. This was no hallucination. They asked the AI about it.

"The navigation system has detected a split in the Solar System's navigational frame of reference. Frame of reference one continues as before. The navigational markers within this system—the Sun, Mercury, Mars, Jupiter, Uranus, Pluto, and some asteroids and Kuiper Belt objects—still satisfy the recognition criteria. Frame of reference two, however, has transformed dramatically. Neptune, Saturn, the Earth, and some asteroids have lost their characteristics as navigational markers. Frame of reference one is moving toward frame of reference two, which leads to the phenomenon you've observed."

In the sky in the other direction, many moving points of light appeared before the stars—the fleet of ships seeking to escape the Solar System. Some of the glowing blue lights dragged long tails behind them. Some of the ships swept by the three of them, fairly close. The bright lights of their engines operating at maximum capacity cast moving shadows of the three observers on the ground. None of the ships tried to land on Pluto.

But it was impossible to escape from the collapsing zone. *Halo*'s AI was trying to say this: The three-dimensional space of the Solar System was like a large carpet that was being pulled by invisible hands into a two-dimensional abyss. These ships were nothing more than worms on the carpet inching along—they couldn't extend their already limited allotment of time by much.

"Go ahead by yourselves," Luo Ji said. "Just take a few more objects. I want to wait here. I don't want to miss it." Cheng Xin and AA understood what he meant by "it," but they had no desire to witness the scene.

After returning to the underground hall, Cheng Xin and AA, not in the mood to pick and choose, randomly gathered a collection of artifacts. Cheng Xin wanted to take along a Neanderthal skull, but AA tossed it aside.

"You'll have plenty of skulls on this picture," AA said.

Cheng Xin acknowledged that she was right. The earliest Neanderthals had lived no more than a few hundred thousand years ago. Optimistically, the flattened Solar System would not have visitors until a few hundred thousand years from now. In their eyes, Neanderthals and modern humans would appear to be the same species. Cheng Xin looked around at the other artifacts, and none excited her. For themselves in the present, and for those unimaginable observers in the far future, nothing here mattered as much as the world that was dying outside.

They took a last look at the dim hall and left with the artifacts. Mona Lisa watched them leave, smiling sinisterly and eerily.

On the surface, they saw that yet another two-dimensional planet had appeared in the sky: Mercury (Venus was on the other side of the Sun at this moment). It looked smaller than the two-dimensional Earth, but the light generated by its recent collapse into two dimensions made it very bright.

After they packed the artifacts in the hold, Cheng Xin and AA came out of *Halo*. Luo Ji, who was waiting outside, leaning on his cane, said, "All right. I think that's enough. It's meaningless to carry more, anyway."

The women agreed. They stood together with Luo Ji on the Plutonian ground and waited for the most magnificent scene of the play: the flattening of the Sun.

At this moment, Pluto was forty-five AU from the Sun. Earlier, since both Pluto and the Sun were in the same region of three-dimensional space, the distance between them hadn't changed. But when the Sun came into contact with the plane, it ceased to move, while Pluto continued to fall toward it, along with the space around it, causing the distance between them to shrink rapidly.

When the Sun began to two-dimensionalize, the naked eye could only see that its brightness and size appeared to increase suddenly. The latter was due to the rapid expansion of the flattened portion of the Sun on the plane, but from a distance it appeared as though the Sun itself was growing. *Halo's* AI projected a large information window outside the ship to show a holographic feed from a telescopic lens, but as Pluto pulled closer to the Sun, even the naked eye could see the grand spectacle of a star collapsing into two dimensions.

As soon as the Sun began to two-dimensionalize, a circle expanded on the plane. Soon, the planar Sun's diameter exceeded the diameter of the remaining part of the Sun. This process took only thirty seconds. Based on the mean solar radius of seven hundred thousand kilometers, the rim of the two-dimensional Sun grew at the rate of twenty thousand kilometers per second. The planar Sun continued to grow, forming a sea of fire on the plane, and the three-dimensional Sun sank slowly into this blood-red sea of fire.

Four centuries ago, Ye Wenjie had stood on the peak of Red Coast Base and watched such a sunset during the last moments of her life. Her heart had struggled to beat like a zither string about to break, and a black fog had begun to cloud her eyes. On the western horizon, the Sun that was falling into the sea of clouds seemed to melt, and the Sun's blood seeped into the clouds and the sky, creating a large crimson swath. She had called it humanity's sunset.

And now, the Sun really was melting, its blood seeping into the deadly plane. This was the last sunset.

In the distance, white fog rose from the ground outside the landing field. Pluto's solid nitrogen and ammonia sublimated, and the fresh, thin atmosphere began to scatter the sunlight. The sky no longer appeared pure black, but showed hints of purple.

While the three-dimensional Sun was setting, the two-dimensional Sun was rising. A flat star could still radiate its light inside the plane, so the two-dimensional Solar System received its first sunlight. The sides of the four two-dimensional planets facing the sun—Neptune, Saturn, the Earth, and Mercury—all took on a golden glow, though the light only fell along a one-dimensional curved edge. The giant snowflakes that surrounded the Earth melted and turned into white vapor, which was blown by two-dimensional solar wind into two-dimensional space. Some of the vapor soaked up the golden sunlight and appeared as if the Earth had hair that drifted with the wind.

An hour later, the Sun had completely collapsed into two dimensions.

From Pluto, the Sun appeared as a giant oval. The two-dimensional planets were tiny fragments compared to it. Unlike the planets, the Sun did not display clear "tree rings" but was separated into three concentric sections around a core. The center was very bright, and no details could be seen—probably corresponding to the core of the original Sun. The wide ring outside the core probably corresponded to the original radiation zone—a boiling, two-dimensional, bright red ocean where countless cell-like structures rapidly formed, split, combined, and disappeared in a manner that seemed chaotic and agitated when viewed locally, but followed grand patterns and order when viewed as a whole. Outside that was the original Sun's convection zone. Like in the original Sun, currents of solar material transferred heat into space. But unlike the chaotic radiation zone, the new convection zone revealed clear structure, as many ring-shaped convection loops, similar in shape and size, arranged themselves side by side in neat order. The outermost layer was the solar atmosphere. Golden currents leapt away from the circular rim and formed a large number of two-dimensional prominences, resembling graceful dancers cavorting wantonly around the Sun. Some of the "dancers" even escaped the Sun and drifted far into the two-dimensional universe.

"Is the Sun still alive in two dimensions?" asked AA. She spoke for the hope of all three. They all wished for the Sun to continue to give light and heat to the planar Solar System, even if there was no more life in it.

But her hope was soon dashed.

The flattened Sun began to dim. The light from the core diminished rapidly and soon it was possible to see fine annular structures within. The radiation zone was also quieting, and the boiling calmed down, turning into a viscous peristalsis. The loops in the convection zone distorted, broke apart, and soon disappeared. The golden dancers around the rim of the Sun wilted like dried leaves and lost their vivaciousness. Now it was possible to tell that at least gravity continued to function in the two-dimensional universe.

The dancing solar prominences lost the support of solar radiation and began to be dragged back to the edge of the Sun by its gravity. Finally, the dancers yielded to gravity and fell lethargically, until the Sun's atmosphere was no more than a thin, smooth ring wrapped around the Sun. As the Sun went out, the golden arcs at the edges of the planets also dimmed, and the Earth's two-dimensional hair, formed from the sublimated ocean, lost its golden glow.

Everything in the three-dimensional world died after collapsing into two dimensions. Nothing survived in a painting with no thickness.

Perhaps a two-dimensional universe could possess its own sun, planets, and life, but they would have to be created and operate under completely different principles.

While the three were focused on the flattening Sun, Venus and Mars collapsed into the plane as well. Compared to the Sun, however, the two-dimensionalization of these two terrestrial planets was rather unremarkable. The flattened Mars and Venus were very similar to the Earth in terms of their "tree ring" structure. There were many hollow areas near the rim of Mars, places in the Martian crust that contained water, suggesting that Mars had possessed far more water than people thought. After a while, the water also turned an opaque white, but no giant snowflakes appeared. There were giant snowflakes around the flattened Venus, but they weren't anywhere as numerous as the ones near the Earth, and the Venusian snowflakes were yellow in hue, indicating that they were not water crystals. A while later, the asteroids on that side of the Sun were also flattened, completing the other half of the Solar System necklace.

Tiny snowflakes—three-dimensional ones—now fell from the light purple Plutonian sky. These were the nitrogen and ammonia that had sublimated in the burst of energy during the Sun's flattening, and which were now freezing into snow as the temperature plummeted following the Sun's extinguishment. The snow fell more heavily, and soon accumulated a thick layer over the monolith and *Halo*. Although there were no clouds, the heavy snow blurred Pluto's sky, and the two-dimensional Sun and the planets turned hazy behind a curtain of snow. The world looked smaller.

"Don't you feel at home?" AA lifted both hands and spun in the snow.

"I was just thinking the same thing," Cheng Xin said, and nodded. She had also thought of snow as something unique to the Earth, and the giant snowflakes around the flattened Earth had confirmed this feeling. The snow falling on this cold, dark world on the edge of the Solar System surprisingly provided her a trace of the warmth of home.

Luo Ji watched as AA and Cheng Xin tried to catch the snow. "Hey, you two! Don't even think about taking off your gloves!"

Cheng Xin did feel an impulse to take off her gloves and catch the snow with her bare hands. She wanted to feel the slight chill, and watch the crystalline snowflakes melt with her own body heat. . . . but of course she had enough presence of mind to not indulge the impulse. The nitrogen-ammonia snowflakes were at a temperature of minus-210-degrees Celsius. If she really took off her gloves, her hand would turn as fragile and hard as glass and the feeling of being on Earth would disappear instantaneously.

"There's no more home," Luo Ji said, shaking his head and leaning against his cane. "Home is now just a picture."

The nitrogen-ammonia snow didn't last long. The snowflakes thinned out and the purple haze from the nitrogen-ammonia atmosphere faded. The sky was once again perfectly transparent and dark. They saw that the Sun and the planets had grown even bigger, indicating that Pluto had moved even closer to that two-dimensional abyss.

When the snow stopped, a bright glowing light appeared near the horizon. The intensity of the light grew rapidly, and soon overwhelmed the fading two-dimensional Sun. Although they couldn't see the details, they knew that it was Jupiter, the Solar System's largest planet, falling into the plane. Pluto spun slowly, and part of the flattened Solar System had fallen below the horizon, so they thought they wouldn't get to witness Jupiter's collapse, but it appeared that the rate of fall into two dimensions was accelerating.

They asked *Halo*'s AI to look for transmissions from Jupiter. Very few images and videos were being transmitted now, and most were indecipherable. Almost all of the messages they got were audio only. Every communication channel was filled with noise, mostly human voices, as though all the remaining space in the Solar System had been filled with a frenzied sea of people. The voices cried, screamed, sobbed, laughed hysterically . . . and some even sang. The chaotic background noise made it impossible to tell what they were singing, only that it was many voices singing in harmony. The music was solemn, slow, like a hymn. Cheng Xin asked the AI whether it was possible to receive any official broadcasts from the Federation Government. The AI said that all official communications from the government had terminated when the Earth was flattened. The Federation Government couldn't fulfill the promise to carry out its duties until the end of the Solar System after all.

Ships trying to escape continued to stream by the vicinity of Pluto.

"Children, it's time to go," said Luo Ji.

"Let's go together," said Cheng Xin.

"What's the point?" Luo Ji shook his head and smiled. He pointed at the monolith with his cane. "I'm more comfortable over there."

"All right. We'll wait until Uranus is flattened so that we get to spend more time with you," AA said. There really didn't seem to be any point in insisting. Even if Luo Ji got on *Halo*, it would only delay the inevitable by another hour. He didn't need that bit of time. Indeed, if Cheng Xin and AA didn't have a mission to carry out, they wouldn't care for that bit of time either.

"No. You must go now!" Luo Ji said. He struck the ground with his cane forcefully, which made him float up under the low gravity. "No one knows how much faster the collapse is happening now. Carry out your mission! We can stay in contact, and that's no different from being together."

Cheng Xin hesitated for a moment, then nodded. "All right. We'll leave. Stay in contact!"

"Of course." Luo Ji lifted his cane in farewell and turned to walk toward the monolith. With the light gravity, he almost floated over the snow on the ground and had to use the cane to slow himself. Cheng Xin and AA watched until the aged figure of this Wallfacer, Swordholder, and humanity's final grave keeper disappeared behind the door of the monolith.

Cheng Xin and AA went back inside *Halo*. The yacht took off right away, its thrusters tossing up snow everywhere. Soon, the ship achieved Pluto's escape velocity—just a hair above one kilometer per second—and reached orbit. From the porthole and the monitor they could see that swaths of white now joined the blue and black patches of the Plutonian surface. The giant words "Earth Civilization," written in multiple scripts and languages, had been covered by the snow and were almost illegible. *Halo* passed through the gap between Pluto and Charon as though flying through a canyon, the two celestial bodies were so close.

In this "canyon" there were now many other moving stars—the escaping spaceships. They all moved far faster than *Halo*. One ship swept past *Halo* at a distance of no more than a hundred kilometers, and the glow from its nozzles lit up Charon's smooth surface. They could clearly see its triangular hull and the nearly ten-kilometer-long blue flame shooting out of its nozzles.

The AI explained, "That's *Mycenae*, a midsized planetary ship without an ecological cycling system. After leaving the Solar System, a passenger would not last five years, even if all the ship's supplies were used to sustain only them."

The AI didn't know that *Mycenae* would not be able to leave the Solar System. Like all the other escaping ships, it would continue to exist for no more than three hours in three-dimensional space.

Halo flew out of the Pluto-Charon canyon and left the two dark worlds for open space. They saw the entirety of the two-dimensionalized Sun and Jupiter, whose flattening process was almost over. Now, except for Uranus, the vast majority of the Solar System had fallen into the plane.

"Oh, heavens! Starry sky!" AA cried out.

Cheng Xin knew that she was referring to Van Gogh's painting. True, the universe really did look like the painting. The painting in her memory was almost a perfect copy of the two-dimensional Solar System before her eyes. Giant planets filled space, the areas of the planets seeming to exceed even the gaps between them. But the immensity of the planets did not give them any sense of substantiality. Rather, they looked like whirlpools in space-time. In the universe, every part of space flowed, churned, trembled between madness and horror like fiery flames that emitted only frost. The Sun and the planets and all substance and existence seemed to be only hallucinations produced by the turbulence of space-time.

Cheng Xin now recalled the strange feeling she had experienced each time she had looked at Van Gogh's painting. Everything else in the painting—the trees that seemed to be on fire, and the village and mountains at night—showed perspective and depth, but the starry sky above had no three-dimensionality at all, like a painting hanging in space.

Because the starry night was two-dimensional.

How could Van Gogh have painted such a thing in 1889? Did he, having suffered a second breakdown, truly leap across five centuries and see the sight before them using only his spirit and delirious consciousness? Or, maybe it was the opposite: He had seen the future, and the sight of this Last Judgment had caused his breakdown and eventual suicide.

"Children, is everything all right? What are you going to do next?" Luo Ji appeared in a pop-up window. He had taken off his space suit, and his white hair and beard floated in the low gravity like in water. Behind him was the tunnel that had been intended to last a hundred million years.

"Hello! We're going to toss the artifacts into space," AA said. "But we want to keep *Starry Night*."

"I think you should hold on to them all. Don't toss any. Take them and leave."

Cheng Xin and AA looked at each other. "Go where?" AA asked.

"Anywhere you like. You can go to any place in the Milky Way. In your lifetimes, you could probably get to the Andromeda Galaxy. *Halo* is capable of lightspeed flight. It is equipped with the world's only curvature propulsion drive."

Utter shock. AA and Cheng Xin couldn't speak.

"I was a part of the group of scientists who worked on curvature propulsion in secret," said Luo Ji. "After Wade died, those who had worked at Halo City didn't give up. After those who had been imprisoned were released, they built another secret research base, and your Halo Group was revived and developed enough to keep it going. Do you know where the base was? Mercury, another place in the Solar System where few set foot. Four centuries ago, another Wallfacer, Manuel Rey Diaz, used giant hydrogen bombs to blast a crater there. The base was built in that crater, and its construction took over thirty years. The whole base was covered with a dome. They claimed that it was a research institute to study solar activity."

A bright shaft of light pierced the porthole. AA and Cheng Xin ignored it, but the ship's AI explained that Uranus had also undergone "state change," meaning that it had also collapsed into two dimensions. By now, nothing stood between them and Pluto.

"Thirty-five years after Wade's death, the research into curvature propulsion picked up at the Mercury base. They continued from the point where they were able to move a two-millimeter segment of your hair two centimeters. The research continued for half a century—though they were interrupted a few times for various reasons—and they gradually moved from theoretical research to technological development. During the last stages of the development process, they had to perform experiments on large-scale curvature propulsion. This was a problem for the Mercury base because the base's resources were limited, and an experiment would produce massive trails, which would expose the Mercury base's true goals. In reality, based on the comings and goings at the base for more than fifty years, it was inconceivable that the Federation Government had no clue what the Mercury base was really up to, but due to the small scale of the experiments and the fact that all the research was done under cover of other projects, the government had tolerated the base's activities. Large-scale experiments, however, required the government's cooperation. We sought it out, and the collaboration went very well."

"Did they repeal the laws proscribing lightspeed ships?" Cheng Xin asked.

"No, not at all. The government collaborated with us because . . ." Luo Ji tapped his cane against the ground and hesitated. "Let's not get into that for now. A few years ago, we completed three curvature engines and conducted three unmanned tests. Engine Number One entered lightspeed about one hundred and fifty astronomical units from the Sun, and returned here after flying at lightspeed for a while. For the engine itself, the experiment lasted only ten minutes or so, but for us, it was three years before the engine returned. The second test involved Engines Number Two and Number Three simultaneously. Right now, both of them are outside the Oort Cloud, and should return to the Solar System in six years.

"Engine Number One, which has already been tested, is installed in *Halo*."

"But how could they have sent Cheng Xin and I alone?" AA shouted. "There should at least be two men with us."

Luo Ji shook his head. "There was no time. The collaboration between the Halo Group and the Federation Government occurred in secret. Very few people knew of the existence of the curvature engines, and even fewer knew where the only engine left in the Solar System was installed. And it was too dangerous. Who knows what people are capable of when the end is nigh? Everyone would fight over *Halo*, and maybe nothing would be left afterward. And so we had to get *Halo* away from the Bunker World before releasing news of the dark forest strike to the public. There really wasn't any time left. Cao Bin sent *Halo* to Pluto because he wanted you to take me with you. He should have just had *Halo* enter lightspeed at Jupiter."

"Why didn't you come with us?" AA shouted.

"I've lived long enough. Even if I get onto the ship, I won't live much longer. I'd rather stay here as a grave keeper."

"We can come back for you!" Cheng Xin said.

"Don't you dare! There's no time!"

The three-dimensional space they were in accelerated toward the two-dimensional plane. The two-dimensional Sun, which had now completely extinguished and appeared as a vast, dark red, dead sea, took up most of the view from *Halo*. Cheng Xin and AA noticed that the plane was not completely flat, but undulating! A long wave slowly rolled across the plane. It was a similar wave in three-dimensional space that had allowed *Blue Space* and *Gravity* to find warp points to enter four-dimensional space. Even in places where there were no two-dimensional objects in the plane, the rippling wave was apparent. The waves were a visualization of two-dimensional space in three dimensions that occurred only when the two-dimensional space was large enough.

On *Halo* itself, the space-time distortion produced by the accelerated fall had started to become apparent as space was stretched in the direction of the fall. Cheng Xin noticed that the circular portholes now appeared as ovals, and the slender AA now looked short and squat. But Cheng Xin and AA felt no discomfort, and the ship's systems were operating normally.

"Return to Pluto!" Cheng Xin ordered the AI. Then she turned to Luo Ji's window. "We're going to come back. There's time—Uranus is still being flattened."

The AI replied stiffly, "Among all authorized users in communication range, Luo Ji has the highest authorization level. Only he can order *Halo* to return to Pluto."

Luo Ji smiled before the tunnel. "If I wanted to go, I would have gotten on the ship with you earlier. I'm too old for voyages far from home. Do not worry about me, children. Like I said, I don't think I've missed anything. Prepare for curvature propulsion!"

Luo Ji's last words were directed at the ship's AI.

"Course parameters?" asked the AI.

"Continue along the current heading. I don't know where you want to go, and I don't think you know, either. If you do think of a destination, just point it out on the star map. The ship is capable of automatic navigation to most stars within fifty thousand light-years."

"Affirmative," said the AI. "Initiating curvature propulsion in thirty seconds."

"Do we need to be immersed in deep-sea fluid?" AA asked—though rationally, she knew that under conventional propulsion, such acceleration would compress her into a pancake no matter what kind of fluid she was immersed in.

"You don't need any kind of preparation. This propulsion method relies on manipulating space, so there's no hypergravity. Curvature propulsion drive online. System is operating within normal parameters. Local space curvature: twenty-three point eight. Forward curvature ratio: three point forty-one to one. *Halo* will enter lightspeed in sixty-four minutes, eighteen seconds."

For Cheng Xin and AA, the AI's announcement was like a Full Stop order, because everything suddenly quieted down. They understood that the silence was due to the nuclear fusion engine being shut off, but the humming produced by the fusion reactor and the thrusters disappeared without being replaced by any other noise. It was hard to believe that some other engine had been started.

But signs of curvature propulsion did appear. The distortion in space gradually disappeared: The portholes returned to being circles, and AA looked slender again. Looking through the portholes, they could still see other escaping ships passing by *Halo*, but they now passed far more slowly.

The ship's AI began to play some of the messages passing between the escaping ships—perhaps because the messages concerned *Halo*.

"Look at that ship! How is it able to accelerate so fast?" a woman screamed.

"Oh! The people inside must have been crushed into meat pies," a man said.

Another man spoke up. "You idiots. The ship itself would be crushed under that kind of acceleration. But look at it: It's perfectly fine. That's not a fusion drive, but something entirely different."

"Curvature propulsion? A lightspeed ship? That's a lightspeed ship!"

"The rumors were true, then. They were building secret lightspeed ships so that they could escape. . . ."

"Aaahhhhh . . ."

"Hey, any ships ahead? Stop that ship! Crash into it. No one should live if we all have to die!"

"They can reach escape velocity! They can run away and live! Ahhhh! I want the lightspeed ship! Stop them; stop them and kill everyone inside!"

Another scream—this one from AA inside the ship. "How can there be two Plutos?"

Cheng Xin turned to the information window AA was looking at. The window showed a view of Pluto taken by the ship's monitoring system. Although Pluto was some distance away, it was clear that both Pluto and Charon had been duplicated, and the twins were lined up side by side. Cheng Xin noticed that some of the flattened objects in the two-dimensional space had also been duplicated. The effect was like selecting a portion of a picture using image-processing software, cloning it, and then moving the clone a bit to the side.

"That's due to the fact that light slows down inside the trail left by *Halo*," Luo Ji said. His image was growing distorted, but his voice still came through clearly. "Pluto is still moving. One of the Plutos you are seeing is the result of slow light. Once Pluto has moved outside of *Halo*'s trail, light traveling at standard speed provides you with a second image. That's why you're seeing double."

"The light slows down?" Cheng Xin sensed a great secret was being revealed.

Luo Ji continued, "I understand that you figured out curvature propulsion from a small boat propelled by soap. Let me ask you: After the ship reached the other side of the bathtub, did you pull it back and try again?"

They hadn't. Due to the fear of sophons, Cheng Xin had tossed the paper boat aside. But it was easy to figure out what would have happened.

"The ship would not move, or at least it would only move slowly," Cheng Xin said. "After the first trip, the surface tension of the water in the tub had already been reduced."

"That's right. It's the same principle with lightspeed ships. The very structure of space itself is changed by the trail of a curvature-propelled ship. If a second curvature-propelled ship were placed inside the trail of the first, it would hardly move. Within the trails of lightspeed ships, one must use a more powerful curvature propulsion drive. It would still be possible to use curvature propulsion to achieve the highest speed possible within such a space, but the maximum velocity is much lower than the maximum velocity of the first ship. In other words, the speed of light through vacuum is lowered within the trail of lightspeed ships."

"How much lower?"

"Theoretically, it could be reduced to zero, but that's not achievable in reality. But if you adjust the curvature ratio of *Halo*'s engine to the maximum, you can lower the speed of light in its trail down to exactly what we've been looking for: sixteen point seven kilometers per second."

"Then you'd have . . ." AA said, staring at Luo Ji.

The black domain, Cheng Xin thought.

"The black domain," Luo Ji said. "Of course, a single ship is insufficient to produce a black domain containing an entire star and its planetary system. We calculated that it would take more than a thousand curvature propulsion ships to accomplish such a thing. If all these ships started near the Sun and spread out in every direction at lightspeed, the trails they produced would expand and connect to each other, forming a sphere that contained the entire Solar System. The speed of light within this sphere would be sixteen point seven kilometers per second—a reduced-lightspeed black hole, or a black domain."

"So the black domain can be a product of lightspeed ships. . . ."

In the cosmos, the trail of a curvature propulsion drive could be a sign of danger, as well as a safety announcement. A trail far away from a world was the former; a trail that shrouded a world the latter. It was like a noose, indicating danger and aggression when held in the hand, but safety when wrapped around the holder's own neck.

"Correct, but we found out about it too late. While studying curvature propulsion, the experimenters plowed ahead of the theoreticians. You should know that was Wade's style. Many experimental discoveries could not be explained by theory, but without a theoretical framework, some phenomena were simply ignored. During the earliest years of research—when their biggest achievement was moving your hair—the trails produced by curvature propulsion were thin and small, and hardly anyone paid any attention, even though there were plenty of signs of something strange going on: For instance, after the trail expanded, the low speed of light caused quantum integrated circuits in nearby computers to malfunction, but no one sought to investigate. Later, after the experiments grew in scale, people finally discovered the secret of lightspeed trails. It was because of this discovery that the Federation Government agreed to collaborate with us. They did, in fact, pour all the resources they could command into the development of lightspeed spaceships, but there just wasn't enough time." Luo Ji shook his head and sighed.

Cheng Xin said what he couldn't bring himself to say. "There were thirty-five years between the Halo City Incident and the completion of the Mercury base. Thirty-five precious years were lost."

Luo Ji nodded. Cheng Xin thought the way he looked at her was no longer kind, but rather resembled the fires of the Last Judgment. His gaze seemed to say, *Child, look at what you've done.*

Cheng Xin now understood that of the three paths of survival presented to humanity—the Bunker Project, the Black Domain Plan, and lightspeed ships—only lightspeed ships were the right choice.

Yun Tianming had pointed this out, but she had blocked it.

If she hadn't stopped Wade, Halo City might have achieved independence. Even if the independence was short-lived, they could have discovered the effects of lightspeed trails and changed the government's attitude toward lightspeed ships. Humanity might have had time to construct a thousand lightspeed ships and build the black domain, to avoid this dimensional strike.

Humanity could have divided into two parts: those who wanted to fly to the stars, and those who wanted to stay within the black domain and live in tranquility. Each would have gotten what they wanted.

In the end, she had committed another grave error.

Twice, she had been placed in a position of authority second only to God, and both times she had pushed the world into the abyss in the name of love. This time, no one could fix her mistake for her.

She began to hate someone: Wade. She hated that he had kept his promise. Why? Out of his masculine pride, or for her? Cheng Xin understood that Wade did not know the effects of curvature propulsion trails. His goal in researching lightspeed ships was stated eloquently by that anonymous Halo City soldier: a fight for freedom, for a chance to live as free men in the cosmos, for the billions and billions of new worlds out there. She believed that if he had known that lightspeed spaceflight was the only path to life for humanity, he would not have kept his promise.

She could not shirk her responsibility. It didn't matter whether she really was second only to God—if she was in that position, she had to carry out her duty.

Not long ago on Pluto, Cheng Xin had experienced one of the most relaxed moments of her life. Indeed, it was easy to face the end of the world: All responsibilities were gone, as were all worries and anxieties. Life was as simple and pure as the moment when one first emerged from the mother's womb. Cheng Xin just had to wait in peace for her poetic, artistic end, for her moment to join the giant painting of the Solar System.

But now, everything had been turned upside down. Early cosmology had presented a paradox: If the universe was infinite, then every spot in the universe would feel the cumulative effects of the infinite gravity exerted by an infinity of celestial bodies. Cheng Xin really did feel an infinite gravity now. The power came from every corner of the universe, ruthlessly tearing at her soul. The horror of her last moments as the Swordholder 127 years ago resurfaced as four billion years of history pressed down on her and suffocated her. The sky was full of eyes staring at her: the eyes of dinosaurs, trilobites, ants, birds, butterflies, bacteria . . . just the number of men and women who had lived on the Earth possessed a hundred billion pairs of eyes.

Cheng Xin saw AA's eyes, and understood the words in her gaze: *You've finally experienced something worse than death.*

Cheng Xin knew that she had no choice but to live on. She and AA were the last two survivors of human civilization. Her death would mean the death of half of all that was left of humanity. Living on was the appropriate punishment for her mistake.

But the course ahead was a blank. In her heart, space was no longer black, but colorless. What was the point of going anywhere?

"Where should we go?" Cheng Xin muttered.

"Go find them," Luo Ji said. His image was even more blurred and now only black and white.

His words illuminated Cheng Xin's dark thoughts like lightning. She and AA looked at each other and immediately understood who "them" meant.

Luo Ji continued, "They're still alive. The Bunker World received a gravitational wave transmission from them five years ago. It was a short message, and didn't explain where they were. *Halo* will periodically hail them with gravitational waves. Maybe you'll find them; maybe they'll find you."

Luo Ji's black-and-white image disappeared as well, but they could still hear his voice. He said one last thing, "Ah, it's time for me to go into the picture. Safe travels, children."

The transmission from Pluto was cut off.

On the monitor, they could see Pluto light up and expand in two dimensions. The part of Pluto containing the museum was the first to touch the plane.

The Doppler effect of *Halo*'s speed was now visible. The light from the stars ahead shifted to bluish, while the light from the stars behind shifted to reddish. The color shift was apparent in the two-dimensional Solar System.

Outside, no other fleeing spaceships could be seen; *Halo* had passed them all. All the fleeing spaceships were now falling onto the two-dimensional space like drops of rain against glass.

Very few transmissions could now be received from the direction of the Solar System. Due to the Doppler effect, the brief bursts of voices sounded strange, like singing.

"We're very close! Are you behind us?" . . . "Don't do this! No!" . . . "There's no pain. I'm telling you, it'll be over in a flash." . . . "You still don't believe me, after all this? Fine, don't believe me." . . . "Yes, sweetie, we'll become very thin." . . . "Come here! We should be together."

Cheng Xin and AA listened. The voices became fewer and fewer, and separated by longer gaps. After thirty minutes, they heard the last voice coming out of the Solar System:

"Ahhhhhhhhh—"

The voice was cut off. The giant painting called the Solar System was complete.

Halo continued to fall toward the plane. The speed it had already achieved was slowing down its fall, but the ship still hadn't achieved escape velocity. By now, *Halo* was the only man-made three-dimensional object in the Solar System, and Cheng Xin and AA were the only people not in the painting. *Halo* was very close to the plane, and from this angle, looking at the two-dimensional Sun was like looking at the sea from shore: the dim, dark red surface stretched into the distance without bounds. The freshly flattened Pluto was now very large, and still expanded at a rate that was visible to the naked eye. Cheng Xin examined the exquisite "tree rings" of Pluto and tried to find traces of the museum, but she couldn't see anything—it was too small. The giant waterfall that was three-dimensional space tumbling into the flat plane seemed inexorable. Cheng Xin began to doubt whether the curvature propulsion engine really was capable of propelling the ship to lightspeed. She hoped for everything to be over.

But then, the ship's AI spoke.

"*Halo* will enter lightspeed in one hundred and eighty seconds. Please select a destination."

"We don't know where to go," said AA.

"You can select a destination after we've entered lightspeed. However, you won't subjectively be spending much time in lightspeed, and it's easy to overshoot your destination. It's best if you select it now."

"We don't know where to find them," Cheng Xin said. Their existence gave the future some light, but she still felt lost.

AA clutched Cheng Xin's hands. "Have you forgotten? Other than them, *he* also exists in the universe."

Yes, he still exists. Cheng Xin was overwhelmed by heartache. She had never yearned to see anyone as much as him.

"You have a date," AA said.

"Yes, we have a date," Cheng Xin repeated mechanically. The torrents of emotion left her numb.

"Then let's go to your star."

"Yes, let's go to our star!" Cheng Xin turned to the ship's AI. "Can you find DX3906? That was the assigned number back at the beginning of the Crisis Era."

"Yes. The star is now numbered S74390E2. Please confirm."

A large holographic star map appeared before them. It showed everything within five hundred light-years of the Solar System. One of the stars glowed bright red, and a white arrow pointed at it. Cheng Xin was very familiar with it.

"That's the one. Let's go there."

"Course set and confirmed. *Halo* will enter lightspeed in fifty seconds."

The holographic star map disappeared. In fact, the ship's entire hull disappeared, and Cheng Xin and AA seemed to be floating in space itself. The AI had never employed this display mode before. In front of them was the starry sea that was the Milky Way, which was now pure blue, reminding them of the real sea. Behind them was the two-dimensional Solar System, suffused with a bloody red.

The universe shuddered and transformed. All the stars in front of them shot straight ahead, as though that half of the universe had transformed into a black bowl and all the stars were falling into the bottom. They clustered ahead of the ship and fused into a single glow, like a giant sapphire in which it was not possible to distinguish individual stars. From time to time, individual stars shot out of the sapphire and swept past the pure black space to fall behind the ship, changing color the whole way: from blue to green, then yellow, and turning red once they were behind the ship. Looking back from the ship, the two-dimensional Solar System and the stars fused into a red ball like a campfire at the end of the universe.

Halo flew at the speed of light toward the star that Yun Tianming had given Cheng Xin.

PART VI

Galaxy Era, Year 409
Our Star

Halo shut off the curvature engine and coasted at lightspeed.

During the voyage, AA tried to comfort Cheng Xin, even though she knew this was a hopeless task.

"It's ridiculous for you to blame yourself for the destruction of the Solar System. Who do you think you are? Do you think if you stand on your hands, you've lifted the Earth? Even if you hadn't stopped Wade, the outcome of that war would have been hard to predict.

"Could Halo City really have achieved independence? Even Wade couldn't be certain of that. Could the Federation Government and Fleet really have been scared of a few antimatter bullets? Maybe Halo City could have destroyed a few warships, or even a space city, but ultimately, Halo City would have been exterminated by the Federation Fleet. And in that version of history, there would be no Mercury base, no second chance.

"Even if Halo City had managed to achieve independence, continued to research curvature propulsion, discovered the slowing effects of the trails, and finally collaborated with the Federation Government to build more than a thousand lightspeed ships in time, do you think people would have agreed to build the black domain? Remember how confident people were that the Bunker World would survive a dark forest strike—why would they have agreed to isolate themselves in the black domain?"

AA's words slid across Cheng Xin's thoughts like drops of water across a lily pad, leaving no trace. Cheng Xin's only thought was to find Yun Tianming and tell him everything. In her mind, a journey of 287 light-years would take a long time, but the ship's AI informed her that the trip would only take fifty-two hours in the ship's frame of reference. Everything felt unreal to Cheng Xin, as though she had already died and gone to another world.

Cheng Xin spent a long time gazing out of the portholes at space. She understood that each time a star leapt out of the blue cluster in front, swept past the ship, and joined the red cluster behind the ship, it meant that *Halo* had passed it. She counted the stars and watched as they turned from blue to red—the sight was hypnotic. Eventually, she fell asleep.

By the time Cheng Xin awakened, *Halo* was close to its destination. It turned 180 degrees and activated the curvature engine for deceleration—in fact, the ship was pushing against its own trail. As the ship decelerated, the blue and red clusters began to spread out like two clusters of exploding fireworks, and soon evolved into a sea of stars distributed evenly around the ship. The slowing down of the ship also gradually erased the red and blue shifts. Cheng Xin and AA saw that the Milky Way ahead of them still looked about the same, but behind them, none of the stars looked familiar. The Solar System was long gone.

"We're now two hundred eighty-six point five light-years from the Solar System," said the ship's AI.

"So two hundred eighty-six years has already passed back there?" AA asked. She looked as if she had just awakened from a dream.

"Yes, if you are using their frame of reference."

Cheng Xin sighed. For the Solar System in its current condition, was there a difference between 286 years and 2.86 million years? But she thought of something.

"When did the collapse into two dimensions stop?"

The question made AA speechless, as well. Right: When—if ever—did it stop? Was there an instruction within that small, packaged two-dimensional foil that would eventually stop it? Cheng Xin and AA had no theoretical understanding of how three-dimensional space collapsed into two dimensions, but they instinctively thought the idea of an instruction embedded into two-dimensional space to halt its infinite expansion was too magical, the kind of magic that seemed impossible.

Would the collapse never stop?

It was best to not think about it too much.

The star called DX3906 was about the Sun's size. As *Halo* began decelerating, it still looked like an ordinary star, but by the time the curvature engine shut off, the star appeared as a disk whose light seemed redder than the Sun's.

Halo engaged the fusion reactor, and the silence on the ship was broken. The humming of the engine filled the ship, and every surface vibrated slightly.

The ship's AI analyzed the data obtained by the monitoring system and confirmed the basic facts about this solar system: DX3906 had two planets, both of them solid. The one farther from the star was about the size of Mars, but it had no atmosphere and appeared gray in color—so Cheng Xin and AA decided to call it Planet Gray. The other planet, closer to the star, was about the size of the Earth, and its surface resembled the Earth's: an atmosphere containing oxygen and many signs of life, but without evidence of agriculture or industry. Since it was blue, like the Earth, they decided to call it Planet Blue.

AA was very happy that her research had been confirmed. More than four hundred years ago, she had discovered the star's planetary system. Before then, people had thought it was a bare star without any planets. Through that work, AA had gotten to know Cheng Xin. Without that coincidence, her life would have turned out completely differently. Fate was such an odd thing: Four centuries ago, when she had gazed at this distant world through the telescope, she could never have imagined that she'd come here one day.

"Were you able to see these two planets back then?" Cheng Xin asked.

"No. They were impossible to see in the visible light range. Maybe those telescopes from the Solar System advance warning system could have seen them, but all I could do was deduce their existence through the data obtained via the solar gravitational lens. . . . I did theorize about the appearance of these two planets, and it looks like I was basically right."

Halo had taken only fifty-two hours (by the ship's frame of reference) to traverse the 286 light-years between the Solar System and the planetary system around DX3906, but it took eight full days to cross the sixty AU between the rim of the planetary system and Planet Blue at sub-light speeds. As *Halo* approached Planet Blue, Cheng Xin and AA discovered that its resemblance to the Earth was only superficial. The blue hue of this planet wasn't the result of an ocean, but the color of the vegetation covering the continents. Planet Blue's oceans were light yellow and took up only about a fifth of the planet's surface. Planet Blue was a cold world; about a third of its continental surface was covered by blue vegetation, with the rest shrouded in snow. Most of the ocean was frozen, and only small patches near the equator were in liquid form.

Halo entered orbit around Planet Blue and began its descent. But the ship's AI announced a new discovery. "An intelligent radio signal has been detected from the surface. It's a landing beacon using communication formats dating from the start of the Crisis Era. Would you like me to follow its instructions?"

Cheng Xin and AA looked at each other excitedly. "Yes!" Cheng Xin said. "Follow its instructions to land."

"Hypergravity will approach 4G. Please enter into secured landing positions. Landing sequence will be initiated once you're secure."

"Do you think it's him?" AA asked.

Cheng Xin shook her head. In her life, moments of happiness were only gaps between mass catastrophes. She was now afraid of happiness.

Cheng Xin and AA sat in hypergravity seats, and the seats closed around them like giant palms squeezing them tight. *Halo* decelerated and descended, entering Planet Blue's atmosphere after a series of powerful jolts. They could see the blue-and-white continents swinging into view in the images captured by the ship's monitoring system.

Twenty minutes later, *Halo* landed near the equator. The ship's AI suggested that Cheng Xin and AA wait ten minutes before getting out of their seats, to give their bodies a chance to adjust to Planet Blue's gravity, which was similar to the Earth's. Out of the porthole and on the monitoring system terminals, they could see that the yacht had landed in the middle of a blue grassland. Not too far away, they could see rolling mountains covered by snow—the landing site was near the foot of the mountain range. The sky was a light yellow, like the ocean when viewed from space. A light red sun shone in the sky. It was noon on Planet Blue, but the sky and the sun's colors made it resemble dusk on the Earth.

Cheng Xin and AA didn't examine the environment around them too carefully. Their attention was taken up by another small vehicle parked near *Halo*. It was a tiny craft, about four to five meters tall, with a dark gray surface. The profile was streamlined, but the tail fins were tiny. It didn't seem to be an aircraft, but rather a ground-to-space shuttle.

A man stood next to the shuttle, dressed in a white jacket and dark-colored pants. The turbulence of *Halo*'s landing disturbed his hair.

"Is that him?" AA asked.

Cheng Xin shook her head. She knew right away that this wasn't Yun Tianming.

The man waded through the blue sea of grass toward *Halo*. He moved slowly, and his posture and movements showed some exhaustion. He didn't show any signs of surprise or excitement, as if the appearance of *Halo* was a perfectly normal occurrence. He stopped a few tens of meters away from the yacht and waited patiently in the grass.

"He's good-looking," said AA.

The man looked to be in his forties. He was East Asian in appearance, and he was indeed more handsome than Yun Tianming, with a broad forehead and wise but gentle eyes. His gaze made you believe he was always thinking, as if nothing in the universe, including *Halo*, could surprise him, but only cause him to think more. He lifted his hands and moved them around his head, indicating a helmet. Then he shook his head and waved one hand, indicating that they didn't need space suits out there.

The ship's AI agreed. "Atmospheric composition: thirty-five percent oxygen, sixty-three percent nitrogen, two percent carbon dioxide, with trace amounts of inert gasses. Breathable. But the atmospheric pressure is only point five three of Earth standard. Do not engage in strenuous exercise."

"What is that biological entity standing next to the ship?" asked AA.

"Standard human being," the AI replied.

Cheng Xin and AA exited the ship. They hadn't adjusted to the gravity yet, and stumbled a bit as they walked. Outside, they breathed easily, not feeling the thinness of the air. A chill breeze blew at them and brought the fragrance of grass, refreshing them. The wide-open view showed the blue-and-white mountains and earth, the light yellow sky and red sun. The whole thing resembled a false-color photograph of the Earth. Other than the strange colors, everything looked familiar. Even the blades of grass looked just like the grass on the Earth, except for their blue hue. The man came to the foot of the stairs.

"Wait a minute. The stairs are too steep. I'll help you down." He climbed up the stairs easily and helped Cheng Xin down. "You should have rested longer before coming out. There's no urgency." Cheng Xin could hear an obvious Deterrence Era accent.

His hand felt warm and strong to Cheng Xin, and his broad body shielded her from the chill wind. She had the impulse to jump into this man's arms, the first man she had met after traveling more than two hundred light-years from the Solar System.

"Did you come from the Solar System?" the man asked.

"Yes." She leaned against the man and descended the stairs. She felt her trust for him grow, and put more of her weight on him.

"There's no more Solar System," AA said as she sat down at the top of the stairs.

"I know. Did anyone else escape?"

Cheng Xin was now on the ground. She sank her feet into the soft grass and sat down on the bottom step. "Probably not."

"Oh . . ." The man nodded and climbed up again to help AA. "My name is Guan Yifan. I've been waiting for you here."

"How did you know we would come?" AA asked, allowing Yifan to hold her hand.

"We received your gravitational wave transmission."

"You're from *Blue Space*?"

"Ha! If you'd asked those who had just left that question, they'd think you very strange. *Blue Space* and *Gravity* are ancient history from more than four centuries ago. But I really am an ancient. I was a civilian astronomer aboard *Gravity*. I've been hibernating for four centuries, and only awakened five years ago."

"Where are *Blue Space* and *Gravity* now?" Cheng Xin struggled to stand, pulling herself up by the railing of the stairs. Yifan continued down with AA.

"In museums."

"Where are the museums?" AA asked. She put her arm around Yifan's shoulder so that Yifan was practically carrying her down.

"On World I and World IV."

"How many worlds are there?"

"Four. And two more are being opened up for settlement."

"Where are all these worlds?"

Guan Yifan gently deposited AA on the ground and laughed. "A word of advice: In the future, no matter who you meet—human or otherwise—don't ask for the location of their worlds. That's a basic bit of manners in the cosmos— like how it's impolite to ask a lady's age. . . . Nonetheless, let me ask you, how old are you now?"

"We're as old as we look," AA said, and sat down on the grass. "She's seven hundred and I'm five hundred."

"Dr. Cheng looks about the same as she did four centuries ago."

"You know her?" AA looked up at Guan Yifan.

"I had seen pictures in transmissions from Earth. Four centuries ago."

"How many people are on this planet?" Cheng Xin asked.

"Just the three of us."

"That must mean that your worlds are all better than this one," AA said.

"You mean the natural environment? Not at all. In some places, the air is barely breathable, even after a century of terraforming. This is one of the best planets we've seen for settlement. Although we welcome you here, Dr. Cheng Xin, we do not recognize your claim of title."

"I'd given that up a long time ago," Cheng Xin said. "So why haven't people settled here?"

"It's too dangerous. Outsiders come here often."

"Outsiders? Extraterrestrials?" AA asked.

"Yes. This is close to the center of the Orion Arm. Two busy shipping lanes flow through here."

"Then what are you doing here? Just waiting for us?"

"No. I came with an exploratory expedition. They've already left, but I stayed to wait for you."

About a dozen hours later, the three welcomed night on Planet Blue. There was no moon, but compared to the Earth, the stars here were far brighter. The Milky Way was like a sea of silver fire that cast their shadows on the ground. This place wasn't much closer to the center of the galaxy than the Solar System. However, the space between here and the Sun was filled with interstellar dust, making the Milky Way appear much dimmer from the Solar System.

In the bright starlight, they could see the grass around them moving. At first, Cheng Xin and AA thought it was an illusion produced by the wind, but then they realized that the grass underfoot was writhing as well, and making a rustling noise. Yifan told them that the blue grass really did move. The roots of the grass were also feet, and as the seasons changed, the grass migrated across the latitudes, mainly at night. As soon as AA heard that, she tossed away the stalks of grass she was playing with in her hands. Yifan explained that the blades of grass really were plants, and relied on photosynthesis, possessing only a basic sense of touch. The other plants in this world were also capable of moving. He pointed to the mountains and they saw the forests moving in the starlight. The trees moved far faster than the grass, and resembled armies marching at night.

Yifan pointed at a spot in the sky where the stars were slightly less dense. "A few days ago we could see the Sun in that direction, much more clearly than you could see this star from the Earth. Of course, what we saw was the Sun of two hundred eighty-seven years ago. The Sun went out on the day the expedition left me here."

"The Sun is no longer emitting light, but its area is huge. Perhaps you can still see it through telescopes," AA said.

"No, you won't be able to see anything." Yifan shook his head and pointed at that patch of sky again. "Even if you go back there now, you wouldn't be able to see anything. That part of space is empty. The two-dimensional Sun and planets you saw were actually just the result of the release of energy when three-dimensional material collapsed into two dimensions. What you saw wasn't two-dimensional material, only the refraction of electromagnetic radiation at the interface between two-dimensional and three-dimensional space. After the energy was released, nothing would be visible. The two-dimensional Solar Space has no contact with three-dimensional space."

"How can that be?" Cheng Xin asked. "It's possible to see the three-dimensional world from four-dimensional space."

"True. I personally got to see three-dimensional space from four-dimensional space, but it's not possible to see the two-dimensional world from three dimensions. This is because three-dimensional space has thickness, meaning that there is a dimension that could stop and scatter the light from four-dimensional space, making it visible from four dimensions. But two-dimensional space has no thickness, so light from three-dimensional space passes through it without hindrance. The two-dimensional world is completely transparent and cannot be seen."

"There's no way at all?" AA asked.

"No. In theory, nothing allows it."

Cheng Xin and AA were silent for a while. The Solar System had disappeared completely. The only hope they had held out for the mother world was gone. But Guan Yifan did bring them a bit of comfort.

"There's only one way to detect the presence of the two-dimensional Solar System from three-dimensional space: gravity. The gravity of the Solar System still has an effect, so, in that empty space ought to be detectable as an invisible source of gravity."

Cheng Xin and AA looked at each other thoughtfully.

"Sounds like dark matter, doesn't it?" Yifan laughed. Then he changed the subject. "Why don't we talk about the date you came for?"

"You know Yun Tianming?" AA asked.

"No."

"What about the Trisolaran Fleet?" Cheng Xin asked.

"We don't know much. The First and Second Trisolaran Fleets never joined together. More than sixty years ago, there was a large-scale space battle near Taurus. It was brutal, and the resulting wreckage formed a new interstellar dust cloud. We know that one of the sides in the battle was the Second Trisolaran Fleet, but we don't know who they were fighting against. We also don't know how the battle ended."

"What happened to the First Trisolaran Fleet?" Cheng Xin asked. Her eyes flickered in the starlight.

"We haven't received any information about them. . . . In any event, you shouldn't stay here too long. This is not a safe place. Why don't you come with me to our world? The terraforming there is over, and life is getting better."

"I agree!" AA said. Then she held Cheng Xin by the arm. "Let's go with him. Even if you wait here for the rest of your life, you most likely won't hear anything. Life shouldn't be a lifetime of waiting."

Cheng Xin nodded silently. She knew that she was chasing a dream.

They decided to wait one more day on Planet Blue before departing.

Guan Yifan had a small spaceship waiting in synchronous orbit. The ship was tiny and didn't have a name, only a number. But Yifan called it *Hunter*, and explained that the name was to honor the memory of a friend who'd lived on *Gravity* more than four hundred years ago. *Hunter* was not equipped with an ecological cycling system, and for long voyages passengers had to enter hibernation. Although *Hunter* was only a few percent of *Halo*'s volume, it was also a lightspeed ship equipped with a curvature engine. They decided to have Yifan ride on *Halo* as well and control *Hunter* as a drone. Cheng Xin and AA didn't ask about the course they would take, and Yifan even refused to answer questions about the duration of the anticipated voyage. He was extremely cautious when it came to information about the location of human worlds.

For the day, the three took short hikes in the vicinity of *Halo*. This was a day of many firsts for Cheng Xin, AA, and all the Solar System humans who had disappeared along with the home world: the first trip to an extrasolar planetary system; the first steps on the surface of an exoplanet; the first voyage to a world with life outside the Solar System.

Compared with the Earth, the ecology of Planet Blue was relatively simple. Other than the mobile blue vegetation, there was not much life to be found, except for a few species of fish in the ocean. There were no complex animals on land, only simple insects. The world resembled a simplified Earth. It was possible for Earth plants to survive here, so humans could live here even without advanced technology.

Guan Yifan was filled with admiration for *Halo*'s design. He said that for Galactic humans, people who had made their home in the Milky Way, there was one quality about Solar System humans that they did not inherit and could not learn: enjoyment of life. He spent much time in the lovely courtyards, and indulged himself with holographic projections of grand sights from ancient Earth. He still looked as thoughtful as ever, but his eyes were moist.

During this time, 艾 AA cast Yifan frequent amorous glances. The relationship between them gradually changed as the day went on. AA thought up all kinds of excuses to be close to Yifan, and listened intently while he spoke, nodding from time to time and smiling. She had never behaved like this in front of any other man. During the centuries Cheng Xin had known her, AA had countless lovers, often dating two or more at the same time, but Cheng Xin knew that AA had never really been in love. However, she was clearly smitten with this cosmologist from the Deterrence Era. Cheng Xin was happy to see this. AA deserved a happy new life in this new world.

As for Cheng Xin, she knew that she was spiritually dead. The only hope that had sustained her was finding Tianming, and now this hope seemed like an impossible dream. Truthfully, she had always known that a date made for four centuries later and 286 light-years away was an impossible dream. She would continue to keep her body alive, but it was just a matter of fulfilling her duty of preventing the death of half of the population to survive the destruction of Earth civilization.

Night fell again. They decided to sleep aboard *Halo* and leave in the morning.

At midnight, Guan Yifan was awakened by his wrist communicator. It was a call from *Hunter* in synchronous orbit. *Hunter* passed on the information gathered by the three small monitoring satellites left by the expedition—two of which orbited around Planet Blue and the last around Planet Gray. The alert had come from the one around Planet Gray.

Thirty-five minutes ago, five unidentified spacecraft had landed on Planet Gray. Twelve minutes later, the spacecraft had lifted off and disappeared without even entering planetary orbit. There was strong interference with the satellite, and the images it transmitted were blurry.

Yifan's expedition was responsible for seeking out and studying traces left in this planetary system by other civilizations. After receiving the alert from the satellite, he immediately decided to take the shuttle up to *Hunter* to investigate. Cheng Xin insisted on coming with him. Yifan initially refused, but agreed after AA spoke to him.

"Let her come with you. She wants to know whether this has anything to do with Yun Tianming."

Before departure, Yifan reminded AA to not communicate with *Hunter* unless it was an emergency. No one knew what other extraterrestrial monitoring equipment might be lurking in this system, and any communication could expose them to danger.

In this lonely world of only three people, even a brief separation was an occasion for anxiety. AA hugged Cheng Xin and Guan Yifan and wished them a safe journey. Before stepping onto the shuttle, Cheng Xin looked back and saw AA waving at them, lit by the watery starlight. Blue grass surged around her, and the cold wind lifted her short hair and made ripples in the grass.

The shuttle took off. In the view from the monitoring system, Cheng Xin saw the grass lit up by the flame from the thruster, and the blue grass scattering in every direction. As the shuttle rose up, the bright patch on the ground quickly dimmed, and soon, the ground sank back into starlight.

An hour later, the shuttle docked with *Hunter* in synchronous orbit. *Hunter* was tetrahedral in shape, like a tiny pyramid. The inside was very cramped and bare, and most of the space was taken up by the hibernation chamber, which had a maximum capacity for four.

Like *Halo*, *Hunter* was equipped with both a curvature engine and a fusion engine. When traveling between planets within the same system, only the fusion engine was used, because the curvature engine would have caused the ship to overshoot the target with no time for deceleration. *Hunter* left orbit and headed for Planet Gray, which appeared as a small spot of light. Out of consideration for Cheng Xin, Guan Yifan initially limited the acceleration to 1.5G, but Cheng Xin told him not to worry about her and just make the trip faster. He increased the acceleration, the blue flame emitted by the nozzles doubled in length, and the hypergravity increased to 3G. At this point, all they could do was to sit in the embrace of the acceleration seats. They were not able to move much, so Yifan switched the ship to surround-holographic display mode, and the ship's hull disappeared. Suspended in space, they watched Planet Blue recede. Cheng Xin imagined the 3G gravity as coming from Planet Blue so that space separated into up and down, and they were flying up toward the galaxy.

It was possible to speak under 3G without too much trouble, so they began to converse. Cheng Xin asked Yifan why he had hibernated for so long. He told her that he had no duties during the long voyage searching for habitable worlds. After the two ships discovered the habitable World I, much of life consisted of opening up the world for settlement and constructing the basics. The first settlement resembled a small town from agrarian times, and the rough conditions did not permit any kind of scientific research. The new world's government passed a resolution to let all scientists enter or remain in hibernation, to be awakened only when conditions permitted basic research. He was the only basic scientist aboard *Gravity*, although *Blue Space* had seven more. He was the last to be awakened of all the hibernators. Two centuries had passed since the day the two ships arrived at World I.

Cheng Xin was mesmerized by Yifan's account of the new human worlds. But she noticed that while he discussed Worlds I, II, and IV, nothing was said about III.

"I've never been there. No one else has, either. Well, it's more accurate to say that anyone who goes there cannot return. That world is sealed inside a light tomb."

"A light tomb?"

"It's a reduced-lightspeed black hole produced by the trails of lightspeed ships. Something happened on World III that caused them to think that their coordinates had been exposed. They had no choice but to turn their world into such a black hole."

"We call such a place a black domain."

"Ah, good name. As a matter of fact, the people of World III initially called it a light curtain, but outsiders referred to it as a light tomb."

"Like a shroud?"[10]

"That's right. Different people see things differently. The inhabitants of World III said it was a happy paradise—though I don't know if they still think that way. After the light tomb was completed, it was impossible for any message from that world to reach the outside. But I think people there are pretty happy. For some people, safety is the sine qua non for happiness."

Cheng Xin asked Yifan when the new world first produced lightspeed ships, and was told it was a century ago. Judging by this, her interpretation of Tianming's secret message had allowed Solar System humans to achieve this stage about two centuries ahead of Galactic humans. Even taking into account the time it took to open up the worlds for settlement, Tianming had accelerated progress by at least a century.

"He's a great man," Yifan said after hearing Cheng Xin's account.

But the civilization of the Solar System hadn't been able to seize this opportunity. Thirty-five precious years had been lost, probably due to her. Her heart no longer felt pain as she thought of this; all she felt was the numbness that indicated a dead heart.

Yifan said, "Lightspeed spaceflight was a tremendous milestone for humankind. It was like another Enlightenment, another Renaissance. Lightspeed flight fundamentally transformed human thinking and changed civilization and culture."

"I can see that. The moment I entered lightspeed, I felt myself change.

[10] *Translator's Note:* This is a wordplay in Chinese. 幕 (*mu*), or "curtain," is a pun for 墓 (*mu*), or "tomb."

I realized that I could, in my lifetime, leap across space-time and reach the edge of the cosmos and the end of the universe. Things that used to seem only philosophical suddenly became concrete and practical."

"Yes. Things like the fate and goal of the universe used to be only ethereal concerns of philosophers, but now every ordinary person must consider them."

"Has anyone in the new world thought of going to the end of the universe?"

"Of course. Five ultimate spaceships have already been launched."

"Ultimate spaceships?"

"Some call them doomsday ships. These lightspeed ships have no destination at all. They turn their curvature engines to maximum and accelerate like crazy, infinitely approaching the speed of light. Their goal is to leap across time using relativity until they reach the heat death of the universe. By their calculations, ten years within their frame of reference would equal fifty billion years in ours. As a matter of fact, you don't even need to plan for it. If some malfunction occurs after a ship has accelerated to lightspeed, preventing the ship from decelerating, then you'd also reach the end of the universe within your lifetime."

"I pity Solar System humans," said Cheng Xin. "Even at the very end, most of them lived lives confined to a tiny portion of space-time, like those old men and women who never left their home villages during the Common Era. The universe remained a mystery to them until the end."

Yifan lifted his head to gaze at Cheng Xin. Under 3G, this was a very strenuous exercise. But he persisted for some time.

"You don't need to pity them. Really, let me tell you: don't. The reality of the universe is not something to envy."

"Why?"

Yifan lifted a hand and pointed at the stars of the galaxy. Then he let the 3G force pull his arm back to this chest.

"Darkness. Only darkness."

"You mean the dark forest state?"

Guan Yifan shook his head, a gesture that appeared to be a struggle in hypergravity. "For us, the dark forest state is all-important, but it's just a detail of the cosmos. If you think of the cosmos as a great battlefield, dark forest strikes are nothing more than snipers shooting at the careless—messengers, mess men, etc. In the grand scheme of the battle, they are nothing. You have not seen what a true interstellar war is like."

"Have you?"

"We've caught a few glimpses. But most things we know are just guesses. . . .

Do you really want to know? The more you possess of this kind of knowledge, the less light remains in your heart."

"My heart is already completely dark. I want to know."

And so, more than six centuries after Luo Ji had fallen through ice into that lake, another dark veil hiding the truth about the universe was lifted before the gaze of one of the only survivors of Earth civilization.

Yifan asked, "Why don't you tell me what the most powerful weapon for a civilization possessing almost infinite technological prowess is? Don't think of this as a technical question. Think philosophy."

Cheng Xin pondered for a while and then struggled to shake her head. "I don't know."

"Your experiences should give you a hint."

What had she experienced? She had seen how a cruel attacker could lower the dimensions of space by one and destroy a solar system. *What are dimensions?*

"The universal laws of physics," Cheng Xin said.

"That's right. The universal laws of physics are the most terrifying weapons, and also the most effective defenses. Whether it's by the Milky Way or the Andromeda Galaxy, at the scale of the local galactic group or the Virgo Supercluster, those warring civilizations possessing godlike technology will not hesitate to use the universal laws of physics as weapons. There are many laws that can be manipulated into weapons, but most commonly, the focus is on spatial dimensions and the speed of light. Typically, lowering spatial dimensions is a technique for attack, and lowering the speed of light is a technique for defense. Thus, the dimensional strike on the Solar System was an advanced attack method. A dimensional strike is a sign of respect. In this universe, respect is not easy to earn. I guess you could consider it an honor for Earth civilization."

"I thought of something I wanted to ask you. When will the collapse of space in the vicinity of the Solar System into two dimensions cease?"

"It will never cease."

Cheng Xin shuddered.

"You are scared? Do you think that in this galaxy, in this universe, only the Solar System is collapsing into two dimensions? Haha . . ."

Guan Yifan's bitter laughter caused Cheng Xin's heart to seize up. She said, "What you're saying makes no sense. At least, it doesn't make sense to lower spatial dimensions as a weapon. In the long run, that's the sort of attack that would kill the attacker as well as the target. Eventually, the side that initiated attack would also see their own space fall into the two-dimensional abyss they created."

Nothing but silence. After a long while, Cheng Xin called out, "Dr. Guan?"

"You're too . . . kind-hearted," Guan Yifan said softly.

"I don't understand—"

"There's a way for the attacker to avoid death. Think about it."

Cheng Xin pondered and then said, "I can't figure it out."

"I know you can't. Because you're too kind. It's very simple. The attacker must first transform themselves into life forms that can survive in a low-dimensional universe. For instance, a four-dimensional species can transform itself into three-dimensional creatures, or a three-dimensional species can transform itself into two-dimensional life. After the entire civilization has entered a lower dimension, they can initiate a dimensional strike against the enemy without concern for the consequences."

Cheng Xin was silent again.

"Are you reminded of anything?" Yifan asked.

Cheng Xin was thinking of more than four hundred years ago, when *Blue Space* and *Gravity* had stumbled into the four-dimensional fragment. Yifan had been a member of the small expedition that conversed with the Ring.

> *Did you build this four-dimensional fragment?*
> *You told me that you came from the sea. Did you build the sea?*
> *Are you saying that for you, or at least for your creators, this four-dimensional space is like the sea for us?*
> *More like a puddle. The sea has gone dry.*
> *Why are so many ships, or tombs, gathered in such a small space?*
> *When the sea is drying, the fish have to gather into a puddle. The puddle is also drying, and all the fish are going to disappear.*
> *Are all the fish here?*
> *The fish responsible for drying the sea are not here.*
> *We're sorry. What you said is really hard to understand.*

The fish that dried out the sea went onto land before they did this. They moved from one dark forest to another dark forest.

"Is it worth it to pay such a price for victory in war?" Cheng Xin asked. She could not imagine how it was possible to live in a world of one fewer dimension.

In two-dimensional space, the visible world consisted of a few line segments of different lengths. Could anyone who was born in three-dimensional space willingly live in a thin sheet of paper with no thickness? Living in three dimensions must be equally confining and unimaginable for those born to a four-dimensional world.

"It's better than death," said Yifan.

While Cheng Xin was still recovering from the shock, Yifan continued, "The speed of light is also frequently used as a weapon. I'm not talking about building light tombs—or, as you call them, black domains. Those are just defensive mechanisms employed by weak worms like us. The gods do not stoop so low. In war, it's possible to make reduced-lightspeed black holes to seal the enemy inside. But more commonly, the technique is used to construct the equivalents of pits and city walls. Some reduced-lightspeed belts are large enough to traverse an entire arm of a galaxy. In places where the stars are dense, many reduced-lightspeed black holes can be connected together into chains that stretch for tens of millions of light-years. That's a Great Wall at the scale of the universe. Even the most powerful fleets, once trapped, would not be able to escape. Those barriers are very difficult to cross."

"What is the ultimate result of all this manipulation of space-time?"

"Dimensional strikes will eventually cause more and more of the universe to become two-dimensional, until one day the entire universe is two-dimensional. Similarly, the construction of fortifications will eventually cause all the reduced-lightspeed areas to connect, until the different lowered lightspeeds all average out: This new average will be the new c for the universe.

"At that time, any scientist from a baby civilization—like us—would think that the speed of light through vacuum is barely a dozen kilometers per second, and this is an ironclad universal constant, just like we now think the same of three hundred thousand kilometers per second.

"Of course, I've only brought up two examples. Other universal laws of physics have been used as weapons as well, though we don't know all of them. It's very possible that every law of physics has been weaponized. It's possible that in some parts of the universe, even . . . Forget it, I don't even believe that."

"What were you going to say?"

"The foundation of mathematics."

Cheng Xin tried to imagine it, but it was simply impossible. "That's . . . madness." Then she asked, "Will the universe turn into a war ruin? Or, maybe it's more accurate to ask: Will the laws of physics turn into war ruins?"

"Maybe they already are. . . . The physicists and cosmologists of the new world are focused on trying to recover the original appearance of the universe before the wars more than ten billion years ago. They've already constructed a fairly clear theoretical model describing the pre-war universe. That was a really lovely time, when the universe itself was a Garden of Eden. Of course, the beauty could only be described mathematically. We can't picture it: Our brains don't have enough dimensions."

Cheng Xin thought back to the conversation with the Ring again.

> *Did you build this four-dimensional fragment?*
> *You told me that you came from the sea. Did you build the sea?*

"You are saying that the universe of the Edenic Age was four-dimensional, and that the speed of light was much higher?"

"No, not at all. The universe of the Edenic Age was ten-dimensional. The speed of light back then wasn't only much higher—rather, it was close to infinity. Light back then was capable of action at a distance, and could go from one end of the cosmos to the other within a Planck time. . . . If you had been to four-dimensional space, you would have some vague hint of how beautiful that ten-dimensional Garden must have been."

"You're saying—"

"I'm not saying anything." Yifan seemed to have awakened from a dream. "We've only seen small hints; everything else is just guessing. You should treat it as a guess, just a dark myth we've made up."

But Cheng Xin continued to follow the course of the discussion taken so far. "—that during the wars after the Edenic Age, one dimension after another was imprisoned from the macroscopic into the microscopic, and the speed of light was reduced again and again. . . ."

"As I said, I'm not saying anything, just guessing." Yifan's voice grew softer. "But no one knows if the truth is even darker than our guesses. . . . We are certain of only one thing: The universe is dying."

The ship stopped accelerating, and weightlessness returned. Before Cheng Xin's eyes, space and the stars appeared more and more hallucinatory, more and more like a nightmare. Only the 3G hypergravity had brought some sense of solidity. She had welcomed the powerful embrace of those arms, an embrace that had provided some protection against the terror and frigidity of the dark myths of the universe. But now the hypergravity was gone, and only nightmare remained. The Milky Way appeared as a patch of ice hiding bloody remains, and DX3906 nearby appeared as a cremator burning over an abyss.

"Can you turn off the holographic display?" Cheng Xin asked.

Yifan turned it off, and Cheng Xin returned from the vastness of space to the cramped eggshell interior of the cabin. Here, she recovered a trace of the security she craved.

"I shouldn't have told you all that," Yifan said. His sorrow was sincere.

"I would have found out sooner or later," Cheng Xin said.

"Let me repeat: They are just guesses. There's no real scientific proof. Don't think about it too much. Focus on what's before your eyes; focus on the life you must live." Yifan put a hand over hers. "Even if what I told you is true, those events are measured at the scale of hundreds of millions of years. Come with me to our world, which is now also your world. Live out your life and stop skipping across the surface of time. As long as you live your life within a hundred thousand years and a thousand light-years, none of those things need concern you. That ought to be enough for anyone."

"Yes, it is enough, thank you." Cheng Xin held Yifan's hand.

Cheng Xin and Guan Yifan spent the rest of the journey in the forced slumber of the sleep-aid machine. The trip lasted four days. By the time they awakened in the hypergravity of deceleration, Planet Gray took up most of their field of view.

Planet Gray was a small planet. It visually resembled the moon, a barren rock, but instead of craters, much of Planet Gray's surface was taken up by desolate plains. *Hunter* entered orbit around Planet Gray. Due to the lack of an atmosphere, the orbit was very low. The ship approached the coordinates provided by the monitoring satellite, where the five unidentified spacecraft had landed and then taken off. Yifan had planned to land the shuttle there and investigate the traces left by the spacecraft, but he and Cheng Xin had not anticipated that the mysterious visitors would leave behind such large signs that they were visible from space.

"What is *that*?" Cheng Xin cried out.

"Death lines." Yifan recognized them right away. "Don't get too close," he said to the AI.

He was referring to five black lines. One end of each line was connected to the surface of the planet, and the other end extended into space, like five black hairs growing out of Planet Gray. Each line stretched higher than *Hunter*'s orbit.

"What are they?"

"Trails left by curvature propulsion. Those lines are the result of extreme curvature manipulation. The speed of light within the trails is zero."

On the next orbit, Guan Yifan and Cheng Xin entered the shuttle and descended toward the surface. Due to the low orbit and the lack of an atmosphere, the descent was smooth and fast. The shuttle landed about three kilometers from the death lines.

They leapt across the surface under 0.2G. A thin layer of dust covered the surface of Planet Gray, along with gravel of various sizes. Due to the lack of atmospheric scattering of sunlight, shadows and lit areas were sharply delineated. When they were about a hundred meters from the death lines, Yifan waved Cheng Xin to a stop. Each death line was about twenty or thirty meters in diameter, and from here, they resembled death columns.

"These are probably the darkest things in the universe," Cheng Xin said. The death lines showed no details except an exceptional blackness showing the boundaries of the zero-lightspeed region, with no real surface. Looking up, the lines showed up clearly even against the dark backdrop of space.

"These are the deadest things in the universe as well," said Guan Yifan. "Zero-lightspeed means absolute, one hundred percent death. Inside it, every fundamental particle, every quark is dead. There is no vibration. Even without a source of gravity inside, each death line is a black hole. A zero-gravity black hole. Anything that falls in cannot reemerge."

Yifan picked up a rock and tossed it toward one of the death lines. The rock disappeared inside the absolute darkness.

"Can your lightspeed ships produce death lines?" Cheng Xin asked.

"Far from it."

"So you've seen these before, then?"

"Yes, but only rarely."

Cheng Xin gazed up at the giant black columns reaching into space. They lifted up the domed sky and seemed to turn the universe into a Palace of Death. *Is this the ultimate end for everything?*

In the sky, Cheng Xin could see the end of the columns. She pointed in that direction. "So the ships entered lightspeed at the end?"

"That's right. These are only about a hundred kilometers high. We've seen columns even shorter than these, presumably left by ships that entered lightspeed almost instantaneously."

"Are these the most advanced lightspeed ships?"

"Maybe. But this is a rarely seen technique. Death lines are usually the products of Zero-Homers."

"Zero-Homers?"

"They're also called Resetters. Maybe they're a group of intelligent individuals, or a civilization, or a group of civilizations. We don't know exactly who they are, but we've confirmed their existence. The Zero-Homers want to reset the universe and return it to the Garden of Eden."

"How?"

"By moving the hour hand of the clock past twelve. Take spatial dimensions as an example. It's practically impossible to drag a universe in lower dimensions back into higher dimensions, so maybe it's better to work forward in the other direction. If the universe can be lowered into zero dimensions and then beyond, the clock might be reset and everything returned to the beginning. The universe might possess ten macroscopic dimensions again."

"Zero dimensions! Have you seen such a thing done?"

"No. We've only witnessed two-dimensionalization. We've never even seen one-dimensionalization. But somewhere, some Zero-Homers must be trying. No one knows if they've ever succeeded. Comparatively, it's easier to lower the speed of light to zero, so we've seen more evidence of such attempts to lower the speed of light past zero and return it to infinity."

"Is that even theoretically possible?"

"We don't know. Maybe the Zero-Homers have theories that say yes, but I don't think so. Zero-lightspeed is an impassable wall. Zero-lightspeed is absolute death for all existence, the cessation of all motion. Under such conditions, the subjective cannot influence the objective in any way, so how can the 'hour hand' be shifted past it? I think the Zero-Homers are practicing a kind of religion, a kind of performance art."

Cheng Xin stared at the death lines, her terror mixed with awe. "If these are trails, why don't they spread?"

Guan Yifan clutched Cheng Xin's arm. "I was just getting to that. We've got to get out of here. Leave not just Planet Gray, but the entire system. This is a very dangerous place. Death lines are not like regular trails. Without disturbance, they'll stay like this, with a diameter equal to the effective surface of the curvature engine. But if they're disturbed, they'll spread very rapidly. A death line of this size can expand to cover a region the size of a solar system. Scientists call this phenomenon a death line rupture."

"Does a rupture make the speed of light zero in the entire region?"

"No, no. After rupture, it turns into a regular trail. The speed of light inside goes up as the trail dissipates over a wider region, but it will never be much more than a dozen meters per second. After these death lines expand, this entire system might turn into a reduced-lightspeed black hole, or a black domain. . . . Let's go."

Cheng Xin and Guan Yifan turned toward the shuttle and began to run and leap.

"What kind of disturbance makes them spread?" Cheng Xin asked. She turned to give the death lines another glance. Behind them, the five death lines cast long shadows that stretched across the plain to the horizon.

"We're not sure. Some theories suggest that the appearance of other curvature trails nearby would cause disturbance. We've confirmed that curvature trails within a short distance can influence each other."

"So, if *Halo* accelerates—"

"That's why we must get farther away using only the fusion engine before engaging the curvature engine. We've got to move . . . using your units of measurement . . . at least forty astronomical units away."

After the shuttle took off, Cheng Xin continued to stare at the receding death lines. She said, "The Zero-Homers give me a bit of hope."

Yifan said, "The universe contains multitudes. You can find any kind of 'people' and world. There are idealists like the Zero-Homers, pacifists, philanthropists, and even civilizations dedicated only to art and beauty. But they're not the mainstream; they cannot change the direction of the universe."

"It's just like the world of humans."

"At least the Zero-Homers' task will ultimately be completed by the cosmos itself."

"You mean the end of the universe?"

"That's right."

"But based on what I know, the universe will continue to expand, and become sparser and colder forever."

"That's the old cosmology you know, but we've disproved it. The amount of dark matter had been underestimated. The universe will stop expanding and then collapse under gravity, finally forming a singularity and initiating another big bang. Everything will return to zero, or home. And so Nature remains the final victor."

"Will the new universe have ten dimensions?"

"Who knows? There are infinite possibilities. That's a brand-new universe, and a brand-new life."

The trip back to Planet Blue was as uneventful as the trip to Planet Gray. Most of the time, Cheng Xin and Guan Yifan remained asleep under the sleep-aid machines. By the time they were awakened, *Hunter* was in orbit around Planet Blue. Looking down at the blue-and-white world, Cheng Xin almost thought she was home.

AA hailed them, and Yifan replied. "*Hunter* here. What's wrong?"

AA's voice was agitated. "I've called you multiple times, and the ship's AI refused to wake you!"

"I told you we have to maintain radio silence. What happened?"

"Yun Tianming is here!"

Cheng Xin was thunderstruck. The last traces of sleep left her, and even Yifan's jaw hung open.

"What?" Cheng Xin said softly.

"Yun Tianming is here! His ship landed three hours ago."

"Oh," Cheng Xin answered mechanically.

"He's still young, as young as you!"

"Really?" Cheng Xin's voice seemed to come from far away, even to herself.

"He brought a gift for you."

"He already gave me a gift. We're inside his gift now."

"That's nothing. Let me tell you, this is an awesome gift, and much bigger. . . . He's outside right now. Let me get him."

Yifan interrupted. "No. We're coming down right now. So much radio transmission is dangerous. I'm cutting it off."

Yifan and Cheng Xin stared at each other, and then laughed. "Are we really awake?" Cheng Xin asked.

Even if it was just a dream, Cheng Xin wanted to be dreaming for longer. She turned on the holographic display, and the starry sky no longer seemed so dark and cold—in fact, it seemed filled with a clear beauty like the sky after a fresh rain. Even the starlight seemed to exude the fragrance of spring buds. It was the feeling of being reborn.

"Let's get into the shuttle and land," Yifan said.

Hunter initiated the shuttle separation sequence. Inside the cramped cabin, Yifan used an interface window to perform the final check prior to atmospheric reentry.

"How did he get here so fast?" Cheng Xin muttered, as if still dreaming.

Yifan was now completely calm. "This confirms our guess. The First Trisolaran Fleet founded a colony nearby, within a hundred light-years of here. They must have received the gravitational wave signal from *Halo*."

The shuttle separated from *Hunter*. They could see the tiny pyramid of *Hunter* recede on the monitoring system.

"What kind of gift is bigger than a sun and its planetary system?" Yifan asked, smiling.

An excited Cheng Xin shook her head.

The shuttle's fusion reactor activated, and the cooling ring outside began to glow red. The thrusters were preheating, and the control interface window showed that deceleration would begin in thirty seconds. The shuttle was about to descend rapidly as it entered Planet Blue's atmosphere.

Cheng Xin heard an abrupt noise, as though something had sliced across the shuttle from bow to stern. Sharp jolts followed. And then, she experienced an eerie moment—eerie, because she couldn't be sure it was just a moment. The moment seemed to be infinitely short but also infinitely long. She had a strange feeling of stepping across time but being situated outside of time.

Later, Yifan would explain to her that she had experienced a "time vacuum." The length of that moment could not be measured in time because, during that moment, time did not exist.

At the same time, she felt herself collapse, as though she was going to turn into a singularity. Meanwhile, the mass of her, Guan Yifan, and the shuttle approached infinity.

And then everything plunged into darkness. At first, Cheng Xin thought something was wrong with her eyes. She couldn't believe the inside of the shuttle could be so dark, so dark that she couldn't see her fingers waving before her eyes. Cheng Xin called for Guan Yifan, but there was only silence in the space suit's earpiece.

Yifan felt around in the darkness until he grabbed Cheng Xin's head. She felt her own face touching his. She did not resist; she only felt comfort. Then she understood that Yifan was only trying to talk to her. The communications system inside the space suits had shut down, and the only way they could talk to each other was to press the visors of their helmets together so that their voices could be transmitted across.

"Don't be scared. Don't panic. Listen to me and don't move!" Cheng Xin heard Yifan's voice from the visor. She could tell from the vibrations that he was shouting, but what she heard was very faint, like a whisper. She felt his hand moving around in the dark until the inside of the cabin lit up. The light came from something held in his hand, a strip about the size of a cigarette. Cheng Xin knew it was some kind of chemical light source. *Halo* was equipped with similar emergency supplies. Bending it caused it to emit a cold light.

"Don't move. The space suits are no longer providing oxygen. Slow down your breathing. I'll repressurize the cabin now. It won't take long!" Yifan handed the glow stick to Cheng Xin, pulled open a storage unit next to his seat, and took out a metal bottle that resembled a small fire extinguisher. He twisted the bottle's opening, and a white gas rushed out of the bottle in raging torrents.

Cheng Xin's breath quickened. All she had left was the air remaining in her helmet, and the harder she inhaled, the more suffocated she felt. Her hand reached instinctively for the visor of her helmet, but Yifan stopped her in time. He embraced her again, this time to calm her down. She imagined that he was trying to rescue her from drowning. In the cold light, she saw his eyes, which seemed to be telling her that they were almost at the surface. Cheng Xin could feel the air pressure in the cabin rising, and just when she was about to pass out from lack of air, Yifan snapped her visor open, as well as his own. The two gulped air.

After she caught her breath, Cheng Xin examined the metal bottle. She noticed the pressure gauge near the neck of the bottle, an ancient analog dial with a swinging needle that was now pointing into the green zone.

Yifan said, "The oxygen from that won't last long, and the cabin is going to get very cold very fast. We need to change space suits." He pushed off from his seat and dragged out two metal boxes from the back of the cabin. He opened one and showed Cheng Xin the space suit inside.

Modern space suits—in the Solar System and here—were very lightweight. If one kept the suit unpressurized, left off the small life-support pack, and took off the helmet, a modern space suit was virtually indistinguishable from ordinary clothes. However, the space suits in the boxes were heavy and clumsy, resembling Common Era space suits.

They could now see their breaths. Cheng Xin took off her original space suit and felt the bone-chilling cold inside the cabin. The heavy space suit was difficult to put on, and Yifan had to help her. She felt like a child dependent on this man, a feeling that she had not experienced in a long time. Before Cheng Xin put on the helmet, Yifan explained the suit's features to her in detail—the oxygen dial, the pressurization toggle, the knob for temperature adjustment, the switches for communications and illumination, and so on. The space suit had no automatic systems, and everything required manual operation.

"There are no computer chips inside this suit at all. Right now, none of our computers—electronic or quantum—work anymore."

"Why?"

"The speed of light right now is less than twenty kilometers per second."

Yifan helped Cheng Xin put on her helmet. Her body was almost frozen. He turned on the oxygen and the heater in her suit, and she felt herself thawing out. Yifan now turned to put on his own suit. He worked fast, but it took some work between when he put on his helmet and the two suits could be connected for communications. Neither was able to speak until their chilled bodies had recovered.

The suits were so heavy and clumsy that Cheng Xin could imagine how difficult it would be to move around in them under 1G. Her suit wasn't so much a suit as a house, the only place where she could find refuge. The light-emitting strip drifting in the cabin was dimming, so Yifan turned on the lamp on his own suit. Inside the cramped space, Cheng Xin thought they were like ancient miners trapped underground.

"What happened?" Cheng Xin asked.

Yifan floated up from his seat and struggled until he managed to open the screen over one of the portholes—the automatic controls for the porthole screens were also nonfunctional. He drifted to the other side of the cabin and repeated the operation with another porthole.

Cheng Xin looked at the transformed universe outside.

She saw two star clusters at the two ends of space: The cluster in front glowed blue and the cluster behind glowed red. Cheng Xin had seen a similar sight earlier when *Halo* was flying at lightspeed, but the two star clusters she saw now were not stable. Their shapes shifted abruptly like two balls of flame in fierce wind. Instead of stars leaping from the blue cluster into the red cluster from time to time, two light belts connected the two ends of the universe, only one of which was visible on each side of the ship.

The wider belt took up half the space on one side. Its two ends were not connected to the blue and red star clusters; instead, the belt ended in two round tips. Cheng Xin could tell that this "belt" was actually an extremely flattened oval—or perhaps a circle that had been stretched out. Colored patches of various sizes flitted across the wide belt: blue, white, and light yellow. Instinctively, Cheng Xin understood that she was looking at Planet Blue.

The light belt on the other side of the ship was thinner but brighter, and its surface showed no details. Unlike Planet Blue, this belt's length cycled rapidly between a bright line that connected the red and blue clusters, and a bright circle. The belt's periodic circular state told Cheng Xin that she was looking at the star DX3906.

"We're orbiting Planet Blue at lightspeed," said Guan Yifan. "Except the speed of light is now very slow."

The shuttle had been moving far faster, but as the speed of light was an absolute speed limit, the shuttle's velocity had been cut down to that.

"The death lines ruptured?"

"Yes. They spread out to cover the entire solar system. We're trapped here."

"Was it due to the disturbance from Tianming's ship?"

"Perhaps. He didn't know the death lines were here."

Cheng Xin didn't want to ask what their next step was, knowing that nothing more could be done. No computer could operate when the speed of light was below twenty kilometers per second. The shuttle's AI and control systems were all dead. Under such conditions, not even a light inside the spacecraft could be turned on—it was just a metal can with no electricity or power. *Hunter* was the same, also dead. Before falling into reduced lightspeed, the shuttle had not yet began decelerating, and so the small spaceship should be nearby—but it might as well be on the other side of the planet. Without the control systems, neither the shuttle nor *Hunter* could open their doors.

Cheng Xin thought about Yun Tianming and 艾 AA. They were both on the ground, and should be safe. But now there was no way for the two sides to communicate. She never even got to say hello to him.

Something light gently struck the visor of her helmet: the metal bottle. Cheng Xin looked at the ancient pressure gauge on it again, and touched her own space suit. Hope, once extinguished, lit up again like a firefly.

"You've been preparing for situations like this?" she asked.

"Yes." Yifan's voice sounded distorted in Cheng Xin's earpiece due to the use of ancient analog signals. "Not for ruptured death lines, of course, but we were prepared for accidentally drifting into the trails of lightspeed ships. The situations are similar: The reduced lightspeed stops everything. . . . Next, we need to start the neurons."

"What?"

"Neural computers. Computers that can operate under reduced lightspeed. The shuttle and *Hunter* both have two control systems, one of which is based on neural computers."

Cheng Xin was amazed that such machines existed.

"The key isn't the speed of light, but the system design. The transmission of chemical signals in the brain is even slower, only two or three meters per second—not much faster than us walking. Neural computers can still work because they imitate the highly parallel processing found in the brains of higher animals. All the chips are designed specifically to function under reduced-lightspeed conditions."

Yifan opened a metal bulkhead decorated with many dots connected in a complex web like the tentacles of an octopus. Inside was a small control panel with a flat display, as well as several switches and indicator lights. The whole assembly was built from components deemed obsolete by the end of the Crisis Era. He toggled a red switch and the screen lit up: text scrolling by. Cheng Xin could tell it was the boot sequence of some operating system.

"The parallel neural mode hasn't been started yet, so we have to load the operating system serially. You'll probably have a hard time believing how slow serial data transmission is under reduced lightspeed: look, the data rate is a few hundred bytes per second. Not even a kilobyte."

"Then the boot sequence will take a long time."

"That's right. But as the parallel mode gradually builds up, the loading will speed up. Still, it really will take a long time to complete the sequence." Yifan pointed to the progress indicator, a line of text on the bottom of the screen.

Remaining load time for boot module: 68 hours 43 minutes *[flickering]* seconds. Total remaining system load time: 297 hours 52 minutes *[flickering]* seconds.

"Twelve days!" Cheng Xin exclaimed. "What about *Hunter*?"

"Its systems will detect the reduced-lightspeed condition and automatically boot the neural computer. But it will take about as long to complete."

Twelve days. They could only get to the survival resources in the shuttle and on *Hunter* after twelve days. Until then, they had to rely on their primitive space suits. If the space suits were powered by nuclear batteries, the electricity should last long enough, but they didn't have enough oxygen.

"We have to hibernate," said Yifan.

"Do we have the equipment for hibernation on the shuttle?" As soon as she asked the question, Cheng Xin realized her error. Even if the shuttle had such equipment, it would be controlled by the computer, which was out of commission right now.

Yifan opened the storage unit from which he had taken the oxygen bottle earlier and took out a small box. He opened it to show Cheng Xin a few capsules. "These are drugs for short-term hibernation. Unlike regular hibernation, you won't need an external life-support system. Once you are in hibernation, your respiration will slow down to the point where you consume very little oxygen. One capsule is enough for fifteen days of hibernation."

Cheng Xin opened her visor and swallowed one of the pills. She watched as Yifan also took one. Then she looked outside the portholes.

Patches of color now moved so fast over Planet Blue—the broad belt that connected the blue and red ends of the lightspeed universe on one side of the ship—that they turned into a blur.

"Can you see the patterns on the belt repeating periodically?" Yifan wasn't looking outside at all. His eyes were half-closed as he strapped himself into the hypergravity seat.

"They're moving too fast."

"Try to follow the motion with your eyes."

Cheng Xin tried to match her moving gaze with the patterns flowing across the belt. For a moment, she could see the blue, white, and yellow patches, but they blurred almost immediately. "I can't," she said.

"That's all right. They're moving too fast. The pattern could be repeating several hundred times per second." Yifan sighed. Cheng Xin noticed his sorrow, despite his effort to hide it. And she knew why.

She understood that every time the pattern repeated on the broad belt, it meant that the shuttle had completed another orbit around Planet Blue at lightspeed. Even at reduced lightspeed, the demonic rules of the theory of special relativity still held. In the planet's frame of reference, time was passing tens of millions of times faster than in here, like blood seeping out of her heart.

A moment here; eons there.

Cheng Xin turned away from the porthole and strapped herself into the seat as well. Light flickered through the porthole on the other side. Outside, the sun of this world was alternately a bright line that connected the two ends of the universe, and a ball of light. It was dancing the mad dance of death.

"Cheng Xin." Yifan called for her softly. "It's possible that when we wake up, we'll find the screen telling us that an error has occurred."

Cheng Xin turned and smiled at him through the visor. "I'm not afraid."

"I know you're not afraid. I just want to tell you something in case we don't . . . I know about your experience as the Swordholder. I want to let you know that you didn't do anything wrong. Humanity chose you, which meant they chose to treat life and everything else with love, even if they had to pay a great price. You fulfilled the wish of the world, carried out their values, and executed their choice. You really didn't do anything wrong."

"Thank you," Cheng Xin said.

"I don't know what happened to you after that, but you still didn't do anything wrong. Love isn't wrong. A single individual cannot destroy a world. If that world was doomed, then it was the result of the efforts of everyone, including those living and those who had already died."

"Thank you," Cheng Xin said. Her eyes felt hot and wet.

"As for what will happen next, I'm not afraid either. When I was on *Gravity*, all those stars in the emptiness made me afraid and tired, and I wanted to stop thinking about the universe. But it was like a drug, and I couldn't stop. Well, now I can stop."

"That's good. You know something? The only thing I'm scared of is that you'll be afraid."

"I'm the same."

They held hands, and as the sun continued its mad dance, they gradually lost consciousness and stopped breathing.

About Seventeen Billion Years
After the Beginning of Time
Our Star

It took a long time to wake up.

Cheng Xin recovered her awareness gradually. After her memory and sight came back, she knew right away that the neural computer had booted successfully. A soft light illuminated the inside of the cabin, and she could hear the machines humming reassuringly. The air was warm. The shuttle had been revived.

But Cheng Xin soon realized that the lights inside the cabin came from different fixtures than before—perhaps these were backups designed specifically for reduced-lightspeed use. There were no information windows in the air. It was possible that the reduced lightspeed meant such holographic displays were no longer operable. The interface of the neural computer was limited to that flat screen, which now resembled a color bitmap display from the Common Era.

Guan Yifan was drifting in front of the display, tapping on it with the fingers of a gloveless hand. He turned and smiled at Cheng Xin, made a hand gesture indicating that it was okay to drink, and then handed her a bottle of water.

"It's been sixteen days," he said.

The bottle felt warm. Cheng Xin saw that she wasn't wearing gloves, either. She realized that although she was still wearing the primitive space suit, her helmet had been removed. The temperature and pressure inside the cabin were comfortable.

Since she had recovered enough to move her hands, Cheng Xin unstrapped herself and drifted next to Yifan to look at the screen with him, their space suits squeezed tightly side by side. Several windows were up on the screen, each showing rapidly scrolling numbers: diagnostics on the shuttle's various systems.

Yifan told Cheng Xin that he had established contact with *Hunter*, whose neural computer had also apparently booted successfully.

Cheng Xin looked up and saw that the two portholes were still open. She drifted over. Guan Yifan dimmed the cabin lights so she could see through them without glare. They anticipated each other's needs now as though they were a single person.

At first, the universe didn't appear to have changed from what she had seen before: The ship continued to orbit around Planet Blue at reduced lightspeed; the two star clusters, blue and red, continued to change their shapes erratically at the two ends of the universe; the sun continued to dance madly between being a line and a circle; and color patches continued to whip across Planet Blue's surface. When Cheng Xin tried to match her gaze to the rapidly flowing surface of Planet Blue, she finally noticed something different: the blue and white patches had been replaced by purple ones.

Yifan pointed to the screen. "The propulsion system self-diagnosis is complete. Everything's basically working. We can decelerate out of lightspeed anytime."

"The fusion drive still works?" Cheng Xin asked. Before they entered hibernation, this question had weighed on her mind. She had not asked because she knew that she was likely to receive a disappointing answer, and she didn't want to give Yifan more to worry about.

"Of course not. With such a reduced lightspeed, nuclear fusion puts out too little power. We have to use the backup antimatter drive."

"Antimatter? But wouldn't the containment field be affected by the reduced lightspeed?"

"No problems there. The antimatter engine was designed specifically for reduced-lightspeed conditions. When we're on long expeditions like this, we equip all our spacecraft with reduced-lightspeed propulsion systems. . . . Our world puts a lot of effort into developing such technologies. The goal isn't to solve the problem of accidentally entering trails left by curvature propulsion; rather, it's because we have to plan for the possibility of having to conceal ourselves inside a light tomb, or a black domain."

Half an hour later, the shuttle and *Hunter* both activated their antimatter engines and began decelerating. Cheng Xin and Guan Yifan were pressed against their seats by the hypergravity, and the porthole screens rose to block out the outside. Violent jolts seized the shuttle, but gradually subsided. The deceleration process took less than twenty minutes. Then the engines shut off, and they were again weightless.

"We're out of lightspeed," Guan Yifan said. He pressed a button, and the screens over the two portholes retracted.

Through the portholes, Cheng Xin saw that the blue and red star clusters were gone, and the sun was now a normal sun. But the sight of Planet Blue in the porthole on the other side surprised her: Planet Blue was now "Planet Purple." Other than the ocean, which was still a light yellow, the rest of the planet was covered by purple—even the snow was gone. She was, however, most shocked by the appearance of space itself.

"What are those lines?" Cheng Xin cried out.

"I think they are . . . stars." Yifan was as amazed as she.

All the stars in space had turned into thin lines of light. Cheng Xin was actually familiar with such a sight: She had seen plenty of long-exposure photographs taken of the starry sky from Earth. Due to the Earth's rotation, the stars in the pictures all became concentric arcs of approximately the same length. But now, the stars she saw were segments of different lengths and aligned every which way. The longest few lines, in fact, took up almost a third of the sky. These lines crossed each other at different angles and made space appear far more confusing and chaotic than before.

"I think they're stars," repeated Yifan. "A star's light must pass through two interfaces before getting to us: First, it must go through the interface between regular lightspeed and reduced lightspeed, and then through the event horizon of the black hole. That's why the stars look so strange to us now."

"We're inside the black domain?"

"That's right. We're inside the light tomb."

The DX3906 solar system was now a reduced-lightspeed black hole completely sealed off from the rest of the universe. The starry sky woven by the multitude of crisscrossing silver threads was a dream that could be seen but would never be achieved.

"Let's go down to the surface," Yifan said after a long silence.

The shuttle decelerated further and lowered its orbit. With a series of powerful jolts, it entered the atmosphere of the planet and descended toward the surface of this world in which the two of them were doomed to spend the rest of their lives.

The purple continents took up most of the view from the monitoring system. They were able to confirm that the purple was due to the color of the vegetation. The change in the sun's radiation had probably caused the plants on Planet Blue to change from blue to purple as they evolved to adapt to the new light.

As a matter of fact, the very existence of the sun puzzled Cheng Xin and Guan Yifan. Since $E = mc^2$, reduced-lightspeed nuclear fusion could produce only small amounts of energy. Perhaps the interior of the sun maintained normal lightspeed?

The shuttle's landing coordinates were set to the same spot from which it had taken off and left *Halo*. As they approached the surface, they saw a dense purple forest at the landing spot. Just when the shuttle was about to lift off again in search of a more open spot, the trees dashed away to escape the flames from the shuttle's thrusters. The shuttle then gently set itself down in the open space vacated by the fleeing trees.

The screen showed that the outside air was breathable. Compared to the last time they had been here, the oxygen content in the atmosphere was substantially higher. Moreover, the atmosphere was denser, and the atmospheric pressure was one and a half times higher than at the last landing.

Cheng Xin and Guan Yifan exited the shuttle and once again stepped onto the surface of Planet Blue. Warm, moist air welcomed them, and a layer of soft, bouncy humus covered the ground. The soil around them was filled with numerous holes left by the roots of the trees that had gotten out of the way. Those trees now huddled around the clearing, their broad leaves rustling in the breeze, like a crowd of whispering giants gathered around them. The clearing was completely covered by their shade. Such dense vegetation made Planet Blue a completely different world than the one they had seen before.

Cheng Xin didn't like purple. She'd always thought of it as a sick, depressing color that reminded her of the lips of invalids whose hearts did not supply them with sufficient oxygen. Yet now she was surrounded by purple everywhere she looked, and she would have to spend the rest of her life in this purple world.

There was no sign of *Halo*, no sign of Yun Tianming's ship, no sign of any human presence.

Guan Yifan and Cheng Xin surveyed the landscape around them and realized that the geographical features were completely different from the last time. They clearly remembered that there had been rolling mountains nearby, but now the forest was growing over a plain. They went back to the shuttle to confirm that the coordinates were really correct—they were. Then they looked even more carefully all around them, but still found no trace of any prior human visit. The site resembled virgin land—it was as though their last visit had occurred on another planet in another space-time that had nothing to do with here.

Yifan returned to the shuttle and established a link with *Hunter*, which was still in near-ground orbit. *Hunter*'s neural computer was very powerful, and its AI was capable of direct natural language communications. Under reduced-lightspeed conditions, the conversation from ground to space suffered a transmission delay of over ten seconds. After dropping out of lightspeed along with the shuttle, *Hunter* had been scanning the surface of the planet from low orbit. By now, it had completed a survey of most of the land on Planet Blue, and it had discovered no trace of humans or signs of any other intelligent life.

Next, Cheng Xin and Guan Yifan had to turn to a task that terrified them but was absolutely necessary: determining how much time had elapsed in this frame of reference. There was a special technique for radiometric dating under reduced-lightspeed conditions: Some elements that did not decay under normal lightspeed decayed at different rates under reduced lightspeed, which could be used to precisely tell the passage of time. Given its scientific mission, the shuttle was equipped with a device for measuring atomic decay, but the instrument required a computer for processing. Yifan had to go to some trouble to connect the instrument to the neural computer on the shuttle. They directed the instrument to test the ten rock samples taken from different parts of the planet one after another so that the results could be compared. The assay required half an hour.

While waiting for the test results, Cheng Xin and Guan Yifan left the shuttle and waited in the clearing. Sunlight illuminated the clearing through gaps in the canopy. Many strange, small creatures flitted through: Some were insects with spinning rotors on top like helicopters; others were like tiny, transparent balloons that drifted through the air, giving off a rainbow sheen as they passed through shafts of sunlight; but none of them had wings.

"Maybe several tens of thousands of years have passed," Cheng Xin muttered.

"Or even longer," said Guan Yifan, looking deep into the woods. "In our current state, tens of thousands of years aren't very different from hundreds of thousands of years."

Then they said no more, but sat on the stairs outside the shuttle, leaning against each other and taking comfort in their heartbeats.

Half an hour later, they climbed back into the shuttle to face facts. The screen on the control panel showed the test results from the ten samples. Many elements had been tested and the charts were complicated. All the samples yielded similar results. Underneath, the average of the results was listed simply:

Average atomic decay dating results (error range: 0.4%): Stellar time
periods lapsed: 6,177,906; Earth years lapsed: 18,903,729.

Cheng Xin counted the digits in the last number three times, turned
around, and quietly exited the shuttle. She descended the stairs and returned to this purple world. Tall purple trees surrounded her, a beam of
sunlight cast a tiny circle of brightness next to her feet, moist wind lifted her
hair, living balloons drifted overhead, and almost nineteen million years followed her.

Yifan came to her. They locked gazes, and their souls embraced.

"Cheng Xin, we missed them."

More than eighteen million years after the DX3906 system turned into a
reduced-lightspeed black hole, seventeen billion years after the birth of the
universe, a man and a woman held each other tightly.

Cheng Xin sobbed her heart out over Yifan's shoulder. In her memories, she
had cried like this only once before, when Tianming's brain had been taken
out of his body. That was . . . 18,903,729 years plus six centuries ago, and those
six centuries were but a rounding error at such geologic timescales. This time,
she cried not only for Tianming. She cried out of a sense of surrender. She
finally understood how she was but a mote of dust in a grand wind, a small
leaf drifting over a broad river. She surrendered completely and allowed the
wind to pass through her, allowed the sunlight to pierce her soul.

Letting the past go, she allowed her growing esteem for Guan Yifan to take
over her heart.

They sat on the yielding humus and continued to hold each other, letting
time flow by. The dappled sunlight gently shifted around them as the planet
continued to rotate. Sometimes Cheng Xin asked herself, *Has another ten million years passed by?* A small, rational part of her mind strangely whispered to
her that such a thing was possible: There really were worlds where one could
step through a thousand years at will. Consider the death lines: If they ruptured and expanded just a bit, the speed of light within would rise from zero to
an extremely small number, like the rate at which continents drifted over the
ocean: a centimeter for every ten thousand years. In such a world, if you got
up from your lover and walked a few steps away, you would be separated from
him by ten million years.

They'd missed each other.

After they knew not how long, Yifan asked her softly, "What should we do?"

"I want to look more. There must be some sign."

"There really won't be anything. Eighteen million years will erase everything: Time is the cruelest force of all."

"Carving words into stone."

Yifan looked at Cheng Xin, confused.

"艾 AA would know to carve words into stone," Cheng Xin muttered.

"I don't understand. . . ."

Cheng Xin didn't explain; instead, she grabbed Yifan by the shoulders:
"Can you have *Hunter* do a deep scan of this area and see if there's anything
under the surface?"

"What are you looking for?"

"Words. I want to see if there are words."

Yifan shook his head. "I understand your desire, but—"

"To better last through the eons, the words ought to be large."

Yifan nodded, but obviously only to appease her. They returned to the shuttle. Although this was a walk of only a few steps, they leaned against each other
as if afraid time would divide them if they were physically separated. Yifan
contacted *Hunter* and directed it to do a deep scan of the area within a circle
centered on this coordinate with a radius of three kilometers. The depth of the
scan was set to be between five and ten meters, focusing on human writing or
other significant markings.

Hunter passed overhead fifteen minutes later and sent back the results about
ten minutes after that: nothing.

Guan Yifan ordered the ship to do another scan at a depth range between
ten and twenty meters. This took another hour, the bulk of which was spent
waiting for the ship to pass overhead. Still nothing. At that depth there was no
more soil, only bedrock.

Guan Yifan adjusted the scanning range to between twenty and thirty meters.
"This is the last time," he said to Cheng Xin. "The sensors can't go deeper
than that."

They waited for the ship to orbit Planet Blue another time. The sun was
setting and the sky was full of lovely, fiery clouds, while the purple woods were
limned with a golden glow.

This time, the shuttle's screen showed the images transmitted back by the
ship. After processing by enhancement software, they could see a few fragments of white words embedded in the dark rock: "e," "liv," "a," "life," "you,"
"little," "side," "Go." The white color was to indicate that the words were carved
into the bedrock; each character was about a meter square, and they were ar-

ranged into four rows. The words were twenty-three to twenty-eight meters below them, carved into a forty-degree incline.

> WE LIVED A HAPPY LIFE TOGETHER
> WE GIVE YOU A LITTLE
> SURVIVE THE COLLAPSE INSIDE
> GO TO THE NEW

Hunter's AI invoked the geological expert system to interpret the results. They found out that the giant characters had initially been carved into the surface of a large sedimentary rock formation on the side of a mountain. The original surface was about 130 square meters. Over the eons, the mountain on which the rock had been located sank, and that was how the carved rock ended up below them. More than four lines of text had been carved into it, but the lower portion of the rock had been broken up during the geological transformations and all the text there lost. The surviving text was incomplete as well—the last three lines all had missing characters at the end.

Cheng Xin and Guan Yifan embraced again. They cried tears of joy at the news concerning 艾AA and Yun Tianming, and shared the happiness that they had enjoyed more than one hundred eighty thousand centuries ago. Their despairing hearts grew peaceful.

"I wonder what their life here was like?" Cheng Xin asked, tears glistening in her eyes.

"Anything was possible," said Yifan.

"Did they have children?"

"Anything was possible. They could have even founded a civilization here."

Cheng Xin knew that was indeed possible. But even if that civilization had lasted ten million years, the eight million-plus years that had come after would have erased all traces of it.

Time really was the cruelest force of all.

Something strange interrupted their meditation: a rectangle limned by faint lines of light, about a man's height, hovered over the clearing like the dashed selection lines marked out by dragging a mouse. It moved through the air, but did not go far before returning to its original position. It was possible that it had been there all along, but the outline was so faint and thin that it was invisible during daytime. Whether it was made by a force field or actual substance, there was no doubt it was the creation of intelligence. The lines making up the rectangle seemed to evoke the line-shaped stars in the sky.

"Do you think this is the . . . gift they left for us?" Cheng Xin asked.

"Seems hard to believe. How could it have survived more than eighteen million years?"

But he was wrong. The object had indeed survived eighteen million years. And, if necessary, it could survive until the end of the universe, because it existed outside of time.

The door remembered that, initially, it had been placed next to the rock carved with text, and it had a real metal frame. But the metal had eroded away after only five hundred thousand years, though the object had always remained brand new. It had no fear of time because its own time had not yet started. It had been thirty meters underground, next to the carved rock, but it had detected the presence of humans and risen to the surface. During the process, it did not interact with the crust, moving like a ghost. It now confirmed that these two were indeed the ones it had been expecting.

"I think it looks like a door," Cheng Xin said.

Yifan picked up a small branch and tossed it at the rectangle. The branch passed through it and landed on the other side. They saw a luminescent flock of little balloon creatures drift over. A few passed through the rectangle and one even crossed the glowing outline.

Yifan reached out and touched the frame. The light and his finger passed through each other, and he felt nothing. Without even thinking, he extended his hand into the space outlined by the rectangle. Cheng Xin screamed. Yifan pulled his hand back, and everything looked unharmed.

"Your hand . . . . It didn't go through." Cheng Xin pointed to the other side of the rectangle.

Yifan tried again. His hand and forearm disappeared as they entered the plane of the rectangle and did not go through. From the other side, Cheng Xin saw the cross section of his forearm, like the surface of a window. All his bones, muscles, and blood vessels were clearly visible. He pulled his hand back and tried again with a branch. It went through the frame without problems. Right after, two insects with spinning rotors passed through the rectangle as well.

"It really is a door—a smart door that recognizes what's going through it," Yifan said.

"It allowed you in."

"Probably you, as well."

Cheng Xin gingerly tried, and her arm also disappeared in the "door." Yifan observed the cross section of her arm from the other side, and had a moment of déjà vu.

"Wait for me here," Yifan said. "I'll go investigate."

"We should go together," Cheng Xin said resolutely.

"No, you wait here."

Cheng Xin grabbed him by both shoulders and turned him to face her. She looked into his eyes. "Do you really want us to also be separated by eighteen million years?"

Yifan stared back into her eyes for a long moment, and finally nodded. "Perhaps we should bring some things with us."

Ten minutes later, they passed through the door, hand in hand.

Outside of Time
Our Universe

━━━━

Primordial darkness.

Cheng Xin and Guan Yifan were once again immersed in a time vacuum. The sensation was similar to when they had entered reduced lightspeed back in the shuttle. Time did not flow here, or maybe it was more accurate to say that time did not exist. They lost all sense of time, and experienced again that feeling of stepping across time, but existing outside of it.

Darkness disappeared; time began.

There is no appropriate expression in human language to express the moment at the start of time. To say that time began after they entered the door would be wrong because "after" required time. There was no time here, and thus no before or after. The time "after" they entered could have been shorter than a billion-billionth of a second, or longer than a billion billion years.

The sun brightened. It did so very gradually: At first it was just a disk, and then the light began to unveil the world. It was like a song that began as barely audible notes, then grew and grew into a mighty chorus. A circle of blue appeared around the sun, expanded, and turned into a blue sky. Under the blue sky, a pastoral scene slowly took shape. There was an unplanted field with black soil; next to it was an exquisite white house. There were also a few trees that brought a hint of the exotic with their broad, strangely shaped leaves. As the sun continued to brighten, the peaceful scene appeared like a welcoming embrace.

"There are people here!" Guan Yifan pointed at the distance.

They could see the backs of two figures standing on the horizon: a man and a woman. The man had just put down his uplifted arm.

"That's us," said Cheng Xin.

In front of those two figures, they could see a distant white house and trees, exact duplicates of the ones nearby. They couldn't see what was at the feet of those figures due to the distance, but they could guess that it was another black field. At the end of the world was a duplicate of it, or maybe a projection.

Duplicates or projections of the world existed all around them. They looked to their sides and saw the same scene repeated. The two of them also existed in those worlds, but all they could see were the backs of those figures, who turned their heads away as Cheng Xin and Yifan turned to look at them. They looked behind them and saw the same thing—except now they were looking at the world from the other direction.

The entrance to the world had disappeared.

They followed a path of stepping-stones, and around them, the copies of themselves in the copies of their world walked along with them. The path was broken by a brook with no bridge over it, but the brook was so small that they could step over it. Only now did they realize that gravity was a standard 1G. They passed the copse of trees and came to the white house. The door was shut and the windows covered by blue curtains. Everything looked brand new, dustless— as a matter of fact, they were brand new, also, as time had just begun to flow.

In front of the house was a pile of simple, primitive farming tools: shovels, rakes, baskets, water pails, and so on. Although some of them were shaped a bit oddly, it was easy to tell their function by appearance. What most drew their attention, though, was a row of metal columns erected next to the farming tools. They were about the height of a person, and the smooth surfaces glinted in the sunlight. Each column had four metal attachments that seemed to be folded limbs. The columns were probably robots in a resting state.

They decided to familiarize themselves with the environment before entering the house, and so they continued to walk past it. After a bit less than a kilometer, they reached the edge of the small world and faced the duplicate world before them. At first, they thought it was just a reflected image of their own world, though it was not mirrored. But after they were halfway there they decided that it couldn't be a reflection: Everything looked so real. They took a step forward and entered the duplicate world without any resistance. Looking around, Cheng Xin was struck with a hint of terror.

Everything looked the same as when they had first entered the world. They were in the same pastoral scene, with duplicates of the scene before them and to the sides, and in those copies, copies of them also existed. They turned around to look back, and they saw copies of themselves at the far end of the world they had just left, looking behind them.

Yifan let out a long sigh. "I don't think we need to go any farther. We'll never reach the end." He pointed up and then down. "I bet that without these barriers, we'd see the same scene above and below us as well."

"Do you know what this is?"

"Are you familiar with the work of Charles Misner?"

"Who was he?"

"A physicist of the Common Era. He was the one who first came up with this concept. The world we're in is actually very simple. It's a regular cube about a kilometer on each side. You can imagine it as a room with four walls and a ceiling as well as a floor. But the room is constructed such that the ceiling is also the floor, and each wall is the same as the opposite wall. In reality, it has only two walls. If you walk through one of the walls, you'll immediately reappear at the opposite wall, and the same is true of the floor and ceiling. Thus, this is a completely enclosed world in which the end is also the beginning. The images we see all around us are the result of light returning to the starting point after crossing the world. We're still in the same world we started from, because this is the only world that exists. Every copy we see around us is just an image of this world."

"So this is . . ."

"Yes!" Yifan swept his arm around to indicate everything. "Yun Tianming once gave you a star, and now he's given you a universe. Cheng Xin, this is an entire universe. It might be small, but it's a complete universe."

Cheng Xin looked around, at a loss for words. Yifan sat down quietly on a ridge in the field and picked up a fistful of black earth, letting the soil slip from between his fingers. He sounded depressed. "He's quite a man to be able to give the woman he loved a star and a universe. But I can't give you anything."

Cheng Xin sat down as well and leaned on his shoulder. She laughed as she said, "You're the only man in this universe. I don't think you need to give me anything."

The feeling of being alone in the universe was soon shattered by the sound of a door opening. A figure in white came out of the house and walked toward them. The world was so small that it was possible to clearly see anyone at any distance. They saw that the newcomer was a woman dressed in a kimono. The kimono, decorated with tiny red flowers, was like a walking flower bush that brought the feeling of spring to the universe.

"Sophon!" Cheng Xin cried out.

"I know her," Yifan said. "She's the robot controlled by sophons."

They walked over to meet the woman under one of the trees. Cheng Xin saw that it really was Sophon: That unparalleled beauty remained unchanged.

Sophon bowed deeply to Cheng Xin and Guan Yifan. When she straightened, she smiled at Cheng Xin. "I said that the universe is grand, but life is grander. Fate has indeed directed us to meet again."

"I couldn't have imagined," Cheng Xin said. "I'm really glad to see you. Really." Sophon brought her to the past—more than eighteen million years ago. But that wasn't really accurate, because they were now in another time stream altogether.

Sophon bowed again. "Welcome to Universe 647. I am its manager."

"The manager of the universe?" Yifan looked at Sophon, astounded. "What a grand title! For a cosmologist like me, that sounds like—"

"Oh no!" Sophon laughed and waved his remark away. "You are the true masters of Universe 647 and have full authority over everything here. I'm just here to serve you."

Sophon made a gesture indicating that they should follow her. They followed her to a refined parlor inside the house. The parlor was decorated in an Eastern style with a few calming brush paintings and calligraphy scrolls hung on the walls. Cheng Xin looked for artifacts taken from Pluto by *Halo* but didn't find any. After they sat down at an antique wooden desk, Sophon poured tea for them—without going through the complicated steps of the Way of Tea. The tea leaves seemed to be Longjing, and they stood up at the bottom of the cups like a tiny green forest, giving off a fresh fragrance.

To Cheng Xin and Guan Yifan, everything seemed to be a dream.

Sophon spoke. "This universe is a gift. Mr. Yun Tianming gave it to the both of you."

"I think it's meant for Cheng Xin," said Yifan.

"No. You're also one of the intended recipients. Your authorization was added to the recognition system later; otherwise you wouldn't have been allowed in. Mr. Yun hoped that you could hide in this tiny universe and avoid the collapse of the great universe—or the big crunch—and, after the next big bang, enter the new universe and see its Edenic Age. Right now, we exist in an independent timeline. Time is passing rapidly in the great universe, and you will certainly be able to see its end within your lifetimes. More specifically, I estimate that the great universe will collapse into a singularity after about ten years here."

"If a new big bang occurs, how will we know?" asked Yifan.

"We'll know. We can sense the conditions in the great universe through the supermembrane."

Sophon's words reminded Cheng Xin of what Yun Tianming and 艾 AA had carved into the rock. But Guan Yifan was reminded of something else. He noticed that Sophon spoke of the "Edenic Age" of the new universe. This was a term invented by the Galactic humans. Two possibilities presented themselves. One was that coincidentally, the Trisolarans had also picked this term. The second possibility was far more terrifying: the Trisolarans had already discovered the Galactic humans. Given how quickly Yun Tianming had arrived on Planet Blue, it was apparent that the First Trisolaran Fleet was very close to the worlds of humankind. And now, the Trisolaran civilization had developed to the point where they were capable of constructing small universes: This was a great threat to humanity.

Then he laughed.

"What are you laughing at?" Cheng Xin asked.

"Myself."

He found himself ridiculous. More than eighteen million years had passed since the day he'd departed World II to come to Planet Blue, and that was before they entered this small universe with its own time. By now, hundreds of millions of years must have passed in the great universe. He was worried about truly ancient history.

"Have you seen Yun Tianming?" Cheng Xin asked.

Sophon shook her head. "No. I've never met him."

"What about 艾 AA?"

"The last time I saw her was on Earth."

"Then how did you come to be here?"

"Universe 647 was a custom order. I've been here since its completion. Remember that I am fundamentally just a collection of digital bits, and many copies of me can be made."

"Did you know that Tianming brought this universe to Planet Blue?"

"I don't know what Planet Blue is. If it's a planet, then Mr. Yun couldn't have brought Universe 647 to it, because this is an independent universe that does not exist within the great universe. He could only bring the entrance to the universe there."

"Why aren't Tianming and AA here?" Yifan asked. This was also the question Cheng Xin most wanted answered. She hadn't asked earlier because she was afraid of hearing an answer she didn't want to know.

Sophon shook her head again. "I don't know. The recognition system has always had Mr. Yun's authorization."

"Is anyone else's authorization in the system?"

"No. Only the three of you."

After a while, Cheng Xin said to Yifan, "AA always cared more than me about the world around her. I don't think she would have been interested in a new universe tens of billions of years later."

"I'm interested," said Yifan. "I really want to see what a new universe is like before it's distorted and tampered with by life and civilization. I think it must exhibit the highest degree of harmony and beauty."

Cheng Xin said, "I also want to go to the new universe. The singularity and the new big bang will erase all memories of our universe. I want to bring some memory of humanity there."

Sophon nodded solemnly at Cheng Xin. "That is a great task you've set yourself. There are others doing similar work, but you're the first human from the Solar System to do this."

"You've always had higher goals in life than I," Yifan whispered to Cheng Xin. She couldn't tell if he was joking or being serious.

Sophon stood up. "Welcome to your new life in Universe 647. Why don't we go outside and take a look around?"

Outside, the spring planting was in full swing. The columnar robots were all working the fields. Some used the rakes to level and smooth out the field—the soil was so loose already that it did not need to be plowed; some were planting seeds in the parts that had already been smoothed. The farming techniques they employed were primitive: There were no drag harrows, so the robots had to use small rakes to level the field a bit at a time; there were no planters, so the robots each carried a bag of seeds and buried the seeds in the field one at a time. The entire scene invoked a sense of ancient simplicity. Here, robots seemed somehow more natural than real farmers.

Sophon explained, "We have only enough food stored here to last two years. After that, you'll need to rely on the food you grow. These seeds are descended from the seeds Cheng Xin sent along with Mr. Yun. Of course, they've all been genetically improved."

Yifan looked somewhat puzzled by the black soil. "I feel that soilless cultivation tanks would be more suitable here."

Cheng Xin said, "Anyone from the Earth has a kind of nostalgia for soil. Remember what Scarlett's father told her in *Gone With the Wind*? 'Why, land is the only thing in the world worth workin' for, worth fightin' for, worth dyin' for, because it's the only thing that lasts.'"

Yifan said, "The Solar System humans spilled their last drop of blood to stay with their land—well, save for two drops: you and AA. But what was the point? They didn't last, and neither did their land. Hundreds of millions of years have passed in the great universe, and do you think anyone still remembers them? This obsession with home and land, this permanent adolescence where you're no longer children but are afraid to leave home—this is the fundamental reason your race was annihilated. I am sorry if I've offended you, but it's the truth."

Cheng Xin smiled at the agitated Yifan. "You haven't offended me. What you said is true. We knew that, but we couldn't help it. You probably can't help it, either. Don't forget that you and all the crew of *Gravity* were prisoners before becoming Galactic humans."

"That is true." Guan Yifan lost some of his fire. "I've never thought of myself as a man qualified for space."

By the standards of space, there were not too many "qualified" men—and it was doubtful Cheng Xin would like any of them. She did think of one person who was probably qualified. His voice still echoed in her ears: *We're going to advance! Advance! We'll stop at nothing to advance!*

"Don't dwell on the past," Sophon said in her sweet voice. "Everything starts anew here."

A year passed in Universe 647.

The wheat had been harvested twice, and Cheng Xin and Guan Yifan had now watched twice as the green seedlings gradually turned into a sea of golden stalks. The vegetable fields next to the wheat had always remained green.

In this tiny world they were provided with all the other necessities of life. None of the objects had manufacturing marks or brand logos—Trisolarans made them—but they looked exactly like human products.

Cheng Xin and Guan Yifan sometimes went into the fields to work alongside the robots. Sometimes they strolled about the universe—as long as they were careful not to leave footprints, they could keep on walking indefinitely and experience the feeling of traversing countless worlds.

They spent most of their time in front of the computer, however. It was possible to invoke a terminal from anywhere in the small universe, but they didn't know where the CPU for the computer was located. The computer had a massive databank of text, image, and video from the Earth, most of which dated from before the Broadcast Era. The Trisolarans had clearly gathered the info as they studied humanity, and the material covered every field in the sciences and the humanities.

But even more information existed in the databank written in the Trisolaran language. This massive ocean of data was what interested them the most. Since they couldn't find any software on the computer for translating Trisolaran writing into human languages, they had to study the Trisolaran script itself. Sophon acted as their teacher, but they soon discovered that this was an extremely difficult endeavor because Trisolaran writing was purely ideographic; unlike human scripts, which were mostly phonetic, Trisolaran writing had no connection to their speech, but expressed ideas directly. In the distant past, humans had also used ideographic scripts—such as some hieroglyphs—but most of these later disappeared.[11] Humans read by decoding speech made visible. However, the difficulty didn't last long. The more they persisted, the easier the learning process became. After struggling for two months, they found themselves making rapid progress. Compared to phonetic scripts, the biggest advantage of an ideographic script was how fast one could read—Cheng Xin and Guan Yifan read at least ten times as fast in Trisolaran as they did with human scripts.

They began to read the Trisolaran material in the databank—at first haltingly, and then faster. They had two initial goals in mind: First, they wanted to know how the Trisolarans had recorded the period of history between their civilization and Earth civilization. Second, they wanted to know how this miniuniverse was constructed. For the latter, they understood that they would likely not achieve a specialist's level of understanding, but they wanted to at least understand it at the level of popular science. Sophon estimated that in order to achieve these two goals, they would need to spend one year to learn how to read Trisolaran better, then take another year to read in depth.

The fundamental principles underlying the small artificial universe seemed unimaginable to them; even the most basic mysteries puzzled them for the longest time. For instance, how could a complete ecological cycle function in a sealed space of only one cubit kilometer? What was the sun? What was its energy source? And most confounding: As a completely sealed system, where did the heat of the mini-universe go?

They asked Sophon these questions. Some she could answer; for others, she referred them to materials in the computer.

They also cared about the answer to one question in particular: Could the

---

[11] *Translator's Note:* Some Anglophone readers may raise an eyebrow at this assertion. The common description of Chinese characters—the script this novel was originally written in—as "ideograms" is inaccurate. The Chinese script is phonetic, like almost every other script still in use, though it still contains a few (very few) ideographic elements that have survived through the ages. An introduction to how Chinese characters really function may be found in John DeFrancis's *Chinese Language: Fact and Fantasy.*

mini-universe communicate with the great universe? Sophon told them that there was no way for the mini-universe to transmit any information to the greater universe, but it was possible for the mini-universe to receive broadcasts from the great universe. She explained that all the universes were bubbles above a supermembrane—this was a fundamental conceptual image from Trisolaran physics and cosmology, and she could explain it no further. The great universe had enough energy to propagate information across the super-membrane. However, this was difficult and required a great expenditure of energy—the great universe would have to convert a Milky Way's worth of matter into pure energy. As a matter of fact, the monitoring systems in Universe 647 often received messages from other great universes on the supermem-brane. Some were natural phenomena; some were messages from intelligent beings that could not be decoded—but they had never received any message from the particular great universe they had come from.

Time flowed by day after day like the smooth, placid water in that little brook.

Cheng Xin began to write her memoir so that she could record the history she knew. She named the book *A Past Outside of Time*.

Sometimes, they also tried to imagine life in the new universe. Sophon told them that according to cosmological theories, the new universe was certain to possess more than four macro dimensions, perhaps even more than ten macro dimensions. After the birth of the new universe, Universe 647 could automatically construct an entrance to it and examine the interior conditions. If the new universe possessed more than four dimensions, the mini-universe's exit could be moved around until a suitable habitable location was found in the great universe. Simultaneously, their mini-universe could establish communications with the refugees of other Trisolaran mini-universes, or even with Galactic human migrants. In the new universe, all the migrants coming from the old universe would practically be one race, and should be able to work together to construct a new world. Sophon emphasized that one characteristic greatly increased the probability of survival in a high-dimensional universe: Out of the many macro dimensions, it was likely that more than one dimension would belong to time.

"Multi-dimensional time?" Cheng Xin couldn't understand the concept at first.

"Even if time were only two-dimensional, it would be a plane instead of a line," Yifan explained. "There would be an infinite number of directions, and we could simultaneously make countless choices."

"And at least one of those choices would turn out to be right," added Sophon.

One night, after the second harvest, Cheng Xin woke up to find Yifan not beside her. She got up, went outside, and saw that the sun had already turned to the moon, and the little world was immersed in the watery, cool light. She saw Yifan sitting by the brook, his posture morose.

In this world of two, each of them had grown especially sensitive to the moods of the other. Cheng Xin had already known that something was troubling Yifan. Earlier, he had been sunny and upbeat. Until a few days ago, he had regularly shared his dream that, if they could find a peaceful life in the new great universe, perhaps their children could re-create the human race. But then he had abruptly changed, frequently going off by himself to ponder something, or to calculate something at a computer terminal.

Cheng Xin sat down next to Yifan, and he pulled her into his arms. The moonlit world was very quiet, and all they heard was the babbling brook. The moon revealed a field of ripe wheat; they'd have to start the harvest tomorrow.

"Loss of mass," Yifan said.

Cheng Xin said nothing. She watched the moonlight dancing in the brook, knowing that Yifan was going to explain.

"I've been reading Trisolaran cosmology, and came across a proof for the elegance of the mathematics behind the great universe we all came from. The design of the total mass in the universe was precise and perfect. The Trisolarans had proved that the total mass of the universe was just enough to allow the big crunch. If the total mass were reduced even slightly, the universe would turn from being closed to open, and expand indefinitely."

"But mass has been lost," Cheng Xin said. She understood right away what he was getting at.

"Yes. The Trisolarans have already constructed several hundred mini-universes. How many more have been constructed by other civilizations in the universe to escape the big crunch, or for some other purpose? Each of these mini-universes took away some matter from the great universe."

"We need to ask Sophon."

"I have. She told me that at the time of Universe 647's completion, the Trisolarans had not observed any influence from the loss of mass in the great universe. That universe was closed and was certain to eventually collapse."

"What about after Universe 647 was constructed?"

"She had no idea, of course. She also mentioned that there was a group of intelligent beings in the universe that resembled the Zero-Homers, but they called themselves the Returners. They advocated against the construction of mini-universes, and called for the mass in completed mini-universes to be returned to the great universe. . . . But she didn't know much else about them. All right, let's forget all this. We're not God."

"But we've long been called on to think about matters that belonged to the province of God."

They sat by the brook until the moon turned into the sun again.

Three days after the harvest, once all the wheat had been threshed and winnowed and stored away, Cheng Xin and Guan Yifan stood at the edge of the field and watched as the robots plowed the field to prepare for the next planting. The granary was now full, so there was no room for more wheat. Before, they would have debated what to plant for the next season. But now, both of them were troubled and had no interest in the topic. Throughout the entire harvest and threshing process, they had stayed in the house and discussed possible futures. They realized that even their individual life choices affected the fate of the universe, or even the fates of multiple universes. They really felt like God. The weight of responsibility made it hard to breathe, and so they left the house.

They saw Sophon walking toward them along one of the field ridges. Sophon rarely disturbed them and only appeared when they needed her. This time, her walk was different—she was in a hurry and did not exhibit her typical grace and dignity. Her anxious expression was also something they had not seen before.

"We've received a supermembrane broadcast from the great universe!" Sophon brought up a window and enlarged it. To make the window easier to see, she also dimmed the sun.

A torrent of symbols scrolled up the screen—the bitmap from the supermembrane broadcast. The symbols were strange and indecipherable. Cheng Xin and Guan Yifan noticed that each row of symbols was different: They rolled past like the surface of a chaotic river.

"The broadcast has been going on for five minutes and is still continuing." Sophon pointed at the window. "In actuality, the message in the broadcast is very simple and brief, but it has lasted this long because it's in many languages. We've seen a hundred thousand languages already!"

"Is the broadcast aimed at all the mini-universes?" Cheng Xin asked.

"Absolutely. Who else would receive it? They expended so much energy that the message must be important."

"Have you seen Trisolaran or Earth languages?"

"No."

Cheng Xin and Guan Yifan realized that this message was a record of which species had survived in the great universe.

By now, tens of billions of years had passed in the great universe. Regardless of the content of the broadcast, if a civilization's language was listed in the broadcast, it meant that the civilization still existed or had existed once and lasted so long that it had left an indelible mark in the great universe.

The river of symbols continued to flow up the screen: two hundred thousand languages, three hundred thousand, four hundred thousand . . . a million. The number continued to go up.

There were no Trisolaran and no Earth languages.

"It doesn't matter," Cheng Xin said. "We know that we existed; we lived." She and Guan Yifan leaned against each other.

"Trisolaran!" Sophon cried out and pointed at the screen. By now, over 1.3 million languages had been broadcast, and one row, written in Trisolaran, flashed by. Cheng Xin and Guan Yifan couldn't catch it, but Sophon did.

"Earth!" Sophon cried out again a few seconds later.

After 1.57 million languages, the broadcast finished.

The window now showed only the message written in Trisolaran and Earth languages. Cheng Xin and Guan Yifan couldn't even read the message because tears blurred their eyes.

On the day of the universe's Last Judgment, two humans and a robot belonging to the Earth and Trisolaran civilizations embraced each other in ecstasy.

They knew that languages and scripts evolved very quickly. If the two civilizations had survived for a long time or even continued to exist now, their scripts were surely very different from what was being shown on the screen. But to allow those hiding in mini-universes to understand, they had to write in ancient scripts. Compared to the total number of civilizations that had lived in the great universe, 1.57 million was a tiny number.

In the eternal night of the Orion Arm of the Milky Way Galaxy, two civilizations had swept through like two shooting stars, and the universe had remembered their light.

After Cheng Xin and Guan Yifan calmed down, they read the message. The content of the message in both scripts was the same, and very simple:

> A notice from the Returners: The total mass of our universe has decreased to below the critical threshold. The universe will turn from being closed to open, and die a slow death in perpetual expansion. All lives and all memories will also die. Please return the mass you have taken away and send only memories to the new universe.

Cheng Xin and Guan Yifan locked gazes. In each other's eyes, they saw the dark future for the great universe. In perpetual expansion, all the galaxies would move farther away from each other until none were visible from any other. By then, standing at any point in the universe, all one would see was darkness in every direction. The stars would go out one by one, and all celestial bodies would turn into thin dust clouds. Coldness and darkness would reign over all, and the universe would become a vast, empty tomb. All civilizations and all memories would be buried in that endless tomb for eternity. Death would be eternal.

The only way to prevent this future was to return the matter locked up in all the mini-universes constructed by all the civilizations. But such a decision meant that the mini-universes would not survive, and all the refugees in the mini-universes had to return to the great universe. That was the meaning of the name of the Returners' movement.

The two said everything they needed to say to each other with their eyes and made their decision wordlessly. But Cheng Xin still spoke aloud. "I want to go back. But if you want to stay here, I'll stay with you."

Yifan shook his head slowly. "I study a grand universe whose diameter is sixteen billion light-years. I don't want to spend the rest of my life in this universe that's only a kilometer in each direction. Let's go back."

"I must advise against that," said Sophon. "We can't precisely determine how fast time is passing in the great universe, but I can be certain that at least ten billion years have passed there since the time you came here. Planet Blue has long since vanished, and the star Mr. Yun gave you was extinguished a long time ago. We know nothing of the conditions in the great universe, and it's possible that it's not even three-dimensional anymore."

"I thought you could move the exit of the mini-universe at lightspeed," Yifan said. "Can't you move it around to find a habitable location?"

"If you insist, I will try. But I still think staying here is the best choice. There are two possible futures if you remain: If the Returners succeed in their mission, the great universe will collapse into a singularity and lead to a new big bang so that we can go to the new universe. But if the Returners fail and the great universe dies, you can live out the rest of your lives in this mini-universe. This isn't too bad."

"If everyone in every mini-universe thinks that way," said Cheng Xin, "then they will have doomed the great universe."

Sophon gazed at Cheng Xin wordlessly. Given the speed of Sophon's thought, perhaps this period of time felt as long as several centuries to her. It was hard to imagine that software and algorithms could produce such a complex expression. Perhaps Sophon's AI software had brought up all the memories accumulated across almost twenty million years since she had met Cheng Xin. All these memories seemed to precipitate in her gaze: sorrow, admiration, surprise, reproach, regret . . . so many complicated feelings mixed together.

"You're still living for your responsibility," Sophon said.

Excerpt from *A Past Outside of Time*
The Stairs of Responsibility

All my life has been spent climbing up a flight of stairs made of responsibility.

When I was little, my only duty was to study hard and obey my parents.

Later, in high school and college, the responsibility to study hard continued, but there was also the added obligation to make myself useful rather than a drain on society.

By the time I started to work toward my doctorate, my responsibilities became more concrete. I needed to contribute to the development of chemical rockets, to build more powerful, more reliable rockets so that more materials and a few men and women could be sent into Earth orbit.

Later, I joined the PIA, and my responsibility was to send a probe into space a light-year away to meet the invading Trisolaran Fleet. This was a distance about ten billion times greater than the distance I had worked with as a rocket engineer.

And then, I received a star. During the new era, it brought me previously unimaginable responsibilities. I became the Swordholder, whose duty was to maintain dark forest deterrence. Looking back on it now, perhaps it was a bit of an exaggeration to claim that I held the fate of humankind; but I really did control the direction of development for two civilizations.

Later, my responsibilities became more complicated: I wanted to endow humans with lightspeed wings, but I also had to thwart that goal to prevent a war.

I don't know how much those catastrophes and the final destruction of the Solar System had to do with me. Those are questions that could never be answered definitively. But I'm certain they had something to do with me, with my responsibilities.

And now, I've climbed to the apex of responsibility: I am responsible for the fate of the universe. Of course this responsibility doesn't belong only to me and Guan Yifan, but we own a share of the responsibility, a share of something that I never could have imagined.

I want to tell all those who believe in God that I am not the Chosen One. I also want to tell all the atheists that I am not a history-maker. I am but an ordinary person. Unfortunately, I have not been able to walk the ordinary person's path. My path is, in reality, the journey of a civilization.

And now we know that this is the journey that must be made by every civilization: awakening inside a cramped cradle, toddling out of it, taking flight, flying faster and farther, and, finally, merging with the fate of the universe as one.

The ultimate fate of all intelligent beings has always been to become as grand as their thoughts.

Outside of Time
Our Universe

────────

Through Universe 647's control system, Sophon managed to move the mini-universe's exit inside the great universe. The door moved quickly through the great universe, searching for a habitable world. The amount of information that the door could transmit to the mini-universe was very limited, and no images or videos were possible. All that could be sent back was a rough analysis of the environment. This was a number between negative ten and ten, indicating the habitability of the environment. Humans could survive only if the number were greater than zero.

The door jumped tens of thousands of times in the great universe. After three months, only once did they discover a habitable planet, with a rating of three. Sophon had to concede that this was probably the best result they could get.

"A rating of three indicates a dangerous and inhospitable world," Sophon warned.

"We're not afraid," said a resolute Cheng Xin. Yifan nodded. "Let's go there."

The door appeared in Universe 647. Like the door Cheng Xin and Guan Yifan had seen on Planet Blue, it was also a rectangle limned by glowing lines. But this door was much bigger, perhaps to make it easier to transport material through it. Initially, the door was not connected to the great universe, and anything could pass through it without leaving the mini-universe. Sophon adjusted its parameters so that anything moving through it would disappear and reappear in the great universe.

Next, it was time to return matter from the mini-universe to the great universe.

Sophon had explained that the mini-universe had no matter of its own. All of its mass had come from material brought out of the great universe. Of the several hundred mini-universes constructed by the Trisolarans, Universe 647 was one of the smallest. In total, it required about five hundred thousand metric tons of matter from the great universe, which was about the carrying capacity of a large oil tanker. It was practically nothing at the scale of the universe.

They began with the soil. After the last harvest, the field had been left fallow. The robots used a wheelbarrow to cart the moist earth; at the door, two of the robots lifted the wheelbarrow to dump the soil through the door; and the soil disappeared. It happened very quickly. Three days later, all the soil in the mini-universe was gone. Even the trees around the house had been returned through the door.

With all the soil removed, they saw the metallic floor of the mini-universe. The floor was pieced together with smooth metal tiles that reflected the sun like a mirror. The robots took off the metal tiles one by one and sent them through the door as well.

Underneath the floor was a small spaceship. Although the ship was less than twenty meters long, it contained the most advanced technologies of the Trisolarans. Designed with human occupants in mind, it could seat three, and was equipped with both a nuclear fusion drive and a curvature drive. There was a miniature ecological cycling system aboard suitable for human needs as well as equipment for hibernation. Like *Halo*, it was capable of landing and taking off from planetary surfaces. It had a slender, streamlined profile, perhaps to make it easier to go through the mini-universe's door. It had been intended for the inhabitants of Universe 647 to enter the new great universe after the next big bang. It could serve as a living base for a considerable amount of time, until they found a suitable location in the new universe. But now, they would use it to return to the old great universe.

As the rest of the metal floor tiles were removed, they also revealed more machinery beneath. These were the first objects Cheng Xin and Guan Yifan had seen in the mini-universe that bore obvious signs of being of Trisolaran origin. Like Cheng Xin had suspected, the design of these machines evinced an aesthetic completely different from human ideals. Cheng Xin and Guan Yifan couldn't even tell at first that they were looking at machinery; rather, the objects resembled strange sculptures or natural geologic formations. The robots began to disassemble the machinery and send the pieces through the door.

Cheng Xin and Sophon busied themselves in a room and wouldn't let Yifan in. They said that they were working on a "women's project" and would surprise him later.

After some machine under the floor was shut off, gravity disappeared from the mini-universe. The white house began to float in air.

The weightless robots disassembled the sky, which was a thin membrane capable of displaying a blue sky and white clouds. Finally, the remnants of the floor below the machinery were also disassembled and sent away.

The water in the mini-universe had evaporated and fog was everywhere. The sun shone from behind a veil of clouds and a spectacular rainbow appeared that crossed from one end of the universe to the other. Whatever liquid water was left in the mini-universe formed spheres of various sizes and drifted around the rainbow, reflecting and refracting sunlight.

Disassembling the machines also meant turning off the ecological cycling system. Cheng Xin and Yifan had to put on space suits.

Sophon adjusted the parameters in the door again to allow gas through. A low rumble shook the mini-universe, caused by air escaping through the door. Below the rainbow, the white fog cloud formed a great maelstrom around the door, like a view of a typhoon from space. And then, the whirling fog turned into a tornado, and let out a high-pitched howl. The drifting balls of water were sucked into the twister, torn apart, and disappeared through the door. Countless small objects drifting in the air were also swallowed up by the cyclone. The sun, the house, the spaceship, and other large objects also drifted in the direction of the door, but robots equipped with thrusters quickly secured them back in place.

As the air thinned, the rainbow disappeared, and the fog dissipated. The air became more transparent, and gradually, the mini-universe's space appeared. Like space in the great universe, it was also dark and deep, but there were no stars. Only three objects floated in space: the sun, the house, and the spaceship, along with about a dozen weightless robots. In Cheng Xin's eyes, this simplified world resembled the naïve, clumsy pictures she had drawn in her childhood.

Cheng Xin and Guan Yifan activated the thrusters on their space suits and flew toward the depths of space. After a kilometer, they reached the end of the universe and, in a flash, found themselves back where they had started. They could see the projected images of every floating object repeated endlessly in every direction. Like two mirrors placed against each other, the images extended in rows into infinity.

The house was disassembled. The last room to be taken apart was the parlor decorated in an Eastern style in which Sophon had welcomed them. All the scrolls, the tea table, and the pieces of the house were sent out the door by the robots.

The sun finally went out. It was a metal sphere where one hemisphere, the part that had emitted light, was transparent. Three robots pushed it through the door. Only lamps now illuminated the mini-universe, and the vacuum that was space soon cooled. What was left of the water and air soon turned into ice fragments that sparkled in the lamplight.

Sophon directed the robots to line up and go through the door, one after the other.

Finally, only the slender ship was left in the mini-universe, along with three figures drifting near it.

Sophon held a metal box. This box would be left behind in the mini-universe, a message in a bottle for the new universe that would be born after the next big bang. The box contained a miniature computer whose quantum memory held all the information in the mini-universe's computer—this was practically the entire memory of the Trisolaran and Earth civilizations. After the birth of the new universe, the metal box would receive a signal from the door, and it would go through the door using its own tiny thrusters and enter the new universe. It would drift through the high-dimensional space of the new universe until the day it was picked up and read. At the same time, it would continuously broadcast its message using neutrinos—assuming the new universe also had neutrinos.

Cheng Xin and Guan Yifan believed that in the other mini-universes, at least those mini-universes that heeded that call of the Returners, the same things were being done. If the new universe were really born, it would contain many bottles containing messages drifting through it. It was believable that a considerable number of bottles contained storage mechanisms that held the memories and thoughts of every individual of that civilization, as well as their complete biological details—maybe the records would be sufficient for a new civilization in the new universe to revive that old civilization.

"Can we keep another five kilograms here?" Cheng Xin asked. She was on the other side of the ship and dressed in her space suit. In her hand, she held a glowing, transparent sphere. The sphere was about half a meter in diameter, and a few balls of water drifted inside it. Inside some of the water spheres were tiny fish, along with green algae. There were also two miniature drifting continents covered with green grass. The light came from the top of the transparent sphere, where there was a tiny glowing emitter, the sun of this miniature world. This was a completely sealed ecological sphere, the result of more than ten days of work by Cheng Xin and Sophon. As long as the tiny sun inside the sphere continued to give off light, this miniature ecological system would persist. As long as it remained here, Universe 647 would not be a lifeless, dark world.

"Of course," said Guan Yifan. "The great universe isn't going to fail to collapse because it misses five kilograms." He had another thought that he did not voice: Perhaps the great universe really would fail to collapse because it lacked a single atom's mass. The precision of Nature can sometimes exceed the imagination. For instance, life itself required the precise collaboration of various universal constants within a billion-billionth of a certain range. But Cheng Xin could still leave behind her ecological sphere. Out of all the countless mini-universes created by the countless civilizations, it was certain that some number of them would not heed the call of the Returners. Ultimately, the great universe was certain to lose at least a few hundred million tons of matter, or perhaps even a million billion billion tons.

Hopefully, the great universe could ignore such a loss.

Cheng Xin and Guan Yifan entered the spaceship, and Sophon came in last. She had long ceased wearing her magnificent kimono and turned once again into that lean and nimble warrior dressed in camouflage. She had all sorts of weapons and survival gear strapped to her body, the most prominent being the katana on her back.

"Don't worry," she said to her two human friends. "As long as I'm alive, no harm will come to you."

The fusion drive activated and the thrusters emitted a dim blue light. The spaceship slowly went through the door of the universe.

The message in a bottle and the ecological sphere were the only things left in the mini-universe. The bottle faded into the darkness so, in this one-cubic-kilometer universe, only the little sun inside the ecological sphere gave off any light. In this minuscule world of life, a few clear watery spheres drifted serenely in weightlessness. One tiny fish leapt out of a watery sphere and entered another, where it effortlessly swam between the green algae. On a blade of grass on one of the miniature continents, a drop of dew took off from the tip of the grass blade, rose spiraling into the air, and refracted a clear ray of sunlight into space.

TRANSLATOR'S POSTSCRIPT

I'm indebted to the following beta readers for their invaluable help during the translation process: Anatoly Belilovsky, John Chu, Elías Combarro, Rachel Cordasco, Derwin Mak, Alex Shvartsman, and Igor Teper. All translators should be so lucky.

I'm also thankful for special assistance from the following individuals: Wang Meizi, for advice on transliterated names; Anna Gustafsson Chen, for pointers on Scandinavian geography; and Emma Osborne, for tracking down books for me on the other side of the globe.

My heartfelt gratitude goes to David Brin for championing the Three-Body series and acting as a wonderful sounding board for me.

I continue to be awed by the genius of Liu Cixin every time I read another passage from this novel. Of the three books in the trilogy, this third one is my favorite. I've been very fortunate to get the chance to work on this book with Da Liu.

Finally, I want to thank the many individuals who played indispensable (though often underappreciated) roles in the epic tale of bringing Three-Body to the English-speaking world: Li Yun and Song Yajuan at China Educational Publications Import & Export Corporation Ltd., for seeing the potential of a global audience for the series and commissioning the translation; Joel Martinsen, who translated *The Dark Forest* and, by example, showed me how to handle some tricky parts in this book; Emily Jiang, Wang Meizi, and Chen Qiufan, for building the bridge that connected Tor Books to Liu Cixin; Joe Monti, for encouraging me to take on this project in the first place; and the many wonderful individuals at Tor Books who worked so hard to make the vision of these books a reality. Among them are: Irene Gallo, Stephan Martinière, and Jamie Stafford-Hill, for extraordinary art direction, artwork, and cover design; Leah Withers and Diana Griffin, for an outstanding publicity campaign; Joe Bendel for his sales and marketing insight; Kevin Sweeney, Heather Saunders, Nathan Weaver, Karl Gold, and Megan Kiddoo, from Tor's production department; Christina MacDonald, who ensured that errors and bugs would not survive in the manuscript; Miriam Weinberg, for assisting with editorial matters; and most of all, Liz Gorinsky, who left an indelible mark on the text with her meticulous and insightful editorial touch, improving this translation in innumerable ways. I hope to continue to make beautiful books with them all in the future.